PENGUIN TWENTIETH-CENTURY CLASSICS

THE PLUMED SERPENT

DAVID HERBERT LAWRENCE was born at Eastwood, Nottinghamshire, in 1885, fourth of the five children of a miner and his middle-class wife. He attended Nottingham High School and Nottingham University College. His first novel, *The White Peacock*, was published in 1911, just a few weeks after the death of his mother to whom he had been abnormally close. At this time he finally ended his relationship with Jessie Chambers (the Miriam of *Sons and Lovers*) and became engaged to Louie Burrows. His career as a schoolteacher was ended in 1911 by the illness which was ultimately diagnosed as tuberculosis. In 1912 Lawrence eloped to Germany with Frieda Weekley, the German wife of his former modern languages tutor. They were married on their return to England in 1914. Lawrence was now living, precariously, by his writing. His greatest novels, *The Rainbow* and *Women in Love*, were completed in 1915 and 1916. The former was suppressed, and he could not find a publisher for the latter.

After the war Lawrence began his 'savage pilgrimage' in search of a more fulfilling mode of life than industrial Western civilization could offer. This took him to Sicily, Ceylon, Australia and, finally, New Mexico. The Lawrences returned to Europe in 1925. Lawrence's last novel, *Lady Chatterley's Lover*, was banned in 1928, and his paintings confiscated in 1929. He died in Vence in 1920 at the age of 44.

Lawrence spent most of his short life living. Nevertheless he produced an amazing quantity of work – novels, stories, poems, plays, essays, travel books, translations and letters ... After his death Frieda wrote: 'What he had seen and felt and known he gave in his writing to his fellow men, the splendour of living, the hope of more and more life ... a heroic and immeasurable gift.'

RONALD G. WALKER received a Ph.D. from the University of Maryland, and is now Associate Professor of English and Chairman of the Division of Arts and Sciences at the Victoria Campus of the University of Houston in Victoria, Texas. He has held a Fulbright Lectureship at the Universidad Nacional Autónoma de México and is the author of *Infernal Paradise: Mexico and the Modern English Novel* (1978).

The Plumed Serpent

(QUETZALCOATL)

D. H. LAWRENCE

EDITED WITH AN

INTRODUCTION AND NOTES

BY RONALD G. WALKER

PENGUIN BOOKS

PENGUIN BOOKS

Published by the Penguin Group
Penguin Books Ltd, 27 Wrights Lane, London W8 5TZ, England
Penguin Books USA Inc., 375 Hudson Street, New York, New York 10014, USA
Penguin Books Australia Ltd, Ringwood, Victoria, Australia
Penguin Books Canada Ltd, 2801 John Street, Markham, Ontario, Canada L3R 1B4
Penguin Books (NZ) Ltd, 182–190 Wairau Road, Auckland 10, New Zealand

Penguin Books Ltd, Registered Offices: Harmondsworth, Middlesex, England

First published by Martin Secker 1926
Published in the Penguin English Library 1983
Reprinted in Penguin Classics 1985
Reprinted in Penguin Books 1990
3 5 7 9 10 8 6 4 2

Printed in England by Clays Ltd, St Ives plc
Filmset in Monophoto Ehrhardt

Contents

Lawrence's Life and Works: a Chronology

1885	David Herbert Richards Lawrence born in Eastwood, Nottinghamshire, the fourth child of Arthur Lawrence, miner, and Lydia, *née* Beardsall, formerly a schoolmistress.
1891–8	He attends Beauvale Board School and becomes the first boy from that school to win a County Council Scholarship to
1898–1901	Nottingham High School, which he attends until 1901.
1901	Begins frequent visits to Chambers family at Haggs Farm, and his relationship with Jessie Chambers (the Miriam of *Sons and Lovers*) which was to develop into an 'unofficial engagement'.
1901–2	Works as a clerk at Haywood's surgical appliances factory. Has to leave after severe attack of pneumonia.
1902–6	Pupil-teacher at British School, Eastwood. Sits the King's Scholarship examination in December 1904 and is placed in the first division of the first class. A few months later he matriculates and qualifies himself to take a two-year teachers' certificate course at Nottingham University College, beginning in September 1906.
1906–8	Writes his first poems and stories and begins his first novel *Laetitia* (later *The White Peacock*). Wins *Nottinghamshire Guardian* Christmas 1907 short story competition with 'A Prelude'. Loses his faith in 'a personal, human God'.
1908–11	Teaches at Davidson Road School, Croydon. Meets Ford Madox Hueffer who begins to publish his poems and stories in the *English Review* and introduces him to the London literary world. In 1910 he writes his second novel, *The Trespasser*, in conjunction with Helen Corke, and begins *Paul Morel* (later *Sons and Lovers*). His relationship with Jessie Chambers comes to an end. He has a brief affair with Alice Dax, wife of an Eastwood chemist, then becomes engaged to Louie Burrows, who had been a fellow-student at college. In December 1910 Mrs Lawrence dies of cancer. In January 1911 *The White Peacock* is published by Heinemann. Edward Garnett becomes Lawrence's mentor. Lawrence becomes seriously ill with pneumonia and has to give up schoolteaching.
1912	In March Lawrence meets Frieda Weekley, wife of his former modern languages tutor, and six weeks later elopes with her to Germany. Lawrence records the vicissitudes of their

relationship in '*Look! We Have Come Through!*'. They walk
over the Alps into Italy and settle at Gárgnano, where Lawrence
finishes *Sons and Lovers* and begins *The Insurrection of Miss
Houghton* (later to be rewritten as *The Lost Girl*).

1913   Begins *The Sisters*, eventually to be split into *The Rainbow*
and *Women in Love*, and *Italian Sketches* (later *Twilight in
Italy*). They return to England in June and begin friendship
with John Middleton Murry and Katherine Mansfield. They
return to Italy (Lerici) in September. Lawrence works mainly

1914   on *The Sisters* until June, when they return to England to marry
(Frieda having at last obtained her divorce) and to find a publisher for *The Rainbow*. The wedding takes place at Kensing-
ton Registry Office on 13 July 1914. Lawrence works on re-
vising his short stories for *The Prussian Officer*. The outbreak
of war the following month prevents the Lawrences from
returning to Italy. At Chesham and Greatham during the next

1915   six months, Lawrence rewrites *The Rainbow*. He begins important friendships with Lady Cynthia Asquith, Lady Otto-
line Morrell, Bertrand Russell and E. M. Forster. In August
they move to Hampstead. Lawrence develops his idea of an
ideal community, Rananim, envisaged, at this stage, in
Florida. His plans to form a revolutionary anti-war party with
Russell and Murry collapse. *The Rainbow* is published by
Methuen and immediately suppressed. This blow, together
with the war, ill-health, increasing poverty, the defection of
several friends, humiliating examinations for military service,
and his inability to get permission to leave the country, brings
Lawrence close to despair and misanthropy – his 'nightmare'.

1916   The Lawrences move to Cornwall where Lawrence writes
Women in Love.

1917   He begins *Studies in Classic American Literature*. The Lawrences are evicted from Cornwall on suspicion of spying. In
London Lawrence begins *Aaron's Rod*.

1918   They move to Newbury, in Berkshire, then to Mountain
Cottage, Middleton-by-Wirksworth, Derbyshire. Lawrence
writes *Movements in European History*.

1919   Lawrence is very ill with influenza. Moves back to Berkshire.
In November the Lawrences leave for Italy and settle in
Capri.

1920   Moves to Fontana Vecchia, Taormina, Sicily. Visits Maurice
Magnus at Monte Cassino.

1920–21 Writes *The Lost Girl*, *Mr Noon*, *Sea and Sardinia* and the two
psychoanalysis books; begins *Birds, Beasts and Flowers*; finishes *Aaron's Rod*.

1922   Translates Verga. Visits the Brewsters in Ceylon on the way
to Australia, where he spends the summer at Thirroul, N. S. W.,

writing *Kangaroo*. Goes to New Mexico in September at the invitation of Mabel Dodge Luhan. In December settles at Del Monte ranch, Questa, near Taos. Finishes *Studies in Classic American Literature*.

1923   Finishes *Birds, Beasts and Flowers*. Spends the summer at Chapala in Mexico where he writes *Quetzalcoatl* (the first version of *The Plumed Serpent*). Rewrites Mollie Skinner's novel *The House of Ellis* as *The Boy in the Bush*. Frieda returns to England in August; Lawrence follows in December.

1924   Dinner at the Café Royal where Lawrence invites his friends to form a community at the ranch in Taos. Only Dorothy Brett accepts and accompanies the Lawrences to New Mexico in March. Frieda acquires Lobo ranch, later renamed Kiowa, from Mabel in exchange for the manuscript of *Sons and Lovers*. That summer at the ranch Lawrence writes *The Woman Who Rode Away*, *St Mawr*, *The Princess* and the New Mexico sections of *Mornings in Mexico*. Lawrence's father dies. In November the Lawrences move to Oaxaca, Mexico, where Lawrence writes the Mexican sections of *Mornings in Mexico* and rewrites *Quetzalcoatl*.

1925   In February Lawrence almost dies of malaria. In Mexico City a doctor tells Frieda that he is dying of consumption. He puts rouge on his cheeks to get back across the border. Recuperates at the ranch and writes *David* and *Reflections on the Death of a Porcupine*. In September the Lawrences return to Europe and settle at Spotorno in Italy, where Lawrence writes *Sun*.

1926   Writes *The Virgin and the Gipsy*. Quarrels with Frieda and leaves her for several weeks. Has an abortive affair with Dorothy Brett. In May the Lawrences move to the Villa Mirenda, Scandicci, near Florence. In the late summer Lawrence makes his last visit to England. On his return he writes *The First Lady Chatterley*. Takes up painting seriously.

1927   Writes second version of *Lady Chatterley's Lover*. Makes Etruscan pilgrimage with Earl Brewster. Writes *The Escaped Cock* and *Etruscan Places*. Begins final version of *Lady Chatterley's Lover*.

1928   In June the Lawrences move to Switzerland and settle at Gsteig. Lawrence is too weak to work, except on newspaper articles and paintings. In October he visits Richard Aldington on Port Cros, then settles in Bandol. Begins *Pansies*. *Lady Chatterley's Lover* published, with consequent furore.

1929   Visits Paris in the spring, then Mallorca. Lawrence's paintings exhibited at the Warren Gallery in London. On the day the show is raided by the police Lawrence collapses at Forte dei Marmi. He goes to Bavaria for treatment, but returns, no better, to Bandol in September. Writes *Nettles* and *Last Poems*. Begins *Apocalypse*.

1930   On Dr Morland's recommendation Lawrence enters Ad Astra sanatorium at Vence in February. After three weeks with no improvement, he is moved by Frieda and Aldous and Maria Huxley to a nearby villa where he dies the following night. He is buried at Vence.

1935   Lawrence's body exhumed, cremated, and the ashes taken to Taos where Frieda's third husband, Angelo Ravagli, has built a small shrine above the ranch.

1956   Frieda dies and is buried outside the shrine.

KEITH SAGAR

Introduction

1

Every continent has its own great spirit of place. Every people is polarised in some particular locality, which is home, the homeland. Different places on the face of the earth have different vital effluence, different vibration, different chemical exhalation, different polarity with different stars: call it what you like. But the spirit of place is a great reality.

(Studies in Classic American Literature)

D. H. LAWRENCE conceived of *The Plumed Serpent* as his 'American novel'. To understand what he meant by this phrase is important because the novel depends, to an extraordinary degree even for Lawrence, upon the evocation of place and the subjective responses that place elicits in character and reader alike. Indeed the simplest way to define an American novel in Lawrence's sense is to say that it must invoke and adequately respond to the American 'spirit of place' – something that, in Lawrence's view, even the 'classic' American writers themselves had realized imperfectly at best.

For Lawrence, the American continent, whether in the south-western part of the United States or in rural Mexico, contained in the remnants of its aboriginal culture an unfulfilled but still attainable religious promise. The promise of redemption for England, for Europe, which he had prophesied at the end of *The Rainbow* (1915), had been destroyed by the inexorable death-drive of the modern industrialized world and its apotheosis, the Great War. A continent's spirit of place could die, and after the war Europe was, for Lawrence, a 'dreadful mummy sarcophagus' inhabited by ghosts and maggots. But America, even during the war and long before he had actually been there, represented – as it had for the Pilgrim Fathers and the Spanish conquistadors – a new beginning.

Lawrence was determined not to make the same mistake that Cortés and Columbus had made. When *he* 'discovered' America he would not impose his European consciousness onto it, thereby denying the aboriginal spirit of place; instead he would find some way to 'take up life where the Red Indian, the Aztec, the Maya, the Inca left it off ... [picking] up the life-thread where the mysterious Red race let it fall' during the Conquest.* These words, written more than two years before Lawrence's arrival in the New World, adumbrate a travel itinerary that already involves the lands of the great pre-Columbian peoples and excludes from serious consideration the more populous urban centres of the United States.

If the Tree of Life was blighted in Europe, and the blight had simply been transplanted to White America, in aboriginal America perhaps life still sprang 'up from the roots, crude but vital'.† In *Fantasia of the Unconscious* (1922) Lawrence formulated a myth of origins that sheds light on his developing vision of America. He describes a kind of Golden Age before the Flood, when the pagan world, both geographically and culturally, was a great monolithic entity. This *Ur*-culture, unlike our atomistic age, 'had a vast and perhaps perfect science of its own, a science in terms of life'; the primal wisdom was esoteric, 'invested in a large priesthood' that spread it round the globe until men everywhere 'were in one complete correspondence over all the earth. Men wandered back and forth from Atlantis to the Polynesian Continent ... The interchange was complete, and knowledge, science was universal over the earth.'‡ Then the glaciers melted, whole continents were drowned, and the monolithic world fragmented into isolate races, each developing its own culture, presumably in response to the now-distinct spirit of place of its autochthonous land. But a few refugees from the lost continents fled to the high ground of Europe, America and Asia; Atlantean priests, for example, settled in Celtic Britain to the north-east or in America to the south-west. There they 'refused to forget, but taught the old wisdom, only in its half-forgotten, symbolic forms. More or less forgotten, as knowledge: remembered as ritual, gesture and myth-story.'§

---

* 'America, Listen to Your Own' (1920), reprinted in *Phoenix: The Posthumous Papers of D. H. Lawrence*, ed. Edward D. McDonald (Heinemann, 1936), p. 90 (hereafter cited as *Phoenix* in the text).

† *The Letters of D. H. Lawrence*, ed. Aldous Huxley (Heinemann, 1932), p. 262.

‡ *Fantasia of the Unconscious and Psychoanalysis and the Unconscious* (Penguin, 1971), pp. 12–13.

§ *Fantasia of the Unconscious*, p. 13.

In modern Europe even these vestiges of the old universal knowledge had largely died out, and with them died what was left of the unitary being of man. First Christianity, with its overemphasis on bodiless spirituality, and then modern science, with its excessive dependence upon finite reason as the instrument of control over a merely mechanistic world, had killed it. Like one of those mystic refugees from a lost continent, Lawrence set out on his 'savage pilgrimage'.

Inevitably the destination of his quest was America, but he approached it by a protracted 'widdershins' movement that took him through the Mediterranean to the Orient and then to Australia before he finally reached San Francisco and moved thence immediately to Taos, New Mexico, arriving in September 1922. All this time America had continued to exercise an increasingly powerful hold on Lawrence's imagination. To say that he had 'high hopes', after more than seven years of intense longing (tinged, to be sure, with fear of disappointment), would be an understatement. His mythic paradigm for the New World had by now taken on a more or less definite form in his mind; he was all but committed to it, imaginatively, before his arrival. Rananim, as he called his much-discussed ideal community of enlightened souls settling together to live in hope for the future, required both the 'unspoilt' isolation and the sense of latent historical mission that primordial America seemed to offer. Lawrence had come to see the Red Indian as the embodiment of the old 'blood-and-vertebrate consciousness', or at least its remnants as expressed in his religion. If the old mode of consciousness could be tapped and somehow brought into fusion with the white 'mental–spiritual consciousness', the result would be the emergence of a 'new germ' or impetus for human life as it entered the next phase of being. But first there would have to be a complete break with the degenerate present phase. His readings in American literature had convinced him that the white and dark modes of consciousness in America resisted fusion, and indeed were mutually annihilating. The first contacts with America suggested to him that for a true rebirth to occur, 'a vast death-happening must come first'.* The 'American novel' he was determined

* *The Collected Letters of D. H. Lawrence*, ed. Harry T. Moore (Heinemann, 1962), II, p. 740. Hereafter the citations to this edition of the letters will appear in the text.

to write could hardly avoid assuming the shape of his apocalyptic vision. For the present, however, he needed to find a place where he could settle to write it. When Taos, for various reasons, proved less than conducive to serious writing, it was natural enough that he turned to the land of the Aztecs.

2

Between March 1923 and March 1925 Lawrence made three trips to Mexico, spending altogether about ten months there. Because travelling, for Lawrence more than for most writers, played a crucial part in his work, and because he always insisted on writing *The Plumed Serpent* only when he was actually in Mexico, his experiences in and feelings about the country during his visits there deserve the attention of any serious reader of the novel.

Almost at once after he had crossed the border he sensed a change of tone in the continent's spirit of place. In New Mexico he had appreciated the bigness, the openness, the 'sense of rough freedom' induced by the pristine mountain landscape. But before long he had come to despise the American 'shove-or-be-shoved' wilfulness, which seemed antipathetic to spontaneous living. Natural beauty abounded, but somehow it resisted his desire for something more, something that would register within: 'It seems to me, in America, for the inside of life, there is just blank nothing. All this outside life – and marvellous country – and it means so little to one' (*Letters*, II, pp. 732–3). The dominant white culture had succeeded in insulating itself from overt contact with the primal spirit of the continent. The remnants of the pure-blooded Indian peoples were safely tucked away on reservations, their ceremonials reduced to sideshows on the tourist circuit. Thus the ambience of New Mexico produced in Lawrence a nervous tautness, an 'unbearable tension' that drove him south in search of release. Mexico, in contrast, still expressed the underlying *daemon* of America directly. There 'the great paleface overlay hasn't gone into the soil half an inch', and the old dark gods – whose fangs and claws have all been pulled, in the States – still snarl and bite and cry out for 'the smoke of a little heart's blood' (*Phoenix*, p. 105). Mexico, he decided, was the true 'solar plexus' of America; immediately it changed his emotional state from nervous tautness to sheer exasperation. And he preferred this exasperation, along with the overt hostility he detected in the natives: at least his feelings were engaged, a prerequisite for him to write. Mexico represented a welcome return to the inner life.

It was not to prove quite so simple, of course. Before very long Mexico posed a host of complications for Lawrence, complications no less imposing, indeed, than the inner life of such a man as he. The first journey lasted four months, March to July 1923. Lawrence and his wife Frieda were joined in Mexico City by the poet Witter Bynner and his associate Willard Johnson. Together they made the rounds of tourist sites, visiting the old Biblioteca Nacional, the frescoes adorning the walls of the university and government buildings, the 'floating gardens' of Xochimilco, the ruined monasteries at San Agustín Acolman and El Desierto de los Leones, the Basílica of Guadalupe, the spectacular pyramids at San Juan Teotihuacán, and the bull-fight. Except for Teotihuacán, where he took due note of the 'ponderous', 'snarling' feathered serpents at the Temple of Quetzalcoatl, Lawrence was not much impressed by what he saw. His response to the bull-fight, presented so powerfully in the opening chapter of *The Plumed Serpent*, was particularly harsh. Like his protagonist Kate Leslie, he was appalled not only by what he felt was the viciousness of the fight itself but also by the bloodlust of the 'degenerate mob' in attendance; like her, too, he left before the end of the first *corrida* without giving the sport a chance to demonstrate its worth. In any event, he had lost all patience with Mexico City, which he now regarded as an inferior version of the European cities he had left behind. He took an active dislike for 'those pale-faced Mexicans of the Capital'. Mexico, he decided (again like Kate), really 'meant the dark-faced men in cotton clothes, big hats: the peasants, peons, pelados, Indians, call them what you will' (p. 108).* Hereafter, though by necessity he stopped many times in transit in the capital, most of his time in Mexico was spent in the western and south-eastern provinces.

In early May, after fruitless jaunts to Cholula, Puebla, Atlixco, Tehuacán and Orizaba, Lawrence finally found in Chapala the place he was looking for, where he could settle long enough to write. Considering the long years of anticipation, he had very little to show so far for his more than seven months in America. As if to make up for

* Quotations from *The Plumed Serpent* are all from this edition.

lost time he now wrote at a furious pace, turning out a nearly complete 100,000-word draft of a novel he called 'Quetzalcoatl' in less than eight weeks. Apart from appeasing his own *daemon*, this creative outburst was no doubt aided by two things that Chapala itself had to offer. First, there was the immediate proximity of Lake Chapala, enormous, many-hued, untainted by modernization. Second, Chapala provided him with his first extended exposure to Mexican village life. Except at weekends, when an influx of tourists and other diversion-seekers from nearby Guadalajara invaded Chapala, it had a combination of natural beauty, isolation and a modicum of both comfort and 'native' culture that he welcomed.

With Lawrence, however, no peace could last for long. Stories of violence and bloodshed, always so prevalent an ingredient in Mexico's mystique among foreign visitors, were very much in the air at that time of political instability just a few years after the bloodiest excesses of the Mexican revolution. That Lawrence – with his mind full of the 'vast death-happening' called for by his prophetic vision of America – took these stories completely seriously, was hardly surprising; according to Witter Bynner he was 'haunted' by them. Rumours of nocturnal raids by gangs of bandits around Chapala troubled his sleep. It did not help matters when one night Lawrence woke to see a dark hand reaching into his room to unlock the door. Thereafter an armed guard was posted outside to protect the house at night. (This incident also finds its way into *The Plumed Serpent*; see Chapter VIII.)

Perhaps this growing preoccupation with violence real or imagined, along with the strain accompanying his intense creative undertaking, accounts for a series of Lawrentian tirades that occurred in Chapala. Perhaps it was something more. For even before his arrival in Chapala, Lawrence had indulged in several verbal outbursts against the Mexican Indians he encountered. Lawrence was beside himself with bewilderment and rage at the sight of the abject worship of the Indian *campesinos* at the Basílica of Guadalupe during Holy Week. Bynner quotes him as complaining that

All this is unreal ... It's all done for the show ... One minute they're groveling in the churches ... The next moment they're gadding in the streets, full of gaiety and pulque, as though they had never heard of Jesus ... They're not thinking of Christ at all ... except for a morbid pleasure in the fact that he was tortured and murdered ... They're out for blood. The

Church is foreign here. They need their own [i.e. Indian] religion, which used to let them kill *ad lib*. That was it.*

In Chapala, Lawrence was infuriated by the servile behaviour of his Indian servants and began to suspect them of covertly expressing defiance of whites such as himself by their dogged silence and reserve. Yet sometimes they were not servile enough, as when they dared to comb their hair for lice in his presence. He continually berated Bynner and Johnson for befriending the ubiquitous bootblacks, mostly Indian children, and when several ragged boys attempted to drum up business in a café where Lawrence happened to be dining he had them arrested as public nuisances. In one of his fulminations against the Indians, he went so far as to insist that they 'need a [dictator like Porfirio] Díaz and they know it ... [That] was the only kind of government they could ever understand or respect ... There must be command; there must be obedience ... These people are devils and always will be.'†

This strain of authoritarian politics and cultural elitism, so at variance with the egalitarian rhetoric of the revolution, would find its way into the visionary Mexico of *The Plumed Serpent*. That it does so is an index of Lawrence's frustration at the disparity between the actual Indians and the Indians he had borne in his imagination for so long. By all accounts his few attempts to establish 'true contact' with various Indians in Chapala and later in Oaxaca were not a success. He peremptorily concluded that for a white man to try to be friends with the Indians was useless, for 'they'll never understand. You can see it in their eyes. These people are volcanoes ... who will erupt again as they have erupted before. What seems laughter in their eyes ... isn't laughter. It's heat turning back into lava.'‡ He had counted on the Indians to 'grin [their] peon grin behind the Cross', confident in the potency of the old dark gods (*Phoenix*, p. 105). But all this indirect subversion and caste-imposed servility, this grovelling before Christian saints alternating with pulque-binges, did not fit into the picture at all. Things were not going as planned in Mexico.

* Witter Bynner, *Journey with Genius: Recollections and Reflections Concerning the D. H. Lawrences* (John Day, N.Y., 1951; Peter Neville, 1953), pp. 46–7.
† *Journey with Genius*, p. 102.
‡ *Journey with Genius*, p. 95.

As if in tacit recognition of this, Lawrence stopped writing 'Quetzalcoatl' before the story had quite reached a conclusion. The draft breaks off with the heroine, still uncommitted to Mexico and the neo-Aztec cult of Don Ramón Carrasco, making preparations to return to Europe.* On 9 or 10 July the Lawrences made their way north, planning to sail from New York to England. But as the time for departure approached, Lawrence demurred: 'I find my soul doesn't want to come to Europe', he wrote to his mother-in-law (*Letters*, II, p. 750). Frieda, intent on seeing her children after a four-year absence, sailed on 18 August. Meanwhile Lawrence, with the siren song of his Mexican Rananim still beckoning and unable in any event to face his native country just then, took the train to Los Angeles en route for the west coast of Mexico.

The second Mexican journey lasted just under two months from 25 September to 11 November 1923. On the whole it was rather uneventful. Lawrence had left his 'Quetzalcoatl' manuscript behind in New York with his agent. Ostensibly his aim on this trip was to locate a site for the Rananim colony, but he soon became too preoccupied by his wife's absence and by his work on Mollie Skinner's Australian novel (which, after his revisions, would be published in 1924 as *The Boy in the Bush*) to pay much attention to Mexico for the time being. When he was offered, gratis, a piece of land outside Guaymas near the Pacific, he turned it down: 'one feels so out of the world: like living on Mars' (*Letters*, II, p. 754). Even Chapala, where he stopped for only a day this time, had lost its magic for him. 'Somehow it becomes unreal to me now,' he told his travelling companion, Kai Gótzsche. 'The life has changed somehow, has gone dead.'† Yet despite his preoccupation he was able to muster some of the old enthusiasm at times. He wrote to Middleton Murry that 'though England may lead the world again, as you say, she's got to find a way first. She's

---

* The 479-page holograph manuscript of the Chapala version of 'Quetzalcoatl' is now housed (along with the 80-page Oaxaca version written longhand in the same copy-books) at the Humanities Research Center of the University of Texas at Austin. For permission to consult these materials I am indebted to the staff of the HRC and, in particular, to Cathy Henderson, research assistant.

† As quoted in Knud Merrild, *A Poet and Two Painters* (Routledge & Sons, 1939); reissued as *With D. H. Lawrence in New Mexico: A Memoir of D. H. Lawrence* (Barnes & Noble, N.Y., 1956), p. 340.

got to pick up a lost trail. And the end of the lost trail is here in Mexico. *Aquí está. Yo lo digo*' ('Here it is. I say so.' *Letters*, II, p. 759). A letter to another old friend and collaborator in the Rananim ideal, S. S. Koteliansky, strikes a more genuine note when Lawrence speaks of 'a sense of suspense, of waiting for something to happen – which something I want to avoid'.* On 22 November he sailed from Veracruz for England to rejoin Frieda.

So far, Lawrence's American experience had been rather tentative and disappointing, raising doubts as to the validity of his earlier vision of the role America and the Indian were to play in the regeneration of the world. The return to Europe that winter of 1923–4, coming in the middle of the American period and while his 'Quetzalcoatl' novel was incubating, proved to be an important turning point. Had this contact with his homeland been happier, it is possible that he might have aborted his plans for America and tried to come to terms directly with the inner tensions that had driven him from England in the first place. As it happened, however, the trip was an exercise in frustration, the kind of frustration which, by eliciting defensive measures, obscures rather than illuminates the real issues. The weather was unremittingly cold and gloomy; he came down with a bad cold; the landscape seemed to him crowded and 'tight' and deathly. Moreover, he repeatedly clashed with old friends, especially Murry, in whose too-solicitous behaviour he saw signs arousing his suspicion that Murry and Frieda had betrayed his trust. In recoil, Lawrence harped on America and Rananim, imploring his friends to join him in the New World. One notorious evening at the Café Royal ended with patently insincere promises to follow him, too many toasts, and an unconscious Lawrence carried home by incipient Rananim drop-outs.

Feeling more homeless than ever, Lawrence once again turned to America for the answer, determined this time not to let it elude his grasp. Accompanied by Frieda and Dorothy Brett, his lone recruit for Rananim, he returned to New Mexico in March 1924. He wanted to move down to Mexico right away to resume work on 'Quetzalcoatl', but when Mabel Dodge Luhan offered them a ranch in the mountains outside Taos they decided to stay there through the autumn.

* See *The Quest for Rananim: D. H. Lawrence's Letters to S. S. Koteliansky, 1914 to 1930*, ed. George J. Zytaruk (McGill-Queen's University Press, Montreal, 1970), p. 261.

The next few months were a time of quiescence and renewal after the turmoil of the last six. Lawrence's letters of this period do not dwell on the vacuity and tension of American life, which was so persistent a complaint during his first stay in New Mexico. Indeed he seems to have been more or less content to attend to the simple domestic tasks of the 'outside' of life – repairing the cabins at the ranch, baking bread, making furniture, riding, milking the cow, and in general absorbing the tonic atmosphere of the mountainous landscape. When he began to write again ('Pan in America', and the three New Mexican sketches later collected in *Mornings in Mexico*, 1927) he drew more heavily upon the Pueblo Indian religion than he had in his earlier efforts, rendering it with a stronger sense of identification. Visits to the Apache, Hopi and Navajo reservations clarified his understanding of the 'Indian way of consciousness' and enabled him to treat these materials, which would later be incorporated into the nascent religion of *The Plumed Serpent*, much more authoritatively. Further evidence of his intensified determination, after the calamitous winter in Europe, not only to seek but to *find* a new basis of life in America can be seen in the three long tales that Lawrence wrote during the summer and early autumn of 1924. 'The Woman Who Rode Away', 'St Mawr' and 'The Princess' all focus, like *The Plumed Serpent*, on female protagonists caught up in the conflict between submission to dark malevolent forces associated with aboriginal America and the rejection of those forces in favour of the white 'mental–spiritual consciousness'. There are many other similarities. Apparently Lawrence, who had dashed off the 'Quetzalcoatl' fragment in Chapala in less than two months, now felt the need for repeated rehearsals before he attempted to take up his American novel again. This period of imaginative and spiritual shoring-up was perhaps as much to prepare him for the renewed descent into the Mexican labyrinth as it was a preparation for rewriting 'Quetzalcoatl'. In any event it suggests how important the whole enterprise had become, and how difficult for him to carry out.

Another index of the seriousness with which Lawrence approached his task is the extensive reading he did to bolster his knowledge of Mexico. References in his letters and in the memoirs of his travelling companions indicate that by the time of his third trip to Mexico he had read such standard works as Bernal Díaz del Castillo's classic *True History of the Conquest of New Spain* (1632), Alexander von

Humboldt's *Vues des cordilleres et monumens des peuples indigenes de l' Amerique* (1810), Frances Calderón de la Barca's *Life in Mexico* (1843) and William Hickling Prescott's *History of the Conquest of Mexico* (1843), as well as the popular *Terry's Guide to Mexico* (1911), and Adolf Bandelier's quasi-historical *The Gilded Man* (1893) and *The Delight Makers* (1890). Not content with these, Lawrence took the trouble to examine several volumes of the *Anales del Museo Nacional de México*; his primary sources of information about pre-Columbian religion, however, were Lewis Spence's *Gods of Mexico* (1923) and *The Fundamental Principles of Old and New World Religions* (1901) by Zelia Nuttall, an archaeologist friend from Mexico City (and model for the character of Mrs Norris in *The Plumed Serpent*). Interestingly enough, the one book that Lawrence is known to have read about contemporary Mexico, *The Mexican People: Their Struggle for Freedom* (1914), is strongly pro-revolution; Lawrence thought enough of this work to want to meet its authors, L. Gutiérrez de Lara and Edcumb Pinchon. He also tried, without success, to meet two very important figures in the revival of Mexican indigenism: José Vasconcelos, then Minister of Education, and Manuel Gamio, regarded as the founder of modern Mexican anthropology. But if such a list is impressive evidence of Lawrence's attempt to flesh out his chimerical vision of Mexico, it should not mislead us into assuming that he had yielded that vision in favour of some form of documentary realism. Never known for fidelity to his sources, he took what he needed from them and adapted it to the apocalyptic nightmare, that 'vast death-happening', which for better or worse still presided over his imagination.

At the end of October 1924 the Lawrences and Dorothy Brett took the train to Mexico City and, after two weeks there, made their way down to Oaxaca. It was the year of a turbulent presidential succession in Mexico, marked by the bitter rebellion led by Adolfo de la Huerta;* the shock-waves had reached as far as Oaxaca, where the state governor, Manuel García Vigil, had been assassinated by the supporters of the Obregón-Calles succession the year before. The little foreign colony had been trapped in Oaxaca throughout the troubles and were full of tales of local violence to share with the newly arrived

* See note 8, Ch. 11.

visitors. Xenophobia was in the air, palpably. Lawrence wrote to Murry that 'everything is so shaky and really so confused. The Indians are queer little savages, and awful agitators pump bits of socialism over them and make everything a mess. It's really a sort of chaos' (*Letters*, II, pp. 819–20). A visit to the archaeological ruins at Mitla only reminded them of how deeply rooted the contemporary lust for 'blood and fierceness' was in Mexico's past.* One can well imagine Lawrence's state of mind as he began to rewrite 'Quetzalcoatl'.

Yet, though he would later regret his decision, Lawrence had quite deliberately chosen to come to Oaxaca. He had determined that Chapala was too much of a tourist resort to express the true spirit of Mexico. Oaxaca, once the centre of the great Zapotecan and Mixtecan civilizations, was more isolated, portentous, and above all more Indian. With his impressions of the Pueblos of the south-west still fresh in his mind, and with the additional information gained from his reading in archaeology, anthropology, and history, Lawrence must have believed that he was better prepared than before to respond to the Mexican Indian with sympathy and understanding.

The four Mexican sketches written in Oaxaca during the Christmas season (later collected, along with the New Mexican sketches, in *Mornings in Mexico*) bear ample testimony to a sincere effort to mollify his antipathy towards the Indians. Though more than once in these pieces he expresses his anger, fear and downright perplexity concerning the occult 'otherness' of the Indian, the overall attempt is to move towards acceptance of and even reconciliation with this 'other' as the correlative of one's own unconscious. Particularly in the fourth sketch, 'Market Day', Lawrence succeeds brilliantly in suggesting the nature of the new mode of consciousness that he believed could emerge from the clash between white and Indian sensibilities in America. Admittedly this new mode – which Don Ramón strives to achieve in *The Plumed Serpent* – is imperfectly realized as yet. It will come, if it comes, not from the futile attempt to collapse the Indian and white consciousnesses into one but from the capacity to 'see both ways' without being absorbed by either. This most elusive of mysteries

* See Dorothy Brett, *Lawrence and Brett: A Friendship* (Lippincott Press, Pa., 1933, p. 184; Secker & Warburg, 1933; new edition Sunstone Press, Santa Fe, 1974).

is compared with the evening star, which partakes of both night and day, moon and sun, and yet remains itself. In these Oaxacan sketches Lawrence was working out, in personal terms, the basic rationale and symbolism of the new religion that would be elaborated and ritually enacted in his novel. At the same time, however, the more deeply engaged he became by this essentially personal religion which he had identified with the Mexican Indian, the more sceptical he became about the real Indians he saw in Oaxaca, susceptible as they still were to both the Church of Rome and the secular ideology of the revolution. 'There are so many wild Indians,' he wrote at the time, 'who don't know anything about anything, except that they are told that every "rich" man is an enemy' (*Letters*, II, p. 818). Never, or not at least since the naïvely hopeful ending of *The Rainbow*, had the breach between vision and attainment been so great.

It took Lawrence about ten weeks of strenuous writing to complete 'Quetzalcoatl' (still the title he preferred; his publishers would later insist on the more accessible and 'lush' translation). The same day that he finished it he was struck down first with malaria and later with acute tuberculosis. The combination of this severe illness – which nearly took his life on this occasion, and did eventually – and the extreme exhaustion attendant upon the completion of such a massive creative effort turned him against Oaxaca for good. 'I hate the place – a let down,' he admitted. 'But the novel is finished' (*Letters*, II, p. 831). The Lawrences left Oaxaca on 24 February for Mexico City. Five weeks later, after much difficulty, they crossed the American border and returned to their ranch in New Mexico. As the summer approached Lawrence was feeling much better, but though he claimed that his 'Quetzalcoatl' novel was 'nearer to my heart than any other work of mine' (*Letters*, II, p. 844), he put off reading the galley proofs for several months. 'I daren't even look at the outside of the Ms. It cost one so much ...' (*Letters*, II, p. 833). His reluctance is as understandable in its own terms as it is portentous of the subsequent shift in his feelings towards the novel. Equally portentous with respect to his old dream of an American Rananim was his valediction to Mexico: 'Altogether I think of Mexico with a sort of nausea ... It gave me a turn that time [in Oaxaca]: doubt if I shall ever come again ... [R]eally feel I never want to see an Indian or an "aboriginee" or anything in

the savage line again.'* In the autumn the Lawrences sailed again for
Europe.

3

Many of the greatest modern literary works – among them *Ulysses*,
The Waste Land, *To the Lighthouse* and *Absalom, Absalom!* – were
greeted initially with charges of 'formlessness' and obscurantism, until
we gradually began to learn how to read them. *The Plumed
Serpent* is also a difficult work, as ambitious and, in its own way, as
audacious as the landmarks of literary modernism. But it may be that
we have not yet learned how to read it.

Part of the problem is that unlike the other works mentioned *The
Plumed Serpent* does not at first appear to be difficult at all. From the
appalling 'show' of the bull-fight to the 'ghastly' cynicism of the tea-
party and the visit to the new revolutionary frescoes at the university,
we find ourselves engaged in what seems a fairly straightforward realistic narrative, a jaundice-eyed parody of both the tourist's guidebook
and the 'classic' American tale of Adventures on the Open Road. To
be sure, the satirical impulse is largely suppressed by the time Kate
leaves the city and arrives in Sayula, but the narrative mode is still
essentially realistic. When symbols are introduced, as during Kate's
initial boat ride on the 'sperm-like' lake, they emerge naturally enough
from the expository descriptions of both place and character that
establish a correspondence between Kate's moods and the dominant
qualities of the landscape through which she moves.

Not until 'Lords of the Day and Night' (Chapter XI), when the
narrative viewpoint abruptly shifts from Kate to Don Ramón, does the
illusion of verisimilitude begin to break down. The chapter is largely
devoted to Ramón's sermon and rites of the Quetzalcoatl cult. While
these are in themselves dramatically convincing and apposite,
thematically, to some of Kate's earlier musings, because of her absence
from the scene we begin to realize that, after all, the symbols are not
contingent upon her moods and impressions but are transferable and
to some extent free-standing. Other authorial intrusions reinforce the

*Letter of 21 May 1925, to Eduardo Rendón, a Mexican acquaintance, in
Harry T. Moore, *The Priest of Love: A Life of D. H. Lawrence* (Farrar,
Straus & Giroux, N.Y., 1974, p. 403; Penguin, 1976, pp. 510–11).

suggestion that ultimately the symbolic perspective is invested in the narrative voice itself. More and more the characters begin to sound alike and to think in similar terms (even those who, like Ramón's wife Carlota, stand for opposing ideas), until the oracular, hieratic voice turns up just about anywhere. Nevertheless the mimetic veneer is retained in page after page of detailed and often brilliant description, and an episode like 'The Attack on Jamiltepec' (Chapter XIX) is as straightforwardly realistic and dramatically 'tight' as any 'action' film could wish.

This shifting and blurring of modes makes *The Plumed Serpent* elusive of classification and leads to uncertainties in its interpretation. From the beginning critics have noted the disjunction between the book's abundant esoteric symbolism and its 'realistic' narrative. The fictional events are laid in a real country whose turbulent history ostensibly offers a degree of plausibility to Lawrence's horrific tale. One reviewer, the novelist L. P. Hartley, observed that the neo-Aztec religion of Quetzalcoatl 'is highly symbolic, but the narrative is told neither romantically, allegorically nor symbolically; it is a plain realistic account of a supposed contemporary religious revolution'.* Another reviewer, Katherine Anne Porter (who spoke with the authority of one who knew Mexico well in the 1920s), offered a similar view:

All of Mexico that can be *seen* is here, evoked clearly with the fervor of things remembered out of impressions that filled the mind to bursting ... [Lawrence] makes you a radiant gift of the place ... A nation-wide political and religious movement provides the framework for a picture that does not omit a leaf, a hanging fruit, an animal, a cloud, a mood, of the visible Mexico.

Yet in the end, she goes on, 'Mexico, the Indians, the cult of the Aztec god Quetzalcoatl – the Plumed Serpent – all these are pretexts, symbols made to the measure of [Lawrence's] preoccupations.'†
To the extent that critics have agreed on anything about *The Plumed Serpent* during what is now nearly six decades since its publication, it is that these realistic and symbolic or mythopoetical elements do not cohere. Even though Lawrence had mixed modes before in other novels (notably in *The Rainbow* and *Women in Love*), it is *The Plumed Serpent*

---

* *Saturday Review*, 30 January 1926, p. 129.
†'Quetzalcoatl' (1926); rpt. in *The Collected Essays and Occasional Writings of Katherine Anne Porter* Delacorte, N.Y., 1970), p. 421.

that has been singled out as, in the words of Lawrence's biographer Harry T. Moore, 'that tremendous volcano of a failure', comparable to 'an opera with magnificent music and a ridiculous libretto'.*

Of course the novel has had its defenders. It is revealing, however, that those who have defended it have generally done so by stressing its symbolic, mythic and religious elements as foremost. William York Tindall, for instance, who believes *The Plumed Serpent* to be Lawrence's 'most brilliant' work of fiction, has argued that the novel amounts to 'a great metaphor for a feeling about reality'. As such it must be judged, says Tindall, less on the merits of its characters than for its intricate pattern of symbols and images which embody the theme of rebirth occurring on the sexual, religious and political levels simultaneously. 'More like a tapestry or a painted window than like the novels we are used to, it triumphs by arrangements of shape and color. Not people but functions, the characters exist like figures in the carpet only by relationship with other parts of the great design.'† A few others have followed suit in subordinating character to a mythic design which offers probably the most fully elaborated expression of Lawrence's religious vision. But most critics have been less willing to ignore the mimetic or realistic elements of the novel, and have found these operating at the expense of the purported religious 'rebirth'.

If Lawrence, who revised his *Studies in Classic American Literature* while in New Mexico, imagined he could take the same sort of liberties with representational modes that Poe and Hawthorne and Melville did, the critical evidence to date suggests that he was in error. For all that Lawrence called *The Plumed Serpent* his 'American novel', it has usually been read as an English novel – or rather as a novel that fails to be English. Unlike the American 'romance-novel', the English novel is firmly rooted in the realistic tradition established by its great nineteenth-century practitioners – Austen, Dickens, Eliot, Meredith, Hardy and James. The modern English novelist departs from such formidable precedents at his peril, and if he does so he would be well advised to warn the reader in some way that the conventions of realism shall not obtain. This Lawrence failed to do in *The Plumed*

* *'The Plumed Serpent: Vision and Language', in D. H. Lawrence: A Collection of Critical Essays*, ed. Mark Spilka (Prentice-Hall, N.J., 1963), pp. 67, 71.

† 'Introduction' to *The Plumed Serpent* (Knopf, N.Y., 1951), pp. xiv, ix.

Serpent. Kate's decision to move to Sayula, for instance, is 'realistically' motivated, notwithstanding the mythic trappings: she is forty; her life in Europe is irretrievably behind her and part of a now-dead phase; Mexico City has left her depressed and in need of a change of scene; the newspaper article about Quetzalcoatl's return to Mexico seems to promise the new start she so desperately seeks (and not a little fears). In practical terms, a novel's mythic design requires only that the fictional events seem *possible*, so that their underlying truth may be entertained; but a fundamental convention of realistic narrative is that the rendering of fictional events be *probable*, the standard of probability being of course the world of actuality. Early on, Lawrence establishes a pattern in which Kate's motivations are explored with equal attention to their psychological plausibility and to her role in the developing symbolic scheme. Since another convention of realistic narrative is consistency, this carefully embedded pattern of motivation gives rise to the expectation that it will recur whenever Kate is faced with an important decision. But the closer Kate comes to immersion in 'a sea of living blood', represented by her growing involvement in the cult of Quetzalcoatl, the less plausible her actions become. For that matter, plausibility itself becomes a meaningless basis for judgement. The probability of realistic motivation yields to the sheer possibility of romance, and character is subsumed by its 'function' in the larger mythic scheme.

Now, if immersion in a sea of living blood were truly *felt* to be the vital 'clue' for both Kate and the civilisation that she represents, as Lawrence repeatedly asserts it to be near the end, this rupture in the logic of narrative causation might not have proved so troublesome. Lawrence is, after all, not to be confused with Henry James. But so unnerved was Lawrence by the failure of the real Mexico, and the real 'aboriginee', to fall into line with his visionary programme of regeneration that he resorted to over-elaborating the vision, as if to suppress his own doubts. As a result the schema became an end in itself, static and ponderous, negating the very things it was designed to celebrate. In an essay written during the summer after his bitter departure from Oaxaca, Lawrence offered what in retrospect seems an admission of his error in the novel:

We know, really, that we can't have life for the asking, nor find it by seeking, nor get it by striving. The river flows into us from behind and below.

We must turn our backs to it, and go ahead. The faster we go ahead, the stronger the river rushes into us. The moment we turn round to embrace the river of life, it ebbs away, and we see nothing but a stony fiumara.*

But in *The Plumed Serpent*, instead of the free and spontaneous realization of this life-flow we have an almost hysterical seeking after it in the form of an institutional religion fully armed with rifles as well as rites. Instead of an intuitive apprehension of sacral mystery we have pat formulae that dissect and rationalize and calcify the mystery, embalming it in the most florid and dogmatic rhetoric. Here is an example from Chapter XXI:

'A man shall take the wine of his spirit and the blood of his heart, the oil of his belly and the seed of his loins, and offer them first to the Morning Star,' said Ramón, in a loud voice, turning to the people.

Four men came to him. One put a blue crown with the bird on his brow, one put a red belt round his breast, another put a yellow belt round his middle, and the last fastened a white belt round his loins. Then the first one pressed a small glass bowl to Ramón's brow, and in the bowl was white liquid like bright water. The next touched a bowl to the breast, and the red shook in the bowl. At the navel the man touched a bowl with yellow fluid, and at the loins a bowl with something dark. They held them all to the light.

Then one by one they poured them into a silver mixing-bowl that Ramón held between his hands.

'For save the Unknown God pours His Spirit over my head and fire into my heart, and sends His power like a fountain of oil into my belly, and His lightning like a hot spring into my loins, I am not. I am nothing. I am a dead gourd.

'And save I take the wine of my spirit and the red of my heart, the strength of my belly and the power of my loins, and mingle them all together, and kindle them to the Morning Star, I betray my body, I betray my soul, I betray my spirit and my God who is Unknown.

'Fourfold is man. But the star is one star. And one man is but one star.'

He took the silver mixing-bowl and slowly circled it between his hands, in the act of mixing.

Then he turned his back to the people, and lifted the bowl high up, between his hands, as if offering it to the image.

Then suddenly he threw the contents of the bowl into the altar fire.

There was a soft puff of explosion, a blue flame leaped high into the air, followed by a yellow flame, and then a rose-red smoke. In three successive instants the faces of the men inside the chancel were lit bluish, then gold, then

*'Him With His Tail in His Mouth' (1925), rpt. in *Phoenix II: Uncollected, Unpublished and Other Prose Works*, ed. Warren Roberts and Harry T. Moore (Viking, N.Y. 1970), p. 429.

dusky red. And in the same moment Ramón had turned to the people and shot up his hand.

'Salute Quetzalcoatl!' ... (pp. 377–8)

Everything in the passage is forced, willed, mechanical – in short, precisely those qualities of the white 'mental–spiritual consciousness' that Lawrence so abhorred. Even the star, a key symbol of the new 'fusion' that Ramón seeks in the novel, is here reduced to a vaudeville trick, merely part of the ersatz religious algebra. And the algebra is contrived so as to apply to revolutionary politics and to sexual relations as well as to the conquering religion of Quetzalcoatl.

Only preoccupation with such an equation, in which individual character is forced to subserve design, can account for Kate's inhuman response to the public executions ritually performed by 'the living Huitzilopochtli' and sanctioned by 'the living Quetzalcoatl'. When Malintzi/Kate

thought of [Cipriano] and his soldiers ... when she remembered his stabbing the three helpless peons, she thought: Why should I judge him? He is of the gods. And when he comes to me he lays his pure, quick flame to mine, and every time I am a young girl again, and every time he takes the flower of my virginity, and I his. It leaves me insouciant like a young girl. What do I care if he kills people? His flame is young and clean. He is Huitzilopochtli, and I am Malintzi. (pp. 429–30)

In this way *The Plumed Serpent* offers us what amounts to a perfect Lawrentian hell but persists in celebrating it as if it were the threshold of paradise.

Indeed, the radical tension between the novel's overt mythic design and the tacit subversion of it, along with the erratic mixture of representational modes, may on consideration offer an important clue to this book's strange power and fascination. The tale is partly parodistic travelogue, and partly mythic quest-journey; partly novel of ideas (or what Lawrence once aptly termed 'thought-adventure'), and partly gothic romance; partly reactionary political diatribe, partly hagiography. The list could go on.

How should we classify such an unstable, hybrid creation? There is no easy answer, but in the last analysis *The Plumed Serpent* is perhaps best understood as a novel of sensibility. The sensibility is none other than Lawrence's, as variously refracted through Kate, Ramón, the Mexican landscape (its power and variety greater than any single character's), and the narrative voice itself. The moods of this composite sensibility are numerous and mercurial to say the least. A few representative samples of how the moods are manifested will give some idea of their range: the horror and outrage provoked by the bull-fight; the utter banality of the suburban tea-party in the second chapter; the quiet humour of 'Casa de las Cuentas' (Chapter IX); the hysterical crescendo of grandiose dogmatism in Chapters XX–XXIV; the muted lyricism of the first half of the concluding chapter, with its almost Keatsean evocation of 'autumnal purity and lull'. Yet volatile as these moods are, they tend to follow a recurrent sequence (especially when Kate is before us), moving from a jeering isolation to a sense of oppressiveness, to dread of violence, to lingering curiosity, to partial identification with and tentative acceptance of the 'dark' mystery, and so back to jeering isolation. With Ramón the range of moods is still more extreme and erratic; his fatigue and disenchantment at the end are particularly revealing of Lawrence on the brink of collapse and retreat. Unquestionably the most eloquent medium for Lawrence's modulating tones of voice in the novel is the landscape. The Mexican countryside can be awesomely beautiful and enticing, yet for that very reason the indwelling spirit of place is all the more cruel and punishing:

... the undertone was like the low angry, snarling purring of some jaguar spotted with night. There was a ponderous, down-pressing weight upon the spirit: the great folds of the dragon of the Aztecs ... winding around one and weighing down the soul. And on the bright sunshine was a dark stream of an angry, impotent blood, and the flowers seemed to have their roots in spilt blood. (p. 81–2)

It should be evident that the pervasive ambiguities in the novel correspond significantly to Lawrence's own troubled responses to Mexico. He had probed far beneath the exotic surface into Mexico's bewildering contradictions. At the same time he had plunged headlong into the dark mysteries of the 'inner life', which, as we have seen, Mexico came to represent for him. In each case the *daemon* within revealed itself as both malevolent and beatific, destructive and creative. Submersion in the 'dark blood' could lead as easily to wholesale murder in the name of religion as to the vital and spontaneous relations between men and women. It is scarcely surprising that Lawrence was unable to reconcile such stark ambiguities in *The Plumed Serpent*. But one must doubt whether such reconciliation, in the end, was actually desirable. Not even the world of romance would seem to hold out *that* possibility. But the major benefit of his courageous attempt was that his 'volcanic' failure revealed, decisively, the disturbing implications of those ambiguities which had so vexed him ever since the war. What W. B. Yeats once said of man – that he can embody truth without actually 'knowing' it – comes close to describing the curious state of affairs in Lawrence's American novel.

In *The Plumed Serpent*, then, Lawrence created out of his inner divisions a dualistic image, the infernal paradise,* and identified it with Mexico. Emerging from the strife between radical contraries, this image fails to resolve them. There is no 'marriage' of heaven and hell here, but there can be no divorce between them either: they coexist, perpetually at war, each dependent upon the opposition that defines them both. Such was the potency of that image, and the resonance of the mystique of Mexico itself, that it would be difficult for writers who subsequently visited the land to react to it without reference to this defining symbol. Writers as different as Aldous Huxley, Graham Greene and Malcolm Lowry all came to Mexico in the 1930s with expectations conditioned at least in part by what Lawrence had said was there. Whatever their own concerns as individuals and their feelings about Lawrence and his work, their own writings about Mexico bear witness to the lasting power and the adaptability of Lawrence's *daemonic*/paradisal vision of Mexico. As for Lawrence himself, just as he had repudiated Mexico after his near-fatal departure, he gradually turned against his novel and the extremes to which it had inexorably led him. In 1928 he wrote to Witter Bynner about *The Plumed Serpent* in terms that strongly suggest what he had learned from his encounter with the only Rananim he would ever know:

The hero is obsolete, and the leader of men is a back number. After all, at the back of the hero is the militant ideal ... We're sort of sick of all forms of

---

* The phrase derives from Malcolm Lowry's letter to his publisher (dated 2 January 1946) defending the choice of setting in *Under the Volcano*: 'We can see [Mexico] as the world itself, or the Garden of Eden, the Tower of Babel and indeed anything else we please. It is paradisal: it is unquestionably infernal. It is, in fact, Mexico.' See *Selected Letters of Malcolm Lowry*, eds. Harvey Breit and Margerie Bonner Lowry (Lippincott Press, N.Y., 1965; Jonathan Cape, 1967), p. 67.

militarism and militantism ... [and] the leader-cum-follower relationship is a bore. And the new relationship will be some sort of tenderness, sensitive, between men and men and men and women, and not the one up one down, lead on I follow, *ich dien* sort of business. (*Letters*, II, p. 1045)

Post-America works such as *The Man Who Died, The Virgin and the Gipsy,* and *Lady Chatterley's Lover* demonstrate that Lawrence's imagination subsequently assumed a different direction, one that celebrated 'tenderness' in personal relations and no longer depended upon grandiose religio-political schemes for world regeneration. In the ancient Etruscans Lawrence discovered a more humane embodiment of the 'dark-blood consciousness' without the vicious elements that haunt *The Plumed Serpent*. In general these late efforts represent a return to materials more congenial to the author of *Sons and Lovers* and *The Rainbow*, and while none quite matches his earlier achievements, taken together they offer evidence of a self-recovery of almost heroic magnitude, coming as it did in the face of imminent death. Yet for this to occur, first it was necessary for Lawrence to live through the Mexican nightmare that finally purged him of the deathly allure of the old American dream. *The Plumed Serpent* is that nightmare.

A NOTE ON THE TEXT

The present text is based on that of the first British edition, published by Martin Secker in January 1926. That edition was printed from the typescript corrected by Lawrence in June 1925 while he was at Kiowa Ranch in New Mexico. Lawrence corrected the proofs in October after returning to England. The corrected proofs are at the University of Texas, along with the manuscripts (see note to p. 18 of the Introduction).

The first American edition was published in January 1926 by Alfred A. Knopf. This edition, though set from the corrected galleys which Secker had sent to Knopf, differs from the Secker first edition in numerous (usually, but not always, minor) ways and is in general less reliable. *The Plumed Serpent* was reprinted before Lawrence's death by William Heinemann in England and Knopf in America, but Lawrence did not make corrections in these editions. Penguin Books first published their edition of *The Plumed Serpent* in 1950.

The misprints which Lawrence overlooked in the first British edition, and his occasionally erroneous Spanish grammar and spelling, have been corrected in this Penguin edition. In a very few instances I have adapted readings from the manuscript of the second or Oaxaca version of the novel.

ACKNOWLEDGEMENTS

I wish to acknowledge with thanks the assistance and support of the following persons: Keith Sagar, Ross Parmenter, L. D. Clark, Wayne Siewert, Donald McFarlan, Kate Hamilton, Kenneth Lavender, Daniel Jaeckle, Paul Carlson, Martha K. Piper, Christine Matyear, and Trudy Chatelle. I am grateful also to Leslie Walker for taking on the tedious but important task of collating, and to her team of helpers: Jill Jaeckle, Neva Carlson, Manuel Zamora, Barbara Moeller, Laura Matyear, Jean McCord, Nancy Bandy, Diane Schadel, Pamela Briones, Michael Megahan, Jo Campbell, Phyllis Malone, and Sherry Culberson.

THE PLUMED SERPENT
(Quetzalcoatl)

Contents

Contents

Beginnings of a Bull-fight

I T was the Sunday after Easter, and the last bull-fight of the season in Mexico City. Four special bulls had been brought over from Spain for the occasion, since Spanish bulls are more fiery than Mexican. Perhaps it is the altitude, perhaps just the spirit of the western Continent which is to blame for the lack of 'pep', as Owen[1] put it, in the native animal.

Although Owen, who was a great socialist, disapproved of bull-fights, 'We have never seen one. We shall have to go,' he said.

'Oh yes, I think we must see it,' said Kate.

'And it's our last chance,' said Owen.

Away he rushed to the place where they sold tickets, to book seats, and Kate went with him. As she came into the street, her heart sank. It was as if some little person inside her were sulking and resisting. Neither she nor Owen spoke much Spanish, there was a fluster at the ticket place, and an unpleasant individual came forward to talk American for them.

It was obvious they ought to buy tickets for the 'Shade'. But they wanted to economise, and Owen said he preferred to sit among the crowd, therefore, against the resistance of the ticket man and the on-lookers, they bought reserved seats in the 'Sun'.

The show was on Sunday afternoon. All the tram-cars and the frightful little Ford omnibuses called *camiones* were labelled *Toreo*, and were surging away towards Chapultepec.[2] Kate felt that sudden dark feeling, that she didn't want to go.

'I'm not very keen on going,' she said to Owen.

'Oh, but why not? I don't believe in them on principle, but we've never seen one, so we shall *have* to go.'

Owen was an American, Kate was Irish. 'Never having seen one' meant 'having to go'. But it was American logic rather than Irish, and Kate only let herself be overcome.

Villiers[3] of course was keen. But then he too was American, and he too had never seen one, and being younger, more than anybody he *had* to go.

They got into a Ford taxi and went. The busted car careered away down the wide dismal street of asphalt and stone and Sunday dreariness. Stone buildings in Mexico have a peculiar hard, dry dreariness.

The taxi drew up in a side street under the big iron scaffolding of the stadium. In the gutters, rather lousy men were selling pulque and sweets, cakes, fruit, and greasy food. Crazy motor-cars rushed up and hobbled away. Little soldiers in washed-out cotton uniforms, pinky drab, hung around an entrance. Above all loomed the network iron frame of the huge, ugly stadium.

Kate felt she was going to prison. But Owen excitedly surged to the entrance that corresponded to his ticket. In the depths of him, he too didn't want to go. But he was a born American, and if anything was on show, he had to see it. That was 'Life'.

The man who took the tickets at the entrance, suddenly, as they were passing in, stood in front of Owen, put both his hands on Owen's chest and pawed down the front of Owen's body. Owen started, bridled, transfixed for a moment. The fellow stood aside. Kate remained petrified.

Then Owen jerked into a smiling composure as the man waved them on. 'Feeling for fire-arms!' he said, rolling his eyes with pleased excitement at Kate.

But she had not got over the shock of horror, fearing the fellow might paw her.

They emerged out of a tunnel in the hollow of the concrete-and-iron amphitheatre. A real gutter-lout came to look at their counterslips, to see which seats they had booked. He jerked his head downwards, and slouched off. Now Kate knew she was in a trap – a big concrete beetle trap.

They dropped down the concrete steps till they were only three tiers from the bottom. That was their row. They were to sit on the concrete, with a loop of thick iron between each numbered seat. This was a reserved place in the 'Sun'.

Kate sat gingerly between her two iron loops, and looked vaguely around.

'I think it's thrilling!' she said.

Like most modern people, she had a will-to-happiness.

'Isn't it thrilling,' cried Owen, whose will-to-happiness was almost a mania. 'Don't you think so, Bud?'

'Why, yes, I think it may be,' said Villiers, non-committal.

But then Villiers was young, he was only over twenty, while Owen was over forty. The younger generation calculates its 'happiness' in a more business-like fashion. Villiers was out after a thrill, but he wasn't going to say he'd got one till he'd got it. Kate and Owen – Kate was also nearly forty – must enthuse a thrill, out of a sort of politeness to the great Show-man, Providence.

'Look here!' said Owen. 'Supposing we try to protect our extremity on this concrete –' and thoughtfully he folded his rain-coat and laid it along the concrete ledge so that both he and Kate could sit on it.

They sat and gazed around. They were early. Patches of people mottled the concrete slope opposite, like eruptions. The ring just below was vacant, neatly sanded; and above the ring, on the encircling concrete, great advertisements for hats, with a picture of a city-man's straw hat, and advertisements for spectacles, with pairs of spectacles supinely folded, glared and shouted.

'Where is the "Shade" then?' said Owen, twisting his neck.

At the top of the amphitheatre, near the sky, were concrete boxes. This was the 'Shade', where anybody who was anything sat.

'Oh but,' said Kate, 'I don't want to be perched right up there, so far away.'

'Why no!' said Owen. 'We're much better where we are, in our "Sun", which isn't going to shine a great deal after all.'

The sky was cloudy, preparing for the rainy season.

It was nearly three o'clock in the afternoon, and the crowd was filling in, but still only occupied patches of the bare concrete. The lower tiers were reserved, so the bulk of the people sat in the mid-way levels, and gentry like our trio were more or less isolated.

But the audience was already a mob, mostly of fattish town men in black tight suits and little straw hats, and a mixing-in of the dark-faced labourers in big hats. The men in black suits were probably employees and clerks and factory hands. Some had brought their women, in sky-blue chiffon with brown chiffon hats and faces powdered to look like white marshmallows. Some were families with two or three children.

The fun began. The game was to snatch the hard straw hat off some fellow's head, and send it skimming away down the slope of humanity, where some smart bounder down below would catch it and send it skimming across in another direction. There were shouts of jeering pleasure from the mass, which rose almost to a yell as seven straw hats were skimming, meteor-like, at one moment across the slope of people.

'Look at that!' said Owen. 'Isn't that fun!'

'No,' said Kate, her little *alter ego* speaking out for once, in spite of her will-to-happiness. 'No, I don't like it. I really hate common people.'

As a socialist, Owen disapproved, and as a happy man, he was disconcerted. Because his own real self, as far as he had any left, hated common rowdiness just as much as Kate did.

'It's awfully smart though!' he said, trying to laugh in sympathy with the mob. 'There now, see that!'

'Yes, it's quite smart, but I'm glad it's not my hat,' said Villiers.

'Oh, it's all in the game,' said Owen largely.

But he was uneasy. He was wearing a big straw hat of native make, conspicuous in the comparative isolation of the lower tiers. After a lot of fidgeting, he took off his hat and put it on his knees. But unfortunately he had a very definitely bald spot on a sunburnt head.

Behind, above, sat a dense patch of people in the unreserved section. Already they were throwing things. *Bum!* came an orange, aimed at Owen's bald spot, and hitting him on the shoulder. He glared round rather ineffectually through his big shell spectacles.

'I'd keep my hat on if I were you,' said the cold voice of Villiers.

'Yes, I think perhaps it's wiser,' said Owen, with assumed nonchalance, putting on his hat again.

Whereupon a banana skin rattled on Villiers' tidy and lady-like little panama. He glared round coldly, like a bird that would stab with its beak if it got the chance, but which would fly away at the first real menace.

'How I detest them!' said Kate.

A diversion was created by the entrance, opposite, of the military bands, with their silver and brass instruments under their arms. There were three sets. The chief band climbed and sat on the right, in the big bare tract of concrete reserved for the Authorities. These musicians wore dark grey uniforms trimmed with rose colour, and made Kate feel almost reassured, as if it were Italy and not Mexico City. A silver band in pale buff uniforms sat opposite our party, high up across the hollow distance, and still a third 'música' threaded away to the left, on the remote scattered hillside of the amphitheatre. The newspapers had said that the President would attend. But the Presidents are scarce at bull-fights in Mexico, nowadays.

There sat the bands, in as much pomp as they could muster, but they did not begin to play. Great crowds now patched the slopes, but there were still bare tracts, especially in the Authorities' section. Only a little distance above Kate's row was a mass of people, as it were impending; a very uncomfortable sensation.

It was three o'clock, and the crowds had a new diversion. The bands, due to strike up at three, still sat there in lordly fashion, sounding not a note.

'La música! La música!' shouted the mob, with the voice of mob authority. They were the People, and the revolutions had been their revolutions, and they had won them all. The bands were their bands, present for their amusement.

But the bands were military bands, and it was the army which had won all the revolutions. So the revolutions were *their* revolutions, and they were present for their own glory alone.

Música pagada toca mal tono.[4]

Spasmodically, the insolent yelling of the mob rose and subsided. *La música! La música!* The shout became brutal and violent. Kate always remembered it. *La música!* The band peacocked its nonchalance. The shouting was a great yell: the degenerate mob of Mexico City![5]

At length, at its own leisure, the band in grey with dark rose facings struck up: crisp, martial, smart.

'That's fine!' said Owen. 'But that's really good! And it's the first time I've heard a good band in Mexico, a band with any backbone.'

The music was smart, but it was brief. The band seemed scarcely to have started, when the piece was over. The musicians took their instruments from their mouths with a gesture of dismissal. They played just to say they'd played, making it as short as possible.

Música pagada toca mal tono.

There was a ragged interval, then the silver band piped up. And at last it was half-past three, or more.

Whereupon, at some given signal, the masses in the middle, unreserved seats, suddenly burst and rushed down on to the lowest, reserved seats. It was a crash like a burst reservoir, and the populace in black Sunday suits poured down round and about our astonished, frightened trio. And in two minutes it was over. Without any pushing or shoving. Everybody careful, as far as possible, not to touch anybody else. You don't elbow your neighbour if he's got a pistol on his hip and a knife at his belly. So all the seats in the lower tiers filled in one rush, like the flowing of water.

Kate now sat among the crowd. But her seat, fortunately, was above one of the track-ways that went round the arena, so at least she would not have anybody sitting between her knees.

Men went uneasily back and forth along this gangway past the feet, wanting to get in next their friends, but never venturing to ask. Three seats away, on the same row, sat a Polish bolshevist fellow who had met Owen. He leaned over and asked the Mexican next to Owen if he might change seats with him. 'No,' said the Mexican. 'I'll sit in my own seat.'

'*Muy bien, Señor, muy bien!*'[6] said the Pole.

The show did not begin, and men like lost mongrels still prowled back and forth on the track that was next step down from Kate's feet. They began to take advantage of the ledge on which rested the feet of our party, to squat there.

Down sat a heavy fellow, plumb between Owen's knees.

'I hope they won't sit on *my* feet,' said Kate anxiously.

'We won't let them,' said Villiers, with bird-like decision. 'Why don't you shove him off, Owen? Shove him off.'

And Villiers glared at the Mexican fellow ensconced between Owen's legs. Owen flushed, and laughed uncomfortably. He was not good at shoving people off. The Mexican began to look round at the three angry white people.

And in another moment, another fat Mexican in a black suit and a little black hat was lowering himself into Villiers' foot-space. But Villiers was too quick for him. He quickly brought his feet together under the man's sinking posterior, so the individual subsided uncomfortably on to a pair of boots, and at the same time felt a hand shoving him quietly but determinedly on the shoulder.

'No!' Villiers was saying in good American. 'This place is for my *feet*! Get off! You get off!'

And he continued, quietly but very emphatically, to push the Mexican's shoulder, to remove him.

The Mexican half raised himself, and looked round murderously at Villiers. Physical violence was being offered, and the only retort was death. But the young American's face was so cold and abstract, only the eyes showing a primitive, bird-like fire, that the Mexican was non-plussed. And Kate's eyes were blazing with Irish contempt.

The fellow struggled with his Mexican city-bred inferiority complex. He muttered an explanation in Spanish that he was only sitting there for a moment, till he could join his friends – waving his hand towards a lower tier. Villiers did not understand a word, but he reiterated:

'I don't care what it is. This place is for my *feet*, and you don't sit there.'

Oh, home of liberty! Oh, land of the free! Which of these two men was to win in the struggle for conflicting liberty? Was the fat fellow free to sit between Villiers' feet, or was Villiers free to keep his foot-space?

There are all sorts of inferiority complex, and the city Mexican has a very strong sort, that makes him all the more aggressive, once it is roused. Therefore the intruder lowered his posterior with a heavy, sudden bounce on Villiers' feet, and Villiers, out of very distaste, had had to extricate his feet from such a compression. The young man's face went white at the nostrils, and his eyes took on that bright abstract look of pure democratic anger. He pushed the fat shoulders more decisively, repeating:

'Go away! Go away! You're not to *sit* there.'

The Mexican, on his own ground, and heavy on his own base, let himself be shoved, oblivious.

'Insolence!' said Kate loudly. 'Insolence!'

She glared at the fat back in the shoddily-fitting black coat, which looked as if a woman dressmaker had made it, with loathing. How could any man's coat-collar look so home-made, so *en famille*!

Villiers remained with a fixed, abstract look on his thin face, rather like a death's head. All his American will was summoned up, the bald eagle of the north bristling in every feather. The fellow *should not* sit there. – But how to remove him?

The young man sat tense with will to annihilate his beetle-like intruder, and Kate used all her Irish malice to help him.

'Don't you wonder who was his tailor?' she asked, with a flicker in her voice.

Villiers looked at the femalish black coat of the Mexican, and made an arch grimace at Kate.

'I should say he hadn't one. Perhaps did it himself.'

'Very likely!' Kate laughed venomously.

It was too much. The man got up and betook himself, rather diminished, to another spot.

'Triumph!' said Kate. 'Can't you do the same, Owen?'

Owen laughed uncomfortably, glançing down at the man between his knees as he might glance at a dog with rabies, when it had its back to him.

'Apparently not yet, unfortunately,' he said, with some constraint, turning his nose away again from the Mexican, who was using him as a sort of chair-back.

There was an exclamation. Two horsemen in gay uniforms[7] and bearing long staffs had suddenly ridden into the ring. They went round the arena, then took up their posts, sentry-wise, on either side the tunnel entrance through which they had come in.

In marched a little column of four toreadors[8] wearing tight uniforms plastered with silver embroidery. They divided, and marched smartly in opposite directions, two and two, around the ring, till they came to the place facing the section of the Authorities, where they made their salute.

So this was a bull-fight! Kate already felt a chill of disgust.

In the seats of the Authorities were very few people, and certainly no sparkling ladies in high tortoise-shell combs and lace mantillas. A few common-looking people, bourgeois with not much taste, and a couple of officers in uniform. The President had not come.

There was no glamour, no charm. A few commonplace people in an expanse of concrete were the elect, and below, four grotesque and effeminate looking fellows in tight, ornate clothes were the heroes. With their rather fat posteriors and their squiffs of pigtails and their clean-shaven faces, they looked like eunuchs, or women in tight pants, these precious toreadors.

The last of Kate's illusions concerning bull-fights came down with a flop. These were the darlings of the mob? These were the gallant toreadors! Gallant? Just about as gallant as assistants in a butcher's shop. Lady-killers? Ugh!

There was an Ah! of satisfaction from the mob. Into the ring suddenly rushed a smallish, dun-coloured bull with long flourishing horns. He ran out, blindly, as if from the dark, probably thinking that now he was free. Then he stopped short, seeing he was not free, but surrounded in an unknown way. He was utterly at a loss.

A toreador came forward and switched out a pink cloak like a fan not far from the bull's nose. The bull gave a playful little prance, neat and pretty, and charged mildly on the cloak. The toreador switched the cloak over the animal's head, and the neat little bull trotted on round the ring, looking for a way to get out.

Seeing the wooden barrier around the arena, finding he was able to look over it, he thought he might as well take the leap. So over he went into the corridor or passage-way which circled the ring, and in which stood the servants of the arena.

Just as nimbly, these servants vaulted over the barrier into the arena, that was now bull-less.

The bull in the gangway trotted inquiringly round till he came to an opening on to the arena again. So back he trotted into the ring.

And back into the gangway vaulted the servants, where they stood again to look on.

The bull trotted waveringly and somewhat irritated. The toreadors waved their cloaks at him, and he swerved on. Till his vague course took him to where one of the horsemen with lances sat motionless on his horse.

Instantly, in a pang of alarm, Kate noticed that the horse was thickly blindfolded with a black cloth. Yes, and so was the horse on which sat the other picador.

The bull trotted suspiciously up to the motionless horse bearing the rider with the long pole; a lean old horse that would never move till Doomsday, unless someone shoved it.

Oh shades of Don Quixote![9] Oh four Spanish horsemen of the Apocalypse![10] This was surely one of them.

The picador pulled his feeble horse round slowly, to face the bull, and slowly he leaned forward and shoved his lance-point into the bull's shoulder. The bull, as if the horse were a great wasp that had stung him deep, suddenly lowered his head in a jerk of surprise and lifted his horns straight up into the horse's abdomen.[11] And without more ado, over went horse and rider, like a tottering monument upset.

The rider scrambled from under the horse and went running away with his lance. The old horse, in complete dazed amazement, struggled to rise, as if overcome with dumb incomprehension. And the bull, with a red place on his shoulder welling a trickle of dark blood, stood looking around in equally hopeless amazement.

But the wound was hurting. He saw the queer sight of the horse half reared from the ground, trying to get to its feet. And he smelled blood and bowels.

So rather vaguely, as if not quite knowing what he ought to do, the bull once more lowered his head and pushed his sharp, flourishing horns in the horse's belly, working them up and down inside there with a sort of vague satisfaction.

Kate had never been taken so completely by surprise in all her life. She had still cherished some idea of a gallant show. And before she knew where she was, she was watching a bull whose shoulders trickled blood goring his horns up and down inside the belly of a prostrate and feebly plunging old horse.

The shock almost overpowered her. She had come for a gallant show. This she had paid to see. Human cowardice and beastliness, a smell of blood, a nauseous whiff of bursten bowels! She turned her face away.

When she looked again, it was to see the horse feebly and dazedly walking out of the ring, with a great ball of its own entrails hanging out of its abdomen and swinging reddish against its own legs as it automatically moved.

And once more, the shock of amazement almost made her lose consciousness. She heard the confused small applause of amusement from the mob. And that Pole, to whom Owen had introduced her, leaned over and said to her, in horrible English:

'Now, Miss Leslie, you are seeing Life! Now you will have something to write about, in your letters to England.'

She looked at his unwholesome face in complete repulsion, and wished Owen would not introduce her to such sordid individuals.

She looked at Owen. His nose had a sharp look, like a little boy who may make himself sick, but who is watching at the shambles with all his eyes, knowing it is forbidden.

Villiers, the younger generation, looked intense and abstract, getting the sensation. He would not even feel sick. He was just getting the thrill of it, without emotion, coldly and scientifically, but very intent.

And Kate felt a real pang of hatred against this Americanism which is coldly and unscrupulously sensational.

'Why doesn't the horse move? Why doesn't it run away from the bull?' she asked in repelled amazement, of Owen.

Owen cleared his throat.

'Didn't you see? It was blindfolded,' he said.

'But can't it *smell* the bull?' she asked.

'Apparently not. – They bring the old wrecks here to finish them off. – I know it's awful, but it's part of the game.'

How Kate hated phrases like 'part of the game'. What do they mean, anyhow! She felt utterly humiliated, crushed by a sense of human indecency, cowardice of two-legged humanity. In this 'brave' show she felt nothing but reeking cowardice. Her breeding and her natural pride were outraged.

The ring servants had cleaned away the mess and spread new sand. The toreadors were playing with the bull, unfurling their foolish cloaks at arm's length. And the animal, with the red sore running on his shoulder, foolishly capered and ran from one rag to the other, here and there.

For the first time, a bull seemed to her a fool. She had always been afraid of bulls, fear tempered with reverence of the great Mithraic beast.[12] And now she saw how stupid he was, in spite of his long horns and his massive maleness. Blindly and stupidly he ran at the rag, each time, and the toreadors skipped like fat-hipped girls showing off. Probably it needed skill and courage, but it *looked* silly.

Blindly and foolishly the bull ran ducking its horns each time at the rag, just because the rag fluttered.

'Run at the *men*, idiot!' said Kate aloud, in her overwrought impatience. 'Run at the men, not at the cloaks.'

'They never do, isn't it curious!' replied Villiers, with cool scientific interest. 'They say no toreador will face a cow, because a cow always goes for *him* instead of the cloak. If a bull did that there'd be no bull-fights. Imagine it!'

She was bored now. The nimbleness and the skipping tricks of the toreadors bored her. Even when one of the banderilleros reared himself on tiptoe, his plump posterior much in evidence, and from his erectness pushed two razor-sharp darts with frills at the top into the bull's shoulder, neatly and smartly, Kate felt no admiration. One of the darts fell out, anyway, and the bull ran on with the other swinging and waggling in another bleeding place.

The bull now wanted to get away, really. He leaped the fence again, quickly, into the attendants' gangway. The attendants vaulted over into the arena. The bull trotted in the corridor, then nicely leaped back. The attendants vaulted once more into the corridor. The bull trotted round the arena, ignoring the toreadors, and leaped once more into the gangway. Over vaulted the attendants.

Kate was beginning to be amused, now that the mongrel men were skipping for safety.

The bull was in the ring again, running from cloak to cloak, foolishly. A banderillero was getting ready with two more darts. But first another picador put nobly forward on his blindfolded old horse. The bull ignored this little lot too, and trotted away again, as if all the time looking for something, excitedly looking for something. He stood still and excitedly pawed the ground, as if he wanted something. A toreador advanced and swung a cloak. Up pranced the bull, tail in air, and with a prancing bound charged – upon the rag, of course. The toreador skipped round with a ladylike skip, then tripped to another point. Very pretty!

The bull, in the course of his trotting and prancing and pawing, had once more come near the bold picador. The bold picador shoved forward his ancient steed, leaned forwards, and pushed the point of his lance in the bull's shoulder. The bull looked up, irritated and arrested. What the devil!

He saw the horse and rider. The horse stood with that feeble monumentality of a milk horse, patient as if between the shafts, waiting while his master delivered the milk. How strange it must have been to him when the bull, giving a little bound like a dog, ducked its head and dived its horns upwards into his belly, rolling him over with his rider as one might push over a hat-stand.

The bull looked with irritable wonder at the incomprehensible medley of horse and rider kicking on the ground a few yards away from him. He drew near to investigate. The rider scrambled out and bolted. And the toreadors running up with their cloaks, drew off the bull. He went caracoling round, charging at more silk-lined rags.

Meanwhile an attendant had got the horse on its feet again, and was leading it totteringly into the gangway and round to the exit, under the Authorities. The horse crawled slowly. The bull, running from pink cloak to red cloak, rag to rag, and never catching anything, was getting excited, impatient of the rag game. He jumped once more into the gangway and started running, alas, on towards where the wounded horse was still limping its way to the exit.

Kate knew what was coming. Before she could look away, the bull had charged on the limping horse from behind, the attendants had fled, the horse was up-ended absurdly, one of the bull's horns between his hind legs and deep in his inside. Down went the horse, collapsing in front, but his rear was still heaved up, with the bull's horn working vigorously up and down inside him, while he lay on his neck all twisted. And a huge heap of bowels coming out. And a nauseous stench. And the cries of pleased amusement among the crowd.[13]

This pretty event took place on Kate's side of the ring, and not far from where she sat, below her. Most of the people were on their feet craning to look down over the edge to watch the conclusion of this delightful spectacle.

Kate knew if she saw any more she would go into hysterics. She was getting beside herself.

She looked swiftly at Owen, who looked like a guilty boy spellbound.

'I'm going!' she said, rising.

'Going!' he cried, in wonder and dismay, his flushed face and his bald flushed forehead a picture, looking up at her.

But she had already turned, and was hurrying away towards the mouth of the exit-tunnel.

Owen came running after her, flustered, and drawn in all directions.

'Really going!' he said in chagrin, as she came to the high, vaulted exit-tunnel.

'I must. I've got to get out,' she cried. 'Don't you come.'

'Really!' he echoed, torn all ways.

The scene was creating a very hostile attitude in the audience. To leave the bull-fight is a national insult.

'Don't come! Really! I shall take a tram-car,' she said hurriedly.

'Really! Do you really think you'll be all right?'

'Perfectly. You stay. Goodbye! I can't smell any more of this stink.'

He turned like Orpheus looking back into hell,[14] and wavering made towards his seat again.

It was not so easy, because many people were now on their feet and crowding to the exit vault. The rain which had sputtered a few drops suddenly fell in a downward splash. People were crowding to shelter; but Owen, unheeding, fought his way back to his seat, and sat in his rain-coat with the rain pouring on his bald head. He was as nearly in hysterics as Kate. But he was convinced that this was life. He was seeing LIFE, and what can an American do more!

'They might just as well sit and enjoy somebody else's diarrhoea' was the thought that passed through Kate's distracted but still Irish mind.

There she was in the great concrete archway under the stadium, with the lousy press of the audience crowding in after her. Facing outwards, she saw the straight downpour of the rain, and a little beyond, the great wooden gates that opened to the free street. Oh to be out, to be out of this, to be free!

But it was pouring tropical rain. The little shoddy soldiers were pressing back under the brick gateway, for shelter. And the gates were almost shut. Perhaps they would not let her out. Oh horror!

She stood hovering in front of the straight downpour. She would have dashed out, but for the restraining thought of what she would look like when her thin gauze dress was plastered to her body by drenching rain. On the brink she hovered.

Behind her, from the inner end of the stadium tunnel, the people were surging in in waves. She stood horrified and alone, looking always out to freedom. The crowd was in a state of excitement, cut off in its sport, on tenterhooks lest it should miss anything. Thank goodness the bulk stayed near the inner end of the vault. She hovered near the outer end, ready to bolt at any moment.

The rain crashed steadily down.

She waited on the outer verge, as far from the people as possible. Her face had that drawn, blank look of a woman near hysterics. She could not get out of her eyes the last picture of the horse lying twisted on its neck with its hindquarters hitched up and the horn of the bull goring slowly and rhythmically in its vitals. The horse so utterly passive and grotesque. And all its bowels slipping on to the ground.

But a new terror was the throng inside the tunnel entrance. The big arched place was filling up, but still the crowd did not come very near her. They pressed towards the inner exit.

They were mostly loutish men in city clothes, the mongrel men of a mongrel city. Two men stood making water against the wall, in the interval of their excitement. One father had kindly brought his little boys to the show, and stood in fat, sloppy paternal benevolence above them. They were pale mites, the elder about ten years old, highly dressed up in Sunday clothes. And badly they needed protecting from that paternal benevolence, for they were oppressed, peaked and a bit wan from the horrors. To those children at least bull-fights did not come natural, but would be an acquired taste. There were other children, however, and fat mammas in black satin that was greasy and grey at the edges with an overflow of face-powder. These fat mammas had a pleased, excited look in their eyes, almost sexual, and very distasteful in contrast to their soft passive bodies.

Kate shivered a little in her thin frock, for the ponderous rain had a touch of ice. She stared through the curtain of water at the big rickety gates of the enclosure surrounding the amphitheatre, at the midget soldiers cowering in their shoddy, pink-white cotton uniforms, and at the glimpse of the squalid street outside, now running with dirty brown streams. The vendors had all taken refuge, in dirty-white clusters, in the pulque shops, one of which was sinisterly named: *A Ver que Sale.*[15]

She was afraid more of the repulsiveness than of anything. She had been in many cities of the world, but Mexico had an underlying ugliness, a sort of squalid evil, which made Naples seem debonair in comparison. She was afraid, she dreaded the thought that anything might really touch her in this town, and give her the contagion of its crawling sort of evil. But she knew that the one thing she must do was to keep her head.

A little officer in uniform, wearing a big, pale-blue cape, made his way through the crowd. He was short, dark, and had a little black beard like an imperial. He came through the people from the inner entrance, and cleared his way with a quiet, silent unobtrusiveness, yet with the peculiar heavy Indian momentum. Even touching the crowd delicately with his gloved hand, and murmuring almost inaudibly the *con permiso!*[16] formula, he seemed to be keeping himself miles away from contact. He was brave too: because there was just the chance some lout might shoot him because of his uniform. The people knew him too. Kate could tell that by the flicker of a jeering, self-conscious smile that passed across many faces, and the exclamation: 'General Viedma! Don Cipriano!'

He came towards Kate, saluting and bowing with a brittle shyness.

'I am General Viedma. Did you wish to leave? Let me get you an automobile,' he said, in very English English, that sounded strange from his dark face, and a little stiff on his soft tongue.

His eyes were dark, quick, with the glassy darkness that she found so wearying. But they were tilted up with a curious slant, under arched black brows. It gave him an odd look of detachment, as if he looked at life with raised brows. His manner was superficially assured, underneath perhaps half-savage, shy and farouche, and deprecating.

'Thank you so much,' she said.

He called to a soldier in the gateway.

'I will send you in the automobile of my friend,' he said. 'It will be better than a taxi. You don't like the bull-fight?'

'No! Horrible!' said Kate. 'But do get me a yellow taxi. That is quite safe.'

'Well, the man has gone for the automobile. You are English, yes?'

'Irish,' said Kate.

'Ah Irish!' he replied, with the flicker of a smile.

'You speak English awfully well,' she said.

'Yes! I was educated there. I was in England seven years.'

'Were you! My name is Mrs Leslie.'

'Ah Leslie! I knew James Leslie in Oxford. Hé was killed in the war.'

'Yes. That was my husband's brother.'

'Oh really!'

'How small the world is!' said Kate.

'Yes indeed!' said the General.

There was a pause.

'And the gentlemen who are with you, they are – ?'

'American,' said Kate.

'Ah Americans! Ah yes!'

'The older one is my cousin – Owen Rhys.'

'Owen Rhys! Ah yes! I think I saw in the newspaper you were here in town – visiting Mexico.'

He spoke in a peculiar quiet voice, rather suppressed, and his quick eyes glanced at her, and at his surroundings, like those of a man perpetually suspecting an ambush. But his face had a certain silent hostility, under his kindness. He was saving his nation's reputation.

'They did put in a not very complimentary note,' said Kate. 'I think they don't like it that we stay in the Hotel San Remo.[17] It is too poor and foreign. But we are none of us rich, and we like it better than those other places.'

'The Hotel San Remo? Where is that?'

'In the Avenida del Peru. Won't you come and see us there, and meet my cousin and Mr Thompson?'

'Thank you! Thank you! I hardly ever go out. But I will call if I may, and then perhaps you will all come to see me at the house of my friend, Señor Ramón Carrasco.'

'We should like to,' said Kate.

'Very well. And shall I call, then?'

She told him a time, and added:

'You mustn't be surprised at the hotel. It *is* small, and nearly all Italians. But we tried some of the big ones, and there is such a feeling of lowness about them, awful! I can't stand the feeling of prostitution. And then the cheap insolence of the servants. No, my little San Remo may be rough, but it's kindly and human, and it's not rotten. It is like Italy as I always knew it, decent, and with a bit of human generosity. I do think Mexico City is evil, underneath.'

'Well,' he said, 'the hotels are bad. It is unfortunate, but the foreigners seem to make the Mexicans worse than they are, naturally. And Mexico, or something in it, certainly makes the foreigners worse than they are at home.'

He spoke with a certain bitterness.

'Perhaps we should all stay away,' she said.

'Perhaps!' he said, lifting his shoulders a little. 'But I don't think so.'

He relapsed into a slightly blank silence. Peculiar how his feelings flushed over him, anger, diffidence, wistfulness, assurance, and an anger again, all in little flushes, and somewhat naïve.

'It doesn't rain so much,' said Kate. 'When will the car come?'

'It is here now. It has been waiting some time,' he replied.

'Then I'll go,' she said.

'Well,' he replied, looking at the sky. 'It is still raining, and your dress is very thin. You must take my cloak.'

'Oh!' she said, shrinking, 'it is only two yards.'

'It is still raining fairly fast. Better either wait, or let me lend you my cloak.'

He swung out of his cloak with a quick little movement, and held it up to her. Almost without realising, she turned her shoulders to him and he put the cape on her. She caught it round her, and ran out to the gate, as if escaping. He followed, with a light yet military stride. The soldiers saluted rather slovenly, and he responded briefly.

A not very new Fiat stood at the gate, with a chauffeur in a short red-and-black check coat. The chauffeur opened the door. Kate slipped off the cloak as she got in, and handed it back. He stood with it over his arm.

'Goodbye!' she said. 'Thank you ever so much. And we shall see you on Tuesday. Do put your cape on.'

'On Tuesday, yes. Hotel San Remo. Calle de Peru,' he added to the chauffeur. Then turning again to Kate: 'The hotel, no?'

'Yes,' she said, and instantly changed. 'No, take me to Sanborn's,[18] where I can sit in a corner and drink tea to comfort me.'

'To comfort you after the bull-fight?' he said, with another quick smile. 'To Sanborn's, Gonzalez.'

He saluted and bowed and closed the door. The car started.

Kate sat back, breathing relief. Relief to get away from that beastly place. Relief even to get away from that nice man. He was awfully nice. But he made her feel she wanted to get away from him too. There was that heavy, black Mexican fatality about him, that put a burden on her. His quietness, and his peculiar assurance, almost aggressive; and at the same time, a nervousness, an uncertainty. His heavy sort of gloom, and yet his quick, naïve, childish smile. Those black eyes, like black jewels, that you couldn't look into, and which were so watchful; yet which, perhaps, were waiting for some sign of recognition and of warmth! Perhaps!

She felt again, as she felt before, that Mexico lay in her destiny almost as a doom. Something so heavy, so oppressive, like the folds of some huge serpent that seemed as if it could hardly raise itself.

She was glad to get to her corner in the tea-house, to feel herself in the cosmopolitan world once more, to drink her tea and eat strawberry shortcake and try to forget.

Tea-party in Tlacolula

OWEN came back to the hotel at about half-past six, tired, excited, a little guilty, and a good deal distressed at having let Kate go alone. And now the whole thing was over, rather dreary in spirit.

'Oh, how did you get on?' he cried, the moment he saw her, afraid almost like a boy of his own sin of omission.

'I got on perfectly. Went to Sanborn's for tea, and had strawberry shortcake – so good!'

'Oh, good for you!' he laughed in relief. 'Then you weren't *too* much overcome! I'm so glad. I had such awful qualms after I'd let you go. Imagined all the things that are supposed to happen in Mexico – chauffeur driving away with you into some horrible remote region, and robbing you and all that – but then I *knew* really you'd be all right. Oh, the time I had – the rain! – and the people throwing things at my bald patch – and those horses – wasn't that horrible? – I wonder I'm still alive.' And he laughed with tired excitement, putting his hand over his stomach and rolling his eyes.

'Aren't you drenched?' she said.

'Drenched!' he replied. 'Or at least I was. I've dried off quite a lot. My rain-coat is no good – I don't know why I don't buy another. Oh, but what a time! The rain *streaming* on my bald head, and the crowd behind throwing oranges at it. Then simply *gored* in my inside about letting you go alone. Yet it was the only bull-fight I shall *ever* see. I came then before it was over. Bud wouldn't come. I suppose he's still there.'

'Was it as awful as the beginning?' she asked.

'No! No! It wasn't. The first was worst – that horse-shambles. Oh, they killed two more horses. And *five* bulls! Yes, a regular butchery. But some of it was very neat work; those toreadors did some very pretty feats. One stood on his cloak while a bull charged him.'

'I think,' interrupted Kate, 'if I knew that some of those toreadors were going to be tossed by the bull, I'd go to see another bull-fight.

Ugh, how I detest them! The longer I live the more loathsome the human species becomes to me. *How* much nicer the bulls are!'

'Oh, quite!' said Owen vaguely. 'Exactly. But still there was some very skilful work, very pretty. Really very plucky.'

'Yah!' snarled Kate. 'Plucky! They with all their knives and their spears and cloaks and darts – and they know just how a bull will behave. It's just a performance of human beings torturing animals, with those common fellows showing off, how smart they are at hurting a bull. Dirty little boys maiming flies – that's what they are. Only grown-up, they are bastards, not boys. Oh, *I* wish I could be a bull, just for five minutes. Bastard, that's what I call it!'

'Well!' laughed Owen uneasily, 'it is rather.'

'Call that manliness!' cried Kate. 'Then thank God a million times that I'm a woman, and know poltroonery and dirty-mindedness when I see it.'

Again Owen laughed uncomfortably.

'Go upstairs and change,' she said. 'You'll die.'

'I think I'd better. I feel I might die any minute, as a matter of fact. Well, till dinner then. I'll tap at your door in half an hour.'

Kate sat trying to sew, but her hand trembled. She could not get the bull-ring out of her mind, and something felt damaged in her inside.

She straightened herself, and sighed. She was really very angry, too, with Owen. He was naturally so sensitive, and so kind. But he had the insidious modern disease of tolerance. He must tolerate everything, even a thing that revolted him. He would call it Life! He would feel he had *lived* this afternoon. Greedy even for the most sordid sensations.

Whereas *she* felt as if she had eaten something which was giving her ptomaine poisoning. If *that* was life!

Ah men, men! They all had this soft rottenness of the soul, a strange perversity which made even the squalid, repulsive things seem part of *life* to them. Life! And what is life? A louse lying on its back and kicking? Ugh!

At about seven o'clock Villiers came tapping. He looked wan, peaked, but like a bird that had successfully pecked a bellyful of garbage.

'Oh it was GREAT!' he said, lounging on one hip. 'GREAT! They killed *seven* BULLS.'[1]

'No calves, unfortunately,' said Kate, suddenly furious again.

He paused to consider the point, then laughed. Her anger was another slight sensational amusement to him.

'No, no calves,' he said. 'The calves have come home to be fattened. But several more horses after you'd gone.'

'I don't want to hear,' she said coldly.

He laughed, feeling rather heroic. After all, one must be able to look on blood and bursten bowels calmly: even with a certain thrill. The young hero! But there were dark rings round his eyes, like a debauch.

'Oh but!' he began, making a rather coy face. 'Don't you want to hear what I did after! I went to the hotel of the chief toreador, and saw him lying on his bed all dressed up, smoking a fat cigar. Rather like a male Venus who is never undressed. So funny!'

'Who took you there?' she said.

'That Pole, you remember? – and a Spaniard who talked English. The toreador was great, lying on his bed in all his get-up, except his shoes, and quite a crowd of men going over it all again – *wawawawawa!* – you never heard such a row!'

'Aren't you wet?' said Kate.

'No, not at all. I'm perfectly dry. You see I had my coat. Only my head, of course. My poor hair was all streaked down my face like streaks of dye.' He wiped his thin hair across his head with rather selfconscious humour. 'Hasn't Owen come in?' he asked.

'Yes, he's changing.'

'Well I'll go up. I suppose it's nearly supper time. Oh yes, it's *after*!' At which discovery he brightened as if he'd received a gift.

'Oh by the way, how did you get on? Rather mean of us to let you go all alone like that,' he said, as he hung poised in the open doorway.

'Not at all,' she said. 'You wanted to stay. And I can look after myself, at my time of life.'

'We-ell!' he said, with an American drawl. 'Maybe you can!' Then he gave a little laugh. 'But you *should* have seen all those men rehearsing in that bedroom, throwing their arms about, and the toreador lying on the bed like Venus with a fat cigar, listening to her lovers.'

'I'm glad I didn't,' said Kate.

Villiers disappeared with a wicked little laugh.

And as she sat her hands trembled with outrage and passion. A-moral! How could one be a-moral, or non-moral, when one's soul was revolted! How could one be like these Americans, picking over the garbage of sensations, and gobbling it up like carrion birds. At the moment, both Owen and Villiers seemed to her like carrion birds, repulsive.

She felt, moreover, that they both hated her first because she was a woman. It was all right so long as she fell in with them in every way. But the moment she stood out against them in the least, they hated her mechanically for the very fact that she was a woman. They hated her womanness.

And in this Mexico, with its great under-drift of squalor and heavy reptile-like evil, it was hard for her to bear up.

She was really fond of Owen. But how could she respect him? So empty, and waiting for circumstance to fill him up. Swept with an American despair of having lived in vain, or of not having *really* lived. Having missed something. Which fearful misgiving would make him rush like mechanical steel filings to a magnet, towards any crowd in the street. And then all his poetry and philosophy gone with the cigarette-end he threw away, he would stand craning his neck in one more frantic effort to *see* – just to *see*. Whatever it was, he must see it. Or he might miss something. And then, after he'd seen an old ragged woman run over by a motor-car and bleeding on the floor, he'd come back to Kate pale at the gills, sick, bewildered, daunted, and yet, yes, glad he'd seen it. It was Life!

'Well,' said Kate, 'I always thank God I'm not Argus.[2] Two eyes are often two too many for me, in all the horrors. I don't feed myself on street-accidents.'

At dinner they tried to talk of pleasanter things than bull-fights. Villiers was neat and tidy and very nicely mannered, but she knew he was keeping a little mocking laugh up his sleeve, because she could not stomach the afternoon's garbage. He himself had black rings under his eyes, but that was because he had 'lived'.

The climax came with the dessert. In walked the Pole and that Spaniard who spoke American. The Pole was unhealthy and unclean-looking. She heard him saying to Owen, who of course had risen with automatic cordiality:

'We thought we'd come here to dinner. Well, how are you?'

Kate's skin was already goose-flesh. But the next instant she heard that dingy voice, that spoke so many languages dingily, assailing her with familiarity:

'Ah, Miss Leslie, you missed the best part of it. You missed all the fun! Oh, I say –'

Rage flew into her heart and fire into her eyes. She got up suddenly from her chair, and faced the fellow behind her.

'Thank you!' she said. 'I don't want to hear. I don't want you to speak to me. I don't want to know you.'

She looked at him once, then turned her back, sat down again, and took a pitahaya from the fruit plate.

The fellow went green, and stood a moment speechless.

'Oh, all right!' he said mechanically, turning away to the Spaniard who spoke American.

'Well – see you later!' said Owen rather hurriedly, and he went back to his seat at Kate's table.

The two strange fellows sat at another table. Kate ate her cactus fruit in silence, and waited for her coffee. By this time she was not so angry, she was quite calm. And even Villiers hid his joy in a new sensation under a manner of complete quiet composure.

When coffee came she looked at the two men at the other table, and at the two men at her own table.

'I've had enough of *canaille*, of any sort,' she said.

'Oh, I understand, perfectly,' said Owen.

After dinner, she went to her room. And through the night she could not sleep, but lay listening to the noises of Mexico City, then to the silence and the strange, grisly fear that so often creeps out on to the darkness of a Mexican night. Away inside her, she loathed Mexico City. She even feared it. In the daytime it had a certain spell – but at night, the underneath grisliness and evil came forth.

In the morning Owen also announced that he had not slept at all.

'Oh, I never slept so well since I was in Mexico,' said Villiers, with a triumphant look of a bird that has just pecked a good morsel from the garbage-heap.

'Look at the frail aesthetic youth!' said Owen, in a hollow voice.

'His frailty and his aestheticism are both bad signs, to me,' said Kate ominously.

'And the youth. Surely that's another!' said Owen, with a dead laugh.

But Villiers only gave a little snort of cold, pleased amusement.

Someone was calling Miss Leslie on the telephone, said the Mexican chambermaid. It was the only person Kate knew in the capital – or in the Distrito Federal – a Mrs Norris,[3] widow of an English ambassador of thirty years ago. She had a big, ponderous old house out in the village of Tlacolula.[4]

'Yes! Yes! This is Mrs Norris. How are you? That's right, that's right. Now, Mrs Leslie, won't you come out to tea this afternoon and see the garden? I wish you would. Two friends are coming in to see me, two Mexicans: Don Ramón Carrasco and General Viedma. They are both *charming* men, and Don Ramón is a great scholar. I assure you, they are both entirely the exception among Mexicans. Oh, but *entirely* the exception! So now, my *dear* Mrs Leslie, won't you come with your cousin? I wish you would.'

Kate remembered the little General; he was a good deal smaller than herself. She remembered his erect, alert little figure, something birdlike, and the face with eyes slanting under arched eyebrows, and the little black tuft of an imperial on the chin: a face with a peculiar Chinese suggestion, without being Chinese in the least, really. An odd, detached, yet cocky little man, a true little Indian, speaking Oxford English in a rapid, low, musical voice, with extraordinarily gentle intonation. Yet those black, inhuman eyes!

Till this minute she had not really been able to recall him to herself, to get any sharp impression. Now she had it. He was an Indian pure and simple. And in Mexico, she knew, there were more generals than soldiers. There had been three generals in the Pullman coming down from El Paso, two, more or less educated, in the 'drawing-room', and the third, a real peasant Indian, travelling with a frizzy half-white woman who looked as if she had fallen into a flour-sack, her face was so deep in powder, and her frizzy hair and her brown silk dress so douched with the white dust of it. Neither this 'general' nor this woman had ever been in a Pullman before. But the general was sharper than the woman. He was a tall wiry fellow with a reddened pock-marked face and sharp little black eyes. He followed Owen to the smokingroom, and watched with sharp eyes, to see how everything was done. And soon he knew. And he would wipe his wash-bowl dry as neatly as anybody. There was something of a real man about him. But the poor, half-white woman, when she wanted the ladies' toilet, got lost in the passage and wailed aloud: *I don't know where to go! No sé adonde! No sé adonde!* – until the general sent the Pullman boy to direct her.

But it had annoyed Kate to see this general and this woman eating chicken and asparagus and jelly in the Pullman, paying fifteen pesos for a rather poor dinner, when for a peso-and-a-half apiece they could have eaten a better meal, and real Mexican, at the meal-stop station. And all the poor, barefoot people clamouring on the platform, while the 'general', who was a man of their own sort, nobly swallowed his asparagus on the other side of the window-pane.

But this is how they save the people, in Mexico and elsewhere. Some tough individual scrambles up out of the squalor and proceeds to save himself. Who pays for the asparagus and jelly and face-powder, nobody asks, because everybody knows.

And so much for Mexican generals: as a rule, a class to be strictly avoided.

Kate was aware of all this. She wasn't much interested in any sort of Mexican in office. There is so much in the world that one wants to avoid, as one wants to avoid the lice that creep on the unwashed crowd.

Being rather late, Owen and Kate bumped out to Tlacolula in a Ford taxi. It was a long way, a long way through the peculiar squalid endings of the town, then along the straight road between trees, into the valley. The sun of April was brilliant, there were piles of cloud about the sky, where the volcanoes would be. The valley stretched away to its sombre, atmospheric hills, in a flat dry bed, parched except where there was some crop being irrigated. The soil seemed strange, dry, blackish, artificially wetted, and old. The trees rose high, and hung bare boughs, or withered shade. The buildings were either new and alien, like the Country Club, or cracked and dilapidated, with all the plaster falling off. The falling of thick plaster from cracked buildings – one could almost hear it!

Yellow tram-cars rushed at express speed away down the fenced-in car-lines, rushing round towards Xochimilco or Tlalpan.[5] The asphalt road ran outside these lines, and on the asphalt rushed incredibly dilapidated Ford omnibuses, crowded with blank dark natives in dirty cotton clothes and big straw hats. At the far edge of the road, on the dust-tracks under the trees, little donkeys under huge loads loitered towards the city, driven by men with blackened faces and bare, blackened legs. Three-fold went the traffic; the roar of the tram-trains, the clatter of the automobiles, the straggle of asses and of outside-seeming individuals.

Occasional flowers would splash out in colour from a ruin of falling plaster. Occasional women with strong, dark-brown arms would be washing rags in a drain. An occasional horseman would ride across to the herd of motionless black-and-white cattle on the field. Occasional maize fields were already coming green. And the pillars that mark the water conduits passed one by one.

They went through the tree-filled plaza of Tlacolula, where natives were squatting on the ground, selling fruits or sweets, then down a road between high walls. They pulled up at last at big gate-doors, beyond which was a heavy pink-and-yellow house, and beyond the house, high, dark cypress trees.

In the road two motor-cars were already standing. That meant other visitors. Owen knocked on the studded fortress doors: there was an imbecile barking of dogs. At last a little footman with a little black moustache opened silently.

The square, inner patio, dark, with sun lying on the heavy arches of one side, had pots of red and white flowers, but was ponderous, as if dead for centuries. A certain dead, heavy strength and beauty seemed there, unable to pass away, unable to liberate itself and decompose. There was a stone basin of clear but motionless water, and the heavy reddish-and-yellow arches went round the courtyard with warrior-like fatality, their bases in dark shadow. Dead, massive house of the Conquistadores, with a glimpse of tall-grown garden beyond, and further Aztec cypresses rising to strange dark heights. And dead silence, like the black, porous, absorptive lava rock. Save when the tram-cars battered past outside the solid wall.

Kate went up the jet-like stone staircase, through the leather doors. Mrs Norris came forward on the terrace of the upper patio to receive her guests.

'I'm so glad, my dear, that you came. I should have rung you up before, but I've had such trouble with my heart. And the doctor wanting to send me down to a lower altitude! I said to him, I've no patience! If you're going to cure me, cure me at an altitude of seven thousand feet or else admit your incompetence at once. Ridiculous, this rushing up and down from one altitude to another. I've lived at this height all these years. I simply refuse to be bundled down to Cuernavaca or some other place where I don't want to go. Well, my dear, and how are you?'

Mrs Norris was an elderly woman, rather like a conquistador herself in her black silk dress and her little black shoulder-shawl of fine cashmere, with a short silk fringe, and her ornaments of black enamel. Her face had gone slightly grey, her nose was sharp and dusky, and her voice hammered almost like metal, a slow, distinct, peculiar hard music of its own. She was an archaeologist, and she had studied the Aztec remains so long, that now some of the black-grey look of the lava rock, and some of the experience of the Aztec idols, with sharp nose and slightly prominent eyes and an expression of tomb-like mockery, had passed into her face. A lonely daughter of culture, with a strong mind and a dense will, she had browsed all her life on the hard stones of archaeological remains, and at the same time she had retained a strong sense of humanity, and a slightly fantastic humorous vision of her fellow men.

From the first instant, Kate respected her for her isolation and her dauntlessness. The world is made up of a mass of people and a few individuals. Mrs Norris was one of the few individuals. True, she played her social game all the time. But she was an odd number; and all alone, she could give the even numbers a bad time.

'But come in. Do come in!' she said, after keeping her two guests out on the terrace that was lined with black idols and dusty native baskets and shields and arrows and tapa, like a museum.

In the dark sitting-room that opened on to the terrace were visitors: an old man in a black morning coat and white hair and beard, and a woman in black crêpe-de-chine, with the inevitable hat of her sort upon her grey hair: a stiff satin turned up on three sides and with black ospreys underneath. She had the baby face and the faded blue eyes and the middle-west accent inevitable.

'Judge and Mrs Burlap.'

The third visitor was a youngish man, very correct and not quite sure. He was Major Law, American military attaché at the moment.

The three people eyed the newcomers with cautious suspicion. They might be shady. There are indeed so many shady people in Mexico that it is taken for granted, if you arrive unannounced and unexpected in the capital, that you are probably under an assumed name, and have some dirty game up your sleeve.

'Been long in Mexico?' snapped the Judge; the police enquiry had begun.

'No!' said Owen, resonantly, his gorge rising. 'About two weeks.'

'You are an American?'

'I,' said Owen, 'am American. Mrs Leslie is English – or rather Irish.'

'Been in the club yet?'

'No,' said Owen, 'I haven't. American clubs aren't much in my line. Though Garfield Spence gave me a letter of introduction.'

'Who? Garfield Spence?' The Judge started as if he had been stung. 'Why the fellow's nothing better than a bolshevist. Why he went to Russia!'

'I should rather like to go to Russia myself,' said Owen. 'It is probably the most interesting country in the world to-day.'

'But weren't you telling me,' put in Mrs Norris, in her clear, metal-musical voice, 'that you loved China so much, Mr Rhys?'

'I *did* like China *very* much,' said Owen.

'And I'm sure you made some wonderful collections. Tell me now, what was your particular fancy?'

'Perhaps, after all,' said Owen, 'it was jade.'

'Ah jade! Yes! Jade! Jade is beautiful! Those wonderful little fairy-lands they carve in jade!'

'And the stone itself! It was the delicate stone that fascinated me,' said Owen. 'The wonderful quality of it!'

'Ah wonderful, wonderful! Tell me now, dear Mrs Leslie, what you have been doing since I saw you?'

'We went to a bull-fight, and hated it,' said Kate. 'At least I did. We sat in the Sun, near the ring, and it was all horrible.'

'Horrible, I am sure. I never went to a bull-fight in Mexico. Only in Spain, where there is wonderful colour. Did you ever try a bull-fight, Major?'

'Yes, I have been several times.'

'You have! Then you know all about it. And how are you liking Mexico, Mrs Leslie?'

'Not much,' said Kate. 'It strikes me as evil.'

'It does! It does!' said Mrs Norris. 'Ah, if you had known it before! Mexico before the revolution! It was different then.[6] What is the latest news, Major?'

'About the same,' said the Major. 'There is a rumour that the new President will be turned down by the army, a few days before he comes into office. But you never know.'

'I think it would be a great shame not to let him have a try,' put in Owen hotly. 'He seems a sincere man, and just because he is honestly a Labour man, they want to shut him out.'

'Ah, my dear Mr Rhys, they *all* talk so nobly beforehand. If only their deeds followed their words, Mexico would be heaven on earth.'

'Instead of hell on earth,' snapped the Judge.

A young man and his wife, also Americans, were introduced as Mr and Mrs Henry. The young man was fresh and lively.

'We were talking about the new President,' said Mrs Norris.

'Well, why not!' said Mr Henry breezily. 'I'm just back from Orizaba. And do you know what they've got pasted up on the walls? – *Hosanna! Hosanna! Hosanna! Viva el Jesús Cristo de Mexico, Socrates Tomás Montes!*'[7]

'Why, did you ever hear of such a thing!' said Mrs Norris.

'*Hosanna! Hosanna! Hosanna!* To the new Labour President! I think it's rich,' said Henry.

The Judge stamped his stick on the ground in a speechless access of irritability.

'They pasted on my luggage,' said the Major, 'when I came through Vera Cruz: *La degenerada media clasa, Será regenerada, por mi, Montes.* The degenerate middle class shall be regenerated by me, Montes.'

'Poor Montes!' said Kate. 'He seems to have got his work cut out.'

'He has indeed!' said Mrs Norris. 'Poor man, I wish he might come in peacefully and put a strong hand on the country. But there's not much hope, I'm afraid.'

There was a silence, during which Kate felt that bitter hopelessness that comes over people who know Mexico well. A bitter barren hopelessness.

'How can a man who comes in on a Labour vote, even a doctored one, put a strong hand on a country!' snapped the Judge. 'Why he came in on the very cry of *Down with the strong hand!*' And again the old man stamped his stick in an access of extreme irritability.

This was another characteristic of the old residents of the city: A state of intense, though often suppressed irritation, an irritation amounting almost to rabies.

'Oh, but mayn't it be possible that he will change his views a little on coming into power?' said Mrs Norris. 'So many Presidents have done so.'

'I should say very probable, if ever he gets into power,' said young Henry. 'He'll have all his work cut out saving Socrates Tomás, he won't have much time left for saving Mexico.'

'He's a dangerous fellow, and will turn out a scoundrel,' said the Judge.

'Myself,' said Owen, 'as far as I have followed him, I believe he is sincere, and I admire him.'

'I thought it was so nice,' said Kate, 'that they received him in New York with loud music by the Street Sweepers' Band. The Street Sweepers' Band they sent to receive him from the ship!'

'You see,' said the Major, 'no doubt the Labour people themselves wished to send that particular band.'

'But to be President Elect, and to be received by the Street Sweepers' Band!' said Kate. 'No, I can't believe it!'

'Oh, it actually was so,' said the Major. 'But that is Labour hailing Labour, surely.'

'The latest rumour,' said Henry, 'is that the army will go over *en bloc* to General Angulo about the twenty-third, a week before the inauguration.'[8]

'But how is it possible?' said Kate, 'when Montes is so popular?'

'Montes popular!' they all cried at once. 'Why!' snapped the Judge, 'he's the most unpopular man in Mexico.'

'Not with the Labour Party!' said Owen, almost at bay.

'The Labour Party!' the Judge fairly spat like a cat. 'There is no such thing. What is the Labour Party in Mexico? A bunch of isolated factory hands here and there, mostly in the State of Vera Cruz. The Labour Party! They've done what they could already. We know them.'

'That's true,' said Henry. 'The Labourites have tried every little game possible. When I was in Orizaba they marched to the Hotel Francia to shoot all the gringoes and the Gachupines. The hotel manager had pluck enough to harangue them, and they went off to the next hotel. When the man came out there to talk to them, they shot him before he got a word out. It's funny, really! If you have to go to the Town Hall, and you're dressed in decent clothes, they let you sit on a hard bench for hours. But if a street-sweeper comes in, or a fellow in dirty cotton drawers, it is *Buenos días! Señor! Pase Usted! Quiere Usted algo?*[9] – while you sit there waiting their pleasure. Oh, it's quite funny.'

The Judge trembled with irritation like an access of gout. The party sat in gloomy silence, that sense of doom and despair overcoming them as it seems to overcome all people who talk seriously about Mexico. Even Owen was silent. He too had come through Vera Cruz, and had had his fright; the porters had charged him twenty pesos to carry his trunk from the ship to the train. Twenty pesos is ten dollars, for ten minutes' work. And when Owen had seen the man in front of him arrested and actually sent to jail, a Mexican jail at that, for refusing to pay the charge, 'the legal charge', he himself had stumped up without a word.

'I walked into the National Museum the other day,' said the Major quietly. 'Just into that room on the patio where the stones are. It was rather a cold morning, with a Norte blowing. I'd been there about ten minutes when somebody suddenly poked me on the shoulder. I turned round, and it was a lout in tight boots. *You spik English?* I said *yes!* Then he motioned me to take my hat off: I'd got to take my hat off. *What for?* said I, and I turned away and went on looking at their idols and things: ugliest set of stuff in the world, I believe. Then up came the fellow with the attendant – the attendant of course wearing his cap. They began gabbling that this was the National Museum, and I must take off my hat to their national monuments. Imagine it: those dirty stones! I laughed at them and jammed my hat on tighter and walked out. They are really only monkeys when it comes to nationalism.'

'Exactly!' cried Henry. 'When they forget all about the Patria and Mexico and all that stuff, they're as nice a people as you'd find. But as soon as they get national, they're just monkeys. A man up from Mixcoatl told me a nice story. Mixcoatl is a capital way in the South,[10] and they've got a sort of Labour bureau there. Well, the Indians come in from the hills, as wild as rabbits. And they get them into that bureau, and the Laboristas, the agitator fellows, say to them: *Now, Señores, have you anything to report from your native village? Haven't you anything for which you would like redress?* Then of course the Indians start complaining about one another, and the Secretary says: *Wait a minute, gentlemen! Let me ring up the Governor and report this.* So he goes to the telephone and starts ringing: ringing: *Ah! Is that the Palace? Is the Governor in? Tell him Señor Fulano[11] wants to speak to him!* The Indians sit gaping with open mouths. To them it's a miracle. *Ah! Is that you, Governor! Good morning! How are you! Can I have your attention for a moment? Many thanks! Well I've got some gentlemen here down from Apaxtle, in the hills: José Garcia, Jesús Querido, etc. – and they wish to report so-and-so. Yes! Yes! That's it! Yes! What? You will see that justice is done and the thing is made right? Ah señor, many thanks! In the name of these gentlemen from the hills, from the village of Apaxtle, many thanks.*

'There sit the Indians staring as if heaven had opened and the Virgin of Guadalupe¹² was standing tiptoe on their chins. And what do you expect? The telephone is a dummy. It isn't connected with anywhere. Isn't that rich? But it's Mexico.'

The moment's fatal pause followed this funny story.

'Oh but!' said Kate, 'it's wicked! It *is* wicked. I'm sure the Indians would be all right, if they were left alone.'

'Well,' said Mrs Norris, 'Mexico isn't like any other place in the world.'

But she spoke with fear and despair in her voice.

'They seem to *want* to betray everything,' said Kate. 'They seem to *love* criminals and ghastly things. They seem to want the ugly things. They seem to *want* the ugly things to come up to the top. All the foulness that lies at the bottom, they want to stir up to the top. They seem to enjoy it. To enjoy making everything fouler. Isn't it curious!'

'It is curious,' said Mrs Norris.

'But that's what it is,' said the Judge. 'They want to turn the country into one big crime. They don't like anything else. They don't like honesty and decency and cleanliness. They want to foster lies and crime. What they call liberty here is just freedom to commit crime. That's what Labour means, that's what they all mean. Free crime, nothing else.'

'I wonder all the foreigners don't go away,' said Kate.

'They have their occupations here,' snapped the Judge.

'And the good people *are* all going away. They have nearly all gone, those that have anything left to go to,' said Mrs Norris. 'Some of us, who have our property here, and who have made our lives here, and who know the country, we stay out of a kind of tenacity. But we know it's hopeless. The more it changes, the worse it is. – Ah, here is Don Ramón and Don Cipriano. So pleased to see you. Let me introduce you.'

Don Ramón Carrasco was a tall, big, handsome man who gave the effect of bigness. He was middle aged, with a large black moustache

and large, rather haughty eyes under straight brows. The General was
in civilian clothes, looking very small beside the other man, and very
smartly built, almost cocky.

'Come,' said Mrs Norris. 'Let us go across and have tea.'

The Major excused himself, and took his departure.

Mrs Norris gathered her little shawl round her shoulders and led
through a sombre antechamber to a little terrace, where creepers and
flowers bloomed thick on the low walls. There was a bell-flower, red
and velvety, like blood that is drying: and clusters of white roses: and
tufts of bougainvillea, papery magenta colour.

'How lovely it is here!' said Kate. 'Having the great dark trees
beyond.'

But she stood in a kind of dread.

'Yes it *is* beautiful,' said Mrs Norris, with the gratification of a
possessor. 'I have such a time trying to keep these apart.' And going
across in her little black shawl, she pushed the bougainvillea away from
the rust-scarlet bell-flowers, stroking the little white roses to make them
intervene.

'I think the two reds together interesting,' said Owen.

'Do you really!' said Mrs Norris, automatically, paying no heed to
such a remark.

The sky was blue overhead, but on the lower horizon was a thick,
pearl haze. The clouds had gone.

'One never sees Popocatepetl nor Ixtaccihuatl,'[13] said Kate, disappointed.

'No, not at this season. But look, through the trees there, you see
Ajusco!'

Kate looked at the sombre-seeming mountain, between the huge dark
trees.

On the low stone parapet were Aztec things, obsidian knives, grim-
acing squatting idols in black lava, and a queer thickish stone stick,
or bâton. Owen was balancing the latter: it felt murderous even to
touch.

Kate turned to the general, who was near her, his face expressionless,
yet alert.

'Aztec things oppress me,' she said.

'They *are* oppressive,' he answered, in his beautiful cultured English,
that was nevertheless a tiny bit like a parrot talking.

'There is no hope in them,' she said.

'Perhaps the Aztecs never asked for hope,' he said, somewhat automatically.

'Surely it is hope that keeps one going?' she said.

'You, maybe. But not the Aztec, nor the Indian to-day.'

He spoke like a man who has something in reserve, who is only half attending to what he hears, and even to his own answer.

'What do they have, if they don't have hope?' she said.

'They have some other strength, perhaps,' he said evasively.

'I would like to give them hope,' she said. 'If they had hope, they wouldn't be so sad, and they would be cleaner, and not have vermin.'

'That of course would be good,' he said, with a little smile. 'But I think they are not so very sad. They laugh a good deal and are gay.'

'No,' she said. 'They oppress me, like a weight on my heart. They make me irritable, and I want to go away.'

'From Mexico?'

'Yes. I feel I want to go away from it and never, never see it again. It is so oppressive and gruesome.'

'Try it a little longer,' he said. 'Perhaps you will feel differently. But perhaps not,' he ended vaguely, driftingly.

She could feel in him a sort of yearning towards her. As if a sort of appeal came to her from him, from his physical heart in his breast. As if the very heart gave out dark rays of seeking and yearning. She glimpsed this now for the first time, quite apart from the talking, and it made her shy.

'And does everything in Mexico oppress you?' he added, almost shyly, but with a touch of mockery, looking at her with a troubled naïve face that had its age heavy and resistant beneath the surface.

'Almost everything!' she said. 'It *always* makes my heart sink. Like the eyes of the men in the big hats – I call them the peons. Their eyes have no middle to them. Those big handsome men, under their big hats, they aren't really there. They have no centre, no real *I*. Their middle is a raging black hole, like the middle of a maelstrom.'

She looked with her troubled grey eyes into the black, slanting, watchful, calculating eyes of the small man opposite her. He had a pained expression, puzzled, like a child. And at the same time something obstinate and mature, a demonish maturity, opposing her in an animal way.

'You mean we aren't real people, we have nothing of our own, except killing and death,' he said, quite matter of fact.

'I don't know,' she said, startled by his interpretation. 'I only say how it makes me feel.'

'You are very clever, Mrs Leslie,' came Don Ramón's quiet, but heavy teasing voice behind her. 'It is quite true. Whenever a Mexican cries *Viva!* he ends up with *Muera!* When he says *Viva!* he really means *Death for Somebody or Other!* I think of all the Mexican revolutions, and I see a skeleton walking ahead of a great number of people, waving a black banner with *Viva la Muerte!* written in large white letters. *Long live Death!* Not *Viva Cristo Rey!* but *Viva Muerte Rey! Vamos! Viva!*'[14]

Kate looked round. Don Ramón was flashing his knowing brown Spanish eyes, and a little sardonic smile lurked under his moustache. Instantly Kate and he, Europeans in essence, understood one another. He was waving his arm to the last *Viva!*

'But,' said Kate, 'I don't want to say *Viva la Muerte!*'

'But when you are real Mexican –' he said, teasing.

'I *never* could be,' she said hotly, and he laughed.

'I'm afraid *Viva la Muerte!* hits the nail on the head,' said Mrs Norris, rather stonily. 'But won't you come to tea! Do!'

She led the way in her black little shawl and neat grey hair, going ahead like a Conquistador herself, and turning to look with her Aztec eyes through her pince-nez, to see if the others were coming.

'We are following,' said Don Ramón in Spanish, teasing her. Stately in his black suit, he walked behind her on the narrow terrace, and Kate followed, with the small, strutting Don Cipriano, also in a black suit, lingering oddly near her.

'Do I call you General or Don Cipriano?' she asked, turning to him.

An amused little smile quickly lit his face, though his eyes did not smile. They looked at her with a black, sharp look.

'As you wish,' he said. 'You know *General* is a term of disgrace in Mexico. Shall we say Don Cipriano?'[15]

'Yes, I like that much the best,' she said.

And he seemed pleased.

It was a round tea-table, with shiny silver tea-service, and silver kettle with a little flame, and pink and white oleanders. The little neat young footman carried the tea-cups, in white cotton gloves. Mrs Norris poured tea and cut cakes with a heavy hand.

Don Ramón sat on her right hand, the Judge on her left. Kate was between the Judge and Mr Henry. Everybody except Don Ramón and the Judge was a little nervous. Mrs Norris always put her visitors uncomfortably at their ease, as if they were captives and she the chieftainess who had captured them. She rather enjoyed it, heavily, archaeologically queening at the head of the table. But it was evident that Don Ramón, by far the most impressive person present, liked her. Cipriano, on the other hand, remained mute and disciplined, perfectly familiar with the tea-table routine, superficially quite at ease, but underneath remote and unconnected. He glanced from time to time at Kate.

She was a beautiful woman, in her own unconventional way, and with a certain richness. She was going to be forty next week. Used to all kinds of society, she watched people as one reads the pages of a novel, with a certain disinterested amusement. She was never *in* any society: too Irish, too wise.

'But of course nobody lives without hope,' Mrs Norris was saying banteringly to Don Ramón. 'If it's only the hope of a *real*, to buy a litre of pulque.'

'Ah, Mrs Norris!' he replied in his quiet, yet curiously deep voice, like a violoncello: 'If pulque is the highest happiness!'

'Then we are fortunate, because a *tostón* will buy paradise,' she said.[16]

'It is a *bon mot, Señora mía*,' said Don Ramón, laughing and drinking his tea.

'Now won't you try these little native cakes with sesame seeds on them!' said Mrs Norris to the table at large. 'My cook makes them, and her national feeling is flattered when anybody likes them. Mrs Leslie, do take one.'

'I will,' said Kate. 'Does one say *Open Sesame!*'[17]

'If one wishes,' said Mrs Norris.

'Won't you have one?' said Kate, handing the plate to Judge Burlap.

'Don't want any,' he snapped, turning his face away as if he had been offered a plate of Mexicans, and leaving Kate with the dish suspended.

Mrs Norris quickly but definitely took the plate, saying:

'Judge Burlap is afraid of *Sesame Seed*, he prefers the cave shut.'
And she handed the dish quietly to Cipriano, who was watching the
old man's bad manners with black, snake-like eyes.

'Did you see that article by Willis Rice Hope, in the *Excelsior?*' suddenly snarled the Judge, to his hostess.

'I did. I thought it very sensible.'

'The only sensible thing that's been said about these Agrarian
Laws.[18] Sensible! I should think so. Why Rice Hope came to me, and
I put him up to a few things. But his article says *everything*, doesn't
miss an item of importance.'

'Quite!' said Mrs Norris, with rather stony attention. 'If only
saying would alter things, Judge Burlap.'

'Saying the wrong thing has done all the mischief!' snapped the
Judge. 'Fellows like Garfield Spence coming down here and talking
a lot of criminal talk. Why the town's full of Socialists and
Sinvergüenzas from New York.'

Mrs Norris adjusted her pince-nez.

'Fortunately,' she said, 'they don't come out to Tlacolula, so we
needn't think about them. Mrs Henry, let me give you some more
tea.'

'Do you read *Spanish?*' the Judge spat out, at Owen. Owen, in his
big shell spectacles, was evidently a red rag to his irritable fellow-
countryman.

'No!' said Owen, round as a cannon-shot.

Mrs Norris once more adjusted her eye-glasses.

'It's such a relief to hear someone who is altogether innocent of
Spanish, and altogether unashamed,' she said. 'My father had us all
speaking four languages by the time we were twelve, and we have none
of us ever quite recovered. My stockings were all dyed blue for me
before I put my hair up.[19] By the way! How have you been for walking,
Judge? You heard of the time I had with my ankle?'

'Of course we heard!' cried Mrs Burlap, seeing dry land at last. 'I've
been trying *so* hard to get out to see you, to ask about it. We were
so *grieved* about it.'

'What happened?' said Kate.

'Why I foolishly slipped on a piece of orange peel in town – just
at the corner of San Juan de Letrán and Madero. And I fell right down.
And of course, the first thing I did when I got up was to push the

piece of orange peel into the gutter. And would you believe it, that lot of Mex –' she caught herself up – 'that lot of fellows standing there at the corner laughed heartily at me, when they saw me doing it. They thought it an excellent joke.'

'Of course they would,' said the Judge. 'They were waiting for the next person to come along and fall.'

'Did nobody help you?' asked Kate.

'Oh no! If anyone has an accident in this country, you must never, *never* help. If you touch them even, you may be arrested for causing the accident.'

'That's the law!' said the Judge. 'If you touch them before the police arrive, you are arrested for complicity. Let them lie and bleed, is the motto.'

'Is that true?' said Kate to Don Ramón.

'Fairly true,' he replied. 'Yes, it is true you must not touch the one who is hurt.'

'How disgusting!' said Kate.

'Disgusting!' cried the Judge. 'A great deal is disgusting in this country, as you'll learn if you stay here long. I nearly lost my life on a banana skin; lay in a darkened room for days, between life and death, and lame for life from it.'

'How awful!' said Kate. 'What did you do when you fell?'

'What did I do? Just smashed my hip.'

It had truly been a terrible accident, and the man had suffered bitterly.

'You can hardly blame Mexico for a banana skin,' said Owen, elated. 'I fell on one in Lexington Avenue;[20] but fortunately I only bruised myself on a soft spot.'

'That wasn't your head, was it?' said Mrs Henry.

'No,' laughed Owen. 'The other extreme.'

'We've got to add banana skins to the list of public menaces,' said young Henry. 'I'm an American, and I may any day turn bolshevist, to save my pesos, so I can repeat what I heard a man saying yesterday. He said there are only two great diseases in the world to-day – Bolshevism and Americanism; and Americanism is the worst of the two, because Bolshevism only smashes your house or your business or your skull, but Americanism smashes your soul.'

'Who was he?' snarled the Judge.

'I forget,' said Henry, wickedly.

'One wonders,' said Mrs Norris slowly, 'what he meant by Americanism.'

'He didn't define it,' said Henry. 'Cult of the dollar, I suppose.'

'Well,' said Mrs Norris. 'The cult of the dollar, in my experience, is far more intense in the countries that haven't got the dollar, than in the United States.'

Kate felt that the table was like a steel disc to which they were all, as victims, magnetised and bound.

'Where *is* your garden, Mrs Norris?' she asked.

They trooped out, gasping with relief, to the terrace. The Judge hobbled behind, and Kate had to linger sympathetically to keep him company.

They were on the little terrace.

'Isn't this strange stuff!' said Kate, picking up one of the Aztec stone knives on the parapet. 'Is it a sort of jade?'

'Jade!' snarled the Judge. 'Jade's *green*, not black. That's obsidian.'

'Jade *can* be black,' said Kate. 'I've got a lovely little black tortoise of jade from China.'

'You can't have. Jade's bright green.'

'But there's white jade too. I know there is.'

The Judge was silent from exasperation for a few moments, then he snapped:

'Jade's bright green.'

Owen, who had the ears of a lynx, had heard.

'What's that?' he said.

'Surely there's more than green jade!' said Kate.

'What!' cried Owen. 'More! Why there's every imaginable tint – white, rose, lavender –'

'And black?' said Kate.

'Black? Oh yes, quite common. Why you should see my collection. The most beautiful range of colour! *Only green jade!* Ha-ha-ha!' – and he laughed a rather stage laugh.

They had come to the stairs, which were old stone, waxed and polished in some way till they were a glittering black.

'I'll catch hold of your arm down here,' said the Judge to young Henry. 'This stair-case is a death-trap.'

Mrs Norris heard without comment. She only tilted her pince-nez on her sharp nose.

In the archway downstairs, Don Ramón and the General took their leave. The rest trailed on into the garden.

Evening was falling. The garden was drawn up tall, under the huge dark trees on the one side, and the tall, reddish-and-yellow house on the other. It was like being at the bottom of some dusky, flowering garden down in Hades.[21] Hibiscus hung scarlet from the bushes, putting out yellow bristling tongues. Some roses were scattering scentless petals on the twilight, and lonely-looking carnations hung on weak stalks. From a huge dense bush the mysterious white bells of the datura were suspended, large and silent, like the very ghosts of sound. And the datura scent was moving thick and noiseless from the tree, into the little alleys.

Mrs Burlap had hitched herself on to Kate, and from her silly, social baby-face was emitting searching questions.

'What hotel are you staying at?'

Kate told her.

'I don't know it. Where is it?'

'In the Avenida del Peru. You wouldn't know it, it is a little Italian hotel.'

'Are you staying long?'

'We aren't certain.'

'Is Mr Rhys on a newspaper?'

'No, he's a poet.'

'Does he make a living by poetry?'

'No, he doesn't try to.'

It was the sort of secret service investigation one is submitted to, in the capital of shady people, particularly shady foreigners.

Mrs Norris was lingering by a flowering arch of little white flowers. Already a firefly was sparking. It was already night.

'Well, good-bye, Mrs Norris! *Won't* you come and lunch with us. I don't mean come out to our house. Only let me know, and lunch with me *anywhere you like*, in town.'

'Thank you my dear! Thank you so much! Well! I'll see!'

Mrs Norris was almost regal, stonily, Aztec-regal.

At last they had all made their adieus, and the great doors were shut behind them.

'How did you come out!' Mrs Burlap asked, impertinent.

'In an old Ford taxi – but where is it?' said Kate, peering into the dark. It should have been under the *fresno* trees opposite, but it wasn't.

'What a curious thing!' said Owen, and he disappeared into the night.

'Which way do you go?' said Mrs Burlap.

'To the Zócalo,' said Kate.

'We have to take a tram, the opposite way,' said the baby-faced, withered woman from the Middle-West.

The Judge was hobbling along the pavement like a cat on hot bricks, to the corner. Across the road stood a group of natives in big hats and white calico clothes, all a little the worse for the pulque they had drunk. Nearer, on this side of the road, stood another little gang, of workmen in town clothes.

'There you have them,' said the Judge, flourishing his stick with utter vindictiveness. 'There's the two lots of 'em.'

'What two lots?' said Kate, surprised.

'Those peon fellows and those obreros, all drunk, the lot of them. The lot of them!' And in a spasm of pure, frustrated hate, he turned his back on her.

At the same time they saw the lights of a tram-car rushing dragon-like up the dark road, between the high wall and the huge trees.

'Here's our car!' said the Judge, beginning to scramble excitedly with his stick.

'You go the other way,' flung the baby-faced, faded woman in the three-cornered satin hat, also beginning to fluster as if she were going to swim off the pavement.

The couple clambered avidly into the brightly-lighted car, first class; hobbling up. The natives crowded into the second class.

Away whizzed the *tren*. The Burlap couple had not even said good-night! They were terrified lest they might have to know somebody whom they might not want to know; whom it might not *pay* to know.

'You common-place little woman!' said Kate aloud, looking after the retreating tram-car. 'You awful ill-bred little pair.'

She was a bit afraid of the natives, not quite sober, who were waiting for the car in the opposite direction. But stronger than her fear was a certain sympathy with these dark-faced silent men in their big straw hats and naïve little cotton blouses. Anyhow they had blood in their veins: they were columns of dark blood.

Whereas the other bloodless, acidulous couple from the Middle-West, with their nasty whiteness . . . !

She thought of the little tale the natives tell. When the Lord was making the first men, he made them of clay and put them into the oven to bake. They came out black. *They're baked too much!* said the Lord. So he made another batch, and put them in. They came out white. *They're baked too little!* He said. So He had a third try. These came out a good warm brown. *They're just right!* said the Lord.

The couple from the Middle-West, that withered baby-face and that limping Judge, they weren't baked. They were hardly baked at all.

Kate looked at the dark faces under the arc-lamp. They frightened her. They were a sort of menace to her. But she felt they were at least baked hot and to a certain satisfactory colour.

The taxi came lurching up, with Owen poking his head out and opening the door.

'I found the man in a *pulquería*,' he said. 'But I don't think he's *quite* drunk. Will you risk driving back with him?'

'The *pulquería* was called *La Flor de un Día* – the Flower of a Day,' said Owen, with an apprehensive laugh.

Kate hesitated, looking at her man.

'We may as well,' she said.

Away gallivanted the Ford, full speed to Hell.

'Do tell him not so fast,' said Kate.

'I don't know how,' said Owen.

He shouted in good English:

'Hey! chauffeur! Not so fast! Don't drive so fast.'

'*No presto. Troppo presto. Va troppo presto!*' said Kate.

The man looked at them with black, dilated eyes of fathomless incomprehension. Then he put his foot on the accelerator.

'He's only going faster!' laughed Owen nervously.

'Ah! Let him alone!' said Kate, with utter weariness.

The fellow drove like a devil incarnate, as if he had the devil in his body. But also, he drove with the devil's own nonchalant skill. There was nothing to do but let him rip.

'Wasn't that a ghastly tea-party!' said Owen.

'Ghastly!' said Kate.

Fortieth Birthday

KATE woke up one morning, aged forty. She did not hide the fact from herself, but she kept it dark from the others.

It was a blow, really. To be forty! One had to cross a dividing line. On this side there was youth and spontaneity and 'happiness'. On the other side something different: reserve, responsibility, a certain standing back from 'fun'.

She was a widow, and a lonely woman now. Having married young, her two children were grown up. The boy was twenty-one, and her daughter nineteen. They stayed chiefly with their father, from whom she had been divorced ten years before, in order to marry James Joachim Leslie. Now Leslie was dead, and all that half of life was over.

She climbed up to the flat roofs of the hotel. It was a brilliant morning, and for once, under the blue sky of the distance, Popocatepetl stood aloof, a heavy giant presence under heaven, with a cape of snow. And rolling a long dark roll of smoke like a serpent.

Ixtaccihuatl, the White Woman, glittered and seemed near, but the other mountain, Popocatepetl,[1] stood further back, and in shadow, a pure cone of atmospheric shadow, with glinting flashes of snow. There they were, the two monsters, watching gigantically and terribly over their lofty, bloody cradle of men, the Valley of Mexico. Alien, ponderous, the white-hung mountains seemed to emit a deep purring sound, too deep for the ear to hear, and yet audible on the blood, a sound of dread. There was no soaring or uplift or exaltation, as there is in the snowy mountains of Europe. Rather a ponderous white-shouldered weight, pressing terribly on the earth, and murmuring like two watchful lions.

Superficially, Mexico might be all right: with its suburbs of villas, its central fine streets, its thousands of motor-cars, its tennis and its bridge-parties. The sun shone brilliantly every day, and big bright flowers stood out from the trees. It was a holiday.

Until you were alone with it. And then the undertone was like the low angry, snarling purring of some jaguar spotted with night. There was a ponderous, down-pressing weight upon the spirit: the great folds of the dragon of the Aztecs, the dragon of the Toltecs[2] winding around one and weighing down the soul. And on the bright sunshine was a dark stream of an angry, impotent blood, and the flowers seemed to have their roots in spilt blood. The spirit of place was cruel, down-dragging, destructive.

Kate could so well understand the Mexican who had said to her: *El grito mexicano es siempre el grito del odio* – The Mexican shout is always a shout of hate. The famous revolutions, as Don Ramón said, began with *Viva!* but ended always with *Muera!* Death to this, death to the other, it was all death! death! death! as insistent as the Aztec sacrifices. Something for ever gruesome and macabre.

Why had she come to this high plateau of death? As a woman, she suffered even more than men suffer: and in the end, practically all men go under. Once, Mexico had had an elaborate ritual of death. Now it has death ragged, squalid, vulgar, without even the passion of its own mystery.

She sat on a parapet of the old roof. The street beyond was like a black abyss, but around her was the rough glare of uneven flat roofs, with loose telephone wires trailing across, and the sudden, deep, dark wells of the patios, showing flowers blooming in shade.

Just behind was a huge old church, its barrel roof humping up like some crouching animal, and its domes, like bubbles inflated, glittering with yellow tiles, and blue and white tiles, against the intense blue heaven. Quiet native women in long skirts were moving on the roofs, hanging out washing or spreading it on the stones. Chickens perched here and there. An occasional bird soared huge overhead, trailing a shadow. And not far away stood the brownish tower-stumps of the Cathedral, the profound old bell trembling huge and deep, so soft as to be almost inaudible, upon the air.

It ought to have been all gay, allegro, allegretto, in that sparkle of bright air and old roof surfaces. But no! There was the dark under-tone, the black, serpent-like fatality all the time.

It was no good Kate's wondering why she had come. Over in England, in Ireland, in Europe, she had heard the *consummatum est*[3] of her own spirit. It was finished, in a kind of death agony. But still this heavy continent of dark-souled death was more than she could bear.

She was forty: the first half of her life was over. The bright page with its flowers and its love and its stations of the Cross ended with a grave. Now she must turn over, and the page was black, black and empty.

The first half of her life had been written on the bright, smooth vellum of hope, with initial letters all gorgeous upon a field of gold. But the glamour had gone from station to station of the Cross, and the last illumination was the tomb.

Now the bright page was turned, and the dark page lay before her. How could one write on a page so profoundly black?

She went down, having promised to go and see the frescoes in the university and schools. Owen and Villiers and a young Mexican were waiting for her. They set off through the busy streets of the town, where automobiles and the little omnibuses called camions run wild, and where the natives in white cotton clothes and sandals and big hats linger like heavy ghosts in the street, among the bourgeoisie, the young ladies in pale pink crêpe de chine and high heels, the men in little shoes and American straw hats. A continual bustle in the glitter of sunshine.

Crossing the great shadeless plaza in front of the Cathedral,[4] where the tram-cars gather as in a corral, and slide away down their various streets, Kate lingered again to look at the things spread for sale on the pavement: the little toys, the painted gourd-shells, brilliant in a kind of lacquer, the *novedades* from Germany, the fruits, the flowers. And the natives squatting with their wares, large-limbed, silent, handsome men looking up with their black, centreless eyes, speaking so softly, and lifting with small sensitive brown hands the little toys they had so carefully made and painted. A strange gentle appeal and wistfulness, strange male voices, so deep, yet so quiet and gentle. Or the women, the small quick women in their blue rebozos, looking up quickly with dark eyes, and speaking in their quick, coaxing voices. The man just setting out his oranges, wiping them with a cloth so carefully, almost tenderly, and piling them in bright tiny pyramids, all neat and exquisite. A certain sensitive tenderness of the heavy blood, a certain chirping charm of the bird-like women, so still and tender with a bud-like femininity. And at the same time, the dirty clothes, and the unwashed skin, the lice, and the peculiar hollow glint of the black eyes, at once so fearsome and so appealing.

Kate knew the Italian fruit vendors, vigorously polishing their oranges on their coat-sleeves. Such a contrast, the big, handsome

Indian, sitting so soft and as it were lonely by the kerb, softly, lingeringly polishing his yellow oranges to a clean gleam, and lingeringly, delicately arranging the little piles, the pyramids for two or three cents each.

Queer work, for a big, handsome, male-looking man. But they seem to prefer these childish jobs.

The University was a Spanish building that had been done up spick and span, and given over to the young artists to decorate. Since the revolutions, nowhere had authority and tradition been so finally overthrown as in the Mexican fields of science and art. Science and art are the sport of the young. Go ahead, my boys!

The boys had gone ahead. But even then, the one artist of distinction was no longer a boy, and he had served a long apprenticeship in Europe.

Kate had seen the reproductions of some of Rivera's frescoes.[5] Now she went round the patios of the University, looking at the originals. They were interesting: the man knew his craft.

But the impulse was the impulse of the artist's hate. In the many frescoes of the Indians, there was sympathy with the Indian, but always from the ideal, social point of view. Never the spontaneous answer of the blood. These flat Indians were symbols in the great script of modern socialism, they were figures of the pathos of the victims of modern industry and capitalism. That was all they were used for: symbols in the weary script of socialism and anarchy.

Kate thought of the man polishing his oranges half-an-hour before: his peculiar beauty, a certain richness of physical being, a ponderous power of blood within him, and a helplessness, a profound unbelief that was fatal and demonish. And all the liberty, all the progress, all the socialism in the world would not help him. Nay, it would only help further to destroy him.

On the corridors of the University, young misses in bobbed hair and boys' jumpers were going around, their chins pushed forward with the characteristic, deliberate youth-and-eagerness of our day. Very much aware of their own youth and eagerness. And very American. Young professors were passing in soft amiability, young and apparently harmless.

The artists were at work on the frescoes, and Kate and Owen were introduced to them. But they were men – or boys – whose very pigments seemed to exist only to *épater le bourgeois*.[6] And Kate was weary of épatisme, just as much as of the bourgeoisie. She wasn't interested in épatant le bourgeois. The épateurs were as boring as the bourgeois, two halves of one dreariness.

The little party passed on to the old Jesuit convent, now used as a secondary school. Here were more frescoes.

But they were by another man.[7] And they were caricatures so crude and so ugly that Kate was merely repelled. They were meant to be shocking, but perhaps the very deliberateness prevents them from being so shocking as they might be. But they were ugly and vulgar. Strident caricatures of the Capitalist and the Church, and of the Rich Woman, and of Mammon painted life-size and as violently as possible, round the patios of the grey old building, where the young people are educated. To anyone with the spark of human balance, the things are a misdemeanour.

'Oh, but how wonderful!' cried Owen.

His susceptibilities were shocked, therefore, as at the bull-fight, he was rather pleased. He thought it was novel and stimulating to decorate your public buildings in this way.

The young Mexican who was accompanying the party was a professor in the University too: a rather short, soft young fellow of twenty-seven or eight, who wrote the inevitable poetry of sentiment, had been in the Government, even as a member of the House of Deputies, and was longing to go to New York. There was something fresh and soft, petulant about him. Kate liked him. He could laugh with real hot young amusement, and he was no fool.

Until it came to these maniacal ideas of socialism, politics, and La Patria. Then he was as mechanical as a mousetrap. Very tedious.

'Oh no!' said Kate in front of the caricatures. 'They are too ugly. They defeat their own ends.'

'But they are meant to be ugly,' said young Garcia.[8] 'They must be ugly, no? Because capitalism is ugly, and Mammon is ugly, and the priest holding his hand to get the money from the poor Indians is ugly. No?' He laughed rather unpleasantly.

'But,' said Kate, 'these caricatures are too intentional. They are like vulgar abuse, not art at all.'

'Isn't that true?' said Garcia, pointing to a hideous picture of a fat female in a tight short dress, with hips and breasts as protuberances, walking over the faces of the poor.

'That is how they are, no?'

'Who is like that?' said Kate. 'It bores me. One must keep a certain balance.'

'Not in Mexico!' said the young Mexican brightly, his plump cheeks flushing. 'In Mexico you can't keep a balance, because things are so bad. In other countries, yes, perhaps you can remain balanced, because things are not so bad as they are here. But here they are so very bad, you can't be human. You have to be Mexican. You have to be more Mexican than human, no? You can't do no other. You have to hate the capitalist, you have to, in Mexico, or nobody can live. We can't live. Nobody can live. If you are Mexican you can't be human, it is impossible. You have to be a socialist Mexican, or you have to be a capitalist Mexican, and you hate. What else is there to be done? We hate the capitalist because he ruins the country and the people. We *must* hate him.'

'But after all,' said Kate, 'what about the twelve million poor – mostly Indians – whom Montes talks about? You can't make them all rich, whatever you do. And they don't understand the very words, capital and socialism. They are Mexico, really, and nobody ever looks at them, except to make a *casus belli*[9] of them. Humanly, they never exist for you.'

'Humanly they can't exist, they are too ignorant!' cried Garcia. 'But when we can kill all the capitalists, then –'

'You'll find somebody killing *you*,' said Kate. 'No, I don't like it. *You* aren't Mexico. You aren't even Mexican, really. You are just half Spaniards full of European ideas, and you care for asserting your own ideas and nothing else. You have no real bowels of compassion. You are no good.'

The young man listened with round eyes, going rather yellow in the face. At the end he lifted his shoulders and spread his hands in a pseudo-Mediterranean gesture.

'Well! It may be!' he said, with a certain jeering flippancy. 'Perhaps you know everything. Maybe! Foreigners, they usually know everything about Mexico.' And he ended on a little cackling laugh.

'I know what I *feel*,' said Kate. 'And now I want a taxi, and I want to go home. I don't want to see any more stupid, ugly pictures.'

Off she drove back to the hotel, once more in a towering rage. She was amazed at herself. Usually she was so good-tempered and easy. But something about this country irritated her and put her into such a violent anger, she felt she would die. Burning, furious rage.

And perhaps, she thought to herself, the white and half-white Mexicans suffered some peculiar reaction in their blood which made them that they too were almost always in a state of suppressed irritation and anger, for which they *must* find a vent. They *must* spend their lives in a complicated game of frustration, frustration of life in its ebbing and flowing.

Perhaps something came out of the earth, the dragon of the earth, some effluence, some vibration which militated against the very composition of the blood and nerves in human beings. Perhaps it came from the volcanoes. Or perhaps even from the silent, serpent-like dark resistance of those masses of ponderous natives whose blood was principally the old, heavy, resistant Indian blood.

Who knows? But something there was, and something very potent. Kate lay on her bed and brooded her own organic rage. There was nothing to be done.

But young Garcia was really nice. He called in the afternoon and sent up his card. Kate, feeling sore, received him unwillingly.

'I came,' he said, with a little stiff dignity, like an ambassador on a mission, 'to tell you that I, too, don't like those caricatures. I, too, don't like them. I don't like the young people, boys and girls, no? – to be seeing them all the time. I, too, don't like. But I think, also, that here in Mexico, we can't help it. People are very bad, very greedy, no? – they only want to get money here, and they don't care. So we must hate them. Yes, we must. But I, too, I don't like it.'

He held his hat in his two hands, and twisted his shoulders in a conflict of feelings.

Kate suddenly laughed, and he laughed too, with a certain pain and confusion in his laughter.

'That's awfully nice of you to come and say so,' she said, warming to him.

'No, not nice,' he said, frowning. 'But I don't know what to *do*. Perhaps you think I am – different – I am not the thing that I am. And I don't want it.'

He flushed and was uncomfortable. There was a curious naïve sincerity about him, since he was being sincere. If he had chosen to play a game of sophistication, he could have played it better. But with Kate he wanted to be sincere.

'I know, really,' laughed Kate, 'you feel a good deal like I do about it. I know you only pretend to be fierce and hard.'

'No!' he said, suddenly making solemn, flashing eyes. 'I do also feel fierce. I do hate these men who take, only take everything from Mexico – money, and all – *everything!*' He spread his hands with finality. 'I hate them because I *must*, no? But also, I am sorry – I am sorry I have to hate so much. Yes, I think I am sorry. I think so.'

He knitted his brows rather tense. And over his plump, young, fresh face was a frown of resentment and hatred, quite sincere too.

Kate could see he wasn't really sorry. Only the two moods, of natural, soft, sensuous flow, and of heavy resentment and hate, alternated inside him like shadow and shine on a cloudy day, in swift, unavoidable succession. What was nice about him was his simplicity, in spite of the complication of his feelings, and the fact that his resentments were not personal, but beyond persons, even beyond himself.

She went out with him to tea, and while she was out, Don Ramón called and left cards with the corners turned down, and an invitation to dinner for her and Owen. There seemed an almost old-fashioned correctness in those cards.

Looking over the newspaper, she came on an odd little item. She could read Spanish without much difficulty. The trouble lay in talking it, when Italian got in her way and caused a continual stumble. She looked on the English page of the *Excelsior* or the *Universal* for the news – if there was any. Then she looked through the Spanish pages for bits of interest.

This little item was among the Spanish information, and was headed: The Gods of Antiquity Return to Mexico.

'There was a ferment in the village of Sayula, Jalisco, on the Lake of Sayula,[10] owing to an incident of more or less comic nature, yesterday morning towards mid-day. The women who inhabit the shores of the lake are to be seen each day soon after sunrise descending to the water's edge with large bundles. They kneel on the rocks and stones, and in little groups, like water-fowl, they wash their dirty linen in the soft water of the lake, pausing at times as an old *canoa* sails by with large single sail. The scene is little changed since the days of Montezuma, when the natives of the lake worshipped the spirit of the waters, and threw in little images and idols of baked clay, which the lake sometimes returns to the descendants of the

dead idolators, to keep them in mind of practices not yet altogether forgotten.

'As the hot sun rises in the sky, the women spread their washing
on the sand and pebbles of the shore, and retire to the shade of the
willow trees that grow so gracefully and retain their verdant hue
through the dryest season of the year. While thus reposing after their
labours, these humble and superstitious women were astonished to
see a man of great stature rise naked from the lake and wade towards the shore. His face, they said, was dark and bearded, but his
body shone like gold.

'As if unaware of any watchful eyes, he advanced calmly and
majestically towards the shore. There he stood a moment, and
selecting with his eye a pair of the loose cotton pants worn by the
peasants in the fields, that was spread whitening in the sun, he stooped
and proceeded to cover his nakedness with the said garment.

'The woman who thus saw her husband's apparel robbed beneath
her eye, rose, calling to the man and summoning the other women.
Whereupon the stranger turned his dark face upon them, and said in
a quiet voice: "Why are you crying? Be quiet! It will be given back
to you. Your gods are ready to return to you. Quetzalcoatl and
Tlaloc,[11] the old gods, are minded to come back to you. Be quiet,
don't let them find you crying and complaining. I have come from
out of the lake to tell you the gods are coming back to Mexico, they
are ready to return to their own home."

'Little comforted by this speech, the woman who had lost her
washing was overcome and said no more. The stranger then appropriated a cotton blouse, which he donned, and disappeared.

'After a while, the simple women gathered courage to return to
their humble dwellings. The story thus reached the ears of the police,
who at once set out to search for the thief.

'The story, however, is not yet concluded. The husband of the poor
woman of the lake-shore, returning from his labours in the field,
approached the gates of the village towards sunset, thinking, no
doubt, of nothing but repose and the evening meal. A man in a black
serape stepped towards him, from the shadows of a broken wall, and
asked: Are you afraid to come with me? The labourer, a man of
spirit, promptly replied; No, señor! He therefore followed the unknown man through the broken wall and through the bushes of a

deserted garden. In a dark room, or cellar, a small light was burning, revealing a great basin of gold, into which four little men, smaller than children, were pouring sweet-scented water. The astounded peasant was now told to wash and put on clean clothes, to be ready for the return of the gods. He was seated in the golden basin and washed with sweet-smelling soap, while the dwarfs poured water over him. *This*, they said, *is the bath of Quetzalcoatl. The bath of fire is yet to come.* They gave him clean clothing of pure white cotton, and a new hat with star embroidery, and sandals with straps of white leather. But beside this, a new blanket, white with bars of blue and black, and flowers like stars at the centre, and two pieces of silver money. *Go*, he was told. *And when they ask you, where did you get your blanket? answer that Quetzalcoatl is young again.* The poor fellow went home in sore fear, lest the police should arrest him for possessing stolen goods.

'The village is full of excitement, and Don Ramón Carrasco, our eminent historian and archaeologist, whose hacienda lies in the vicinity, has announced his intention of proceeding as soon as possible to the spot to examine the origin of this new legend. Meanwhile, the police are watching attentively the development of affairs, without taking any steps for the moment. Indeed, these little fantasies create a pleasant diversion in the regular order of banditry, murder, and outrage, which it is usually our duty to report.'

Kate wondered what was at the back of this: if anything more than a story. Yet, strangely, a different light than the common light seemed to gleam out of the words of even this newspaper paragraph.

She wanted to go to Sayula. She wanted to see the big lake where the gods had once lived, and whence they were due to emerge. Amid all the bitterness that Mexico produced in her spirit, there was still a strange beam of wonder and mystery, almost like hope. A strange darkly-iridescent beam of wonder, of magic.

The name Quetzalcoatl, too, fascinated her. She had read bits about the god. Quetzal is the name of a bird that lives high up in the mists of tropical mountains, and has very beautiful tail-feathers, precious to the Aztecs. Coatl is a serpent. Quetzalcoatl[12] is the Plumed Serpent, so hideous in the fanged, feathered, writhing stone of the National Museum.

But Quetzalcoatl was, she vaguely remembered, a sort of fair-faced bearded god; the wind, the breath of life, the eyes that see and are unseen, like the stars by day. The eyes that watch behind the wind, as the stars beyond the blue of day. And Quetzalcoatl must depart from Mexico to merge again into the deep bath of life. He was old. He had gone eastwards, perhaps into the sea, perhaps he had sailed into heaven, like a meteor returning, from the top of the Volcano of Orizaba: gone back as a peacock streaming into the night, or as a bird of Paradise, its tail gleaming like the wake of a meteor. Quetzalcoatl! Who knows what he meant to the dead Aztecs, and to the older Indians, who knew him before the Aztecs raised their deity to heights of horror and vindictiveness?

All a confusion of contradictory gleams of meaning, Quetzalcoatl. But why not? Her Irish spirit was weary to death of definite meanings, and a God of one fixed purport. Gods should be iridescent, like the rainbow in the storm. Man creates a God in his own image, and the gods grow old along with the men that made them. But storms sway in heaven, and the god-stuff sways high and angry over our heads. Gods die with men who have conceived them. But the god-stuff roars eternally, like the sea, with too vast a sound to be heard. Like the sea in storm, that beats against the rocks of living, stiffened men, slowly to destroy them. Or like the sea of the glimmering, ethereal plasm of the world, that bathes the feet and the knees of men as earthsap bathes the roots of trees. Ye must be born again. Even the gods must be born again. We must be born again.[13]

In her vague, woman's way, Kate knew this. She had lived her life. She had had her lovers, her two husbands. She had her children.

Joachim Leslie, her dead husband, she had loved as much as a woman can love a man: that is, to the bounds of human love. Then she had realised that human love has its limits, that there is a beyond. And Joachim dead, willy nilly her spirit had passed the bounds. She was no longer in love with love. She no longer yearned for the love of a man, or the love even of her children. Joachim had gone into eternity in death, and she had crossed with him into a certain eternity in life. There, the yearning for companionship and sympathy and human love had left her. Something infinitely intangible but infinitely blessed took its place: a peace that passes understanding.

At the same time, a wild and angry battle raged between her and the thing that *Owen* called life: such as the bull-fight, the tea-party, the enjoyments; like the arts in their modern aspect of hate effusion. The powerful, degenerate thing called life, wrapping one or other of its tentacles round her.

And then, when she could escape into her true loneliness, the influx of peace and soft, flower-like potency which was beyond understanding. It disappeared even if you thought about it, so delicate, so fine. And yet, the only reality.

Ye must be born again. Out of the fight with the octopus of life, the dragon of degenerate or of incomplete existence, one must win this soft bloom of being, that is damaged by a touch.

No, she no longer wanted love, excitement, and something to fill her life. She was forty, and in the rare, lingering dawn of maturity, the flower of her soul was opening. Above all things, she must preserve herself from worldly contacts. Only she wanted the silence of other unfolded souls around her, like a perfume. The presence of that which is forever unsaid.

And in the horror and climax of death-rattles, which is Mexico, she thought she could see it in the black eyes of the Indians. She felt that Don Ramón and Don Cipriano both had heard the soundless call, across all the hideous choking.

Perhaps this had brought her to Mexico: away from England and her mother, away from her children, away from everybody. To be alone with the unfolding flower of her own soul, in the delicate, chiming silence that is at the midst of things.

The thing called 'Life' is just a mistake we have made in our own minds. Why persist in the mistake any further?

Owen was the mistake itself: so was Villiers: so was that Mexico City.

She wanted to get out, to disentangle herself again.

They had promised to go out to dinner to the house of Don Ramón. His wife was away in the United States with her two boys, one of whom had been ill, not seriously, at his school in California. But Don Ramón's aunt would be hostess.

The house was out at Tlalpam. It was May, the weather was hot, the rains were not yet started. The shower at the bull-fight had been a sort of accident.

'I wonder,' said Owen, 'whether I ought to put on a dinner-coat.

Really, I feel humiliated to the earth every time I put on evening dress.'

'Then don't do it!' said Kate, who was impatient of Owen's kicking at these very little social pricks, and swallowing the whole porcupine.

She herself came down in a simple gown with a black velvet top and a loose skirt of delicate brocaded chiffon, of a glimmering green and yellow and black. She also wore a long string of jade and crystal.

It was a gift she had, of looking like an Ossianic goddess,[14] a certain feminine strength and softness glowing in the very material of her dress. But she was never 'smart'.

'Why you're dressed up to the eyes!' cried Owen in chagrin, pulling at his soft collar. 'Bare shoulders notwithstanding!'

They went out to the distant suburb in the tram-car, swift in the night, with big clear stars overhead, dropping and hanging with a certain gleam of menace. In Tlalpan there was a heavy scent of nightflowers, a feeling of ponderous darkness, with a few sparks of intermittent fireflies. And always the heavy calling of nightflower scents. To Kate, there seemed a faint whiff of blood in all tropical-scented flowers: of blood or sweat.

It was a hot night. They banged on the iron doors of the entrance, dogs barked, and a mozo opened to them, warily, closing fast again the moment they had entered the dark garden of trees.

Don Ramón was in white, a white dinner-jacket: Don Cipriano the same. But there were other guests, young Garcia, another pale young man called Mirabal, and an elderly man in a black cravat, named Toussaint. The only other woman was Doña Isabel, aunt to Don Ramón. She wore a black dress with a high collar of black lace, and some strings of pearls, and seemed shy, frightened, absent as a nun before all these men. But to Kate she was very kind, caressive, speaking English in a plaintive faded voice. This dinner was a sort of ordeal and ritual combined, to the cloistered, elderly soul.

But it was soon evident that she was trembling with fearful joy. She adored Ramón with an uncritical, nun-like adoration. It was obvious she hardly heard the things that were said. Words skimmed the surface of her consciousness without ever penetrating. Underneath, she was trembling in nun-like awareness of so many men, and in almost sacred excitement at facing Don Ramón as hostess.

The house was a fairly large villa, quietly and simply furnished, with natural taste.

'Do you always live here?' said Kate to Don Ramón. 'Never at your hacienda?'

'How do you know I have a hacienda?' he asked.

'I saw it in a newspaper – near Sayula.'

'Ah!' he said, laughing at her with his eyes. 'You saw about the returning of the Gods of Antiquity.'

'Yes,' she said. 'Don't you think it is interesting?'

'I think so,' he said.

'I love the *word* Quetzalcoatl.'

'The *word*!' he repeated.

His eyes laughed at her teasingly all the time.

'What do you think, Mrs Leslie,' cried the pale-faced young Mirabal,[15] in curiously resonant English, with a French accent. 'Don't you think it would be wonderful if the gods came back to Mexico? our own gods?' He sat in intense expectation, his blue eyes fixed on Kate's face, his soup-spoon suspended.

Kate's face was baffled with incomprehension.

'Not those Aztec horrors!' she said.

'The Aztec horrors! The Aztec horrors! Well, perhaps they were not so horrible after all. But if they were, it was because the Aztecs were all tied up. They were in a cul de sac, so they saw nothing but death. Don't you think so?'

'I don't know enough!' said Kate.

'Nobody knows any more. But if you like the *word* Quetzalcoatl, don't you think it would be wonderful if he came back again? Ah, the *names* of the gods! Don't you think the *names* are like seeds, so full of magic, of the unexplored magic? Huitzilopochtli![16] – how wonderful! And Tlaloc! Ah! I love them! I say them over and over, like they say *Mani padma Om!*[17] in Tibet. I believe in the fertility of sound. *Itzpapalotl* – the Obsidian Butterfly! Itzpapalotl![18] But say it, and you will see it does good to your soul. Itzpapalotl! Tezcatlipoca![19] They were old when the Spaniards came, they needed the bath of life again. But now, re-bathed in youth, how wonderful they must be! Think of *Jehovah! Jehovah!* Think of *Jesus Christ!* How thin and poor they sound! Or *Jesucristo!* They are dead names, all the life withered out of them. Ah, it is time now for Jesus to go back to the place of the death of the gods, and take the long bath of being made young again. He is an old-old young god, don't you think?' He looked long at Kate, then dived for his soup.

Kate widened her eyes in amazement at this torrent from the young Mirabal. Then she laughed.

'I think it's a bit overwhelming!' she said, non-committal.

'Ah! Yes! Exactly! Exactly! But how good to be overwhelmed! How splendid if something will overwhelm me! Ah, I am so glad!'

The last word came with a clapping French resonance, and the young man dived for his soup again. He was lean and pale, but burning with an intense, crazy energy.

'You see,' said young Garcia, raising his full, bright dark eyes to Kate, half aggressive and half bashful: 'we must do something for Mexico. If we don't, it will go under, no? You say you don't like socialism. I don't think I do either. But if there is nothing else but socialism, we will have socialism. If there is nothing better. But perhaps there is.'

'Why should Mexico go under?' said Kate. 'There are lots of children everywhere.'

'Yes. But the last census of Porfirio Díaz[20] gave seventeen million people in Mexico, and the census of last year gave only thirteen millions. Maybe the count was not quite right. But you count four million people fewer, in twenty years, then in sixty years there will be no Mexicans: only foreigners, who don't die.'

'Oh, but figures always lie!' said Kate. 'Statistics are always misleading.'

'Maybe two and two don't make four,' said Garcia. 'I don't know if they do. But I know, if you take two away from two, it leaves none.'

'Do you think Mexico might die out?' she said to Don Ramón.

'Why!' he replied. 'It might. Die out and become Americanised.'

'I quite see the danger of Americanisation,' said Owen. 'That *would* be ghastly. Almost better die out.'

Owen was so American, he invariably said these things.

'But!' said Kate. 'The Mexicans look so strong!'

'They are strong to carry heavy loads,' said Don Ramón. 'But they die easily. They eat all the wrong things, they drink the wrong things, and they don't mind dying. They have many children, and they like their children very much. But when the child dies, the parents say: *Ah, he will be an angelito!* So they cheer up and feel as if they had been given a present. Sometimes I think they enjoy it when their children die. Sometimes I think they would like to transfer Mexico *en bloc* into Paradise, or whatever lies behind the walls of death. It would be better there!'

There was a silence.

'But how sad you are!' said Kate, afraid.

Doña Isabel was giving hurried orders to the manservant.

'Whoever knows Mexico below the surface, is sad!' said Julio Toussaint, rather sententiously, over his black cravat.

'Well,' said Owen, 'it seems to me, on the contrary, a gay country. A country of gay, irresponsible children. Or rather, they *would* be gay, if they were properly treated. If they had comfortable homes, and a sense of real freedom. If they felt that they could control their lives and their own country. But being in the grip of outsiders, as they have been for hundreds of years, life of course seems hardly worth while to them. Naturally, they don't care if they live or die. They don't feel *free*.'

'Free for what?' asked Toussaint.

'To make Mexico their own. Not to be so poor and at the mercy of outsiders.'

'They are at the mercy of something worse than outsiders,' said Toussaint. 'Let me tell you. They are at the mercy of their own natures. It is this way. Fifty per cent. of the people in Mexico are pure Indian: more or less.[21] Of the rest, a small proportion are foreigners or Spaniard. You have then the mass which is on top, of mixed blood, Indian and Spaniard mixed, chiefly. These are the Mexicans, those with the mixed blood. Now, you take us at this table. Don Cipriano is pure Indian. Don Ramón is almost pure Spaniard, but most probably he has the blood of Tlaxcalan Indians in his veins as well.[22] Señor Mirabal is mixed French and Spanish. Señor Garcia most probably has a mixture of Indian blood with Spanish. I myself have French, Spanish, Austrian, and Indian blood. Very well! Now you mix blood of the same race, and it may be all right. Europeans are all Aryan stock, the race is the same. But when you mix European and American Indian, you mix different blood races, and you produce the half-breed. Now, the half-breed is a calamity. For why? He is neither one thing nor another, he is divided against himself. His blood of one race tells him one thing, his blood of another race tells him another. He is an unfortunate, a calamity to himself. And it is hopeless.

'And this is Mexico. The Mexicans of mixed blood are hopeless.

Well then! There are only two things to be done. All the foreigners and the Mexicans clear out and leave the country to the Indians, the pure-blooded Indians. But already you have a difficulty. How can you distinguish the pure-blooded Indian, after so many generations? Or else the half-breed or mixed-blood Mexicans who are all the time on top shall continue to destroy the country till the Americans from the United States flood in and we are as California and New Mexico now are, swamped under the dead white sea.

'But let me tell you something further. I hope we are not Puritans. I hope I may say that it depends on the moment of coition. At the moment of coition, either the spirit of the father fuses with the spirit of the mother, to create a new being with a soul, or else nothing fuses but the germ of procreation.

'Now consider. How have these Mexicans of mixed blood been begotten, for centuries? In what spirit? What was the moment of coition like? Answer me that, and you have told me the reason for this Mexico which makes us despair and which will go on making everybody despair, till it destroys itself. In what spirit have the Spanish and other foreign fathers gotten children of the Indian women? What sort of spirit was it? What sort of coition? And then, what sort of race do you expect?'

'But what sort of a spirit is there between white men and white women!' said Kate.

'At least,' replied the didactic Toussaint, 'the blood is homogeneous, so that consciousness automatically unrolls in continuity.'

'I hate its unrolling in automatic continuity,' said Kate.

'Perhaps! But it makes life possible. Without developing continuity in consciousness, you have chaos. And this comes of mixed blood.'

'And then,' said Kate, 'surely the Indian men are fond of their women! The men seem manly, and the women seem very lovable and womanly.'

'It is possible that the Indian children are pure-blooded, and there is the continuity of blood. But the Indian consciousness is swamped under the stagnant water of the white man's Dead Sea consciousness. Take a man like Benito Juárez,[23] a pure Indian. He floods his old consciousness with the new white ideas, and there springs up a whole forest of verbiage, new laws, new constitutions and all the rest. But it is a sudden weed. It grows like a weed on the surface, saps the strength of the Indian soil underneath, and helps the process of ruin. No, madam! There is no hope for Mexico short of a miracle.'

'Ah!' cried Mirabal, flourishing his wine-glass. 'Isn't that wonderful, when only the miracle will save us! When we must produce the miracle? *We! We!* We must make the miracle!' He hit his own breast emphatically. 'Ah, I think that is marvellous!' And he returned to his turkey in black sauce.

'Look at the Mexicans!' Toussaint flared on. 'They don't care about anything. They eat food so hot with chili, it burns holes in their insides. And it has no nourishment. They live in houses that a dog would be ashamed of, and they lie and shiver with cold. But they don't *do* anything. They could make, easily, easily, a bed of maize leaves or similar leaves. But they don't do it. They don't do anything. They roll up in a thin serape and lie on a thin mat on the bare ground, whether it is wet or dry. And Mexican nights are cold. But they lie down like dogs, anyhow, as if they lay down to die. I say dogs! But you will see the dogs looking for a dry sheltered place. The Mexicans, no! Anywhere, nothing, nothing! And it is terrible. It is terrible! As if they wanted to punish themselves for being alive!'

'But then, why do they have so many children?' said Kate.

'Why do they? The same, because they don't care. They don't care. They don't care about money, they don't care about making anything, they don't care about nothing, nothing, nothing. Only they get an excitement out of women, as they do out of chili. They like to feel the red pepper burning holes in their insides, and they like to feel the other thing, the sex, burning holes in them too. But after the moment, they don't care. They don't care a bit.

'And that is bad. I tell you, excuse me, but all, everything, depends on the moment of coition. At that moment many things can come to a crisis: all a man's hope, his honour, his faith, his trust, his belief in life and creation and God, all these things can come to a crisis in the moment of coition. And these things will be handed on in continuity to the child. Believe me, I am a crank on this idea, but it is true. It is certainly absolutely true.'

'I believe it is true,' said Kate, rather coldly.

'Ah! you do! Well then! Look at Mexico! The only *conscious* people are half-breeds, people of mixed blood, begotten in greed and selfish brutality.'

'Some people believe in the mixed blood,' said Kate.

'Ah! They do, do they? Who?'

'Some of your serious-minded men. They say the half-breed is better than the Indian.'

'Better! Well! The Indian has his hopelessness. The moment of coition is his moment of supreme hopelessness, when he throws himself down the pit of despair.'

The Austrian, European blood, which fans into fire of conscious understanding, died down again, leaving what was Mexican in Julio Toussaint sunk in irredeemable gloom.

'It is true,' said Mirabal, out of the gloom. 'The Mexicans who have any feeling always prostitute themselves, one way or another, and so they can never *do* anything. And the Indians can never do anything either, because they haven't got hope in anything. But it is always darkest before the dawn. We must make the miracle come. The miracle is superior even to the moment of coition.'

It seemed, however, as if he said it by an effort of will.

The dinner was ending in silence. During the whirl of talk, or of passionate declaration, the servants had carried round the food and wine. Doña Isabel, completely oblivious of the things that were being said, watched and directed the servants with nervous anxiety and excitement, her hands with their old jewellery trembling with agitation. Don Ramón had kept his eye on his guests' material comfort, at the same time listening, as it were, from the back of his head. His big brown eyes were inscrutable, his face impassive. But when he had anything to say, it was always with a light laugh and a teasing accent. And yet his eyes brooded and smouldered with an incomprehensible, unyielding fire.

Kate felt she was in the presence of men. Here were men face to face not with death and self-sacrifice, but with the life-issue. She felt for the first time in her life, a pang almost like fear, of men who were passing beyond what she knew, beyond her depth.

Cipriano, his rather short but intensely black, curved eyelashes lowering over his dark eyes, watched his plate, only sometimes looking up with a black, brilliant glance, either at whomsoever was speaking, or at Don Ramón, or at Kate. His face was changeless and intensely serious, serious almost with a touch of childishness. But the curious blackness of his eyelashes lifted so strangely, with such intense unconscious maleness from his eyes, the movement of his hand was so odd, quick, light as he ate, so easily a movement of shooting, or of flashing a knife into the body of some adversary, and his dark-coloured lips were so helplessly savage, as he ate or briefly spoke, that her heart stood still. There was something undeveloped and intense in him, the intensity and the crudity of the semi-savage. She could well understand the potency of the snake upon the Aztec and Maya imagination. Something smooth, undeveloped, yet vital in this man suggested the heavy-ebbing blood of reptiles in his veins. That was what it was, the heavy-ebbing blood of powerful reptiles, the dragon of Mexico.

So that unconsciously she shrank when his black, big, glittering eyes turned on her for a moment. They were not, like Don Ramón's, *dark* eyes. They were black, as black as jewels into which one could not look without a sensation of fear. And her fascination was tinged with fear. She felt somewhat as the bird feels when the snake is watching it.

She wondered almost that Don Ramón was not afraid. Because she had noticed that usually, when an Indian looked to a white man, both men stood back from actual contact, from actual meeting of each other's eyes. They left a wide space of neutral territory between them. But Cipriano looked at Ramón with a curious intimacy, glittering, steady, warrior-like, and at the same time betraying an almost menacing trust in the other man.

Kate realised that Ramón had a good deal to stand up to. But he kept a little, foiling laugh on his face, and lowered his beautiful head with the black hair touched with grey, as if he would put a veil before his countenance.

'Do you think one can make this miracle come?' she asked of him.

'The miracle is always there,' he said, 'for the man who can pass his hand through to it, to take it.'

They finished dinner, and went to sit out on the verandah, looking into the garden where the light from the house fell uncannily on the blossoming trees and the dark tufts of Yucca and the strange great writhing trunks of the Laurel de India.

Cipriano had sat down next to her, smoking a cigarette.

'It is a strange darkness, the Mexican darkness!' she said.

'Do you like it?' he asked.

'I don't know yet,' she said. 'Do you?'

'Yes. Very much. I think I like best the time when the day is falling and the night coming on like something else. Then, one feels more free, don't you think? Like the flowers that send out their scent at night, but in the daytime they look at the sun and don't have any smell.'

'Perhaps the night here scares me,' she laughed.

'Yes. But why not? The smell of the flowers at night may make one feel afraid, but it is a good fear. One likes it, don't you think?'

'I am afraid of fear,' she said.

He laughed shortly.

'You speak such English English,' she said. 'Nearly all the Mexicans who speak English speak American English. Even Don Ramón does, rather.'

'Yes. Don Ramón graduated in Columbia University. But I was sent to England, to school in London, and then to Oxford.'

'Who sent you?'

'My god-father. He was an Englishman: Bishop Severn, Bishop of Oaxaca. You have heard of him?'

'No,' said Kate.

'He was a very well-known man. He died only about ten years ago. He was very rich, too, before the revolution. He had a big hacienda in Oaxaca, with a very fine library. But they took it away from him in the revolution, and they sold the things, or broke them. They didn't know the value of them, of course.'

'And did he adopt you?'

'Yes! In a way. My father was one of the overseers on the hacienda. When I was a little boy[24] I came running to my father, when the Bishop was there, with something in my hands – so!' – and he made a cup of his hand. 'I don't remember. This is what they tell me. I was a small child – three or four years of age – somewhere there. What I had in my hands was a yellow scorpion, one of the small ones, very poisonous, no?'

And he lifted the cup of his small, slender, dark hands, as if to show Kate the creature.

'Well, the Bishop was talking to my father, and he saw what I had got before my father did. So he told me at once, to put the scorpion in his hat – the Bishop's hat, no? Of course I did what he told me, and I put the scorpion in his hat, and it did not bite me. If it had stung me I should have died, of course. But I didn't know, so I suppose the alacrán was not interested. The Bishop was a very good man, very kind. He liked my father, so he became my god-father. Then he always took an interest in me, and he sent me to school, and then to England. He hoped I should be a priest. He always said that the one hope for Mexico was if she had really fine native priests.' He ended rather wistfully.

'And didn't you want to become a priest?' said Kate.

'No!' he said sadly. 'No!'

'Not at all?' she asked.

'No! When I was in England it was different from Mexico. Even God was different, and the Blessed Mary. They were changed so much, I felt I didn't know them any more. Then I came to understand better, and when I understood I didn't believe any more. I used to think it was the images of Jesus, and the Virgin, and the Saints, that were doing everything in the world. And the world seemed to me so strange, no? I couldn't see that it was bad, because it was all so very strange and mysterious, when I was a child, in Mexico. Only in England I learned about the laws of life, and some science. And then when I knew why the sun rose and set, and how the world really was, I felt quite different.'

'Was your god-father disappointed?'

'A little, perhaps. But he asked me if I would rather be a soldier, so I said I would. Then when the revolution came, and I was twenty-two years old, I had to come back to Mexico.'

'Did you like your god-father?'

'Yes, very much. But the revolution carried everything away. I felt I must do what my god-father wished. But I could see that Mexico was not the Mexico he believed in. It was different. He was too English, and too good to understand. In the revolutions, I tried to help the man I believed was the best man. So you see, I have always been half a priest and half a soldier.'

'You never married?'

'No. I couldn't marry, because I always felt my god-father was there, and I felt I had promised him to be a priest – all those things, you know. When he died he told me to follow my own conscience, and to remember that Mexico and all the Indians were in the hands of God, and he made me promise never to take sides against God. He was an old man when he died, seventy-five.'

Kate could see the spell of the old Bishop's strong, rather grandiose personality upon the impressionable Indian. She could see the curious recoil into chastity, perhaps characteristic of the savage. And at the same time she felt the intense masculine yearning, coupled with a certain male ferocity, in the man's breast.

'Your husband was James Joachim Leslie, the famous Irish leader?' he asked her: and added:

'You had no children?'

'No. I wanted Joachim's children so much, but I didn't have any. But I have a boy and a girl from my first marriage. My first husband was a lawyer, and I was divorced from him for Joachim.'

'Did you like him – that first one?'

'Yes. I liked him. But I never felt anything very deep for him. I married him when I was young, and he was a good deal older than I. I was fond of him, in a way. But I had never realised that one could be more than fond of a man, till I knew Joachim. I thought that was all one could ever expect to feel – that you just liked a man, and that he was in love with you. It took me years to understand that a woman *can't* love a man – at least a woman like I am can't – if he is only the sort of good, decent citizen. With Joachim I came to realise that a woman like me *can* only love a man who is fighting to *change* the world, to make it freer, more alive. Men like my first husband, who are good and trustworthy and who work to keep the world going on well in the same state they found it in, they let you down horribly, somewhere. You feel so terribly sold. Everything is just a sell: it becomes so small. A woman who isn't quite ordinary herself can only love a man who is fighting for something beyond the ordinary life.'

'And your husband fought for Ireland.'

'Yes – for Ireland, and for something he never quite realised. He ruined his health. And when he was dying, he said to me: *Kate, perhaps I've let you down. Perhaps I haven't really helped Ireland. But I couldn't help myself. I feel as if I'd brought you to the doors of life, and was leaving you there. Kate, don't be disappointed in life because of me. I didn't really get anywhere. I haven't really got anywhere. I feel as if I'd made a mistake. But perhaps when I'm dead I shall be able to do more for you than I have done while I was alive. Say you'll never feel disappointed!*'

There was a pause. The memory of the dead man was coming over her again, and all her grief.

'And I don't feel disappointed,' she went on, her voice beginning to shake. 'But I loved him. And it was bitter, that he had to die, feeling he hadn't – hadn't.'

She put her hands before her face, and the bitter tears came through her fingers.

Cipriano sat motionless as a statue. But from his breast came that dark, surging passion of tenderness the Indians are capable of. Perhaps it would pass, leaving him indifferent and fatalistic again. But at any rate for the moment he sat in a dark, fiery cloud of passionate male tenderness. He looked at her soft, wet white hands over her face, and at the one big emerald on her finger, in a sort of wonder. The wonder, the mystery, the magic that used to flood over him as a boy and a youth, when he kneeled before the babyish figure of the Santa Maria de la Soledad,²⁵ flooded him again. He was in the presence of the goddess, white-handed, mysterious, gleaming with a moon-like power and the intense potency of grief.

Then Kate hastily took her hands from her face and with head ducked looked for her handkerchief. Of course she hadn't got one. Cipriano lent her his, nicely folded. She took it without a word, and rubbed her face and blew her nose.

'I want to go and look at the flowers,' she said in a strangled voice.

And she dashed into the garden with his handkerchief in her hand. He stood up and drew aside his chair, to let her pass, then stood a moment looking at the garden, before he sat down again and lighted a cigarette.

CHAPTER IV

To Stay or Not to Stay

OWEN had to return to the United States, and he asked Kate whether she wanted to stay on in Mexico.

This put her into a quandary. It was not an easy country for a woman to be alone in. And she had been beating her wings in an effort to get away. She felt like a bird round whose body a snake has coiled itself. Mexico was the snake.

The curious influence of the country, pulling one down, pulling one down. She had heard an old American, who had been forty years in the Republic, saying to Owen: 'No man who hasn't a strong moral backbone should try to settle in Mexico. If he does, he'll go to pieces, morally and physically, as I've seen hundreds of young Americans do.'

To pull one down. It was what the country wanted to do all the time, with a slow, reptilian insistence, to pull one down. To prevent the spirit from soaring. To take away the free, soaring sense of liberty.

'There is no such thing as liberty,' she heard the quiet, deep, dangerous voice of Don Ramón repeating. 'There is no such thing as liberty. The greatest liberators are usually slaves of an idea. The freest people are slaves to convention and public opinion, and more still, slaves to the industrial machine. There is no such thing as liberty. You only change one sort of domination for another. All we can do is to choose our master.'

'But surely that *is* liberty – for the mass of people.'

'They don't choose. They are tricked into a new form of servility, no more. They go from bad to worse.'

'You yourself – aren't you free?' she asked.

'I?' he laughed. 'I spent a long time trying to pretend. I thought I could have my own way. Till I realised that having my own way meant only running about smelling all the things in the street, like a dog that will pick up something. Of myself, I have no way. No man has any way in himself. Every man who goes along a way is led by one of three things: by an appetite – and I class ambition among appetites; or by an idea; or by an inspiration.'

'I used to think my husband was inspired about Ireland,' said Kate doubtfully.

'And now?'

'Yes! Perhaps he put his wine in old, rotten bottles that wouldn't hold it. No! – Liberty is a rotten old wine-skin. It won't hold one's wine of inspiration or passion any more,' she said.

'And Mexico!' he said. 'Mexico is another Ireland. Ah no, no man can be his own master. If I must serve, I will not serve an idea, which cracks and leaks like an old wine-skin. I will serve the God that gives me my manhood. There is no liberty for a man, apart from the God of his manhood. Free Mexico is a bully, and the old, colonial, ecclesiastical Mexico was another sort of bully. When man has nothing but his *will* to assert – even his good-will – it is always bullying. Bolshevism is one sort of bullying, capitalism another: and liberty is a change of chains.'

'Then what's to be done?' said Kate. 'Just nothing?'

And with her own will, she wanted nothing to be done. Let the skies fall!

'One is driven, at last, back to the far distance, to look for God,' said Ramón uneasily.

'I rather hate this search-for-God business, and religiosity,' said Kate.

'I know!' he said, with a laugh. 'I've suffered from would-be-cock-sure religion myself.'

'And you can't *really* "find God"!' she said. 'It's a sort of sentimentalism, and creeping back into old, hollow shells.'

'No!' he said slowly. 'I can't *find God*, in the old sense. I know it's a sentimentalism if I pretend to. But I am nauseated with humanity and the human will: even with my own will. I have realised that *my will*, no matter how intelligent I am, is only another nuisance on the face of the earth, once I start exerting it. And other people's *wills* are even worse.'

'Oh! isn't human life horrible!' she cried. 'Every human being exerting his will all the time – over other people, and over himself, and nearly always self-righteous!'

Ramón made a grimace of repulsion.

'To me,' he said, 'that is just the weariness of life! For a time, it can be amusing: exerting your own will, and resisting all the other people's wills, that they try to put over you. But at a certain point a nausea sets in at the very middle of me: my *soul* is nauseated. My soul is nauseated, and there is nothing but death ahead, unless I find something else.'

Kate listened in silence. She knew the road he had gone, but she herself had not yet come to the end of it. As yet she was still strong in the pride of her own – her very own *will*.

'Oh, people are repulsive!' she cried.

'My own will becomes even more repulsive at last,' he said. 'My own will, merely as my own will, is even more distasteful to me than other people's wills. From being the god in my own machine, I must either abdicate, or die of disgust – self-disgust, at that.'

'How amusing!' she cried.

'It is rather funny,' he said sardonically.

'And then?' she asked, looking at him with a certain malevolent challenge.

He looked back at her slowly, with an ironical light in his eyes.

'Then!' he repeated. 'Then! – I ask, what else is there in the world, besides human will, human appetite? because ideas and ideals are only instruments of human will and appetite.'

'Not entirely,' said Kate. 'They may be disinterested.'

'May they? If the appetite *isn't* interested, the will is.'

'Why not?' she mocked. 'We can't be mere detached blocks.'

'It nauseates me – I look for something else.'

'And what do you find?'

'My own manhood!'

'What does that mean?' she cried, jeering.

'If you looked, and found your own womanhood, you would know.'

'But I *have* my own womanhood!' she cried.

'And then – when you find your own manhood – your womanhood,' he went on, smiling faintly at her – 'then you know it is not your own, to do as you like with. You don't have it of your own will. It comes from – from the middle – from the God. Beyond me, at the middle, is the God. And the God gives me my manhood, then leaves me to it. I have nothing but my manhood. The God gives it me, and leaves me to do further.'

Kate would not hear any more. She broke off into banalities.

The immediate question, for her, was whether she would stay in

Mexico or not. She was not really concerned with Don Ramón's soul – or even her own. She was concerned with her immediate future. Should she stay in Mexico? Mexico meant the dark-faced men in cotton clothes, big hats: the peasants, peons, pelados, Indians, call them what you will. The mere natives.

Those pale-faced Mexicans of the Capital, politicians, artists, professionals, and business people, they did not interest her. Neither did the hacendados and the ranch-owners, in their tight trousers and weak, soft sensuality, pale victims of their own emotional undiscipline. Mexico still meant the mass of silent peons, to her. And she thought of them again, these silent, stiff-backed men, driving their strings of asses along the country roads, in the dust of Mexico's infinite dryness, past broken walls, broken houses, broken haciendas, along the endless desolation left by the revolutions; past the vast stretches of maguey, the huge cactus, or aloe, with its gigantic rosette of upstarting, pointed leaves, that in its iron rows covers miles and miles of ground in the Valley of Mexico, cultivated for the making of that bad-smelling drink, pulque. The Mediterranean has the dark grape, old Europe has malted beer, and China has opium from the white poppy. But out of the Mexican soil a bunch of black-tarnished swords bursts up, and a great unfolded bud of the once-flowering monster begins to thrust at the sky. They cut the great phallic bud and crush out the sperm-like juice for the pulque. *Agua miel! Pulque!* [1]

But better pulque than the fiery white brandy distilled from the maguey: mescal, tequila: or in the low lands, the hateful sugar-cane brandy, aguardiente.

And the Mexican burns out his stomach with those beastly fire-waters and cauterises the hurt with red-hot chili. Swallowing one hell-fire to put out another.

Tall fields of wheat and maize. Taller, more brilliant fields of bright-green sugar-cane. And threading in white cotton clothes, with dark, half-visible face, the eternal peón of Mexico, his great white calico drawers flopping round his ankles as he walks, or rolled up over his dark, handsome legs.

The wild, sombre, erect men of the north! The too-often degenerate men of Mexico Valley, their heads through the middle of their ponchos! The big men in Tlaxcala, selling ice-cream or huge half-sweetened buns and fancy bread! The quick little Indians, quick as spiders, down in Oaxaca! The queer-looking half-Chinese natives towards Vera Cruz! The dark faces and the big black eyes on the coast of Sinaloa! The handsome men of Jalisco, with a scarlet blanket folded on one shoulder!

They were of many tribes and many languages, and far more alien to one another than Frenchmen, English, and Germans are. Mexico! It is not really even the beginnings of a nation: hence the rabid assertion of nationalism in the few. And it is not a race.

Yet it is a people. There is some Indian quality which pervades the whole. Whether it is men in blue overalls and a slouch, in Mexico City, or men with handsome legs in skin-tight trousers, or the floppy, white, cotton-clad labourers in the fields, there is something mysteriously in common. The erect, prancing walk, stepping out from the base of the spine with lifted knees and short steps. The jaunty balancing of the huge hats. The thrown-back shoulders with a folded serape like a royal mantle. And most of them handsome, with dark, warm-bronze skin so smooth and living, their proudly-held heads, whose black hair gleams like wild, rich feathers. Their big, bright black eyes that look at you wonderingly, and have no centre to them. Their sudden, charming smile, when you smile first. But the eyes unchanged.

Yes, and she had to remember, too, a fair proportion of smaller, sometimes insignificant looking men, some of them scaly with dirt, who looked at you with a cold, mud-like antagonism as they stepped cattishly past. Poisonous, thin, stiff little men, cold and unliving like scorpions, and as dangerous.

And then the truly terrible faces of some creatures in the city, slightly swollen with the poison of tequila, and with black, dimmed, swivel eyes swinging in pure evil. Never had she seen such faces of pure brutish evil, cold and insect-like, as in Mexico City.

The country gave her a strange feeling of hopelessness and of dauntlessness. Unbroken, eternally resistant, it was a people that lived without hope, and without care. Gay even, and laughing with indifferent carelessness.

They were something like her own Irish, but gone to a much greater length. And also, they did what the self-conscious and pretentious Irish rarely do, they touched her bowels with a strange fire of compassion.

At the same time, she feared them. They would pull her down, pull her down, to the dark depths of nothingness.

It was the same with the women. In their full long skirts and bare feet, and with the big dark-blue scarf or shawl called a rebozo over their womanly small heads and tight round their shoulders, they were images of wild submissiveness, the primitive womanliness of the world, that is so touching and so alien. Many women kneeling in a dim church, all hooded in their dark-blue rebozos, the pallor of their skirts on the floor, their heads and shoulders wrapped dark and tight, as they swayed with devotion of fear and ecstasy! A churchful of dark-wrapped women sunk there in wild, humble supplication of dread and of bliss filled Kate with tenderness and revulsion. They crouched like people not quite created.

Their soft, untidy black hair, which they scratched for lice; the round-eyed baby joggling like a pumpkin in the shawl slung over the woman's shoulder, the never-washed feet and ankles, again somewhat reptilian under the long, flounced, soiled cotton skirt; and then, once more, the dark eyes of half-created women, soft, appealing, yet with a queer void insolence! Something lurking, where the womanly centre should have been; lurking snake-like. Fear! The fear of not being able to find full creation. And the inevitable mistrust and lurking insolence, insolent against a higher creation, the same thing that is in the striking of a snake.

Kate, as a woman, feared the women more than the men. The women were little and insidious, the men were bigger and more reckless. But in the eyes of each, the uncreated centre, where the evil and the insolence lurked.

And sometimes she wondered whether America really was the great death-continent, the great *No!* to the European and Asiatic and even African *Yes!* Was it really the great melting-pot, where men from the creative continents were smelted back again, not to a new creation, but down into the homogeneity of death? Was it the great continent of the undoing, and all its peoples the agents of the mystic destruction! Plucking, plucking at the created soul in a man, till at last it plucked out the growing germ, and left him a creature of mechanism and automatic reaction, with only one inspiration, the desire to pluck the quick out of every living spontaneous creature.

Was that the clue to America, she sometimes wondered. Was it the great death-continent, the continent that destroyed again what the other continents had built up. The continent whose spirit of place fought purely to pick the eyes out of the face of God. Was that America?

And all the people who went there, Europeans, Negroes, Japanese, Chinese, all the colours and the races, were they the spent people, in whom the God impulse had collapsed, so they crossed to the great continent of the negation, where the human will declares itself 'free', to pull down the soul of the world? Was it so? And did this account for the great drift to the New World, the drift of spent souls passing over to the side of Godless democracy, energetic negation? The negation which is the life-breath of materialism. And would the great negative pull of the Americans at last break the heart of the world?

This thought would come to her, time and again.

She herself, what had she come to America for?

Because the flow of her life had broken, and she knew she could not re-start it in Europe.

These handsome natives! Was it because they were death-worshippers, Moloch-worshippers,[2] that they were so uncowed and handsome? Their pure acknowledgement of death, and their undaunted admission of nothingness kept so erect and careless.

White men had had a soul, and lost it. The pivot of fire had been quenched in them, and their lives had started to spin in the reversed direction, widdershins.[3] That reversed look which is in the eyes of so many white people, the look of nullity, and life wheeling in the reversed direction. Widdershins.

But the dark-faced natives, with their strange soft flame of life wheeling upon a dark void: were they centreless and widdershins too, as so many white men now are?

The strange, soft flame of courage in the black Mexican eyes. But still it was not knit to a centre, that centre which is the soul of a man in a man.

And all the efforts of white men to bring the soul of the dark men of Mexico into final clinched being has resulted in nothing but the collapse of the white man. Against the soft, dark flow of the Indian the white man at last collapses, with his God and his energy he collapses. In attempting to convert the dark man to the white man's way of life, the white man has fallen helplessly down the hole he wanted to fill up. Seeking to save another man's soul, the white man lost his own, and collapsed upon himself.

Mexico! The great, precipitous, dry, savage country, with a handsome church in every landscape, rising as it were out of nothing. A revolution broken landscape, with lingering, tall, handsome churches whose domes are like inflations that are going to burst, and whose pinnacles and towers are like the trembling pagodas of an unreal race. Gorgeous churches waiting, above the huts and straw hovels of the natives, like ghosts to be dismissed.

And noble ruined haciendas, with ruined avenues approaching their broken splendour.

And the cities of Mexico, great and small, that the Spaniards conjured up out of nothing. Stones live and die with the spirit of the builders. And the spirit of Spaniards in Mexico dies, and the very stones in the building die. The natives drift into the centre of the plazas again, and in unspeakable empty weariness the Spanish buildings stand around, in a sort of dry exhaustion.

The conquered race! Cortés[4] came with his iron heel and his iron will, a conqueror. But a conquered race, unless grafted with a new inspiration, slowly sucks the blood of the conquerors, in the silence of a strange night and the heaviness of a hopeless will. So that now, the race of the conquerors in Mexico is soft and boneless, children crying in helpless hopelessness.

Was it the dark negation of the continent?

Kate could not look at the stones of the National Museum in Mexico without depression and dread. Snakes coiled like excrement, snakes fanged and feathered beyond all dreams of dread. And that was all.

The ponderous pyramids of San Juan Teotihuacan,[5] the House of Quetzalcoatl wreathed with the snake of all snakes, his huge fangs white and pure to-day as in the lost centuries when his makers were alive. He has not died. He is not so dead as the Spanish churches, this all-enwreathing dragon of the horror of Mexico.

Cholula,[6] with its church where the altar was! And the same ponderousness, the same unspeakable sense of weight and downward pressure of the blunt pyramid. Down-sinking pressure and depression. And the great market-place with its lingering dread and fascination.

Mitla[7] under its hills, in the parched valley where a wind blows the dust and the dead souls of the vanished race in terrible gusts. The carved courts of Mitla, with a hard, sharp-angled, intricate fascination, but the fascination of fear and repellence. Hard, four-square, sharp-edged, cutting, zig-zagging Mitla, like continual blows of a stone axe.

Without gentleness or grace or charm. Oh America, with your unspeakable hard lack of charm, what then is your final meaning! Is it forever the knife of sacrifice, as you put out your tongue at the world?

Charmless America! With your hard, vindictive beauty, are you waiting forever to smite death? Is the world your everlasting victim?

So long as it will let itself be victimised.

But yet! But yet! The gentle voices of the natives. The voices of the boys, like birds twittering among the trees of the plaza of Tehuacan! The soft touch, the gentleness. Was it the dark-fingered quietness of death, and the music of the presence of death in their voices?

She thought again of what Don Ramón had said to her.

'They pull you down! Mexico pulls you down, the people pull you down like a great weight! But it may be they pull you down as the earth's pull of gravitation does, that you can balance on your feet. Maybe they draw you down as the earth draws down the roots of a tree, so that it may be clinched deep in soil. Men are still part of the Tree of Life,[8] and the roots go down to the centre of the earth. Loose leaves, and aeroplanes, blow away on the wind, in what they call freedom. But the Tree of Life has fixed, deep, gripping roots.

'It may be you need to be drawn down, down, till you send roots into the deep places again. Then you can send up the sap and the leaves back to the sky, later.

'And to me, the men in Mexico are like trees, forests that the white men felled in their coming. But the roots of the trees are deep and alive and forever sending up new shoots.

'And each new shoot that comes up overthrows a Spanish church or an American factory. And soon the dark forest will rise again, and shake the Spanish buildings from the face of America.

'All that matters to me are the roots that reach down beyond all destruction. The roots and the life are there. What else it needs is the word, for the forest to begin to rise again. And some man among men must speak the word.'

The strange doom-like sound of the man's words! But in spite of the sense of doom on her heart, she would not go away yet. She would stay longer in Mexico.

The Lake

OWEN left, Villiers stayed on a few days to escort Kate to the lake. If she liked it there, and could find a house, she could stay by herself. She knew sufficient people in Mexico and in Guadalajara to prevent her from being lonely. But she still shrank from travelling alone in this country.

She wanted to leave the city. The new President had come in quietly enough, but there was an ugly feeling of uppishness in the lower classes, the bottom dog clambering mangily to the top. Kate was no snob. Man or woman, she cared nothing about the social class. But meanness, sordidness she hated. She hated bottom dogs. They all were mangy, they all were full of envy and malice, many had the rabies. Ah no, let us defend ourselves from the bottom dog, with its mean growl and its yellow teeth.

She had tea with Cipriano before leaving.

'How do you get along with the Government?' she asked.

'I stand for the law and the constitution,' he said. 'They know I don't want anything to do with cuartelazos or revolutions. Don Ramón is my chief.'

'In what way?'

'Later, you will see.'

He had a secret, important to himself, on which he was sitting tight. But he looked at her with shining eyes, as much as to say that soon she would share the secret, and then he would be much happier.

He watched her curiously, from under his wary black lashes. She was one of the rather plump Irishwomen, with soft brown hair and hazel eyes, and a beautiful, rather distant repose. Her great charm was her soft repose, and her gentle, unconscious inaccessibility. She was taller and bigger than Cipriano: he was almost boyishly small. But he was all energy, and his eyebrows tilted back and with a barbarian conceit, above his full, almost insolent black eyes.

He watched her continually, with a kind of fascination: the same spell that the absurd little figures of the doll Madonna had cast over him as a boy. She was the mystery, and he the adorer, under the semi-ecstatic spell of the mystery. But once he rose from his knees, he rose in the same strutting conceit of himself as before he knelt: with all his adoration in his pocket again. But he had a good deal of magnetic power. His education had not diminished it. His education lay like a film of white oil on the black lake of his barbarian consciousness. For this reason, the things he said were hardly interesting at all. Only what he *was*. He made the air around him seem darker, but richer and fuller. Sometimes his presence was extraordinarily grateful, like a healing of the blood. And sometimes he was an intolerable weight on her. She gasped to get away from him.

'You think a great deal of Don Ramón?' she said to him.

'Yes,' he said, his black eyes watching her. 'He is a very fine man.'

How trivial the words sounded! That was another boring thing about him: his English seemed so trivial. He wasn't really expressing himself. He was only flipping at the white oil that lay on his surface.

'You like him better than the Bishop, your god-father?'

He lifted his shoulders in a twisted, embarrassed shrug.

'The same!' he said. 'I like him the same.'

Then he looked away into the distance, with a certain hauteur and insolence.

'Very different, no?' he said. 'But in some ways, the same. He knows better what is Mexico. He knows better what I am. Bishop Severn did not know the real Mexico: how could he, he was a sincere Catholic! But Don Ramón knows the real Mexico, no?'

'And what is the real Mexico?' she asked.

'Well – you must ask Don Ramón. I can't explain.'

She asked Cipriano about going to the lake.

'Yes!' he said. 'You can go! You will like it. Go first to Orilla, no? – you take a ticket on the railway to Ixtlahuacan. And in Orilla is an hotel with a German manager.[1] Then from Orilla you can go in a motor-boat, in a few hours, to Sayula. And there you will find a house to live in.'

He wanted her to do this, she could tell.

'How far is Don Ramón's hacienda from Sayula?' she asked.

'Near! About an hour in a boat. He is there now. And at the beginning of the month I am going with my division to Guadalajara: now there is a new Governor. So I shall be quite near too.'

'That will be nice,' she said.

'You think so?' he asked quickly.

'Yes,' she said, on her guard, looking at him slowly. 'I should be sorry to lose touch with Don Ramón and you.'

He had a little tension on his brow, haughty, unwilling, conceited, and at the same time, yearning and desirous.

'You like Don Ramón very much?' he said. 'You want to know him more?'

There was a peculiar anxiety in his voice.

'Yes,' she said. 'One knows so few people in the world nowadays, that one can respect – and fear a little. I am a little afraid of Don Ramón: and I have the *greatest* respect for him –' She ended on a hot note of sincerity.

'It is good!' he said. 'It is very good. You may respect him more than any other man in the world.'

'Perhaps that is true,' she said, turning her eyes slowly to his.

'Yes! Yes!' he cried impatiently. 'It is true. You will find out later. And Ramón likes you. He told me to ask you to come to the lake. When you come to Sayula, when you are coming, write to him, and no doubt he can tell you about a house, and all those things.'

'Shall I?' she said, hesitant.

'Yes. Yes! of course, we say what we mean.'

Curious little man, with his odd, inflammable *hauteur* and conceit, something burning inside him, that gave him no peace. He had an almost childish faith in the other man. And yet she was not sure that he did not, in some corner of his soul, resent Ramón somewhat.

Kate set off by the night train for the west, with Villiers. The one Pullman coach was full: people going to Guadalajara and Colima and the coast. There were three military officers, rather shy in their new uniforms, and rather swaggering at the same time, making eyes at the empty air, as if they felt they were conspicuous, and sitting quickly in their seats, as if to obliterate themselves. There were two country farmers or ranchers, in tight trousers and cart-wheel hats stitched with silver. One was a tall man with a big moustache, the other was a smaller, grey man. But they both had the handsome, alive legs of the Mexicans, and the rather quenched faces. There was a widow buried in crape, accompanied by a criada, a maid. The rest were townsmen, Mexicans on business, at once shy and fussy, unobtrusive and self-important.

The Pullman was clean and neat, with its hot green-plush seats. But, full of people, it seemed empty compared with a Pullman in the United States. Everybody was very quiet, very soft and guarded. The farmers folded their beautiful serapes and laid them carefully on the seats, sitting as if their section were a lonely little place. The officers folded their cloaks and arranged dozens of little parcels, little cardboard hatboxes and heterogeneous bundles, under the seats and on the seats. The business men had the oddest luggage, canvas hold-alls embroidered in wool, with long, touching mottoes.

And in all the crowd, a sense of guardedness and softness and self-effacement: a curious soft *sensibilité*, touched with fear. It was already a somewhat conspicuous thing to travel in the Pullman, you had to be on your guard.

The evening for once was grey: the rainy season really approaching. A sudden wind whirled dust and a few spots of rain. The train drew out of the formless, dry, dust-smitten areas fringing the city, and wound mildly on for a few minutes, only to stop in the main street of Tacubaya, the suburb-village. In the grey approach of evening the train halted heavily in the street, and Kate looked out at the men who stood in groups, with their hats tilted against the wind and their blankets folded over their shoulders and up to their eyes, against the dust, motionless standing like sombre ghosts, only a glint of eyes showing between the dark serape and the big hat-brim; while donkey-drivers in a dust-cloud ran frantically, with uplifted arms like demons, uttering short, sharp cries to prevent their donkeys from poking in between the coaches of the train. Silent dogs trotted in-and-out under the train, women, their faces wrapped in their blue rebozos, came to offer tortillas folded in a cloth to keep them warm, or pulque in an earthenware mug, or pieces of chicken smothered in red, thick, oily sauce; or oranges or bananas or pitahayas, anything. And when few people bought, because of the dust, the women put their wares under their arm, under the blue rebozo, and covered their faces and motionless watched the train.

It was about six o'clock. The earth was utterly dry and stale. Somebody was kindling charcoal in front of a house. Men were hurrying down the wind, balancing their great hats curiously. Horsemen on quick, fine little horses, guns slung behind, trotted up to the train, lingered, then trotted quickly away again into nowhere.

Still the train stood in the street. Kate and Villiers got down. They watched the sparks blowing from the charcoal which a little girl was kindling in the street, to cook tortillas.

The train had a second-class coach and a first-class. The second class was jam-full of peasants, Indians, piled in like chickens with their bundles and baskets and bottles, endless things. One woman had a fine peacock under her arm. She put it down and in vain tried to suppress it beneath her voluminous skirts. It refused to be suppressed. She took it up and balanced it on her knee and looked round again over the medley of jars, baskets, pumpkins, melons, guns, bundles and human beings.

In the front was a steel car with a guard of little scrubby soldiers in their dirty cotton uniforms. Some soldiers were mounted on top of the train with their guns: the look-out.

And the whole train, seething with life, was curiously still, subdued. Perhaps it is the perpetual sense of danger which makes the people so hushed, without clamour or stridency. And with an odd, hushed politeness among them. A sort of demon-world.

At last the train moved on. If it had waited forever, no one would have been deeply surprised. For what might not be ahead? Rebels, bandits, bridges blown up – anything.

However, quietly, stealthily, the train moved out and along the great weary valley. The circling mountains, so relentless, were invisible save near at hand. In a few broken adobe huts, a bit of fire sparked red. The adobe was grey-black, of the lava dust, depressing. Into the distance the fields spread dry, with here and there patches of green irrigation. There was a broken hacienda with columns that supported nothing. Darkness was coming, dust still blew in the shadow; the valley seemed encompassed in a dry, stale, weary gloom.

Then there came a heavy shower. The train was passing a pulque hacienda. The rows of the giant maguey stretched bristling their iron-black barbs in the gloom.

All at once, the lights came on, the Pullman attendant came swiftly lowering the blinds, so that the brilliance of the windows should attract no bullets from the dark outside.

There was a poor little meal at exorbitant prices, and when this was cleared away, the attendant came with a clash to make the beds, pulling down the upper berths. It was only eight o'clock, and the passengers looked up in resentment. But no good. The pug-faced Mexican in charge and his smallpox-pitted assistant insolently came in between the seats, inserted the key over-head, and brought down the berth with a crash. And the Mexican passengers humbly crawled away to the smoking-room or the toilet, like whipped dogs.

At half-past eight everybody was silently and with intense discretion going to bed. None of the collar-stud-snapping bustle and 'homely' familiarity of the United States. Like subdued animals they all crept in behind their green serge curtains.

Kate hated a Pullman, the discreet indiscretion, the horrible nearness of other people, like so many larvae in so many sections, behind the green serge curtains. Above all, the horrible intimacy of the noise of going to bed. She hated to undress, struggling in the oven of her berth, with her elbow butting into the stomach of the attendant who was buttoning up the green curtain outside.

And yet, once she was in bed and could put out her light and raise the window-blind, she had to admit it was better than a *wagon-lit* in Europe: and perhaps the best that can be done for people who must travel through the night in trains.

There was a rather cold wind, after the rain, up there on that high plateau. The moon had risen, the sky was clear. Rocks, and tall organ cactus, and more miles of maguey. Then the train stopped at a dark little station on the rim of the slope, where men swathed in dark serapes held dusky, ruddy lanterns that lit up no faces at all, only dark gaps. Why did the train stay so long? Was something wrong?

At last they were going again. Under the moon she saw beyond her a long downslope of rocks and cactus, and in the distance below, the lights of a town. She lay in her berth watching the train wind slowly down the wild, rugged slope. Then she dozed.

To wake at a station that looked like a quiet inferno, with dark faces coming near the windows, glittering eyes in the half-light, women in their rebozos running along the train balancing dishes of meat, tamales, tortillas on one hand, black-faced men with fruit and sweets, and all calling in a subdued, intense, hushed hubbub. Strange and glaring, she saw eyes at the dark screen of the Pullman, sudden hands thrusting up something to sell. In fear, Kate dropped her window. The wire screen was not enough.

The platform below the Pullman all was dark. But at the back of the train she could see the glare of the first-class windows, on the dark station. And a man selling sweetmeats - *Cajetas! Cajetas! Las de Celaya!*

She was safe inside the Pullman, with nothing to do but to listen to an occasional cough behind the green curtains, and to feel the faint bristling apprehension of all the Mexicans in their dark berths. The dark Pullman was full of a subdued apprehension, fear lest there might be some attack on the train.

She went to sleep and woke at a bright station: probably Queretaro. The green trees looked theatrical in the electric light. *Opales!* she heard the men calling softly. If Owen had been there he would have got up in his pyjamas to buy opals. The call would have been too strong.

She slept fitfully, in the shaken saloon, vaguely aware of stations and the deep night of the open country. Then she started from a complete sleep. The train was dead still, no sound. Then a tremendous jerking as the Pullman was shunted. It must be Irapuato, where they branched to the west.

She would arrive at Ixtlahuacan soon after six in the morning. The man woke her at daybreak, before the sun had risen. Dry country with mesquite bushes, in the dawn: then green wheat alternating with ripe wheat. And men already in the pale, ripened wheat reaping with sickles, cutting short little handfuls from the short straw. A bright sky, with a bluish shadow on earth. Parched slopes with ragged maize stubble. Then a forlorn hacienda and a man on horseback, in a blanket, driving a silent flock of cows, sheep, bulls, goats, lambs, rippling a bit ghostly in the dawn, from under a tottering archway. A long canal beside the railway, a long canal paved with bright green leaves from which poked the mauve heads of the lirio, the water hyacinth. The sun was lifting up, red. In a moment, it was the full, dazzling gold of a Mexican morning.

Kate was dressed and ready, sitting facing Villiers, when they came to Ixtlahuacan. The man carried out her bags. The train drifted in to a desert of a station. They got down. It was a new day.

In the powerful light of morning, under a turquoise blue sky, she gazed at the helpless-looking station, railway lines, some standing trucks, and a remote lifelessness. A boy seized their bags and ran across the lines to the station yard, which was paved with cobblestones, but overgrown with weeds. At one side stood an old tram-car with two mules, like a relic. One or two men, swathed up to the eyes in scarlet blankets, were crossing on silent white legs.

'Adonde?' said the boy.

But Kate went to see her big luggage taken out. It was all there.

'Orilla Hotel,' said Kate.

The boy said they must go in the tram-car, so in the tram-car they went. The driver whipped his mules, they rolled in the still, heavy morning light away down an uneven, cobbled road with holes in it, between walls with falling mortar and low, black adobe houses, in the peculiar *vacuous* depression of a helpless little Mexican town, towards the plaza. The strange emptiness, everything empty of life!

Occasional men on horseback clattered suddenly by, occasional big men in scarlet serapes went noiselessly on their own way, under the big hats. A boy on a high mule was delivering milk from red globe-shaped jars slung on either side his mount. The street was stony, uneven, vacuous, sterile. The stones seemed dead, the town seemed made of dead stone. The human life came with a slow, sterile unwillingness, in spite of the low-hung power of the sun.

At length they were in the plaza, where brilliant trees flowered in a blaze of pure scarlet, and some in pure lavender, around the basins of milky-looking water. Milky-dim the water bubbled up in the basins, and women, bleary with sleep, uncombed, came from under the dilapidated arches of the portales, and across the broken pavement, to fill their water-jars.

The tram stopped and they got down. The boy got down with the bags, and told them they must go to the river to take a boat.

They followed obediently down the smashed pavements, where every moment you might twist your ankle or break your leg. Everywhere the same weary indifference and brokenness, a sense of dirt and of helplessness, squalor of far-gone indifference, under the perfect morning sky, in the pure sunshine and the pure Mexican air. The sense of life ebbing away, leaving dry ruin.

They came to the edge of the town, to a dusty, humped bridge, a broken wall, a pale-brown stream flowing full. Below the bridge a cluster of men.

Each one wanted her to hire his boat. She demanded a motor-boat: the boat from the hotel. They said there wasn't one. She didn't believe

it. Then a dark-faced fellow with his black hair down his forehead, and
a certain intensity in his eyes, said: Yes, yes; the hotel had a boat, but
it was broken. She must take a row-boat. In an hour and a half he
would row her there.

'How long?' said Kate.

'An hour and a half.'

'And I am so hungry!' cried Kate. 'How much do you charge?'

'Two pesos.' He held up two fingers.

Kate said yes, and he ran down to his boat. Then she noticed he
was a cripple with inturned feet. But how quick and strong!

She climbed with Villiers down the broken bank to the river, and
in a moment they were in the boat. Pale green willow trees fringed
from the earthen banks to the fuller-flowing, pale-brown water. The
river was not very wide, between deep banks. They slipped under the
bridge, and past a funny high barge with rows of seats. The boatman said
it went up the river to Jocotlan: and he waved his hand to show the direction. They were slipping down-stream, between lonely banks of willow-
trees.

The crippled boatman was pulling hard, with great strength and
energy. When she spoke to him in her bad Spanish and he found it
hard to understand, he knitted his brow a little, anxiously. And when
she laughed he smiled at her with such a beautiful gentleness, sensitive,
wistful, quick. She felt he was naturally honest and truthful, and generous. There was a beauty in these men, a wistful beauty and a great
physical strength. Why had she felt so bitterly about the country?

Morning was still young on the pale buff river, between the silent
earthen banks. There was a blue dimness in the lower air, and black
water-fowl ran swiftly, unconcernedly back and forth from the river's
edge, on the dry, baked banks that were treeless now, and wider. They
had entered a wide river, from the narrow one. The blueness and moist-
ness of the dissolved night seemed to linger under the scattered pepper-
trees of the far shore.

The boatman rowed short and hard upon the flimsy, soft, sperm-like
water, only pausing at moments swiftly to smear the sweat from his
face with an old rag he kept on the bench beside him. The sweat ran
from his bronze-brown skin like water, and the black hair on his high-
domed, Indian head smoked with wetness.

'There is no hurry,' said Kate, smiling to him.

'What does the Señorita say?'

'There is no hurry,' she repeated.

He paused, smiling, breathing deeply, and explained that now he was rowing against stream. This wider river flowed out of the lake, full and heavy. See! even as he rested a moment, the boat began to turn and drift! He quickly took his oars.

The boat moved slowly, in the hush of departed night, upon the soft, full-flowing buff water, that carried little tufts of floating water hyacinth. Some willow-trees stood near the edge, and some pepper trees of most delicate green foliage. Beyond the trees and the level of the shores, big hills rose up to high, blunt points, baked incredibly dry, like biscuit. The blue sky settled against them nakedly, they were leaf-less and lifeless save for the iron-green shafts of the organ cactus, that glistered blackly, yet atmospherically, in the ochreous aridity. This was Mexico again, stark-dry and luminous with powerful light, cruel and unreal.

On a flat near the river a peon, perched on the rump of his ass, was slowly driving five luxurious cows towards the water to drink. The big black-and-white animals stepped in a dream-pace past the pepper-trees to the bank, like moving pieces of light-and-shade: the dun cows trailed after, in the incredible silence and brilliance of the morning.

Earth, air, water were all silent with new light, the last blue of night dissolving like a breath. No sound, even no life. The great light was stronger than life itself. Only, up in the blue, some turkey-buzzards were wheeling with dirty-edged wings, as everywhere in Mexico.

'Don't hurry!' Kate said again to the boatman, who was again mop-ping his face, while his black hair ran sweat. 'We can go slowly.'

The man smiled deprecatingly.

'If the Señorita will sit in the back,' he said.

Kate did not understand his request at first. He had rowed in to-wards a bend in the right bank, to be out of the current. On the left bank Kate had noticed some men bathing: men whose wet skins flashed with the beautiful brown-rose colour and glitter of the naked natives, and one stout man with the curious creamy-biscuit skin of the city Mexicans. Low against the water across-stream she watched the glitter of naked men, half-immersed in the river.

She rose to step back into the stern of the boat, where Villiers was. As she did so, she saw a dark head and the flashing ruddy shoulders of a man swimming towards the boat. She wavered – and as she was sitting down, the man stood up in the water and was wading near, the water washing at the loose little cloth he had round his loins. He was smooth and wet and of a lovely colour, with the rich smooth-muscled physique of the Indians. He was coming towards the boat, pushing back his hair from his forehead.

The boatman watched him, transfixed, without surprise, a little subtle half-smile, perhaps of mockery, round his nose. As if he had expected it!

'Where are you going?' asked the man in the water, the brown river running softly at his strong thighs.

The boatman waited a moment for his patrons to answer, then, seeing they were silent, replied in a low, unwilling tone:

'Orilla.'

The man in the water took hold of the stern of the boat, as the boatman softly touched the water with the oars to keep her straight, and he threw back his longish black hair with a certain effrontery.

'Do you know whom the lake belongs to?' he asked, with the same effrontery.

'What do you say?' asked Kate, haughty.

'If you know whom the lake belongs to?' the young man in the water repeated.

'To whom?' said Kate, flustered.

'To the old gods of Mexico,' the stranger said. 'You have to make a tribute to Quetzalcoatl, if you go on the lake.'

The strange calm effrontery of it! But truly Mexican.

'How?' said Kate.

'You can give me something,' he said.

'But why should I give something to you, if it is a tribute to Quetzalcoatl?' she stammered.

'I am Quetzalcoatl's man, I,' he replied, with calm effrontery.

'And if I don't give you anything?' she said.

He lifted his shoulders and spread his free hand, staggering a little, losing his footing in the water as he did so.

'If you wish to make an enemy of the lake! –' he said, coolly, as he recovered his balance.

And then for the first time he looked straight at her. And as he did so, the demonish effrontery died down again, and the peculiar American tension slackened and left him.

He gave a slight wave of dismissal with his free hand, and pushed the boat gently forward.

'But it doesn't matter,' he said, with a slight insolent jerk of his head sideways, and a faint, insolent smile. 'We will wait till the Morning Star[2] rises.'

The boatman softly but powerfully pulled the oars. The man in the water stood with the sun on his powerful chest, looking after the boat in half-seeing abstraction. His eyes had taken again the peculiar gleaming far-awayness, suspended between the realities, which, Kate suddenly realized, was the central look in the native eyes. The boatman, rowing away, was glancing back at the man who stood in the water, and his face, too, had the abstracted, transfigured look of a man perfectly suspended between the world's two strenuous wings of energy. A look of extraordinary, arresting beauty, the silent, vulnerable centre of all life's quivering, like the nucleus gleaming in tranquil suspense, within a cell.

'What does he mean,' said Kate, 'by "We will wait till the Morning Star rises"?'

The man smiled slowly.

'It is a name,' he said.

And he seemed to know no more. But the symbolism had evidently the power to soothe and sustain him.

'Why did he come and speak to us?' asked Kate.

'He is one of those of the god Quetzalcoatl, Señorita.'

'And you? are you one too?'

'Who knows!' said the man, putting his head on one side. Then he added: 'I think so. We are many.'

He watched Kate's face with that gleaming, intense semi-abstraction, a gleam that hung unwavering in his black eyes, and which suddenly reminded Kate of the morning star, or the evening star, hanging perfect between night and the sun.

'You have the morning star in your eyes,' she said to the man.

He flashed her a smile of extraordinary beauty.

'The Señorita understands,' he said.

His face changed again to a dark-brown mask, like semitransparent stone, and he rowed with all his might. Ahead, the river was widening, the banks were growing lower, down to the water's level, like shoals planted with willow trees and with reeds. Above the willow trees a square white sail was standing, as if erected on the land.

'Is the lake so near?' said Kate.

The man hastily mopped his running wet face.

'Yes, Señorita! The sailing boats are waiting for the wind, to come into the river. We will pass by the canal.'

He indicated with a backward movement of the head a narrow, twisting passage of water between deep reeds. It made Kate think of the little river Anapo: the same mystery unbroken. The boatman, with creases half of sadness and half of exaltation in his bronze, still face, was pulling with all his might. Water-fowl went swimming into the reeds, or rose on wing and wheeled into the blue air. Some willow trees hung a dripping, vivid green, in the stark dry country. The stream was narrow and winding. With a nonchalant motion, first of the right then of the left hand, Villiers was guiding the boatman, to keep him from running aground in the winding, narrow water-way.

And this put Villiers at his ease, to have something practical and slightly mechanical to do and to assert. He was striking the American note once more, of mechanical dominance.

All the other business had left him incomprehending, and when he asked Kate, she had pretended not to hear him. She sensed a certain delicate, tender mystery in the river, in the naked man in the water, in the boatman, and she could not bear to have it subjected to the tough American flippancy. She was weary to death of American automatism and American flippant toughness. It gave her a feeling of nausea.

'Quite a well-built fellow, that one who laid hold of the boat. What did he want, anyway?' Villiers insisted.

'Nothing!' said Kate.

They were slipping out past the clay-coloured, loose stony edges of the land, through a surge of ripples, into the wide white light of the lake. A breeze was coming from the east, out of the upright morning, and the surface of the shallow, flimsy, dun-coloured water was in motion. Shoal-water rustled near at hand. Out to the open, large, square white sails were stepping gingerly forward, and beyond the buff-coloured, pale desert of water rose far-away blue, sharp hills of the other side, many miles away, pure pale blue with distance, yet sharp-edged and clear in form.

'Now,' said the boatman, smiling to Kate, 'it is easier. Now we are out of the current.'

He pulled rhythmically through the frail-rippling, sperm-like water, with a sense of peace. And for the first time Kate felt she had met the mystery of the natives, the strange and mysterious gentleness between a scylla and a charybdis of violence;[3] the small poised, perfect body of the bird that waves wings of thunder and wings of fire and night, in its flight. But central between the flash of day and the black of night, between the flash of lightning and the break of thunder, the still, soft body of the bird poised and soaring, forever. The mystery of the evening-star brilliant in silence and distance between the downward-surging plunge of the sun and the vast, hollow seething of inpouring night. The magnificence of the watchful morning-star, that watches between the night and the day, the gleaming clue to the two opposites.

This kind of frail, pure sympathy she felt at the moment between herself and the boatman, between herself and the man who had spoken from the water. And she was not going to have it broken by Villiers' American jokes.

There was a sound of breaking water. The boatman drew away, and pointed across to where a *canoa*, a native sailing-boat, was lying at an angle. She had run aground in a wind, and now must wait till another wind would carry her off the submerged bank again. Another boat was coming down the breeze, steering cautiously among the shoals, for the river outlet. She was piled high with petates, the native leaf mats, above her hollowed black sides. And bare-legged men with loose white drawers rolled up, and brown chests showing, were running with poles as the shallows heaved up again, pushing her off, and balancing their huge hats with small, bird-like shakes of the head.

Beyond the boats, sea-wards, were rocks outcropping and strange birds like pelicans standing in silhouette, motionless.

They had been crossing a bay of the lake-shore, and were nearing the hotel. It stood on a parched dry bank above the pale-brown water, a long, low building amid a tender green of bananas and pepper-trees. Everywhere the shores rose up pale and cruelly dry, dry to cruelty, and on the little hills the dark statues of the organ cactus poised in nothingness.

There was a broken-down landing-place, and a boat-house in the distance, and someone in white flannel trousers was standing on the broken masonry. Upon the filmy water ducks and black water-fowl bobbed like corks. The bottom was stony. The boatman suddenly backed the boat, and pulled round. He pushed up his sleeve and hung over the bows, reaching into the water. With a quick motion he grabbed something, and scrambled into the boat again. He was holding in the pale-skinned hollow of his palm a little earthenware pot, crusted by the lake deposit.

'What is it?' she said.

'Ollita of the gods,' he said. 'Of the old dead gods. Take it, Señorita.'

'You must let me pay for it,' she said.

'No, Señorita. It is yours,' said the man, with that sensitive, masculine sincerity which comes sometimes so quickly from a native.

It was a little, rough round pot with protuberances.

'Look!' said the man, reaching again for the little pot. He turned it upside-down, and she saw cut-in eyes and the sticking-out ears of an animal's head.

'A cat!' she exclaimed. 'It is a cat.'

'Or a coyote!'

'A coyote!'

'Let's look!' said Villiers. 'Why how awfully interesting! Do you think it's old?'

'It is old?' Kate asked.

'The time of the old gods,' said the boatman. Then with a sudden smile: 'The dead gods don't eat much rice, they only want little casseroles while they are bone under the water.' And he looked her in the eyes.

'While they are bone?' she repeated. And she realised he meant the skeletons of gods that cannot die.

They were at the landing stage; or rather, at the heap of collapsed masonry which had once been a landing stage. The boatman got out and held the boat steady while Kate and Villiers landed. Then he scrambled up with the bags.

The man in white trousers, and a *mozo* appeared. It was the hotel manager. Kate paid the boatman.

'Adiós, Señorita!' he said with a smile. 'May you go with Quetzalcoatl.'

'Yes!' she cried. 'Goodbye!'

They went up the slope between the tattered bananas, whose ragged leaves were making a hushed, distant patter in the breeze. The green fruit curved out its bristly-soft bunch, the purple flower-bud depending stiffly.

The German manager came to talk to them: a young man of about forty, with his blue eyes going opaque and stony behind his spectacles, though the centres were keen. Evidently a German who had been many years out in Mexico – out in the lonely places. The rather stiff look, the slight look of fear in the *soul* – not physical fear – and the look of defeat, characteristic of the European who has long been subjected to the unbroken spirit of place! But the defeat was in the soul, not the will.

He showed Kate to her room in the unfinished quarter, and ordered her breakfast. The hotel consisted of an old low ranch-house with a verandah – and this was the dining-room, lounge, kitchen, and office. Then there was a two-storey new wing, with a smart bath-room between each two bedrooms, and almost up-to-date fittings: very incongruous.

But the new wing was unfinished – had been unfinished for a dozen years and more, the work abandoned when Porfirio Díaz fled.[4] Now it would probably never be finished.

And this is Mexico. Whatever pretentiousness and modern improvements it may have, outside the capital, they are either smashed or raw and unfinished, with rusty bones of iron girders sticking out.

Kate washed her hands and went down to breakfast. Before the long verandah of the old ranch-house, the green pepper-trees dropped like green light, and small cardinal birds with scarlet bodies and blazing impertinent heads like poppy-buds flashed among the pinkish pepper-heads, closing their brown wings upon the audacity of their glowing redness. A train of geese passed in the glaring sun, automatic, towards the eternal tremble of pale, earth-coloured water beyond the stones.

It was a place with a strange atmosphere: stony, hard, broken, with round cruel hills and the many-fluted bunches of the organ cactus behind the old house, and an ancient road trailing past, deep in ancient dust. A touch of mystery and cruelty, the stoniness of fear, a lingering, cruel sacredness.

Kate loitered hungrily, and was glad when the Mexican in shirt-sleeves and patched trousers, another lingering remnant of Don Porfirio's day, brought her her eggs and coffee.

He was muted as everything about the place seemed muted, even the very stones and the water. Only those poppies on wing, the cardinal birds, gave a sense of liveliness: ánd they were uncanny.

So swiftly one's moods changed! In the boat, she had glimpsed the superb rich stillness of the morning-star, the poignant intermediate flashing its quiet between the energies of the cosmos. She had seen it in the black eyes of the natives, in the sunrise of the man's rich, still body, Indian-warm.

And now again already the silence was of vacuity, arrest, and cruelty: the uncanny empty unbearableness of many Mexican mornings. Already she was uneasy, suffering from the malaise which tortures one inwardly in that country of cactuses.

She went up to her room, pausing at the corridor window to look out at the savage little hills that stood at the back of the hotel in desiccated heaps, with the dark-green bulks of organ-cactus sticking up mechanically and sinister, sombre in all the glare. Grey ground-squirrels like rats slithered ceaselessly around. Sinister, strangely dark and sinister, in the great glare of the sun!

She went to her room to be alone. Below her window, in the bricks and fallen rubble of unfinished masonry, a huge white turkey-cock, dim-white, strutted with his brown hens. And sometimes he stretched out his pink wattles and gave vent to fierce, powerful turkey-yelps, like some strong dog yelping; or else he ruffled all his feathers like a great, soiled white peony, and chuffed, hissing here and there, raging the metal of his plumage.

Below him, the eternal tremble of pale-earth, unreal waters, far beyond which rose the stiff resistance of mountains losing their pristine blue. Distinct, frail distances far off on the dry air, dim-seeing, yet sharp and edged with menace.

Kate took her bath in the filmy water that was hardly like water at all. Then she went and sat on the collapsed masonry, in the shade of the boat-house below. Small white ducks bobbed about on the shallow water below her, or dived, raising clouds of submarine dust. A canoe came paddling in; a lean fellow with sinewy brown legs. He answered Kate's nod with the aloof promptness of an Indian, made fast his canoe inside the boat-house, and was gone, stepping silent and barefoot over the bright green water-stones, and leaving a shadow, cold as flint, on the air behind him.

No sound on the morning save a faint touching of water, and the occasional powerful yelping of the turkey-cock. Silence, an aboriginal, empty silence, as of life *withheld*. The vacuity of a Mexican morning. Resounding sometimes to the turkey-cock.

And the great, lymphatic expanse of water, like a sea, trembling, trembling, trembling to a far distance, to the mountains of substantial nothingness.

Near at hand, a ragged shifting of banana trees, bare hills with immobile cactus, and to the left, a hacienda with peons' square mud boxes of houses. An occasional ranchero in skin-tight trousers and big hat rode trotting through the dust on a small horse, or peons on the rump of their asses, in floppy white cotton, going like ghosts.

Always something ghostly. The morning passing all of a piece, empty, vacuous. All sound withheld, all life withheld, everything *holding back*. The land so dry as to have a quality of invisibility, the water earth-filmy, hardly water at all. The lymphatic milk of fishes, somebody said.

CHAPTER VI

The Move Down the Lake

IN Porfirio Díaz' day the Lake-side began to be the Riviera of Mexico, and Orilla was to be the Nice, or at least the Mentone of the country. But revolutions started erupting again, and in 1911 Don Porfirio fled to Paris with, it is said, thirty million gold pesos in his pocket: a peso being half a dollar, nearly half-a-crown. But we need not believe all that is said, especially by a man's enemies.

During the subsequent revolutions, Orilla, which had begun to be a winter paradise for the Americans, lapsed back into barbarism and broken brickwork. In 1921 a feeble new start had been made.

The place belonged to a German-Mexican family, who also owned the adjacent hacienda. They acquired the property from the American Hotel Company, who had undertaken to develop the lake-shore, and who had gone bankrupt during the various revolutions.

The German-Mexican owners were not popular with the natives. An angel from heaven would not have been popular, these years, if he had been known as the owner of property. However, in 1921 the hotel was very modestly opened again, with an American manager.

Towards the end of the year, José, son of the German-Mexican owner, came to stay with his wife and children in the hotel, in the new wing. José was a bit of a fool, as most foreigners are, after the first generation in Mexico. Having business to settle, he went into Guadalajara to the bank and returned with a thousand gold pesos in a bag, keeping the matter, as he thought, a dead secret.

Everyone had just gone to bed, on a brilliant moonlight night in winter, when two men appeared in the yard calling for José: they had to speak to him. José, suspecting nothing, left his wife and two children, and went down. In a moment he called for the American manager. The manager, thinking it was some bargaining to be done, also came down. As he came out of the door, two men seized him by the arms, and said: '*Don't make a noise!*'

'What's amiss?' said Bell, who had built up Orilla, and had been twenty years on the lake.

Then he noticed that two other men had hold of José. 'Come,' they said.

There were five Mexicans – Indians, or half-Indians – and the two captives. They went, the captives in slippers and shirt-sleeves, to the little office away at the end of the other part of the hotel, which had been the old ranch-house.

'What do you want,' said Bell.

'Give us the money,' said the bandits.

'Oh, all right,' said the American. There were a few pesos only in the safe. He opened, showed them, and they took the money.

'Now give us the rest,' they said.

'There is no more,' said the manager, in all sincerity; for José had not confessed to the thousand pesos.

The five peons then began to search the poor little office. They found a pile of red blankets – which they appropriated – and a few bottles of red wine – which they drank.

'Now,' they said, 'give us the money.'

'I can't give you what there isn't to give,' said the manager.

'Good!' they said, and pulled out the hideous machetes, the heavy knives of the Mexicans.

José, intimidated, produced the suit-case with the thousand pesos. The money was wrapped up in the corner of a blanket.

'Now, come with us,' said the bandits.

'Where to?' asked the manager, beginning at last to be scared.

'Only out on to the hill, where we will leave you, so that you cannot telephone to Ixtlahuacan before we have time to get away,' said the Indians.

Outside, in the bright moon, the air was chill. The American shivered, in his trousers and shirt and a pair of bedroom slippers.

'Let me take a coat,' he said.

'Take a blanket,' said the tall Indian.

He took a blanket, and with two men holding his arms, he followed José, who was likewise held captive, out of the little gate, across the dust of the road, and up the steep little round hill on which the organ cactus thrust up their sinister clumps, like bunches of cruel fingers, in the moonlight. The hill was stony and steep, the going, slow. José, a fat young man of twenty-eight, protested in the feeble manner of the well-to-do Mexicans.

At last they came to the top of the hill. Three men took José apart, leaving Bell alone near a cactus clump. The moon shone in a perfect Mexican heaven. Below, the big lake glimmered faintly, stretching its length towards the west. The air was so clear, the mountains across, thirty miles away, stood sharp and still in the moonlight. And not a sound nor a motion anywhere! At the foot of the hill was the hacienda, with the peons asleep in their huts. But what help was there in them?

José and the three men had gone behind a cactus tree that stuck up straight like a great black bundle of poles, poised on one central foot, and cast a sharp, iron shadow. The American could hear the voices, talking low and rapidly, but could not distinguish the words. His two guards drew away from him a little, to hear what the others were saying, behind the cactus.

And the American, who knew the ground he stood on and the sky that hung over him, felt again the black vibration of death in the air, the black thrill of the death-lust. Unmistakable he felt it seething in the air, as any man may feel it, in Mexico. And the strange aboriginal fiendishness, awake now in the five bandits, communicated itself to his blood.

Loosening his blanket, he listened tensely in the moonlight. And came the *thud! thud! thud!* of a machete striking with lust in a human body, then the strange voice of José: '*Perdóneme! – Forgive me!*' the murdered man cried as he fell.

The American waited for no more. Dropping his blanket, he jumped for the cactus cover, and stooping, took the down-slope like a rabbit. The pistol-shots rang out after him, but the Mexicans don't as a rule take good aim. His bedroom slippers flew off, and barefoot, the man, thin and light, sped down over the stones and the cactus, down to the hotel.

When he got down, he found everyone in the hotel awake and shouting.

'They are killing José!' he said, and he rushed to the telephone, expecting every moment the five bandits would be on him.

The telephone was in the old ranch-building, in the dining-room. There was no answer – no answer – no answer. In her little bedroom over the kitchen, the cook-woman, the traitress, was yelling. Across in the new wing, a little distance away, José's Mexican wife was screaming. One of the servant boys appeared.

'Try and get the police in Ixtlahuacan,' said the American, and he ran to the new wing, to get his gun and to barricade the doors. His daughter, a motherless girl, was crying with José's wife.

There was no answer on the telephone. At dawn, the cook, who said the bandits would not hurt a woman, went across to the hacienda to fetch the peons. And when the sun rose, a man was sent for the police.

They found the body of José, pierced with fourteen holes. The American was carried to Ixtlahuacan, and kept in bed, having cactus spines dug out of his feet by two native women.

The bandits fled across the marshes. Months later, they were identified by the stolen blankets, away in Michoacan; and, pursued, one of them betrayed the others.

After this, the hotel was closed again, and had been re-opened only three months, when Kate arrived.

But Villiers came with another story. Last year the peons had murdered the manager of one of the estates across the lake. They had stripped him and left him naked on his back, with his sexual organs cut off and put into his mouth, his nose slit and pinned back, the two halves, to his cheeks, with long cactus spines.

'Tell me no more!' said Kate.

She felt there was doom written on the very sky, doom and horror.

She wrote to Don Ramón in Sayula, saying she wanted to go back to Europe. True, she herself had seen no horrors, apart from the bull-fight. And she had had some exquisite moments, as coming to this hotel in the boat. The natives had a certain mystery and beauty, to her. But she could not bear the unease, and the latest sense of horror.

True, the peons were poor. They used to work for twenty cents, American, a day; and now the standard price was fifty cents, or one peso. But then in the old days they received their wage all the year round. Now, only at harvest time or sowing time. No work, no pay. And in the long dry season, it was mostly no work.

'Still,' said the German manager of the hotel, a man who had run a rubber plantation in Tabasco, a sugar plantation in the state of Vera Cruz, and a hacienda growing wheat, maize, oranges, in Jalisco: 'Still, it isn't a question of money with the peons. It doesn't start with the peons. It starts in Mexico City, with a lot of malcontents who want to put their spoke in the wheel, and who lay hold of pious catchwords,

to catch the poor. There's no more in it than that. Then the agitators
go round and infect the peons. It is nothing but a sort of infectious
disease, like syphilis, all this revolution and socialism.'

'But why does no one oppose it,' said Kate. 'Why don't the
hacendados put up a fight, instead of caving in and running away?'

'The Mexican hacendado!' The man's German eyes gave out a spark.
'The Mexican *gentleman* is such a brave man, that while the soldier
is violating his wife on the bed, he is hiding under the bed and holding
his breath so they shan't find him. He's as brave as that.'

Kate looked away uncomfortably.

'They all want the United States to intervene. They hate the
Americans; but they want the United States to intervene, to save them
their money and their property. That's how brave they are! They hate
the Americans personally, but they love them because they can look
after money and property. So they want the United States to annex
Mexico, the beloved patria; leaving the marvellous green and white and
red flag, and the eagle with the snake in its claws, for the sake of appear-
ances and *honour*! They're simply bottled full of honour; of that sort.'

Always the same violence of bitterness, Kate thought to herself. And
she was so weary of it. How, how weary she was of politics, of the very
words 'Labour' and '*Socialism!*' and all that sort! It suffocated her.

'Have you heard of the men of Quetzalcoatl?' asked Kate.

'Quetzalcoatl!' exclaimed the manager, giving a little click of the final
'l', in a peculiar native fashion. 'That's another try-on of the Bolshevists. They thought socialism needed a god, so they're going to fish
him out of this lake. He'll do for another pious catchword in another
revolution.'

The man went away, unable to stand any more.

'Oh dear!' thought Kate. 'It really is hard to bear.'

But she wanted to hear more of Quetzalcoatl.

'Did you know,' she said to the man later, showing him the little
pot, 'that they find those things in the lake?'

'They're common enough!' he said. 'They used to throw them in,
in the idolatrous days. May still do so, for what I know. Then get them
out again to sell to tourists.'

'They call them ollitas of Quetzalcoatl.'

'That's a new invention.'

'Why, do you think?'

'They're trying to start a new thing, that's all. They've got this society on the lake here, of the Men of Quetzalcoatl, and they go round singing songs. It's another dodge for national-socialism, that's all.'

'What do they do, the Men of Quetzalcoatl?'

'I can't see they do anything, except talk and get excited over their own importance.'

'But what's the idea?'

'I couldn't say. Don't suppose they have any. But if they have, they won't let on to you. You're a gringo – or a gringita, at the best. And this is for pure Mexicans. For los señores, the workmen, and los caballeros, the peons. Every peon is a caballero nowadays, and every workman is a señor. So I suppose they're going to get themselves a special god, to put the final feather in their caps.'

'Where did it start, the Quetzalcoatl thing?'

'Down in Sayula. They say Don Ramón Carrasco is at the back of it. Maybe he wants to be the next President – or maybe he's aiming higher, and wants to be the first Mexican Pharaoh.'

Ah, how tired it made Kate feel; the hopelessness, the ugliness, the cynicism, the emptiness. She felt she could cry aloud, for the unknown gods to put the magic back into her life, and to save her from the dry-rot of the world's sterility.

She thought again of going back to Europe. But what was the good? She knew it! It was all politics or jazzing or slushy mysticism or sordid spiritualism. And the magic had gone. The younger generation, so smart and *interesting*, but so without any mystery, any background. The younger the generation, the flatter and more jazzy, more and more devoid of wonder.

No, she could not go back to Europe.

And no! She refused to take the hotel manager's estimate of Quetzalcoatl. How should an hotel manager judge? – even if he was not really an hotel manager, but a ranch-overseer. She had seen Ramón Carrasco, and Cipriano. And they were men. They wanted something beyond. She would believe in them. Anything, anything rather than this sterility of nothingness which was the world, and into which her life was drifting.

She would send Villiers away, too. He was nice, she liked him. But he, too, was widdershins, unwinding the sensations of disintegration

and anti-life. No, she must send him away. She must, she must free
herself from these mechanical connections.

Every one of them, like Villiers, was like a cog-wheel in contact with
which all one's workings were reversed. Everything he said, everything
he did, reversed her real life flow, made her go against the sun.

And she did not want to go against the sun. After all, in spite of
the horrors latent in Mexico, when you got these dark-faced people
away from wrong contacts like agitators and socialism, they made one
feel that life was vast, if fearsome, and death was fathomless.

Horrors might burst out of them. But something must burst out,
sometimes, if men are not machines.

No! no! no! no! no! she cried to her own soul. *Let me still believe
in some human contact. Let it not be all cut off for me!*

But she made up her mind, to be alone, and to cut herself off from
all the mechanical widdershin contacts.[1] Villiers must go back to his
United States. She would be alone in her own milieu. Not to be
touched by any, any of the mechanical cog-wheel people. To be left
alone, not to be touched. To hide, and be hidden, and never really be
spoken to.

Yet at the same time, with her blood flowing softly sunwise, to let
the sunwise sympathy of unknown people steal in to her. To shut doors
of iron against the mechanical world. But to let the sunwise world steal
across to her, and add its motion to her, the motion of the stress of
life, with the big sun and the stars like a tree holding out its leaves.

She wanted an old Spanish house, with its inner patio of flowers
and water. Turned inwards, to the few flowers walled in by shadow.
To turn one's back on the cog-wheel world. Not to look out any more
on to that horrible machine of the world. To look at one's own quiet
little fountain and one's own little orange trees, with only heaven above.

So, having soothed her heart, she wrote Don Ramón again, that she
was coming to Sayula to look for a house. She sent Villiers away. And
the next day she set off with a man-servant, in the old motor-boat of
the hotel, down to the village of Sayula.

It was thirty-five miles to travel, down the long lake. But the
moment she set off, she felt at peace. A tall dark-faced fellow sat in
the stern of the boat, steering and attending to the motor. She sat on
cushions in the middle. And the young man-servant perched in the
prow.

They started before sunrise, when the lake was bathed in motionless light. Odd tufts of water-hyacinth were travelling on the soft spermy water, holding up a green leaf like a little sail of a boat, and nodding a delicate, mauve blue flower.

Give me the mystery and let the world live again for me! Kate cried to her own soul. *And deliver me from man's automatism.*

The sun rose, and a whiteness of light played on the tops of the mountains. The boat hugged the north shore, turning the promontory on which the villas had started so jauntily, twenty years ago, but now were lapsing back to wilderness. All was still and motionless in the light. Sometimes, on the little bare patches high up on the dry hills were white specks; birds? No, men in their white cotton, peons hoeing. They were so tiny and so distinct, they looked like white birds settled.

Round the bend were the hot springs, the church, the inaccessible village of the pure Indians, who spoke no Spanish. There were some green trees, under the precipitous, dry mountain-side.

So on and on, the motor-boat chugging incessantly, the man in the bows coiled up like a serpent, watching; the fish-milk water gleaming and throwing off a dense light, so that the mountains away across were fused out. And Kate, under the awning, went into a kind of sleep.

They were passing the island, with its ruins of fortress and prison. It was all rock and dryness, with great broken walls and the shell of a church among its hurtful stones and its dry grey herbage. For a long time the Indians had defended it against the Spaniards. Then the Spaniards used the island as a fortress against the Indians. Later, as a penal settlement. And now the place was a ruin, repellent, full of scorpions, and otherwise empty of life. Only one or two fishermen lived in the tiny cove facing the mainland, and a flock of goats, specks of life creeping among the rocks. And an unhappy fellow put there by the Government to register the weather.

No, Kate did not want to land. The place looked too sinister. She took food from the basket, and ate a little lunch, and dozed.

In this country, she was afraid. But it was her soul more than her body that knew fear. She had realized, for the first time, with finality and fatality, what was the illusion she laboured under. She had thought that each individual had a complete self, a complete soul, an accomplished I. And now she realised as plainly as if she had turned into a new being, that this was not so. Men and women had incomplete selves, made up of bits assembled together loosely and somewhat haphazard. Man was not created ready-made. Men to-day were half-made, and women were half-made. Creatures that existed and functioned with certain regularity, but which ran off into a hopeless jumble of inconsequence.

Half-made, like insects that can run fast and be so busy and suddenly grow wings, but which are only winged grubs after all. A world full of half-made creatures on two legs, eating food and degrading the one mystery left to them, sex. Spinning a great lot of words, burying themselves inside the cocoons of words and ideas that they spin round themselves, and inside the cocoons, mostly perishing inert and overwhelmed.

Half-made creatures, rarely more than half-responsible and half-accountable, acting in terrible swarms, like locusts.

Awful thought! And with a collective insect-like will, to avoid the responsibility of achieving any more perfected being or identity. The queer, rabid hate of being urged on into purer self. The morbid fanaticism of the non-integrate.

In the great seething light of the lake, with the terrible blue-ribbed mountains of Mexico beyond, she seemed swallowed by some grisly skeleton, in the cage of his death-anatomy. She was afraid, mystically, of the man crouching there in the bows with his smooth thighs and supple loins like a snake, and his black eyes watching. A half-being, with a will to disintegration and death. And the tall man behind her at the tiller, he had the curious smoke-grey phosphorus eyes under black lashes, sometimes met among the Indians. Handsome, he was, and quiet and seemingly self-contained. But with that peculiar devilish half-smile lurking under his face, the half jeering look of a part-thing, which knows its power to destroy the purer thing.

And yet, Kate told herself, both these men were manly fellows. They would not molest her, unless she communicated the thought to them, and by a certain cowardliness, prompted them. Their souls were nascent, there was no fixed evil in them, they could sway both ways.

So in her soul she cried aloud to the greater mystery, the higher power that hovered in the interstices of the hot air, rich and potent. It was as if she could lift her hands and clutch the silent, stormless potency that roved everywhere, waiting. 'Come then!' she said, drawing a long slow breath, and addressing the silent life-breath which hung unrevealed in the atmosphere, waiting.

And as the boat ran on, and her fingers rustled in the warm water of the lake, she felt the fulness descend into her once more, the peace, and the power. The fulfilment filling her soul like the fulness of ripe grapes. And she thought to herself: 'Ah, how wrong I have been, not to turn sooner to the other presence, not to take the life-breath sooner! How wrong to be afraid of these two men.'

She did what she had been half-afraid to do before; she offered them the oranges and sandwiches still in the basket. And each of the men looked at her, the smoke-grey eyes looked her in the eyes, and the black eyes looked her in the eyes. And the man with the smoke-grey eyes, who was cunninger than the other man, but also prouder, said to her with his eyes: *We are living! I know your sex, and you know mine. The mystery we are glad not to meddle with. You leave me my natural honour, and I thank you for the grace.*

In his look, so quick and proud, and in his quiet *Muchas gracias!* she heard the touch of male recognition, a man glad to retain his honour, and to feel the communion of grace. Perhaps it was the Spanish word *Gracias!* But in her soul she was thinking of the communion of grace.

With the black-eyed man it was the same. He was humbler. But as he peeled his orange and dropped the yellow peel on the water, she could see the stillness, the humility, and the pathos of grace in him; something very beautiful and truly male, and very hard to find in a civilised white man. It was not of the spirit. It was of the dark, strong, unbroken blood, the flowering of the soul.

Then she thought to herself: After all, it is good to be here. It is very good to be in this boat on this lake with these two silent, semi-barbarous men. They can receive the gift of grace, and we can share it like a communion, they and I. I am very glad to be here. It is so much better than love: the love I knew with Joachim. This is the fulness of the vine.

'Sayula!' said the man in the bows, pointing ahead.

She saw, away off, a place where there were green trees, where the shore was flat, and a biggish building stood out.

'What is the building?' she asked.

'The railway station.'

She was suitably impressed, for it was a new-looking, imposing structure.

A little steamer was smoking, lying off from a wooden jetty in the loneliness, and black, laden boats were poling out to her, and merging back to shore. The vessel gave a hoot, and slowly yet busily set off on the bosom of the water, heading in a slanting line across the lake, to which the tiny high white twin-towers of Tuliapán showed above the water-line, tiny and far-off, on the other side.

They had passed the jetty, and rounding the shoal where the willows grew, she could see Sayula; white fluted twin-towers of the church, obelisk shaped above the pepper trees; beyond, a mound of a hill standing alone, dotted with dry bushes, distinct and Japanese looking; beyond this, the corrugated, blue-ribbed, flat-flanked mountains of Mexico.

It looked peaceful, delicate, almost Japanese. As she drew nearer she saw the beach with the washing spread on the sand; the fleecy green willow trees and pepper trees, and the villas in foliage and flowers, hanging magenta curtains of bougainvillea, red dots of hibiscus, pink abundance of tall oleander trees; occasional palm-trees sticking out.

The boat was steering round a stone jetty, on which, in black letters, was painted an advertisement for motor-car tyres. There were a few seats, some deep fleecy trees growing out of the sand, a booth for selling drinks, a little promenade, and white boats on a sandy beach. A few women sitting under parasols, a few bathers in the water, and trees in front of the few villas deep in green or blazing scarlet blossoms.

'This is very good,' thought Kate. 'It is not too savage, and not over-civilised. It isn't broken, but it is rather out of repair. It is in contact with the world, but the world has got a very weak grip on it.'

She went to the hotel, as Don Ramón had advised her.

'Do you come from Orilla? You are Mrs Leslie? Don Ramón Carrasco sent us a letter about you.'

There was a house. Kate paid her boatmen and shook hands with them. She was sorry to be cut off from them again. And they looked at her with a touch of regret as they left. She said to herself:

'There is something rich and alive in these people. They want to be able to breathe the Great Breath. They are like children, helpless. And then they're like demons. But somewhere, I believe, they want the breath of life and the communion of the brave, more than anything.'

She was surprised at herself, suddenly using this language. But her weariness and her sense of devastation had been so complete, that the Other Breath in the air, and the bluish dark power in the earth had become, almost suddenly, more real to her than so-called reality. Concrete, jarring, exasperating reality had melted away, and a soft world of potency stood in its place, the velvety dark flux from the earth, the delicate yet supreme life-breath in the inner air. Behind the fierce sun the dark eyes of a deeper sun were watching, and between the bluish ribs of the mountains a powerful heart was secretly beating, the heart of the earth.

Her house was what she wanted; a low, L-shaped, tiled building with rough red floors and deep verandah, and the other two sides of the patio completed by the thick, dark little mango-forest outside the low wall. The square of the patio, within the precincts of the house and the mango trees, was gay with oleanders and hibiscus, and there was a basin of water in the seedy grass. The flower-pots along the verandah were full of flowering geranium and foreign flowers. At the far end of the patio, the chickens were scratching under the silent motionlessness of ragged banana trees.

There she had it; her stone, cool, dark house, every room opening on to the verandah; her deep, shady verandah, or piazza, or corridor, looking out to the brilliant sun, the sparkling flowers and the seed grass, the still water and the yellowing banana trees, the dark splendour of the shadow-dense mango trees.

With the house went a Mexican Juana with two thick-haired daughters and one son. This family lived in a den at the back of the projecting bay of the dining-room. There, halfscreened, was the well and the toilet, and a little kitchen and a sleeping room where the family slept on mats on the floor. There the paltry chickens paddled, and the banana trees made a chitter as the wind came.

Kate had four bedrooms to choose from. She chose the one whose low, barred window opened on the rough, grass and cobble-stone street, closed her doors and windows, and went to sleep, saying to herself as she lay down: Now I am alone. And now I have only one thing to do; not to get caught up into the world's cog-wheels any more, and not to lose my hold on the hidden greater thing.

She was tired with a strange weariness, feeling she could make no further effort. She woke up at tea-time, but there was no tea. Juana hastened off to the hotel to buy a bit.

Juana was a woman of about forty, rather short, with full dark face, centreless dark eyes, untidy hair, and a limping way of walking. She

spoke rapidly, a rather plum-in-the-mouth Spanish, adding 'n' to all
her words. Something of a sloven, down to her speech.

'*No, Niña, no hay masn*'[2] – *masn* instead of *mas*. And calling Kate,
in the old Mexican style, *Niña*, which means *child*. It is the honourable title for a mistress.

Juana was going to be a bit of a trial. She was a widow of doubtful
antecedents, a creature with passion, but not much control, strong with
a certain indifference and looseness. The hotel owner assured Kate that
she was honest, but that if Kate would rather find another *criada*, all
well and good.

There was a bit of a battle to be fought between the two women.
Juana was obstinate and reckless; she had not been treated very well
by the world. And there was a touch of bottom-dog insolence about
her.

But also, sudden touches of passionate warmth and the peculiar self-
less generosity of the natives. She would be honest out of rough defiance and indifference, so long as she was not in a state of antagonism.

As yet, however, she was cautiously watching her ground, with that
black-eyed touch of malice and wariness to be expected. And Kate felt
that the cry: *Niña* – child! by which she was addressed, held in it
a slight note of malevolent mockery.

But there was nothing to do but to go ahead and trust the dark-
faced, centreless woman.

The second day, Kate had the energy to cast out one suite of bent-
wood and cane furniture from her salon, remove pictures and little
stands.

If there is one social instinct more dreary than all the other social
instincts in the world, it is the Mexican. In the centre of Kate's red-
tiled salon were two crescents: a black bent-wood cane settee flanked
on each side by two black bent-wood cane chairs, exactly facing a brown
bent-wood cane settee flanked on each side by two brown bent-wood
cane chairs. It was as if the two settees and the eight chairs were occupied by the ghosts of all the Mexican banalities ever uttered, sitting
facing one another with their knees towards one another, and their feet
on the terrible piece of green-with-red-roses carpet, in the weary centre
of the salon. The very sight of it was frightening.

Kate shattered this face-to-face symmetry, and had the two girls,
Maria and Concha, assisted by the ironic Juana, carrying off the brown

bent-wood chairs and the bamboo stands into one of the spare bed-rooms. Juana looked on cynically, and assisted officiously. But when Kate had her trunk, and fished out a couple of light rugs and a couple of fine shawls and a few things to make the place human, the criada began to exclaim:

  '*Qué bonita! Qué bonita, Niña! Mire qué bonita!*'[3]

The Plaza

SAYULA was a little lake resort; not for the idle rich, for Mexico has few left; but for tradespeople from Guadalajara, and week-enders. Even of these, there were few.

Nevertheless, there were two hotels, left over, really, from the safe quiet days of Don Porfirio, as were most of the villas. The outlying villas were shut up, some of them abandoned. Those in the village lived in a perpetual quake of fear. There were many terrors, but the two regnant were bandits and bolshevists.

Bandits are merely men who, in the outlying villages, having very often no money, no work, and no prospects, take to robbery and murder for a time – occasionally for a lifetime – as a profession. They live in their wild villages until troops are sent after them, when they retire into the savage mountains, or the marshes.

Bolshevists, somehow, seem to be born on the railway. Wherever the iron rails run, and passengers are hauled back and forth in railway coaches, there the spirit of rootlessness, of transitoriness, of first and second class in separate compartments, of envy and malice, and of iron and demonish panting engines, seems to bring forth the logical children of materialism, the bolshevists.

Sayula had her little branch of railway, her one train a day. The railway did not pay, and fought with extinction. But it was enough.

Sayula also had that real insanity of America, the automobile. As men used to want a horse and a sword, now they want a car. As women used to pine for a home and a box at the theatre, now it is a 'machine'. And the poor follow the middle class. There was a perpetual rush of 'machines', motor-cars and motor-buses – called camions – along the one forlorn road coming to Sayula from Guadalajara. One hope, one faith, one destiny; to ride in a camion, to own a car.

There was a little bandit scare when Kate arrived in the village, but she did not pay much heed. At evening she went into the plaza, to be with the people. The plaza was a square with big trees and a dis-used bandstand in the centre, a little promenade all round, and then the cobbled streets where the donkeys and the camions passed. There was a further little section of real market-place, on the north side.

The band played no more in Sayula, and the *elegancia* strolled no more on the inner pavement around the plaza, under the trees. But the pavement was still good, and the benches were still more-or-less sound. Oh Don Porfirio's day! And now it was the peons and Indians, in their blankets and white clothes, who filled the benches and monopolised the square. True, the law persisted that the peons must wear trousers in the plaza, and not the loose great floppy drawers of the fields. But then the peons also *wanted* to wear trousers, instead of the drawers that were the garb of their humble labour.

The plaza now belonged to the peons. They sat thick on the benches, or slowly strolled round in their sandals and blankets. Across the cobbled road on the north side, the little booths selling soup and hot food were crowded with men, after six o'clock; it was cheaper to eat out, at the end of a day's work. The women at home could eat tortillas, never mind the *caldo*, the soup or the meat mess. At the booths which sold tequila, men, women, and boys sat on the benches with their elbows on the board. There was a mild gambling game, where the man in the centre turned the cards, and the plaza rang to his voice: *Cinco de 'spadas! Rey de Copas!*[1] A large, stout, imperturbable woman, with a cigarette on her lip and danger in her lowering black eye, sat on into the night, selling tequila. The sweet-meat man stood by his board and sold sweets at one centavo each. And down on the pavement, small tin torch-lamps flared upon tiny heaps of mangoes or nauseous tropical red plums, two or three centavos the little heap, while the vendor, a woman in the full wave of her skirt, or a man with curious patient humility, squatted waiting for a purchaser, with that strange fatal indifference and that gentle sort of patience so puzzling to a stranger. To have thirty cents' worth of little red plums to sell; to pile them on the pavement in tiny pyramids, five in a pyramid; and to wait all day and on into the night, squatting on the pavement and looking up from the feet to the far-off face of the passer-by and potential purchaser, this, apparently, is an occupation and a living. At night by the flare of the tin torch, blowing its flame on the wind.

Usually there would be a couple of smallish young men with guitars of different sizes, standing close up facing one another like two fighting cocks that are uttering a long, endless swansong, singing in tense subdued voices the eternal ballads, not very musical, mournful, endless, intense, audible only within close range; keeping on and on till their throats were scraped. And a few tall, dark men in red blankets standing around, listening casually, and rarely, very rarely making a contribution of one *centavo*.

In among the food booths would be another trio, this time two guitars and a fiddle, and two of the musicians blind; the blind ones singing at a high pitch, full speed, yet not very audible. The very singing seemed secretive, the singers pressing close in, face to face, as if to keep the wild, melancholy ballad re-echoing in their private breasts, their backs to the world.

And the whole village was in the plaza, it was like a camp, with the low, rapid sound of voices. Rarely, very rarely a voice rose above the deep murmur of the men, the musical ripple of the women, the twitter of children. Rarely any quick movement; the slow promenade of men in sandals, the sandals, called huaraches, making a slight cockroach shuffle on the pavement. Sometimes, darting among the trees, bare-legged boys went sky-larking in and out of the shadow, in and out of the quiet people. They were the irrepressible boot-blacks, who swarm like tiresome flies in a barefooted country.

At the south end of the plaza, just across from the trees and cornerwise to the hotel, was a struggling attempt at an out-door café, with little tables and chairs on the pavement. Here, on weekdays, the few who dared flaunt their prestige would sit and drink a beer or a glass of tequila. They were mostly strangers. And the peons, sitting immobile on the seats in the background, looked on with basilisk eyes from under the great hats.

But on Saturdays and Sundays there was something of a show. Then the camions and motor-cars came in lurching and hissing. And, like strange birds alighting, you had slim and charming girls in organdie frocks and face powder and bobbed hair, fluttering into the plaza. There they strolled, arm in arm, brilliant in red organdie and blue chiffon and white muslin and pink and mauve and tangerine frail stuffs, their black hair bobbed out, their dark slim arms interlaced, their dark faces curiously macabre in the heavy make-up; approximating to white, but the white of a clown or a corpse.

In a world of big, handsome peon men, these flappers flapped with butterfly brightness and an incongruous shrillness, manless. The supply of fifis, the male young elegants who are supposed to equate the flappers, was small. But still, fifis there were, in white flannel trousers and white shoes, dark jackets, correct straw hats, and canes. Fifis far more lady-like than the reckless flappers; and far more nervous, wincing. But fifis none the less, gallant, smoking a cigarette with an elegant flourish, talk-ing elegant Castilian, as near as possible, and looking as if they were going to be sacrificed to some Mexican god within a twelvemonth; when they were properly plumped and perfumed. The sacrificial calves being fattened.

On Saturday, the fifis and the flappers and the motor-car people from town – only a forlorn few, after all – tried to be butterfly-gay, in sinister Mexico. They hired the musicians with guitars and fiddle, and the jazz music began to quaver, a little too tenderly, without enough kick.

And on the pavement under the trees of the alameda – under the trees of the plaza, just near the little tables and chairs of the café, the young couples began to gyrate *à la mode*. The red and the pink and the yellow and the blue organdie frocks were turning sharply with all the white flannel trousers available, and some of the white flannel trou-sers had smart shoes, white with black strappings or with tan brogue bands. And some of the organdie frocks had green legs and green feet, some had legs *à la nature*, and white feet. And the slim, dark arms went around the dark blue fifi shoulders – or dark blue with a white thread. And the immeasurably soft faces of the males would smile with a self-conscious fatherliness at the whitened, pretty, reckless little faces of the females; soft, fatherly, sensuous smiles, suggestive of a victim's luxuriousness.

But they were dancing on the pavement of the plaza, and on this pavement the peons were slowly strolling, or standing in groups watch-ing with black, inscrutable eyes the uncanny butterfly twitching of the dancers. Who knows what they thought? – whether they felt any ad-miration and envy at all, or only just a silent, cold dark-faced opposition. Opposition there was.

The young peons in their little white blouses, and the scarlet serape folded jauntily on one shoulder, strolled slowly on under their big, heavy, poised hats, with a will to ignore the dancers. Slowly, with a heavy, calm balance, they moved irresistibly through the dance, as if the dance did not exist. And the fifis in white trousers, with organdie in their arms, steered as best they might, to avoid the heavy relentless passage of the young peons, who went on talking to one another, smiling and flashing powerful white teeth, in a black, heavy sang-froid that settled like a blight even on the music. The dancers and the passing peons never touched, never jostled. In Mexico you do not run into people accidentally. But the dance broke against the invisible opposition.

The Indians on the seats, they too watched the dancers for a while. Then they turned against them the heavy negation of indifference, like a stone on the spirit. The mysterious faculty of the Indians, as they sit there, so quiet and dense, for killing off any ebullient life, for quenching any light and colourful effervescence.

There was indeed a little native dance-hall. But it was shut apart within four walls. And the whole rhythm and meaning was different, heavy, with a touch of violence. And even there, the dancers were artisans and mechanics or railway-porters, the half-urban people. No peons at all – or practically none.

So, before very long, the organdie butterflies and the flannel-trouser fifis gave in, succumbed, crushed once more beneath the stone-heavy passivity of resistance in the demonish peons.

The curious, radical opposition of the Indians to the thing we call the spirit. It is spirit which makes the flapper flap her organdie wings like a butterfly. It is spirit, which creases the white flannel trousers of the fifi and makes him cut his rather pathetic dash. They try to talk the elegancies and flippancies of the modern spirit.

But down on it all, like a weight of obsidian, comes the passive negation of the Indian. He understands soul, which is of the blood. But spirit, which is superior, and is the quality of our civilisation, this, in the mass, he darkly and barbarically repudiates. Not until he becomes an artisan or connected with machinery does the modern spirit get him.

And perhaps it is this ponderous repudiation of the modern spirit which makes Mexico what it is.

But perhaps the automobile will make roads even through the inaccessible soul of the Indian.

Kate was rather sad, seeing the dance swamped. She had been sitting at a little table, with Juana for dueña, sipping a glass of absinthe.

The motor-cars returning to town left early, in a little group. If bandits were out, they had best keep together. Even the fifis had a pistol on their hips.

But it was Saturday, so some of the young 'elegance' was staying on, till the next day; to bathe and flutter in the sun.

It was Saturday, so the plaza was very full, and along the cobble streets stretching from the square many torches fluttered and wavered upon the ground, illuminating a dark salesman and an array of straw hats, or a heap of straw mats called petates, or pyramids of oranges from across the lake.

It was Saturday, and Sunday morning was market. So, as it were suddenly, the life in the plaza was dense and heavy with potency. The Indians had come in from all the villages, and from far across the lake. And with them they brought the curious heavy potency of life which seems to hum deeper and deeper when they collect together.

In the afternoon, with the wind from the south, the big *canoas*, sailing-boats with black hulls and one huge sail, had come drifting across the waters, bringing the market-produce and the natives to their gathering ground. All the white specks of villages on the far shore, and on the far-off slopes, had sent their wild quota to the throng.

It was Saturday, and the Indian instinct for living on into the night, once they are gathered together, was now aroused. The people did not go home. Though market would begin at dawn, men had no thought of sleep.

At about nine o'clock, after the fifi dance was shattered, Kate heard a new sound, the sound of a drum, or tom-tom, and saw a drift of the peons away to the dark side of the plaza, where the side market would open to-morrow. Already places had been taken, and little stalls set up, and huge egg-shaped baskets, big enough to hold two men, were lolling against the wall.

There was a rippling and a pulse-like thudding of the drum, strangely arresting on the night air, then the long note of a flute playing a sort of wild, unemotional melody, with the drum for a syncopated rhythm. Kate, who had listened to the drums and the wild singing of the Red Indians in Arizona and New Mexico, instantly felt that timeless, primeval passion of the prehistoric races, with their intense and complicated religious significance, spreading on the air.

She looked inquiringly at Juana, and Juana's black eyes glanced back at her furtively.

'What is it?' said Kate.

'Musicians, singers,' said Juana evasively.

'But it's *different*,' said Kate.

'Yes, it is new.'

'New?'

'Yes, it has only been coming for a short time.'

'Where does it come from?'

'Who knows!' said Juana, with an evasive shrug of her shoulders

'I want to hear,' said Kate.

'It's purely men,' said Juana.

'Still, one can stand a little way off.'

Kate moved towards the dense, silent throng of men in big hats. They all had their backs to her.

She stood on the step of one of the houses, and saw a little clearing at the centre of the dense throng of men, under the stone wall over which bougainvillea and plumbago flowers were hanging, lit up by the small, brilliantly flaring torches of sweet-smelling wood, which a boy held in his two hands.

The drum was in the centre of the clearing, the drummer standing facing the crowd. He was naked from the waist up, wore snow-white cotton drawers, very full, held round the waist by a red sash, and bound at the ankles with red cords. Round his uncovered head was a red cord, with three straight scarlet feathers rising from the back of his head, and on his forehead, a torquoise ornament, a circle of blue with a round blue stone in the centre. The flute player was also naked to the waist, but over his shoulder was folded a fine white serape with blue-and-dark edges, and fringe. Among the crowd, men with naked shoulders were giving little leaflets to the onlookers. And all the time, high and pure, the queer clay flute was repeating a savage, rather difficult melody, and the drum was giving the blood-rhythm.

More and more men were drifting in from the plaza. Kate stepped from her perch and went rather shyly forward. She wanted one of the papers. The man gave her one without looking at her. And she went into the light to read. It was a sort of ballad, but without rhyme, in Spanish. At the top of the leaflet was a rough print of an eagle within the ring of a serpent that had its tail in its mouth; a curious deviation from the Mexican emblem, which is an eagle standing on a nopal, a cactus with great flat leaves, and holding in its beak and claws a writhing snake.

This eagle stood slim upon the serpent, within the circle of the snake, that had black markings round its back, like short black rays pointing inwards. At a little distance, the emblem suggested an eye.

'In the place of the west
In peace, beyond the lashing of the sun's bright tail,
In the stillness where waters are born
Slept I, Quetzalcoatl.

In the cave which is called Dark Eye,
Behind the sun, looking through him as a window
Is the place. There the waters rise,
There the winds are born.

On the waters of the after-life
I rose again, to see a star falling, and feel a breath on my face.
The breath said: Go! And lo!
I am coming.

The star that was falling was fading, was dying.
I heard the star singing like a dying bird;
My name is Jesus, I am Mary's Son.
I am coming home.
My mother the Moon is dark.
Oh brother, Quetzalcoatl
Hold back the dragon of the sun,
Bind him with shadow while I pass
Homewards. Let me come home.

I bound the bright fangs of the Sun
And held him while Jesus passed
Into the lidless shade,
Into the eye of the Father,
Into the womb of refreshment.

And the breath blew upon me again.
So I took the sandals of the Saviour
And started down the long slope
Past the mount of the sun.
Till I saw beneath me
White breast-tips of my Mexico
My bride.

Jesus the Crucified
Sleeps in the healing waters
The long sleep.

Sleep, sleep, my brother, sleep.
My bride between the seas
Is combing her dark hair,
Saying to herself: Quetzalcoatl.'

There was a dense throng of men gathered now, and from the centre, the ruddy glow of ocote torches rose warm and strong, and the sweet scent of the cedar-like resin was on the air. Kate could see nothing, for the mass of men in big hats.

The flute had stopped its piping, and the drum was beating a slow, regular thud, acting straight on the blood. The incomprehensible hollow barking of the drum was like a spell on the mind, making the heart burst each stroke, and darkening the will.

The men in the crowd began to subside, sitting and squatting on the ground, with their hats between their knees. And now it was a little sea of dark, proud heads leaning a little forward above the soft, strong male shoulders.

Near the wall was a clear circle, with the drum in the centre. The drummer with the naked torso stood tilting his drum towards him, his shoulders gleaming smooth and ruddy in the flare of light. Beside him stood another man holding a banner that hung from a light rod. On the blue field of the banneret was the yellow sun with a black centre, and between the four greater yellow rays, four black rays emerging, so that the sun looked like a wheel spinning with a dazzling motion.

The crowd having all sat down, the six men with naked torsos, who had been giving out the leaflets and ordering the crowd, now came back and sat down in a ring, of which the drummer, with the drum tilted between his knees as he squatted on the ground, was the key. On his right hand sat the banner-bearer, on his left the flautist. They were nine men in the ring, the boy, who sat apart watching the two ocote torches, which he had laid upon a stone supported on a long cane tripod, being the tenth.

The night seemed to have gone still. The curious seed-rattling hum of voices that filled the plaza was hushed. Under the trees, on the pavements, people were still passing unconcerned, but they looked curiously lonely, isolated figures drifting in the twilight of the electric lamps, and going about some exceptional business. They seemed outside the nucleus of life.

Away on the north side, the booths were still flaring, people were buying and selling. But this quarter too, looked lonely, and outside the actual reality, almost like memory.

When the men sat down, the women began to drift up shyly, and seat themselves on the ground at the outer rim, their full cotton skirts flowering out around them, and their dark rebozos drawn tight over their small, round, shy heads, as they squatted on the ground. Some, too shy to come right up, lingered on the nearest benches of the plaza. And some had gone away. Indeed, a good many men and women had disappeared as soon as the drum was heard.

So that the plaza was curiously void. There was the dense clot of people round the drum, and then the outer world, seeming empty and hostile. Only in the dark little street that gave on to the darkness of the lake, people were standing like ghosts, half lit-up, the men with their serapes over their faces, watching erect and silent and concealed, from the shadow.

But Kate, standing back in the doorway, with Juana sitting on the doorstep at her feet, was fascinated by the silent, half-naked ring of men in the torchlight. Their heads were black, their bodies soft and ruddy with the peculiar Indian beauty that has at the same time something terrible in it. The soft, full, handsome torsos of silent men with heads softly bent a little forward; the soft, easy shoulders, that are yet so broad, and which balance upon so powerful a backbone; shoulders drooping a little, with the relaxation of slumbering, quiescent power; the beautiful ruddy skin, gleaming with a dark fineness; the strong breasts, so male and so deep, yet without the muscular hardening that belongs to white men; and the dark, closed faces, closed upon a darkened consciousness, the black moustaches and delicate beards framing the closed silence of the mouth; all this was strangely impressive, moving strange, frightening emotions in the soul. Those men who sat there in their dark, physical tenderness, so still and soft, they looked at the same time frightening. Something dark, heavy, and reptilian in their silence and their softness. Their very naked torsos were clothed with a subtle shadow, a certain secret obscurity. White men sitting there would have been strong-muscled and frank, with an openness in their very physique, a certain ostensible presence. But not so these men. Their very nakedness only revealed the soft, heavy depths of their natural secrecy, their eternal invisibility. They did not belong to the realm of that which comes forth.

Everybody was quite still; the expectant hush deepened to a kind of dead, night silence. The naked-shouldered men sat motionless, sunk into themselves, and listening with the dark ears of the blood. The red sash went tight round their waists, the wide white trousers, starched rather stiff, were bound round the ankles with red cords, and the dark feet in the glare of the torch looked almost black, in huaraches that had red thongs. What did they want then, in life, these men who sat so softly and without any assertion, yet whose weight was so ponderous, arresting?

Kate was at once attracted and repelled.[2] She was attracted, almost fascinated by the strange *nuclear* power of the men in the circle. It was like a darkly glowing, vivid nucleus of new life. Repellent the strange heaviness, the sinking of the spirit into the earth, like dark water. Repellent the silent, dense opposition to the pale-faced spiritual direction.

Yet here and here alone, it seemed to her, life burned with a deep new fire. The rest of life, as she knew it, seemed wan, bleached and sterile. The pallid wanness and weariness of her world! And here, the dark, ruddy figures in the glare of a torch, like the centre of the everlasting fire, surely this was a new kindling of mankind!

She knew it was so. Yet she preferred to be on the fringe, sufficiently out of contact. She could not bear to come into actual contact.

The man with the banner of the sun lifted his face as if he were going to speak. And yet he did not speak. He was old; in his sparse beard were grey hairs, grey hairs over his thick dark mouth. And his face had the peculiar thickness, with a few deep-scored lines, of the old among these people. Yet his hair rose vigorous and manly from his forehead, his body was smooth and strong. Only, perhaps, a little smoother, heavier, softer than the shoulders of the younger men.

His black eyes gazed sightless for some time. Perhaps he was really blind; perhaps it was a heavy abstraction, a sort of heavy memory working in him, which made his face seem sightless.

Then he began, in a slow, clear, far-off voice, that seemed strangely to echo the vanished barking of the drum:

'Listen to me, men! Listen to me, women of these men! A long time ago, the lake started calling for men, in the quiet of the night. And there were no men. The little charales were swimming round the shore, looking for something, and the bágari and the other big fish would jump out of the water, to look around. But there were no men.

'So one of the gods with hidden faces walked out of the water, and climbed the hill –' he pointed with his hand in the night towards the invisible round hill at the back of the village – 'and looked about. He looked up at the sun, and through the sun he saw the dark sun, the same that made the sun and the world, and will swallow it again like a draught of water.

'He said: *Is it time?* And from behind the bright sun the four dark arms of the greater sun shot out, and in the shadow men arose. They could see the four dark arms of the sun in the sky. And they started walking.

'The man on the top of the hill, who was a god, looked at the mountains and the flat places, and saw men very thirsty, their tongues hanging out. So he said to them: Come! Come here! Here is my sweet water!

'They came like dogs running with their tongues out, and kneeled on the shore of the lake. And the man on the top of the hill heard them panting with having drunk much water. He said to them: Have you drunk too much into yourselves? Are your bones not dry enough?

'The men made houses on the shore, and the man on the hill, who was a god, taught them to sow maize and beans, and build boats. But he said to them: No boat will save you, when the dark sun ceases to hold out his dark arms abroad in the sky.

'The man on the hill said: I am Quetzalcoatl, who breathed moisture on your dry mouths. I filled your breasts with breath from beyond the sun. I am the wind that whirls from the heart of the earth, the little winds that whirl like snakes round your feet and your legs and your thighs, lifting up the head of the snake of your body, in whom is your power. When the snake of your body lifts its head, beware! It is I, Quetzalcoatl, rearing up in you, rearing up and reaching beyond the bright day, to the sun of darkness beyond, where is your home at last. Save for the dark sun at the back of the day-sun, save for the four dark arms in the heavens, you were bone, and the stars were bone, and the moon an empty sea-shell on a dry beach, and the yellow sun were an empty cup, like the dry thin bone of a dead coyote's head. So beware!

'Without me you are nothing. Just as I, without the sun that is back of the sun, am nothing.

'When the yellow sun is high in the sky, then say: Quetzalcoatl will lift his hand and screen me from this, else I shall burn out, and the land will wither.

'For, say I, in the palm of my hand is the water of life, and on the back of my hand is the shadow of death. And when men forget me, I lift the back of my hand, farewell! Farewell, and the shadow of death.

'But men forgot me. Their bones were moist, their hearts weak. When the snake of their body lifted its head, they said: This is the tame snake that does as we wish. And when they could not bear the fire of the sun, they said: The sun is angry. He wants to drink us up. Let us give him blood of victims.

'And so it was, the dark branches of shade were gone from heaven, and Quetzalcoatl mourned and grew old, holding his hand before his face, to hide his face from men.

'He mourned and said: Let me go home. I am old, I am almost bone. Bone triumphs in me, my heart is a dry gourd. I am weary in Mexico.

'So he cried to the Master-Sun, the dark one, of the unuttered name: I am withering white like a perishing gourd-vine. I am turning to bone. I am denied of these Mexicans. I am waste and weary and old. Take me away.

'Then the dark sun reached an arm, and lifted Quetzalcoatl into the sky. And the dark sun beckoned with a finger, and brought white men out of the east. And they came with a dead god on the Cross, saying: Lo! This is the Son of God! He is dead, he is bone! Lo, your god is bled and dead, he is bone. Kneel and sorrow for him, and weep. For your tears he will give you comfort again, from the dead, and a place among the scentless rose-trees of the after-life, when you are dead.

'Lo! His mother weeps, and the waters of the world are in her hands. She will give you drink, and heal you, and lead you to the land of God. In the land of God you shall weep no more. Beyond the gates of death, when you have passed from the house of bone into the garden of white roses.

'So the weeping Mother brought her Son who was dead on the Cross to Mexico, to live in the temples. And the people looked up no more, saying: The Mother weeps. The Son of her womb is bone. Let us hope for the place of the west, where the dead have peace among the scentless rose-trees, in the Paradise of God.

'For the priests would say: It is beautiful beyond the grave.

'And then the priests grew old, and the tears of the Mother were exhausted, and the Son on the Cross cried out to the dark sun far beyond the sun: *What is this that is done to me? Am I dead for ever, and only dead? Am I always and only dead, but bone on a Cross of bone?*

'So this cry was heard in the world, and beyond the stars of the night, and beyond the sun of the day.

'Jesus said again: *Is it time? My Mother is old like a sinking moon, the old bone of her can weep no more. Are we perished beyond redeem?*

'Then the greatest of the great suns spoke aloud from the back of the sun: I will take my Son to my bosom, I will take His Mother on my lap. Like a woman I will put them in my womb, like a mother I will lay them to sleep, in mercy I will dip them in the bath of forgetting and peace and renewal.

'That is all. So hear now, you men, and you women of these men.

'Jesus is going home, to the Father, and Mary is going back, to sleep in the belly of the Father. And they both will recover from death, during the long long sleep.

'But the Father will not leave us alone. We are not abandoned.

'The Father has looked around, and has seen the Morning Star, fearless between the rush of the oncoming yellow sun, and the backward reel of the night. So the Great One, whose name has never been spoken, says: Who art thou, bright watchman? And the dawn-star answering: It is I, the Morning Star, who in Mexico was Quetzalcoatl. It is I, who look at the yellow sun from behind, have my eye on the unseen side of the moon. It is I, the star, midway between the darkness and the rolling of the sun. I, called Quetzalcoatl, waiting in the strength of my days.

'The Father answered: It is well. It is well. And again: It is time.

'Thus the big word was spoken behind the back of the world. The Nameless said: It is time.

'Once more the word has been spoken: It is time.

'Listen, men, and the women of men: It is time. Know now it is time. Those that left us are coming back. Those that came are leaving again. Say welcome, and then farewell!

'Welcome! Farewell!'

The old man ended with a strong, suppressed cry, as if really calling to the gods:

'Bienvenido! Bienvenido! Adiós! Adiós!'

Even Juana, seated at Kate's feet, cried out without knowing what she did:

'Bienvenido! Bienvenido! Adiós! Adiós! Adiós-n!'

On the last adiós! she trailed out to a natural human 'n'.

The drum began to beat with an insistent, intensive rhythm, and the flute, or whistle, lifted its odd, far-off calling voice. It was playing again and again the peculiar melody Kate had heard at first.

Then one of the men in the circle lifted his voice, and began to sing the hymn. He sang in the fashion of the old Red Indians, with intensity and restraint, singing inwardly, singing to his own soul, not outward to the world, nor yet even upward to God, as the Christians sing. But with a sort of suppressed, tranced intensity, singing to the inner mystery, singing not into space, but into the other dimension of man's existence, where he finds himself in the infinite room that lies inside the axis of our wheeling space. Space, like the world, cannot but move. And like the world, there is an axis. And the axis of our worldly space, when you enter, is a vastness where even the trees come and go, and the soul is at home in its own dream, noble and unquestioned.

The strange, inward pulse of the drum, and the singer singing inwardly, swirled the soul back into the very centre of time, which is older than age. He began on a high, remote note, and holding the voice at a distance, ran on in subtle, running rhythms, apparently unmeasured, yet pulsed underneath by the drum, and giving throbbing, three-fold lilts and lurches. For a long time, no melody at all was recognisable: it was just a lurching, running, far-off crying, something like the distant faint howling of a coyote. It was really the music of the old American Indian.

There was no recognisable rhythm, no recognisable emotion, it was hardly music. Rather a far-off, perfect crying in the night. But it went straight through to the soul, the most ancient and everlasting soul of all men, where alone can the human family assemble in immediate contact.

Kate knew it at once, like a sort of fate. It was no good resisting. There was neither urge nor effort, nor any speciality. The sound sounded in the innermost far-off place of the human core, the ever-present, where there is neither hope nor emotion, but passion sits with folded wings on the nest, and faith is a tree of shadow.

Like fate, like doom. Faith is the Tree of Life itself,[3] inevitable, and the apples are upon us, like the apples of the eye, the apples of the chin, the apple of the heart, the apples of the breast, the apple of the belly, with its deep core, the apples of the loins, the apples of the knees, the little, side-by-side apples of the toes. What do change and evolution matter? We are the Tree with the fruit forever upon it. And we are faith forever. Verbum Sat.[4]

The one singer had finished, and only the drum kept on, touching the sensitive membrane of the night subtly and knowingly. Then a voice in the circle rose again on the song, and like birds flying from a tree, one after the other, the individual voices arose, till there was a strong, intense, curiously weighty soaring and sweeping of male voices, like a dark flock of birds flying and dipping in unison. And all the dark birds seemed to have launched out of the heart, in the inner forest of the masculine chest.

And one by one, voices in the crowd broke free, like birds launching and coming in from a distance, caught by the spell. The words did not matter. Any verse, any words, no words, the song remained the same: a strong, deep wind rushing from the caverns of the breast, from the everlasting soul! Kate herself was too shy and wincing to sing: too blenched with disillusion. But she heard the answer away back in her soul, like a far-off mocking-bird at night. And Juana was singing in spite of herself, in a crooning feminine voice, making up the words unconsciously.

The half-naked men began to reach for their serapes: white serapes, with borders of blue and earth-brown bars, and dark fringe. A man rose from the crowd and went towards the lake. He came back with ocote and with faggots that a boat had brought over. And he started a little fire. After a while, another man went for fuel, and started another fire in the centre of the circle, in front of the drum. Then one of the women went off soft and barefoot, in her full cotton skirt. And she made a little bonfire among the women.

The air was bronze with the glow of flame, and sweet with smoke like incense. The song rose and fell, then died away. Rose, and died. The drum ebbed on, faintly touching the dark membrane of the night. Then ebbed away. In the absolute silence could be heard the soundless stillness of the dark lake.

Then the drum started again, with a new, strong pulse. One of the seated men, in his white poncho with the dark blackish-and-blue border, got up, taking off his sandals as he did so, and began softly to dance the dance step. Mindless, dancing heavily and with a curious bird-like sensitiveness of the feet, he began to tread the earth with his bare soles, as if treading himself deep into the earth. Alone, with a curious pendulum rhythm, leaning a little forward from a powerful backbone, he trod to the drum-beat, his white knees lifting and lifting alternately against the dark fringe of his blanket, with a queer dark splash. And another man put his huaraches into the centre of the ring, near the fire, and stood up to dance. The man at the drum lifted up his voice in a wild, blind song. The men were taking off their ponchos. And soon, with the firelight on their breasts and on their darkly abstracted faces, they were all afoot, with bare torsos and bare feet, dancing the savage bird-tread.

'*Who sleeps shall wake! Who sleeps shall wake!* Who treads down the path of the snake in the dust shall arrive at the place; in the path of the dust shall arrive at the place and be dressed in the skin of the snake: shall be dressed in the skin of the snake of the earth, that is father of stone; that is father of stone and the timber of earth; of the silver and gold, of the iron, the timber of earth from the bone of the father of earth, of the snake of the world, of the heart of the world, that beats as a snake beats the dust in its motion on earth, from the heart of the world.

'Who slee-eeps, sha-all wake! Who slee-eeps, sha-all wake! Who sleeps, sha-ll wake in the way of the snake of the dust of the earth, of the stone of the earth, of the bone of the earth.'

The song seemed to take new wild flights, after it had sunk and rustled to a last ebb. It was like waves that rise out of the invisible, and rear up into form and a flying, disappearing whiteness and a rustle of extinction. And the dancers, after dancing in a circle in a slow, deep absorption, each man changeless in his own place, treading the same dust with the soft churning of bare feet, slowly, slowly began to revolve, till the circle was slowly revolving round the fire, with always the same soft, down-sinking, churning tread. And the drum kept the changeless living beat, like a heart, and the song rose and soared and fell, ebbed and ebbed to a sort of extinction, then heaved up again.

Till the young peons could stand it no more. They put off their sandals and their hats and their blankets, and shyly, with inexpert feet that yet knew the old echo of the tread, they stood behind the wheeling dancers, and danced without changing place. Till soon the revolving circle had a fixed yet throbbing circle of men outside.

Then suddenly one of the naked-shouldered dancers from the inner circle stepped back into the outer circle and with a slow leaning, slowly started the outer circle revolving in the reverse direction from the inner. So now there were two wheels of the dance, one within the other, and revolving in different directions.

They kept on and on, with the drum and the song, revolving like wheels of shadow-shapes around the fire. Till the fire died low, and the drum suddenly stopped, and the men suddenly dispersed, returning to their seats again.

There was silence, then the low hum of voices and the sound of laughter. Kate had thought, so often, that the laughter of the peons broke from them in a sound almost like pain. But now the laughs came like little invisible flames, suddenly from the embers of the talk.

Everybody was waiting, waiting. Yet nobody moved at once, when the thud of the drum struck again like a summons. They sat still talking, listening with a second consciousness. Then a man arose and threw off his blanket, and threw wood on the central fire. Then he walked through the seated men to where the women clustered in the fullness of their skirts. There he waited, smiling with a look of abstraction. Till a girl rose and came with utmost shyness towards him, holding her rebozo tight over her lowered head with her right hand, and taking the hand of the man in her left. It was she who lifted the motionless hand of the man in her own, shyly, with a sudden shy snatching. He laughed, and led her through the now risen men, towards the inner fire. She went with dropped head, hiding her face in confusion. But side by side and loosely holding hands, they began to tread the soft, heavy dance-step, forming the first small segment of the inner, stationary circle.

And now all the men were standing facing outwards, waiting to be chosen. And the women quickly, their shawled heads hidden, were slipping in and picking up the loose right hand of the man of their choice. The inner men with the naked shoulders were soon chosen. The inner circle, of men and women in pairs, hand in hand, was closing.

'Come, Niña, come!' said Juana, looking up at Kate with black, gleaming eyes.

'I am afraid!' said Kate. And she spoke the truth.

One of the bare-breasted men had come across the street, out of the crowd, and was standing waiting, near the doorway in which Kate stood, silently, with averted face.

'Look! Niña! This master is waiting for you. Then come! Oh, Niña, come!'

The voice of the criada had sunk to the low, crooning, almost magical appeal of the women of the people, and her black eyes glistened strangely, watching Kate's face. Kate, almost mesmerised, took slow, reluctant steps forward, towards the man who was standing with averted face.

'Do you mind?' she said in English, in great confusion. And she touched his fingers with her own.

His hand, warm and dark and savagely suave, loosely, almost with indifference, and yet with the soft barbaric nearness, held her fingers, and he led her to the circle. She dropped her head, and longed to be able to veil her face. In her white dress and green straw hat, she felt a virgin again, a young virgin. This was the quality these men had been able to give back to her.

Shyly, awkwardly, she tried to tread the dance-step. But in her shoes she felt inflexible, insulated, and the rhythm was not in her. She moved in confusion.

But the man beside her held her hand in the same light, soft grasp, and the slow, pulsing pendulum of his body swayed untrammelled. He took no notice of her. And yet he held her fingers in his soft, light touch.

Juana had discarded her boots and stockings, and with her dark, creased face like a mask of obsidian, her eyes gleaming with the timeless female flame, dark and unquenchable, she was treading the step of the dance.

'As the bird of the sun treads the earth at the dawn of the day like a brown hen under his feet, like a hen and the branches of her belly droop with the apples of birth, with the eggs of gold, with the eggs that hide the globe of the sun in the waters of heaven, in the purse of the shell of earth that is white from the fire of the blood, tread the earth, and the earth will conceive like the hen 'neath the feet of the bird of the sun; 'neath the feet of the heart, 'neath the heart's twin feet. Tread the earth, tread the earth that squats as a pullet with wings closed in –'

The circle began to shift, and Kate was slowly moving round between two silent and absorbed men, whose arms touched her arms. And the one held her fingers softly, loosely, but with transcendent nearness.

And the wild song rose again like a bird that has alighted for a second, and the drum changed rhythm incomprehensibly.

The outer wheel was all men. She seemed to feel the strange dark glow of them upon her back. Men, dark, collective men, non-individual. And herself woman, wheeling upon the great wheel of womanhood.

Men and women alike danced with faces lowered and expressionless, abstract, gone in the deep absorption of men into the greater manhood, women into the great womanhood. It was sex, but the greater, not the lesser sex. The waters over the earth wheeling upon the waters under the earth, like an eagle silently wheeling above its own shadow.

She felt her sex and her womanhood caught up and identified in the slowly revolving ocean of nascent life, the dark sky of the men lowering and wheeling above. She was not herself, she was gone, and her own desires were gone in the ocean of the great desire. As the man whose fingers touched hers was gone in the ocean that is male, stooping over the face of the waters.

The slow, vast, soft-touching revolution of the ocean above upon ocean below, with no vestige of rustling or foam. Only the pure sliding conjunction. Herself gone into her greater self, her womanhood consummated in the greater womanhood. And where her fingers touched the fingers of the man, the quiet spark, like the dawn-star, shining between her and the greater manhood of men.

How strange, to be merged in desire beyond desire, to be gone in the body beyond the individualism of the body, with the spark of contact lingering like a morning star between her and the man, her woman's greater self, and the greater self of man. Even of the two men next to her. What a beautiful slow wheel of dance, two great streams streaming in contact, in opposite directions.

She did not know the face of the man whose fingers she held. Her personal eyes had gone blind, his face was the face of dark heaven, only the touch of his fingers a star that was both hers and his.

Her feet were feeling the way into the dance-step. She was beginning to learn softly to loosen her weight, to loosen the uplift of all her life, and let it pour slowly, darkly, with an ebbing gush, rhythmical in soft, rhythmic gushes from her feet into the dark body of the earth. Erect, strong like a staff of life, yet to loosen all the sap of her strength and let it flow down into the roots of the earth.

- She had lost count of time. But the dance of itself seemed to be wheeling to a close, though the rhythm remained exactly the same to the end.

The voice finished singing, only the drum kept on. Suddenly the drum gave a rapid little shudder, and there was silence. And immediately the hands were loosened, the dance broke up into fragments. The man gave her a quick, far-off smile and was gone. She would never know him by sight. But by presence she might know him.

The women slipped apart, clutching their rebozos tight round their shoulders. The men hid themselves in their blankets. And Kate turned to the darkness of the lake.

'Already you are going, Niña?' came Juana's voice of mild, aloof disappointment.

'I must go now,' said Kate hurriedly.

And she hastened towards the dark of the lake, Juana running behind her with shoes and stockings in her hand.

Kate wanted to hurry home with her new secret, the strange secret of her greater womanhood, that she could not get used to. She would have to sink into this mystery.

She hastened along the uneven path of the edge of the lake shore, that lay dark in shadow, though the stars gave enough light to show the dark bulks and masts of the sailing-canoes against the downy obscurity of the water. Night, timeless, hourless night! She would not look at her watch. She would lay her watch face down, to hide its phosphorus figures. She would not be timed.

And as she sank into sleep, she could hear the drum again, like a pulse inside a stone beating.

CHAPTER VIII

Night in the House

OVER the gateway of Kate's house was a big tree called a cuenta tree, because it dropped its fruits, that were little, round, hard balls like little dark marbles, perfect in shape, for the natives to gather up and string for beads, cuentas, or, more particularly, for the Pater Noster beads of the rosary. At night, the little road outside was quite dark, and the dropping of the cuentas startled the silence.

The nights, which at first had seemed perfectly friendly, began to be full of terrors. Fear had risen again. A band of robbers had gathered in one of the outlying villages on the lake, a village where the men had bad characters, as being ready to turn bandit at any moment. And this gang, invisible in the daytime, consisting during the day of lake fishermen and labourers on the land, at night would set off on horseback to sack any lonely, or insufficiently-protected house.

Then the fact that a gang of bandits was out always set the isolated thieves and scoundrels in action. Whatever happened, it would be attributed to the bandits. And so, many an unsuspected, seemingly honest man, with the old lust in his soul, would steal out by night with his machete and perhaps a pistol, to put his fingers in the pie of the darkness.

And again Kate felt the terror clot and thicken in the black silence of the Mexican night, till the sound of a cuenta falling was terrible. She would lie and listen to the thickening darkness. A little way off would sound the long, shrill whistle of the police watch. And in a while, the police patrol, on horseback, would go clattering lightly by. But the police in most countries are never present save where there is no trouble.

The rainy season was coming, and the night-wind rose from the lake, making strange noises in the trees, and shaking the many loose doors of the house. The servants were away in their distant recess. And in Mexico, at night, each little distance isolates itself absolutely, like a man in a black coat turning his back.

In the morning, Juana would appear from the plaza, her eyes blob-like and inky, and the old, weary, monkey look of subjection to fear, settled on her bronze face. A race old in subjection to fear, and unable to shake it off. She would immediately begin to pour forth to Kate, in a babbling, half intelligent stream, some story of a house broken into and a woman stabbed. And she would say, the owner of the hotel had sent word that it was not safe for Kate to sleep alone in the house. She must go to the hotel to sleep.

The whole village was in that state of curious, reptile apprehension which comes over dark people. A panic fear, a sense of devilment and horror thick in the night air. When blue morning came they would cheer up. But at night, like clotting blood the air would begin to thicken again.

The fear, of course, was communicated from one person to another. Kate was sure that if Juana and her family had not been huddled in reptile terror away at the far end of the house, she herself would have been unafraid. As it was, Juana was like a terror-struck lizard.

There was no man about the place. Juana had two sons, Jesús, who was about twenty, and Ezequiel, about seventeen. But Jesús – she pronounced it *Hezoosn* – ran the little gasoline motor for the electric light, and he and Ezequiel slept together on the floor of the little engine house. So that Juana huddled with her two girls, Concha and Maria, in the den at the end of Kate's house, and seemed to sweat a rank odour of fear.

The village was submerged. Usually the plaza kept alive till ten o'clock, with the charcoal fires burning and the ice-cream man going round with his bucket on his head, endlessly crying: *Nieve! Nieve!* and the people gossiping on the streets or listening to the young men with guitars.

Now, by nine o'clock, the place was deserted, curiously stony and vacuous. And the Jefe sent out the order that anybody in the streets after ten o'clock would be arrested.

Kate hurried to her house and locked herself in. It is not easy to withstand the panic fear of a black-eyed, semi-barbaric people. The thing communicates itself like some drug on the air, wringing the heart and paralysing the soul with a sense of evil; black, horrible evil.

She would lie in her bed in the absolute dark: the electric light was cut off completely, everywhere, at ten o'clock, and primitive darkness reigned. And she could feel the demonish breath of evil moving on the air in waves.

She thought of the grisly stories of the country, which she had heard. And she thought again of the people, outwardly so quiet, so nice, with a gentle smile. But even Humboldt[1] had said of the Mexicans, that few people had such a gentle smile, and at the same time, such fierce eyes. It was not that their eyes were exactly fierce. But their blackness was inchoate, with a dagger of white light in it. And in the inchoate blackness the blood-lust might arise, out of the sediment of the uncreated past.

Uncreated, half-created, such a people was at the mercy of old black influences that lay in a sediment at the bottom of them. While they were quiet, they were gentle and kindly, with a sort of limpid naïveté. But when anything shook them at the depths, the black clouds would arise, and they were gone again in the old grisly passions of death, blood-lust, incarnate hate. A people incomplete, and at the mercy of old, upstarting lusts.

Somewhere at the bottom of their souls, she felt, was a fathomless resentment, like a raw wound. The heavy, bloody-eyed resentment of men who have never been able to win a soul for themselves, never been able to win themselves a nucleus, an individual integrity out of the chaos of passions and potencies and death. They are caught in the toils of old lusts and old activities as in the folds of a black serpent that strangles the heart. The heavy, evil-smelling weight of an unconquered past.

And under this weight they live and die, not really sorry to die. Clogged and tangled in the elements, never able to extricate themselves. Blackened under a too-strong sun, surcharged with the heavy sundering electricity of the Mexican air, and tormented by the bubbling of volcanoes away below the feet. The tremendous potent elements of the American continent, that give men powerful bodies, but which weigh the soul down and prevent its rising into birth. Or, if a man arrives with a soul, the maleficent elements gradually break it, gradually, till he decomposes into ideas and mechanistic activities, in a body full of mechanical energy, but with his blood-soul dead and putrescent.

So, these men, unable to overcome the elements, men held down by the serpent tangle of sun and electricity and volcanic emission, they are subject to an ever-recurring, fathomless lust of resentment, a demonish hatred of life itself. Then, the instriking thud of a heavy knife, stabbing into a living body, this is the best. No lust of women can equal that lust. The clutching throb of gratification as the knife strikes in and the blood spurts out!

It is the inevitable supreme gratification of a people entangled in the past, and unable to extricate itself. A people that has never been redeemed, that has not known a Saviour.

For Jesus is no Saviour to the Mexicans. He is a dead god in their tomb. As a miner who is entombed underground by the collapsing of the earth in the gangways, so do whole nations become entombed under the slow subsidence of their past. Unless there comes some Saviour, some Redeemer to drive a new way out, to the sun.

But the white men brought no salvation to Mexico. On the contrary, they find themselves at last shut in the tomb along with their dead god and the conquered race.

Which is the *status quo*.

Kate lay and thought hard, in the black night. At the same time, she was listening intensely, with a clutch of horror. She could not control her heart. It seemed wrenched out of place, and really hurt her. She was, as she had never been before, absolute physically afraid, blood afraid. Her blood was wrenched in a paralysis of fear.

In England, in Ireland, during the war and the revolution she had known *spiritual* fear. The ghastly fear of the rabble; and during the war, nations were nearly all rabble. The terror of the rabble that, mongrel-like, wanted to break the free *spirit* in individual men and women. It was the cold, collective lust of millions of people, to break the spirit in the outstanding individuals. They wanted to break this spirit, so that they could start the great downhill rush back to old underworld levels, old gold-worship and murder lust. The rabble.

In those days, Kate had known the agony of cold social fear, as if a democracy were a huge, huge cold centipede which, if you resisted it, would dig every claw into you. And the flesh would mortify around every claw.

That had been her worst agony of fear. And she had survived.

Now she knew the real heart-wrench of blood fear. Her heart seemed pulled out of place, in a stretched pain.

She dozed, and wakened suddenly, at a small noise. She sat up in bed. Her doors on to the verandah had shutters. The doors themselves were fastened, but the shutters were open for air, leaving the upper space, like the window of the door, open. And against the dark grey of the night she saw what looked like a black cat crouching on the bottom of the panel-space.

'What is that?' she said automatically.

Instantly, the thing moved, slid away, and she knew it was the arm of a man that had been reaching inside to pull the bolt of the door. She lay for a second paralysed, prepared to scream. There was no movement. So she leaned and lit a candle.

The curious panic fear was an agony to her. It paralysed her and wrenched her heart out of place. She lay prostrate in the anguish of night-terror. The candle blazed duskily. There was a far-off mutter of thunder. And the night was horrible, horrible, Mexico was ghastly to her beyond description.

She could not relax, she could not get her heart into place. 'Now,' she thought to herself, 'I am at the mercy of this thing, and I have lost myself.' And it was a terrible feeling, to be lost, scattered, as it were, from herself in a horror of fear.

'What can I do?' she thought, summoning her spirit. 'How can I help myself?' She knew she was all alone.

For a long time she could do nothing. Then a certain relief came to her as she thought: 'I am believing in evil. I mustn't believe in evil. Panic and murder never start unless the leading people let slip the control. I don't really believe in evil. I don't believe the old Pan² can wrench us back into the old, evil forms of consciousness, unless we wish it. I do believe there is a greater power, which will give us the greater strength, while we keep the faith in it, and the spark of contact. Even the man who wanted to break in here, I don't think he really had the power. He was just trying to be mean and wicked, but something in him would have to submit to a greater faith and a greater power.'

So she re-assured herself, till she had the courage to get up and fasten her door-shutters at the top. After which she went from room to room, to see that all was made fast. And she was thankful to realise that she was afraid of scorpions on the floor, as well as of the panic horror.

Now she had seen that the five doors and the six windows of her wing of communicating rooms were fast. She was sealed inside the darkness, with her candle. To get to the other part of the house, the dining-room and kitchen, she had to go outside on the verandah.

She grew quieter, shut up with the dusky glow of her candle. And her heart, still wrenched with the pain of fear, was thinking: 'Joachim said that evil was the lapsing back to old life-modes that have been surpassed in us. This brings murder and lust. But the drums of Saturday night are the old rhythm, and that dancing round the drum is the old savage form of expression. Consciously reverting to the savage. So perhaps it is evil.'

But then again her instinct to believe came up.

'No! It's not a helpless, panic reversal. It is conscious, carefully chosen. We must go back to pick up old threads. We must take up the old, broken impulse that will connect us with the mystery of the cosmos again, now we are at the end of our own tether. We must do it. Don Ramón is right. He must be a great man, really. I thought there *were* no really great men any more: only great financiers and great artists and so on, but no great *men*. He must be a great man.'

She was again infinitely reassured by this thought.

But again, just as she had blown out the candle, vivid flares of white light spurted through all the window-cracks, and thunder broke in great round balls, smashing down. The bolts of thunder seemed to fall on her heart. She lay absolutely crushed, in a kind of quiescent hysterics, tortured. And the hysterics held her listening and tense and abject, until dawn. And then she was a wreck.

In the morning came Juana, also looking like a dead insect, with the conventional phrase: 'How have you passed the night, Niña?'

'Badly!' said Kate. Then she told the story of the black cat, or the man's arm.

'*Mire!*' said Juana, in a hushed voice. 'The poor innocent will be murdered in her bed. No, Niña, you must go and sleep in the hotel. No, no, Niña, you can't leave your window shutter open. No, no, impossible. See now, will you go to the hotel to sleep? The other señora does it.'

'I don't want to,' said Kate.

'You don't want to, Niña? Ah! *Entonces! Entonces*, Niña, I will tell Ezequiel to sleep here outside your door, with his pistol. He has a pistol, and he will sleep outside your door, and you can leave your shutter open, for air in the hot night. Ah, Niña, we poor women, we need a man and a pistol. We ought not to be left alone all the night. We are afraid, the children are afraid. And imagine it, that there was a robber trying to open the bolt of your door! Imagine it to yourself! No, Niña, we will tell Ezequiel at mid-day.'

Ezequiel came striding proudly in, at mid-day. He was a wild, shy youth, very erect and proud, and half savage. His voice was breaking, and had a queer resonance.

He stood shyly while the announcement was being made to him. Then he looked at Kate with flashing black eyes, very much the man to the rescue.

'Yes! Yes!' he said. 'I will sleep here on the corridor. Don't have any fear. I shall have my pistol.'

He marched off, and returned with the pistol, an old long-barrelled affair.

'It has five shots,' he said, showing the weapon. 'If you open the door in the night, you must say a word to me first. Because if I see anything move, I shall fire five shots. *Pst! Pst!*'

She saw by the flash of his eyes *what* satisfaction it would give him to fire five shots at something moving in the night. The thought of shots being fired at *him* gave him not the least concern.

'And Niña,' said Juana, 'if you come home late, after the light is out, you must call *Ezequiel!* Because if not, *Brumm! Brumm!* – and who knows who will be killed!'

Ezequiel slept on a straw mat on the brick verandah outside Kate's door, rolled up in his blanket, and with the pistol at his side. So she could leave her shutter open for air. And the first night she was kept awake once more by his fierce snoring. Never had she heard such a tremendous resonant sound! What a chest that boy must have! It was sound from some strange, savage other world. The noise kept her awake, but there was something in it which she liked. Some sort of wild strength.

CHAPTER IX

Casa de las Cuentas

KATE was soon fond of the limping, untidy Juana, and of the girls. Concha was fourteen, a thick, heavy, barbaric girl with a mass of black waving hair which she was always scratching. Maria was eleven, a shy, thin bird-like thing with big eyes that seemed almost to absorb the light round her.

It was a reckless family. Juana admitted a different father for Jesús, but to judge from the rest, one would have suspected a different father for each of them. There was a basic, sardonic carelessness in the face of life, in all the family. They lived from day to day, a stubborn, heavy, obstinate life of indifference, careless about the past, careless about the present, careless about the future. They had even no interest in money. Whatever they got they spent in a minute, and forgot it again.

Without aim or purpose, they lived absolutely *à terre*, down on the dark, volcanic earth. They were not animals, because men and women and their children *cannot* be animals. It is not granted us. *Go, for once gone, thou never canst return!* says the great Urge which drives us creatively on. When man tries brutally to return to the older, previous levels of evolution, he does so in the spirit of cruelty and misery.

So in the black eyes of the family, a certain vicious fear and wonder and misery. The misery of human beings who squat helpless outside their own unbuilt selves, unable to win their souls out of the chaos, and indifferent to all other victories.

White people are becoming soulless too. But they have conquered the lower worlds of metal and energy, so they whizz around in machines, circling the void of their own emptiness.

To Kate, there was a great pathos in her family. Also a certain repulsiveness.

Juana and her children, once they accepted their Niña as their own, were honest with intensity. Point of honour, they were honest to the least little plum in the fruit bowl. And almost intensely eager to serve.

Themselves indifferent to their surroundings, they would live in squalor. The earth was the great garbage bowl. Everything discarded was flung on the earth and they did not care. Almost they liked to live in a milieu of fleas and old rags, bits of paper, banana skins and mango stones. Here's a piece torn off my dress! Earth, take it. Here's the combings of my hair! Earth, take them!

But Kate could not bear it. She cared. And immediately, the family was quite glad, thrilled that *she* cared. They swept the patio with the twig broom till they swept the very surface of the earth away. Fun! The Niña had feelings about it.

She was a source of wonder and amusement to them. But she was never a class superior. She was a half-incomprehensible, half-amusing wonder-being.

The Niña wanted the *aguador* to bring two *botes* of hot water, quick, from the hot springs, to wash herself all over every morning. Fun! Go, Maria, tell the aguador to *run* with the Niña's water.

Then they almost resented it that she shut herself off to have her bath. She was a sort of goddess to them, to provide them with fun and wonder; but she ought always to be accessible. And a god who is forever accessible to human beings has an unenviable time of it, Kate soon discovered.

No, it was no sinecure, being a Niña. At dawn began the scrape-scrape of the twig broom outside. Kate stayed on in bed, doors fastened but shutters open. Flutter outside! Somebody wanted to sell two eggs. Where is the Niña? She is sleeping! The visitor does not go. Continual flutter outside.

The *aguador!* Ah, the water for the Niña's bath! She is sleeping, she is sleeping. 'No!' called Kate, slipping into a dressing-gown and unbolting the door. In come the children with the bathtub, in comes the aguador with the two square kerosene cans full of hot water. Twelve centavos! Twelve centavos for the aguador! *No hay!* We haven't got twelve centavos. Later! Later! Away trots the aguador, pole over his shoulder. Kate shuts her doors and shutters and starts her bath.

'Niña? Niña?'

'What do you want?'

'Eggs boiled or fried or rancheros? Which do you want?'

'Boiled.'

'Coffee or chocolate?'

'Coffee.'

'Or do you want tea?'

'No, coffee.'

Bath proceeds.

'Niña?'

'Yes.'

'There is no coffee. We are going to buy some.'

'I'll take tea.'

'No, Niña! I am going. Wait for me.'

'Go then.'

Kate comes out to breakfast on the verandah. The table is set, heaped with fruit and white bread and sweet buns.

'Good morning, Niña. How have you passed the night? Well! Ah, praised be God! Maria, the coffee. I'm going to put the eggs in the water. Oh, Niña, that they may not be boiled hard! – Look, what feet of the Madonna! Look! *Bonitos!*'

And Juana stooped down, fascinated to touch with her black finger Kate's white soft feet, that were thrust in light sandals, just a thong across the foot.

The day had begun. Juana looked upon herself as dedicated entirely to Kate. As soon as possible she shooed her girls away, to school. Sometimes they went: mostly they didn't. The Niña said they must go to school. Listen! Listen now! Says the Niña that you must go to school! Away! Walk!

Juana would limp back and forth down the long verandah from kitchen to the breakfast table, carrying away the dishes one by one. Then, with a great splash, she was washing up.

Morning! Brilliant sun pouring into the patio, on the hibiscus flowers and the fluttering yellow and green rags of the banana trees. Birds swiftly coming and going, with tropical suddenness. In the dense shadow of the mango-grove, white clad Indians going like ghosts. The sense of fierce sun and almost more impressive, of dark, intense shadow. A twitter of life, yet a certain heavy weight of silence. A dazzling flicker and brilliance of light, yet the feeling of weight.

Kate would sit alone, rocking on her verandah, pretending to sew. Silently appears an old man with one egg held up mysteriously, like some symbol. Would the patrona buy it for five centavos. La Juana only gives four centavos. All right? Where is Juana?

Juana appears from the plaza with more purchases. The egg! The four centavos! The account of the spendings. *Entonces! Entonces! Luego!*

Luego! Ah, Niña, no tengo memoria![1] Juana could not read nor write. She scuffled off to the market with her pesos, bought endless little things at one or two centavos each, every morning. And every morning there was a reckoning up. Ah! Ah! Where are we? I have no memory. Well then – ah – yes – I bought ocote for three centavos! How much? How much, Niña? How much is it now?

It was a game which thrilled Juana to the marrow, reckoning up the centavos to get it just right. If she was a centavo short in the change, she was paralysed. Time after time she would re-appear. *There is a centavo short, Niña? Ah, how stupid I am. But I will give you one of mine!*

'Don't bother,' said Kate. 'Don't think of it any more.'

'But yes. But yes!' and away she limped in distraction.

Till an hour later, loud cry from the far end of the house. Juana waving a scrap of greenery.

'Mire! Niña! Compré perejil a un centavo – I bought parsley for one cent. Is it right?'

'It is right,' said Kate.

And life could proceed once more.

There were two kitchens, the one next the dining-room, belonging to Kate, and the narrow little shed under the banana trees, belonging to the servants. From her verandah Kate looked away down to Juana's kitchen shed. It had a black window hole.

Clap! Clap! Clap! Clap! Why I thought Concha was at school! said Kate to herself.

No! – there, in the darkness of the window hole was Concha's swarthy face and mane, peering out like some animal from a cave, as she made the tortillas. Tortillas are flat pancakes of maize dough, baked dry on a flat earthen-ware plate over the fire. And the making consists of clapping a bit of new dough from the palm of one hand to the other, till the tortilla is of the requisite thinness, roundness, and so-called lightness.

Clap! Clap! Clap! Clap! Clap! Clap! Clap! It was as inevitable as the tick of some spider, the sound of Concha making tortillas in the heat of the morning, peering out of her dark window hole. And some time after mid-day, the smoke would be coming out of the window hole; Concha was throwing the raw tortillas on the big earthen plate over the slow wood fire.

Then Ezequiel might or might not stride in, very much the man, serape poised over one shoulder and big straw hat jauntily curled, to eat the mid-day tortillas. If he had work in the fields at any distance, he would not appear till nightfall. If he had appeared, he sat on the doorstep and the women served him his tortillas and fetched him his drink of water as if he was a king, boy though he might be. And his rough, breaking voice was heard in quiet command.

Command was the word. Though he was quiet and gentle, and very conscientious, there was calm, kingly command in his voice when he spoke to his mother or sisters. The old male prerogative. Somehow, it made Kate want to ridicule him.

Came her own meal: one of her trials. Hot, rather greasy soup. Inevitable hot, greasy, rather peppery rice. Inevitable meat in hot, thick, rather greasy sauce. Boiled calabacitas or egg-plant, salad, perhaps some dulce made with milk – and the big basket of fruit. Overhead, the blazing tropical sun of late May.

Afternoon, and greater heat. Juana set off with the girls and the dishes. They would do the washing up in the lake. Squatting on the stones, they would dabble the plates one by one, the spoons and the forks one by one in the filmy water of the lake, then put them in the sun to dry. After which Juana might wash a couple of towels in the lake and the girls might bathe. Sauntering the day away – sauntering the day away.

Jesús, the eldest son, a queer, heavy, greasy fellow, usually appeared in the afternoon, to water the garden. But he ate his meals at the hotel, and really lived there, had his home there. Not that he had any home, any more than a zopilote had a home. But he ran the *planta*, and did odd jobs about the hotel, and worked every day in the year till half past ten at night, earning twenty-two pesos, eleven dollars, a month. He wore a black shirt, and his thick, massive black hair dropped over his low brow. Very near to an animal. And though, to order, he wore a black Fascisti shirt, he had the queer, animal jeering of the socialists, an instinct for pulling things down.

His mother and he had a funny little intimacy of quiet and indifferent mutual taunting of one another. He would give her some money if she were in a strait. And there was a thin little thread of blood-bondage between them. Apart from that, complete indifference.

Ezequiel was a finer type. He was slender and so erect that he almost curved backwards. He was very shy, farouche. Proud also, and more responsible to his family. He would not go to work in an hotel. No. He was a worker in the fields, and he was proud of it. A man's work. No equivocal sort of half-service for him.

Though he was just a hired labourer, yet working on the land he never felt he was working for a master. It was the land he worked for. Somewhere inside himself he felt that the land was his, and he belonged in a measure to it. Perhaps a lingering feeling of tribal, communal land-ownership and service.

When there was work, he was due to earn a peso a day. There was often no work: and often only seventy-five centavos a day for wage. When the land was dry, he would try to get work on the road, though this he did not like. But he earned his peso a day.

Often, there was no work. Often, for days, sometimes for weeks, he would have to hang about, nothing to do, nothing to do. Only, when the Socialist Government had begun giving the peasants bits of land, dividing up the big haciendas, Ezequiel had been allotted a little piece outside the village.[2] He would go and gather the stones together there, and prepare to build a little hut. And he would break the earth with a hoe, his only implement, as far as possible. But he had no blood connection with this square allotment of unnatural earth, and he could not get himself into relations with it. He was fitful and diffident about it. There was no incentive, no urge.

On workdays he would come striding in about six o'clock, shyly greeting Kate as he passed. He was a gentleman in his barbarism. Then, away in the far recess, he would rapidly fold tortilla after tortilla, sitting on the floor with his back to the wall, rapidly eating the leathery things that taste of mortar, because the maize is first boiled with lime to loosen the husk, and accepting another little pile, served on a leaf, from the cook, Concha. Juana, cook for the Niña, would no longer condescend to cook for her own family. And sometimes there was a mess of meat and chile for Ezequiel to scoop up out of the earthenware casserole, with his tortillas. And sometimes there was not. But always, he ate with a certain blind, rapid indifference, that also seems to be Mexican. They seem to *eat* even with a certain hostile reluctance, and have a strange indifference to what or when they eat.

His supper finished, as a rule he was off again like a shot, to the plaza, to be among men. And the women would sit desultorily about, on the ground. Sometimes Kate would come in at nine o'clock to an empty place – Ezequiel in the plaza, Juana and Maria disappeared somewhere or other, and Concha lying asleep like a heap of rags on the gravel of the patio. When Kate called her, she would raise her head, stupefied and hopeless; then get up like a dog and crawl away to the gate. The strange stupor of boredom and hopelessness that was always sinking upon them would make Kate's heart stand still with dread.

The peculiar indifference to everything, even to one another. Juana washed a cotton shirt and a pair of cotton trousers for each of her sons, once a week, and there her maternal efforts ended. She saw hardly anything of them, and was often completely unaware of what Ezequiel was doing, where he was working, or at what. He had just gone off to work, no more.

Yet again, sometimes she had hot, fierce pangs of maternal protectiveness, when the boy was unjustly treated, as he often was. And if she thought he were ill, a black sort of fatalistic fear came over her. But Kate had to rouse her into getting some simple medicine.

Like animals, yet not at all like animals. For animals are complete in their isolation and their insouciance. With them it is not indifference. It is completeness in themselves. But with the family there was always a kind of bleeding of incompleteness, a terrible stupor of boredom settling down.

The two girls could not be apart: they must always be running after one another. Yet Concha continually teased the big-eyed, naïve simpleton of a Maria. And Maria was always in tears. Or the two were suddenly throwing stones at one another. But with no real aim to hit. And Juana was abusing them with sudden vehemence, that flickered in a minute to complete indifference again.

Queer, the savage ferocity with which the girls would suddenly be throwing stones at one another. But queerer still, they always aimed *just to miss*. Kate noticed the same in the savage attacks the boys made on one another, on the beach; hurling large stones with intense, terrible ferocity. But almost always, aiming with a curious cast in the eyes, just to miss.

But sometimes not. Sometimes hitting with a sharp cut. And then the wounded one would drop right down, with a howl, as if dead. And the other boys would edge away, in a silent kind of dread. And the wounded boy would be prostrate, not really much hurt, but as if he was killed.

Then, maybe, suddenly he would be up, with a convulsion of murder in his face, pursuing his adversary with a stone. And the adversary would abjectly flee.

Always the same thing among the young: a ceaseless, endless taunting and tormenting. The same as among the Red Indians. But the Pueblo Indians rarely lapsing from speech into violence. The Mexican boys almost always. And almost always, one boy in murderous rage, pursuing his taunter till he had hurt him: then an abject collapse of the one hurt. Then, usually, a revival of the one hurt, the murderous frenzy transferred to him, and the first attacker fleeing abjectly, in terror. One or the other always abject.

They were a strange puzzle to Kate. She felt something must be done. She herself was inspired to help. So she had the two girls for an hour a day, teaching them to read, to sew, to draw. Maria wanted to learn to read: that she did want. For the rest, they began well. But soon, the regularity and the slight insistence of Kate on their attention made them take again that peculiar invisible jeering tone, something peculiar to the American Continent. A quiet, invisible, malevolent mockery, a desire to wound. They would press upon her, trespassing upon her privacy, and with a queer effrontery, doing all they could to walk over her. With their ugly little wills, trying to pull her will down.

'No, don't lean on me, Concha. Stand on your own feet.'

The slight grin of malevolence on Concha's face, as she stood on her own feet. Then:

'Do you have lice in your hair, Niña?'

The question asked with a peculiar, subtle, Indian insolence.

'No!' said Kate, suddenly angry. 'And now go! Go! Go away from me! Don't come near me.'

They slunk out, abject. So much for educating them.

Kate had visitors from Guadalajara – great excitement. But while the visitors were drinking tea with Kate on the verandah, at the other side of the patio, full in view, Juana, Concha, Maria, and Felipa, a cousin of about sixteen, squatted on the gravel with their splendid black hair down their backs, displaying themselves as they hunted in each other's hair for lice. They wanted to be full in view. And they were it. They wanted the basic fact of lice to be thrust under the noses of those white people.

Kate strode down the verandah.

'If you must pick lice,' she said in a shaking voice to Juana, shaking
with anger, 'pick them there, in your own place, where you can't be
seen.'

One instant, Juana's black inchoate eyes gleamed with a malevolent
ridicule, meeting Kate's. The next instant, humble and abject, the four
with their black hair down their backs slunk into the recess out of
sight.

But it pleased Juana that she had been able to make Kate's eyes blaze
with anger. It pleased her. She felt a certain low power in herself. True,
she was a little afraid of that anger. But that was what she wanted.
She would have no use for a Niña of whom she was not a bit afraid.
And she wanted to be able to provoke that anger, of which she felt
a certain abject twinge of fear.

Ah the dark races! Kate's own Irish were near enough for her to
have glimpsed some of the mystery. The dark races belong to a bygone
cycle of humanity. They are left behind in a gulf out of which they have
never been able to climb. And on to the particular white man's levels
they never will be able to climb. They can only follow as servants.

While the white man keeps the impetus of his own proud, onward
march, the dark races will yield and serve, perforce. But let the white
man once have a misgiving about his own leadership, and the dark races
will at once attack him, to pull him down into the old gulfs. To engulf
him again.

Which is what is happening. For the white man, let him bluster as
he may, is hollow with misgiving about his own supremacy.

Full speed ahead, then, for the débâcle.

But once Kate had been roused to a passion of revulsion from these
lice-picking, down-dragging people, they changed again, and served her
with a certain true wistfulness that could not but touch her. Juana cared
really about nothing. But just that last thread of relationship that connected her with Kate and the upper world of daylight and fresh air,
she didn't want to break. No, no, she didn't want finally to drive her
Niña away. No, no, the only one thing she did want, ultimately, was
to serve her Niña.

But at the same time, she cherished a deep malevolent grudge against
rich people, white people, superior people. Perhaps the white man has
finally betrayed his own leadership. Who knows! But it is a thing of

the brave, on-marching soul, and perhaps this has been betrayed already by the white man. So that the dark are rising upon him.

Juana would come to Kate, telling her stories from the past. And the sinister mocking film would be on her black eyes, and her lined copper face would take on its reptile mask as she would continue: 'Usted sabe, Niña, los gringos, los gringuitos llevan todo – you know, Niña, the *gringos* and the *gringuitos* take away everything ...'

The *gringos* are the Americans. But Kate herself was included by Juana in the *gringuitos*: the white foreigners. The woman was making another sliding, insolent attack.

'It is possible,' said Kate coldly. 'But tell me what I take away from Mexico.'

'No, Niña, No!' The subtle smile of satisfaction lurked under the bronze tarnish of Juana's face. She had been able to get at the other woman, touch the raw. 'I don't speak of you, Niña!' But there was too much protest in it.

Almost, they wanted to drive her away: to insult her and drag her down and make her want to go away. They couldn't help it. Like the Irish, they could cut off their nose to spite their face.

The backward races!

At the same time there was a true pathos about them. Ezequiel had worked for a man for two months, building a house, when he was a boy of fourteen, in order to get a serape. At the end of the two months, the man had put him off, and he had not got the serape: had never got it. A bitter disappointment.

But, then, Kate was not responsible for that. And Juana seemed almost to make her so.

A people without the energy of *getting on*, how could they fail to be hopelessly exploited. They had been hopelessly and cruelly exploited, for centuries. And their backbones were locked in malevolent resistance.

'But,' as Kate said to herself, 'I don't want to exploit them. Not a bit. On the contrary, I am willing to give more than I get. But that nasty insinuating insultingness is not fair in the game. I never insult them. I am so careful not to hurt them. And then they *deliberately* make these centipede attacks on me, and are pleased when I am hurt.'

But she knew her own Irish at the game. So she was able to put

Juana and the girls away from her, and isolate herself from them. Once they were put away, their malevolence subsided and they remembered what Kate wanted. While she stayed amiable, they forgot. They forgot to sweep the patio, they forgot to keep themselves clean. Only when they were shoved back, into isolation, did they remember again.

The boy, Ezequiel, seemed to her to have more honour than the women. He never made these insidious attacks.

And when her house was clean and quiet and the air seemed cleaned again, the soul renewed, her old fondness for the family came back. Their curious flitting, coming and going, like birds: the busy clap – clap – clapping of tortillas, the excited scrunching of tomatoes and chile on the metate, as Juana prepared sauce. The noise of the bucket in the well. Jesús, come to water the garden.

The game, the game of it all! Everything they did must be fun, or they could not do it. They could not abstract themselves to a routine. Never. Everything must be fun, must be variable, must be a bit of an adventure. It was confusion, but after all, a living confusion, not a dead, dreary thing. Kate remembered her English servants in the English kitchens: so mechanical and somehow inhuman. Well, this was the other extreme.

Here there was no discipline nor method at all. Although Juana and her brats really wanted to do the things Kate wished, they must do them their own way. Sometimes Kate felt distracted: after all, the mechanical lines are so much *easier* to follow. But as far as possible, she let the family be. She had to get used, for example, to the vagaries of her dining-table: a little round table that always stood on the verandah. At breakfast time it would be discreetly set under the *plantas* by the salon; for dinner, at one o'clock, it would have travelled way down the verandah; for tea it might be under a little tree on the grass. And then Juana would decide that the Niña must take supper, two eggs, *rancheros*, in the dining-room itself, isolated at the corner of the long dining-table meant for fourteen people.

The same with the dishes. Why they should, after washing up in the big bowls in the kitchen for several days, suddenly struggle way down to the lake with the unwashed pots in a basket on Concha's shoulder, Kate never knew. Except for the fun of the thing.

Children! But, then, not at all children. None of the wondering insouciance of childhood. Something dark and cognisant in their souls all the time: some heavy weight of resistance. They worked in fits and starts, and could be very industrious; then came days when they lay about on the ground like pigs. At times they were merry, seated round on the ground in groups, like Arabian nights, and laughing away. Then suddenly resisting even merriment in themselves, relapsing into the numb gloom. When they were busily working, suddenly for no reason, throwing away the tool, as if resenting having given themselves. Careless in their morals, always changing their loves, the men at least resisted all the time any real giving of themselves. They didn't want the thing they were pursuing. It was the women who drew them on. And a young man and a girl going down the road from the lake in the dark, teasing and poking each other in excitement, would startle Kate because of their unusualness – the men and women never walked their sex abroad, as white people do. And the sudden, sexual laugh of the man, so strange a sound of pain and desire, obstinate reluctance and helpless passion, a noise as if something was tearing in his breast, was a sound to remember.

Kate felt her household a burden. In a sense, they were like parasites, they wanted to live on her life, and pull her down, pull her down. Again, they were so generous with her, so good and gentle, she felt they were wonderful. And then once more she came up against that unconscious, heavy, reptilian indifference in them, indifference and resistance.

Her servants were the clue to all the native life, for her. The men always together, erect, handsome, balancing their great hats on the top of their heads and sitting, standing, crouching with a snake-like impassivity. The women together separately, soft, and as if *hidden*, wrapped tight in their dark rebozos. Men and women seemed always to be turning their backs on one another, as if they didn't want to see one another. No flirting, no courting. Only an occasional quick, dark look, the signal of a weapon-like desire, given and taken.

The women seemed, on the whole, softly callous and determined to go their own way: to change men if they wished. And the men seemed not to care very profoundly. But it was the women who wanted the men.

The native women, with their long black hair streaming down their full, ruddy backs, would bathe at one end of the beach, usually wearing their chemise, or a little skirt. The men took absolutely no notice. They didn't even look the other way. It was the women bathing, that was all. As if it were, like the charales swimming, just a natural part of the lake life. The men just left that part of the lake to the women. And the women sat in the shallows of the lake, isolated in themselves like moor-fowl, pouring water over their heads and over their ruddy arms from a gourd scoop.

The quiet, unobtrusive, but by no means down-trodden women of the peon class. They went their own way, enveloped in their rebozos as in their own darkness. They hurried nimbly along, their full cotton skirts swinging, chirping and quick like birds. Or they sat in the lake with long hair streaming, pouring water over themselves: again like birds. Or they passed with a curious slow inevitability up the lake-shore, with a heavy red jar of water perched on one shoulder, one arm over the head, holding the rim of the jar. They had to carry all water from the lake to their houses. There was no town supply. Or, especially on Sunday afternoons, they sat in their doorways de-lousing one another. The most resplendent *belles*, with magnificent black wavy hair, were most thoroughly de-loused. It was as if it were a meritorious public act.

The men were the obvious figures. They assert themselves on the air. They are the dominant. Usually they are in loose groups, talking quietly, or silent: always standing or sitting apart, rarely touching one another. Often a single man would stand alone at a street corner in his serape, motionless for hours, like some powerful spectre. Or a man would lie on the beach as if he had been cast up dead from the waters. Impassive, motionless, they would sit side by side on the benches of the plaza, not exchanging a word. Each one isolated in his own fate, his eyes black and quick like a snake's, and as blank.

It seemed to Kate that the highest thing this country might produce would be some powerful relationship of man to man. Marriage itself would always be a casual thing. Though the men seemed very gentle and protective to the little children. Then they forgot them.

But sex itself was a powerful, potent thing, not to be played with or paraded. The one mystery. And a mystery greater than the individual. The individual hardly counted.

It was strange to Kate to see the Indian huts on the shore, little holes built of straw or corn-stalks, with half-naked children squatting on the naked earth floor, and a lousy woman-squalor around, a litter of rags and bones, and a sharp smell of human excrement. The people have no noses. And standing silent and erect not far from the hole of the doorway, the man, handsome and impassive. How could it be, that such a fine-looking human male should be so absolutely indifferent, content with such paltry squalor?

But there he was, unconscious. He seemed to have life and passion in him. And she knew he was strong. No men in the world can carry heavier loads on their backs, for longer distances, than these Indians. She had seen an Indian trotting down a street with a piano on his back: holding it, also, by a band round his forehead. From his forehead, and on his spine he carried it, trotting along. The women carry with a band round the breast.

So there is strength. And *apparently*, there is passionate life. But no energy. Nowhere in Mexico is there any sign of energy. This is, as it were, switched off.

Even the new artisan class, though it imitates the artisan class of the United States, has no real energy. There are workmen's clubs. The workmen dress up and parade a best girl on their arm. But somehow, it seems what it is, only a weak imitation.

Kate's family was increased, without her expecting it. One day there arrived from Ocotlan a beautiful ox-eyed girl of about fifteen, wrapped in her black cotton rebozo, and somewhat towny in her Madonna-meekness: Maria del Carmen. With her, Julio, a straight and fierce young man of twenty-two. They had just been married, and had come to Sayula for a visit. Julio was Juana's cousin.

Might they sleep in the patio with herself and the girls, was Juana's request. They would stay only two days.

Kate was amazed. Maria del Carmen must have had some Spanish blood, her beauty was touched with Spain. She seemed even refined and superior. Yet she was to sleep out on the ground like a dog, with her young husband. And he, so erect and proud-looking, possessed nothing in the world but an old serape.

'There are three spare bedrooms,' said Kate. 'They may sleep in one of those.'

The beds were single beds. Would they need more blankets? she asked Juana.

No! They would manage with the one serape of Julio's.

The new family had arrived. Julio was a bricklayer. That is to say, he worked building the adobe walls of the little houses. He belonged to Sayula, and had come back for a visit.

The visit continued. Julio would come striding in at mid-day and at evening; he was looking for work. Maria del Carmen, in her one black dress, would squat on the floor and pat tortillas. She was allowed to cook them in Juana's kitchen hole. And she talked and laughed with the girls. At night, when Julio was home, he would lie on the ground with his back to the wall, impassive, while Maria del Carmen fondled his thick black hair.

They were in love. But even now, he was not yielding to his love.

She wanted to go back to Ocotlan, where she was at home, and more a señorita than here in Sayula. But he refused. There was no money: the young ménage lived on about five American cents a day.

Kate was sewing. Maria del Carmen, who didn't even know how to put a chemise together, watched with great eyes. Kate taught her, and bought a length of cotton material. Maria del Carmen was sewing herself a dress!

Julio had got work at a peso a day. The visit continued. Kate thought Julio wasn't very nice with Maria del Carmen: his quiet voice was so overbearing in command when he spoke to her. And Maria del Carmen, who was a bit towny, did not take it well. She brooded a little.

The visit stretched into weeks. And now Juana was getting a bit tired of her relative.

But Julio had got a bit of money. He had rented a little one-room adobe house, at one peso fifty per week. Maria del Carmen was going to move into her own home.

Kate saw the new outfit got together. It consisted of one straw mat, three cooking plates of earthenware, five bits of native crockery, two wooden spoons, one knife and Julio's old blanket. That was all. But Maria del Carmen was moving in.

Kate presented her with a large old eiderdown, whose silk was rather worn, a couple of bowls, and a few more bits of crockery. Maria del Carmen was set up. *Good! Good! Oh Good!* Kate heard her voice down the patio. *I have got a coverlet! I have got a coverlet!*

In the rainy season, the nights can be very cold, owing to evaporation. Then the natives lie through the small hours like lizards, numb and prostrate with cold. They are lying on the damp earth on a thin straw mat, with a corner of an old blanket to cover them. And the same terrible inertia makes them endure it, without trying to make any change. They could carry in corn husks or dry banana leaves for a bed. They could even cover themselves with banana leaves.

But no! On a thin mat on damp cold earth they lie and tremble with cold, night after night, night after night, night after night.

But Maria del Carmen was a bit towny. *Oh good! Oh good! I've got a coverlet!*

Don Ramón and Doña Carlota

KATE had been in Sayula ten days before she had any sign from Don Ramón. She had been out in a boat on the lake, and had seen his house, round the bend of the western point. It was a reddish-and-yellow two-storey house with a little stone basin for the boats, and a mango grove between it and the lake. Among the trees, away from the lake, were the black adobe huts, two rows, of the peons.

The hacienda had once been a large one. But it had been irrigated from the hills, and the revolutions had broken all the aqueducts. Only a small supply of water was available. Then Don Ramón had had enemies in the Government. So that a good deal of his land was taken away to be divided among the peons.[1] Now, he had only some three hundred acres. The two hundred acres along the lake shore were mostly lost to him. He worked a few acres of fruit land round the house, and in a tiny valley just in the hills, he raised sugar-cane. On the patches of the mountain slope little patches of maize were to be seen.

But Doña Carlota had money. She was from Torreon and drew still a good income from the mines.

A mozo came with a note from Don Ramón: might he bring his wife to call on Kate?

Doña Carlota was a thin, gentle, wide-eyed woman, with a slightly startled expression, and soft, brownish hair. She was pure European in extraction, of a Spanish father and French mother: very different from the usual stout, over-powdered, ox-like Mexican matron. Her face was pale, faded, and without any make-up at all. Her thin, eager figure had something English about it, but her strange, wide brown eyes were not English. She spoke only Spanish – or French. But her Spanish was so slow and distinct and slightly plaintive, that Kate understood her at once.

The two women understood one another quickly, but were a little nervous of one another. Doña Carlota was delicate and sensitive like a Chihuahua dog, and with the same slightly prominent eyes. Kate felt she had rarely met a woman with such a doglike finesse of gentleness.

And the two women talked. Ramón, large and muted, kept himself in reserve. It was as if the two women rushed together to unite against his silence and his powerful, different significance.

Kate knew at once that Doña Carlota loved him, but with a love that was now nearly all *will*. She had worshipped him, and she had had to leave off worshipping him. She had had to question him. And she would never now cease from questioning.

So he sat apart, a little constrained, his handsome head hanging a little, and his dark, sensitive hands dangling between his thighs.

'I had such a wonderful time!' Kate said suddenly to him. 'I danced a dance round the drum with the Men of Quetzalcoatl.'

'I heard,' he said, with a rather stiff smile.

Doña Carlota understood English, though she would not speak it.

'You danced with the men of Quetzalcoatl!' she said in Spanish, in a pained voice. 'But, Señora, why did you do such a thing? Oh why?'

'I was fascinated,' said Kate.

'No, you must not be fascinated. No! No! It is not good. I tell you. I am *so sorry* my husband interests himself in this thing. I am so sorry.'

Juana was bringing a bottle of vermouth: all that Kate had to offer her visitors, in the morning.

'You went to see your boys in the United States?' said Kate to Doña Carlota. 'How were they?'

'Oh, better, thank you. They are well; that is, the younger is very delicate.'

'You didn't bring him home?'

'No! No! I think they are better at school. Here – here – there are so many things to trouble them. No! But they will come home next month, for the vacation.'

'How nice!' said Kate. 'Then I shall see them. They will be here, won't they? – on the lake?'

'Well! – I am not sure. Perhaps for a little while. You see I am so busy in Mexico with my Cuna.'

'What is a Cuna?' said Kate; she only knew it was the Spanish for cradle.

It turned out to be a foundlings' home, run by a few obscure Carmelite sisters. And Doña Carlota was the director. Kate gathered that Don Ramón's wife was an intense, almost exalted Catholic. She exalted herself in the Church, and in her work for the Cuna.

'There are so many children born in Mexico,' said Doña Carlota, 'and so many die. If only we could save them, and equip them for life. We do a little, all we can.'

It seemed the waste, unwanted babies could be delivered in at the door of the Cuna, like parcels. The mother had only to knock, and hand in the little living bundle.

'It saves so many mothers from neglecting their babies, and letting them die,' said Doña Carlota. 'Then we do what we can. If the mother doesn't leave a name, I name the child. Very often I do. The mothers just hand over a little naked thing, sometimes without a name or a rag to cover it. And we never ask.'

The children were not all kept in the Home. Only a small number. Of the others, some decent Indian woman was paid a small sum to take the child into her home. Every month she must come with the little one to the Cuna, to receive her wage. The Indians are so very rarely unkind to children. Careless, yes. But rarely, rarely unkind.

In former days, Doña Carlota said, nearly every well-born lady in Mexico would receive one or more of these foundlings into her home, and have it brought up with the family. It was the loose, patriarchal generosity innate in the bosoms of the Spanish-Mexicans. But now, few children were adopted. Instead, they were taught as far as possible to be carpenters or gardeners, or house-servants, or, among the girls, dress-makers, even school-teachers.

Kate listened with uneasy interest. She felt there was so much real human feeling in this Mexican charity: she was almost rebuked. Perhaps what Doña Carlota was doing was the best that could be done, in this half-wild, helpless country. At the same time, it was such a forlorn hope, it made one's heart sink.

And Doña Carlota, confident as she was in her good works, still had just a bit the look of a victim; a gentle, sensitive, slightly startled victim. As if some secret enemy drained her blood.

Don Ramón sat there impassive, listening without heeding; solid and unmoving *against* the charitable quiver of his wife's emotion. He let her do as she would. But against her work and against her flow he was in silent, heavy, unchanging opposition. She knew this, and trembled in her nervous eagerness, as she talked to Kate about the Cuna, and won Kate's sympathy. Till it seemed to her that there was something cruel in Don Ramón's passive, masked poise. An impassive male cruelty, changeless as a stone idol.

'Now won't you come and spend the day with me while I am here with Don Ramón?' said Doña Carlota. 'The house is very poor and rough. It is no longer what it used to be. But it is your house if you will come.'

Kate accepted, and said she would prefer to walk out. It was only four miles, and surely she would be safe, with Juana.

'I will send a man to come with you,' said Don Ramón. 'It might not be quite safe.'

'Where is General Viedma?' asked Kate.

'We shall try to get him out when you come,' replied Doña Carlota. 'I am so very fond of Don Cipriano, I have known him for many years, and he is the godfather of my younger son. But now he is in command of the Guadalajara division, he is not very often able to come out.'

'I wonder why he is a general?' said Kate. 'He seems to me too human.'

'Oh, but he is very human too. But he is a general; yes, yes, he wants to be in command of the soldiers. And I tell you, he is very strong. He has great power with his regiments. They believe in him, oh, they believe in him. He has that power, you know, that some of the higher types of Indians have, to make many others want to follow them and fight for them. You know? Don Cipriano is like that. You can never change him. But I think a woman might be wonderful for him. He has lived so without any woman in his life. He won't care about them.'

'What does he care about?' asked Kate.

'Ah!' Doña Carlota started as if stung. Then she glanced quickly, involuntarily at her husband, as she added: 'I don't know. Really, I don't know.'

'The Men of Quetzalcoatl,' said Don Ramón heavily, with a little smile.

But Doña Carlota seemed to be able to take all the ease and the banter out of him. He seemed stiff and a bit stupid.

'Ah, there! There! There you have it! The Men of Quetzalcoatl — that is a nice thing for him to care about! A nice thing, I say,' fluttered Doña Carlota, in her gentle, fragile, scolding way. And it was evident to Kate that she adored both the men, and trembled in opposition to their wrongness, and would never give in to them.

To Ramón it was a terrible burden, his wife's quivering, absolute, blind opposition, taken in conjunction with her helpless adoration.

A man-servant appeared at nine o'clock one morning, to accompany Kate to the hacienda, which was called Jamiltepec.² He had a basket, and had been shopping in the market. An elderly man, with grey in his moustache, he had bright young eyes and seemed full of energy. His bare feet in the huaraches were almost black with exposure, but his clothes were brilliantly white.

Kate was glad to be walking. The one depressing thing about life in the villages was that one could not walk out into the country. There was always the liability to be held up or attacked. And she had walked already, as far as possible, in every direction, in the neighbourhood of the village, accompanied usually by Ezequiel. Now she was beginning to feel a prisoner.

She was glad, then, to be setting off. The morning was clear and hot, the pale brown lake quite still, like a phantom. People were moving on the beach, in the distance tiny, like dots of white: white dots of men following the faint dust of donkeys. She wondered often why humanity was like specks in the Mexican landscape; just specks of life.

They passed from the lake shore to the rough, dusty road going west, between the steep slope of the hills and the bit of flat by the lake. For almost a mile there were villas, most of them shut up fast, some of them smashed, with broken walls and smashed windows. Only flowers bloomed in masses above the rubble.

In the empty places were flimsy straw huts of the natives, haphazard, as if blown there. By the road under the hill were black-grey adobe huts, like boxes, and fowls running about, and brown pigs or grey pigs spotted with black careered and grunted, and half-naked children, dark orange-brown, trotted or lay flat on their faces in the road, their little naked posteriors hutched up, fast asleep. Already asleep again.

The houses were many of them being re-thatched, or the tiled roofs were being patched by men who assumed a great air of importance at having undertaken such a task. They were pretending to hurry, too, because the real rains might begin any day. And in the little stony levels by the lake, the land was being scratch-ploughed by a pair of oxen and a lump of pointed wood.

But this part of the road Kate knew. She knew the fine villa on the

knoll, with its tufts of palms, and the laid-out avenues that were laid
out, indeed, as the dead are, to crumble back again. She was glad to
be past the villas, where the road came down to the lake again, under
big shady trees that had twisted, wriggly beans. On the left was the
water, the colour of turtle doves, lapping the pale fawn stones. At a
water-hole of a stream in the beach, a cluster of women were busily
washing clothes. In the shallows of the lake itself two women sat
bathing, their black hair hanging dense and wet. A little further along,
a man was wading slowly, stopping to throw his round net skilfully
upon the water, then slowly stooping and gathering it in, picking
out the tiny, glittery fish called charales. Strangely silent and remote
everything, in the gleaming morning, as if it were some distant period
of time.

A little breeze was coming from the lake, but the deep dust under-
foot was hot. On the right the hill rose precipitous, baked and yellowish,
giving back the sun and the intense dryness, and exhaling the faint,
desiccated, peculiar smell of Mexico, that smells as if the earth had
sweated itself dry.

All the time strings of donkeys trotted laden through the dust, their
drivers stalking erect and rapid behind, watching with eyes like black
holes, but always answering Kate's salute with a respectful *Adiós–!*[3] And
Juana echoed her laconic *Adiósn!* She was limping, and she thought it
horrible of Kate to walk four miles, when they might have struggled
out in an old hired motor-car, or gone in a boat, or even ridden donkey-
back.

But to go on foot! Kate could hear all her criada's feelings in the
drawled, sardonic *Adiósn!* But the man behind strode bravely and called
cheerfully. His pistol was prominent in his belt.

A bluff of yellow rock came jutting at the road. The road wound
round it, and into a piece of flat open country. There were fields of
dry stone, and hedges of dusty thorn and cactus. To the left the bright
green of the willows by the lake-shore. To the right the hills swerved
inland, to meet the sheer, fluted sides of dry mountains. Away ahead,
the hills curved back at the shore, and a queer little crack or niche
showed. This crack in the hills led from Don Ramón's shore-property
to the little valley where he grew the sugar cane. And where the hills
approached the lake again, there was a dark clustering of mango trees,
and the red upper-storey of the hacienda house.

'There it is!' cried the man behind. 'Jamiltepec, Señorita. La hacienda de Don Ramón!'

And his eyes shone as he said the name. He was a proud peon, and he really seemed happy.

'Look! How far!' cried Juana.

'Another time,' said Kate, 'I shall come alone, or with Ezequiel.'

'No, Niña! Don't say so. Only my foot hurts this morning.'

'Yes. Better not to bring you.'

'No, Niña! I like to come, very much!'

The tall windmill fan for drawing up water from the lake was spinning gaily. A little valley came down from the niche in the hills, and at the bottom a little water running. Towards the lake, where this valley flattened out, was a grove of banana plants, screened a little from the lake breeze by a vivid row of willow-trees. And on the top of the slope, where the road ran into the shade of mango trees, were the two rows of adobe huts, like a village, set a little back from the road.

Women were coming up between the trees, on the patch from the lake, with jars of water on their shoulders; children were playing around the doors, squatting with little naked posteriors in deep dust; and here and there a goat was tethered. Men in soiled white clothes were lounging, with folded arms and one leg crossed in front of the other, against the corner of a house, or crouching under the walls. Not by any means *dolce far niente*.[4] They seemed to be waiting, eternally waiting for something.

'That way, Señorita!' called the man with the basket, running to her side and indicating the smoother road sloping down between some big trees, towards the white gate of the hacienda. 'We are here!'

Always he spoke with pleased delight, as if the place were a wonder-place to him.

The big doors of the zaguán, the entrance, stood open, and in the shade of the entrance-way a couple of little soldiers were seated. Across the cleared, straw-littered space in front of the gates two peons were trotting, each with a big bunch of bananas on his head. The soldiers said something, and the two peons halted in their trotting, and slowly turned under their yellow-green load, to look back at Kate and Juana and the man Martin, approaching down the road. Then they turned again and trotted into the courtyard, barefoot.

The soldiers stood up. Martin, trotting at Kate's side again, ushered

her into the arched entrance, where the ox-wagons rumbling through
had worn deep ruts. Juana came behind, making a humble noise.

Kate found herself in a big, barren yard, that seemed empty. There
were high walls on the three sides, with sheds and stables. The fourth
side, facing, was the house, with heavily-barred windows looking on
to the courtyard, but with no door. Instead, there was another zaguán,
or passage with closed doors, piercing the house.

Martin trotted ahead to knock on the closed doors. Kate stood looking
round at the big yard. In a shed in one corner, four half-naked men
were packing bunches of bananas. A man in the shade was sawing poles,
and two men in the sun were unloading tiles from a donkey. In a corner
was a bullock wagon, and a pair of big black-and-white oxen standing
with heads pressed down, waiting.

The big doors opened, and Kate entered the second zaguán. It was
a wide entrance way, with stairs going up on one side, and Kate lingered
to look through the open iron gates in front of her, down a formal garden
hemmed in with huge mango trees, to the lake, with its little artificial
harbour where two boats were moored. The lake seemed to give off
a great light, between dark walls of mango.

At the back of the new-comers the servant woman closed the big
doors on to the yard, then waved Kate to the stairs.

'Pass this way, Señorita.'

A bell tinkled above. Kate climbed the stone stairs. And there above
her was Doña Carlota, in white muslin and with white shoes and stockings, her face looking curiously yellow and faded by contrast. Her soft
brown hair was low over her ears, and she held out her thin brownish
arms with queer effusiveness.

'So, you have come! And you have walked, walked all the way? Oh,
imagine walking in so much sun and dust! Come, come in and rest.'

She took Kate's hands and led her across the open terrace at the
top of the stairs.

'It is beautiful here,' said Kate.

She stood on the terrace, looking out past the mango trees at the
lake. A distant sailing canoe was going down the breeze, on the pallid,
unreal water. Away across rose the bluish, grooved mountains, with
the white speck of a village: far away in the morning it seemed, in
another world, in another life, in another mode of time.

'What is that village?' Kate asked.

'That one? That one there? It is San Ildefonso,' said Doña Carlota, in her fluttering eagerness.

'But it is beautiful here!' Kate repeated.

'Hermoso – si! Sí, bonito!'[5] quavered the other woman uneasily, always answering in Spanish.

The house, reddish and yellow in colour, had two short wings towards the lake. The terrace, with green plants on the terrace wall, went round the three sides, the roof above supported by big square pillars that rose from the ground. Down below, the pillars made a soi. of cloisters around the three sides, and in the little stone court was a pool of water. Beyond, the rather neglected formal garden with a strong sun and deep mango-shade.

'Come, you will need to rest!' said Doña Carlota.

'I would like to change my shoes,' said Kate.

She was shown into a high, simple, rather bare bedroom with red-tiled floor. There she changed into the shoes and stockings Juana had carried, and rested a little.

As she lay resting, she heard the dulled thud-thud of the tom-tom drum, but, save the crowing of a cock in the distance, no other sound on the bright, yet curiously hollow Mexican morning. And the drum, thudding with its dulled, black insistence, made her uneasy. It sounded like something coming over the horizon.

She rose, and went into the long, high salon where Doña Carlota was sitting talking to a man in black. The salon, with its three window-doors open on to the terrace, its worn, red floor tiled with old square bricks, its high walls colour-washed a faint green, and the many-beamed ceiling white-washed; and with its bareness of furniture, seemed like part of the out-of-doors, like some garden-arbour put for shade. The sense, which houses have in hot climates, of being just three walls wherein one lingers for a moment, then goes away again.

As Kate entered the room, the man in black rose and shook hands with Doña Carlota, bowing very low and deferential. Then with a deferential sideways sort of bow to Kate, he vanished out of doors.

'Come!' said Doña Carlota to Kate. 'Are you sure now you are rested?' And she pulled forward one of the cane rocking-chairs that had poised itself in the room, en route to nowhere.

'Perfectly!' said Kate. 'How still it seems here! Except for the drum.

Perhaps it is the drum that makes it seem so still. Though I always think the lake *makes* a sort of silence.'

'Ah, the drum!' cried Doña Carlota, lifting her hand with a gesture of nervous, spent exasperation. 'I cannot hear it. No, I cannot, I cannot bear to hear it.'

And she rocked herself in a sudden access of agitation.

'It does hit one rather below the belt,' said Kate. 'What is it?'

'Ah, do not ask me! It is my husband.'

She made a gesture of despair, and rocked herself almost into un-consciousness.

'Is Don Ramón drumming?'

'Drumming?' Doña Carlota seemed to start. 'No! Oh no! He is not drumming, himself. He brought down two Indians from the north to do that.'

'Did he!' said Kate, non-committal.

But Doña Carlota was rocking in a sort of semi-consciousness. Then she seemed to pull herself together.

'I *must talk* to somebody, I must!' she said, suddenly straightening herself in her chair, her face creamy and creased, her soft brown hair sagging over her ears, her brown eyes oddly desperate. 'May I talk to you?'

'Do!' said Kate, rather uneasy.

'You know what Ramón is doing?' she said, looking at Kate almost furtively, suspiciously.

'Does he want to bring back the old gods?' said Kate vaguely.

'Ah!' cried Doña Carlota, again with that desperate, flying jerk of her hand. 'As if it were *possible*! As if it were possible! The old gods! Imagine it, Señora! The old gods! Why, what are they? Nothing but dead illusions. And ugly, repulsive illusions! Ah! I always thought my husband such a clever man, so superior to me! Ah, it is terrible to have to change one's idea! This is such *nonsense*. How dare he! How dare he take such nonsense seriously! How does he dare!'

'Does he believe in it himself?' asked Kate.

'Himself? But, Señora –' and Doña Carlota gave a pitiful, pitying smile of contempt. 'How could he! As if it were possible. After all he is an educated man! How could he believe in such nonsense!'

'Then why does he do it?'

'Why? Why?' There was a tone of unspeakable weariness in Doña

Carlota's voice. 'I wish I knew. I think he has gone insane, as Mexicans do. Insane like Francisco Villa, the bandit.'[6]

Kate thought of the pug-faced notorious Pancho Villa in wonder, unable to connect him with Don Ramón.

'All the Mexicans, as soon as they rise above themselves, go that way,' said Doña Carlota. 'Their pride gets the better of them. And then they understand nothing, nothing but their own foolish will, their will to be very, very important. It is just the male vanity. Don't you think, Señora, that the beginning and the end of a man is his vanity? Don't you think it was just against this danger that Christ came, to teach men a proper humility? To teach them the sin of pride. But that is why they hate Christ so much, and His teaching. First and last, they want their own vanity.'

Kate had often thought so herself. Her own final conclusion about men was that *they* were the vanity of vanities, nothing but vanity. They must be flattered and made to feel great: Nothing else.

'And now, my husband wants to go to the other extreme of Jesus. He wants to exalt pride and vanity higher than God. Ah, it is terrible, terrible! And foolish like a little boy! Ah, what is a man but a little boy who needs a nurse and a mother! Ah, Señora, I can't bear it.'

Doña Carlota covered her face with her hand, as if swooning.

'But there is something wonderful, too, about Don Ramón,' said Kate coaxingly: though at the moment she hated him.

'Wonderful! Ah yes, he has gifts. He has great gifts! But what are gifts to a man who perverts them!'

'Tell me what you think he really wants,' said Kate.

'Power! Just power! Just foolish, wicked power. As if there had not been enough horrible, wicked power let loose in this country. But he – he – he wants to be beyond them all. He – he – he wants to be worshipped. To be worshipped! To be worshipped! A God! He, whom I've held, I've held in my arms! He is a child, as all men are children. And now he wants – to be worshipped – !' She went off into a shrill, wild laughter, covering her face with her hands, and laughing shrilly, her laughter punctuated by hollow, ghastly sobs.

Kate sat in absolute dismay, waiting for the other woman to recover herself. She felt cold against these hysterics, and exerted all her heavy female will to stop them.

'After all,' she said, when Doña Carlota became quiet, her face in her hands, 'it isn't your fault. We can't be responsible, even for our husbands. I know *that*, since my husband died, and I couldn't prevent him dying. And then – then I learned that no matter how you love another person, you can't really do anything, you are helpless when it comes to the last things. You have to leave them to themselves, when they want to die: or when they want to do things that seem foolish, so, so foolish, to a woman.'

Doña Carlota looked up at the other woman.

'You loved your husband very much – and he died?' she said softly.

'I *did* love him. And I shall never, never love another man. I couldn't. I've lost the power.'

'And why did he die?'

'Ah, even that was really his own fault. He broke his own soul and spirit, in those Irish politics. I knew it was wrong. What does Ireland matter, what does nationalism and all that rubbish matter, really! And revolutions! They are so, so stupid and *vieux jeu*.[7] Ah! It would have been *so* much better if Joachim had been content to live his life in peace, with me. It could be so jolly, so lovely. And I tried and tried and tried with him. But it was no good. He *wanted* to kill himself with that beastly Irish business, and I tried in vain to prevent him.'

Doña Carlota stared slowly at Kate.

'As a woman *must* try to prevent a man, when he is going wrong,' she said. 'As I try to prevent Ramón. As he will get himself killed, as surely as they all do, down to Francisco Villa. And when they are dead, what good is it all?'

'When they *are* dead,' said Kate, 'then you *know* it's no good.'

'You do! Oh, Señora, if you think you can help me with Ramón, *do* help me, *do*! For it means the death either of me or him. And *I* shall die, though he is wrong. Unless he gets killed.'

'Tell me what he wants to do,' said Kate. 'What does he *think* he wants to do, anyhow? – Like my husband thought he wanted to make a free Ireland and a great Irish people. But I knew all the time, the Irish aren't a great people any more, and you *can't* make them free. They are only good at destroying – just mere stupid destroying. How can you make a people free, if they *aren't* free. If something inside them compels them to go on destroying!'

'I know! I know! And that is Ramón. He wants to destroy even

Jesus and the Blessed Virgin, for this people. Imagine it! To destroy
Jesus and the Blessed Virgin! the last thing they've got!'

'But what does he say himself, that he wants to do?'

'He says he wants to make a new connection between the people
and God. He says himself, God is always God. But man loses his connection with God. And then he can never recover it again, unless some
new Saviour comes to give him his new connection. And every new
connection is different from the last, though God is always God. And
now, Ramón says, the people have lost God. And the Saviour cannot
lead them to Him any more. There must be a new Saviour with a new
vision. But ah, Señora, that is not true for me. God is love, and if
Ramón would only submit to love, he would know that he had found
God. But he is perverse. Ah, if we could be together, quietly loving,
and enjoying the beautiful world, and *waiting in the love of God*! Ah,
Señora, *why*, why, why can't he see it? Oh, why can't he see it! Instead
of doing all these –'

The tears came to Doña Carlota's eyes, and spilled over her cheeks.
Kate also was in tears, mopping her face.

'It's no good!' she said, sobbing. 'I know it's no good, no matter
what we do. They don't *want* to be happy and peaceful. They *want*
this strife and these other false, horrible connections. It's no good whatever we do! That's what's so bitter, so bitter!'

The two women sat in their bent-wood rocking-chairs and just
sobbed. And as they sobbed, they heard a step coming along the terrace,
the faint swish of the sandals of the people.

It was Don Ramón, drawn unconsciously by the emotional dis-
turbance of the two women.

Doña Carlota hastily dabbed her eyes and her sniffing nose, Kate
blew her nose like a trumpet, and Don Ramón stood in the doorway.

He was dressed in white, dazzling, in the costume of the peons, the
white blouse jacket and the white, wide pantaloon trousers. But the
white was linen, slightly starched, and brilliant, almost unnatural in
its whiteness. From under his blouse, in front, hung the ends of a narrow
woollen sash, white, with blue and black bars, and a fringe of scarlet.
And on his naked feet were the plaited huaraches, of blue and black
strips of leather, with thick, red-dyed soles. His loose trousers were
bound round the ankles with blue, red, and black woollen braids.

Kate glanced at him as he stood in the sun, so dazzlingly white, that his black hair and dark face looked like a hole in the atmosphere. He came forward, the ends of his sash swinging against his thighs, his sandals slightly swishing.

'I am pleased to see you,' he said, shaking hands with Kate. 'How did you come?'

He dropped into a chair, and sat quite still. The two women hung their heads, hiding their faces. The presence of the man seemed to put their emotion out of joint. He ignored all the signs of their discomfort, overlooking it with a powerful will. There was a certain strength in his presence. They all cheered up a bit.

'You didn't know my husband had become one of the people – a real peon – a Señor Peon, like Count Tolstoy[8] became a Señor Moujik?' said Doña Carlota, with an attempt at raillery.

'Anyway it suits him,' said Kate.

'There!' said Don Ramón. 'Give the devil his dues.'

But there was something unyielding, unbending about him. He laughed and spoke to the women only from a surface self. Underneath, powerful and inscrutable, he made no connection with them.

So it was at lunch. There was a flitting conversation, with intervals of silence. It was evident that Ramón was thinking in another world, in the silence. And the ponderous stillness of his will, working in another sphere, made the women feel overshadowed.

'The Señora is like me, Ramón,' said Doña Carlota. 'She cannot bear the sound of that drum. Must it play any more this afternoon?'

There was a moment's pause, before he answered:

'After four o'clock only.'

'*Must* we have that noise to-day?' Carlota persisted.

'Why not to-day like other days!' he said. But a certain darkness was on his brow, and it was evident he wanted to leave the presence of the two women.

'Because the Señora is here: and I am here: and we neither of us like it. And to-morrow the Señora will not be here, and I shall be gone back to Mexico. So why not spare us to-day! Surely you can show us this consideration.'

Ramón looked at her, and then at Kate. There was anger in his eyes. And Kate could almost feel, in his powerful chest, the big heart swelling with a suffocation of anger. Both women kept mum. But it pleased them, anyhow, that they could make him angry.

'Why not row with Mrs Leslie on the lake!' he said, with quiet control.

But under his dark brows was a level, indignant anger.

'We may not want to,' said Carlota.

Then he did what Kate had not known anyone to do before. He withdrew his consciousness away from them as they all three sat at table, leaving the two women, as it were, seated outside a closed door, with nothing more happening. Kate felt for the first time startled and forlorn, then a slow anger burned in her warm ivory cheek.

'Oh, yes,' she said. 'I can start home before then.'

'No! No!' said Doña Carlota, with a Spanish wail. 'Don't leave me. Stay with me till evening, and help me to amuse Don Cipriano. He is coming to supper.'

CHAPTER XI

Lords of the Day and Night

WHEN lunch was over, Ramón went to his room, to sleep for an hour. It was a hot, still afternoon. Clouds were standing erect and splendid, at the west end of the lake, like messengers. Ramón went into his room and closed the window-doors and the shutters, till it was quite dark, save for yellow pencils of light that stood like substance on the darkness, from the cracks of the shutters.

He took off his clothes, and in the darkness thrust his clenched fists upwards above his head, in a terrible tension of stretched, upright prayer. In his eyes was only darkness, and slowly the darkness revolved in his brain, too, till he was mindless. Only a powerful will stretched itself and quivered from his spine in an immense tension of prayer. Stretched the invisible bow of the body in the darkness with inhuman tension, erect, till the arrows of the soul, mindless, shot to the mark, and the prayer reached its goal.

Then suddenly, the clenched and quivering arms dropped, the body relaxed into softness. The man had reached his strength again. He had broken the cords of the world, and was free in the other strength.

Softly, delicately, taking great care not to think, not to remember, not to disturb the poisonous snakes of mental consciousness, he picked up a thin, fine blanket, wrapped it round him, and lay down on the pile of mats on the floor. In an instant he was asleep.

He slept in complete oblivion for about an hour. Then suddenly he opened his eyes wide. He saw the velvety darkness, and the pencils of light gone frail. The sun had moved. Listening, there seemed not a sound in the world: there was no world.

Then he began to hear. He heard the faint rumble of an ox-wagon: then leaves in a wind: then a faint tapping noise: then the creak of some bird calling.

He rose and quickly dressed in the dark, and threw open the doors. It was mid-afternoon, with a hot wind blowing, and clouds reared up dark and bronze in the west, the sun hidden. But the rain would not fall yet. He took a big straw hat and balanced it on his head. It had a round crest of black and white and blue feathers, like an eye, or a sun, in front. He heard the low sound of women talking. Ah, the strange woman! He had forgotten her. And Carlota! Carlota was here! He thought of her for a moment, and of her curious opposition. Then, before he could be angry, he lifted his breast again in the black, mindless prayer, his eyes went dark, and the sense of opposition left him.

He went quickly, driftingly along the terrace to the stone stairs that led down to the inner entrance-way. Going through to the courtyard, he saw two men packing bales of bananas upon donkeys, under a shed. The soldiers were sleeping in the zaguán. Through the open doors, up the avenue of trees, he could see an ox-wagon slowly retreating. Within the courtyard there was the sharp ringing of metal hammered on an anvil. It came from a corner where was a smithy, where a man and a boy were working. In another shed a carpenter was planing wood.

Don Ramón stood a moment to look around. This was his own world. His own spirit was spread over it like a soft, nourishing shadow, and the silence of his own power gave it peace.

The men working were almost instantly aware of his presence. One after the other the dark, hot faces glanced up at him, and glanced away again. They were men, and his presence was wonderful to them; but they were afraid to approach him, even by staring at him. They worked the quicker for having seen him, as if it gave them new life.

He went across to the smithy, where the boy was blowing the old-fashioned bellows, and the man was hammering a piece of metal, with quick, light blows. The man worked on without lifting his head, as the *patrón* drew near.

'It is the bird?' said Ramón, standing watching the piece of metal, now cold upon the anvil.

'Yes, *Patrón*! It is the bird. Is it right?' And the man looked up with black, bright, waiting eyes.

The smith lifted with the tongs the black, flat, tongue-shaped piece of metal, and Ramón looked at it a long time.

'I put the wings on after,' said the smith.

Ramón traced with his dark, sensitive hand an imaginary line, outside the edge of the iron. Three times he did it. And the movement fascinated the smith.

'A little more slender – so!' said Ramón.

'Yes, *Patrón*! Yes! Yes! I understand,' said the man eagerly.

'And the rest?'

'Here it is!' The man pointed to two hoops of iron, one smaller than the other, and to some flat discs of iron, triangular in shape.

'Lay them on the ground.'

The man put the hoops on the ground, one within the other. Then, taking the triangular discs, he placed them with quick, sensitive hands, so that their bases were upon the outer circle, and their apices touched the inner. There were seven. And thus they made a seven-pointed sun of the space inside.

'Now the bird,' said Ramón.

The man quickly took the long piece of iron: it was the rudimentary form of a bird, with two feet, but as yet without wings. He placed it in the centre of the inner circle, so that the feet touched the circle and the crest of the head touched opposite.

'So! It fits,' said the man.

Ramón stood looking at the big iron symbol on the ground. He heard the doors of the inner entrance: Kate and Carlota walking across the courtyard.

'I take it away?' asked the workman quickly.

'Never mind,' Ramón answered quietly.

Kate stood and stared at the great wreath of iron on the ground.

'What is it?' she asked brightly.

'The bird within the sun.'

'Is that a bird?'

'When it has wings.'

'Ah, yes! When it has wings. And what is it for?'

'For a symbol to the people.'

'It is pretty.'

'Yes.'

'Ramón!' said Doña Carlota, 'will you give me the key for the boat? Martin will row us out.'

He produced the key from under his sash.

'Where did you get that beautiful sash?' asked Kate.

It was the white sash with blue and brown-black bars, and with a heavy red fringe.

'This?' he said. 'We wove it here.'

'And did you make the sandals too?'

'Yes! They were made by Manuel. Later I will show you.'

'Oh, I should like to see! – They are beautiful, don't you think, Doña Carlota?'

'Yes! Yes! It is true. But whether beautiful things are wise things, I don't know. So much I don't know, Señora. Ay, so much! – And you, do you know what is wise?'

'I?' said Kate. 'I don't care very much.'

'Ah! You don't care! – You think Ramón is wise, to wear the peasants' clothes, and the huaraches?' For once Doña Carlota was speaking in slow English.

'Oh, yes!' cried Kate. 'He looks so handsome! – Men's clothes are so hideous, and Don Ramón looks so handsome in those!' With the big hat poised on his head, he had a certain air of nobility and authority.

'Ah!' cried Doña Carlota, looking at the other woman with intelligent, half-scared eyes, and swinging the key of the boat. 'Shall we go to the lake?'

The two women departed. Ramón, laughing to himself, went out of the gate and across the outer yard, to where a big, barn-like building stood near the trees. He entered the barn, and gave a low whistle. It was answered from the loft above, and a trap-door opened. Don Ramón went up the steps, and found himself in a sort of studio and carpenter's shop. A fattish young man with curly hair, wearing an artist's blouse, and with mallet and chisels in his hand, greeted him.

'How is it going?' asked Ramón.

'Yes – well –'

The artist was working on a head, in wood. It was larger than life, conventionalised. Yet under the conventional lines the likeness to Ramón revealed itself.

'Sit for me for half an hour,' said the sculptor.

Ramón sat in silence, while the other man bent over his model, working in silent concentration. And all the time, Ramón sat erect, almost motionless, with a great stillness of repose and concentration, thinking about nothing, but throwing out the dark aura of power, in the spell of which the artist worked.

'That is enough,' he said at last, quietly rising.

'But give me the pose before you go,' said the artist.

Ramón slowly took off his blouse-skirt, and stood with naked torso, the sash with its blue and black bars tight round his naked waist. For some moments he stood gathering himself together. Then suddenly, in a concentration of intense, proud prayer, he flung his right arm up above his head, and stood transfixed, his left arm hanging softly by his side, the fingers touching his thigh. And on his face that fixed, intense look of pride which was at once a prayer.

The artist gazed with wonder, and with an appreciation touched with fear. The other man, large and intense, with big dark eyes staring with intense pride, yet prayerful, beyond the natural horizons, sent a thrill of dread and of joy through the artist. He bowed his head as he looked.

Don Ramón turned to him.

'Now you!' he said.

The artist was afraid. He seemed to quail. But he met Ramón's eyes. And instantly, that stillness of concentration came over him, like a trance. And then suddenly, out of the trance, he shot his arm aloft, and his fat, pale face took on an expression of peace, a noble, motionless transfiguration, the blue-grey eyes calm, proud, reaching into the beyond, with prayer. And though he stood in his blouse, with a rather pudgy figure and curly hair, he had the perfect stillness of nobility.

'It is good!' said Ramón, bowing his head.

The artist suddenly changed; Ramón held out his two hands; the artist took them in his two hands. Then he lifted Ramón's right hand and placed the back of it on his brow.

'Adiós!' said Ramón, taking his blouse again.

'Adiós, Señor!' said the artist.

And with a proud, white look of joy in his face, he turned again to his work.

Ramón visited the adobe house, its yard fenced with cane and over-shadowed by a great mango tree, where Manuel and his wife and children, and two assistants, were spinning and weaving. Two little girls were assiduously carding white wool and brown wool under a cluster of banana trees: the wife and a young maiden were spinning fine, fine thread. On the line hung dyed wool, red, and blue, and green. And under the shed stood Manuel and a youth, weaving at two heavy hand-looms.

'How is it going?' called Don Ramón.

'*Muy bien! Muy bien!*' answered Manuel, with that curious look of transfiguration glistening in his black eyes and in the smile of his face. 'It is going well, very well, Señor!'

Ramón paused to look at the fine white serape on the loom. It had a zig-zag border of natural black wool and blue, in little diamonds, and the ends a complication of blackish and blue diamond-pattern. The man was just beginning to do the centre – called the *boca*, the mouth: and he looked anxiously at the design that was tacked to the loom. But it was simple: the same as the iron symbol the smith was making: a snake with his tail in his mouth, the black triangles on his back being the outside of the circle: and in the middle, a blue eagle standing erect, with slim wings touching the belly of the snake with their tips, and slim feet upon the snake, within the hoop.

Ramón went back to the house, to the upper terrace, and round to the short wing where his room was. He put a folded serape over his shoulder, and went along the terrace. At the end of this wing, projecting to the lake, was a square terrace with a low, thick wall and a tiled roof, and a coral-scarlet bignonia dangling from the massive pillars. The terrace, or loggia, was strewn with the native palm-leaf mats, petates, and there was a drum in one corner, with the drum-stick upon it. At the far inner corner went down an enclosed stone staircase, with an iron door at the bottom.

Ramón stood a while looking out at the lake. The clouds were dissolving again, the sheet of water gave off a whitish light. In the distance he could see the dancing speck of a boat, probably Martin with the two women.

He took off his hat and his blouse, and stood motionless, naked to the waist. Then he lifted the drum-stick, and after waiting a moment or two, to become still in soul, he sounded the rhythmic summons, rather slow, yet with a curious urge in its strong-weak, one-two rhythm. He had got the old barbaric power into the drum.

For some time he stood alone, the drum, or tom-tom, lifted by its thong against his legs, his right hand drumming, his face expressionless. A man entered, bareheaded, running from the inner terrace. He was in the white cotton clothes, snow white, but with a dark serape folded on his shoulder, and he held a key in his hand. He saluted Ramón by putting the back of his right hand in front of his eyes for a moment, then he went down the stone stairway and opened the iron door.

Immediately men were coming up, all dressed alike, in the white cotton clothes and the huaraches, each with a folded serape over his shoulder. But their sashes were all blue, and their sandals blue and white. The sculptor came too, and Mirabal was there, also dressed in the cotton clothes.

There were seven men, besides Ramón. At the top of the stairs, one after another, they saluted. Then they took their serapes, dark brown, with blue eyes filled with white, along the edges, and threw them down along the wall, their hats beside them. Then they took off their blouses, and flung them on their hats.

Ramón left the drum, and sat down on his own serape, that was white with the blue and black bars, and the scarlet fringe. The drummer sat down and took the drum. The circle of men sat cross-legged, naked to the waist, silent. Some were of a dark, ruddy coffee-brown, two were white, Ramón was of a soft creamy brown. They sat in silence for a time, only the monotonous, hypnotic sound of the drum pulsing, touching the inner air. Then the drummer began to sing, in the curious, small, inner voice, that hardly emerges from the circle, singing in the ancient falsetto of the Indians:

'Who sleeps – shall wake! Who sleeps – shall wake! Who treads down the path of the snake shall arrive at the place; in the path of the dust shall arrive at the place and be dressed in the skin of the snake –'

One by one the voices of the men joined in, till they were all singing in the strange, blind infallible rhythm of the ancient barbaric world. And all in the small, inward voices, as if they were singing from the oldest, darkest recess of the soul, not outwards, but inwards, the soul singing back to herself.

They sang for a time, in the peculiar unison like a flock of birds that fly in one consciousness. And when the drum shuddered for an end, they all let their voices fade out, with the same broad, clapping sound in the throat.

There was silence. The men turned, speaking to one another, laughing in a quiet way. But their daytime voices, and their daytime eyes had gone.

Then Ramón's voice was heard, and the men were suddenly silent, listening with bent heads. Ramón sat with his face lifted, looking far away, in the pride of prayer.

'There is no Before and After, there is only Now,' he said, speaking in a proud, but inward voice.

'The great Snake coils and uncoils the plasm of his folds, and stars appear, and worlds fade out. It is no more than the changing and easing of the plasm.

'*I always am*, says his sleep.

'As a man in a deep sleep knows not, but is, so is the Snake of the coiled cosmos, wearing its plasm.

'As a man in a deep sleep has no to-morrow, no yesterday, nor to-day, but only *is*, so is the limpid, far-reaching Snake of the eternal Cosmos, Now, and forever Now.

'Now, and only Now, and forever Now.

'But dreams arise and fade in the sleep of the Snake.

'And worlds arise as dreams, and are gone as dreams.

'And man is a dream in the sleep of the Snake.

'And only the sleep that is dreamless breathes *I Am!*

'In the dreamless Now, *I Am*.

'Dreams arise as they must arise, and man is a dream arisen.

'But the dreamless plasm of the Snake is the plasm of a man, of his body, his soul, and his spirit at one.

'And the perfect sleep of the Snake *I Am* is the plasm of a man, who is whole.

'When the plasm of the body, and the plasm of the soul, and the plasm of the spirit are at one, in the Snake *I Am*.

'I am Now.

'Was-not is a dream, and shall-be is a dream, like two separate, heavy feet.

'But Now, I Am.

'The trees put forth their leaves in their sleep, and flowering emerge out of dreams, into pure I Am.

'The birds forget the stress of their dreams, and sing aloud in the Now, I Am! I Am!

'For dreams have wings and feet, and journeys to take, and efforts to make.

'But the glimmering Snake of the Now is wingless and footless, and undivided, and perfectly coiled.

'It is thus the cat lies down, in the coil of Now, and the cow curves round her nose to her belly, lying down.

'In the feet of a dream the hare runs uphill. But when he pauses, the dream has passed, he has entered the timeless Now, and his eyes are the wide I Am.

'Only man dreams, dreams, and dreams, and changes from dream to dream, like a man who tosses on his bed.

'With his eyes and his mouth he dreams, with his hands and his feet, with phallos and heart and belly, with body and spirit and soul, in a tempest of dreams.

'And rushes from dream to dream, in the hope of the perfect dream.

'But I, I say to you, there is no dream that is perfect, for every dream has an ache and an urge, an urge and an ache.

'And nothing is perfect, save the dream pass out into the sleep, I Am.

'When the dream of the eyes is darkened, and encompassed with Now.

'And the dream of the mouth resounds in the last I Am.

'And the dream of the hands is a sleep like a bird on the sea, that sleeps and is lifted and shifted, and knows not.

'And the dreams of the feet and the toes touch the core of the world, where the Serpent sleeps.

'And the dream of the phallos reaches the great I Know Not.

'And the dream of the body is the stillness of a flower in the dark.

'And the dream of the soul is gone in the perfume of Now.

'And the dream of the spirit lapses, and lays down its head, and is still with the Morning Star.

'For each dream starts out of Now, and is accomplished in Now.

'In the core of the flower, the glimmering, wakeless Snake.

'And what falls away is a dream, and what accrues is a dream. There is always and only Now, Now and I Am.'

There was silence in the circle of men. Outside, the sound of the bullock-wagon could be heard, and from the lake, the faint knocking of oars. But the seven men sat with their heads bent, in the semi-trance, listening inwardly.

Then the drum began softly to beat, as if of itself. And a man began to sing, in a small voice:

> The Lord of the Morning Star
> Stood between the day and the night:
> As a bird that lifts its wings, and stands
> With the bright wing on the right

And the wing of the dark on the left,
The Dawn Star stood into sight.

Lo! I am always here!
Far in the hollow of space
I brush the wing of the day
And put light on your face.
The other wing brushes the dark.
But I, I am always in place.

Yea, I am always here. I am Lord
In every way. And the lords among men
See me through the flashing of wings.
They see me and lose me again.
But lo! I am always here
Within ken.

The multitudes see me not.
They see only the waving of wings,
The coming and going of things.
The cold and the hot.

But ye that perceive me between
The tremors of night and the day,
I make you the Lords of the Way
Unseen.

The path between gulfs of the dark and the steeps of the light;
The path like a snake that is gone, like the length of a fuse to ignite
The substance of shadow, that bursts and explodes into sight.

I am here undeparting. I sit tight
Between wings of the endless flight,
At the depths of the peace and the fight.

Deep in the moistures of peace,
And far down the muzzle of the fight
You shall find me, who am neither increase
Nor destruction, different quite.

I am far beyond
The horizons of love and strife.
Like a star, like a pond
That washes the lords of life.

'Listen!' said Ramón, in the stillness. 'We will be masters among men, and lords among men. But lords of men and masters of men we will not be. Listen! We are lords of the night. Lords of the day and night. Sons of the Morning Star, sons of the Evening Star. Men of the Morning and the Evening Star.

'We are not lords of men: how can men make us lords? Nor are we masters of men, for men are not worth it.

'But I am the Morning and the Evening Star, and lord of the day and the night. By the power that is put in my left hand, and the power that I grasp in my right, I am lord of the two ways.

'And my flower on earth is the jasmine flower, and in heaven the flower Hesperus.

'I will not command you, nor serve you, for the snake goes crooked to his own house.

'Yet I will be with you, so you depart not from yourselves.

'There is no giving, and no taking. When the fingers that give touch the fingers that receive, the Morning Star shines at once, from the contact, and the jasmine gleams between the hands. And thus there is neither giving nor taking, nor hand that proffers nor hand that receives, but the star between them is all, and the dark hand and the light hand are invisible on each side. The jasmine takes the giving and the receiving in her cup, and the scent of the oneness is fragrant on the air.

'Think neither to give nor to receive, only let the jasmine flower.

'Let nothing spill from you in excess, let nothing be reived from you.

'And reive nothing away. Not even the scent from the rose, nor the juice from the pomegranate, nor the warmth from the fire.

'But say to the rose: Lo! I take you away from your tree, and your breath is in my nostrils, and my breath is warm in your depths. Let it be a sacrament between us.

'And beware when you break the pomegranate; it is sunset you take in your hands. Say: I am coming, come thou. Let the Evening Star stand between us.

'And when the fire burns up and the wind is cold and you spread your hands to the blaze, listen to the flame saying: Ah! Is it thou? Comest thou to me? Lo, I was going the longest journey, down the path of the greatest snake. But since thou comest to me, I come to thee. And where thou fallest into my hands, fall I into thine, and jasmine flowers on the burning bush between us. Our meeting is the burning bush, whence the jasmine flowers.

'Reive nothing away, and let nothing be reived from you. For reiver and bereaved alike break the root of the jasmine flower, and spit upon the Evening Star.

'Take nothing, to say: *I have it!* For you can possess nothing, not even peace.

'Nought is possessible, neither gold, nor land, nor love, nor life, nor peace, nor even sorrow nor death, nor yet salvation.

'Say of nothing: It is mine.

'Say only: It is with me.

'For the gold that is with thee lingers as a departing moon, looking across space thy way, saying: Lo! We are beholden of each other. Lo! for this little while, to each other thou and I are beholden.

'And thy land says to thee: Ah, my child of a far-off father! Come, lift me, lift me a little while, that poppies and wheat may blow on the level wind that moves between my breast and thine! Then sink with me, and we will make one mound.

'And listen to thy love saying: Beloved! I am mown by thy sword like mown grass, and darkness is upon me, and the tremble of the Evening Star. And to me thou art darkness and nowhere. Oh thou, when thou risest up and goest thy way, speak to me, only say: The star rose between us.

'And say to thy life: Am I thine? Art thou mine? Am I the blue curve of day around thine uncurved night? Are my eyes the twilight of neither of us, where the star hangs? Is my upper lip the sunset and my lower lip the dawn, does the star tremble inside my mouth?

'And say to thy peace: Ah! risen, deathless star! Already the waters of dawn sweep over thee, and wash me away on the flood!

'And say to thy sorrow: Axe, thou art cutting me down!

'Yet did a spark fly from out of thy edge and my wound!

'Cut then, while I cover my face, father of the Star.

'And say to thy strength: Lo, the night is foaming up my feet and my loins, day is foaming down from my eyes and my mouth to the sea of my breast. Lo, they meet! My belly is a flood of power, that races in down the sluice of bone at my back, and a star hangs low on the flood, over a troubled dawn.

'And say to thy death: Be it so! I, and my soul, we come to thee, Evening Star. Flesh, go thou into the night. Spirit, farewell, 'tis thy day. Leave me now. I go in last nakedness now to the nakedest Star.'

The First Waters

THE men had risen and covered themselves, and put on their hats, and covered their eyes for a second, in salute before Ramón, as they departed down the stone stair. And the iron door at the bottom had clanged, the doorkeeper had returned with the key, laid it on the drum, and softly, delicately departed.

Still Ramón sat on his serape, leaning his naked shoulders on the wall, and closing his eyes. He was tired, and in that state of extreme separateness which makes it very hard to come back to the world. On the outside of his ears he could hear the noises of the hacienda, even the tinkle of tea-spoons, and the low voice of women, and later, the low, labouring sound of a motor-car struggling over the uneven road, then swirling triumphantly into the courtyard.

It was hard to come back to these things. The noise of them sounded on the outside of his ears, but inside them was the slow, vast, inaudible roar of the cosmos, like in a sea-shell. It was hard to have to bear the contact of commonplace daily things, when his soul and body were naked to the cosmos.

He wished they would leave him the veils of his isolation awhile. But they would not: especially Carlota. She wanted him to be present to her: in familiar contact.

She was calling: 'Ramón! Ramón! Have you finished? Cipriano is here.' And even so, in her voice was fear, and an over-riding temerity.

He pushed back his hair and rose, and very quickly went out, as he was, with naked torso. He didn't want to dress himself into everyday familiarity, since his soul was unfamiliar.

They had a tea-table out on the terrace, and Cipriano, in uniform, was there. He got up quickly, and came down the terrace with outstretched arms, his black eyes gleaming with an intensity almost like pain, upon the face of the other man. And Ramón looked back at him with wide, seeing, yet unchanging eyes.

The two men embraced, breast to breast, and for a moment Cipriano laid his little blackish hands on the naked shoulders of the bigger man, and for a moment was perfectly still on his breast. Then very softly, he stood back and looked at him, saying not a word.

Ramón abstractedly laid his hand on Cipriano's shoulder, looking down at him with a little smile.

'Qué tal?' he said, from the edge of his lips. 'How goes it?'

'Bien! Muy bien!' said Cipriano, still gazing into the other man's face with black, wondering, childlike, searching eyes, as if he, Cipriano, were searching for *himself*, in Ramón's face. Ramón looked back into Cipriano's black, Indian eyes with a faint, kind smile of recognition, and Cipriano hung his head as if to hide his face, the black hair, which he wore rather long and brushed sideways, dropping over his forehead.

The women watched in absolute silence. Then, as the two men began slowly to come along the terrace to the tea-table, Carlota began to pour tea. But her hand trembled so much, the teapot wobbled as she held it, and she had to put it down and clasp her hands in the lap of her white muslin dress.

'You rowed on the lake?' said Ramón abstractedly, coming up.

'It was lovely!' said Kate. 'But hot when the sun came.'

Ramón smiled a little, then pushed his hand through his hair. Then, leaning one hand on the parapet of the terrace wall, he turned to look at the lake, and a sigh lifted his shoulders unconsciously.

He stood thus, naked to the waist, his black hair ruffled and splendid, his back to the women, looking out at the lake. Cipriano stood lingering beside him.

Kate saw the sigh lift the soft, quiescent, cream-brown shoulders. The soft, cream-brown skin of his back, of a smooth, *pure* sensuality, made her shudder. The broad, square, rather high shoulders, with neck and head rising steep, proudly. The full-fleshed, deep-chested, rich body of the man made her feel dizzy. In spite of herself, she could not help imagining a knife stuck between those pure, male shoulders. If only to break the arrogance of their remoteness.

That was it. His nakedness was so aloof, far-off and intangible, in another day. So that to *think* of it was almost a violation, even to look at it with prying eyes. Kate's heart suddenly shrank in her breast. This was how Salome had looked at John.[1] And this was the beauty of John, that he had had; like a pomegranate on a dark tree in the distance, naked, but not undressed! Forever still and clothe-less, and with another light about it, of a richer day than our paltry, prying, sneak-thieving day.

The moment Kate had imagined a knife between his shoulders, her heart shrank with grief and shame, and a great stillness came over her. Better to take the hush into one's heart, and the sharp, prying beams out of one's eyes. Better to lapse away from one's own prying, assertive self, into the soft, untrespassing self, to whom nakedness is neither shame nor excitement, but clothed like a flower in its own deep, soft consciousness, beyond cheap awareness.

The evening breeze was blowing very faintly. Sailing boats were advancing through the pearly atmosphere, far off, the sun above had a golden quality. The opposite shore, twenty miles away, was distinct, and yet there seemed an opalescent, spume-like haze in the air, the same quality as in the filmy water. Kate could see the white specks of the far-off church towers of Tuliapan.[2]

Below, in the garden below the house, was a thick grove of mango trees. Among the dark and reddish leaves of the mangoes, scarlet little birds were bustling, like suddenly-opening poppy-buds, and pairs of yellow birds, yellow underneath as yellow butterflies, so perfectly clear, went skimming past. When they settled for a moment and closed their wings, they disappeared, for they were grey on top. And when the cardinal birds settled, they too disappeared, for the outside of their wings was brown, like a sheath.

'Birds in this country have all their colour below,' said Kate.

Ramón turned to her suddenly.

'They say the word *Mexico* means *below this!*' he said, smiling, and sinking into a rocking-chair.

Doña Carlota had made a great effort over herself, and with eyes fixed on the tea-cups, she poured out the tea. She handed him his cup without looking at him. She did not trust herself to look at him. It made her tremble with a strange, hysterical anger: she, who had been married to him for years, and knew him, ah, knew him: and yet, and yet, had not got him at all. None of him.

'Give me a piece of sugar, Carlota,' he said, in his quiet voice.

But at the sound of it, his wife stopped as if some hand had suddenly grasped her.

'Sugar! Sugar!' she repeated abstractedly to herself.

Ramón sat forward in his rocking-chair, holding his cup in his hand, his breasts rising in relief. And on his thighs the thin linen seemed to reveal him almost more than his own dark nakedness revealed him.

She understood why the cotton pantaloons were forbidden on the plaza. The living flesh seemed to emanate through them.

He was handsome, almost horribly handsome, with his black head poised as it were without weight, above his darkened, smooth neck. A pure sensuality, with a powerful purity of its own, hostile to her sort of purity. With the blue sash round his waist, pressing a fold in the flesh, and the thin linen seeming to gleam with the life of his hips and his thighs, he emanated a fascination almost like a narcotic, asserting his pure, fine sensuality against her. The strange, soft, still sureness of him, as if he sat secure within his own dark aura. And as if this dark aura of his militated against her presence, and against the presence of his wife. He emitted an effluence so powerful, that it seemed to hamper her consciousness, to bind down her limbs.

And he was utterly still and quiescent, without desire, soft and un-roused, within his own *ambiente*. Cipriano going the same, the pair of them so quiet and dark and heavy, like a great weight bearing the women down.

Kate knew now how Salome felt. She knew now how John the Baptist had been, with his terrible, aloof beauty, inaccessible, yet so potent.

'Ah!' she said to herself. 'Let me close my eyes to him, and open only my soul. Let me close my prying, *seeing* eyes, and sit in dark still-ness along with these two men. They have got more than I, they have a richness that I haven't got. They have got rid of that itching of the eye, and the desire that works through the eye. The itching, prurient, *knowing*, imagining eye, I am cursed with it, I am hampered up in it. It is my curse of curses, the curse of Eve. The curse of Eve is upon me, my eyes are like hooks, my knowledge is like a fish-hook through my gills, pulling me in spasmodic desire. Oh, who will free me from the grappling of my eyes, from the impurity of sharp sight! Daughter of Eve, of greedy vision, why don't these men save me from the sharpness of my own eyes!'

She rose and went to the edge of the terrace. Yellow as daffodils underneath, two birds emerged out of their own invisibility. In the little shingle bay, with a small breakwater, where the boat was pulled up and chained, two men were standing in the water, throwing out a big, fine round net, catching the little silvery fish called *charales*, which flicked out of the brownish water sometimes like splinters of glass.

'Ramón!' Kate heard Doña Carlota's voice. 'Won't you put something on?'

The wife had been able to bear it no more.

'Yes! Thank you for the tea,' said Ramón, rising.

Kate watched him go down the terrace, in his own peculiar silence, his sandals making a faint swish on the tiles.

'Oh, Señora Caterina!' came the voice of Carlota. 'Come and drink your tea. Come!'

Kate returned to the table, saying:

'It seems so wonderfully peaceful here.'

'Peaceful!' echoed Carlota. 'Ah, I do not find it peaceful. There is a horrible stillness, which makes me afraid.'

'Do you come out very often?' said Kate, to Cipriano.

'Yes. Fairly often. Once a week. Or twice,' he replied, looking at her with a secret consciousness which she could not understand, lurking in his black eyes.

These men wanted to take her *will* away from her, as if they wanted to deny her the light of day.

'I must be going home now,' she said. 'The sun will be setting.'

'*Ya va?*' said Cipriano, in his soft, velvety Indian voice, with a note of distant surprise and reproach. 'Will you go already?'

'Oh, no, Señora!' cried Carlota. 'Stay until to-morrow. Oh, yes, stay until to-morrow, with me.'

'They will expect us home,' she said, wavering.

'Ah, no! I can send a boy to say you will come to-morrow. Yes? You will stay? Ah, good, good!'

And she laid her hand caressively on Kate's arm, then rose to hurry away to the servants.

Cipriano had taken out his cigarette case. He offered it to Kate.

'Shall I take one?' she said. 'It is my vice.'

'Do take one,' he said. 'It isn't good, to be perfect.'

'It isn't, is it?' she laughed, puffing her cigarette.

'Now would you call it peace?' he asked with incomprehensible irony.

'Why?' she cried.

'Why do white people always want peace?' he asked.

'Surely peace is natural! Don't all people want it? Don't you?'

'Peace is only the rest after war,' he said. 'So it is not more natural than fighting: perhaps not so natural.'

'No, but there is another peace: the peace that passes all understanding. Don't you know that?'

'I don't think I do,' he said.

'What a pity!' she cried.

'Ah!' he said. 'You want to teach me! But to me it is different. Each man has two spirits in him. The one is like the early morning in the time of rain, very quiet, and sweet, moist, no? – with the mocking-bird singing, and birds flying about, very fresh. And the other is like the dry season, the steady, strong hot light of the day, which seems as if it will never change.'

'But you like the first better,' she cried.

'I don't know!' he replied. 'The other lasts longer.'

'I am sure you like the fresh morning better,' she said.

'I don't know! I don't know!' He smiled a crumpled sort of smile, and she could tell he really did *not* know. 'In the first time, you can feel the flowers on their stem, the stem very strong and full of sap, no? – and the flower opening on top like a face that has the perfume of desire. And a woman might be like that. – But this passes, and the sun begins to shine very strong, very hot, no? Then everything inside a man changes, goes dark, no? And the flowers crumple up, and the breast of a man becomes like a steel mirror. And he is all darkness inside, coiling and uncoiling like a snake. All the flowers withered up on shrunk stems, no? And then women don't exist for a man. They disappear like the flowers.'

'And then what does he want?' said Kate.

'I don't know. Perhaps he wants to be a very big man, and master all the people.'

'Then why doesn't he?' said Kate.

He lifted his shoulders.

'And you,' he said to her. 'You seem to me like that morning I told you about.'

'I am just forty years old,' she laughed shakily.

Again he lifted his shoulders.

'It doesn't matter,' he said. 'It is the same. Your body seems to me like the stem of the flower I told you about, and in your face it will always be morning, of the time of the rains.'

'Why do you say that to me?' she said, as an involuntary strange shudder shook her.

'Why not say it!' he replied. 'You are like the cool morning, very fresh. In Mexico, we are the end of the hot dry day.'

He watched her, with a strange lingering desire in his black eyes, and what seemed to her a curious, lurking sort of insolence. She dropped her head to hide from him, and rocked in her chair.

'I would like to marry you,' he said; 'if ever you will marry. I would like to marry you.'

'I don't think I shall *ever* marry again,' she flashed, her bosom heaving like suffocation, and a dark flush suffusing over her face, against her will.

'Who knows!' said he.

Ramón was coming down the terrace, his fine white serape folded over his naked shoulder, with its blue-and-dark pattern at the borders, and its long scarlet fringe dangling and swaying as he walked. He leaned against one of the pillars of the terrace, and looked down at Kate and Cipriano. Cipriano glanced up with that peculiar glance of primitive intimacy.

'I told the Señora Caterina,' he said, 'if ever she wanted to marry a man, she should marry me.'

'It is plain talk,' said Ramón, glancing at Cipriano with the same intimacy, and smiling.

Then he looked at Kate, with a slow smile in his brown eyes, and a shadow of curious knowledge on his face. He folded his arms over his breast, as the natives do when it is cold and they are protecting themselves; and the cream-brown flesh, like opium, lifted the bosses of his breasts, full and smooth.

'Don Cipriano says that white people always want peace,' she said, looking up at Ramón with haunted eyes. 'Don't you consider yourselves white people?' she asked, with a slight, deliberate impertinence.

'No whiter than we are,' smiled Ramón. 'Not lily-white, at least.'

'And don't you want peace?' she asked.

'I? I shouldn't think of it. The meek have inherited the earth, according to prophecy. But who am I, that I should envy them their peace! No, Señora. Do I look like a gospel of peace? – or a gospel of war either? Life doesn't split down that division, for me.'

'I don't know what you want,' said she, looking up at him with haunted eyes.

'We only half know ourselves,' he replied, smiling with changeful eyes. 'Perhaps not so much as half.'

There was a certain vulnerable kindliness about him, which made her wonder, startled, if she had ever realised what real fatherliness meant. The mystery, the nobility, the inaccessibility, and the vulnerable compassion of man in his separate fatherhood.

'You don't like brown-skinned people?' he asked her gently.

'I think it is beautiful to look at,' she said. 'But' – with a faint shudder – 'I am glad I am white.'

'You feel there could be no contact?' he said, simply.

'Yes!' she said. 'I mean that.'

'It is as you feel,' he said.

And as he said it, she knew he was more beautiful to her than any blond white man, and that, in a remote, far-off way, the contact with him was more precious than any contact she had known.

But then, though he cast over her a certain shadow, he would never encroach on her, he would never seek any close contact. It was the incompleteness in Cipriano that sought her out, and seemed to trespass on her.

Hearing Ramón's voice, Carlota appeared uneasily in a doorway. Hearing him speak English, she disappeared again, on a gust of anger. But after a little while, she came once more, with a little vase containing the creamy-coloured, thick flowers that are coloured like freesias, and that smell very sweet.

'Oh, how nice!' said Kate. 'They are temple flowers! In Ceylon the natives tiptoe into the little temples and lay one flower on the table at the foot of the big Buddha statues. And the tables of offering are all covered with these flowers, all put so neatly. The natives have that delicate oriental way of putting things down.'

'Ah!' said Carlota, setting the vase on the table. 'I did not bring them for any gods, especially strange ones. I brought them for you, Señora. They smell so sweet.'

'Don't they!' said Kate.

The two men went away, Ramón laughing.

'Ah, Señora!' said Carlota, sitting down tense at the table. 'Could you follow Ramón? Could *you* give up the Blessed Virgin? – I could sooner die!'

'Ha!' said Kate, with a little weariness. 'Surely we don't want any *more* gods.'

'More gods, Señora!' said Doña Carlota, shocked. 'But how is it possible! – Don Ramón is in mortal sin.'

Kate was silent.

'And he wants to lead more and more people into the same,' continued Carlota. 'It is the sin of pride. Men wise in their own conceit! – The cardinal sin of men. Ah, I have told him. – And I am so glad, Señora, that you feel as I feel. I am so afraid of American women, women like that. They wish to have men's minds, so they accept all the follies and wickedness of men. – You are Catholic, Señora?'

'I was educated in a convent,' said Kate.

'Ah, of course! Of course! – Ah, Señora, as if a woman who had ever known the Blessed Virgin could ever part from her again. Ah, Señora, what woman would have the heart to put Christ back on the Cross, to crucify him twice! But men, men! This Quetzalcoatl business! What buffoonery, Señora; if it were not horrible sin! And two clever, well-educated men! Wise in their own conceit!'

'Men usually are,' said Kate.

It was sunset, with a big level cloud like fur overhead, only the sides of the horizon fairly clear. The sun was not visible. It had gone down in a thick, rose-red fume behind the wavy ridge of the mountains. Now the hills stood up bluish, all the air was a salmon-red flush, the fawn water had pinkish ripples. Boys and men, bathing a little way along the shore, were the colour of deep flame.

Kate and Carlota had climbed up to the azotea, the flat roof, from the stone stairway at the end of the terrace. They could see the world: the hacienda with its courtyard like a fortress, the road between deep trees, the black mud huts near the broken highroad, and little naked fires already twinkling outside the doors. All the air was pinkish, melting to a lavender blue, and the willows on the shore, in the pink light, were apple-green and glowing. The hills behind rose abruptly, like mounds, dry and pinky. Away in the distance, down the lake, the two white obelisk towers of Sayula glinted among the trees, and villas peeped out. Boats were creeping into the shadow, from the outer brightness of the lake.

And in one of these boats was Juana, being rowed, disconsolate, home.

CHAPTER XIII

The First Rain

RAMÓN and Cipriano were out by the lake. Cipriano also had changed into the white clothes and sandals, and he looked better than when in uniform.

'I had a talk with Montes when he came to Guadalajara,' Cipriano said to Ramón. Montes was the President of the Republic.

'And what did he say?'

'He is careful. But he doesn't like his colleagues. I think he feels lonely. I think he would like to know you better.'

'Why?'

'Perhaps that you could give him your moral support. Perhaps that you might be Secretary, and President when Montes' term is up.'

'I like Montes,' said Ramón. 'He is sincere and passionate. Did you like him?'

'Yes!' said Cipriano. 'More or less. He is suspicious, and jealous for fear anyone else might want to share in his power. He has the cravings of a dictator. He wanted to find out if I would stick to him.'

'You let him know you would?'

'I told him that all I cared for was for you and for Mexico.'

'What did he say?'

'Well, he is no fool. He said: "Don Ramón sees the world with different eyes from mine. Who knows which of us is right. I want to save my country from poverty and unenlightenment, he wants to save its soul. I say, a hungry and ignorant man has no place for a soul. An empty belly grinds upon itself, so does an empty mind, and the soul doesn't exist. Don Ramón says, if a man has no soul, it doesn't matter whether he is hungry or ignorant. Well, he can go his way, and I mine. We shall never hinder one another, I believe. I give you my word I won't have him interfered with. He sweeps the patio and I sweep the street."'

'Sensible!' said Ramón. 'And honest in his convictions.'

'Why should you not be Secretary in a few months' time? And follow to the Presidency?' said Cipriano.

'You know I don't want that. I must stand in another world, and act in another world. – Politics must go their own way, and society must do as it will. Leave me alone, Cipriano. I know you want me to be another Porfirio Diaz, or something like that. But for me that would be failure pure and simple.'

Cipriano was watching Ramón with black, guarded eyes, in which was an element of love, and of fear, and of trust, but also incomprehension, and the suspicion that goes with incomprehension.

'I don't understand, myself, *what* you want,' he muttered.

'Yes, yes, you do. Politics and all this *social* religion that Montes has got is like washing the outside of the egg, to make it look clean. But I, myself, I want to get inside the egg, right to the middle, to start it growing into a new bird. Ay! Cipriano! Mexico is like an old, old egg that the bird of Time laid long ago; and she has been sitting on it for centuries, till it looks foul in the nest of the world. But still, Cipriano, it is a good egg. It is not addled. Only the spark of fire has never gone into the middle of it, to start it. – Montes wants to clean the nest and wash the egg. But meanwhile, the egg will go cold and die. The more you save these people from poverty and ignorance, the quicker they will die: like a dirty egg that you take from under the hen-eagle, to wash it. While you wash the egg, it chills and dies. Poor old Montes, all his ideas are American and European. And the old Dove of Europe will never hatch the egg of dark-skinned America. The United States can't die, because it isn't alive. It is a nestful of china eggs, made of pot. So they can be kept clean. – But here, Cipriano, here, let us hatch the chick before we start cleaning up the nest.'

Cipriano hung his head. He was always testing Ramón, to see if he could change him. When he found he couldn't, then he submitted, and new little fires of joy sprang up in him. But meanwhile, he had to try, and try again.

'It is no good, trying to mix the two things. At this stage of affairs, at least, they won't mix. We have to shut our eyes and sink down, sink away from the surface, away, like shadows, down to the bottom. Like the pearl divers. But you keep bobbing up like a cork.'

Cipriano smiled subtly. He knew well enough.

'We've got to open the oyster of the cosmos, and get our manhood out of it. Till we've got the pearl, we are only gnats on the surface of the ocean,' said Ramón.

'My manhood is like a devil inside me,' said Cipriano.

'It's very true,' said Ramón. 'That's because the old oyster has him shut up, like a black pearl. You must let him walk out.'

'Ramón,' said Cipriano, 'wouldn't it be good to be a serpent, and be big enough to wrap one's folds round the globe of the world, and crush it like that egg?'

Ramón looked at him and laughed.

'I believe we could do that,' said Cipriano, a slow smile curling round his mouth. 'And wouldn't it be good?'

Ramón shook his head, laughing.

'There would be *one* good moment, at least,' he said.

'Who asks for more!' said Cipriano.

A spark flashed out of Ramón's eyes too. Then he checked himself, and gathered himself together.

'What would be the good!' he said heavily. 'If the egg was crushed, and we remained, what could we do but go howling down the empty passages of darkness. What's the good, Cipriano?'

Ramón got up and walked away. The sun had set, the night was falling. And in his soul the great, writhing anger was alive again. Carlota provoked it into life: the two women seemed to breathe life into the black monster of his inward rage, till it began to lash again. And Cipriano stirred it up till it howled with desire.

'My manhood is like a demon howling inside me,' said Ramón to himself, in Cipriano's words.

And he admitted the justice of the howling, his manhood being pent up, humiliated, goaded with insult inside him. And rage came over him, against Carlota, against Cipriano, against his own people, against all mankind, till he was filled with rage like the devil.

His people would betray him, he knew that. Cipriano would betray him. Given one little vulnerable chink, they would pierce him. They would leap at the place out of nowhere, like a tarantula, and bite in the poison.

While ever there was one little vulnerable chink. And what man can be invulnerable?

He went upstairs by the outer stairway, through the iron door at the side of the house, under the heavy trees, up to his room, and sat on his bed. The night was hot, heavy, and ominously still.

'The waters are coming,' he heard a servant say. He shut the doors of his room till it was black dark inside. Then he threw aside his clothing, saying: I put off the world with my clothes. And standing nude and invisible in the centre of his room he thrust his clenched fist upwards, with all his might, feeling he would break the walls of his chest. And his left hand hung loose, the fingers softly curving downwards.

And tense like the gush of a soundless fountain, he thrust up and reached down in the invisible dark, convulsed with passion. Till the black waves began to wash over his consciousness, over his mind, waves of darkness broke over his memory, over his being, like an incoming tide, till at last it was full tide, and he trembled, and fell to rest. Invisible in the darkness, he stood soft and relaxed, staring with wide eyes at the dark, and feeling the dark fecundity of the inner tide washing over his heart, over his belly, his mind dissolved away in the greater, dark mind, which is undisturbed by thoughts.

He covered his face with his hands, and stood still, in pure unconsciousness, neither hearing nor feeling nor knowing, like a dark seaweed deep in the sea. With no Time and no World, in the deeps that are timeless and worldless.

Then when his heart and his belly were restored, his mind began to flicker again softly, like a soft flame flowing without departing.

So he wiped his face with his hands, and put his serape over his head, and, silent inside an aura of pain, he went out and took the drum, carrying it downstairs.

Martin, the man who loved him, was hovering in the zaguán.

'*Ya*, Patrón?' he said.

'*Ya!*' said Ramón.

The man ran indoors, where a lamp was burning in the big, dark kitchen, and ran out again with an armful of the woven straw mats.

'Where, *Patrón*?' he said.

Ramón hesitated in the centre of the courtyard, and looked at the sky.

'*Viene el agua?*' he said.

'*Creo que sí, Patrón.*'[1]

They went to the shed where the bananas had been packed and carried away on donkeys. There the man threw down the petates. Ramón
arranged them. Guisleno ran with canes. He was going to make lights,
the simplest possible. Three pieces of thick cane, tied at the neck with
a cord, stood up three-legged, waist high. In the three-pronged fork
at the top he laid a piece of flat, slightly hollow lava stone. Then he
came running from the house with a bit of burning ocote wood. Three
or four bits of ocote, each bit no bigger than a long finger, flickered
and rose in quick flames from the stone, and the courtyard danced with
shadow.

Ramón took off his serape, folded it, and sat upon it. Guisleno lit
another tripod-torch. Ramón sat with his back to the wall, the fire-light
dancing on his dark brows, that were sunk in a sort of frown. His breast
shone like gold in the flame. He took the drum and sounded the summons, slow, monotonous, rather sad. In a moment two or three men
came running. The drummer came, Ramón stood up and handed him
the drum. He ran with it to the great outer doorway, and out into the
dark lane, and there sounded the summons, quick, sharp.

Ramón put on his serape, whose scarlet fringe touched his knees,
and stood motionless, with ruffled hair. Round his shoulders went the
woven snake, and his head was through the middle of the blue, woven
bird.

Cipriano came from the house. He was wearing a serape all
scarlet and dark brown, a great scarlet sun at the centre, deep scarlet
zigzags at the borders, and dark brown fringe at his knees. He came
and stood at Ramón's side, glancing up into Ramón's face. But the
other man's brows were low, his eyes were fixed in the darkness of
the sheds away across the courtyard. He was looking into the heart of
the world; because the faces of men, and the hearts of men are helpless
quicksands. Only in the heart of the cosmos man can look for strength.
And if he can keep his soul in touch with the heart of the world, then
from the heart of the world new blood will beat in strength and stillness into him, fulfilling his manhood.

Cipriano turned his black eyes to the courtyard. His soldiers had
drawn near, in a little group. Three or four men were standing in
dark serapes, round the fire. Cipriano stood brilliant like a cardinal
bird, next to Ramón. Even his sandals were bright, sealing-wax red,

and his loose linen trousers were bound at the ankles with red and black bands. His face looked very dark and ruddy in the firelight, his little black tuft of a beard hung odd and devilish, his eyes were glittering sardonically. But he caught Ramón's hand in his small hand, and stood holding it.

The peons were coming through the entrance-way, balancing their big hats. Women were hurrying barefoot, swishing their full skirts, carrying babies inside the dark wrap of their rebozos, children running after. They all clustered towards the flame-light, like wild animals gazing in at the circle of men in dark serapes, Ramón, magnificent in his white and blue and shadow, poising his beautiful head, Cipriano at his side like a glittering cardinal bird.

Carlota and Kate emerged from the inner doorway of the house. But there Carlota remained, wrapped in a black silk shawl, seated on a wooden bench where the soldiers usually sat, looking across at the ruddy flare of light, the circle of dark men, the tall beauty of her husband, the poppy-petal glitter of red, of Cipriano, the group of little, dust-coloured soldiers, and the solid throng of peons and women and children, standing gazing like animals. While through the gate men still came hurrying, and from outside, the drum sounded, and a high voice sang again and again:

> Someone will enter between the gates,
>   Now, at this moment, Ay!
> See the light on the man that waits.
>   Shall you? Shall I?
>
> Someone will come to the place of fire,
>   Now, at this moment, Ay!
> And hark to the words of their heart's desire.
>   Shall you? Shall I?
>
> Someone will knock when the door is shut,
>   Ay! in a moment, Ay!
> Hear a voice saying: I know you not!
>   Shall you? Shall I?[2]

There was a queer, wild yell each time on the *Ay!* and like a bugle refrain: *Shall you? Shall I?* It made Carlota shiver.

Kate, wrapping her yellow shawl round her, walked slowly towards the group.

The drum outside gave a rapid shudder, and was finished. The drummer came in, the great doors were shut and barred, the drummer took his place in the ring of standing men. A dead silence supervened.

Ramón continued to gaze from under lowered brows, into space. Then in a quiet, inward voice, he said:

'As I take off this cover, I put away the day that is gone from upon me.'

He took off his serape, and stood with it over his arm. All the men in the circle did the same, till they stood with naked breasts and shoulders, Cipriano very dark and strong-looking, in his smallness, beside Ramón.

'I put away the day that is gone,' Ramón continued, in the same still, inward voice, 'and stand with my heart uncovered in the night of the gods.'

Then he looked down at the ground.

'Serpent of the earth,' he said; 'snake that lies in the fire at the heart of the world, come! Come! Snake of the fire of the heart of the world, coil like gold round my ankles, and rise like life around my knee, and lay your head against my thigh. Come, put your head in my hand, cradle your head in my fingers, snake of the deeps. Kiss my feet and my ankles with your mouth of gold, kiss my knees and my inner thigh, snake branded with flame and shadow, come! and rest your head in my finger-basket! So!'

The voice was soft and hypnotic. It died upon a stillness. And it seemed as if really a mysterious presence had entered unseen from the underworld. It seemed to the peons as if really they saw a snake of brilliant gold and living blackness softly coiled around Ramón's ankle and knee, and resting its head in his fingers, licking his palm with forked tongue.

He looked out at the big, dilated, glittering eyes of his people, and his own eyes were wide and uncanny.

'I tell you,' he said, 'and I tell you truly. At the heart of this earth sleeps a great serpent, in the midst of fire. Those that go down in mines feel the heat and the sweat of him, they feel him move. It is the living fire of the earth, for the earth is alive. The snake of the world is huge, and the rocks are his scales, trees grow between them. I tell you the earth you dig is alive as a snake that sleeps. So vast a serpent you walk on, this lake lies between his folds as a drop of rain in the folds of a sleeping rattlesnake. Yet he none the less lives. The earth is alive.

'And if he died, we should all perish. Only his living keeps the soil sweet, that grows you maize. From the roots of his scales we dig silver and gold, and the trees have root in him, as the hair of my face has root in my lips.

'The earth is alive. But he is very big, and we are very small, smaller than dust. But he is very big in his life, and sometimes he is angry. *These people, smaller than dust*, he says, *they stamp on me and say I am dead. Even to their asses they speak, and shout Harreh! Burro! But to me they speak no word. Therefore I will turn against them, like a woman who lies angry with her man in bed, and eats away his spirit with her anger, turning her back to him.*

'That is what the earth says to us. He sends sorrow into our feet, and depression into our loins.

'Because as an angry woman in the house can make a man heavy, taking his life from him, so the earth can make us heavy, make our souls cold, and our life dreary in our feet.

'Speak then to the snake of the heart of the world, put oil on your fingers and lower your fingers for him to taste the oil of the earth, and let him send life into your feet and ankles and knees, like sap in the young maize pressing against the joint and making the milk of the maize bud among its hair.

'From the heart of the earth man feels his manhood rise up in him, like the maize that is proud, turning its green leaves outwards. Be proud like the maize, and let your roots go deep, deep, for the rains are here, and it is time for us to be growing in Mexico.'

Ramón ceased speaking, the drum softly pulsed. All the men of the ring were looking down at the earth and softly letting their left hands hang.

Carlota, who had not been able to hear, drifted up to Kate's side, spell-bound by her husband. Kate unconsciously glanced down at the earth, and secretly let her fingers hang softly against her dress. But then she was afraid of what might happen to her, and she caught her hand up into her shawl.

Suddenly the drum began to give a very strong note, followed by a weak: a strange, exciting thud.

Everybody looked up. Ramón had flung his right arm tense into the air, and was looking up at the black dark sky. The men of the ring did the same, and the naked arms were thrust aloft like so many rockets.

'Up! Up! Up!' said a wild voice.

'Up! Up!' cried the men of the ring, in a wild chorus.

And involuntarily the men in the crowd twitched, then shot their arms upwards, turning their faces to the dark heavens. Even some of the women boldly thrust up their naked arms, and relief entered their hearts as they did so.

But Kate would not lift her arm.

There was dead silence, even the drum was silent. Then the voice of Ramón was heard, speaking upwards to the black sky:

'Your big wings are dark, Bird, you are flying low to-night. You are flying low over Mexico, we shall soon feel the fan of your wings on our face.

'Ay, Bird! You fly about where you will. You fly past the stars, and you perch on the sun. You fly out of sight, and are gone beyond the white river of the sky. But you come back like the ducks of the north, looking for water and winter.

'You sit in the middle of the sun, and preen your feathers. You crouch in the river of stars, and make the star-dust rise around you. You fly away into the deepest hollow place of the sky, whence there seems no return.

'You come back to us, and hover overhead, and we feel your wings fanning our faces –'

Even as he spoke the wind rose, in sudden gusts, and a door could be heard slamming in the house, with a shivering of glass, and the trees gave off a tearing sound.

'Come then, Bird of the great sky!' Ramón called wildly. 'Come! Oh Bird, settle a moment on my wrist, over my head, and give me power of the sky, and wisdom. Oh Bird! Bird of all the wide heavens, even if you drum your feathers in thunder, and drop the white snake of fire from your beak back to the earth again, where he can run in, deep down the rocks again, home: even if you come as the Thunderer, come! Settle on my wrist a moment, with the clutch of the power of thunder, and arch your wings over my head, like a shadow of clouds; and bend your breast to my brow, and bless me with the sun. Bird, roaming Bird of the Beyond, with thunder in your pinions and the snake of lightning in your beak, with the blue heaven in the socket of your wings and cloud in the arch of your neck, with sun in the burnt feathers of your breast and power in your feet, with terrible wisdom in your flight, swoop to me a moment, swoop!'

Sudden gusts of wind tore at the little fires of flame, till they could be heard to rustle, and the lake began to speak in a vast hollow noise, beyond the tearing of trees. Distant lightning was beating far off, over the black hills.

Ramón dropped his arm, which had been bent over his head. The drum began to beat. Then he said:

'Sit down a moment, before the Bird shakes water out of his wings. It will come soon. Sit down.'

There was a stir. Men put their serapes over their faces, women clutched their rebozos tighter, and all sat down on the ground. Only Kate and Carlota remained standing, on the outer edge. Gusts of wind tore at the flames, the men put their hats on the ground in front of them.

'The earth is alive, and the sky is alive,' said Ramón in his natural voice, 'and between them, we live. Earth has kissed my knees, and put strength in my belly. Sky has perched on my wrist, and sent power into my breast.

'But as in the morning the Morning-star stands between earth and sky, a star can rise in us, and stand between the heart and the loins.

'That is the manhood of man, and for woman, her womanhood.

'You are not yet men. And women, you are not yet women.

'You run about and toss about and die, and still you have not found the star of your manhood rise within you, the stars of your womanhood shine out serene between your breasts, women.

'I tell you, for him that wishes it, the star of his manhood shall rise within him, and he shall be proud, and perfect even as the Morning-star is perfect.

'And the star of a woman's womanhood can rise at last, from between the heavy rim of the earth and the lost grey void of the sky.

'But how? How shall we do it? How shall it be?

'How shall we men become Men of the Morning Star? And the women the Dawn-Star Women?

'Lower your fingers to the caress of the Snake of the earth.

'Lift your wrist for a perch to the far-lying Bird.

'Have the courage of both, the courage of lightning and the earth-quake.

'And wisdom of both, the wisdom of the snake and the eagle.

'And the peace of both, the peace of the serpent and the sun.

'And the power of both, the power of the innermost earth and the outermost heaven.

'But on your brow, Men! the undimmed Morning Star, that neither day nor night, nor earth nor sky can swallow and put out.

'And between your breasts, Women! the Dawn-Star, that cannot be dimmed.

'And your home at last is the Morning Star. Neither heaven nor earth shall swallow you up at the last, but you shall pass into the place beyond both, into the bright star that is lonely yet feels itself never alone.

'The Morning Star is sending you a messenger, a god who died in Mexico. But he slept his sleep, and the invisible Ones washed his body with water of resurrection. So he has risen, and pushed the stone from the mouth of the tomb, and has stretched himself. And now he is striding across the horizons even quicker than the great stone from the tomb is tumbling back to the earth, to crush those that rolled it up.

'The Son of the Star is coming back to the Sons of Men, with big, bright strides.

'Prepare to receive him. And wash yourselves, and put oil on your hands and your feet, on your mouth and eyes and ears and nostrils, on your breast and navel and on the secret places of your body, that nothing of the dead days, no dust of skeletons and evil things may pass into you and make you unclean.

'Do not look with the eyes of yesterday, nor like yesterday listen, nor breathe, nor smell, nor taste, nor swallow food and drink. Do not kiss with the mouths of yesterday, nor touch with the hands, nor walk with yesterday's feet. And let your navel know nothing of yesterday, and go into your women with a new body, enter the new body in her.

'For yesterday's body is dead, and carrion, the xopilote[3] is hovering above it.

'Put yesterday's body from off you, and have a new body. Even as your God who is coming. Quetzalcoatl is coming with a new body, like a star, from the shadows of death.

'Yes, even as you sit upon the earth this moment, with the round of your body touching the round of the earth, say: Earth! Earth! you are alive as the globes of my body are alive. Breathe the kiss of the inner earth upon me, even as I sit upon you.

'And so, it is said. The earth is stirring beneath you, the sky is rushing its wings above. Go home to your homes, in front of the waters that will fall and cut you off forever from your yesterdays.

'Go home, and hope to be Men of the Morning Star, Women of the Star of Dawn.

'You are not yet men and women —'

He rose up and waved to the people to be gone. And in a moment they were on their feet, scurrying and hastening with the quiet Mexican hurry, that seems to run low down upon the surface of the earth.

The black wind was all loose in the sky, tearing with the thin shriek of torn fabrics, in the mango trees. Men held their big hats on their heads and ran with bent knees, their serapes blowing. Women clutched their rebozos tighter and ran barefoot to the zaguán.

The big doors were open, a soldier stood with a gun across his back, holding a hurricane lamp. And the people fled like ghosts through the doors, and away up the black lane like bits of paper veering away into nothingness, blown out of their line of flight. In a moment, they had all silently gone.

Martin barred the great doors. The soldier put down his lamp on the wooden bench, and he and his comrades sat huddled in their dark shawls, in a little bunch like toadstools in the dark cavern of the zaguán. Already one had curled himself up on the wooden bench, wrapped like a snail in his blanket, head disappeared.

'The water is coming!' cried the servants excitedly, as Kate went upstairs with Doña Carlota.

The lake was quite black, like a great pit. The wind suddenly blew with violence, with a strange ripping sound in the mango trees, as if some membrane in the air were being ripped. The white-flowered oleanders in the garden below leaned over quite flat, their white flowers ghostly, going right down to the earth, in the pale beam of the lamp — like a street lamp — that shone on the wall at the front entrance. A young palm-tree bent and spread its leaves on the ground. Some invisible juggernaut car rolling in the dark over the outside world.

Away across the lake, south-west, lightning blazed and ran down the sky like some portentous writing. And soft, velvety thunder broke inwardly, strangely.

'It frightens me!' cried Doña Carlota, putting her hand over her eyes and hastening into a far corner of the bare salon.

Cipriano and Kate stood on the terrace, watching the coloured flowers in the pots shake and fly to bits, disappearing up into the void of darkness. Kate clutched her shawl. But the wind suddenly got under Cipriano's blanket, and lifted it straight up in the air, then dropped it in a scarlet flare over his head. Kate watched his deep, strong Indian chest lift as his arms quickly fought to free his head. How dark he was, and how primitively physical, beautiful, and deep-breasted, with soft, full flesh! But all, as it were, for himself. Nothing that came forth from him to meet with one outside. All oblivious of the outside, all for himself.

'Ah! the water!' he cried, holding down his serape.

The first great drops were flying darkly at the flowers, like arrows. Kate stood back into the doorway of the salon. A pure blaze of lightning slipped three-fold above the black hills, seemed to stand a moment, then slip back into the dark.

Down came the rain with a smash, as if some great vessel had broken. With it, came a waft of icy air. And all the time, first in one part of the sky, then in another, in quick succession the blue lightning, very blue, broke out of heaven and lit up the air for a blue, breathless moment, looming trees and ghost of a garden, then was gone, while thunder dropped and exploded continually.

Kate watched the dropping masses of water in wonder. Already, in the blue moments of lightning, she saw the garden below a pond, the walks were rushing rivers. It was cold. She turned indoors.

A servant was going round the rooms with a lantern, to look if scorpions were coming out. He found one scuttling across the floor of Kate's room, and one fallen from the ceiling beams on to Carlota's bed.

They sat in the salon in rocking chairs, Carlota and Kate, and rocked, smelling the good wetness, breathing the good, chilled air. Kate had already forgotten what really chill air was like. She wrapped her shawl tighter round her.

'Ah, yes, you feel cold! You must take care in the nights, now. Sometimes in the rainy season the nights are very cold. You must be ready with an extra blanket. And the servants, poor things, they just lie and shudder, and they get up in the morning like corpses. – But the sun soon warms them again, and they seem to think they must bear what comes. So they complain sometimes, but still they don't provide.'

The wind had gone, suddenly. Kate was uneasy, uneasy, with the smell of water, almost of ice, in her nostrils, and her blood still hot and dark. She got up and went again to the terrace. Cipriano was still standing there, motionless and inscrutable, like a monument, in his red and dark serape.

The rain was abating. Down below in the garden, two bare-footed women-servants were running through the water, in the faint light of the zaguán lamp, running across the garden and putting ollas and square gasoline cans under the arching spouts of water that seethed down from the roof, then darting away while they filled, then struggling in with the frothy vessel. It would save making trips to the lake, for water.

'What do you think of us?' Cipriano said to her.

'It is strange to me,' she replied, wondering and a little awed by the night.

'Good, no?' he said, in an exultant tone.

'A little scaring,' she replied, with a slight laugh.

'When you are used to it,' he said, 'it seems natural, no? It seems natural so – as it is. And when you go to a country like England, where all is so safe and ready-made, then you miss it. You keep saying to yourself: "What am I missing? What is it that is not here?"'

He seemed to be gloating in his native darkness. It was curious, that though he spoke such good English, it seemed always foreign to her, more foreign than Doña Carlota's Spanish.

'I can't understand that people want to have everything, all life, no? – so safe and ready-made as in England and America. It is good to be *awake*. On the *qui vive*,[4] no?'

'Perhaps,' she said.

'So I like it,' he said, 'when Ramón tells the people the earth is alive, and the sky has a big bird in it, that you don't see. I think it is true. Certainly! And it is good to know it, because then one is on the *qui vive*, no?'

'But it's tiring to be always on the *qui vive*,' she said.

'Why? Why tiring? No, I think, on the contrary, it is refreshing. –

Ah, you should marry, and live in Mexico. At last, I am sure, you would like it. You would keep waking up more and more to it.'

'Or else going more and more deadened,' she said. 'That is how most foreigners go, it seems to me.'

'Why deadened?' he said to her. 'I don't understand. Why deadened? Here you have a country where night is night, and rain comes down and you know it. And you have a people with whom you must be on the *qui vive* all the time, all the time. And that is very good, no? You don't go sleepy. Like a pear! Don't you say a pear goes sleepy, no? – cuando se echa a perder?'⁵

'Yes!' she said.

'And here you have also Ramón. How does Ramón seem to you?'

'I don't know. I don't want to say anything. But I do think he is almost too much: too far. – And I *don't* think he is Mexican.'

'Why not? Why not Mexican? He is Mexican.'

'Not as you are.'

'How not as I am? He is Mexican.'

'He seems to me to belong to the old, old Europe,' she said.

'And he seems to me to belong to the old, old Mexico – and also to the new,' he added quickly.

'But you don't believe in him.'

'How?'

'You – yourself. You don't believe in him. You think it is like everything else, a sort of game. Everything is a sort of game, a put-up job, to you Mexicans. You don't *really* believe, in anything.'

'How not believe? I not believe in Ramón? – Well, perhaps not, in that way of kneeling before him and spreading out my arms and shedding tears on his feet. But I – I believe in him, too. Not in your way, but in mine. I tell you why. Because he has the power to compel me. If he hadn't the power to *compel* me, how should I believe?'

'It is a queer sort of belief that is compelled,' she said.

'How else should one believe, except by being compelled? I like Ramón for that, that he can compel me. When I grew up, and my god-father could not compel me to believe, I was very unhappy. It made me very unhappy. – But Ramón *compels* me, and that is very good. It makes me very happy, when I know I can't escape. It would make you happy too.'

'To know I could not escape from Don Ramón?' she said ironically.

'Yes, that also. And to know you could not escape from Mexico. And even from such a man as me.'

She paused in the dark before she answered, sardonically:

'I don't think it would make me happy to feel I couldn't escape from Mexico. No, I feel, unless I was sure I could get out any day, I couldn't bear to be here.'

In her mind she thought: And perhaps Ramón is the only one I couldn't quite escape from, because he really touches me somewhere inside. But from you, you little Cipriano, I should have no need even to escape, because I could not be caught by you.

'Ah!' he said quickly. 'You think so. But then you don't know. You can only think with American thoughts. It is natural. From your education, you have only American thoughts, U.S.A. thoughts, to think with. Nearly all women are like that: even Mexican women of the Spanish-Mexican class. They are all thinking nothing but U.S.A. thoughts, because those are the ones that go with the way they dress their hair. And so it is with you. You think like a modern woman, because you belong to the Anglo-Saxon or Teutonic world, and dress your hair in a certain way, and have money, and are altogether free. – But you only think like this because you have had these thoughts put in your head, just as in Mexico you spend centavos and pesos, because that is the Mexican money you have put in your pocket. It's what they give you at the bank. – So when you say you are free, you are *not* free. You are compelled all the time to be thinking U.S.A. thoughts – *compelled*, I must say. You have not as much choice as a slave. As the peons must eat tortillas, tortillas, tortillas, because there is nothing else, you must think these U.S.A. thoughts, about being a woman and being free. Every day you must eat those tortillas, tortillas. – Till you don't know how you would like something else.'

'What else should I like?' she said, with a grimace at the darkness.

'Other thoughts, other feelings. – You are afraid of such a man as me, because you think I should not treat you *à l'américaine*. You are quite right. I should not treat you as an American woman must be treated. Why should I? I don't wish to. It doesn't seem good to me.'

'You would treat a woman like a real old Mexican, would you? Keep her ignorant, and shut her up?' said Kate sarcastically.

'I could not keep her ignorant if she did not start ignorant. But what more I had to teach her wouldn't be in the American style of teaching.'

'What then?'

'Quién sabe! Ça reste à voir.'

'Et continuera à y rester,'[6] said Kate, laughing.

CHAPTER XIV

Home to Sayula

THE morning came perfectly blue, with a freshness in the air and a blue luminousness over the trees and the distant mountains, and birds so bright, absolutely like new-opened buds sparking in the air.

Cipriano was returning to Guadalajara in the automobile, and Carlota was going with him. Kate would be rowed home on the lake.

To Ramón, Carlota was still, at times, a torture. She seemed to have the power still to lacerate him, inside his bowels. Not in his mind or spirit, but in his old emotional, passional self: right in the middle of his belly, to tear him and make him feel he bled inwardly.

Because he had loved her, he had cared for her: for the affectionate, passionate, whimsical, sometimes elfish creature she had been. He had made much of her, and spoiled her, for many years.

But all the while, gradually, his nature was changing inside him. Not that he ceased to care for her, or wanted other women. That she could have understood. But inside him was a slow, blind imperative, urging him to cast his emotional and spiritual and mental self into the slow furnace, and smelt them into a new, whole being.

But he had Carlota to reckon with. She loved him, and that, to her, was the outstanding factor. She loved him, emotionally. And spiritually, she loved mankind. And mentally, she was sure she was quite right.

Yet as time went on, he had to change. He had to cast that emotional self, which she loved, into the furnace, to be smelted down to another self.

And she felt she was robbed, cheated. Why couldn't he go on being gentle, good, and loving, and trying to make the whole world more gentle, good, and loving?

He couldn't, because it was borne in upon him that the world had gone as far as it could go in the good, gentle, and loving direction, and anything further in that line meant perversity. So the time had come for the slow, great change to something else – what, he didn't know.

The emotion of love, and the greater emotion of liberty for mankind seemed to go hard and congeal upon him, like the shell on a chrysalis. It was the old caterpillar stage of Christianity evolving into something else.

But Carlota felt this was all she had, this emotion of love, for her husband, her children, for her people, for the animals and birds and trees of the world. It was her all, her Christ, and her Blessed Virgin. How could she let it go?

So she continued to love him, and to love the world, steadily, pathetically, obstinately and devilishly. She prayed for him, and she engaged in works of charity.

But her love had turned from being the spontaneous flow, subject to the unforeseen comings and goings of the Holy Ghost, and had turned into will. She loved now with her *will*: as the white world now tends to do. She became filled with charity: that cruel kindness.

Her winsomeness and her elfishness departed from her, she began to wither, she grew tense. And she blamed him, and prayed for him. Even as the spontaneous mystery died in her, the will hardened, till she was nothing but a will: a lost will.

She soon succeeded in drawing the life of her young boys all to herself, with her pathos and her subtle will. Ramón was too proud and angry to fight for them. They were her children. Let her have them.

They were the children of his old body. His new body had no children: would probably never have any.

'But remember,' he said to her, with southern logic, 'you do not love, save with your will. I don't like the love you have for your god: it is an assertion of your own will. I don't like the love you have for me: it is the same. I don't like the love you have for your children. If ever I see in them a spark of desire to be saved from it, I shall do my best to save them. Meanwhile have your love, have your will. But you know I dislike it. I dislike your insistence. I dislike your monopoly of one feeling, I dislike your charity works. I disapprove of the whole trend of your life. You are weakening and vitiating the boys. You do *not* love them, you are only putting your love-will over them. One day they will turn and hate you for it. Remember I have said this to you.'

Doña Carlota had trembled in every fibre of her body, under the shock of this. But she went away to the chapel of the Annunciation Convent, and prayed. And, praying for his soul, she seemed to gain a victory over him, in the odour of sanctity. She came home in frail, pure triumph, like a flower that blooms on a grave: his grave.

And Ramón henceforth watched her in her beautiful, rather fluttering, rather irritating gentleness, as he watched his closest enemy.

Life had done its work on one more human being, quenched the spontaneous life and left only the will. Killed the god in the woman, or the goddess, and left only charity, with a will.

'Carlota,' he had said to her, 'how happy you would be if you could wear deep, deep mourning for me. – I shall not give you this happiness.'

She gave him a strange look from her hazel-brown eyes.

'Even that is in the hands of God,' she had replied, as she hurried away from him.

And now, on this morning after the first rains, she came to the door of his room as he was sitting writing. As yesterday, he was naked to the waist, the blue-marked sash tied round his middle confined the white linen, loose trousers – like big, wide pyjama trousers crossed in front and tied round his waist.

'May I come in?' she said nervously.

'Do!' he replied, putting down his pen and rising.

There was only one chair – he was offering it her, but she sat down on the unmade bed, as if asserting her natural right. And in the same way she glanced at his naked breast – as if asserting her natural right.

'I am going with Cipriano after breakfast,' she said.

'Yes, so you said.'

'The boys will be home in three weeks.'

'Yes.'

'Don't you want to see them?'

'If they want to see me.'

'I am sure they do.'

'Then bring them here.'

'Do you think it is pleasant for me?' she said, clasping her hands.

'You do not make it pleasant for me, Carlota.'

'How can I? You know I think you are wrong. When I listened to you last night – there is something so beautiful in it all – and yet so monstrous. So *monstrous*! – Oh! I think to myself: What is this man doing? This man of all men, who might be such a blessing to his country and mankind –'

'Well,' said Ramón. 'And what is he instead?'

'You know! You know! I can't bear it. – It *isn't* for you to save Mexico, Ramón. Christ has already saved it.'

'It seems to me not so.'

'He has! He has! And He made you the wonderful being that you are, so that you should *work out* the salvation, in the name of Christ and of love. Instead of which –'

'Instead of which, Carlota, I try something else. – But believe me, if the real Christ has not been able to save Mexico – and He hasn't – then I am sure the white Anti-Christ of charity, and socialism, and politics, and reform, will only succeed in finally destroying her. That, and that alone makes me take my stand. – You, Carlota, with your charity works and your *pity*: and men like Benito Juárez,[1] with their Reform and their Liberty: and the rest of the benevolent people, politicians and socialists and so forth, surcharged with pity for living men, in their mouths, but really with hate – the hate of the materialist *have-nots* for the materialist *haves*: they are the Anti-Christ. The old world, that's just the world. But the new world, that wants to save the People, this is the Anti-Christ. This is Christ with real poison in the communion cup. – And for this reason I step out of my ordinary privacy and individuality. I don't want everybody poisoned. About the great mass I don't care. But I don't want everybody poisoned.'

'How can you be so sure that you yourself are not a poisoner of the people? – I think you are.'

'Think it then. I think of you, Carlota, merely that you have not been able to come to your complete, final womanhood: which is a different thing from the old womanhoods.'

'Womanhood is always the same.'

'Ah, no it isn't! Neither is manhood.'

'But what do you think you can do? What do you think this Quetzalcoatl nonsense amounts to?'

'Quetzalcoatl is just a living word, for these people, no more. All I want them to do is to find the beginnings of the way to their own manhood, their own womanhood. Men are not yet men in full, and women are not yet women. They are all half and half, incoherent, part horrible, part pathetic, part good creatures. Half arrived. – I mean you as well, Carlota. I mean all the world. – But these people don't assert any righteousness of their own, these Mexican people of ours. That makes me think that grace is still with them. And so, having got hold of some kind of clue to my own whole manhood, it is part of me now to try with them.'

'You will fail.'

'I shan't. Whatever happens to me, there will be a new vibration, a new call in the air, and a new answer inside some men.'

'They will betray you. – Do you know what even your friend Toussaint said of you? – Ramón Carrasco's future is just the past of mankind.'

'A great deal of it is the past. Naturally Toussaint sees that part.'

'But the boys don't believe in you. Instinctively, they disbelieve. Cyprian said to me, when I went to see him: "Is father doing any more of that silly talk about old gods coming back, mother? I wish he wouldn't. It would be pretty nasty for us if he got himself into the newspapers with it."'

Ramón laughed.

'Little boys,' he said, 'are like little gramophones. They only talk according to the record that's put into them.'

'*You* don't believe out of the mouths of babes and sucklings,' said Carlota bitterly.

'Why, Carlota, the babes and sucklings don't get much chance. Their mothers and their teachers turn them into little gramophones from the first, so what can they do, but say and feel according to the record the mother and teacher puts into them. Perhaps in the time of Christ, babes and sucklings were not so perfectly exploited by their elders.'

Suddenly, however, the smile went off his face. He rose up, and pointed to the door.

'Go away,' he said in a low tone. 'Go away! I have smelt the smell of your spirit long enough.'

She sat on the bed, spell-bound, gazing at him with frightened, yet obstinate, insolent eyes, wincing from his outstretched arm as if he had threatened to strike her.

Then again the fire went out of his eyes, and his arm sank. The still, far-away look came on his face.

'What have I to do with it!' he murmured softly.

And taking up his blouse and his hat, he went silently out on to the terrace, departing from her in body and in soul. She heard the soft swish of his sandals. She heard the faint resonance of the iron door to the terrace, to which he alone had access. And she sat like a heap of

ash on his bed, ashes to ashes, burnt out, with only the coals of her will
still smouldering.

Her eyes were very bright, as she went to join Kate and Cipriano.

After breakfast, Kate was rowed home down the lake. She felt a
curious depression at leaving the hacienda: as if, for her, life now was
there, and not anywhere else.

Her own house seemed empty, banal, vulgar. For the first time in
her life, she felt the banality and emptiness even of her own milieu.
Though the Casa de las Cuentas was not purely her own milieu.

'Ah Niña, how good! How good that you have come! Ay, in the
night, how much water! Much! Much! But you were safe in the hacienda, Niña. Ah, how nice, that hacienda of Jamiltepec. Such a good
man, Don Ramón – isn't he, Niña? He cares a great deal for his people.
And the Señora, ah, how sympathetic she is!'

Kate smiled and was pleasant. But she felt more like going into her
room and saying: For God's sake, leave me alone, with your cheap rattle.

She suffered again from the servants. Again that quiet, subterranean
insolence against life, which seems to belong to modern life. The unbearable note of flippant jeering, which is underneath almost all modern
utterance. It was underneath Juana's constant cry. – Niña! Niña!

At meal-times Juana would seat herself on the ground at a little
distance from Kate, and talk, talk in her rapid mouthfuls of conglo-
merate words with trailing, wistful endings: and all the time watch her
mistress with those black, unseeing eyes on which the spark of light
would stir with the peculiar slow, malevolent jeering of the Indian.

Kate was not rich – she had only her moderate income.

'Ah, the rich people –!' Juana would say.

'I am not rich,' said Kate.

'You are not rich, Niña?' came the singing, caressive bird-like voice:
'Then, you are poor?' – this was indescribable irony.

'No, I am not poor either. I am not rich, and I am not poor,' said Kate.

'You are not rich, and you are not poor, Niña!' repeated Juana, in
her bird-like voice, that covered the real bird's endless, vindictive jeering.

For the words meant nothing to her. To her, who had nothing,
could never have anything, Kate was one of that weird class, the rich.
And, Kate felt, in Mexico it was a crime to be rich, or to be classed with
the rich. Not even a crime, really, so much as a freak. The rich class

was a freak class, like dogs with two heads or calves with five legs. To be looked upon, not with envy, but with the slow, undying antagonism and curiosity which 'normals' have towards 'freaks'. The slow, powerful, corrosive Indian mockery, issuing from the lava-rock Indian nature, against anything which strives to be above the grey, lava-rock level.

'Is it true, Niña, that your country is through there?' Juana asked, jabbing her finger downward, towards the bowels of the earth.

'Not quite!' said Kate. 'My country is more there –' and she slanted her finger at the earth's surface.

'Ah – that way!' said Juana. And she looked at Kate with a subtle leer, as if to say: what could you expect from people who came out of the earth sideways, like sprouts of camote!

'And is it true, that over there, there are people with only one eye – here!' Juana punched herself in the middle of her forehead.

'No. That isn't true. That is just a story.'

'Ah!' said Juana. 'Isn't it true! Do you know? Have you been to the country where they are, these people?'

'Yes,' said Kate. 'I have been to all the countries, and there are no such people.'

'Verdad! Verdad!' breathed Juana awestruck. 'You have been to all the countries, and there are no such people! – But in your country, they are all *gringos*? Nothing but *gringos*?'

She meant, no real people and salt of the earth like her own Mexican self.

'They are all people like me,' said Kate coldly.

'Like you, Niña? And they all talk like you?'

'Yes! Like me.'

'And there are many?'

'Many! Many!'

'Look now!' breathed Juana, almost awestruck to think that there could be whole worlds of these freak, mockable people.

And Concha, that young, belching savage, would stare through her window-grating at the strange menagerie of the Niña and the Niña's white visitors. Concha, slapping tortillas, was real.

Kate walked down towards the kitchen. Concha was slapping the *masa*, the maize dough which she bought in the plaza at eight centavos a kilo.

'Niña!' she called in her raucous voice. 'Do you eat tortillas?'

'Sometimes,' said Kate.

'Eh?' shouted the young savage.

'Sometimes.'

'Here! Eat one now!' And Concha thrust a brown paw with a pinkish palm, and a dingy-looking tortilla, at Kate.

'Not now,' said Kate.

She disliked the heavy plasters that tasted of lime.

'Don't you want it? Don't you eat it?' said Concha, with an impudent, strident laugh. And she flung the rejected tortilla on the little pile.

She was one of those who won't eat bread: say they don't like it, that it is not food.

Kate would sit and rock on her terrace, while the sun poured in the green square of the garden, the palm-tree spread its great fans translucent at the light, the hibiscus dangled great double-red flowers, rosy red, from its very dark tree, and the dark green oranges looked as if they were sweating as they grew.

Came lunch time, madly hot: and greasy hot soup, greasy rice, splintery little fried fishes, bits of boiled meat and boiled egg-plant vegetables, a big basket piled with mangoes, papayas, zapotes – all the tropical fruits one did not want, in hot weather.

And the barefoot little Maria, in a limp, torn, faded red frock, to wait at table. She was the loving one. She would stand by Juana as Juana bubbled with talk, like dark bubbles in her mouth, and she would stealthily touch Kate's white arm; stealthily touch her again. Not being rebuked, she would stealthily lay her thin little black arm on Kate's shoulder, with the softest, lightest touch imaginable, and her strange, wide black eyes would gleam with ghostly black beatitude, very curious, and her childish, pock-marked, slightly imbecile face would take on a black, arch, beatitudinous look. Then Kate would quickly remove the thin, dark, pock-marked arm, the child would withdraw half a yard, the beatitudinous look foiled, but her very black eyes still shining exposed and absorbedly, in a rapt, reptilian sort of ecstasy.

Till Concha came to hit her with her elbow, making some brutal, savage remark which Kate could not understand. So the glozing black eyes of the child would twitch, and Maria would break into meaningless tears, Concha into a loud, brutal, mocking laugh, like some violent bird. And Juana interrupted her black and gluey flow of words to glance at her daughters and throw out some ineffectual remark.

The victim, the inevitable victim, and the inevitable victimiser.

The terrible, terrible hot emptiness of the Mexican mornings, the weight of black *ennui* that hung in the air! It made Kate feel as if the bottom had fallen out of her soul. She went out to the lake, to escape that house, that family.

Since the rains, the trees in the broken gardens of the lake front had flamed into scarlet, and poured themselves out into lavender flowers. Rose red, scarlet and lavender, quick, tropical flowers. Wonderful splashes of colour. But that was all: splashes! They made a splash, like fireworks.

And Kate thought of the black-thorn puffing white, in the early year, in Ireland, and hawthorn with coral grains, in a damp still morning in the lanes, and foxgloves by the bare rock, and tufts of ling and heather, and a ravel of harebells. And a terrible, terrible longing for home came over her. To escape from these tropical brilliancies and meaninglessnesses.

In Mexico, the wind was a hard draught, the rain was a sluice of water, to be avoided, and the sun hit down on one with hostility, terrific and stunning. Stiff, dry, unreal land, with sunshine beating on it like metal. Or blackness and lightning and crashing violence of rain.

No lovely fusion, no communion. No beautiful mingling of sun and mist, no softness in the air, never. Either hard heat or hard chill. Hard, straight lies and zigzags, wounding the breast. No soft, sweet smell of earth. The smell of Mexico, however subtle, suggested violence and things in chemical conflict.

And Kate felt herself filled with an anger of resentment. She would sit under a willow tree by the lake, reading a Pío Baroja[2] novel that was angry and full of No! No! No! – ich bin der Geist der stets verneint![3] But she herself was so much angrier and fuller of repudiation than Pío Baroja. Spain cannot stand for No! as Mexico can.

The tree hung fleecy above her. She sat on the warm sand in the shadow, careful not to let even her ankles lie in the biting shine of the sun. There was a faint, old smell of urine. The lake was so still and filmy as to be almost invisible. In the near distance, some dark women were kneeling on the edge of the lake, dressed only in their long wet chemises in which they had bathed. Some were washing garments, some were pouring water over themselves, scooping it up in gourd scoops and pouring it over their black heads and ruddy-dark shoulders, in the intense pressure of the sunshine. On her left were two big trees, and a cane fence, and little straw huts of Indians. There the beach itself ended, and the little Indian plots of land went down to the lake-front.

Glancing around in the great light, she seemed to be sitting isolated in a dark core of shadow, while the world moved in inconsequential specks through the hollow glare. She noticed a dark urchin, nearly naked, marching with naked, manly solemnity down to the water's edge. He would be about four years old, but more manly than an adult man. With sex comes a certain vulnerability which these round-faced, black-headed, stiff-backed infant men have not got. Kate knew the urchin. She knew his tattered rag of a red shirt, and the weird rags that were his little man's white trousers. She knew his black round head, his stiff, sturdy march of a walk, his round eyes, and his swift, scuttling run, like a bolting animal.

'What's the brat got,' she said to herself, gazing at the moving little figure within the great light.

Dangling from his tiny outstretched arm, held by the webbed toe, head down and feebly flapping its out-sinking wings, was a bird, a water-fowl. It was a black mud-chick with a white bar across the under-wing, one of the many dark fowl that bobbed in little flocks along the edge of the sun-stunned lake.

The urchin marched stiffly down to the water's edge, holding the upside-down bird, that seemed big as an eagle in the tiny fist. Another brat came scuttling after. The two infant men paddled a yard into the warm, lapping water, under the great light, and gravely stooping, like old men, set the fowl on the water. It floated, but could hardly paddle. The lift of the ripples moved it. The urchins dragged it in, like a rag, by a string tied to its leg.

So quiet, so still, so dark, like tiny, chubby little infant men, the two solemn figures with the rag of a bird!

Kate turned uneasily to her book, her nerves on edge. She heard the splash of a stone. The bird was on the water, but apparently the string that held it by the leg was tied to a stone. It lay wavering, a couple of yards out. And the two little he-men, with sober steadfastness and a quiet, dark lust, were picking up stones, and throwing them with the fierce Indian aim at the feebly fluttering bird: right down upon it. Like a little warrior stood the mite in the red rag, his arm upraised, to throw the stone with all his might down on the tethered bird.

In a whiff, Kate was darting down the beach.

'Ugly boys! Ugly children! Go! Go away, ugly children, ugly boys!' she said on one breath, with quiet intensity.

The round-headed dot gave her one black glance from his manly eyes, then the two of them scuttled up the beach into invisibility.

Kate went into the water, and lifted the wet, warm bird. The bit of coarse fibre-string hung from its limp, greenish, water-fowl's ankle. It feebly tried to bite her.

She rapidly stepped out of the water and stood in the sun to unfasten the string. The bird was about as big as a pigeon. It lay in her hand with the absolute motionlessness of a caught wild thing.

Kate stooped and pulled off her shoes and stockings. She looked round. No sign of life from the reed huts dark in the shadow of the trees. She lifted her skirts and staggered out barefoot in the hot shallows of the water, almost falling on the cruel stones under the water. The lake-side was very shallow. She staggered on and on, in agony, holding up her skirts in one hand, holding the warm, wet, motionless bird in the other. Till at last she was up to her knees. Then she launched the greeny-black bird, and gave it a little push to the uprearing expanse of filmy water, that was almost dim, invisible with the glare of light.

It lay wet and draggled on the pale, moving sperm of the water, like a buoyant rag.

'Swim then! Swim!' she said, trying to urge it away into the lake.

Either it couldn't or wouldn't. Anyhow it didn't.

But it was out of reach of those urchins. Kate struggled back from those stones, to her tree, to her shade, to her book, away from the rage of the sun. Silent with slow anger, she kept glancing up at the floating bird, and sideways at the reed huts of the Indians in the black shadow.

Yes, the bird was dipping its beak in the water, and shaking its head. It was coming to itself. But it did not paddle. It let itself be lifted, lifted on the ripples, and the ripples would drift it ashore.

'Fool of a thing!' said Kate nervously, using all her consciousness to make it paddle away into the lake.

Two companions, two black dots with white specks of faces, were coming out of the pale glare of the lake. Two mud-chicks swam busily forward. The first swam up and poked its beak at the inert bird, as if to say *Hello! What's up?* Then immediately it turned away and paddled in complete oblivion to the shore, its companion following.

Kate watched the rag of feathered misery anxiously. Would it not rouse itself, wouldn't it follow?

No! There it lay, slowly, inertly drifting on the ripples, only sometimes shaking its head.

The other two alert birds waded confidently, busily among the stones. Kate read a bit more.

When she looked again, she could not see her bird. But the other two were walking among the stones, jauntily.

She read a bit more.

The next thing was a rather loutish youth of eighteen or so, in overall trousers, running with big strides towards the water, and the stiff little man-brat scuttling after with determined bare feet. Her heart stood still.

The two busy mud-chicks rose in flight and went low over the water into the blare of light. Gone!

But the lout in the big hat and overall trousers and those stiff Indian shoulders she sometimes hated so much, was peering among the stones. She, however, was sure her bird had gone.

No! Actually no! The stiff-shoulder lout stooped and picked up the damp thing. It had let itself drift back.

He turned, dangling it like a rag from the end of one wing, and handed it to the man-brat. Then he stalked self-satisfied up the shore.

Ugh! and that moment how Kate hated these people: their terrible lowness, *à terre, à terre.* Their stiff broad American shoulders, and high chests, and above all, their walk, their prancing, insentient walk. As if some motor-engine drove them at the bottom of their back.

Stooping rather forward and looking at the ground so that he could turn his eyes sideways to her, without showing her his face, the lout returned to the shadow of the huts. And after him, diminutive, the dot of a man marched stiffly, hurriedly, dangling the wretched bird, that stirred very feebly, downwards from the tip of one wing. And from time to time turning his round, black-eyed face in Kate's direction, vindictively, apprehensively, lest she should swoop down on him again. Black, apprehensive male defiance of the great, white, weird female.

Kate glared back from under her tree.

'If looks would kill you, brat, I'd kill you,' she said. And the urchin turned his face like clockwork at her from time to time, as he strutted palpitating towards the gap in the cane hedge, into which the youth had disappeared.

Kate debated whether to rescue the foolish bird again. But what was the good!

This country would have its victim. America would have its victim. As long as time lasts, it will be the continent divided between Victims and Victimisers. What is the good of trying to interfere!

She rose up in detestation of the flabby bird, and of the sulky-faced brat turning his full moon on her in apprehension.

Lumps of women were by the water's edge. Westwards, down the glare, rose the broken-looking villas and the white twin towers of the church, holding up its two fingers in mockery above the scarlet flame-trees and the dark mangoes. She saw the rather lousy shore, and smelt the smell of Mexico, come out in the hot sun after the rains: excrement, human and animal dried in the sun on a dry, dry earth; and dry leaves; and mango leaves; and pure air with a little refuse-smoke in it.

'But the day will come when I shall go away,' she said to herself.

And sitting rocking once more on her verandah, hearing the clap-clap of tortillas from the far end of the patio, the odd, metallic noises of birds, and feeling the clouds already assembling in the west, with a weight of unborn thunder upon them, she felt she could bear it no more: the vacuity, and the pressure: the horrible uncreate elementality, so uncouth, even sun and rain uncouth, uncouth.

And she wondered over the black vision in the eyes of that urchin. The curious void.

He could not see that the bird was a real living creature with a life of its own. This, his race had never seen. With black eyes they stared out on an elemental world, where the elements were monstrous and cruel, as the sun was monstrous, and the cold, crushing black water of the rain was monstrous, and the dry, dry, cruel earth.

And among the monstrosity of the elements flickered and towered other presences: terrible uncouth things called *gringos*, white people, and dressed up monsters of rich people, with powers like gods, but uncouth, demonish gods. And uncouth things like birds that could fly and snakes that could crawl and fish that could swim and bite. An uncouth, monstrous universe of monsters big and little, in which man held his own by sheer resistance and guardedness, never, never going forth from his own darkness.

And sometimes, it was good to have revenge on the monsters that fluttered and strode. The monsters big and the monsters little. Even the monster of that bird, which had its own monstrous bird-nature. On this the mite could wreak the long human vengeance, and for once be master.

Blind to the creature as a soft, struggling thing finding its own fluttering way through life. Seeing only another monster of the outer void.

Walking forever through a menace of monsters, blind to the sympathy in things, holding one's own, and not giving in, nor going forth. Hence the lifted chests and the prancing walk. Hence the stiff, insentient spines, the rich physique, and the heavy, dreary natures, heavy like the dark-grey mud-bricks, with a terrible obstinate ponderosity and a dry sort of gloom.

The Written Hymns of Quetzalcoatl

THE electric light in Sayula was as inconstant as everything else. It would come on at half-past six in the evening, and it *might* bravely burn till ten at night, when the village went dark with a click. But usually it did no such thing. Often it refused to sputter into being till seven, or half-past, or even eight o'clock. But its worst trick was that of popping out just in the middle of supper, or just when you were writing a letter. All of a sudden, the black Mexican night came down on you with a thud. And then everybody running blindly for matches and candles, with a calling of frightened voices. Why were they always frightened? Then the electric light, like a wounded thing, would try to revive, and a red glow would burn in the bulbs, sinister. All held their breath – was it coming or not? Sometimes it expired for good, sometimes it got its breath back and shone, rather dully, but better than nothing.

Once the rainy season had set in, it was hopeless. Night after night it collapsed. And Kate would sit with her weary, fluttering candle, while blue lightning revealed the dark shapes of things in the patio. And half-seen people went swiftly down to Juana's end of the patio, secretly.

On such a night Kate sat on her verandah facing the deepness of the black night. A candle shone in her desert salon. Now and again she saw the oleanders and the papaya in the patio garden, by the blue gleam of lightning that fell with a noiseless splash into the pitch darkness. There was a distant noise of thunder, several storms prowling round like hungry jaguars, above the lake.

And several times the gate clicked, and crunching steps came along the gravel, someone passed on the gravel walk, saluting her, going down to Juana's quarters, where the dull light of a floating oil wick shone through the grated window-hole. Then there was a low, monotonous sound of a voice, reciting or reading. And as the wind blew and the lightning alighted again like a blue bird among the plants, there would come the sharp noise of the round *cuentas* falling from the cuenta tree.

Kate was uneasy and a bit forlorn. She felt something was happening down in the servants' corner, something secret in the dark. And she was stranded in her isolation on her terrace.

But after all, it was her house, and she had a right to know what her own people were up to. She rose from her rocking chair and walked down the verandah and round the dining-room bay. The dining-room, which had its own two doors on the patio, was already locked up.

In the far corner beyond the well, she saw a group sitting on the ground, outside the doorway of Juana's kitchen-hole. Out of this little kitchen-shed shone the light of the floating-wick lamp, and a voice was slowly intoning, all the faces were looking into the dim light, the women dark-hooded in rebozos, the men with their hats on, their serapes over their shoulders.

When they heard Kate's footsteps, the faces looked her way, and a voice murmured in warning. Juana struggled to her feet.

'It is the Niña!' she said. 'Come, then, Niña, you poor innocent all alone in the evening.'

The men in the group rose to their feet – she recognized the young Ezequiel, taking his hat off to her. And there was Maria del Carmen, the bride. And inside the little shed, with the wick lamp on the floor, was Julio, the bridegroom of a few weeks ago. Concha and little Maria were there, and a couple of strangers.

'I could hear the voice –' said Kate. 'I didn't know it was you, Julio. How do you do? – And I wondered so much what it was.'

There was a moment's dead silence. Then Juana plunged in.

'Yes, Niña! Come! It's very nice that you come. Concha, the chair for the Niña!'

Concha got up rather unwillingly, and fetched the little low chair which formed Juana's sole article of furniture, save the one bed.

'I don't disturb you?' said Kate.

'No, Niña, you are a friend of Don Ramón, *verdad?*'

'Yes,' said Kate.

'And we – we are reading the Hymns.'

'Yes?' said Kate.

'The Hymns of Quetzalcoatl,' said Ezequiel, in his barking young voice, with sudden bravado.

'Do go on! May I listen!'

'You hear! The Niña wants to listen. Read, Julio, read! Read then.'

They all sat down once more on the ground, and Julio sat down by the lamp, but he hung his head, hiding his face in the shadow of his big hat.

'*Entonces!* – Read then,' said Juana.

'He is afraid,' murmured Maria del Carmen, laying her hand on the young man's knee. 'However, read, Julio! Because the Niña wants to hear.'

And after a moment's struggle, Julio said in a muffled voice:

'Do I begin from the beginning.'

'Yes, from the beginning! Read!' said Juana.

The young man took a sheet of paper, like an advertisement leaflet, from under his blanket. At the top it had the Quetzalcoatl symbol, called the Eye, the ring with the bird-shape standing in the middle.

He began to read in a rather muffled voice:

'I am Quetzalcoatl with the dark face, who lived in Mexico in other days.

'Till there came a stranger from over the seas, and his face was white, and he spoke with strange words. He showed his hands and his feet, that in both there were holes. And he said: "My name is Jesus, and they called me Christ. Men crucified me on a Cross till I died. But I rose up out of the place where they put me, and I went up to heaven to my Father. Now my Father has told me to come to Mexico."

'*Quetzalcoatl said:* You alone?

'*Jesus said:* My mother is here. She shed many tears for me, seeing me crucify. So she will hold the Sons of Mexico on her lap, and soothe them when they suffer, and when the women of Mexico weep, she will take them on her bosom and comfort them. And when she cries to the Father for her people, He will make everything well.

'*Quetzalcoatl said:* That is well. And Brother with the name Jesus, what will you do in Mexico?

'*Jesus said:* I will bring peace into Mexico. And on the naked I will put clothes, and food between the lips of the hungry, and gifts in all men's hands, and peace and love in their hearts.

'*Quetzalcoatl said:* It is very good. I am old. I could not do so much. I must go now. Farewell, people of Mexico. Farewell, strange brother called Jesus. Farewell, woman called Mary. It is time for me to go.

'So Quetzalcoatl looked at his people; and he embraced Jesus, the Son of Heaven; and he embraced Maria, the Blessed Virgin, the Holy Mother of Jesus, and he turned away. Slowly he went. But in his ears was the sound of the tearing down of his temples in Mexico. Nevertheless he went on slowly, being old, and weary with much living. He climbed the steep of the mountain, and over the white snow of the volcano. As he went, behind him rose a cry of people dying, and a flame of places burning. He said to himself: Surely those are Mexicans crying! Yet I must not hear, for Jesus has come to the land, and he will wipe the tears from all eyes, and his Mother will make them all glad.

'He also said: Surely that is Mexico burning. But I must not look, for all men will be brothers, now Jesus has come to the land, and the women will sit by the blue skirts of Mary, smiling with peace and with love.

'So the old god reached the top of the mountain, and looked up into the blue house of heaven. And through a door in the blue wall he saw a great darkness, and stars and a moon shining. And beyond the darkness he saw one great star, like a bright gateway.

'Then fire rose from the volcano around the old Quetzalcoatl, in wings and glittering feathers. And with the wings of fire and the glitter of sparks Quetzalcoatl flew up, up, like a wafting fire, like a glittering bird, up, into the space, and away to the white steps of heaven, that lead to the blue walls, where is the door to the dark. So he entered in and was gone.

'Night fell, and Quetzalcoatl was gone, and men in the world saw only a star travelling back into heaven, departing under the low branches of darkness.

'Then men in Mexico said: Quetzalcoatl has gone. Even his star has departed. We must listen to this Jesus, who speaks in a foreign tongue.

'So they learned a new speech from the priests that came from upon the great waters to the east. And they became Christians.'

Julio, who had become absorbed, ended abruptly, as the tale of the leaflet was ended.

'It is beautiful,' said Kate.

'And it is true!' cried the sceptical Juana.

'It seems to me true,' said Kate.

'Señora!' yelled Concha. 'Is it true that heaven is up there, and you come down steps like clouds to the edge of the sky, like the steps from the mole into the lake? Is it true that El Señor comes and stands on the steps and looks down at us like we look down into the lake to see the charales?'

Concha shoved up her fierce swarthy face, and shook her masses of hair, glaring at Kate, waiting for an answer.

'I don't know everything,' laughed Kate. 'But it seems to me true.'

'She believes it,' said Concha, turning her face to her mother.

'And is it true,' asked Juana, 'that El Señor, El Cristo del Mundo, is a gringo, and that He comes from your country, with His Holy Mother?'

'Not from my country, but from a country near.'

'Listen!' exclaimed Juana, awestruck. 'El Señor is a gringuito, and His Holy Mother is a gringuita. Yes, one really knows. Look! Look at the feet of the Niña! Pure feet of the Santísima! Look!' Kate was barefoot, wearing sandals with a simple strap across the foot. Juana touched one of the Niña's white feet, fascinated. 'Feet of the Santísima. And She, the Holy Mary, is a gringuita. She came over the sea, like you, Niña?'

'Yes, she came over the sea!'

'Ah! You know it?'

'Yes. We know that.'

'Think of it! The Santísima is a gringuita, and She came over the Sea like the Niña, from the countries of the Niña!' Juana spoke in a wicked wonder, horrified, delighted, mocking.

'And the Lord is a Gringuito – pure Gringuito?' barked Concha.

'And Niña – it was the gringos who killed El Señor? It wasn't the Mexicans? It was those other gringos who put Him on the Cross?'

'Yes!' said Kate. 'It wasn't the Mexicans.'

'The gringos?'

'Yes, the gringos.'

'And He Himself was a Gringo?'

'Yes!' said Kate, not knowing what else to say.

'Look!' said Juana, in her hushed, awed, malevolent voice. 'He was a Gringo, and the gringos put him on the Cross.'

'But a long time ago,' said Kate hastily.

'A long time ago, says the Niña,' echoed Juana, in her awed voice.

There was a moment of silence. The dark faces of the girls and men seated on the ground were turned up to Kate, watching her fixedly, in the half light, counting every word. In the outer air, thunder muttered in different places.

'And now, Niña,' came the cool, clear voice of Maria del Carmen,

'El Señor is going back again to His Father, and our Quetzalcoatl is coming back to us?'

'And the Santísima is leaving us?' put in the hurried voice of Juana. 'Think of it! The Santísima is leaving us, and this Quetzalcoatl is coming! He has no mother, he!'

'Perhaps he has a wife,' said Kate.

'Quién sabe!' murmured Juana.

'They say,' said the bold Concha, 'that in Paradise he has grown young.'

'Who?' asked Juana.

'I don't know how they call him,' muttered Concha, ashamed to say the word.

'Quetzalcoatl!' said Ezequiel, in his barking strong young voice. 'Yes, he is young. He is a god in the flower of life, and finely built.'

'They say so! They say so!' murmured Juana. 'Think of it!'

'Here it says so!' cried Ezequiel. 'Here it is written. In the second Hymn.'

'Read it then, Julio.'

And Julio, now nothing loth, took out a second paper.

'I, Quetzalcoatl, of Mexico, I travelled the longest journey.

'Beyond the blue outer wall of heaven, beyond the bright place of the Sun, across the plains of darkness where the stars spread out like trees, like trees and bushes, far away to the heart of all the worlds, low down like the Morning Star.

'And at the heart of all the worlds those were waiting whose faces I could not see. And in voices like bees they murmured among themselves: *This is Quetzalcoatl whose hair is white with fanning the fires of life. He comes alone, and slowly.*

'Then with hands I could not see, they took my hands, and in their arms that I could not see, at last I died.

'But when I was dead, and bone, they cast not my bones away, they did not give me up to the four winds, nor to the six. No, not even to the wind that blows down to the middle of earth, nor to him that blows upward like a finger pointing, did they give me.

'*He is dead*, they said, *but unrelinquished.*

'So they took the oil of the darkness, and laid it on my brow and my eyes, they put it in my ears and nostrils and my mouth, they put it on the two-fold silence of my breasts, and on my sunken navel, and on my secret places, before and behind: and in the palms of my hands, and on the mounds of my knees, and under the tread of my feet.

'Lastly, they anointed all my head with the oil that comes out of the darkness. Then they said: He is sealed up. Lay him away.

'So they laid me in the fountain that bubbles darkly at the heart of the worlds, far, far behind the sun, and there lay I, Quetzalcoatl, in warm oblivion.

'I slept the great sleep, and dreamed not.

'Till a voice was calling: Quetzalcoatl!

'I said: Who is that?

'No one answered, but the voice said: Quetzalcoatl!

'I said: Where art thou?

'So! he said. I am neither here nor there. I am thyself. Get up.

'Now all was very heavy upon me, like a tomb-stone of darkness.

'I said: Am I not old? How shall I roll this stone away?

'How art thou old, when I am new man? I will roll away the stone. Sit up!

'I sat up, and the stone went rolling, crashing down the gulfs of space.

'I said to myself: I am new man. I am younger than the young and older than the old. Lo! I am unfolded on the stem of time like a flower, I am at the midst of the flower of my manhood. Neither do I ache with desire, to tear, to burst the bud; neither do I yearn away like a seed that floats into heaven. The cup of my flowering is unfolded, in its middle the stars float balanced with array. My stem is in the air, my roots are in all the dark, the sun is no more than a cupful within me.

'Lo! I am neither young nor old, I am the flower unfolded, I am new.

'So I rose and stretched my limbs and looked around. The sun was below me in a daze of heat, like a hot humming-bird hovering at mid-day over the worlds. And his beak was long and very sharp, he was like a dragon.

'And a faint star was hesitating wearily, waiting to pass.

'I called aloud, saying: "Who is that?"

> *My name is Jesus, I am Mary's son.*
> *I am coming home.*
> *My mother the Moon is dark.*

Brother, Quetzalcoatl,
Hold back the wild hot sun.
Bind him with shadow while I pass.
Let me come home.

'I caught the sun and held him, and in my shade the faint star slipped past, going slowly into the dark reaches beyond the burning of the sun. Then on the slope of silence he sat down and took off his sandals, and I put them on.

' "How do they wear the wings of love, Jesus, the Mexican people?"

' "The souls of the Mexican people are heavy for the wings of love, they have swallowed the stone of despair."

' "Where is your Lady Mother in the mantle of blue, she with comfort in her lap?"

' "Her mantle faded in the dust of the world, she was weary without sleep, for the voices of people cried night and day, and the knives of the Mexican people were sharper than the pinions of love, and their stubbornness was stronger than hope. Lo! the fountain of tears dries up in the eyes of the old, and the lap of the aged is comfortless, they look for rest. Quetzalcoatl, Sir, my mother went even before me, to her still white bed in the moon."

' "She is gone, and thou art gone, Jesus, the Crucified. Then what of Mexico?"

' "The images stand in their churches, Oh Quetzalcoatl, they don't know that I and my Mother have departed. They are angry souls, Brother, my Lord! They vent their anger. They broke my Churches, they stole my strength, they withered the lips of the Virgin. They drove us away, and we crept away like a tottering old man and a woman, tearless and bent double with age. So we fled while they were not looking. And we seek but rest, to forget forever the children of men who have swallowed the stone of despair."

'Then said I: It is good, pass on. I, Quetzalcoatl, will go down. Sleep thou the sleep without dreams. Farewell at the cross-roads, Brother Jesus.

'He said: Oh, Quetzalcoatl! They have forgotten thee. The feathered snake! The serpent – silent bird! They are asking for none of thee.

'I said: Go thy way, for the dust of earth is in thy eyes and on thy lips. For me the serpent of middle-earth sleeps in my loins and my belly, the bird of the outer air perches on my brow and sweeps her bill across my breast. But I, I am lord of two ways. I am master of up and down. I am as a man who is a new man, with new limbs and life, and the light of the Morning Star in his eyes. Lo! I am I! The lord of both ways. Thou wert lord of the one way. Now it leads thee to the sleep. Farewell!

'So Jesus went on towards the sleep. And Mary the Mother of Sorrows lay down on the bed of the white moon, weary beyond any more tears.

'And I, I am on the threshold. I am stepping across the border. I am Quetzalcoatl, lord of both ways, star between day and the dark.'

There was silence as the young man finished reading.

CHAPTER XVI

Cipriano and Kate

ON Saturday afternoons the big black canoes with their large square sails came slowly approaching out of the thin haze across the lake, from the west, from Tlapaltepec,[1] with big straw hats and with blankets and earthenware stuff, from Ixtlahuacan and Jaramay[2] and Las Zemas with mats and timber and charcoal and oranges, from Tuliapan and Cuxcueco and San Cristobal with boatloads of dark-green, globular watermelons, and piles of red tomatoes, mangoes, vegetables, oranges: and boat-loads of bricks and tiles, burnt red, but rather friable; then more charcoal, more wood, from the stark dry mountains over the lake.

Kate nearly always went out about five o'clock, on Saturdays, to see the boats, flat-bottomed, drift up to the shallow shores, and begin to unload in the glow of the evening. It pleased her to see the men running along the planks with the dark-green melons, and piling them in a mound on the rough sand, melons dark-green like creatures with pale bellies. To see the tomatoes all poured out into a shallow place in the lake, bobbing about while the women washed them, a bobbing scarlet upon the water.

The long, heavy bricks were piled in heaps along the scrap of demolished break-water, and little gangs of asses came trotting down the rough beach, to be laden, pressing their little feet in the gravelly sand, and flopping their ears.

The cargadores were busy at the charcoal boats, carrying out the rough sacks.

'Do you want charcoal, Niña?' shouted a grimy cargador, who had carried the trunks from the station on his back.

'At how much?'

'Twenty-five reales the two sacks.'

'I pay twenty reales.'

'At twenty reales then, Señorita. But you give me two reales for the transport?'

'The owner pays the transport,' said Kate. 'But I will give you twenty centavos.'

Away went the man, trotting barelegged, barefoot, over the stony ground, with two large sacks of charcoal on his shoulders. The men carry huge weights, without seeming ever to think they are heavy. Almost as if they liked to feel a huge weight crushing on their iron spines, and to be able to resist it.

Baskets of spring guavas, baskets of sweet lemons called limas, basket of tiny green and yellow lemons, big as walnuts; orange-red and greenish mangoes, oranges, carrots, cactus fruits in great abundance, a few knobby potatoes, flat, pearl-white onions, little calabacitas and speckled green calabacitas like frogs, camotes cooked and raw – she loved to watch the baskets trotting up the beach past the church.

Then, rather late as a rule, big red pots, bulging red ollas for water-jars, earthenware casseroles and earthenware jugs with cream and black scratched pattern in glaze, bowls, big flat earthenware discs for cooking tortillas – much earthenware.

On the west shore, men were running up the beach wearing twelve enormous hats at once, like a trotting pagoda. Men trotting with finely woven huaraches and rough strip sandals. And men with a few dark serapes, with gaudy rose-pink patterns, in a pile on their shoulders.

It was fascinating. But at the same time, there was a heavy, almost sullen feeling on the air. These people came to market to a sort of battle.[3] They came, not for the joy of selling, but for the sullen contest with those who wanted what they had got. The strange, black resentment always present.

By the time the church bells clanged for sunset, the market had already begun. On all the pavements round the plaza squatted the Indians with their wares, pyramids of green water-melons, arrays of rough earthenware, hats in piles, pairs of sandals side by side, a great array of fruit, a spread of collar-studs and knick-knacks, called *nove-dades*, little trays with sweets. And people arriving all the time out of the wild country, with laden asses.

Yet never a shout, hardly a voice to be heard. None of the animation and the frank wild clamour of a Mediterranean market. Always the heavy friction of the will; always, always, grinding upon the spirit, like the grey-black grind of lava-rock.

When dark fell, the vendors lighted their tin torch-lamps, and the flames wavered and streamed as the dark-faced men squatted on the ground in their white clothes and big hats, waiting to sell. They never asked you to buy. They never showed their wares. They didn't even look at you. It was as if their static resentment and indifference would hardly let them sell at all.

Kate sometimes felt the market cheerful and easy. But more often she felt an unutterable weight slowly, invisibly sinking on her spirits. And she wanted to run. She wanted above all, the comfort of Don Ramón and the Hymns of Quetzalcoatl. This seemed to her the only escape from a world gone ghastly.

There was talk of revolution again, so the market was uneasy and grinding the black grit into the spirit. Foreign-looking soldiers were about, with looped hats, and knives and pistols, and savage northern faces: tall, rather thin figures. They would loiter about in pairs, talking in a strange northern speech, and seeming more alien even than Kate herself.

The food-stalls were brilliantly lighted. Rows of men sat at the plank boards, drinking soup and eating hot food with their fingers. The milk-man rode in on horseback, his two big cans of milk slung before him, and he made his way slowly through the people to the food-stalls. There, still sitting unmoved on horseback, he delivered bowls of milk from the can in front of him, and then, on horseback like a monument, took his supper, his bowl of soup, and his plate of tamales, or of minced, fiery meat spread on tortillas. The peons drifted slowly round. Guitars were sounding, half-secretly. A motor-car worked its way in from the city, choked with people, girls, young men, city papas, children, in a pile.

The rich press of life, above the flare of torches upon the ground! The throng of white-clad, big-hatted men circulating slowly, the women with dark rebozos slipping silently. Dark trees overhead. The doorway of the hotel bright with electricity. Girls in organdie frocks, white, cherry-red, blue, from the city. Groups of singers singing inwardly. And all the noise subdued, suppressed.

The sense of strange, heavy suppression, the dead black power of negation in the souls of the peons. It was almost pitiful to see the pretty, pretty slim girls from Guadalajara going round and round, their naked arms linked together, so light in their gauzy, scarlet, white, blue, orange dresses, looking for someone to look at them, to take note of them. And the peon men only emitting from their souls the black vapour of nega-tion, that perhaps was hate. They seemed, the natives, to have the power of blighting the air with their black, rock-bottom resistance.

Kate almost wept over the slim, eager girls, pretty as rather papery flowers, eager for attention, but thrust away, victimised.

Suddenly there was a shot. The market-place was on its feet in a moment, scattering, pouring away into the streets and the shops. Another shot! Kate, from where she stood, saw across the rapidly-emptying plaza a man sitting back on one of the benches, firing a pistol into the air. He was a lout from the city, and he was half drunk. The people knew what it was. Yet any moment he might lower the pistol and start firing at random. Everybody hurried silently, melting away, leaving the plaza void.

Two more shots, pap–pap! still into the air. And at the same moment a little officer in uniform darted out of the dark street where the military station was, and where now the big hats were piled on the ground; he rushed straight to the drunkard, who was spreading his legs and waving the pistol: and before you could breathe, *slap!* and again *slap!* He had slapped the pistol-firer first on one side of the face, then on the other, with slaps that resounded almost like shots. And in the same breath he seized the arm that held the pistol and wrested the weapon away.

Two of the strange soldiers instantly rushed up and seized the man by the arms. The officer spoke two words, they saluted and marched off their prisoner.

Instantly the crowd was ebbing back into the plaza, unconcerned. Kate sat on a bench with her heart beating. She saw the prisoner pass under a lamp, streaks of blood on his cheek. And Juana, who had fled, now came scuttling back and took Kate's hand, saying:

'Look! Niña! It is the General!'

She rose startled to her feet. The officer was saluting her.

'Don Cipriano!' she said.

'The same!' he replied. 'Did that drunken fellow frighten you?'

'Not much! Only startled me. I didn't *feel* any evil intention behind it.'

'No, only drunk.'

'But I shall go home now.'

'Shall I walk with you?'

'Would you care to?'

He took his place at her side, and they turned down by the church, to the lake shore. There was a moon above the mountain and the air was coming fresh, not too strong, from the west. From the Pacific. Little lights were burning ruddy by the boats at the water's edge, some outside, and some inside, under the roof-tilt of the boat's little inward shed. Women were preparing a mouthful of food.

'But the night is beautiful,' said Kate, breathing deep.

'With the moon clipped away just a little,' he said.

Juana was following close on her heels: and behind, two soldiers in slouched hats.

'Do the soldiers escort you?' she said.

'I suppose so,' said he.

'But the moon,' she said, 'isn't lovely and friendly as it is in England or Italy.'

'It is the same planet,' he replied.

'But the moonshine in America isn't the same. It doesn't make one feel glad as it does in Europe. One feels it would like to hurt one.'

He was silent for some moments. Then he said:

'Perhaps there is in you something European, which hurts our Mexican Moon.'

'But I come in good faith.'

'European good faith. Perhaps it is not the same as Mexican.'

Kate was silent, almost stunned.

'Fancy your Mexican moon objecting to me!' she laughed ironically.

'Fancy your objecting to our Mexican moon!' said he.

'I wasn't,' said she.

They came to the corner of Kate's road. At the corner was a group of trees, and under the trees, behind the hedge, several reed huts. Kate often laughed at the donkey looking over the dry-stone low wall, and at the black sheep with curved horns, tied to a bitten tree, and at the lad, naked but for a bit of a shirt, fleeing into the corner under the thorn screen.

Kate and Cipriano sat on the verandah of the House of the Cuentas. She offered him vermouth, but he refused.

They were still. There came the faint pip!–pip! from the little electric plant just up the road, which Jesús tended. Then a cock from beyond the bananas crowed powerfully and hoarsely.

'But how absurd!' said Kate. 'Cocks don't crow at this hour.'

'Only in Mexico,' laughed Cipriano.

'Yes! Only here!'

'He thinks your moon is the sun, no?' he said, teasing her.

The cock crowed powerfully, again and again.

'This is very nice, your house, your patio,' said Cipriano.

But Kate was silent.

'Or don't you like it?' he said.

'You see,' she answered, 'I have nothing to *do*! The servants won't let me do anything. If I sweep my room, they stand and say *Qué Niña! Qué Niña!* As if I was standing on my head for their benefit. I sew, though I've no interest in sewing. – What is it, for a life?'

'And you read!' he said, glancing at the magazines and books.

'Ah, it is all such stupid, lifeless stuff, in the books and papers,' she said.

There was a silence. After which he said:

'But what would you like to do? As you say, you take no interest in sewing. You know the Navajo women, when they weave a blanket, leave a little place for their soul to come out, at the end: not to weave their soul into it. – I always think England has woven her soul into her fabrics, into all the things she has made. And she never left a place for it to come out. So now all her soul is in her goods, and nowhere else.'

'But Mexico *has* no soul,' said Kate. 'She's swallowed the stone of despair, as the hymn says.'

'Ah! You think so? I think not. The soul is also a thing you make, like a pattern in a blanket. It is very nice while all the wools are rolling their different threads and different colours, and the pattern is being made. But once it is finished – then finished it has ño interest any more. Mexico hasn't started to weave the pattern of her soul. Or she is only just starting: with Ramón. Don't you believe in Ramón?'

Kate hesitated before she answered.

'Ramón, yes! I do! But whether it's any good trying here in Mexico, as he is trying –' she said slowly.

'He *is* in Mexico. *He* tries here. Why should not you?'

'I?'

'Yes! You! Ramón doesn't believe in womanless gods, he says. Why should you not be the woman in the Quetzalcoatl pantheon? If you will, the goddess!'

'I, a goddess in the Mexican pantheon?' cried Kate, with a burst of startled laughter.

'Why not?' said he.

'But I am not Mexican,' said she.

'You may easily be a goddess,' said he, 'in the same pantheon with Don Ramón and me.'

A strange, inscrutable flame of desire seemed to be burning on Cipriano's face, as his eyes watched her glittering. Kate could not help feeling that it was a sort of intense, blind *ambition*, of which she was partly an object: a passionate object also: which kindled the Indian to the hottest pitch of his being.

'But I don't feel like a goddess in a Mexican pantheon,' she said. 'Mexico is a bit horrible to me. Don Ramón is *wonderful*: but I'm so afraid they will destroy him.'

'Come, and help to prevent it.'

'How?'

'You marry me. You complain you have nothing to do. Then marry me. Marry me, and help Ramón and me. We need a woman, Ramón says, to be with us. And you are the woman. There is a great deal to do.'

'But can't I help without marrying anybody?' said Kate.

'How can you?' he said simply.

And she knew it was true.

'But you see,' she said, 'I have no *impulse* to marry you, so how can I?'

'Why?' he said.

'You see, Mexico is *really* a bit horrible to me. And the black eyes of the people really make my heart contract, and my flesh shrink. There's a bit of horror in it. And I don't want horror in my soul.'

He was silent and unfathomable. She did not know in the least what he was thinking, only a black cloud seemed over him.

'Why not?' he said at last. 'Horror is real. Why not a bit of horror, as you say, among all the rest?'

He gazed at her with complete, glittering earnestness, something heavy upon her.

'But –' she stammered in amazement.

'You feel a bit of horror for me too – But why not? Perhaps I feel a bit of horror for you too, for your light-coloured eyes and your strong white hands. But that is good.'

Kate looked at him in amazement. And all she wanted was to flee, to flee away beyond the bounds of this gruesome continent.

'Get used to it,' he said. 'Get used to it that there must be a bit of fear, and a bit of horror in your life. And marry me, and you will find many things that are not horror. The bit of horror is like the sesame seed in the nougat, it gives the sharp wild flavour. It is good to have it there.'

He sat watching her with black, glittering eyes, and talking with strange, uncanny reason. His desire seemed curiously impersonal, physical, and yet not personal at all. She felt as if, for him, she had some other name, she moved within another species. As if her name were, for example, Itzpapalotl,[4] and she had been born in unknown places, and was a woman unknown to herself.

Yet surely, surely he was only putting his will over her?

She was breathless with amazement, because he had made her see the physical possibility of marrying him: a thing she had never even glimpsed before. But surely, surely it would not be *herself* who could marry him. It would be some curious female within her, whom she did not know and did not own.

He was emanating a dark, exultant sort of passion.

'I can't believe,' she said, 'that I could do it.'

'Do it,' he said. 'And then you will know.'

She shuddered slightly, and went indoors for a wrap. She came out again in a silk Spanish shawl, brown, but deeply embroidered in silver-coloured silk. She tangled her fingers nervously in the long brown fringe.

Really, he seemed sinister to her, almost repellent. Yet she hated to think that she merely was afraid: that she had not the courage. She sat with her head bent, the light falling on her soft hair and on the heavy, silvery-coloured embroidery of her shawl, which she wrapped round her tight, as the Indian women do their rebozos. And his black eyes watched her, and watched the rich shawl, with a peculiar intense glitter. The shawl, too, fascinated him.

'Well!' he said suddenly. 'When shall it be?'

'What?' she said, glancing up into his black eyes with real fear.

'The marriage.'

She looked at him, almost hypnotised with amazement that he should have gone so far. And even now, she had not the power to make him retreat.

'I don't know,' she said.

'Will you say in August? On the first of August?'

'I won't say any time,' she said.

Suddenly the black gloom and anger of the Indians came over him. Then again he shook it off, with a certain callous indifference.

'Will you come to Jamiltepec to-morrow to see Ramón?' he asked. 'He wants to speak with you.'

Kate also wanted to see Ramón: she always did.

'Shall I?' she said.

'Yes! Come with me in the morning in the automobile. Yes?'

'I would like to see Don Ramón again,' she said.

'You are not afraid of him, eh? Not the bit of horror, eh?' he said, smiling peculiarly.

'No. But Don Ramón isn't really Mexican,' she said.

'Not really Mexican?'

'No! – He feels European.'

'Really! To me he is – Mexico.'

She paused and gathered herself together.

'I will row in a boat to Jamiltepec to-morrow, or I will take Alonso's motor-boat. I will come about ten o'clock.'

'Very good!' said Cipriano, rising to leave.

When he had gone, she heard the sound of the drum from the plaza. It would be another meeting of the men of Quetzalcoatl. But she had not the desire nor the courage to set out afresh that day.

Instead, she went to bed, and lay breathing the inner darkness. Through the window-cracks she saw the whiteness of the moon, and through the walls she heard the small pulse of the drum. And it all oppressed her and made her afraid. She lay forming plans to escape. She must escape. She would hurriedly pack her trunks and disappear: perhaps take the train to Manzanillo, on the coast, and thence sail up to California, to Los Angeles or to San Francisco. Suddenly escape, and flee away to a white man's country, where she could once more breathe freely. How good it would be! – Yes, this was what she would do.

The night grew late, the drum ceased, she heard Ezequiel come home and lie down on the mattress outside her door. The only sound was the hoarse crowing of cocks in the moonlit night. And in her room, like someone striking a match, came the greenish light of a firefly, intermittent, now here, now there.

Thoroughly uneasy and cowed, she went to sleep. But then she slept deeply.

And curiously enough, she awoke in the morning with a new feeling of strength. It was six o'clock, the sun was making yellow pencils through her shutter-cracks. She threw open her window to the street, and looked through the iron grating at the little lane with deep shadow under the garden wall, and above the wall, banana leaves fraying translucent green, and shaggy mops of palm-trees perching high, towards the twin white tower-tips of the church, crowned by the Greek cross with four equal arms.

In the lane it was already motion: big cows marching slowly to the lake, under the bluish shadow of the wall, and a small calf, big-eyed and adventurous, trotting aside to gaze through her gate at the green watered grass and the flowers. The silent peon, following, lifted his two arms with a sudden swoop upwards, noiselessly, and the calf careered on. Only the sound of the feet of calves.

Then two boys vainly trying to urge a young bull-calf to the lake. It kept on jerking up its sharp rump, and giving dry little kicks, from which the boys ran away. They pushed its shoulder, and it butted them with its blunt young head. They were in the state of semi-frenzied bewilderment which the Indians fall into when they are opposed and frustrated. And they took the usual recourse of running to a little distance, picking up heavy stones, and hurling them viciously at the animal.

'No!' cried Kate from her window. 'Don't throw stones. Drive it sensibly!'

They started as if the skies had opened, dropped their stones, and crept very much diminished after the see-sawing bull-calf.

An ancient crone appeared at the window with a plate of chopped-up young cactus leaves, for three centavos. Kate didn't like cactus vegetable, but she bought it. An old man was thrusting a young cockerel through the window-bars.

'Go,' said Kate, 'into the patio.'

And she shut her window on the street, for the invasion had begun.

But it had only changed doors.

'Niña! Niña!' came Juana's voice. 'Says the old man that you buy this chicken?'

'At how much?' shouted Kate, slipping on a dressing gown.

'At ten reales.'

'Oh, no!' said Kate, flinging open her patio doors, and appearing in her fresh wrap of pale pink cotton crepe, embroidered with heavy white flowers. 'Not more than a peso!'

'A peso and ten centavos!' pleaded the old man, balancing the staring-eyed red cock between his hands. 'He is nice and fat, Señorita. See!'

And he held out the cock for Kate to take it and balance it between her hands, to try its weight. She motioned to him to hand it to Juana. The red cock fluttered, and suddenly crowed in the transfer. Juana balanced him, and made a grimace.

'No, only a peso!' said Kate.

The man gave a sudden gesture of assent, received the *peso*, and disappeared like a shadow. Concha lurched up and took the cock, and instantly she bawled in derision:

'Está muy flaco! He is very thin.'

'Put him in the pen,' said Kate. 'We'll let him grow.'

The patio was liquid with sunshine and shadows. Ezequiel had rolled up his mattress and gone. Great rose-coloured hibiscus dangled from the tips of their boughs, there was a faint scent from the half-wild, creamy roses. The great mango trees were most sumptuous in the morning, like cliffs, with their hard green fruits dropping like the organs of some animal from the new bronze leaves, so curiously heavy with life.

'Está muy flaco!' the young Concha was bawling still in derision as she bore off the young cock to the pen under the banana trees. 'He's very scraggy.'

Everybody watched intent while the red cock was put in among the few scraggy fowls. The grey cock, elder, retreated to the far end of the pen, and eyed the newcomer with an eye of thunder. The red cock, *muy flaco*, stood diminished in a dry corner. Then suddenly he stretched himself and crowed shrilly, his red gills lifted like an aggressive beard. And the grey cock stirred around, preparing the thunders of his vengeance. The hens took not the slightest notice.

Kate laughed, and went back to her room to dress, in the powerful newness of the morning. Outside her window the women were passing quietly, the red water-jar on one shoulder, going to the lake for water. They always put one arm over their head, and held the jar on the other shoulder. It had a contorted look, different from the proud way the women carried water in Sicily.

'Niña! Niña!' Juana was crying outside.

'Wait a minute,' said Kate.

It was another of the hymn-sheets, with a Hymn of Quetzalcoatl.

'See, Niña, the new hymn from last evening.'

Kate took the leaflet and sat upon her bed to read it.

QUETZALCOATL LOOKS DOWN ON MEXICO

Jesus had gone far up the dark slope, when he looked back.
Quetzalcoatl, my brother! he called. Send me my images,
And the images of my mother, and the images of my saints.
Send me them by the swift way, the way of the sparks,
That I may hold them like memories in my arms when I go to sleep.

And Quetzalcoatl called back: I will do it.

Then he laughed, seeing the sun dart fiercely at him.
He put up his hand, and held back the sun with his shadow.
So he passed the yellow one, who lashed like a dragon in vain.
And having passed the yellow one, he saw the earth beneath.
And he saw Mexico lying like a dark woman with white breast-tips.

Wondering he stepped nearer, and looked at her,
At her trains, at her railways and her automobiles,
At her cities of stone and her huts of straw.
And he said: Surely this looks very curious!

He sat within the hollow of a cloud, and saw the men that worked in the fields,
   with foreign overseers.
He saw the men that were blind, reeling with aguardiente.
He saw the women that were not clean.
He saw the hearts of them all, that were black, and heavy, with a stone of anger
   at the bottom.

Surely, he said, this is a curious people I have found!

So leaning forward on his cloud, he said to himself:
I will call to them.
Hola! Hola! Mexicanos! Glance away a moment towards me.
Just turn your eyes this way, Mexicanos!

They turned not at all, they glanced not one his way.

Holala! Mexicanos! Holala!

They have gone stone deaf! he said.

So he blew down on them, to blow his breath in their faces.
But in the weight of their stupefaction, none of them knew.

Holala! What a pretty people!
All gone stupefied!

A falling star was running like a white dog over a plain.
He whistled to it loudly, twice, till it fell to his hand.
In his hand it lay and went dark.
It was the Stone of Change.

This is the stone of change! he said.

So he tossed it awhile in his hand, and played with it.
Then suddenly he spied the old lake, and he threw it in.
It fell in.
And two men looked up.

Holala! he said. *Mexicanos!*
Are there two of you awake?
So he laughed, and one heard him laughing.

Why are you laughing? asked the first man of Quetzalcoatl.
I hear the voice of my First Man ask me why I am laughing?
Holala, Mexicanos! It is funny!
To see them so glum and so lumpish!

Hey! First Man of my name! Hark here!
Here is my sign.
Get a place ready for me.

Send Jesus his images back, Mary and the saints and all.
Wash yourself, and rub oil in your skin.
On the seventh day, let every man wash himself, and put oil on his skin; let
  every woman.
Let him have no animal walk on his body, nor through the shadow of his hair.
  Say the same to the women.
Tell them they all are fools, that I'm laughing at them.
The first thing I did when I saw them, was to laugh at the sight of such fools.
Such lumps, such frogs with stones in their bellies.
Tell them they are like frogs with stones in their bellies, can't hop!
Tell them they must get the stones out of their bellies,
Get rid of their heaviness,
Their lumpishness,
Or I'll smother them all.

I'll shake the earth, and swallow them up, with their cities.
I'll send fire and ashes upon them, and smother them all.
I'll turn their blood like sour milk rotten with thunder,
They will bleed rotten blood, in pestilence.
Even their bones shall crumble.

Tell them so, First Man of my Name.

For the sun and the moon are alive, and watching with gleaming eyes.
And the earth is alive, and ready to shake off his fleas.
And the stars are ready with stones to throw in the faces of men.
And the air that blows good breath in the nostrils of people and beasts
Is ready to blow bad breath upon them, to perish them all.

The stars and the earth and the sun and the moon and the winds
Are about to dance the war dance round you, men!
When I say the word, they will start.
For sun and stars and earth and the very rains are weary
Of tossing and rolling the substance of life to your lips.
They are saying to one another: Let us make an end
Of those ill-smelling tribes of men, these frogs that can't jump,
These cocks that can't crow
These pigs that can't grunt
This flesh that smells
These words that are all flat
These money vermin.
These white men, and red men, and yellow men, and brown men, and black
   men
That are neither white, nor red, nor yellow, nor brown, nor black
But everyone of them dirtyish.
Let us have a spring cleaning in the world.
For men upon the body of the earth are like lice,
Devouring the earth into sores.
This is what stars and sun and earth and moon and winds and rain
Are discussing with one another; they are making ready to start.
So tell the men I am coming to,
To make themselves clean, inside and out.
To roll the grave-stone off their souls, from the cave of their bellies,
To prepare to be men.

Or else prepare for the other things.

   Kate read this long leaflet again and again, and a swift darkness like
a whirlwind seemed to envelop the morning. She drank her coffee on
the verandah, and the heavy papayas in their grouping seemed to be
oozing like great drops from the invisible spouting of the fountain of

non-human life. She seemed to see the great sprouting and urging of the cosmos, moving into weird life. And men only like green-fly clustering on the tender tips, an aberration there. So monstrous the rolling and unfolding of the life of the cosmos, as if even iron could grow like lichen deep in the earth, and cease growing, and prepare to perish. Iron and stone render up their life, when the hour comes. And men are less than the green-fly sucking the stems of the bush, so long as they live by business and bread alone. Parasites on the face of the earth.

She strayed to the shore. The lake was blue in the morning light, the opposite mountains pale and dry and ribbed like mountains in the desert. Only at their feet, next the lake, the dark strip of trees and white specks of villages.

Near her against the light five cows stood with their noses to the water drinking. Women were kneeling on the stones, filling red jars. On forked sticks stuck up on the foreshore, frail fishing nets were hung out, drying, and on the nets a small bird sat facing the sun; he was red as a drop of new blood, from the arteries of the air.

From the straw huts under the trees, her urchin of the mud-chick was scuttling towards her, clutching something in his fist. He opened his hand to her, and on the palm lay three of the tiny cooking-pots, the ollitas which the natives had thrown into the water long ago, to the gods.

'Muy chiquitas!'[5] he said, in his brisk way, a little, fighting trades-man; 'do you buy them?'

'I have no money. Tomorrow!' said Kate.

'Tomorrow!' he said, like a pistol shot.

'Tomorrow.'

He had forgiven her, but she had not forgiven him.

Somebody in the fresh Sunday morning was singing rather beauti-fully, letting the sound, as it were, produce itself.

A boy was prowling with a sling, prowling like a cat, to get the little birds. The red bird like a drop of new blood twittered upon the almost invisible fish-nets, then in a flash was gone. The boy prowled under the delicate green of the willow trees, stumbling over the great roots in the sand.

Along the edge of the water flew four dark birds, their necks pushed out, skimming silent near the silent surface of the lake, in a jagged level rush.

Kate knew these mornings by the lake. They hypnotised her almost like death. Scarlet birds like drops of blood, in very green willow trees. The aguador trotting to her house with a pole over his shoulder, and two heavy square gasoline cans, one at each end of the pole, filled with hot water. He had been to the hot spring for her daily supply. Now barefoot, with one bare leg, the young man trotted softly beneath the load, his dark, handsome face sunk beneath the shadows of the big hat, as he trotted in a silence, mindlessness that was like death.

Dark heads out on the water in little groups, like black water-fowl bobbing. Were they birds? Were they heads? Was this human life, or something intermediate, that lifted its orange, wet, glistening shoulders a little out of the lake, beneath the dark head?

She knew so well what the day would be. Slowly the sun thickening and intensifying in the air overhead. And slowly the electricity clotting invisibly as afternoon approached. The beach in the blind heat, strewn with refuse, smelling of refuse and the urine of creatures.

Everything going vague in the immense sunshine, as the air invisibly thickened, and Kate could feel the electricity pressing like hot iron on the back of her head. It stupefied her like morphine. Meanwhile the clouds rose like white trees from behind the mountains, as the afternoon swooned in silence, rose and spread black branches, quickly, in the sky, from which the lightning stabbed like birds.

And in the midst of the siesta stupor, the sudden round bolts of thunder, and the crash and the chill of rain.

Tea-time, and evening coming. The last sailing-boats making to depart, waiting for the wind. The wind was from the west, the boats going east and south had gone, their sails were lapsing far away on the lake. But the boats towards the west were waiting, waiting, while the water rattled under their black, flat keels.

The big boat from Tlapaltepec, bringing many people from the west, waited on into the night. She was anchored a few yards out, and in the early night her passengers came down the dark beach, weary of the day, to go on board. They clustered in a group at the edge of the flapping water.

The big, wide, flat-bottomed canoe, with her wooden awning and her one straight mast, lay black, a few yards out, in the dark night. A lamp was burning under the wooden roof; one looked in, from the shore. And this was home for the passengers.

A short man with trousers rolled up came to carry the people on board. The men stood with their backs to him, legs apart. He suddenly dived at them, ducked his head between the fork of their legs, and rose, with a man on his shoulders. So he waded out through the water to the black boat, and heaved his living load on board.

For a woman, he crouched down before her, and she sat on one of his shoulders. He clasped her legs with his right arm, she clasped his dark head. So he carried her to the ship, as if she were nothing.

Soon the boat was full of people. They sat on the mats on the floor, with their backs to the sides of the vessel, baskets hanging from the pent roof, swaying as the vessel swayed. Men spread their serapes and curled up to sleep. The light of the lantern lit them up, as they sat and lay, and slept, or talked in murmurs.

A little woman came up out of the darkness; then suddenly ran back again. She had forgotten something. But the vessel would not sail without her, for the wind would not change yet.

The tall mast stood high, the great sail lay in folds along the roof, ready. Under the roof, the lantern swayed, the people slept and stretched. Probably they would not sail till midnight. Then down the lake to Tlapaltepec, with its reeds at the end of the lake, and its dead, dead plaza, its dead dry houses of black adobe, its ruined streets, its strange, buried silence, like Pompeii.

Kate knew it. So strange and deathlike, it frightened her, and mystified her.

But to-day! To-day she would not loiter by the shore all morning. She must go to Jamiltepec in a motor-boat, to see Ramón. To talk to him even about marrying Cipriano.

Ah, how could she marry Cipriano, and give her body to this death? Take the weight of this darkness on her breast, the heaviness of this strange gloom. Die before dying, and pass away whilst still beneath the sun?

Ah no! Better to escape to the white men's lands.

But she went to arrange with Alonso for the motor-boat.

CHAPTER XVII

Fourth Hymn and the Bishop

THE President of the Republic, as a new broom, had been sweeping perhaps a little too clean for the common liking, so there was a 'rebellion'. It was not a very large one. But it meant, of course, banditry, robbery, and cowed villages.

Ramón was determined to keep free from the taint of politics. But already the Church, and with the Church, the Knights of Cortés[1] and a certain 'black' faction, was preparing against him. The priests began to denounce him from the pulpits – but not very loudly – as an ambitious Anti-Christ. With Cipriano beside him, however, and with Cipriano the army of the west, he had not much to fear.

But it was possible Cipriano would have to march away in defence of the government.

'Above all things,' said Ramón, 'I don't want to acquire a political smell. I don't want to be pushed in the direction of any party. Unless I can stand uncontaminated, I had better abandon everything. But the Church will push me over to the socialists – and the socialists will betray me on the first opportunity. It is not myself. It is the new spirit. The surest way to kill it – and it can be killed, like any other living thing – is to get it connected with any political party.'

'Why don't you see the Bishop?' said Cipriano. 'I will see him too. Am I to be chief of the division in the west for nothing?'

'Yes,' said Ramón slowly. 'I will see Jimenez. I have thought of it. Yes, I intend to use every means in my power. – Montes will stand for us, because he hates the Church and hates any hint of dictation from outside. He sees the possibility of a "national" church. Though myself, I don't care about national churches. Only one has to speak the language of one's own people. You know the priests are forbidding the people to read the Hymns?'

'What does that matter?' said Cipriano. 'These people are nothing if not perverse, nowadays. They will read them all the more.'

'Maybe! – I shall take no notice. I'll let my new legend, as they call it, grow while the earth is moist. But we have to keep our eye very close on all the little bunches of "interests".'

'Ramón!' said Cipriano. 'If you can turn Mexico entirely into a Quetzalcoatl country, what then?'

'I shall be First Man of Quetzalcoatl – I know no more.'

'You won't trouble about the rest of the world?'

Ramón smiled. Already he saw in Cipriano's eye the gleam of a Holy War.

'I would like,' he said, smiling, 'to be one of the Initiates of the Earth. One of the Initiators. Every country its own Saviour, Cipriano: or every people its own Saviour. And the First Men of every people, forming a Natural Aristocracy of the World. One must have aristocrats, that we know. But natural ones, not artificial. And in some way the world must be organically united: the world of man. But in the concrete, not in the abstract. Leagues and Covenants and International Programmes. Ah! Cipriano! it's like an international pestilence. The leaves of one great tree can't hang on the boughs of another great tree. The races of the earth are like trees, in the end they neither mix nor mingle. They stand out of each other's way, like trees. Or else they crowd on one another, and their roots grapple, and it is the fight to the death. – Only from the flowers there is commingling. And the flowers of every race are the natural aristocrats of that race. And the spirit of the world can fly from flower to flower, like a humming-bird, and slowly fertilize the great trees in their blossoms. Only the Natural Aristocrats can rise above their nation; and even then they do not rise beyond their race. Only the Natural Aristocrats of the World can be international, or cosmopolitan, or cosmic. It has always been so. The peoples are no more capable of it than the leaves of the mango tree are capable of attaching themselves to the pine. – So if I want Mexicans to learn the name of Quetzalcoatl, it is because I want them to speak with the tongues of their own blood. I wish the Teutonic world would once more think in terms of Thor[2] and Wotan,[3] and the tree Igdrasil.[4] And I wish the Druidic world would see, honestly, that in the mistletoe[5] is their mystery, and that they themselves are the Tuatha De Danaan,[6] alive, but submerged. And a new Hermes[7] should come back to the Mediterranean, and a new Ashtaroth[8] to Tunis; and Mithras[9] again to Persia, and Brahma unbroken[10] to India, and the oldest of dragons[11] to China. Then I, Cipriano, I, First Man of Quetzalcoatl, with you, First Man of Huitzilopochtli, and perhaps your wife, First Woman of Itzpapalotl, could we not meet, with sure souls, the other great aristocrats of the world, the First Man of Wotan and the First Woman of Freya,[12] First Lord of Hermes, and the Lady of Astarte,[13] the Best-Born of Brahma, and the Son of the Greatest Dragon? I tell you, Cipriano, then the earth might rejoice, when the First Lords of the West met the First Lords of South and East, in the Valley of the Soul. Ah, the earth has Valleys of the Soul, that are not cities of commerce and industry. And the mystery is one mystery, but men must see it differently. The hibiscus and the thistle and the gentian all flower on the Tree of Life,[14] but in the world they are far apart; and must be. And I am hibiscus and you are a yucca flower, and your Caterina is a wild daffodil, and my Carlota is a white pansy. Only four of us, yet we make a curious bunch. So it is. The men and women of the earth are not manufactured goods, to be interchangeable. But the Tree of Life is one tree, as we know when our souls open in the last blossoming. We can't change ourselves, and we don't want to. But when our souls open out in the final blossoming, then as blossoms we share one mystery with all blossoms, beyond the knowledge of any leaves and stems and roots: something transcendent.

'But it doesn't matter. At the present time I have to fight my way in Mexico, and you have to fight yours. So let us go and do it.'

He went away to his workshops and his men who were labouring under his directions, while Cipriano sat down to his correspondence and his military planning.

They were both interrupted by the thudding of a motor-boat entering the little bay. It was Kate, escorted by the black-scarved Juana.

Ramón, in his white clothes with the blue-and-black figured sash, and the big hat with the turquoise-inlaid Eye of Quetzalcoatl, went down to meet her. She was in white, too, with a green hat and the shawl of pale yellow silk.

'I was so glad to come again,' she said, holding out her hand to him. 'Jamiltepec has become a sort of Mecca to me, my inside yearns for it.'

'Then why don't you come oftener? I wish you would come.'

'I am afraid of intruding.'

'No! You could help if you would.'

'Oh!' she said. 'I am so frightened, and so sceptical of big undertakings. I think it is because, at the very bottom of me, I dislike the masses of people – anywhere. I'm afraid I rather despise people; I don't want them to touch me, and I don't want to touch them. – So how could I pretend to join any – any – any sort of Salvation Army? – which is a horrid way of putting it.'

Don Ramón laughed.

'I do myself,' he said. 'I detest and despise masses of people. But these are my own people.'

'I, ever since I was a child, since I can remember. – They say of me, when I was a little girl of four, and my parents were having a big dinner party, they had the nurse bring me in to say goodnight to all the people they had there dressed up and eating and drinking. And I suppose they all said nice things to me, as they do. I only answered: *You are all monkeys!* It was a great success! – But I felt it even as a child, and I feel it now. People are all monkeys to me, performing in different ways.'

'Even the people nearest you?'

Kate hesitated. Then she confessed, rather unwillingly:

'Yes! I'm afraid so. Both my husbands – even Joachim – they seemed, somehow, so *obstinate* in their little stupidities – rather like monkeys. I felt a terrible revulsion from Joachim when he was dead. I thought: What peaked monkey is that, that I have been losing my blood about. – Do you think it's rather awful?'

'I do! But then I think we *all* feel like that, at moments. Or we would if we dared. It's only one of our moments.'

'Sometimes,' said she, 'I think that is my *permanent* feeling towards people. I like the world, the sky and the earth and the greater mystery beyond. But people – yes, they are all monkeys to me.'

He could see that, at the bottom of her soul, it was true.

'Puros monos!' he said to himself in Spanish. 'Y lo que hacen, puras monerías.'[15]

'Pure monkeys! And the things they do, sheer monkeydom!' Then he added: 'Yet you have children!'

'Yes! Yes!' she said, struggling with herself. 'My first husband's children.'

'And they? – *monos y no más?*'[16]

'No!' she said, frowning and looking angry with herself. 'Only partly.'

'It is bad,' he said, shaking his head. 'But then!' he added. – 'What are my own children to me, but little monkeys? And their mother – and their mother – Ah, no! Señora Caterina! It is no good. One must be able to disentangle oneself from persons, from people. If I go to a rose-bush, to be intimate with it, it is a nasty thing that hurts me. One must disentangle oneself from persons and personalities, and see people as one sees the trees in the landscape. People in some way *dominate* you. In some way, humanity dominates your consciousness. So you must hate people and humanity, and you want to escape. But there is only one way of escape: to turn beyond them, to the greater life.'

'But I do!' cried Kate. 'I do nothing else. When I was with Joachim absolutely alone in a cottage, doing all the work myself, and knowing nobody at all, just living, and *feeling* the greater thing all the time; then I was free, I was happy.'

'But he?' said Ramón. 'Was he free and happy?'

'He was *really*. But that's where the monkeyishness comes in. He wouldn't let himself be content. He insisted on having *people* and a *cause*, just to torture himself with.'

'Then why didn't you live in your cottage *quite* alone, and without him?' he said. 'Why do you travel, and see people?'

She was silent, very angry. She knew she could not live quite alone. The vacuity crushed her. She needed a man there, to stop the gap, and to keep her balanced. But even when she had him, in her heart of hearts she despised him, as she despised the dog and the cat. Between herself and humanity there was the bond of subtle, helpless antagonism.

She was naturally quite free-handed and she left people their liberty. Servants would get attached to her, and casual people all liked and admired her. She had a strong life-flow of her own, and a certain assertive *joie de vivre*.

But underneath it all was the unconquerable dislike, almost *disgust* of people. More than hate, it was disgust. Whoever it was, wherever it was, however it was, after a little while this disgust overcame her. Her mother, her father, her sisters, her first husband, even her children whom she loved, and Joachim, for whom she had felt such passionate love, even these, being near her, filled her with a certain disgust and repulsion after a little while, and she longed to fling them down the great and final oubliette.

But there is no great and final oubliette: or at least, it is never final, until one has flung *oneself* down.

So it was with Kate. Till she flung herself down the last dark oubliette of death, she would never escape from her deep, her bottomless disgust with human beings. Brief contacts were all right, thrilling even. But close contacts, or long contacts, were short and long revulsions of violent disgust.

She and Ramón had sat down on a bench under the white-flowering oleander of the garden downstairs. His face was impassive and still. In the stillness, with a certain pain and nausea, he realized the state she was in, and realized that his own state, as regards *personal* people, was the same. Mere *personal* contact, mere human contact filled him, too, with disgust. Carlota disgusted him. Kate herself disgusted him. Sometimes, Cipriano disgusted him.

But this was because, or when, he met them on a merely human, personal plane. To do so was disaster; it filled him with disgust of them and loathing of himself.

He had to meet them on another plane, where the contact was different; intangible, remote, and without *intimacy*. His soul was concerned elsewhere. So that the quick of him need not be bound to anybody. The quick of a man must turn to God alone: in some way or other.

With Cipriano he was most sure. Cipriano and he, even when they embraced each other with passion, when they met after an absence, embraced in the recognition of each other's eternal and abiding loneliness; like the Morning Star.

But women would not have this. They wanted intimacy – and intimacy means disgust. Carlota wanted to be eternally and closely identified with Ramón, consequently she hated him and hated everything which she thought drew him away from this eternal close identification with herself. It was just a horror, and he knew it.

Men and women should know that they cannot, absolutely, meet on earth. In the closest kiss, the dearest touch, there is the small gulf which is none the less complete because it is so narrow, so *nearly* nonexistent. They must bow and submit in reverence, to the gulf. Even though I eat the body and drink the blood of Christ, Christ is Christ and I am I, and the gulf is impassable. Though a woman be dearer to a man than his own life, yet he is he and she is she, and the gulf can never close up. Any attempt to close it is a violation, and the crime against the Holy Ghost.

That which we get from the beyond, we get it alone. The final me I am, comes from the farthest off, from the Morning Star. The rest is assembled. All that of me which is assembled from the mighty cosmos can meet and touch all that is assembled in the beloved. But this is never the quick. Never can be.

If we would meet in the quick, we must give up the assembled self, the daily I, and putting off ourselves one after the other, meet unconscious in the Morning Star. Body, soul and spirit can be transfigured into the Morning Star. But without transfiguration we shall never get there. We shall gnash at the leash.

Ramón knew what it was to gnash at his leashes. He had gnashed himself almost to pieces, before he had found the way to pass out in himself, in the quick of himself, to the Quick of all being and existence, which he called the Morning Star, since men must give all things names. To pass in the quick of himself, with transfiguration, to the Morning Star, and there, there alone meet his fellow man.

He knew what it was to fail even now, and to keep on failing. With Carlota he failed absolutely. She claimed him and he restrained himself in resistance. Even his very naked breast, when Carlota was there, was self-conscious and assertively naked. But then that was because she claimed it as her property.

When men meet at the quick of all things, they are neither naked nor clothed; in the transfiguration they are just complete, they are not seen in part. The final perfect strength has also the power of innocence.

Sitting on the seat beside Kate, Ramón was sad with the sense of heaviness and inadequacy. His third Hymn was angry and bitter. Carlota almost embittered his soul. In Mexico, turbulent fellows had caught at his idea and burlesqued it. They had invaded one of the churches of the city, thrown out the sacred images, and hung in their place the grotesque papier-mâché Judas figures which the Mexicans explode at Easter time. This of course made a scandal. And Cipriano, whenever he was away on his own for some time, slipped back into the inevitable Mexican General, fascinated by the opportunity for furthering his own personal ambition and imposing his own personal will. Then came Kate, with this centre of sheer repudiation deep in the middle of her, the will to explode the world.

He felt his spirits sinking again, his limbs going like lead. There is only one thing that a man really wants to do, all his life; and that is, to find his way to his God, his Morning Star, and be alone there. Then afterwards, in the Morning Star, salute his fellow man, and enjoy the woman who has come the long way with him.

But to find the way, far, far along, to the bright Quick of all things, this is difficult, and requires all a man's strength and courage, for himself. If he breaks a trail alone, it is terrible. But if every hand pulls at him, to stay him in the human places; if the hands of love drag at his entrails and the hands of hate seize him by the hair, it becomes almost impossible.

This was how Ramón felt at the moment: – I am attempting the impossible. I had better either go and take my pleasure of life while it lasts, hopeless of the pleasure which is beyond all pleasures. Or else I had better go into the desert and take my way all alone, to the Star where at last I have my wholeness, holiness. The way of the anchorites and the men who went into the wilderness to pray. For surely my soul is craving for her consummation, and I am weary of the thing men call life. Living, I want to depart to where *I am*.

Yet, he said to himself, the woman that was with me in the Morning Star, how glad I should be of her! And the man that was with me there, what a delight his presence would be! Surely the Morning Star is a meeting-ground for us, for the joy!

Sitting side by side on the bench, Ramón and Kate forgot one another, she thinking back on the past, with the long disgust of it all, he thinking on into his future, and trying to revive his heavy spirits.

In the silence, Cipriano came out on to the balcony above, looking around. He almost started as he saw the two figures seated on the bench below, under the white oleander tree, miles apart, worlds apart, in their silence.

Ramón heard the step, and glanced up.

'We are coming up!' he called, rising and looking round at Kate. 'Shall we go upstairs? Will you drink something cool, tepache, or squeezed oranges? There is no ice.'

'I would like orange juice and water,' she said.

He called to his servant and gave the order.

Cipriano was in the white pantaloons and blouse, like Ramón. But his sash was scarlet, with black curves, something like the markings on a snake.

'I heard you come. I thought perhaps you had gone away again,' he said, looking at her with a certain black reproachfulness: an odd, hesitating wistfulness of the barbarian, who feels himself at a loss. Then also a certain resentment.

'Not yet,' she said.

Ramón laughed, and flung himself into a chair.

'The Señora Caterina thinks we are all monkeys, but perhaps this particular monkey-show is the most amusing after all,' he said. 'So she will see a little more of it.'

Cipriano, a real Indian, was offended in his pride, and the little black *imperial* on his chin seemed to become portentous.

'That's *rather* an unfair way of putting it!' laughed Kate.

The black eyes of Cipriano glanced at her in hostility. He thought she was laughing at him. And so, at the depths of her female soul, she was. She was jeering at him inwardly. Which no man can stand, least of all a dark-skinned man.

'No!' she said. 'There's something else besides that.'

'Ah!' said Ramón. 'Take care! A little mercy is a dangerous thing.'

'No! Not mercy!' she said, flushing. 'Why are you being horrid to me?'

'Monkeys always end by being horrid to the spectators,' said Ramón.

She looked up at him, and caught the flash of anger in his eyes.

'I came,' she said, 'to hear about the Mexican pantheon. I was even given to understand I might be admitted.'

'Ah, that is good!' laughed Ramón. 'A rare specimen of the female monkey has been added to the Ramón menagerie! I am sure you would be a good draw. There have been some pretty goddesses, I assure you, in the Aztec pantheon.'

'How horrid!' she said.

'Come! Come!' he cried. 'Let us keep to the bedrock of things, Señora mía. We are all monkeys. Monos somos. – Ihr seid alle Affen![17] Out of the mouths of babes and sucklings was it spoken, as Carlota said. You see that little male monkey, Cipriano. He had the monkey's idea of marrying you. Say the word. Marriage is a monkey's game. Say the word. He will let you go when you've had enough; and he's had enough. He is a *general* and a very great *jefe*. He can make you monkey-queen of monkey-Mexico, if it please you. And what should monkeys do, but amuse themselves! *Vamos! Embobémonos!*[18] Shall I be priest? *Vamos! Vamos!*'

He rose with sudden volcanic violence, and rushed away.

Cipriano looked at Kate in wonder. She had gone pale.

'What have you been saying to him?' he asked.

'Nothing!' she said, rising. 'I'd better go now.'

Juana was collected; and Alonso and Kate set off back down the lake. She sat with a certain obstinate offendedness under the awning of the boat. The sun was terrifically hot, and the water blinded her. She put on black spectacles, in which she looked a monster.

'Mucho calor, Niña! Mucho calor!'[19] Juana was repeating behind her. The criada had evidently imbibed tepache.

On the pale-brown water little tufts of water-hyacinth were vaguely sailing, holding up the hand of a leaf for a sail. Everywhere the lake was dotted with these sailing tufts. The heavy rains had washed in flood down the Lerma river into the lake, washing the acres of *lirio* loose from the marshy end of the waters, thirty miles away, and slowly setting them travelling over all the expanse of the inland sea, till the shores began to be piled, and the far-off Santiago river, which flowed out of the lake, was choked.

That day Ramón wrote his Fourth Hymn.

WHAT QUETZALCOATL SAW IN MEXICO

Who are these strange faces in Mexico?
Palefaces, yellowfaces, blackfaces? These are no Mexicans!
Where do they come from, and why?

Lord of the Two Ways, these are the foreigners.
They come out of nowhere.
Sometimes they come to tell us things,
Mostly they are the greedy ones.

What then do they want?

They want gold, they want silver from the mountains,
And oil, much oil from the coast.
They take sugar from the tall tubes of the cane,
Wheat from the high lands, and maize;
Coffee from the bushes in the hot lands, even the juicy rubber.
They put up tall chimneys that smoke,
And in the biggest houses they keep their machines, that talk
And work iron elbows up and down,
And hold myriad threads from their claws!
Wonderful are the machines of the greedy ones!

And you, Mexicans and peons, what do you do?

We work with their machines, we work in their fields,
They give us pesos made of Mexican silver.
They are the clever ones.

Do you love them then?

We love them not, and never.
Their faces are ugly, yet they make wonderful things.
And their wills are like their machines of iron.
What can we do?

I see dark things rushing across the country.

Yea, Lord! Even trains and camions and automobiles.

Trains and camions, automobiles and aeroplanes.
How nice! says the peon, to go rushing in a train!
How nice, to get in the camion, and for twenty centavos, to be gone!
How nice, in the great cities, where all things rush, and huge lights flare bright,
    to wander and do nothing!
How nice to sit in the cine, where the picture of all the world dances before
    the eyes!
How nice if we could take all these things away from the foreigners, and possess
    them!
Take back our lands and silver and oil, take the trains and the factories and
    the automobiles
And play with them all the time!
How nice!

Oh, fools! Mexicans and peons!
Who are you, to be masters of machines which you cannot make?
Which you can only break!
Those that can make are masters of these machines.
Not you, poor boobs.

How have these palefaces, yellowfaces crossed the waters of the world?
Oh, fools! Mexicans and peons, with muddy hearts!
Did they do it by squatting on their hams?
You do nothing but squat on your hams, and stare with vacant eyes, and drink
    fire-waters, and quarrel and stab.
And then run like surly dogs at the bidding of paleface masters.

Oh, dogs and fools, Mexicans and peons!
Watery-hearted, with wishy-washy knees.
Sulky in spirit, and inert.
What are you good for, but to be slaves, and rot away?

You are not worth a god!
Lo! the universe tangles its great dragons,
The dragons in the cosmos are stirring with anger again.

The dragon of the disappointed dead, that sleeps in the snow-white north
Is lashing his tail in his sleep; the winds howl, the cold rocks round.
The spirits of the cold dead whistle in the ears of the world.
Prepare for doom.

For I tell you, there are no dead dead, not even your dead.
There are dead that sleep in the waves of the Morning Star, with freshening
    limbs.
There are dead that weep in bitter rains.
There are dead that cluster in the frozen north, shuddering and chattering
    among the ice
And howling with hate.
There are dead that creep through the burning bowels of the earth,
Stirring the fires to acid of bitterness.
There are dead that sit under the trees, watching with ash-grey eyes for their
    victims.
There are dead that attack the sun like swarms of black flies, to suck his life.
There are dead that stand upon you, when you go in to your women,
And they dart to her womb, they fight for the chance to be born, they struggle
    at the gate you have opened,
They gnash when it closes, and hate the one that got in, to be born again,
Child of the living dead, the dead that live and are not refreshed.
I tell you, sorrow upon you; you shall all die.
And being dead, you shall not be refreshed.
There are no dead dead.
Being dead, you shall rove like dogs with broken haunches
Seeking the offal and garbage of life, in the invisible lanes of the air.

The dead that have mastered fire live on, salamanders, in fire.
The dead of the water-lords rock and glimmer in the seas.
The dead of the steel machines go up in motion, *away*!
The dead of electric masters are electricity itself.

But the dead of those who have mastered nothing, nothing at all,
Crawl like masterless dogs in the back streets of the air,
Creeping for the garbage of life, and biting with venomous mouths.

Those that have mastered the forces of the world, die into the forces, they have
    homes in death.
But you! what have you mastered, among the dragon hosts of the cosmos?
There are dragons of sun and ice, dragons of the moon and the earth, dragons
    of salty waters, dragons of thunder;

There is the spangled dragon of the stars at large.
And far at the centre, with one unblinking eye, the dragon of the Morning Star.

Conquer! says the Morning Star. Pass the dragons, and pass on to me.
For I am sweet, I am the last and the best, the pool of new life.
But lo! you inert ones, I will set the dragons upon you.
They shall crunch your bones.
And even then they shall spit you out, as broken-haunched dogs,
You shall have nowhere to die into.

Lo! in the back streets of the air, dead ones are crawling like curs!
Lo! I release the dragons! The great white one of the north,
Him of the disappointed dead, he is lashing and turning round.
He is breathing cold corruption upon you, you shall bleed in your chests.

I am going to speak to the dragon of the inner fires,
He who housels the dead of the guns,
To withdraw his warmth from your feet, so your feet turn cold with death.

I am about to tell the dragon of the waters to turn round on you
And spew out corrosion into your streams, on your rains.

And I wait for the final day, when the dragon of thunder, waking under the
    spider-web nets
Which you've thrown upon him, shall suddenly shake with rage,
And dart his electric needles into your bones, and curdle your blood like milk
    with electric venom.

Wait! Only wait! Little by little it all shall come upon you.

Ramón put on his black city clothes, and a black hat, and went himself with this hymn to the printer in the city. The sign of Quetzalcoatl he had printed in black and red, and the sign of the dragon, at the end, in green and black and red. And the sheet was folded.

Six soldiers of Cipriano's command took the bundles of hymns by train; one to the capital, one to Puebla and Jalapa, one to Tampico and Monterrey, one to Torreon and Chihuahua, one to Sinaloa and Sonora, and one to the mines in Pachucha, Guanajuato, and the central region. Each soldier took only a hundred sheets. But in every town there was a recognized Reader of the Hymns; or two, or three, or four, or even ten Readers in one city. And readers who went round to the villages.

Because there was a strange, submerged desire in the people for things beyond the world. They were weary of events, and weary of news and the newspapers, weary even of the things that are taught in education. Weary is the spirit of man with man's importunity. Of all things human, and humanly invented, we have had enough, they seemed to say. And though they took not much active notice of the Hymns, they craved for them, as men crave for alcohol, as a relief from the weariness and ennui of mankind's man-made world.

Everywhere, in all the towns and villages, at night-time the little flames would be seen flickering, a cluster of people was seen, sometimes standing, sometimes sitting upon the ground, listening to the slow voice of some Reader.

More rarely, in some small, out-of-the-way plaza, would sound the sinister thud of the tom-tom, beating out of the hollow of the ages. And there would be two men with white serapes with the blue edges. Then the singing of the Songs of Quetzalcoatl, and perhaps the slow round dance, with the ancient rhythm of the feet on the earth, belonging to aboriginal America.

For the old dances of the Aztecs and the Zapotecs, of all the submerged Indian races, are based upon the old, sinking birdstep of the Red Indians of the north.[20] It is in the blood of the people; they cannot quite forget it. It comes back to them, with a sense of fear, and joy, and relief.

Of themselves, they dared not revive the old motion, nor stir the blood in the old way. The spell of the past is too terrible. But in the Songs and the Hymns of Quetzalcoatl, there spoke a new voice, the voice of a master and authority. And though they were slow to trust, the slowest and the most untrusting, they seized upon the new-old thrill, with a certain fear, and joy, and relief.

The Men of Quetzalcoatl avoided the great market-places and centres of activity. They took their stand in the little side places. On the rim of a fountain a man in a dark blanket with blue borders, or with the sign of Quetzalcoatl in his hat, would sit down and begin to read aloud. It was enough. The people lingered to listen. He would read to the end, then say: 'I have finished this reading of the Fourth Hymn of Quetzalcoatl. Now I will begin again.'

In this way, by a sort of far-away note in the voice, and by the slow monotony of repetition, the thing would drift darkly into the consciousness of the listeners.

Already in the beginning there had been the scandal of the Judases.

Holy Week, in Mexico City, is, to all appearance, the great week of Judas. Everywhere you see men carrying home in triumph the great, gaudily-varnished dolls of papier-mâché. They are all men-dolls, more or less life-like grotesque. Most frequently it is a fat Mexican-Spanish hacendado, landowner and big farmer, who is represented with his tight trousers, sticking-out belly, and huge upturned moustaches. The old-fashioned *patrón*. Some of the figures are like Punch, some are like harlequin. But they all have rosy faces and the white man's get-up. You never see the dark-faced image of a native-blooded Mexican; always a stiff, haughty grotesque of a white man.

And all these are Judases. Judas is the fun of the fair, the victim, the big man of Holy Week, just as the Skeleton, and the skeleton on horse-back, is the idol of the first week in November, the days of the dead and of all the saints.[21]

On Easter Saturday the Judases are hung from the balconies, the string is lighted, and at length, *bang!* Shrieks of joy, Judas has exploded into nothingness, from a big cracker in the middle of him! – All the town is popping with Judases.

There was the scandal of the Holy Images thrown out of one of the churches in Mexico City, and these Judases put in their place.[22] The Church began to move.

But then the Church in Mexico has to move gingerly; it is not popular, and its claws are cut. The priest may not ring the church bells for more than three minutes. Neither priests nor monks may wear any habit in the street, beyond the hideous black vest and white collar of the Pro-testant clergy. So that the priest shows himself as little as possible in the street, and practically never in the chief streets and the chief plazas.

Nevertheless, he still has influence. Processions in the streets are for-bidden, but not sermons from the pulpit, nor advice from the con-fessional. Montes, the President, had no love for the Church, and was meditating the expulsion of all foreign priests.[23] The Archbishop him-self was an Italian. But he was also a fighter.

He gave orders to all the priests, to forbid the people from listening to anything concerned with Quetzalcoatl, to destroy any hymn-sheet that might fall into their hands, and to prevent as far as possible the Hymns from being read, and the Songs from being sung, in the parishes.

But Montes had given orders to the police and the military to afford such protection to the Men of Quetzalcoatl as was accorded to any other law-abiding citizen.

Mexico is not Mexico for nothing, however, and already blood had been shed on both sides. This Ramón particularly wanted to avoid, as he felt that violent death was not so easily wiped out of the air and out of the souls of men, as spilt blood was washed off the pavements.

Therefore, when he was in the City, he asked the Bishop of the West if he would consent to an interview with himself and Don Cipriano, and would he name the place. The Bishop – who was an old friend and adviser of Carlota, and who knew Ramón well enough, replied that he should be pleased to see Don Ramón and the *Señor General* the next day, if they would be so good as to come to his house.

The Bishop no longer occupied the great episcopal palace. This was turned into the post-office building. But he had a large house not far from the Cathedral, which had been presented by the faithful.

Ramón and Cipriano found the thin old man in a dusty, uninteresting library, waiting. He wore a simple black cassock, not too clean, with purple buttons. He received Ramón, who was in a black town suit, and Cipriano, who was in uniform, with an affable manner and suspicious looks. But he played at being the lively, genial old bird.

'Ah, Don Ramón, it is long since I saw you! How goes it, eh? Well, well? That is good! That is very good!' And he patted Ramón on the sleeve like a fussy old uncle. 'Ah, my General, much honour, much honour! Welcome to this poor house of yours. It is the house of your Honour! To serve you! Gentlemen! Won't you take a seat?'

They all sat down, in the dusty, dreary room, in the old leather chairs. The Bishop nervously looked at his thin old hands, at the fine, but rather dull amethyst ring he wore.

'Good! Señores!' he said, glancing up with his little black eyes. 'At your service! Entirely at the service of your Honours.'

'Doña Carlota is in the city, Father. You have seen her?' said Ramón.

'Yes, son of mine,' said the Bishop.

'Then you know the latest news about me. She told you everything.'

'Somewhat! Somewhat! She spoke somewhat of you, the poor little thing. Thanks to God she has her sons with her. They are safely back in their native country, in good health.'

'Did you see them?'

'Yes! Yes! Two of my dearest children! Very sympathetic, very intelligent, like their father; and, like him, promising to be of very handsome presence. Yes! Yes! Smoke if you will, my General. Don't hesitate.'

Cipriano lit a cigarette. From old associations, he was nervous, albeit amused.

'You know all about what I want to do, Father?' said Ramón.

'I don't know all, son of mine, but I know enough. I wouldn't want to hear more. Eh!' he sighed. 'It is very sad.'

'Not so very sad, Father, if we don't make it sad. Why make a sad thing out of it, Father? We are in Mexico for the most part Indians. They cannot understand the high Christianity, Father, and the Church knows it. Christianity is a religion of the spirit, and must needs be understood if it is to have any effect. The Indians cannot understand it, any more than the rabbits of the hills.'

'Very good! Very good! Son of mine! But we can convey it to them. The rabbits of the hills are in the hands of God.'

'No, Father, it is impossible. And without a religion that will connect them with the universe, they will all perish. Only religion will serve; not socialism, nor education, nor anything.'

'Thou speakest well,' said the Bishop.

'The rabbits of the hills may be in the hands of God, Father. But they are at the mercy of men. The same with Mexico. The people sink heavier and heavier into inertia, and the Church cannot help them, because the Church does not possess the key-word to the Mexican soul.'

'Doesn't the Mexican soul know the Voice of God?' said the Bishop.

'Your own children may know your voice, Father. But if you go out to speak to the birds on the lake, or the deer among the mountains, will they know your voice? Will they wait and listen?'

'Who knows? It is said they waited to listen to the Holy Francisco of Assisi.'

'Now, Father, we must speak to the Mexicans in their own language, and give them the clue-word to their own souls. I shall say *Quetzalcoatl*. If I am wrong, let me perish. But I am not wrong.'

The Bishop fidgeted rather restlessly. He didn't want to hear all this. And he did not want to answer. He was impotent anyhow.

'Your Church is the Catholic Church, Father?'

'Surely!' said the Bishop.

'And Catholic Church means the Church of All, the Universal Church?'

'Surely, son of mine.'

'Then why not let it be really catholic? Why call it catholic, when it is not only just one among many churches, but is even hostile to all the rest of the churches? Father, why not let the Catholic Church become really the Universal Church?'

'It is the Universal Church of Christ, my son.'

'Why not let it be the Universal Church of Mohammed as well; since ultimately, God is One God, but the peoples speak varying languages, and each needs its own prophet to speak with its own tongue. The Universal Church of Christ, and Mohammed, and Buddha, and Quetzalcoatl, and all the others – *that* would be a Catholic Church, Father.'

'You speak of things beyond me,' said the Bishop, turning his ring.

'Not beyond any man,' said Don Ramón. 'A Catholic Church is a church of all the religions, a home on earth for all the prophets and the Christs. A big tree under which every man who acknowledges the greater life of the soul can sit and be refreshed. Isn't *that* the Catholic Church, Father?'

'Alas, my son, I know the Apostolic Church of Christ in Rome, of which I am a humble servant. I do not understand these clever things you are saying to me.'

'I am asking you for peace, Father. I am not one who hates the Church of Christ, the *Roman* Catholic Church. But in Mexico I think it has no place. When my heart is not bitter, I am grateful forever to Christ, the Son of God. The affair of the Judases grieves me more than it does you, and the affairs of bloodshed are far bitterer to me.'

'I am no innovator, my son, to provoke bloodshed.'

'Listen! I am going to remove the holy images from the church at Sayula, with reverence, and with reverence burn them upon the lake. Then I shall put the image of Quetzalcoatl in the church at Sayula.'

The Bishop looked up furtively. For some moments he said nothing. But his silence was furtive, cornered.

'Would you dare do that, Don Ramón?' he said.

'Yes! And I shall not be prevented. General Viedma is with me.'

The Bishop glanced sideways at Cipriano.

'Certainly,' said Cipriano.

'Nevertheless it is illegal,' said the Bishop, with acid bitterness.

'What is illegal in Mexico?' said Ramón. 'What is weak is illegal. I will not be weak, My Lord.'

'Lucky you!' said the Bishop, lifting his shoulders.

There was a break of silence.

'No!' said Ramón. 'I come to ask you for peace. Tell the Archbishop what I say. Let him tell the Cardinals and the Pope that the time has come for a Catholic Church of the Earth, the Catholic Church of All the Sons of Men. The Saviours are more than one, and let us pray they will still be increased. But God is one God, and the Saviours are the Sons of the One God. Let the Tree of the Church spread its branches over all the earth, and shelter the prophets in its shade, as they sit and speak their knowledge of the beyond.'

'Are you one of these prophets, Don Ramón?'

'I surely am, Father. And I would speak about Quetzalcoatl in Mexico, and build his Church here.'

'Nay! You would invade the Churches of Christ and the Blessed Virgin, I heard you say.'

'You know my intentions. But I do not want to quarrel with the Church of Rome, nor have bloodshed and enmity, Father. Can you not understand me? Should there not be peace between the men who strive down their different ways to the God-Mystery?'

'Once more desecrate the altars! Bring in strange idols. Burn the images of Our Lord and Our Lady, and ask for peace?' said the poor Bishop, who helplessly longed to be left alone.

'All that, Father,' said Ramón.

'Son, what can I answer? You are a good man smitten with the madness of pride. Don Cipriano is one more Mexican general. I am the poor old Bishop of this diocese, faithful servant of the Holy Church, humble child of the Holy Father in Rome. What can I do? What can I answer? Take me out to the cemetery and shoot me at once, General!'

'I don't want to,' said Cipriano.

'It will end like that,' said the Bishop.

'But why?' cried Don Ramón. 'Is there no sense in what I say? Cannot you understand?'

'My son, my understanding goes no farther than my faith, my duty, will allow. I am not a clever man. I live by faith, and my duty to my sacred office. Understand that I do not understand.'

'Good-day, Father!' said Ramón, suddenly rising.

'Go with God, my son,' said the Bishop, rising and lifting his fingers.

'Adiós, Señor!' said Cipriano, clicking his spurs, and putting his hand on his sword as he turned to the door.

'Adiós, Señor General,' said the Bishop, darting after them his eyes of old malice, which they could feel in their backs.

'He will say nothing,' said Cipriano, as he and Ramón went down the steps. 'The old jesuit, he only wants to keep his job and his power, and prevent the heart's beating. I know them. All they treasure, even more than their money, is their centipede power over the frightened people; especially over the women.'

'I didn't know you hated them,' laughed Ramón.

'Waste no more breath on them, my dear one,' said Cipriano. 'Go forward, you can walk over broken snakes such as those.'

As they went on foot past the post-office square, where the modern scribes at little tables under the arches sat tapping out letters on their typewriters for the poor and illiterate, who waited with their few centavos to have their messages turned into florid Castilian, Ramón and Cipriano met with an almost startled respect.

'Why talk to the Bishop? – he doesn't exist any more. I hear his Knights of Cortés had a big dinner the other evening, and it is said – I don't believe it – that they drank oaths in blood to have my life and yours. But I think the oaths of the Catholic Dames would frighten me more. Why, if a man stops to unfasten his trousers to make water, the Knights of Cortés run for their lives, thinking the pistol is pointed at them. Don't think about them, man! Don't try to conciliate them. They will only puff up and become insolent, thinking you are afraid of them. Six soldiers will trample down all that dirt,' said the General.

It was the city, and the spirit of the city.

Cipriano had a suite in the big Palace on the Plaza de Armas.

'If I marry,' he said, as they passed into the stone patio, where soldiers stood at attention, 'I shall take a house in the colony, to be more private.'

Cipriano in town was amusing. He seemed to exude pride and arrogant authority as he walked about. But his black eyes, glancing above his fine nose and that little goat beard, were not to be laughed at. They seemed to get everything, in the stab of a glance. A demoniacal little fellow.

Auto da Fé[1]

RAMÓN saw Carlota and his boys in the city, but it was a rather fruitless meeting. The elder boy was just uncomfortable in the presence of his father, but the younger, Cyprian, who was delicate and very intelligent, had a rather lofty air of displeasure with his parent.

'Do you know what they sing, papa?' he said.

'Not all the things they sing,' said Ramón.

'They sing –' the boy hesitated. Then, in his clear young voice, he piped up, to the tune of *La Cucaracha*:[2]

> 'Don Ramón don't drink, don't smoke.
> Doña Carlota wished he would.
> He's going to wear the sky-blue cloak
> That he's stole from the Mother of God.'

'No, I'm not,' said Ramón, smiling. 'Mine's got a snake and a bird in the middle, and black zigzags and a red fringe. You'd better come and see it.'

'No, papa! I don't want to.'

'Why not?'

'I don't want to be mixed up in this affair. It makes us all look ridiculous.'

'But how do you think you look, anyhow, in your striped little sailor suit and your little saintly look? We'd better dress you as the Infant Jesus.'

'No, papa! You are in bad taste. One doesn't say those things.'

'Now you'll have to confess to a fib. You say one doesn't say those things, when I, who am your father, said them only a moment ago, and you heard me.'

'I mean good people don't. Decent people.'

'Now you'll have to confess again, for calling your father indecent. – Terrible child!'

The child flushed, and tears rose to his eyes. There was silence for a while.

'So you don't want to come to Jamiltepec?' said Ramón, to his boys.

'Yes!' said the elder boy, slowly. 'I want to come and bathe in the lake, and have a boat. But – they say it is impossible.'

'Why?'

'They say you make yourself a peon, in your clothes.' – The boy was shy.

'They're very nice clothes, you know. Nicer than those little breeches of yours.'

'They say, also, that you pretend to be the Aztec god Quetzalcoatl.'

'Not at all. I only pretend that the Aztec god Quetzalcoatl is coming back to the Mexicans.'

'But, papa, it is not true.'

'How do you know?'

'Because it is impossible.'

'Why?'

'There never was any Quetzalcoatl, except idols.'

'Is there any Jesus, except images?'

'Yes, papa.'

'Where?'

'In heaven.'

'Then in heaven there is also Quetzalcoatl. And what is in heaven is capable of coming back to earth. Don't you believe me?'

'I can't.'

'Then go on unbelieving,' said the father, laughing at them and rising to leave them.

'It is very bad that they sing songs about you, and put mama in; like about Pancho Villa,' said the younger boy. 'It hurts me very much.'

'Rub it with *Vapour-rub*, my pet,' said Ramón. 'Rub it with *Vapour-rub*, where it hurts you.'

'What a real bad man you are, papa!'

'What a real good child are you, my son! Isn't that so?'

'I don't know, papa. I only know you are bad.'

'Oh! Oh! Is that all they teach thee at thy American school?'

'Next term,' said Ciprianito, 'I want to change my name. I don't want to be called Carrasco any more. When thou art in the newspapers, they will laugh at us.'

'Oh! Oh! I am laughing at thee *now*, little frog! What name wilt thou choose then? Espina, perhaps. Thou knowest Carrasco is a wild bush, on the moors in Spain, where we come from. Wilt thou be the little thorn on the bush? Call thyself Espina, thou art a sprig of the old tree. Entonces, adiós! Señor Espina Espinita!'

'Adiós!' said the boy abruptly, flushing with rage.

Ramón took a motor-car to Sayula, for there was a made road. But already the rains were washing it away. The car lurched and bumped in the great gaps. In one place, a camión lay on its back, where it had overturned.

On the flat desert, there were already small smears of water, and the pink cosmos flowers, and the yellow, were just sprouting their tufts of buds. The hills in the distance were going opaque, as leaves came out on the invisible trees and bushes. The earth was coming to life.

Ramón called in Sayula at Kate's house. She was out, but the wild Concha came scouring across the beach, to fetch her. – 'There is Don Ramón! There is Don Ramón!'

Kate hurried home, with sand in her shoes.

She thought Ramón looked tired, and, in his black suit, sinister.

'I didn't expect you,' she said.

'I am on my way back from town.'

He sat very still, with that angry look on his creamy dark face, and he kept pushing back his black moustache from his closed, angry lips.

'Did you see anybody in town?' she asked.

'I saw Don Cipriano – and Doña Carlota, and my boys!'

'Oh, how nice for you! Are they quite well?'

'In excellent health, I believe.'

She laughed suddenly.

'You are still cross,' she said. 'Is it about the monkeys still?'

'Señora,' he said, leaning forward, so that his black hair dropped a little on his brow, 'in monkeydom, I don't know who is prince. But in the kingdom of fools, I believe it is I.'

'Why?' she said.

And as he did not answer, she added:

'It must be a comfort to be a prince, even of fools.'

He looked daggers at her, then burst into a laugh.

'Oh, Señora mía! What ails us men, when we are always wanting to be *good*?'

'Are you repenting of it?' she laughed.

'Yes!' he said. 'I am a prince of fools! Why have I started this Quetzalcoatl business? Why? Pray tell me why?'

'I suppose you wanted to.'

He pondered for a time, pushing up his moustache.

'Perhaps it is better to be a monkey than a fool. I object to being called a monkey, nevertheless. Carlota is a monkey, no more; and my two boys are prize young monkeys in sailor suits. And I am a fool. Yet what is the difference between a fool and a monkey?'

'Quién sabe?' said Kate.

'One wants to be good, and the other is sure he *is* good. So I make a fool of myself. They are sure they are always good, so that makes monkeys of them. Oh, if only the world would blow up like a bomb!'

'It won't!' said Kate.

'True enough. – Ah, well!'

He drew himself erect, pulling himself together.

'Do you think, Señora Caterina, you might marry our mutual General?' Ramón had put himself aside again.

'I – I don't know!' stammered Kate. 'I hardly think so.'

'He is not sympathetic to you at all?'

'Yes. He is. He is alive, and there is even a certain fascination about him. – But one shouldn't try marrying a man of another race, do you think, even if he were more sympathetic?'

'Ah!' sighed Ramón. 'It's no good generalizing. It's no good marrying anybody, unless there will be a real fusion somewhere.'

'And I feel there wouldn't,' said Kate. 'I feel he just wants something of me; and perhaps I just want something of him. But he would never meet me. He would never come forward himself, to meet me. He would come to take something from me and I should have to let him. And I don't want merely that. I want a man who will come half-way, just half-way, to meet me.'

Don Ramón pondered, and shook his head.

'You are right,' he said. 'Yet, in these matters, one never knows what is half-way, nor where it is. A woman who just wants to be taken, and then to cling on, is a parasite. And a man who wants just to take, without giving, is a creature of prey.'

'And I'm afraid Don Cipriano might be that,' said Kate.

'Possibly,' said Ramón. 'He is not so with me. But perhaps he would be, if we did not meet – perhaps it is our half-way – in some physical belief that is at the very middle of us, and which we recognize in one another. Don't you think there might be that between you and him?'

'I doubt if he'd feel it necessary, with a woman. A woman wouldn't be important enough.'

Ramón was silent.

'Perhaps!' he said. 'With a woman, a man always wants to let himself go. And it is precisely with a woman that he should never let himself go. It is precisely with a woman that he should never let himself go, but stick to his innermost belief, and meet her just there. Because when the innermost belief coincides in them both, if it's physical, there, and then, and nowhere else, they can meet. And it's no good unless there is a meeting. It's no good a man ravishing a woman, and it's absolutely no good a woman ravishing a man. It's a sin, that is. There is such a thing as sin, and that's the centre of it. Men and women keep on ravishing one another. Absurd as it may sound, it is not I who would ravish Carlota. It is she who would ravish me. Strange and absurd and a little shameful, it is true. – Letting oneself go, is either ravishing or being ravished. Oh, if we could only abide by our own souls, and meet in the abiding place. – Señora, I have not a very great respect for myself. Woman and I have failed with one another, and it is a bad failure to have in the middle of oneself.'

Kate looked at him in wonder, with a little fear. Why was he confessing to her? Was he going to love her? She almost suspended her breathing. He looked at her with a sort of sorrow on his brow, and in his dark eyes, anger, vexation, wisdom, and a dull pain.

'I am sorry,' he went on, 'that Carlota and I are as we are with one another. Who am I, even to talk about Quetzalcoatl, when my heart is hollow with anger against the woman I have married and the children she bore me? – We never met in our souls, she and I. At first I loved her, and she wanted me to ravish her. Then after a while a man becomes uneasy. He can't keep on wanting to ravish a woman, the same woman. He has revulsions. Then she loved me, and she wanted to ravish me. And I liked it for a time. But she had revulsions too. The eldest boy is really my boy, when I ravished her. And the youngest is her boy, when she ravished me. See how miserable it is! And now we can never meet; she turns to her crucified Jesus, and I to my uncrucified and uncrucifiable Quetzalcoatl, who at least cannot be ravished.'

'And I'm sure you won't make him a ravisher,' she said.

'Who knows? If I err, it will be on that side. But you know, Señora,

Quetzalcoatl is to me only the symbol of the best a man may be, in the next days. The universe is a nest of dragons, with a perfectly unfathomable life-mystery at the centre of it. If I call the mystery the Morning Star, surely it doesn't matter! A man's blood can't beat in the abstract. And man is a creature who wins his own creation inch by inch from the nest of the cosmic dragons. Or else he loses it little by little, and goes to pieces. Now we are all losing it, in the ravishing and ravished disintegration. We must pull ourselves together, hard, both men and women, or we are all lost. – We must pull ourselves together, hard.'

'But are you a man who needs a woman in his life?' she said.

'I am a man who yearns for the sensual fulfilment of my soul, Señora,' he said. 'I am a man who has no belief in abnegation of the blood desires. I am a man who is always on the verge of taking wives and concubines to live with me, so deep is my desire for that fulfilment. Except that now I know that is useless – not momentarily useless, but in the long run – my ravishing a woman with hot desire. No matter how much she is in love with me and desires me to ravish her. It is no good, and the very inside of me knows it is no good. Wine, woman, and song – all that – all that game is up. Our insides won't really have it any more. Yet it is hard to pull ourselves together.'

'So that you really want a woman to be with you?' said Kate.

'Ah, Señora! If I could trust myself; and trust her! I am no longer a young man, who can afford to make mistakes. I am forty-two years old, and I am making my last – and perhaps in truth, my first great effort as a man. I hope I may perish before I make a big mistake.'

'Why should you make a mistake? You needn't?'

'I? It is very easy for me to make a mistake. Very easy, on the one hand, for me to become arrogant and a ravisher. And very easy, on the other hand, for me to deny myself, and make a sort of sacrifice of my life. Which is being ravished. Easy to let myself, in a certain sense, be ravished. I did it to a small degree even yesterday, with the Bishop of Guadalajara. And it is bad. If I had to end my life in a mistake, Señora, I had rather end it in being a ravisher, than in being ravished. As a hot ravisher, I can still slash and cut at the disease of the other thing, the horrible pandering and the desire men have to be ravished, the hateful, ignoble desire they have.'

'But why don't you do as you say, stick by the innermost soul that

is in you, and meet a woman there, meet her, as you say, where your
two souls coincide in their deepest desire? Not always that horrible
unbalance that you call ravishing.'

'Why don't I? But which woman can I meet in the body, without
that slow degradation of ravishing, or being ravished, setting in? If
I marry a Spanish woman or a dark Mexican, she will give herself
up to me to be ravished. If I marry a woman of the Anglo-Saxon or
any blonde northern stock, she will want to ravish me, with the will
of all the ancient white demons. Those that want to be ravished are
parasites on the soul, and one has revulsions. Those that want to ravish
a man are vampires. And between the two, there is nothing.'

'Surely there are *some* really good women?'

'Well, show me them. They are all potential Carlotas or – or – yes,
Caterinas. I am sure you ravished your Joachim till he died. No doubt
he wanted it; even more than you wanted it. It is not just sex. It lies
in the will. Victims and victimisers. The upper classes, craving to be
victims to the lower classes; or else craving to make victims of the
lower classes. The politicians, craving to make one people victims to
another. The Church, with its evil will for turning the people into
humble, writhing things that shall crave to be victimised, to be ravished.
– I tell you, the earth is a place of shame.'

'But if *you* want to be different,' said Kate, 'surely a few other people
do – really.'

'It may be,' he said, becoming calm. 'It may be. I wish I kept myself
together better. I must keep myself together, keep myself within the
middle place, where I am still. My Morning Star. Now I am ashamed
of having talked like this to you, Señora Caterina.'

'Why?' she cried. And for the first time, the flush of hurt and
humiliation came into her face.

He saw it at once, and put his hand on hers for a moment.

'No,' he said. 'I am not ashamed. I am relieved.'

She flushed deeply at his touch, and was silent. He rose hastily, to
leave, craving to be alone again with his own soul.

'On Sunday,' he said, 'will you come into the plaza, in the morning,
when the drum sounds? Will you come?'

'What for?' she said.

'Well! Come, and you will see.'

He was gone in a flash.

There were many soldiers in the village. When she went to the post-office, she saw the men in their cotton uniforms lying about in the entrance to the military station. There must have been fifty or more, little men, not the tall soldiers in slouched hats. These were little, quick, compact men, like Cipriano, and they talked in a strange Indian language, very subdued. They were very rarely seen in the streets. They kept out of sight.

But at night, everyone was requested to be indoors by ten o'clock, and through the darkness Kate heard the patrols of horse-soldiers riding round.

There was an air of excitement and mystery in the place. The parish priest, a rather overbearing, fat man of fifty or so, had preached a famous Saturday evening sermon against Ramón and Quetzalcoatl, forbidding the heathen name to be mentioned, threatening with all the penalties any parishioner who read the Hymns, or even listened.

So, of course, he was attacked when he left the church, and had to be rescued by soldiers who were in the doorway. They marched him safely home. But his criada, the old woman who served him, was told by more women than one that the next time the padre opened his mouth against Quetzalcoatl, he would have a few inches of machete in his fat guts.

So his reverence stayed at home, and a curate officiated.

Practically all the people who came over the lake in boats on Saturdays went to mass in Sayula church. The great doors stood open all the day. Men as they passed to and fro to the lake, took off their big hats, with a curious cringing gesture, as they went by the gateway of the church. All day long, scattered people were kneeling in the aisles or among the benches, the men kneeling erect, their big hats down by their knees, their curious tall-shaped Indian heads with the thick black hair also erect; only the kneeling legs, close together, humble. The women hooded themselves in their dark rebozos and spread their elbows as they kneeled at a bench, in a slack sort of voluptuousness.

On Saturday night, a great ruddy flickering of many candle-points, away down the dark cavern of the church; and a clustering of dark men's heads, a shuffling of women, a come and go of men arriving from the lake, of men departing to the market. A hush, not exactly of worship, but of a certain voluptuous admiration of the loftiness and glitter, a sensual, almost victimised self-abandon to the god of death, the Crucified streaked with blood, or to the pretty white woman in a blue mantle, with her little doll's face under her crown, Mary, the doll of dolls, Niña of Niñas.

It was not worship. It was a sort of numbness and letting the soul sink uncontrolled. And it was a luxury, after all the week of unwashed dullness in their squalid villages of straw huts. But it irritated Kate.

The men got up and tiptoed away in their sandals, crossing themselves front and back, on the navel and on the back of the head, with holy water. And their black eyes shone with a loose, sensuous look. Instead of having gathered themselves together and become graver, stronger, more collected and deep in their own integrity, they emerged only the more loose and sloppy and uncontrolled.

Oh, if there is one thing men need to learn, but the Mexican Indians especially, it is to collect each man his own soul together deep inside him, and to abide by it. The Church, instead of helping men to this, pushes them more and more into a soft, emotional helplessness, with the unpleasant sensuous gratification of feeling themselves victims, victimised, victimised, but at the same time with the lurking sardonic consciousness that in the end a victim is stronger than the victimiser. In the end, the victims pull down their victimiser, like a pack of hyænas on an unwary lion. They know it. Cursed are the falsely meek, for they are inheriting the earth.

On Sunday morning there was early mass at sunrise, another mass at seven o'clock, another at nine, another at eleven. Then there was a little band of violins and 'cellos, playing old-fashioned dance music; there was, especially early in the morning, a solid mass of peons and women, kneeling on the floor; and a flapping of dusky candles, a smell of the exhaust air of candles, a heavy, rolling fume of incense, and the heavy choir of men's voices, solid, powerful, impressive, from the gallery.

And the people went away in sensuous looseness, which soon turned, in the market, to hate, the old, unfathomable hate which lies at the bottom of the Indian heart, and which always rises black and turbid when they have swayed awhile in sensuous gratification.

The church inside was a dead interior, like all Mexican churches, even the gorgeous Puebla cathedral. The interior of almost any Mexican church gives the impression of cynical barrenness, cynical meaningless-ness, an empty, cynical, mocking shell. The Italian churches are built much in the same style, and yet in them lingers a shadow and stillness of old, mysterious holiness. The hush.

But not in Mexico. The churches outside are impressive. Inside, and it is curious to define it, they are blatant; void of sound and yet with no hush, simple, and yet completely vulgar, barren, sterile. More barren than a bank or a schoolroom or an empty concert-hall, less mysterious than any of these. You get a sense of plaster, of mortar, of whitewash, of smeared blue-wash or grey-wash; and of gilt laid on and ready to peel off. Even in the most gorgeous churches, the gilt is hatefully gilt, never golden. Nothing is soft nor mellow.

So the interior of Sayula church; and Kate had often been in. The white exterior was charming, and so valuable in the landscape, with the twin white pagoda-towers peering out of the green willow trees. But inside, it seemed nothing but whitewash, stencilled over with grey scroll-work decorations. The windows were high, and many, letting in the light as into a schoolroom. Jesus, streaked with blood, was in one of the transepts, and the Virgin, a doll in faded satin, stood startled inside a glass case. There were rag flowers and paper flowers, coarse lace and silver that looked like tin.

Nevertheless, it was quite clean, and very much frequented.

The Month of Mary had gone by, the blue and white paper ribbons were all taken down, the palm trees in pots were all removed from the aisle, the little girls in white dresses and little crowns of flowers no longer came with posies in their hand, at evening. Curious, the old gentle ceremonials of Europe, how trashy they seem in Mexico, just a cheap sort of charade.

The day of Corpus Christi came, with high mass and the church full to the doors with kneeling peons, from dawn till noon. Then a feeble little procession of children within the church, because the law forbids religious processions outside. But all, somehow, for nothing. Just so that the people could call it a fiesta, and so have an excuse to be more slack, more sloshy and uncontrolled than ever. The one Mexican desire; to let themselves go in sloppy inertia.

And this was the all-in-all of the religion. Instead of doing as it should, collecting the soul into its own strength and integrity, the religious day left it all the more decomposed and degenerate.

However, the weeks passed, the crowd in the church seemed the same as ever. But the crowd in the church one hour was the crowd of Quetzalcoatl the next hour. Just a sensation.

Till the more socialistic Readers mingled a little anti-clerical bitterness in their reading. And all the peons began to say: was El Señor a gringo, and the Santísima, was she nothing but a gringuita?

This provoked retaliation on the part of the priests, first mere admonitions, then at last the loud denunciations and threat of that sermon. Which meant war.

Everybody waited for Saturday. Saturday came, and the church remained shut. Saturday night, the church was dark and closed. Sunday, the church was silent and the doors blank fastened.

Something like consternation spread through the market host. They had nowhere to go! – But among the consternation was a piqued curiosity. Perhaps something exciting was going to happen.

Things had happened before. In the revolutions, many of the churches in Mexico have been used for stables and for barracks. And churches are turned into schools, and concert halls, and cinematograph theatres. The convents and the monasteries are most of them barracks for the rag-tag-and-bobtail soldiers. The world changes, is bound to change.

The second Saturday of the closed church was, as it happened, a big market. Much fruit and stuff had come up the lake, from the south from far distances, even from Colima. There were men with lacquer wooden bowls, and women with glazed pottery. And as usual, men crouching in guard over twenty centavos worth of nauseous tropical plums, or chiles, or mangoes, in tiny pyramids along the roadway.

A crowded market, with the much and the little of the Indians. And the church doors shut and locked, the church bells silent, even the clock stopped. True, the clock was always stopping. But not with such a final arrest.

No mass, no confession, no little orgy of incense and slack emotion! The low rumble of murmuring tones, the quick, apprehensive glances around. Vendors by the causeway squatted tight, as if to make themselves dense and small, squatting down on their haunches with their knees up to their shoulders, like the Aztec idols. And soldiers in twos and threes sprinkled everywhere. And Señoras and Señoritas, in their black gauze scarves or mantillas, tripping to the church for mass and shrilling round the gateway of the church, all a bubble and a froth of chatter; though they had known quite well the church was shut.

But it was Sunday morning, and something was due to happen.

At about half-past ten, a boat appeared, and men in snow-white clothes got out, one carrying a drum. They marched quickly through the people, under the old trees on the sand, across to the church. They passed through the broken iron gates into the stone courtyard in front of the church.

At the church doors, which were still shut, they took off their blouses, and stood in a ring, with dark naked shoulders and the blue-and-black sashes of Quetzalcoatl round their waists.

The drum began to beat, with a powerful, pounding note, as the men stood bare-headed and bare-breasted in a circle outside the church doors; a strange ring of lustrous, bluey-black heads and dark shoulders, above the snowy white pantaloons. Monotonously the drum beat, on and on. Then the little clay flute with the husky sound wheezed a clear melody.

The whole market pressed densely towards the gateways of the church. But there, soldiers stood guard. And on the inside of the stone yard in front of the church, soldiers quietly guarded the low walls, letting nobody mount. So that outside, under the old willow and pepper trees, in the hot morning sun, the dense crowd stood gazing at the church doors. They were mostly men in big hats; but some townsmen were there, and some women, and Kate with a parasol lined with dark blue. A close, silent, tense throng under the spangled shade, pressing round the trunks of the palm trees, climbing on the roots of the pepper trees. And behind were the camions and the motor-cars drawn up.

The drum shuddered and went still, and the earthen flute was silent. The lake could be heard lapping, and a clink of glasses and a sound of chauffeurs' voices at the little cantina-booth. For the rest, the silent breathing of the crowd. – Soldiers were quickly distributing a few leaflets among the crowd. A strong, far-carrying male voice began to sing to the softened thud of the drum.

Jesus' Farewell

Farewell, Farewell, *Despedida!*
The last of my days is gone.
To-morrow Jesus and Holy Mary
Will be bone.

It is a long, long way
From Mexico to the Pool of Heaven.

Look back the last time, Mary Mother.
Let us call the eleven.

James, and John, and Mark,
Felipe and San Cristobal,
All my saints, and Anna, Teresa,
Guadalupe whose face is oval.

Come then, now, it is finished for all of us.
Let us all be gone.
Follow me now up the ladders of sparks,
Every one.

Joaquin, Francis, and Anthony
And many-named Maria,
Purísima, Refugio, and Soledad
Follow here.

Ho! all my saints and my Virgins
Troop out of your shrines,
After your master, the Crucified;
Bring all your signs.

Run up the flames, and with feet on the sparks
Troop into the sky.
Once more following the Master,
Back again now, on high.

Farewell, let all be forgotten
In Mexico.
To the pool of peace and forgetting in heaven
We go.

While this was singing, another boat had arrived, and soldiers made
way through the crowd for Ramón, in his white serape with the blue
edges and scarlet fringe, and a young priest of the church in a black
cassock, and six men in dark serapes with the blue borders of Quetzalcoatl. This strange procession marched through the crowd and
through the gateways of the yard.

As they approached, the ring of men round the drum opened, and
spread into a crescent. Ramón stood tall behind the drum, the six
men in dark serapes divided and went to the wings of the crescent,
the young, slim priest in a black cassock stood alone, in front of the
crescent, facing the crowd.

He lifted his hand; Ramón took off his hat; all the men in the crowd took off their hats.

The priest turned, met Ramón at the centre of the crescent, and, across the drum, handed him the key of the church. Then the priest waited.

Ramón unlocked the church doors and flung them open. The men in front of the crowd kneeled down suddenly, seeing the church dark like a cavern, but a trembling blaze of many candles, away, seemingly far down the mysterious darkness, shuddering with dark, rippling flame, like the Presence of the burning bush.

The crowd swayed and rustled, and subsided, kneeling. Only here and there a labourer, a chauffeur or a railway man stood erect.

The priest raised his hand a little higher, re-turning towards the people.

'My children,' he said; and as he spoke the lake seemed to rustle; 'God the Almighty has called home His Son, and the Holy Mother of the Son. Their days are over in Mexico. They go back to the Father.

> Jesus, the Son of God, bids you farewell.
> Mary, the Mother of God, bids you farewell.
> For the last time they bless you, as they leave you.
> Answer *Adiós!*
> Say *Adiós!* my children.'

The men in the circle said a deep *Adiós!* And from the soldiers, and from the kneeling crowd, a ragged, muttered, strange repeating of *Adiós!* again and again, like a sort of storm.

Suddenly, in a blast, down the darkness of the church into which the kneeling people were staring, the burning bush of candles was gone, there was only darkness. Across the sunshine, lit here and there by a frail light of a taper, was a cave of darkness.

Men in the crowd exclaimed and groaned.

Then the drum softly touched, and two men in the crescent began to sing, in magnificent, terrible voices, the Farewell Hymn again. They were men whom Ramón, or his followers, had found in low drinking dens in Mexico City, men with trained and amazing voices, the powerful Mexican tenor that seemed to tear the earth open. Men whom the 'times' have reduced to singing in low city dives. And now they sang with all the terrible desperation that was in them, the hopeless, demonish recklessness.

When they finished, the priest again lifted his hand, and gave the benediction; adding in a quiet voice:

'And now, with all the saints, let Me go, saith Jesus. For I go back to my Father which is in heaven, and I lead my Mother in my right hand, home to peace.'

He turned and went into the church. Ramón followed. Then slowly, all the men of the crescent. Overhead the church bell rang a little while, on the deathly silence. It ceased.

And in a moment, from the depths of the church sounded a drum, with a remote, fearsome thud, and a slow monotony.

The priest, in his white vestments with rich lace, appeared in the doorway of the church, bearing a tall crucifix. He hesitated, then came into the sun. The kneeling people clasped their hands.

Candles in the dark church were clustering towards the door, lonely flames. Don Ramón came out of the dark, naked to the waist, his serape over one shoulder, bearing the front pole of the great bier whereon lies, within a glass case, the lifelike, terrible dead Christ of Holy Week. A tall, dark man, naked to the waist, held the other end of the pole on his shoulder. The crowd moaned and crossed themselves. The lifelike Dead Christ seemed really dead, as he passed the gate. As He entered the crowd, kneeling men and women lifted sightless faces and flung their arms wide apart, and so remained, arms rigid and outflung, in an unspeakable ecstasy of fear, supplication, acknowledgement of death.

After the bier of the Dead Christ, a slow procession of men naked to the waist, carrying litter after litter. First the terrible scourged Christ, with naked body striped like a tiger with blood. Then the image of the Saviour of the Sacred Heart, the well-known figure from the side altar, with long hair and outstretched hands. Then the image of Jesus of Nazareth, with a crown of Thorns.

Then the Virgin with the blue mantle and lace, and the golden crown. The women began to moan as she emerged rather trashily into the blazing sunlight. Behind her, in the church, the candles were one by one going out.

Then came brown Saint Anthony of Padua, with a child in his arms. Then Saint Francis, looking strangely at a cross in his hand. Then Saint Anna. And last, Saint Joaquin. And as he emerged, the last candles in the dark church went out, there were only open doors upon a darkness.

The images on the shoulders of the brown-skinned men rode rather childishly out through the blazing sun, into the shadow of trees. The drum followed last, slowly thudding. On the glass case of the big Dead Christ the sun flashed with startling flashes, as the powerful men carrying it turned towards the water. The crowd murmured and swayed on its knees. Women cried: *Purísima! Purísima! Don't leave us!* and some men ejaculated in strangled anguish, over and over again: *Señor! Señor! Señor!*

But the strange procession made its way slowly under the trees, to the coarse sands, and descended again into the great light towards the lake. There was a little breeze under a blaze of sun. Folded serapes on naked, soft shoulders swung unevenly, the images rocked and tottered a little. But onwards to the edge of the water went the tall crucifix, then the flashing glass box. And after, came Jesus in a red silk robe, fluttering, then a wooden Jesus all paint and streaks, then Jesus in white with a purple mantle that blew like a kerchief, Mary in lace that fluttered upon stiff white and blue satin. But the Saints were only painted; painted wood.

The slim, lace-smocked priest staggered down the sand under the heavy crucifix, which had a white Christ Crucified stretched aloft, facing the lake. By the little wall was a large black *canoa*, sailing boat, with a broad plank gangway up to her stern. Two bare-legged, white-clad men walked by the slim priest, whose white sleeves blew like flags as he slowly climbed the gangway to the ship. Men helped him on board, and he walked away to the prow, where at length he stood the big crucifix, with the Christ still facing outwards.

The ship was open, without deck or hatches, but with fixed tables for the images. Slowly Ramón ascended and descended into the boat, the great glass case was laid down on its rest, the two men could wipe their wet brows and their hot, black hair. Ramón put on his blanket and his hat, against the sun. The boat heaved very slightly. The wind was from the west. The lake was pale and unreal, sun-blinded.

One after another the images rose over the stern of the boat, against the sky, then descended into the vessel, to be set down on their rests, where they rose above the black sides of the *canoa*, in view of the throng on the shore.

It was a strange and tawdry collection of images. And yet, each image had a certain pathos of its own, and a certain touch of horror, as they were grouped together for their last ride, upon the trestle-supports within the vessels. By each image stood the bearers, in hats and serapes, keeping a steady hand on the poles.

There was a little line of soldiers on the shore, and three motor-boats with soldiers waited by the big *canoa*. The shore was covered with a mass of people. Many row-boats came rowing inquisitively round, like fishes. But none came too near.

Bare-legged sailors began to pole the ship from the shore. They leaned heavily on the poles, and walked along the rims of the vessel. Slowly she began to move upon the waters, in the shallows. Slowly, she was leaving the shore, and the throng.

Two other sailors swiftly began to hoist the huge, square white sail. Quickly, yet heavily it rose in the air, and took the wind. It had the great sign of Quetzalcoatl, the circling blue snake and the blue eagle upon a yellow field, at the centre, like a great eye.

The wind came from the west, but the boat was steering south-east, for the little Island of the Scorpions, which rose like a small dim hummock from the haze of the lake. So the sail reached out, and the great eye seemed to be glancing back, at the village with the green willows and the empty white church, the throng on the shore.

Motor-boats circled the huge, slow canoe, small boats like insects followed and ranged round at a distance, never coming too close. The running water clucked and spoke, the men by the images steadied the poles with one hand, their hats with the other, the great eye on the sail ever looked back at the land, the sweep of the white canvas sweeping low above the glass case of death, the Christ caked with gore, the images in their fluttering mantles.

On the shore, the people wandered away, or sat on the sands waiting and watching in a sort of dumb patience that was half indifference. The canoe grew smaller, more inconspicuous, lapsing into the light, the little boats circled around it like mere dots. The lake tired the eyes with its light.

Away under the trees, in a half silence, a half vacancy, a woman bought a dark water-melon, smashed it open on a stone, and gave the big pinky fragments to her children. In silence, men sprinkled salt on the thick slice of cucumber sold by the woman under the tree. In silence they wandered into the church, past the soldiers on guard at the door.

The church was absolutely dark, save for the light that entered the doorway, and absolutely bare; walls, floor, altar, transepts, all stark bare and empty. The people wandered away again, in silence.

It was noon, and a hot day. The *canoa* slowly ranged to the small hummock of the island amid the waters, where lived one family of Indians – fishers, with a few goats and one dry little place where they grew a few beans and heads of maize. For the rest, the island was all dry rock and thorny bushes, and scorpions.

The vessel was poled round to the one rocky bay. Slowly she drew near the island. The motor-boats and the little boats hurried ahead. Already brown, naked men were bathing among the rocks.

The great sail sank, the *canoa* edged up to the rocky shore, men sprang from her into the water, the images were lowered and slowly carried on to the rocks. There they waited for the bearers.

Slowly the procession went again up the bank of the dishevelled island, past the couple of huts, where a red cock was crowing among the litter, and over to rocks, beyond the bushes, on the far side.

The side facing Sayula was all rock, naked and painful to tread on. In a rocky hollow at the water's edge, tall stones had been put up on end, with iron bars across the top, like a grill. Underneath, a pile of faggots ready; and at the side, a pile of faggots.

The images, the glass box of the great Dead Christ, were laid on the iron bars of the grill, in a pathetic cluster all together. The crucifix was leaned against them. It was noon, the heat and the light were fierce and erect. But already down the lake clouds were pushing up fantastically.

Beyond the water, beyond the glare, the village looked like a mirage, with its trees and villages and white church towers.

Men who had come in boats crowded on the rocks of the little amphitheatre. In silence, Ramón kindled shreds of cane and ocote, with a burning-glass. Little hasty flames like young snakes arose in the solid sunlight, with vapour of smoke. He set fire to the carefully-arranged pyramid of faggots beneath the grill-table of the images.

There was a crackling, and a puffing of whitish smoke, the sweet scent of ocote, and orange-red tongues of half-substantial flame were leaping up in the hot white air. Hot breaths blew suddenly, sudden flames gushed up, and the ocote, full of sweet resin, began to roar. The glass of the great box emitted strange, painful yelps as it splintered and fell tinkling. Between the iron bars, brownish flames pushed up among the images, which at once went black. The little vestments of silk and satin withered in a moment to blackness, the caked wounds of paint bubbled black.

The young priest took off his linen vestment, his stole and his chasuble, and with flushed face flung them in the flame. Then he stripped off his black cassock, and emerged in the white cotton of the men of Quetzalcoatl, his white drawers rolled up to the knee. He threw his cassock in the fire. Someone handed him a big hat, and a white serape with blue ends.

There was a smell of burning paint, and wool, and ocote. The fire rushed in a dusky mass upon the blackened, flickering images, till nothing was to be seen but a confused bush of smoke and brown-red flames, puthering, reeking, roaring. The flaming crucifix slipped aside, and fell. A man seized it and pushed it into the fire, under the images. Men in a sort of ecstasy threw on more of the heavy, resinous wood, that almost exploded into flame. Rocks cracked and exploded like guns. Everybody drew back from that roaring tree of flame, which rose ever higher and higher, its dark smoke and its sparks unfolding into heaven.

One of the supporting stones burst with a bang, bars of iron and blazing stumps of images tumbled in a confused roar. The glass case had disappeared, but ribbons of iron waved, then curled over red, into the torrent of the sudden fire. Strange rods of iron appeared out of nowhere, protruding from solid red coals.

And soon, all that was left was a fierce glow of red coals of wood, with a medley of half-fused iron.

Ramón stood aside and watched in silence, his dark brow quite expressionless.

Then, when only the last bluish flames flickered out of a tumble of red fire, from the eminence above, rockets began to shoot into the air with a swish, exploding high in the sightless hot blue, with a glimmer of bluish showers, and of gold.

The people from the shore had seen the tree of smoke with its trunk of flame. Now they heard the heavy firing of the rockets, they looked again, exclaiming, half in dismay, half in the joyful lust of destruction:

'Señor! Señor! La Purísima! La Santísima!'

The flame and the smoke and the rockets melted as if by miracle, into nothingness, leaving the hot air unblemished. The coals of fire were shovelled and dropped down a steep hole.

As the *canoa* sailed back, the side of the lake, through filmy air, looked brownish and changeless. A cloud was rising in the south-west, from behind the dry, silent mountains, like a vast white tail, like the vast white fleecy tail of some squirrel, that had just dived out of sight behind the mountains. This wild white tail fleeced up and up, to the zenith, straight at the sun. And as the *canoa* spread her sail to tack back, already a delicate film of shadow was over the chalk-white lake.

Only on the low end of the isle of Scorpions, hot air still quivered.

Ramón returned in one of the motor-boats. Slowly the sky was clouding for the thunder and the rain. The *canoa*, unable to make her way across, was sailing for Tuliapan. The little boats hurried in silence.

They landed before the wind rose. Ramón went and locked the doors of the church.

The crowd scattered in the wind, rebozos waving wildly, leaves torn, dust racing. Sayula was empty of God, and, at heart, they were glad.

CHAPTER XIX

The Attack on Jamiltepec

SUDDENLY, nearly all the soldiers disappeared from the village, there was a 'rebellion' in Colima. A train had been held up, people killed. And somebody, Generals Fulano and Tulano, had 'pronounced' against the government.

Stir in the air, everybody enjoying those periodical shivers of fear! But for these shivers, everything much the same as usual. The church remained shut up, and dumb. The clock didn't go. Time suddenly fell off, the days walked naked and timeless, in the old, uncounted manner of the past. The strange, old, uncounted, unregistered, unreckoning days of the ancient heathen world.

Kate felt a bit like a mermaid trying to swim in a wrong element. She was swept away in some silent tide, to the old, ante-diluvian silence, where things moved without contact. She moved and existed without contact. Even the striking of the hours had ceased. As a drowning person sees nothing but the waters, so Kate saw nothing but the face of the timeless waters.

So, of course, she clutched at her straw. She couldn't bear it. She ordered an old, rickety Ford car, to take her bumping out to Jamiltepec, over the ruinous roads in the afternoon.

The country had gone strange and void, as it does when these 'rebellions' start. As if the life-spirit were sucked away, and only some empty, anti-life void remained in the wicked hollow countryside. Though it was not far to Jamiltepec, once outside the village, the chauffeur and his little attendant lad began to get frightened, and to go frog-like with fear.

There is something truly mysterious about the Mexican quality of fear. As if man and woman collapsed and lay wriggling on the ground like broken reptiles, unable to rise. Kate used all her will, against this cringing nonsense.

They arrived without ado at Jamiltepec. The place seemed quiet, but normal. An oxen wagon stood empty in the courtyard. There were no soldiers on guard. They had all been withdrawn, against the rebellion. But several peons were moving round, in a desultory fashion. The day was a fiesta, when not much work was doing. In the houses of the peons, the women were patting tortillas, and preparing hot chile sauce, grinding away on the metates. A fiesta! Only the windmill that pumped up water from the lake was spinning quickly, with a little noise.

Kate drove into the yard in silence, and two mozos with guns and belts of cartridges came to talk in low tones to the chauffeur.

'Is Doña Carlota here?' asked Kate.

'No, Señora. The patrona is not here.'

'Don Ramón?'

'Sí, Señora! Está.'

Even as she hesitated, rather nervous, Ramón came out of the inner doorway of the courtyard, in his dazzling white clothes.

'I came to see you,' said Kate. 'I don't know if you'd rather I hadn't. But I can go back in the motor-car.'

'No,' he said. 'I am glad. I was feeling deserted, I don't know why. Let us go upstairs.'

'Patrón!' said the chauffeur, in a low voice. 'Must I stay?'

Ramón said a few words to him. The chauffeur was uneasy, and didn't want to stay. He said he had to be back in Sayula at such and such a time. Excuses, anyhow. But it was evident he wanted to get away.

'Then best let him go,' said Ramón to Kate. 'You do not mind going home in the boat?'

'I don't want to give you trouble.'

'It is least trouble to let this fellow go, and you can leave by boat just whenever you wish to. So we shall all be more free.'

Kate paid the chauffeur, and the Ford started rattling. After rattling a while, it moved in a curve round the courtyard, and lurched through the zaguán, disappearing as fast as possible.

Ramón spoke to his two mozos with the guns. They went to the outer doorway, obediently.

'Why do you have to have armed men?' she said.

'Oh, they're afraid of bandits,' he said. 'Whenever there's a rebellion anywhere, everybody is afraid of bandits. So of course that calls bandits into life.'

'But where do they come from?' said Kate, as they passed into the inner doorways.

'From the villages,' he said, closing the heavy door of that entrance behind him, and putting the heavy iron bars across, from wall to wall.

The inner archway was now a little prison, for the strong iron gates at the lake end of the passage were shut fast. She looked through, at the little round pond. It had some blue water-lilies on it. Beyond, the pallid lake seemed almost like a ghost, in the glare of the sun.

A servant was sent to the kitchen quarters, Rámón and Kate climbed the stone stairs to the upper terrace. How lonely, stonily lonesome and forlorn the hacienda could feel! The very stone walls could give off emptiness, loneliness, negation.

'But which villages do the bandits come from?' she insisted.

'Any of them. Mostly, they say, from San Pablo or from Ahuajijic.'¹

'Quite near!' she cried.

'Or from Sayula,' he added. 'Any of the ordinary men in big hats you see around the plaza may possibly be bandits, when banditry pays, as a profession, and isn't punished with any particular severity.'

'It is hard to believe!' she said.

'It is so obvious!' he said, dropping into one of the rocking-chairs opposite her, and smiling across the onyx table.

'I suppose it is!' she said.

He clapped his hands, and his mozo Martin came up. Ramón ordered something, in a low, subdued tone. The man replied in an even lower, more subdued tone. Then the master and man nodded at one another, and the man departed, his huaraches swishing a little on the terrace.

Ramón had fallen into the low, crushed sort of voice so common in the country, as if everyone were afraid to speak aloud, so they murmured guardedly. This was unusual, and Kate noticed it in him with displeasure. She sat looking past the thick mango-trees, whose fruit was changing colour like something gradually growing hot, to the ruffled, pale-brown lake. The mountains of the opposite shore were very dark. Above them lay a heavy, but distant black cloud, out of which lightning flapped suddenly and uneasily.

'Where is Don Cipriano?' she asked.

'Don Cipriano is very much General Viedma at the moment,' he replied. 'Chasing rebels in the State of Colima.'

'Will they be very hard to chase?'

'Probably not. Anyhow Cipriano will enjoy chasing them. He is

Zapotec, and most of his men are Zapotecans, from the hills. They love chasing men who aren't.'

'I wondered why he wasn't there on Sunday when you carried away the images,' she said. 'I think it was an awfully brave thing to do.'

'Do you?' he laughed. 'It wasn't. It's never half so brave, to carry something off, and destroy it, as to set a new pulse beating.'

'But you have to destroy those old things, first.'

'Those frowsty images – why, yes. But it's no good until you've got something else moving, from the inside.'

'And have you?'

'I think I have. Don't you?'

'Yes,' she said, a little doubtful.

'I think I have,' he said. 'I feel there's a new thing moving inside me.' He was laughing at her, for her hesitation. 'Why don't you come and join us?' he added.

'How?' she said. 'By being married off to Don Cipriano?'

'Not necessarily. Not necessarily. Not necessarily by being married to anybody.'

'What are you going to do next?' she said.

'I? I am going to re-open the church, for Quetzalcoatl to come in. But I don't like lonely gods. There should be several of them, I think, for them to be happy together.'

'Does one need gods?' she said.

'Why yes. One needs manifestations, it seems to me.'

Kate sat in unwilling silence.

'One needs goddesses too. That is also a dilemma,' he added, with a laugh.

'How I would *hate*,' said Kate, 'to have to be a goddess for people.'

'For the monkeys?' he said, smiling.

'Yes! Of course.'

At that moment, he sat erect, listening. There had been a shot, which Kate had heard, but which she had hardly noticed; to her ears, it might have been a motor-car back-firing, or even a motor-boat.

Suddenly, a sharp little volley of shots.

Ramón rose swiftly, swift as a great cat, and slammed to the iron door at the top of the stair-way, shooting the bars.

'Won't you go into that room?' he said to her, pointing to a dark doorway. 'You will be all right there. Just stay a few minutes till I come back.'

As he spoke, there came a shriek from the courtyard at the back, and a man's death-voice yelled *Patrón!*

Ramón's eyes dilated with terrible anger, the anger of death. His face went pale and strange, as he looked at her without seeing her, the black flame filling his eyes. He had drawn a long-barrelled steel revolver from his hip.

Still without seeing her, he strode rapidly, soft and catlike, along the terrace, and leaped up the end staircase on to the roof. The soft, eternal passion of anger in his limbs.

Kate stood in the doorway of the room, transfixed. The light of day seemed to have darkened before her face.

'*Hola!* You there!' she heard his voice from the roof, in such anger it was almost a laugh, from far away.

For answer, a confused noise from the courtyard, and several shots. The slow, steady answer of shots!

She started as a rushing hiss broke on the air. In terror she waited. Then she saw it was a rocket bursting with a sound like a gun, high over the lake, and emitting a shower of red balls of light. A signal from Ramón!

Unable to go into the dark room, Kate waited as if smitten to death. Then something stirred deep in her, she flew along the terrace and up the steps to the roof. She realised that she didn't mind dying so long as she died with that man. Not alone.

The roof was glaring with sunshine. It was flat, but its different levels were uneven. She ran straight out into the light, towards the parapet wall, and had nearly come in sight of the gateway of the court-yard below, when something gave a slight smack, and bits of plaster flew in her face and her hair. She turned and fled back like a bee to the stairway.

The stairs came up in a corner, where there was a little sort of stone turret, square, with stone seats. She sank on one of these seats, looking down in terror at the turn of the stairs. It was a narrow little stone stairway, between the solid stone walls.

She was almost paralysed with shock and with fear. Yet something within her was calm. Leaning and looking out across calm sunshine of the level roof, she could not believe in death.

She saw the white figure and the dark head of Ramón within one of the small square turrets across the roof. The little tower was open, and hardly higher than his head. He was standing in a corner, looking sideways down a loop-hole, perfectly motionless. Snap! went his revolver, deliberately. There was a muffled cry below, and a sudden volley of shots.

Ramón stood away from the loop-hole and took off his white blouse, so that it should not betray him. Above his sash was a belt of cartridges. In the shadow of the turret, his body looked curiously dark, rising from the white of his trousers. Again he took his stand quietly at the side of the long, narrow, slanting aperture. He lifted his revolver carefully, and the shots, one, two, three, slow and deliberate, startled her nerves. And again there was a volley of shots from below, and bits of stone and plaster smoking against the sky. Then again, silence, long silence. Kate pressed her hands against her body, as she sat.

The clouds had shifted, the sun shone yellowish. In the heavier light, the mountains beyond the parapet showed a fleece of young green, smoky and beautiful.

All was silent. Ramón in the shadow did not move, pressing himself against the wall, and looking down. He commanded, she knew, the big inner doors.

Suddenly, however, he shifted. With his revolver in his hand he stooped and ran, like some terrible cat, the sun gleaming on his naked back as he crouched under the shelter of the thick parapet wall, running along the roof to the corresponding front turret.

This turret was roofless, and it was nearer to Kate, as she sat spellbound, in a sort of eternity, on the stone seat at the head of the stairs, watching Ramón. He pressed himself against the wall, and lifted his revolver to the slit. And again, one, two, three, four, five, the shots exploded deliberately. Some voice below yelled *Ay-ee! Ay-ee! Ay-ee!* in yelps of animal pain. A voice was heard shouting command. Ramón kneeled on one knee, re-loading his revolver. Then he struck a match, and again Kate almost started out of her skin, as a rocket rushed ferociously up into the sky, exploded like a gun, and let fall the balls of red flame that lingered as if loth to die away, in the high, remote air.

She sighed, wondering what it all was. It was death, she knew. But so strange, so vacant. Just these noises of shots! And she could see nothing outside. She wanted to see what was in the courtyard.

Ramón was at his post, pressing himself close to the wall, looking down, with bent head, motionless. There were shots, and a spatter of lead from below. But he did not move. She could not see his face, only part of his back; the proud, heavy, creamy-brown shoulders, the black head bent a little forward, in concentration, the cartridge-belt dropping above his loins, over the white, floppy linen of the trousers. Still and soft in watchful concentration, almost like silence itself. Then with soft, diabolic swiftness in his movements, he changed his position, and took aim.

He was utterly unaware of her; even of her existence. Which was as it should be, no doubt. She sat motionless, waiting. Waiting, waiting, waiting, in that yellowish sunlight of eternity, with a certain changeless suspense of stillness inside her. Someone would come from the village. There would be an end. There would be an end.

At the same time, she started every time he fired, and looked at him. And she heard his voice saying: 'One needs manifestations, it seems to me.' Ah, how she hated the noise of shots.

Suddenly she gave a piercing shriek, and in one leap was out of her retreat. She had seen a black head turning the stairs.

Before she knew it, Ramón jumped past her like a great cat, and two men clashed in mid-air, as the unseen fellow leaped up from the stairs. Two men in a crash went down on the floor, a revolver went off, terrible limbs were writhing.

Ramón's revolver was on the floor. But again there was a shot from the tangled men, and a redness of blood suddenly appearing out of nowhere, on the white cotton clothing, as the two men twisted and fought on the floor.

They were both big men. Struggling on the ground, they looked huge. Ramón had the bandit's revolver-hand by the wrist. The bandit, with a ghastly black face with rolling eyes and sparse moustache, had got Ramón's naked arm in his white teeth, and was hanging on, showing his red gums, while with his free hand he was feeling for his knife.

Kate could not believe that the black, ghastly face with the sightless eyes and biting mouth was conscious. Ramón had him clasped round the body. The bandit's revolver fell, and the fellow's loose black hand scrabbled on the concrete, feeling for it. Blood was flowing over his teeth. Yet some blind super-consciousness seemed to possess him, as if he were a devil, not a man.

His hand nearly touched Ramón's revolver. In horror Kate ran and snatched the weapon from the warm concrete, running away as the bandit gave a heave, a great sudden heave of his body, under the body of Ramón. Kate raised the revolver. She hated that horrible devil under Ramón as she had never hated in her life. Yet she dared not fire.

Ramón shouted something, glancing at her. She could not understand. But she ran round, to be able to shoot the man under Ramón. Even as she ran, the bandit twisted with a great lunge of his body, heaved Ramón up, and with his short free hand got Ramón's own knife from the belt at the groin, and stabbed.

Kate gave a cry! Oh, how she wanted to shoot! She saw the knife strike sideways, slanting in a short jab into Ramón's back. At the same moment there was a stumble on the stairs, and another black-headed man was leaping on to the roof from the turret.

She stiffened her wrist and fired without looking, in a sudden second of pure control. The black head came crashing at her. She recoiled in horror, lifted the revolver and fired again, and missed. But even as it passed her, she saw red blood among the black hairs of that head. It crashed down, the buttocks of the body heaving up, the whole thing twitching and jerking along, the face seeming to grin in a mortal grin.

Glancing from horror to horror, she saw Ramón, his face still as death, blood running down his arm and his back, holding down the head of the bandit by the hair and stabbing him with short stabs in the throat, one, two, while blood shot out like a red projectile; there was a strange sound like a soda-syphon, a ghastly bubbling, one final terrible convulsion from the loins of the stricken man, throwing Ramón off, and Ramón lay twisted, still clutching the man's hair in one hand, the bloody knife in the other, and gazing into the livid, distorted face, in which ferocity seemed to have gone frozen, with a steady, intent, inhuman gaze.

Then, without letting go his victim's hair, he looked up, cautiously. To see Kate's man, with black hair wet with blood, and blood running down into his glazed, awful eyes, slowly rising to his knees. It was the strangest face in the world; the high, domed head with blood-soddened hair, blood running in several streams down the narrow, corrugated brow and along the black eyebrows above the glazed, black, numb eyes, in which the last glazing was of ferocity, stranger even than wonder, the glazed and absolute ferocity which the man's last consciousness showed.

It was a long, thin, handsome face, save for those eyes of glazed ferocity, and for the longish white teeth under the sparse moustache.

The man was reduced to his last, blank term of being; a glazed and ghastly ferocity.

Ramón dropped the hair of his victim, whose head dropped sideways with a gaping red throat, and rose to a crouching position. The second bandit was on his knees, but his hand already clasped his knife. Ramón crouched. They were both perfectly still. But Ramón had got his balance, crouching between his feet.

The bandit's black, glazed eyes of blank ferocity took a glint of cunning. He was stretching. He was going to leap to his feet for his stroke.

And even as he leaped, Ramón shot the knife, that was all bright red as a cardinal bird. It flew red like a bird, and the drops of Ramón's handful of blood flew with it, splashing even Kate, who kept her revolver ready, watching near the stairway.

The bandit dropped on his knees again, and remained for a moment kneeling as if in prayer, the red pommel of the knife sticking out of his abdomen, from his white trousers. Then he slowly bowed over, doubled up, and went on his face again, once more with his buttocks in the air.

Ramón still crouched at attention, almost supernatural, his dark eyes glittering with watchfulness, in pure, savage attentiveness. Then he rose, very smooth and quiet, crossed the blood-stained concrete to the fallen man, picked up the clean, fallen knife that belonged to the fellow, lifted the red-dripping chin, and with one stroke drove the knife into the man's throat. The man subsided with the blow, not even twitching.

Then again, Ramón turned to look at the first man. He gazed a moment attentively. But that horrible black face was dead.

And then Ramón glanced at Kate, as she stood near the stairs with the revolver. His brow was like a boy's, very pure and primitive, and the eyes underneath had a certain primitive gleaming look of virginity. As men must have been, in the first awful days, with that strange beauty that goes with pristine rudimentariness.

For the most part, he did not recognise her. But there was one remote glint of recognition.

'Are they both dead?' she asked, awestruck.

'*Creo que sí!*' he replied in Spanish.

He turned to look once more, and to pick up the pistol that lay on the concrete. As he did so, he noticed that his right hand was bright red, with the blood that flowed still down his arm. He wiped it on the jacket of the dead man. But his trousers on his loins were also sodden with blood, they stuck red to his hips. He did not notice.

He was like a pristine being, remote in consciousness, and with far, remote sex.

Curious rattling, bubbling noises still came from the second man, just physical sounds. The first man lay sprawling in a ghastly fashion, his evil face fixed above a pool of blackening blood.

'Watch the stairs!' said Ramón in Spanish to her, glancing at her with farouche eyes, from some far remote jungle. Yet still the glint of recognition sparked furtively out of the darkness.

He crept to the turret, and stealthily looked out. Then he crept back, with the same stealth, and dragged the nearest dead man to the parapet, raising the body till the head looked over. There was no sound. Then he raised himself, and peeped over. No sign, no sound.

He looked at the dead body as he let it drop. Then he went to Kate, to look down the stairs.

'You grazed that man with your first shot, you only stunned him, I believe,' he said.

'Are there any more?' she asked, shuddering.

'I think they are all gone.'

He was pale, almost white, with that same pristine clear brow, like a boy's, a sort of twilight changelessness.

'Are you much hurt?' she said.

'I? No!' and he put his fingers round to his back, to feel the slowly welling wound, with his bloody fingers.

The afternoon was passing towards yellow, heavy evening.

He went again to look at the terrible face of the first dead man.

'Did you know him?' she said.

He shook his head.

'Not that I am aware,' he said. Then: 'Good that he is dead. Good that he is dead. – Good that we killed them both.'

He looked at her with that glint of savage recognition from afar.

'Ugh! No! It's terrible!' she said, shuddering.

'Good for me that you were there! Good that we killed them between us! Good they are dead.'

The heavy, luxurious yellow light from below the clouds gilded the mountains of evening. There was the sound of a motor-car honking its horn.

Ramón went in silence to the parapet, the blood wetting his pantaloons lower and lower, since they stuck to him when he bent down. Rich yellow light flooded the blood-stained roof. There was a terrible smell of blood.

'There is a car coming,' he said.

She followed, frightened, across the roof.

She saw the hills and lower slopes inland swimming in gold light like lacquer. The black huts of the peons, the lurid leaves of bananas showed up uncannily, the trees green-gold stood up, with boughs of shadow. And away up the road was a puther of dust, then the flash of glass as the automobile turned.

'Stay here,' said Ramón, 'while I go down.'

'Why didn't your peons come and help you?' she said.

'They never do!' he replied. 'Unless they are armed on purpose.'

He went, picking up his blouse and putting it on. And immediately the blood came through.

He went down. She listened to his steps. Below, the courtyard was all shadow, and empty, save for two dead white-clothed bodies of men, one near the zaguán, one against a pillar of the shed.

The motor-car came sounding its horn wildly all the way between the trees. It lurched into the zaguán. It was full of soldiers, soldiers standing on the running-boards, hanging on.

'Don Ramón! Don Ramón!' shouted the officer, leaping out of the car. 'Don Ramón!' He was thundering at the doors of the inner zaguán.

Why did not Ramón open? Where was he?

She leaned over the parapet and screamed like a wild bird:

'Viene! Viene Don Ramón! Él viene!'[2]

The soldiers all looked up at her. She drew back in terror. Then, in a panic, she turned downstairs, to the terrace. There was blood on the stone stairs, at the bottom, a great pool. And on the terrace near the rocking-chairs, two dead men in a great pool of blood.

One was Ramón! For a moment she went unconscious. Then slowly she crept forward. Ramón had fallen, reeking with blood from his wound, his arms round the body of the other man, who was bleeding too. The second man opened his eyes, wildly, and in a rattling voice, blind and dying, said:

'*Patrón!*'

It was Martin, Ramón's own mozo. He was stiffening and dying in Ramón's arms. And Ramón, lifting him, had made his own wound gush with blood, and had fainted. He lay like dead. But Kate could see the faintest pulse in his neck.

She ran blindly down the stairs, and fought to get the great iron bars from across the door, screaming all the time:

'Come! Somebody! Come to Don Ramón! He will die.'

A terrified boy and a woman appeared from the kitchen quarters. The door was opened, just as six horse-soldiers galloped into the court-yard. The officer leaped from his horse and ran like a hare, his revolver drawn, his spurs flashing, straight through the doors and up the stairs, like a madman. When Kate got up the stairs again, the officer was standing with drawn revolver, gazing down at Ramón.

'He is dead?' he said, stupefied, looking at Kate.

'No!' she said. 'It is only loss of blood.'

The officers lifted Ramón and laid him on the terrace. Then quickly they got off his blouse. The wound was bleeding thickly in the back.

'We've got to stop this wound,' said the lieutenant. 'Where is Pablo?'

Instantly there was a cry for Pablo.

Kate ran into a bedroom for water, and she switched an old linen sheet from the bed. Pablo was a young doctor among the soldiers. Kate gave him the bowl of water and the towel, and was tearing the sheet into bands. Ramón lay naked on the floor, all streaked with blood. And the light was going.

'Bring light!' said the young doctor.

With swift hands he washed the wound, peering with his nose almost touching it.

'It is not much!' he said.

Kate had prepared bandages and a pad. She crouched to hand them to the young man. The woman-servant set a lamp with a white shade on the floor by the doctor. He lifted it, peering again at the wound.

'No!' he said. 'It is not much.'

Then glancing up at the soldiers who stood motionless, peering down, the light on their dark faces.

'*Tu!*' he said, making a gesture.

Quickly the lieutenant took the lamp, holding it over the inert body, and the doctor, with Kate to help, proceeded to staunch and bind the wound. And Kate, as she touched the soft, inert flesh of Ramón, was thinking to herself: This too is he, this silent body! And that face that stabbed the throat of the bandit was he! And that twilit brow, and those remote eyes, like a death-virgin, was he. Even a savage out of the twilight! And the man that knows me, where is he? One among these many men, no more! Oh God! give the man his soul back, into this bloody body. Let the soul come back, or the universe will be cold for me and for many men.

The doctor finished his temporary bandage, looked at the wound in the arm, swiftly wiped the blood off the loins and buttocks and legs, and said:

'We must put him in bed. Lift his head.'

Quickly Kate lifted the heavy, inert head. The eyes were half open. The doctor pressed the closed lips, under the sparse black moustache. But the teeth were firmly shut.

The doctor shook his head.

'Bring a mattress,' he said.

The wind was suddenly roaring, the lamp was leaping with a long, smoky needle of flame, inside its chimney. Leaves and dust flew rattling on the terrace, there was a splash of lightning. Ramón's body lay there uncovered and motionless, the bandage was already soaked with blood, under the darkening, leaping light of the lamp.

And again Kate saw, vividly, how the body is the flame of the soul, leaping and sinking upon the invisible wick of the soul. And now the soul, like a wick, seemed spent, the body was a sinking, fading flame.

'Kindle his soul again, oh God!' she cried to herself.

All she could see of the naked body was the terrible absence of the living soul of it. All she wanted was for the soul to come back, the eyes to open.

They got him upon the bed and covered him, closing the doors against the wind and the rain. The doctor chafed his brow and hands with cognac. And at length the eyes opened; the soul was there, but standing far back.

For some moments Ramón lay with open eyes, without seeing or moving. Then he stirred a little.

'What's the matter?' he said.

'Keep still, Don Ramón,' said the doctor, who with his slim dark hands was even more delicate than a woman. 'You have lost much blood. Keep still.'

'Where is Martin?'

'He is outside.'

'How is he?'

'He is dead.'

The dark eyes under the black lashes were perfectly steady and changeless. Then came the voice:

'Pity we did not kill them all. Pity we did not kill them all. We have got to kill them all. – Where is the Señora Inglesa?'[3]

'Here she is.'

His black eyes looked up at Kate. Then more of his consciousness came back.

'Thank you for my life,' he said, closing his eyes. Then: 'Put the lamp aside.'

Soldiers were tapping at the glass pane, for the lieutenant. A black little fellow entered, wiping the rain from his black face and pushing his thick black hair back.

'There are two more dead on the azotea,' he announced to his officer.

The lieutenant rose, and followed him out. Kate too went on to the terrace. In the early darkness the rain was threshing down. A lantern was coming down from the roof: it came along the terrace to the stairs, and after it two soldiers in the pouring rain, carrying a dead body, then behind, two more, with the other body. The huaraches of the soldiers clicked and shuffled on the wet terrace. The dismal cortège went downstairs.

Kate stood on the terrace facing the darkness, while the rain threshed down. She felt uneasy here, in this house of men and of soldiers. She found her way down to the kitchen, where the boy was fanning a charcoal fire, and the woman was crushing tomatoes on the metate, for a sauce.

'Ay, Señora!' cried the woman. 'Five men dead, and the *Patrón* wounded to death! Ay! Ay!'

'Seven men dead!' said the boy. 'Two on the azotea!'

'Seven men! Seven men!'

Kate sat on her chair, stunned, unable to hear anything but the threshing rain, unable to feel anything more. Two or three peons came in, and two more women, the men wrapped to their noses in their blankets. The women brought masa, and began a great clapping of tortillas. The people conversed in low, rapid tones, in the dialect, and Kate could not listen.

At length the rain began to abate. She knew it would leave off suddenly. There was a great sound of water running, gushing, splashing, pouring into the cistern. And she thought to herself: The rain will wash the blood off the roof and down the spouts into the cistern. There will be blood in the water.

She looked at her own blood-smeared white frock. She felt chilly. She rose to go upstairs again, into the dark, empty, masterless house.

'Ah, Señora! You are going upstairs? Go, Daniel, carry the lantern for the Señora!'

The boy lit a candle in a lantern, and Kate returned to the upper terrace. The light shone out of the room where Ramón was. She went into the salon and got her hat and her brown shawl. The lieutenant heard her, and came to her quickly, very kindly and respectful.

'Won't you come in, Señora?' he said, holding the door to the room where Ramón lay; the guest-room.

Kate went in. Ramón lay on his side, his black, rather thin moustache pushed against the pillow. He was himself.

'It is very unpleasant for you here, Señora Caterina,' he said. 'Would you like to go to your house? The lieutenant will send you in the motor-car.'

'Is there nothing I can do here?' she said.

'Ah no! Don't stay here! It is too unpleasant for you. — I shall soon get up, and I shall come to thank you for my life.'

He looked at her, into her eyes. And she saw that his soul had come back to him, and with his soul he saw her and acknowledged her; though always from the peculiar remoteness that was inevitable in him.

She went downstairs with the young lieutenant.

'Ah, what a horrible affair! They were not bandits, Señora!' said the young man, with passion. 'They didn't come to rob. They came to murder Don Ramón, you know, Señora! simply to murder Don Ramón. And but for your being here, they would have done it! — Ah, think of it, Señora! Don Ramón is the most precious man in Mexico. It is possible that in the world there is not a man like him. And personally, he hasn't got enemies. As a man among men, he hasn't got enemies.

No, Señora. Not one! But do you know who it will be? the priests,
and the Knights of Cortés.'⁴

'Are you sure?' said Kate.

'Sure, Señora!' cried the lieutenant indignantly. 'Look! There are
seven men dead. Two were the mozos with guns, watching in the
zaguán. One was Don Ramón's own mozo Martin! – ah, what a faithful
man, what a brave one! Never will Don Ramón pardon his death. Then
moreover, the two men killed on the azotea, and two men in the courtyard, shot by Don Ramón. Besides these, a man whom Martin wounded,
who fell and broke his leg, so we have got him. Come and see them,
Señora.'

They were down in the wet courtyard. Little fires had been lighted
under the sheds, and the little, black, devil-may-care soldiers were
crouching round them, with a bunch of peons in blankets standing
round. Across the courtyard, horses stamped and jingled their harness.
A boy came running with tortillas in a cloth. The dark-faced little
soldiers crouched like animals, sprinkled salt on the tortillas, and de-
voured them with small, white, strong teeth.

Kate saw the great oxen tied in their sheds, lying down, the wagons
standing inert. And a little crowd of asses was munching alfalfa in a
corner.

The officer marched beside Kate, his spurs sparkling in the firelight. He went to the muddy car, that stood in the middle of the yard;
then to his horse. From a saddle-pocket he took an electric torch, and
led Kate across to the end shed.

There he suddenly flashed his light upon seven dead bodies, laid
side by side. The two from the roof were wet. Ramón's dead man
lay with his dark, strong breast bare, and his blackish, thick, devilish
face sideways; a big fellow. Kate's man lay rigid. Martin had been
stabbed in the collar bone; he looked as if he were staring at the roof
of the shed. The others were two more peons, and two fellows in black
boots and grey trousers and blue overall jackets. They were all inert
and straight and dead, and somehow, a little ridiculous. Perhaps it is
clothing that makes dead people gruesome and absurd. But also, the
grotesque fact that the bodies are vacant, is always present.

'Look!' said the lieutenant, touching a body with his toe. 'This is a
chauffeur from Sayula; this is a boatman from Sayula. These two are
peons from San Pablo. This man –' the lieutenant kicked the dead

body – 'we don't know.' It was Ramón's dead man. 'But this man –'
he kicked her dead man, with the tall domed head – 'is from Ahuajijic,
and he was married to the woman that now lives with a peon here.
– You see, Señora! A chauffeur and a boatman from Sayula – they are
Knights-of-Cortés men; and those two peons from San Pablo are
priests' men. – These are not bandits. It was an attempt at assassination.
But of course they would have robbed everything, everything, if they
had killed Don Ramón.'

Kate was staring at the dead men. Three of them were handsome;
one, the boatman, with a thin line of black beard framing his shapely
face, was beautiful. But dead, with the mockery of death in his face.
All of them men who had been in the flush of life. Yet dead, they did
not even matter. They were gruesome, but it did not matter that they
were dead men. They were vacant. Perhaps even in life there had been
a certain vacancy, nothingness, in their handsome physique.

For a pure moment, she wished for men who were not handsome
as these dark natives were. Even their beauty was suddenly repulsive
to her; the dark beauty of half-created, half-evolved things, left in the
old, reptile-like smoothness. It made her shudder.

The soul! If only the soul in man, in woman, would speak to her,
not always this strange, perverse materialism, or a distorted animalism.
If only people were souls, and their bodies were gestures from the
soul! If one could but forget both bodies and facts, and be present
with strong, living souls!

She went across the courtyard, that was littered with horse-
droppings, to the car. The lieutenant was choosing the soldiers who
should stay behind. The horse-soldiers would stay. A peon on a delicate
speckled horse, a flea-bitten roan, came trotting past the soldiers in
the zaguán. He had been to Sayula for doctor's stuff, and to give
messages to the Jefe.

At last the car, with little soldiers clinging on to it all round, moved
slowly out of the courtyard. The lieutenant sat beside Kate. He stopped
the car again at the big white barn under the trees, to talk to two
soldiers picketed there.

Then they moved slowly on, under the wet trees, in the mud that
crackled beneath the wheels, up the avenue to the highroad, where
were the little black huts of the peons. Little fires were flapping in
front of one or two huts, women were baking tortillas on the flat earthen-

ware plates, upon the small wood fires. A woman was going to her hut with a blazing brand, like a torch, to kindle her fire. A few peons in dirty-white clothes squatted silent against the walls of their houses, utterly silent. As the motor-car turned its great glaring headlights upon the highroad, little sandy pigs with short, curly hair started up squealing, and faces and figures stood out blindly, as in a searchlight.

There was a hut with a wide opening in the black wall, and a grey old man was standing inside. The car stopped for the lieutenant to call to the peons under the wall. They came to the car with their black eyes glaring and glittering apprehensively. They seemed very much abashed, and humble, answering the lieutenant.

Meanwhile Kate watched a boy buy a drink for one centavo and a piece of rope for three centavos, from the grey old man at the dark hole, which was a shop.

The car went on, the great lights glaring unnaturally upon the hedges of cactus and mesquite and palo blanco trees, and upon the great pools of water in the road. It was a slow progress.

CHAPTER XX

Marriage by Quetzalcoatl

KATE hid in her own house, numbed. She could not bear to talk to people. She could not bear even Juana's bubbling discourse. The common threads that bound her to humanity seemed to have snapped. The little human things didn't interest her any more. Her eyes seemed to have gone dark, and blind to individuals. They were all just individuals, like leaves in the dark, making a noise. And she was alone under the trees.

The egg-woman wanted six centavos for an egg.

'And I said to her – I said to her – we buy them at five centavos!' Juana went on.

'Yes!' said Kate. She didn't care whether they were bought at five or fifty, or not bought at all.

She didn't care, she didn't care, she didn't care. She didn't even care about life any more. There was no escaping her own complete indifference. She felt indifferent to everything in the whole world, almost she felt indifferent to death.

'Niña! Niña! Here is the man with the sandals! Look! Look how nicely he has made them for you, Niña! Look what Mexican huaraches the Niña is going to wear!'

She tried them on. The man charged her too much. She looked at him with her remote, indifferent eyes. But she knew, in the world one must live, so she paid him less than he asked, though more than he really would have accepted.

She sat down again in her rocking-chair in the shade of the room. Only to be alone! Only that no one should speak to her. Only that no one should come near her! Because in reality her soul and spirit were gone, departed into the middle of some desert, and the effort of reaching across to people to effect an apparent meeting, or contact, was almost more than she could bear.

Never had she been so alone, and so inert, and so utterly without desire; plunged in a wan indifference, like death. Never had she passed her days so blindly, so unknowingly, in stretches of nothingness.

Sometimes, to get away from her household, she sat under a tree by the lake. And there, without knowing it, she let the sun scorch her foot and burn her face inflamed. Juana made a great outcry over her. The foot blistered and swelled, her face was red and painful. But it all seemed to happen merely to her shell. And she was wearily, wanly indifferent.

Only at the very centre of her sometimes a little flame rose, and she knew that what she wanted was for her soul to live. The life of days and facts and happenings was dead on her, and she was like a corpse. But away inside her a little light was burning, the light of her innermost soul. Sometimes it sank and seemed extinct. Then it was there again.

Ramón had lighted it. And once it was lighted the world went hollow and dead, all the world-activities were empty weariness to her. Her soul! Her frail, innermost soul! She wanted to live *its* life, not her own life.

The time would come again when she would see Ramón and Cipriano, and the soul that was guttering would kindle again in her, and feel strong. Meanwhile she only felt weak, weak, weak, weak as the dying. She felt that afternoon of bloodshed had blown all their souls into the twilight of death, for the time. But they would come back. They would come back. Nothing to do but to submit, and wait. Wait, with a soul almost dead, and hands and heart of uttermost inert heaviness, indifference.

Ramón had lost much blood. And she, too, in other ways, had been drained of the blood of the body. She felt bloodless and powerless.

But wait, wait, wait, the new blood would come.

One day Cipriano came. She was rocking in her salon, in a cotton housedress, and her face red and rather swollen. She saw him, in uniform, pass by the window. He stood in the doorway on the terrace, a dark, grave, small, handsome man.

'Do come in,' she said with effort.

Her eyelids felt burnt. He looked at her with his full black eyes, that always had in them so many things she did not understand. She felt she could not look back at him.

'Have you chased all your rebels?' she said.

'For the present,' he replied.

He seemed to be watching, watching for something.

'And you didn't get hurt?'

'No, I didn't get hurt.'

She looked away out of the door, having nothing to say in the world

'I went to Jamiltepec yesterday evening,' he said.

'How is Don Ramón?'

'Yes, he is better.'

'Quite better?'

'No. Not quite better. But he walks a little.'

'Wonderful how people heal.'

'Yes. We die very easily. But we also come quickly back to life.'

'And you? Did you fight the rebels, or didn't they want to fight?'

'Yes, they wanted to. We fought once or twice; not very much.'

'Men killed?'

'Yes! Some! Not many, no? Perhaps a hundred. We can never tell, no? Maybe two hundred.'

He waved his hand vaguely.

'But you had the worst rebellion at Jamiltepec, no?' he said suddenly, with heavy Indian gravity, gloom suddenly settling down.

'It didn't last long, but it was rather awful while it did.'

'Rather awful, no? – If I had known! I said to Ramón, won't you keep the soldiers? – the guard, no? He said they were not necessary. But here – you never know, no?'

'Niña!' cried Juana, from the terrace. 'Niña! Don Antonio says he is coming to see you.'

'Tell him to come to-morrow.'

'Already he is on the way!' cried Juana, in helplessness. Don Antonio was Kate's fat landlord; and, of course, Juana's permanent master, more important in her eyes, then, even than Kate.

'Here he is!' she cried, and fled.

Kate leaned forward in her chair, to see the stout figure of her landlord on the walk outside the window, taking off his cloth cap and bowing low to her. A cloth cap! – She knew he was a great Fascista, the reactionary Knights of Cortés held him in great esteem.

Kate bowed coldly.

He bowed low again, with the cloth cap.

Kate said not a word.

He stood on one foot, then on the other, and then marched forward up the gravel walk, towards the kitchen quarters, as if he had not seen either Kate or General Viedma. In a few moments he marched back, as if he could not see either Kate or the General, through the open door.

Cipriano looked at the passing stout figure of Don Antonio in a cloth cap as if it were the wind blowing.

'It is my landlord!' said Kate. 'I expect he wants to know if I am taking on the house for another three months.'

'Ramón wanted me to come and see you – to see how you are, no? – and to ask you to come to Jamiltepec. Will you come with me now? The car is here.'

'Must I?' said Kate, uneasily.

'No. Not unless you wish. Ramón said, not unless you wished. He said, perhaps it would be painful to you, no? – to go to Jamiltepec again – so soon after –'

How curious Cipriano was! He stated things as if they were mere bare facts with no emotional content at all. As for its being painful to Kate to go to Jamiltepec, that meant nothing to him.

'Lucky thing you were there that day, no?' he said. 'They might have killed him. Very likely they would! Very likely! Awful, no?'

'They might have killed me too,' she said.

'Yes! Yes! They might!' he acquiesced.

Curious he was! With a sort of glaze of the ordinary world on top, and underneath a black volcano with hell knows what depths of lava. And talking half-abstractedly from his glazed, top self, the words came out small and quick, and he was always hesitating, and saying: *No?* It wasn't himself at all talking.

'What would you have done if they had killed Ramón?' she said, tentatively.

'I?' – He looked up at her in a black flare of apprehension. The volcano was rousing. 'If they had killed him? –' His eyes took on that fixed glare of ferocity, staring her down.

'Would you have cared very much?' she said.

'I? Would I?' he repeated, and the black suspicious look came into his Indian eyes.

'Would it have meant *very* much to you?'

He still watched her with a glare of ferocity and suspicion.

'To me!' he said, and he pressed his hand against the buttons of his tunic. 'To me Ramón is *more* than life. *More* than life.' His eyes seemed to glare and go sightless, as he said it, the ferocity melting in a strange blind, confiding glare, that seemed sightless, either looking inward, or out at the whole vast void of the cosmos, where no vision is left.

'More than anything?' she said.

'Yes!' he replied abstractedly, with a blind nod of the head.

Then abruptly he looked at her and said:

'You saved his life.'

By this he meant that *therefore* – But she could not understand the therefore.

She went to change, and they set off to Jamiltepec. Cipriano made her a little uneasy, sitting beside him. He made her physically aware of him, of his small but strong and assertive body, with its black currents and storms of desire. The range of him was very limited, really. The great part of his nature was just inert and heavy, unresponsive, limited as a snake or a lizard is limited. But within his own heavy, dark range he had a curious power. Almost she could *see* the black fume of power which he emitted, the dark, heavy vibration of his blood, which cast a spell over her.

As they sat side by side in the motor-car, silent, swaying to the broken road, she could feel the curious tingling heat of his blood, and the heavy power of the *will* that lay unemerged in his blood. She could see again the skies go dark, and the phallic mystery rearing itself like a whirling dark cloud, to the zenith, till it pierced the sombre, twilit zenith; the old, supreme phallic mystery. And herself in the everlasting twilight, a sky above where the sun ran smokily, an earth below where the trees and creatures rose up in blackness, and man strode along naked, dark, half-visible, and suddenly whirled in supreme power, towering like a dark whirlwind column, whirling to pierce the very zenith.

The mystery of the primeval world! She could feel it now in all its shadowy, furious magnificence. She knew now what was the black, glinting look in Cipriano's eyes. She could understand marrying him, now. In the shadowy world where men were visionless, and winds of fury rose up from the earth, Cipriano was still a power. Once you entered his mystery the scale of all things changed, and he became a living male power, undefined, and unconfined. The smallness, the limitations ceased to exist. In his black, glinting eyes the power was limitless, and it was as if, from him, from his body of blood could rise up that pillar of cloud which swayed and swung, like a rearing serpent or a rising tree, till it swept the zenith, and all the earth below was dark and prone, and consummated. Those small hands, that little natural tuft of black goats' beard hanging light from his chin, the tilt of his brows and the slight slant of his eyes, the domed Indian head with its thick black hair, they were like symbols to her, of another mystery, the bygone mystery of the twilit, primitive world, where shapes that are small suddenly loom up huge, gigantic on the shadow, and a face like Cipriano's is the face at once of a god and a devil, the undying Pan face. The bygone mystery, that has indeed gone by, but has not passed away. Never shall pass away.

As he sat in silence, casting the old, twilit Pan-power over her, she felt herself submitting, succumbing. He was once more the old dominant male, shadowy, intangible, looming suddenly tall, and covering the sky, making a darkness that was himself and nothing but himself, the Pan male. And she was swooned prone beneath, perfect in her proneness.

It was the ancient phallic mystery, the ancient god-devil of the male Pan.[1] Cipriano unyielding forever, in the ancient twilight, keeping the ancient twilight around him. She understood now his power with his soldiers. He had the old gift of demon-power.

He would never woo; she saw this. When the power of his blood rose in him, the dark aura streamed from him like a cloud pregnant with power, like thunder, and rose like a whirlwind that rises suddenly in the twilight and raises a great pliant column, swaying and leaning with power, clear between heaven and earth.

Ah! and what a mystery of prone submission, on her part, this huge erection would imply! Submission absolute, like the earth under the sky. Beneath an over-arching absolute.

Ah! what a marriage! How terrible! and how complete! With the finality of death, and yet more than death. The arms of the twilit Pan. And the awful, half-intelligible voice from the cloud.

She could conceive now her marriage with Cipriano; the supreme passivity, like the earth below the twilight, consummate in living lifelessness, the sheer solid mystery of passivity. Ah, what an abandon, what an abandon, what an abandon! – of so many things she wanted to abandon.

Cipriano put his hand, with its strange soft warmth and weight, upon her knee, and her soul melted like fused metal.

'En poco tiempo, verdad?' he said to her, looking into her eyes with the old, black, glinting look, of power about to consummate itself.

'In a little while, no?'

She looked back at him, wordless. Language had abandoned her, and she leaned silent and helpless in the vast, unspoken twilight of the Pan world. Her self had abandoned her, and all her day was gone. Only she said to herself:

'My demon lover!'[2]

Her world could end in many ways, and this was one of them. Back to the twilight of the ancient Pan world, where the soul of woman was dumb, to be forever unspoken.

The car had stopped, they had come to Jamiltepec. He looked at her again, as reluctantly he opened the door. And as he stepped out, she realised again his uniform, his small figure in uniform. She had lost it entirely. She had only known his face, the face of the supreme god-demon; with the arching brows and slightly slanting eyes, and the loose, light tuft of a goat-beard. The Master. The everlasting Pan.

He was looking back at her again, using all his power to prevent her seeing in him the little general in uniform, in the worldly vision. And she avoided his eyes, and saw nothing.

They found Ramón sitting in his white clothes in a long chair on the terrace. He was creamy-brown in his pallor.

He saw at once the change in Kate. She had the face of one waking from the dead, curiously dipped in death, with a tenderness far more new and vulnerable than a child's. He glanced at Cipriano. Cipriano's face seemed darker than usual, with that secret *hauteur* and aloofness of the savage. He knew it well.

'Are you better?' Kate asked.

'Very nearly!' he said, looking up at her gently. 'And you?'

'Yes, I am all right.'

'You are?'

'Yes, I think so. – I have felt myself all lost, since that day. Spiritually, I mean. Otherwise I am all right. Are you healing well?'

'Oh, yes! I always heal quickly.'

'Knives and bullets are horrible things.'

'Yes – in the wrong place.'

Kate felt rather as if she were coming to, from a swoon, as Ramón spoke to her and looked at her. His eyes, his voice seemed kind. Kind? The word suddenly was strange to her, she had to try to get its meaning.

There was no kindness in Cipriano. The god-demon Pan preceded kindness. She wondered if she wanted kindness. She did not know. Everything felt numb.

'I was wondering whether to go to England,' she said.

'Again?' said Ramón, with a slight smile. 'Away from the bullets and the knives, is that it?'

'Yes! – to get away.' And she sighed deeply.

'No!' said Ramón. 'Don't go away. You will find nothing in England.'

'But *can* I go on here?'

'Can you help it?'

'I wish I knew what to do.'

'How can one know? Something happens inside you, and all your decisions are smoke. – Let happen what will happen.'

'I can't *quite* drift as if I had no soul of my own, can I?'

'Sometimes it is best.'

There was a pause. Cipriano stayed outside the conversation altogether, in a dusky world of his own, apart and secretly hostile.

'I have been thinking so much about you,' she said to Ramón, 'and wondering whether it is worth while.'

'What?'

'What you are doing; trying to change the religion of these people. If they have any religion to change. I don't think they are a religious people. They are only superstitious. I have no use for men and women who go crawling down a church aisle on their knees, or holding up their arms for hours. There's something stupid and wrong about it. They never worship a God. Only some little evil power. I have been wondering so much if it is worth while giving yourself to them, and exposing yourself to them. It would be horrible if you were really killed. I have seen you *look* dead.'

'Now you see me look alive again,' he smiled.

But a heavy silence followed.

'I believe Don Cipriano knows them better than you do. I believe he knows best, if it is any good,' she said.

'And what does he say?' asked Ramón.

'I say I am Ramón's man,' replied Cipriano stubbornly.

Kate looked at him, and mistrusted him. In the long run he was nobody's man. He was that old, masterless Pan-male, that could not even conceive of service; particularly the service of mankind. He saw only glory; the black mystery of glory consummated. And himself like a wind of glory.

'I feel they'll let you down,' said Kate to Ramón.

'Maybe! But I shan't let myself down. I do what I believe in. Possibly I am only the first step round the corner of change. But: ce n'est que le premier pas qui coute[3] – Why will you not go round the corner with us? At least it is better than sitting still.'

Kate did not answer his question. She sat looking at the mango trees and the lake, and the thought of that afternoon came over her again.

'How did those two men get in; those two bandits on the roof?' she asked wonderingly.

'It was a woman this time; a girl whom Carlota brought here from the Cuna in Mexico City, to be a sewing girl and to teach the peons' wives to sew and do little things. She had a little room at the end of the terrace there –' Ramón pointed to the terrace projecting towards the lake, opposite the one where his own room was, and the covered balcony. 'She got entangled with one of the peons; a sort of second overseer, called Guillermo. Guillermo had got a wife and four children, but he came to me to say could he change and take Maruca – the sewing girl. I said no, he could stay with his family. And I sent Maruca back to Mexico. But she had had a smattering of education, and thought she was equal to anything. She got messages through to Guillermo, and he ran away and joined her in Mexico, leaving wife and four children here. The wife then went to live with another peon – the blacksmith – whose wife had died and who was supposed to be a good match; a decent fellow.

'One day appeared Guillermo, and said: could he come back? I said not with Maruca. He said he didn't want Maruca, he wanted to come back. His wife was willing to go back to him again with the children. The blacksmith was willing to let her go. I said very well; but he had forfeited his job as sub-overseer, and must be a peon again.

'And he seemed all right – satisfied. But then Maruca came and stayed in Sayula, pretending to make her living as a dressmaker. She was in with the priest; and she got Guillermo again.

'It seems the Knights of Cortés had promised a big reward for the man who would bring in my scalp; secretly, of course. The girl got Guillermo: Guillermo got those two peons, one from San Pablo and one from Ahuajijic; somebody else arranged for the rest.

'The bedroom the girl used to have is that one, on the terrace not far from where the stairs go up to the roof. The bedroom has a lattice window, high up, looking out on the trees. There's a big *laurel de India* grows outside. It appears the girl climbed on a table and knocked the iron lattice of the window loose, while she was living here, and that Guillermo, by taking a jump from the bough – a very risky thing, but then he was one of that sort – could land on the window-sill and pull himself into the room.

'Apparently he and the other two men were going to get the scalp and pillage the house before the others could enter. So the first one, the man I killed, climbed the tree, and with a long pole shoved in the lattice of the window, and so got into the room, and up the terrace stairs.

'Martin, my man, who was waiting on the other stairs, ready if they tried to blow out the iron door, heard the smash of the window and rushed round just as the second bandit – the one you shot – was crouching on the window-sill to jump down into the room. The window is quite small, and high up.

'Before Martin could do anything the man had jumped down on top of him and stabbed him twice with his machete. Then he took Martin's knife and came up the stairs, when you shot him in the head.

'Martin was on the floor when he saw the hands of a third man gripping through the window. Then the face of Guillermo. Martin got up and gave the hands a slash with the heavy machete, and Guillermo fell smash back down on to the rocks under the wall.

'When I came down, I found Martin lying outside the door of that room. He told me – *They came through there, Patrón. Guillermo was one of them.*

'Guillermo broke his thigh on the rocks, and the soldiers found him. He confessed everything, and said he was sorry, and begged my pardon. He's in the prison hospital now.'

'And Maruca?' said Kate.

'They've got her too.'

'There will always be a traitor,' said Kate gloomily.

'Let us hope there will also be a Caterina,' said Ramón.

'But will you go on with it – your Quetzalcoatl?'

'How can I leave off? It's my *métier* now. Why don't you join us? Why don't you help me?'

'How?'

'You will see. Soon you will hear the drums again. Soon the first day of Quetzalcoatl will come. You will see. Then Cipriano will appear – in the red serape – and Huitzilopochtli will share the Mexican Olympus with Quetzalcoatl. Then I want a goddess.'

'But will Don Cipriano be the god Huitzilopochtli?' she asked, taken aback.

'First Man of Huitzilopochtli, as I am First Man of Quetzalcoatl.'

'Will you?' said Kate to Cipriano. 'That horrible Huitzilopochtli?'[4]

'Yes, Señora!' said Cipriano, with a subtle smile of hauteur, the secret savage coming into his own.

'Not the old Huitzilopochtli – but the new,' said Ramón. 'And then there must come a goddess; wife or virgin, there must come a goddess. Why not you, as the First Woman of – say Itzpapalotl,[5] just for the sound of the name?'

'I?' said Kate. 'Never! I should die of shame.'

'Shame?' laughed Ramón. 'Ah, Señora Caterina, why shame? This is a thing that *must* be done. There must be manifestations. We *must* change back to the vision of the living cosmos; we *must*. The oldest Pan is in us, and he will not be denied. In cold blood and in hot blood both, we must make the change. That is how man is made. I accept the *must* from the oldest Pan in my soul, and from the newest *me*. Once a man gathers his whole soul together and arrives at a conclusion, the time of alternatives has gone. I *must*. No more than that. I *am* the First Man of Quetzalcoatl. I am Quetzalcoatl himself, if you like. A manifestation, as well as a man. I accept myself entire, and proceed to make destiny. Why, what else can I do?'

Kate was silent. His loss of blood seemed to have washed him curiously fresh again, and he was carried again out of the range of human emotion. A strange sort of categorical imperative! She saw now his power over Cipriano. It lay in this imperative which he acknowledged in his own soul, and which really was like a messenger from the beyond.

She looked on like a child looking through a railing; rather wistful, and rather frightened.

Ah, the soul! The soul was always flashing and darkening into new shapes, each one strange to the other. She had thought Ramón and she had looked into each other's souls. And now, he was this pale, distant man, with a curious gleam, like a messenger from the beyond, in his soul. And he was remote, remote from any woman.

Whereas Cipriano had suddenly opened a new world to her, a world of twilight, with the dark, half-visible face of the god-demon Pan, who can never perish, but ever returns upon mankind from the shadows. The world of shadows and dark prostration, with the phallic wind rushing through the dark.

Cipriano had to go to the town at the end of the lake, near the State of Colima; to Jaramay. He was going in a motor-boat with a couple of soldiers. Would Kate go with him?

He waited, in heavy silence, for her answer.

She said she would. She was desperate. She did not want to be sent back to her own empty, dead house.

It was one of those little periods when the rain seems strangled, the air thick with thunder, silent, ponderous thunder latent in the air from day to day, among the thick, heavy sunshine. Kate, in these days in Mexico, felt that between the volcanic violence under the earth, and the electric violence of the air above, men walked dark and incalculable, like demons from another planet.

The wind on the lake seemed fresh, from the west, but it was a running mass of electricity, that burned her face and her eyes and the roots of her hair. When she had wakened in the night and pushed the sheets, heavy sparks fell from her fingertips. She felt she could not live.

The lake was like some frail milk of thunder; the dark soldiers curled under the awning of the boat, motionless. They seemed dark as lava and sulphur, and full of a dormant, diabolic electricity. Like salamanders. The boatman in the stern, steering, was handsome, almost like the man she had killed. But this one had pale greyish eyes, phosphorescent with flecks of silver.

Cipriano sat in silence in front of her. He had removed his tunic, and his neck rose almost black from his white shirt. She could see how different his blood was from hers, dark, blackish, like the blood of lizards among hot black rocks. She could feel its changeless surge, holding up his light, bluey-black head as on a fountain. And she would feel her own pride dissolving, going.

She felt he wanted his blood-stream to envelop hers. As if it could possibly be. He was so still, so unnoticing, and the darkness of the nape of his neck was so like invisibility. Yet he was always waiting, waiting, waiting, invisibly and ponderously waiting.

She lay under the awning in the heat and light without looking out. The wind made the canvas crackle.

Whether the time was long or short, she knew not. But they were coming to the silent lake-end, where the beach curved round in front of them. It seemed sheer lonely sunlight.

But beyond the shingle there were willow trees, and a low ranch-house. Three anchored *canoas* rode with their black, stiff lines. There were flat lands, with maize half grown and blowing its green flags sideways. But all was as if invisible, in the intense hot light.

The warm, thin water ran shallower and shallower, to the reach of shingle beyond. Black water-fowl bobbed like corks. The motor stopped. The boat ebbed on. Under the thin water were round stones, with thin green hair of weed. They would not reach the shore – not by twenty yards.

The soldiers took off their huaraches, rolled their cotton trousers up their black legs, and got into the water. The tall boatman did the same, pulling forward the boat. She would go no farther. He anchored her with a big stone. Then with his uncanny pale eyes, under the black lashes, he asked Kate in a low tone if he could carry her ashore, offering her his shoulder.

'No, no!' she said. 'I'll paddle.'

And hastily she took off her shoes and stockings and stepped into the shallow water, holding up her thin skirt of striped silk. The man laughed; so did the soldiers.

The water was almost hot. She went blindly forward, her head dropped. Cipriano watched her with the silent, heavy, changeless patience of his race, then when she reached the shingle he came ashore on the boatman's shoulders.

They crossed the hot shingle to the willow trees by the maize-fields, and sat upon boulders. The lake stretched pale and unreal, far, far away into the invisible, with dimmed mountains rising on either side, bare and abstract. The *canoas* were black and stiff, their masts motionless. The white motor-boat rode near. Black birds were bobbing like corks, at this place of the water's end and the world's end.

A lonely woman went up the shingle with a water-jar on her shoulder. Hearing a sound, Kate looked, and saw a group of fishermen holding a conclave in a dug-out hollow by a tree. They saluted, looking at her with black, black eyes. They saluted humbly, and yet in their black eyes was that ancient remote hardness and hauteur.

Cipriano had sent the soldiers for horses. It was too hot to walk.

They sat silent in the invisibility of this end of the lake, the great light taking sight away.

'Why am I not the living Huitzilopochtli?' said Cipriano quietly, looking full at her with his black eyes.

'Do you feel you are?' she said, startled.

'Yes,' he replied, in the same low, secret voice. 'It is what I feel.'

The black eyes looked at her with a rather awful challenge. And the small, dark voice seemed to take all her will away. They sat in silence, and she felt she was fainting, losing her consciousness for ever.

The soldiers came, with a black Arab horse for him; a delicate thing; and for her a donkey, on which she could sit sideways. He lifted her into the saddle, where she sat only half-conscious. A soldier led the donkey, and they set off, past the long, frail, hanging fishing nets, that made long filmy festoons, into the lane.

Then out into the sun and the grey-black dust, towards the grey-black, low huts of Jaramay, that lined the wide, desert road.

Jaramay was hot as a lava oven. Black low hut-houses with tiled roofs lined the broken, long, dilapidated street. Broken houses. Blazing sun. A brick pavement all smashed and sun-worn. A dog leading a blind man along the little black walls, on the broken pavement. A few goats. And unspeakable lifelessness, emptiness.

They came to the broken plaza, with sun-decayed church and ragged palm trees. Emptiness, sun, sun-decay, sun-dilapidation. One man on a dainty Arab horse trotting lightly over the stones, gun behind, big hat making a dark face. For the rest, the waste space of the centre of life. Curious how dainty the horse looked, and the horseman sitting erect, amid the sun-roasted ruin.

They came to a big building. A few soldiers were drawn up at the entrance. They saluted Cipriano as if they were transfixed, rolling their dark eyes.

Cipriano was down from his horse in a moment. Emitting the dark rays of dangerous power, he found the Jefe all obsequious; a fat man in dirty white clothes. They put their wills entirely in his power.

He asked for a room where his *esposa* could rest. Kate was pale and all her will had left her. He was carrying her on his will.

He accepted a large room with a brick-tiled floor and a large, new brass bed with a coloured cotton cover thrown over it, and with two chairs. The strange, dry, stark emptiness, that looked almost cold in the heat.

'The sun makes you pale. Lie down and rest. I will close the windows,' he said.

He closed the shutters till only a darkness remained.

Then in the darkness, suddenly, softly he touched her, stroking her hip.

'I said you were my wife,' he said, in his small, soft Indian voice. 'It is true, isn't it?'

She trembled, and her limbs seemed to fuse like metal melting down. She fused into a molten unconsciousness, her will, her very self gone, leaving her lying in molten life, like a lake of still fire, unconscious of everything save the eternality of the fire in which she was gone. Gone in the fadeless fire, which has no death. Only the fire can leave *us*, and we can die.

And Cipriano the master of fire. The Living Huitzilopochtli, he had called himself. The living firemaster. The god in the flame; the salamander.

One cannot have one's own way, and the way of the gods. It has to be one or the other.

When she went out into the next room, he was sitting alone, waiting for her. He rose quickly, looking at her with black, flashing eyes from which dark flashes of light seemed to play upon her. And he took her hand, to touch her again.

'Will you come to eat at the little restaurant?' he said.

In the uncanny flashing of his eyes she saw a gladness that frightened her a little. His touch on her hand was uncannily soft and inward. His words said nothing; would never say anything. But she turned aside her face, a little afraid of that flashing, primitive gladness, which was so impersonal and beyond her.

Wrapping a big yellow-silk shawl around her, Spanish fashion, against the heat, and taking her white sunshade lined with green, she stepped out with him past the bowing Jefe and the lieutenant, and the saluting soldiers. She shook hands with the Jefe and the lieutenant. They were men of flesh and blood, they understood her presence, and bowed low, looking up at her with flashing eyes. And she knew what it was to be a goddess in the old style, saluted by the real fire in men's eyes, not by their lips.

In her big, soft velour hat of jade green, her breast wrapped round with the yellow brocade shawl, she stepped across the sun-eaten plaza, a sort of desert made by man, softly, softly beside her Cipriano, soft as a cat, hiding her face under her green hat and her sunshade, keeping her body secret and elusive. And the soldiers and the officers and clerks of the Jefatura, watching her with fixed black eyes, saw, not the physical woman herself, but the inaccessible, voluptuous mystery of man's physical consummation.

They ate in the dusky little cavern of a *fonda* kept by a queer old woman with Spanish blood in her veins. Cipriano was very sharp and imperious in his orders, the old woman scuffled and ran in a sort of terror. But she was thrilled to her soul.

Kate was bewildered by the new mystery of her own elusiveness. She was elusive even to herself. Cipriano hardly talked to her at all; which was quite right. She did not want to be talked to, and words addressed straight at her, without the curious soft veiling which these people knew how to put into their voices, speaking only to the unconcerned, third person in her, came at her like blows. Ah, the ugly blows of direct, brutal speech! She had suffered so much from them. Now she wanted this veiled elusiveness in herself, she wanted to be addressed in the third person.

After the lunch they went to look at the serapes which were being spun for Ramón. Their two soldiers escorted them a few yards up a broken, sun-wasted wide street of little, low black houses, then knocked at big doors.

Kate entered the grateful shade of the zaguán. In the dark shade of the inner court, or patio, where sun blazed on bananas beyond, was a whole weaver's establishment. A fat, one-eyed man sent a little boy to fetch chairs. But Kate wandered, fascinated.

In the zaguán was a great heap of silky white wool, very fine, and in the dark corridor of the patio all the people at work. Two boys with flat square boards bristling with many little wire bristles were carding the white wool into thin films, which they took off the boards in fine rolls like mist, and laid beside the two girls at the end of the shed.

These girls stood by their wheels, spinning, standing beside the running wheel, which they set going with one hand, while with the other hand they kept a long, miraculous thread of white wool-yarn dancing at the very tip of the rapidly-spinning spool-needle, the filmy rolls of the carded wool just touching the point of the spool, and at once running out into a long, pure thread of white, which wound itself on to the spool, and another piece of carded wool was attached. One of the girls, a beautiful oval-faced one, who smiled shyly at Kate, was very clever. It was almost miraculous the way she touched the spool and drew out the thread of wool almost as fine as sewing cotton.

At the other end of the corridor, under the black shed, were two looms, and two men weaving. They treadled at the wooden tread-looms, first with one foot and then the other, absorbed and silent, in the shadow of the black mud walls. One man was weaving a brilliant scarlet serape, very fine, and of the beautiful cochineal red. It was difficult work. From the pure scarlet centre zigzags of black and white were running in a sort of whorl, away to the edge, that was pure black. Wonderful to see the man, with small bobbins of fine red and white yarn, and black, weaving a bit of the ground, weaving the zigzag of black up to it, and, up to that, the zigzag of white, with deft, dark fingers, quickly adjusting his setting needle, quick as lightning threading his pattern, then bringing down the beam heavily to press it tight. The serape was woven on a black warp, long fine threads of black, like a harp. But beautiful beyond words the perfect, delicate scarlet weaving in.

'For whom is that?' said Kate to Cipriano. 'For you?'

'Yes,' he said. 'For me!'

The other weaver was weaving a plain white serape with blue and natural-black ends, throwing the spool of yarn from side to side, between the white harp-strings, pressing down each thread of his woof heavily, with the wooden bar, then treadling to change the long, fine threads of the warp.

In the shadow of the mud shed, the pure colours of the lustrous wool looked mystical, the cardinal scarlet, the pure, silky white, the lovely blue, and the black, gleaming in the shadow of the blackish walls.

The fat man with the one eye brought serapes, and two boys opened them one by one. There was a new one, white, with close flowers of blue on black stalks, and with green leaves, forming the borders, and at the *boca*, the mouth, where the head went through, a whole lot of little, rainbow-coloured flowers, in a coiling blue circle.

'I love that!' said Kate. 'What is that for?'

'It is one of Ramón's; they are Quetzalcoatl's colours, the blue and white and natural black. But this one is for the day of the opening of the flowers, when he brings in the goddess who will come,' said Cipriano.

Kate was silent with fear.

There were two scarlet serapes with a diamond at the centre, all black, and a border-pattern of black diamonds.

'Are these yours?'

'Well, they are for the messengers of Huitzilopochtli. Those are my colours: scarlet and black. But I myself have white as well, just as Ramón has a fringe of my scarlet.'

'Doesn't it make you afraid?' she said to him, looking at him rather blenched.

'How make me afraid?'

'To do this. To be the living Huitzilopochtli,' she said.

'I *am* the living Huitzilopochtli,' he said. 'When Ramón dares to be the living Quetzalcoatl, I dare to be the living Huitzilopochtli. I *am* he. – Am I not?'

Kate looked at him, at his dark face with the little hanging tuft of beard, the arched brows, the slightly slanting black eyes. In the round, fierce gaze of his eyes there was a certain silence, like tenderness, for her. But beyond that, an inhuman assurance, which looked far, far beyond her, in the darkness.

And she hid her face from him, murmuring:

'I know you are.'

'And on the day of flowers,' he said, 'you, too, shall come, in a green dress they shall weave you, with blue flowers at the seam, and on your head the new moon of flowers.'

She hid her face, afraid.

'Come and look at the wools,' he said, leading her across the patio to the shade where, on a line, the yarn hung in dripping tresses of colour, scarlet and blue and yellow and green and brown.

'See!' he said. 'You shall have a dress of green, that leaves the arms bare, and a white under-dress with blue flowers.'

The green was a strong apple-green colour.

Two women under the shed were crouching over big earthenware vessels, which sat over a fire which burned slowly in a hole dug in the ground. They were watching the steaming water. One took dried, yellow-brown flowers, and flung them in her water as if she were a witch brewing decoctions. She watched as the flowers rose, watched as they turned softly in the boiling water. Then she threw in a little white powder.

'And on the day of flowers you, too, will come. Ah! If Ramón is the centre of a new world, a world of new flowers shall spring up round him, and push the old world back. I call you the First Flower.'

They left the courtyard. The soldiers had brought the black Arab stallion for Cipriano, and for her the donkey, on which she could perch sideways, like a peasant woman. So they went through the hot, deserted silence of the mud-brick town, down the lane of deep, dark-grey dust, under vivid green trees that were bursting into flower, again to the silent shore of the lake-end, where the delicate fishing nets were hung in long lines and blowing in the wind, loop after loop striding above the shingle and blowing delicately in the wind, as away on the low places the green maize was blowing, and the fleecy willows shook like soft green feathers hanging down.

The lake stretched pale and unreal into nowhere; the motor-boat rode near in, the black *canoas* stood motionless a little further out. Two women, tiny as birds, were kneeling on the water's edge, washing.

Kate jumped from her donkey on to the shingle.

'Why not ride through the water to the boat?' said Cipriano.

She looked at the boat, and thought of the donkey stumbling and splashing.

'No,' she said. 'I will wade again.'

He rode his black Arab to the water. It sniffed, and entered with delicate feet into the warm shallows. Then, a little way in, it stood and suddenly started pawing the water, as a horse paws the ground, in the oddest manner possible, very rapidly striking the water with its fore-foot, so that little waves splashed up over its black legs and belly.

But this splashed Cipriano too. He lifted the reins and touched the creature with his spurs. It jumped, and went half-stumbling, half-dancing through the water, prettily, with a splashing noise. Cipriano quieted it, and it waded gingerly on through the shallows of the vast lake, bending its black head down to look, to look in a sort of fascination at the stony bottom, swaying its black tail as it moved its glossy, raven haunches gingerly.

Then again it stood still, and suddenly, with a rapid beating of its fore-paw, sent the water hollowly splashing up, till its black belly glistened wet like a black serpent, and its legs were shiny wet pillars. And again Cipriano lifted its head and touched it with the spurs, so the delicate creature danced in a churn of water.

'Oh, it looks so pretty! It looks so pretty when it paws the water!' cried Kate from the shore. 'Why does it do it?'

Cipriano turned in the saddle and looked back at her with the sudden, gay Indian laugh.

'It likes to be wet – who knows?' he said.

A soldier hurried wading through the water and took the horse's bridle. Cipriano dismounted neatly from the stirrup, with a little backward leap into the boat, a real savage horseman. The barefoot soldier leaped into the saddle, and turned the horse to shore. But the black horse, male and wilful, insisted on stopping to paw the waters and splash himself, with a naïve, wilful sort of delight.

'Look! Look!' cried Kate. 'It's so pretty.'

But the soldier was perching in the saddle, drawing up his legs like a monkey, and shouting at the horse. It would wet its fine harness.

He rode the Arab slanting through the water, to where an old woman, sitting in her own silence and almost invisible before, was squatted in the water with brown bare shoulders emerging, ladling water from a half gourd-shell over her matted grey head. The horse splashed and danced, the old woman rose with her rag of chemise clinging to her, scolding in a quiet voice and bending forward with her calabash cup; the soldier laughed, the black horse joyfully and excitedly pawed the water and made it splash high up, the soldier shouted again. – But the soldier knew he could make Cipriano responsible for the splashings.

Kate waded slowly to the boat, and stepped in. The water was warm, but the wind was blowing with strong, electric heaviness. Kate quickly dried her feet and legs on her handkerchief, and pulled on her biscuit-coloured silk stockings and brown shoes.

She sat looking back, at the lake-end, the desert of shingle, the blowing, gauzy nets, and, beyond them, the black land with green maize standing, a further fleecy green of trees, and the broken lane leading deep into the rows of old trees, where the soldiers from Jaramay were now riding away on the black horse and the donkey. On the right there was a ranch, too; a long, low black building and a cluster of black huts with tiled roofs, empty gardens with reed fences, clumps of banana and willow trees. All in the changeless, heavy light of the afternoon, the long lake reaching into invisibility, between its unreal mountains.

'It is beautiful here!' said Kate. 'One could almost live here.'

'Ramón says he will make the lake the centre of a new world,' said Cipriano. 'We will be the gods of the lake.'

'I'm afraid I am just a woman,' said Kate.

His black eyes came round at her swiftly.

'What does it mean, just a woman?' he said, quickly, sternly.

She hung her head. What did it mean? What indeed did it mean? Just a woman! She let her soul sink again into the lovely elusiveness where everything is possible, even that oneself is elusive among the gods.

The motor-boat, with waves slapping behind, was running quickly along the brownish pale water. The soldiers, who were in the front, for balance, crouched on the floor with the glazed, stupefied mask-faces of the people when they are sleepy. And soon they were a heap in the bottom of the boat, two little heaps lying in contact.

Cipriano sat behind her, his tunic removed, spreading his white-sleeved arms on the back of his seat. The cartridge-belt was heavy on his hips. His face was completely expressionless, staring ahead. The wind blew his black hair on his forehead, and blew his little beard. He met her eyes with a far-off, remote smile, far, far down his black eyes. But it was a wonderful recognition of her.

The boatman in the stern sat tall and straight, watching with pale eyes of shallow, superficial consciousness. The great hat made his face dark, the chin-ribbon fell black against his cheek. Feeling her look at him, he glanced at her as if she were not there.

Turning, she pushed her cushion on to the floor and slid down. Cipriano got up, in the running, heaving boat, and pulled her another seat-cushion. She lay, covering her face with her shawl, while the motor chugged rapidly, the awning rattled with sudden wind, the hurrying waves rose behind, giving the boat a slap and throwing her forward, sending spray sometimes, in the heat and silence of the lake.

Kate lost her consciousness, under her yellow shawl, in the silence of men.

She woke to the sudden stopping of the engine, and sat up. They were near shore; the white towers of San Pablo among near trees. The boatman, wide-eyed, was bending over the engine, abandoning the tiller. The waves pushed the boat slowly round.

'What is it?' said Cipriano.

'More gasoline, Excellency!' said the boatman.

The soldiers woke and sat up.

The breeze had died.

'The water is coming,' said Cipriano.

'The rain?' said Kate.

'Yes —' and he pointed with his fine black finger, which was pale on the inside, to where black clouds were rushing up behind the mountains, and in another place farther off, great heavy banks were rising with strange suddenness. The air seemed to be knitting together overhead. Lightning flashed in various places, muffled thunder spoke far away.

Still the boat drifted. There was a smell of gasoline. The man pottered with the engine. The motor started again, only to stop again in a moment.

The man rolled up his trousers, and, to Kate's amazement, stepped into the lake, though they were a mile from the shore. The water was not up to his knees. They were on a bank. He slowly pushed the boat before him, wading in the silence.

'How deep is the lake further in?' asked Kate.

'There, Señorita, where the birds with the white breasts are swimming, it is eight and a half metres,' he said, pointing as he waded.

'We must make haste,' said Cipriano.

'Yes, Excellency!'

The man stepped in again, with his long, handsome brown legs. The motor spluttered. They were under way, running fast. A new chill wind was springing up.

But they rounded a bend, and saw ahead the flat promontory with the dark mango-trees, and the pale yellow upper storey of the hacienda house of Jamiltepec rising above the trees. Palm-trees stood motionless, the bougainvillea hung in heavy sheets of magenta colour. Kate could see huts of peons among the trees, and women washing, kneeling on stones at the lake side where the stream ran in, and a big plantation of bananas just above.

A cool wind was spinning round in the heavens. Black clouds were filling up. Ramón came walking slowly down to the little harbour as they landed.

'The water is coming,' he said in Spanish.

'We are in time,' said Cipriano.

Ramón looked them both in the face, and knew. Kate, in her new elusiveness, laughed softly.

'There is another flower opened in the garden of Quetzalcoatl,' said Cipriano in Spanish.

'Under the red cannas of Huitzilopochtli,' said Ramón.

'Yes, there, Señor,' said Cipriano. 'Pero una florecita tan zarca! Y abrió en mi sombra, amigo.'

'Eres hombre de la alta fortuna.'

'Verdad!'[6]

It was about five in the afternoon. The wind hissed in the leaves, and suddenly the rain was streaming down in a white smoke of power. The ground was a solid white smoke of water, the lake was gone.

'You will have to stay here to-night,' said Cipriano to Kate, in Spanish, in the soft, lapping Indian voice.

'But the rain will leave off,' she said.

'You will have to stay here,' he repeated, in the same Spanish phrase, in a curious voice like a breath of wind.

Kate looked at Ramón, blushing. He looked back at her, she thought, very remote, as if looking at her from far, far away.

'The bride of Huitzilopochtli,' he said, with a faint smile.

'Thou, Quetzalcoatl, thou wilt have to marry us,' said Cipriano.

'Do you wish it?' said Ramón.

'Yes!' she said. 'I want you to marry us, only you.'

'When the sun goes down,' said Ramón.

And he went away to his room. Cipriano showed Kate to her room, then left her and went to Ramón.

The cool water continued to come down, rushing with a smoke of speed down from heaven.

As the twilight came through the unceasing rain, a woman-servant brought Kate a sleeveless dress or chemise of white linen, scalloped at the bottom and embroidered with stiff blue flowers upside-down on the black stalks, with two stiff green leaves. In the centre of the flowers was the tiny Bird of Quetzalcoatl.

'The Patrón asks that you put this on!' said the woman, bringing also a lamp and a little note.

The note was from Ramón, saying in Spanish: 'Take the dress of the bride of Huitzilopochtli, and put it on, and take off everything but this. Leave no thread nor thing that can touch you from the past. The past is finished. It is the new twilight.'

Kate did not quite know how to put on the slip, for it had no sleeves nor arm-holes, but was just a straight slip with a running string. Then she remembered the old Indian way, and tied the string over her left shoulder; rather, slipped the tied string over her left shoulder, leaving her arms and part of her right breast bare, the slip gathered full over her breasts. And she sighed. For it was but a shirt with flowers upturned at the bottom.

Ramón, barefoot, in his white clothes, came for her and took her in silence downstairs into the garden. The zaguán was dark, the rain fell steadily in the twilight, but was abating. All was dark twilight.

Ramón took off his blouse and threw it on the stairs. Then with naked breast he led her into the garden, into the massive rain. Cipriano came forward, barefoot, with naked breast, bareheaded, in the floppy white pantaloons.

They stood barefoot on the earth, that still threw back a white smoke of waters. The rain drenched them in a moment.

'Barefoot on the living earth, with faces to the living rain,' said Ramón in Spanish, quietly; 'at twilight, between the night and the day; man, and woman, in presence of the unfading star, meet to be perfect in one another. Lift your face, Caterina, and say: *This man is my rain from heaven.*'

Kate lifted her face and shut her eyes in the downpour.

'This man is my rain from heaven,' she said.

'This woman is the earth to me – say that, Cipriano,' said Ramón, kneeling on one knee and laying his hand flat on the earth.

Cipriano kneeled and laid his hand on the earth.

'This woman is the earth to me,' he said.

'I, woman, kiss the feet and the heels of this man, for I will be strength to him, throughout the long twilight of the Morning Star.'

Kate kneeled and kissed the feet and heels of Cipriano, and said her say.

'I, man, kiss the brow and the breast of this woman, for I will be her peace and her increase, through the long twilight of the Morning Star.'

Cipriano kissed her, and said his say.

Then Ramón put Cipriano's hand over the rain-wet eyes of Kate, and Kate's hand over the rain-wet eyes of Cipriano.

'I, a woman, beneath the darkness of this covering hand, pray to this man to meet me in the heart of the night, and never deny me,' said Kate. 'But let it be an abiding place between us, for ever.'

'I, a man, beneath the darkness of this covering hand, pray to this woman to receive me in the heart of the night, in the abiding place that is between us for ever.'

'Man shall betray a woman, and woman shall betray a man,' said Ramón, 'and it shall be forgiven them, each of them. But if they have met as earth and rain, between day and night, in the hour of the Star; if the man has met the woman with his body and the star of his hope, and the woman has met the man with her body and the star of her yearning, so that a meeting has come to pass, and an abiding place for the two where they are as one star, then shall neither of them betray the abiding place where the meeting lives like an unsetting star. For if either betray the abiding place of the two, it shall not be forgiven, neither by day nor by night nor in the twilight of the star.'

The rain was leaving off, the night was dark.

'Go and bathe in the warm water, which is peace between us all. And put oil on your bodies, which is the stillness of the Morning Star. Anoint even the soles of your feet, and the roots of your hair.'

Kate went up to her room and found a big earthenware bath with steaming water, and big towels. Also, in a beautiful little bowl, oil, and a soft bit of white wool.

She bathed her rain-wet body in the warm water, dried and anointed herself with the clear oil, that was clear as water. It was soft, and had a faint perfume, and was grateful to the skin. She rubbed all her body, even among her hair and under her feet, till she glowed softly.

Then she put on another of the slips with the inverted blue flowers, that had been laid on the bed for her, and over that a dress of green, hand-woven wool, made of two pieces joined openly together down the sides, showing a bit of the white, full under-dress, and fastened on the left shoulder. There was a stiff flower, blue, on a black stem, with two black leaves, embroidered at the bottom, at each side. And her white slip showed a bit at the breast, and hung below the green skirt, showing the blue flowers.

It was strange and primitive, but beautiful. She pushed her feet into the plaited green huaraches. But she wanted a belt. She tied a piece of ribbon round her waist.

A mozo tapped to say supper was ready.

Laughing rather shyly, she went along to the salon.

Ramón and Cipriano were both waiting, in silence, in their white clothes. Cipriano had his red serape loosely thrown over his shoulders.

'So!' said Cipriano, coming forward. 'The bride of Huitzilopochtli, like a green morning. But Huitzilopochtli will put on your sash, and you will put on his shoes, so that he shall never leave you, and you shall be always in his spell.'

Cipriano tied round her waist a narrow woollen sash of white wool, with white, terraced towers upon a red and black ground. And she stooped and put on his small, dark feet the huaraches of woven red strips of leather, with a black cross on the toes.

'One more little gift,' said Ramón.

He made Kate put over Cipriano's head a blue cord bearing a little symbol of Quetzalcoatl, the snake in silver and the bird in blue turquoise. Cipriano put over her head the same symbol, but in gold, with a bird in black dull jet, and hanging on a red cord.

'There!' said Ramón. 'That is the symbol of Quetzalcoatl, the Morning Star. Remember the marriage is the meeting-ground, and the meeting-ground is the star. If there be no star, no meeting-ground, no true coming together of man with the woman, into a wholeness, there is no marriage. And if there is no marriage, there is nothing but an agitation. If there is no honourable meeting of man with woman and woman with man, there is no good thing come to pass. But if the meeting come to pass, then whosoever betrays the abiding place, which is the meeting-ground, which is that which lives like a star between day and night, between the dark of woman and the dawn of man, between man's night and woman's morning, shall never be forgiven, neither here nor in the hereafter. For man is frail and woman is frail, and none can draw the line down which another shall walk. But the star that is between two people and is their meeting-ground shall not be betrayed.

'And the star that is between three people, and is their meeting-ground, shall not be betrayed.

'And the star that is between all men and all women, and between all the children of men, shall not be betrayed.

'Whosoever betrays another man, betrays a man like himself, a fragment. For if there is no star between a man and a man, or even a man and a wife, there is nothing. But whosoever betrays the star that is between him and another man, betrays all, and all is lost to the traitor.

'Where there is no star and no abiding place, nothing is, so nothing can be lost.'

The Opening of the Church

KATE went back to her house in Sayula, and Cipriano went back to his command in the city.

'Will you not come with me?' he said. 'Shall we not make a civil marriage, and live in the same house together?'

'No,' she said. 'I am married to you by Quetzalcoatl, no other. I will be your wife in the world of Quetzalcoatl, no other. And if the star has risen between us, we will watch it.'

Conflicting feelings played in his dark eyes. He could not bear even to be the least bit thwarted. Then the strong, rather distant look came back.

'It is very good,' he said. 'It is the best.'

And he went away without looking back.

Kate returned to her house, to her servants and her rocking-chair. Inside herself she kept very still and almost thoughtless, taking no count of time. What was going to unfold must unfold of itself.

She no longer feared the nights, when she was shut alone in her darkness. But she feared the days a little. She shrank so mortally from contact.

She opened her bedroom window one morning, and looked down to the lake. The sun had come, and queer blotty shadows were on the hills beyond the water. Way down at the water's edge a woman was pouring water from a calabash bowl over a statuesque pig, dipping rapidly and assiduously. The little group was seen in silhouette against the pale, dun lake.

But impossible to stand at her open window looking on the little lane. An old man suddenly appeared from nowhere, offering her a leaf full of tiny fish, charales, like splinters of glass, for ten centavos, and a girl was unfolding three eggs from the ragged corner of her rebozo, thrusting them imploringly forward to Kate. An old woman was shambling up with a sad story, Kate knew. She fled from her window and the importunity.

At the same instant, the sound that always made her heart stand still woke on the invisible air. It was the sound of drums, of tom-toms rapidly beaten. The same sound she had heard in the distance, in the tropical dusk of Ceylon, from the temple at sunset. The sound she had heard from the edge of the forests in the north, when the Red Indians were dancing by the fire. The sound that wakes dark, ancient echoes in the heart of every man, the thud of the primeval world.

Two drums were violently throbbing against one another. Then grad-ually they were slowing down, in a peculiar uneven rhythm, till at last there was only left one slow, continual, monotonous note, like a great drop of darkness falling heavily, continually, dripping in the bright morning.

The re-evoked past is frightening, and if it be re-evoked to overwhelm the present, it is fiendish. Kate felt a real terror of the sound of a tom-tom. It seemed to beat straight on her solar plexus, to make her sick.

She went to her window. Across the lane rose a tall garden-wall of adobe brick, and above that, the sun on the tops of the orange trees, deep gold. Beyond the orange garden rose three tall, handsome, shaggy palm trees, side by side on slim stems. And from the very top of the two outer palms, rose the twin tips of the church towers. She had noticed it so often; the two ironwork Greek crosses seeming to stand on the mops of the palms.

Now in an instant she saw the glitter of the symbol of Quetzalcoatl in the places where the cross had been; two circular suns, with the dark bird at the centre. The gold of the suns – or the serpents – flashed new in the light of the sun, the bird lifted its wings dark in outline within the circle.

Then again the two drums were speeding up, beating against one another with the peculiar uneven savage rhythm, which at first seems no rhythm, and then seems to contain a summons almost sinister in its power, acting on the helpless blood direct. Kate felt her hands flutter on her wrists, in fear. Almost, too, she could hear the heart of Cipriano beating; her husband in Quetzalcoatl.

'Listen, Niña! Listen, Niña!' came Juana's frightened voice from the verandah.

Kate went to the verandah. Ezequiel had rolled up his mattress and was hitching up his pants. It was Sunday morning, when he sometimes lay on after sunrise. His thick black hair stood up, his dark face was blank with sleep, but in his quiet aloofness and his slightly bowed head Kate could see the secret satisfaction he took in the barbarous sound of the drums.

'It comes from the Church!' said Juana.

Kate caught the other woman's black, reptilian eyes unexpectedly. Usually, she forgot that Juana was dark, and different. For days she would not realise it. Till suddenly she met that black, void look with the glint in it, and she started inwardly, involuntarily asking herself: 'Does she hate me?'

Or was it only the unspeakable difference in blood?

Now, in the dark glitter which Juana showed her for one moment, Kate read fear, and triumph, and a slow, savage, nonchalant defiance. Something very inhuman.

'What does it mean?' Kate said to her.

'It means, Niña, that they won't ring the bells any more. They have taken the bells away, and they beat the drums in the church. Listen! Listen!'

The drums were shuddering rapidly again.

Kate and Juana went across to the open window.

'Look! Niña! The Eye of the Other One! No more crosses on the church. It is the Eye of the Other One. Look! How it shines! How nice!'

'It means,' said Ezequiel's breaking young voice, which was just turning deep, 'that it is the church of Quetzalcoatl. Now it is the temple of Quetzalcoatl; our own God.'

He was evidently a staunch Man of Quetzalcoatl.

'Think of it!' murmured Juana, in an awed voice. She seemed like a heap of darkness low at Kate's side.

Then again she glanced up, and the eyes of the two women met for a moment.

'See the Niña's eyes of the sun!' cried Juana, laying her hand on Kate's arm. Kate's eyes were a sort of hazel, changing, grey-gold, flickering at the moment with wonder, and a touch of fear and dismay. Juana sounded triumphant.

A man in a white serape, with the blue and black borders, suddenly appeared at the window, lifting his hat, on which was the sign of Quetzalcoatl, and pushing a little card through the window.

The card said: Come to the church when you hear the one big drum; about seven o'clock. – It was signed with the sign of Quetzalcoatl.

'Very well!' said Kate. 'I will come.'

It was a quarter to seven already. Outside the room was the noise of Juana sweeping the verandah. Kate put on a white dress and a yellow hat, and a long string of pale-coloured topaz that glimmered with yellow and mauve.

The earth was all damp with rain, the leaves were all fresh and tropical thick, yet many old leaves were on the ground, beaten down.

'Niña! You are going out already! Wait! Wait! The coffee. Concha! quick!'

There was a running of bare feet, the children bringing cup and plate and sweet buns and sugar, the mother hastily limping with the coffee. Ezequiel came striding along the walk, lifting his hat. He went down to the servants' quarters.

'Ezequiel says – !' Juana came crying. When suddenly a soft, slack thud seemed to make a hole in the air, leaving a gap behind it. Thud! – Thud! – Thud! – rather slowly. It was the big drum, irresistible.

Kate rose at once from her coffee.

'I am going to the church,' she said.

'Yes, Niña – Ezequiel says – I am coming, Niña –'

And Juana scuttled away, to get her black rebozo.

The man in the white serape with the blue and black ends was waiting by the gate. He lifted his hat, and walked behind Kate and Juana.

'He is following us!' whispered Juana.

Kate drew her yellow shawl around her shoulders.

It was Sunday morning, sailing-boats lined the water's edge, with their black hulls. But the beach was empty. As the great drum let fall its slow, bellowing note, the last people were running towards the church.

In front of the church was a great throng of natives, the men with their dark serapes, or their red blankets over their shoulders; the nights of rain were cold; and their hats in their hands. The high, dark Indian heads! – Women in blue rebozos were pressing along. The big drum slowly, slackly exploded its note from the church-tower. Kate had her heart in her mouth.

In the middle of the crowd, a double row of men in the scarlet serapes of Huitzilopochtli with the black diamond on the shoulders, stood with rifles, holding open a lane through the crowd.

'Pass!' said her guard to her. And Kate entered the lane of scarlet and black serapes, going slow and dazed between watchful black eyes of the men. Her guard followed her. But Juana had been turned back.

Kate looked at her feet, and stumbled. Then she looked up.

In the gateway of the yard before the church stood a brilliant figure in a serape whose zig-zag whorls of scarlet, white, and black ran curving, dazzling, to the black shoulders; above which was the face of Cipriano, calm, superb, with the little black beard and the arching brows. He lifted his hand to her in salute.

Behind him, stretching from the gateway to the closed door of the church, was a double row of the guard of Quetzalcoatl, in their blankets with the blue and black borders.

'What shall I do?' said Kate.

'Stand here with me a moment,' said Cipriano, in the gateway.

It was no easy thing to do, to face all those dark faces and black, glittering eyes. After all, she was a gringuita, and she felt it. A sacrifice? Was she a sacrifice? She hung her head, under her yellow hat, and watched the string of topaz twinkling and shaking its delicate, bog-watery colours against her white dress. Joachim had given it her. He had had it made up for her, the string, in Cornwall. So far away! In another world, in another life, in another era! Now she was condemned to go through these strange ordeals, like a victim.

The big drum overhead ceased, and suddenly the little drums broke like a shower of hail on the air, and as suddenly ceased.

In low, deep, inward voices, the guard of Quetzalcoatl began to speak, in heavy unison:

'Oye! Oye! Oye! Oye!'[1]

The small, inset door within the heavy doors of the church opened and Don Ramón stepped through. In his white clothes, wearing the Quetzalcoatl serape, he stood at the head of his two rows of guards, until there was a silence. Then he raised his naked right arm.

'What is God, we shall never know!' he said, in a strong voice, to all the people.

The Guard of Quetzalcoatl turned to the people, thrusting up their right arm.

'What is God, you shall never know!' they repeated.

Then again, in the crowd, the words were re-echoed by the Guard of Huitzilopochtli.

After which there fell a dead silence, in which Kate was aware of a forest of black eyes glistening with white fire.

'But the Sons of God come and go.
They come from beyond the Morning Star;
And thither they return, from the land of men.'

It was again the solemn, powerful voice of Ramón. Kate looked at his face; it was creamy-brown in its pallor, but changeless in expression, and seemed to be sending a change over the crowd, removing them from their vulgar complacency.

The Guard of Quetzalcoatl turned again to the crowd, and repeated Ramón's words to the crowd.

'Mary and Jesus have left you, and gone to the place of renewal.
And Quetzalcoatl has come. He is here.
He is your lord.'

With his words, Ramón was able to put the power of his heavy, strong will over the people. The crowd began to fuse under his influence. As he gazed back at all the black eyes, his eyes seemed to have no expression, save that they seemed to be seeing the heart of all darkness in front of him, where his unknowable God-mystery lived and moved.

'Those that follow me, must cross the mountains of the sky,
And pass the houses of the stars by night.
They shall find me only in the Morning Star.

But those that will not follow, must not peep.
Peeping, they will lose their sight, and lingering, they will fall very lame.'

He stood a moment in silence, gazing with dark brows at the crowd. Then he dropped his arm, and turned. The big doors of the church opened, revealing a dim interior. Ramón entered the church alone. Inside the church, the drum began to beat. The guard of Quetzalcoatl slowly filed into the dim interior, the scarlet guard of Huitzilopochtli filed into the yard of the church, taking the place of the guard of Quetzalcoatl. Cipriano remained in the gateway of the churchyard. His voice rang out clear and military.

'Hear me, people. You may enter the house of Quetzalcoatl. Men must go to the right and left, and remove their shoes, and stand erect. To the new God no man shall kneel.

'Women must go down the centre, and cover their faces. And they may sit upon the floor.

'But men must stand erect.

'Pass now, those who dare.'

Kate went with Cipriano into the church.

It was all different, the floor was black and polished, the walls were in stripes of colour, the place seemed dark. Two files of the white-clad men of Quetzalcoatl stood in a long avenue down the centre of the church.

'This way,' said one of the men of Quetzalcoatl, in a low voice, drawing her into the centre between the motionless files of men.

She went alone and afraid over the polished black floor, covering her face with her yellow shawl. The pillars of the nave were dark green, like trees rising to a deep, blue roof. The walls were vertically striped in bars of black and white, vermilion and yellow and green, with the windows between rich with deep blue and crimson and black glass, having specks of light. A strange maze, the windows.

The daylight came only from small windows, high up under the deep blue roof, where the stripes of the walls had run into a maze of green, like banana leaves. Below, the church was all dark, and rich with hard colour.

Kate went forward to the front, near the altar steps. High at the back of the chancel, above where the altar had been, burned a small but intense bluey-white light, and just below and in front of the light stood a huge dark figure, a strange looming block, apparently carved in wood. It was a naked man, carved archaic and rather flat, holding his right arm over his head, and on the right arm balanced a carved wooden eagle with outspread wings whose upper surface gleamed with gold, near the light, whose under surface was black shadow. Round the heavy left leg of the man-image was carved a serpent, also glimmering gold, and its golden head rested in the hand of the figure, near the thigh. The face of the figure was dark.

This great dark statue loomed stiff like a pillar, rather frightening in the white-lit blue chancel.

At the foot of the statue was a stone altar with a small fire of ocote-wood burning. And on a low throne by the altar sat Ramón.

People were beginning to file into the church. Kate heard the strange sound of the naked feet of the men on the black, polished floor, the white figures stole forward towards the altar steps, the dark faces gazing round in wonder, men crossing themselves involuntarily. Throngs of men slowly flooded in, and women came half running, to crouch on the floor and cover their faces. Kate crouched down too.

A file of the men of Quetzalcoatl came and stood along the foot of the altar steps, like a fence with a gap in the middle, facing the people. Beyond the gap was the flickering altar, and Ramón.

Ramón rose to his feet. The men of Quetzalcoatl turned to face him, and shot up their naked right arms, in the gesture of the statue, Ramón lifted his arm, so that his blanket fell in towards his shoulder, revealing the naked side and the blue sash.

'All men salute Quetzalcoatl!' said a clear voice in command.

The scarlet men of Huitzilopochtli were threading among the men of the congregation, pulling the kneeling ones to their feet, causing all to thrust up their right arm, palm flat to heaven, face uplifted, body erect and tense. It was the statue receiving the eagle.

So that around the low dark shrubs of the crouching women stood a forest of erect, upthrusting men, powerful and tense with inexplicable passion. It was a forest of dark wrists and hands up-pressing, with the striped wall vibrating above, and higher, the maze of green going to the little, iron-barred windows that stood open, letting in the light and air of the roof.

'I am the living Quetzalcoatl,' came the solemn, impassive voice of Ramón.

'I am the Son of the Morning Star, and child of the deeps.
No man knows my Father, and I know Him not.
My Father is deep within the deeps, whence He sent me forth.
He sends the eagle of silence down on wide wings
To lean over my head and my neck and my breast
And fill them strong with strength of wings.
He sends the serpent of power up my feet and my loins
So that strength wells up in me like water in hot springs.
But midmost shines as the Morning Star midmost shines
Between night and day, my Soul-star in one,
Which is my Father whom I know not.
I tell you, the day should not turn into glory,
And the night should not turn deep,
Save for the morning and evening stars, upon which they turn.
Night turns upon me, and Day, who am the star between.
Between your breast and belly is a star.
If it be not there
You are empty gourd-shells filled with dust and wind.
When you walk, the star walks with you, between your breast and your belly.
When you sleep, it softly shines.
When you speak true and true, it is bright on your lips and your teeth.

When you lift your hands in courage and bravery, its glow is clear in your
  palms.
When you turn to your wives as brave men turn to their women
The Morning Star and the Evening Star shine together.
For man is the Morning Star.
And woman is the Star of Evening.
I tell you, you are not men alone.
The star of the beyond is within you.
But have you seen a dead man, how his star has gone out of him?
So the star will go out of you, even as a woman will leave a man if his warmth
  never warms her.
Should you say: *I have no star; I am no star.*
So it will leave you, and you will hang like a gourd on the vine of life
With nothing but rind:
Waiting for the rats of the dark to come and gnaw your inside.
Do you hear the rats of the darkness gnawing at your inside?
Till you are as empty as rat-gnawed pomegranates hanging hollow on the Tree
  of Life?
If the star shone, they dare not, they could not.
If you were men with the Morning Star.
If the star shone within you
No rat of the dark dared gnaw you.
But I am Quetzalcoatl, of the Morning Star.
I am the living Quetzalcoatl.
And you are men who should be men of the Morning Star.
See you be not rat-gnawed gourds.
I am Quetzalcoatl of the eagle and the snake.
The earth and air.
Of the Morning Star.
I am Lord of the Two Ways –'

The drum began to beat, the men of Quetzalcoatl suddenly took off
their serapes, and Ramón did the same. They were now men naked to
the waist. The eight men from the altar-steps filed up to the altar
where the fire burned, and one by one kindled tall green candles, which
burned with a clear light. They ranged themselves on either side the
chancel, holding the lights high, so that the wooden face of the image
glowed as if alive, and the eyes of silver and jet flashed most curiously.

'A man shall take the wine of his spirit and the blood of his heart,
the oil of his belly and the seed of his loins, and offer them first to
the Morning Star,' said Ramón, in a loud voice, turning to the people.

Four men came to him. One put a blue crown with the bird on
his brow, one put a red belt round his breast, another put a yellow
belt round his middle, and the last fastened a white belt round his

loins. Then the first one pressed a small glass bowl to Ramón's brow, and in the bowl was white liquid like bright water. The next touched a bowl to the breast, and the red shook in the bowl. At the navel the man touched a bowl with yellow fluid, and at the loins a bowl with something dark. They held them all to the light.

Then one by one they poured them into a silver mixing-bowl that Ramón held between his hands.

'For save the Unknown God pours His Spirit over my head and fire into my heart, and sends His power like a fountain of oil into my belly, and His lightning like a hot spring into my loins, I am not. I am nothing. I am a dead gourd.

'And save I take the wine of my spirit and the red of my heart, the strength of my belly and the power of my loins, and mingle them all together, and kindle them to the Morning Star, I betray my body, I betray my soul, I betray my spirit and my God who is Unknown.

'Fourfold is man.[2] But the star is one star. And one man is but one star.'

He took the silver mixing-bowl and slowly circled it between his hands, in the act of mixing.

Then he turned his back to the people, and lifted the bowl high up, between his hands, as if offering it to the image.

Then suddenly he threw the contents of the bowl into the altar fire.

There was a soft puff of explosion, a blue flame leaped high into the air, followed by a yellow flame, and then a rose-red smoke. In three successive instants the faces of the men inside the chancel were lit bluish, then gold, then dusky red. And in the same moment Ramón had turned to the people and shot up his hand.

'Salute Quetzalcoatl!' cried a voice, and men began to thrust up their arms, when another voice came moaning strangely:

'No! Ah no! Ah no!' – the voice rose in a hysterical cry.

It came from among the crouching women, who glanced round in fear, to see a woman in black, kneeling on the floor, her black scarf falling back from her lifted face, thrusting up her white hands to the Madonna, in the old gesture.

'No! No! It is not permitted!' shrieked the voice. 'Lord! Lord! Lord Jesus! Holy Virgin! Prevent him! Prevent him!'

The voice sank again to a moan, the white hands clutched the breast, and the woman in black began to work her way forward on her knees, through the throng of women who pressed aside to make her way, towards the altar steps. She came with her head lowered, working her way on her knees, and moaning low prayers of supplication.

Kate felt her blood run cold. Crouching near the altar steps, she looked round. And she knew, by the shape of the head bent in the black scarf, it was Carlota, creeping along on her knees to the altar steps.

The whole church was frozen in horror. 'Saviour! Saviour! Jesus! Oh Holy Virgin!' Carlota was moaning to herself as she crawled along.

It seemed hours before she reached the altar steps. Ramón still stood below the great Quetzalcoatl image with arm upflung.

Carlota crouched black at the altar steps and flung up the white hands and her white face in the frenzy of the old way.

'Lord! Lord!' she cried, in a strange ecstatic voice that froze Kate's bowels with horror: 'Jesus! Jesus! Jesus! Jesus! Jesus! Jesus!'

Carlota strangled in her ecstasy. And all the while, Ramón, the living Quetzalcoatl, stood before the flickering altar with naked arm upraised, looking with dark, inalterable eyes down upon the woman.

Throes and convulsions tortured the body of Carlota. She gazed sightlessly upwards. Then came her voice, in the mysterious rhapsody of prayer:

'Lord! Lord! Forgive!

'God of love, forgive! He knows not what he does.

'Lord! Lord Jesus! Make an end. Make an end, Lord of the world, Christ of the cross, make an end. Have mercy on him, Father. Have pity on him!

'Oh, take his life from him now, now, that his soul may not die.'

Her voice had gathered strength till it rang out metallic and terrible.

'Almighty God, take his life from him, and save his soul.'

And in the silence after that cry her hands seemed to flicker in the air like flames of death.

'The Omnipotent,' came the voice of Ramón, speaking quietly, as if to her, 'is with me, and I serve Omnipotence!'

She remained with her white clasped hands upraised, her white arms and her white face showing mystical, like onyx, from her thin black dress. She was absolutely rigid. And Ramón, with his arm too upraised, looked down on her abstractedly, his black brows a little contracted.

A strong convulsion seized her body. She became tense again, making inarticulate noises. Then another convulsion seized her. Once more she recovered herself, and thrust up her clenched hands in frenzy. A third convulsion seized her as if from below, and she fell with a strangling moan in a heap on the altar steps.[3]

Kate had risen suddenly and ran to her, to lift her up. She found her stiff, with a little froth on her discoloured lips, and fixed, glazed eyes.

Kate looked up in consternation at Ramón. He had dropped his arm, and stood with his hands against his thighs, like a statue. But he remained with his wide, absorbed dark eyes watching without any change. He met Kate's glance of dismay, and his eyes quickly glanced, like lightning, for Cipriano. Then he looked back at Carlota, across a changeless distance. Not a muscle of his face moved. And Kate could see that his heart had died in its connection with Carlota, his heart was quite, quite dead in him; out of the deathly vacancy he watched his wife. Only his brows frowned a little, from his smooth, male forehead. His old connections were broken. She could hear him say: *There is no star between me and Carlota.* – And how terribly true it was!

Cipriano came quickly, switched off his brilliant serape, wrapped it round the poor, stiff figure, and picking up the burden lightly, walked with it through the lane of women to the door, and out into the brilliant sun; Kate following. And as she followed, she heard the slow, deep voice of Ramón:

'I am the Living Quetzalcoatl.
Naked I come from out of the deep
From the place which I call my Father,
Naked have I travelled the long way round
From heaven, past the sleeping sons of God.

Out of the depths of the sky, I came like an eagle.
Out of the bowels of the earth like a snake.

All things that lift in the lift of living between earth and sky, know me.

But I am the inward star invisible.
And the star is the lamp in the hand of the Unknown Mover.
Beyond me is a Lord who is terrible, and wonderful, and dark to me forever.
Yet I have lain in his loins, ere he begot me in Mother space.

Now I am alone on earth, and this is mine.
The roots are mine, down the dark, moist path of the snake.
And the branches are mine, in the paths of the sky and the bird,
But the spark of me that is me is more than mine own.

And the feet of men, and the hands of the women know me.
And knees and thighs and loins, and the bowels of strength and seed are lit with me.
The snake of my left-hand out of the darkness is kissing your feet with his mouth of caressive fire,
And putting his strength in your heels and ankles, his flame in your knees and your legs and your loins, his circle of rest in your belly.
For I am Quetzalcoatl, the feathered snake,
And I am not with you till my serpent has coiled his circle of rest in your belly.

And I, Quetzalcoatl, the eagle of the air, am brushing your faces with vision.
I am fanning your breasts with my breath.
And building my nest of peace in your bones.
I am Quetzalcoatl, of the Two Ways.'

Kate lingered to hear the end of this hymn. Cipriano also had lingered in the porch, with the strange figure in the brilliant serape in his arms. His eyes met Kate's. In his black glance was a sort of homage, to the mystery of the Two Ways; a sort of secret. And Kate was uneasy.

They crossed quickly under the trees to the hotel, which was very near, and Carlota was laid in bed. A soldier had gone already to find a doctor; they sent also for a priest.

Kate sat by the bed. Carlota lay on the bed, making small, horrible moaning noises. The drums outside on the church-roof started to roll, in a savage, complicated rhythm. Kate went to the window and looked out. People were streaming dazzled from the church.

And then, from the church-roof, came the powerful singing of men's voices, fanning like a dark eagle in the bright air; a deep relentless chanting, with an undertone of passionate assurance. She went to the window to look. She could see the men on the church-roof, the people swarming down below. And the roll of that relentless chanting, with its undertone of exultance in power and life, rolled through the air like an invisible dark presence.

Cipriano came in again, glancing at Carlota and at Kate.

'They are singing the song of Welcome to Quetzalcoatl,' said he.

'Is that it?' said Kate. 'What are the words?'

'I will find you a song-sheet,' he said.

He stood beside her, putting the spell of his presence over her. And she still struggled a little, as if she were drowning. When she wasn't drowning, she wanted to drown. But when it actually came, she fought for her old footing.

There was a crying noise from Carlota. Kate hurried to the bed.

'Where am I?' said the white-faced, awful, deathly-looking woman.

'You are resting in bed,' said Kate. 'Don't trouble.'

'Where was I?' came Carlota's voice.

'Perhaps the sun gave you a touch of sunstroke,' said Kate.

Carlota closed her eyes.

Then suddenly outside the noise of drums rolled again, a powerful sound. And outside in the sunshine life seemed to be rolling in powerful waves.

Carlota started, and opened her eyes.

'What is that noise?'

'It is a fiesta,' said Kate.

'Ramón, he's murdered me, and lost his own soul,' said Carlota. 'He has murdered me, and lost his own soul. He is a murderer, and one of the damned. The man I married! The man I married! A murderer among the damned!'

It was evident she no longer heard the sounds outside.

Cipriano could not bear the sound of her voice. He came quickly to the side of the bed.

'Doña Carlota!' he said, looking down at her dulled hazel eyes, that were fixed and unseeing: 'Do not die with wrong words on your lips. If you are murdered, you have murdered yourself. You were never married to Ramón. You were married to your own way.'

He spoke fiercely, avengingly.

'Ah!' said the dying woman. 'Ah! I never married Ramón. No! I never married him! How could I? He was not what I would have him be. How could I marry him? Ah! I thought I married him. Ah! I am so glad I didn't – so glad.'

'You are glad! You are glad!' said Cipriano in anger, angry with the very ghost of the woman, talking to the ghost. 'You are glad because you never poured the wine of your body into the mixing-bowl! Yet in your day you have drunk the wine of his body and been soothed with his oil. You are glad you kept yours back? You are glad you kept back the wine of your body and the secret oil of your soul? That you gave only the water of your charity? I tell you the water of charity, the hissing water of the spirit is bitter at last in the mouth and in the breast and in the belly; it puts out the fire. You would have put out the fire, Doña Carlota. – But you cannot. You shall not. You have been charitable and compassionless to the man you called your own. So you have put out your own fire.'

'Who is talking?' said the ghost of Carlota.

'I, Cipriano Viedma, am talking.'

'The oil and the wine! The oil and the wine and the bread! They are the sacrament! They are the body and the blessing of God! Where is the priest? I want the sacrament. Where is the priest? I want to confess, and take the sacrament, and have the peace of God,' said the ghost of Carlota.

'The priest is coming. – But you can take no sacrament, unless you give it. The oil and the wine and the bread! They are not for the priest to give. They are to be poured into the mixing-bowl, which Ramón calls the cup of the star. If you pour neither oil nor wine into the mixing-bowl, from the mixing-bowl you cannot drink. So you have no sacrament.'

'The sacrament! The bread!' said the ghost of Carlota.

'There is no bread. There is no body without blood and oil, as Shylock found out.'[4]

'A murderer, lost among the damned!' murmured Carlota. 'The father of my children! The husband of my body! Ah no! It is better for me to call to the Holy Virgin, and die.'

'Call then, and die!' said Cipriano.

'My children!' murmured Carlota.

'It is well you must leave them. With your beggar's bowl of charity you have stolen their oil and their wine as well. It is good for you to steal from them no more, you stale virgin, you spinster, you born widow, you weeping mother, you impeccable wife, you just woman. You stole the very sunshine out of the sky and the sap out of the earth. Because back again, what did you pour? Only the water of dead dilution into the mixing-bowl of life, you thief. Oh die! – die! – die! Die and be a thousand times dead! Do nothing but utterly die!'

Doña Carlota had relapsed into unconsciousness; even her ghost refused to hear. Cipriano flung his sinisterly-flaming serape over his shoulders and his face, over his nose, till only his black, glittering eyes were visible as he blew out of the room.

Kate sat by the window, and laughed a little. The primeval woman inside her laughed to herself, for she had known all the time about the two thieves on the Cross with Jesus; the bullying, marauding thief of the male in his own rights, and the much more subtle, cold, sly, charitable thief of the woman in *her* own rights, forever chanting her beggar's whine about the love of God and the God of pity.

But Kate, too, was a modern woman and a woman in her own right. So she sat on with Carlota. And when the doctor came, she accepted the obsequiousness of the man as part of her rights. And when the priest came, she accepted the obsequiousness from him, just the same, as part of her woman's rights. These two ministers of love, what were they for, but to be obsequious to her? As for herself, she could hardly be called a thief, and a sneak-thief of the world's virility, when these men came forcing their obsequiousness upon her, whining to her to take it and relieve them of the responsibility of their own manhood. No, if women are thieves, it is only because men want to be thieved from. If women thieve the world's virility, it is only because men want to have it thieved, since for men to be responsible for their own manhood seems to be the last thing men want.

So Kate sat on in the room of the dying Carlota, smiling a little cynically. Outside she heard the roll of the tom-toms and the deep chanting of the men of Quetzalcoatl. Beyond, under the trees, in the smoothed, cleared space before the church, she saw the half-naked men dancing in a circle, to the drum; the round dance. Then later, dancing a religious dance of the return of Quetzalcoatl. It was the old, bare-footed, absorbed dancing of the Indians, the dance of downward-sinking absorption. It was the dance of these people too, just the same: the dance of the Aztecs and Zapotecs and the Huicholes, just the same in essence, indigenous to America; the curious, silent, absorbed dance of the softly-beating feet and ankles, the body coming down softly, but with deep weight, upon powerful knees and ankles, to the tread of the earth, as when a male bird treads the hen. And women softly stepping in unison.

And Kate, listening to the drums, and the full-throated singing, and watching the rich, soft bodies in the dance, thought to herself a little sceptically: Yes! For these it is easier. But all the white men, of the dominant race, what are they doing at this moment?

In the afternoon there was a great dance of the *Welcome of Quet-zalcoatl*. Kate could only see a little of it, in front of the church.

The drums beat vigorously all the time, the dance wound strangely to the water's edge. Kate heard afterwards that the procession of women with baskets on their heads, filled with bread and fruits all wrapped in leaves, went down to the shore and loaded the boats. Then dancers and all got into the boats and *canoas*, and rowed to the island.

They made a feast on the island, and learned the dance of the *Welcome of Quetzalcoatl*, which they would dance every year on that day. And they learned the Song of the Welcome of Quetzalcoatl; which later on Cipriano brought to Kate, as she sat in that dim room with the unconscious woman, who made small, terrible, mechanical noises.

The doctor came hastening, and the priest came after a while. Neither could do anything. They came in the afternoon again, and Kate walked out and wandered on the half-deserted beach, looking at the flock of boats drawing near the island, and feeling that life was a more terrible issue even than death. One could die and have done. But living was never done, it could never be finished, and the responsibility could never be shifted.

She went back again to the sick-room, and with the aid of a woman she undressed poor Carlota and put a nightdress on her. Another doctor came from the city. But the sick woman was dying. And Kate was alone with her again.

The men, where were they?

The business of living? Were they really gone about the great business of living, abandoning her here to this business of dying?

It was nightfall before she heard the drums returning. And again that deep, full, almost martial singing of men, savage and remote, to the sound of the drum. Perhaps after all life would conquer again, and men would be men, so that women could be women. Till men are men indeed, women have no hope to be women. She knew that fatally enough.

Cipriano came to her, smelling of sun and sweat, his face darkly glowing, his eyes flashing. He glanced at the bed, at the unconscious woman, at the medicine bottles.

'What do they say?' he asked.

'The doctors think she may come round.'

'She will die,' he said.

Then he went with her to the window.

'See!' he said. 'This is what they are singing.'

It was the Song-sheet of the *Welcome to Quetzalcoatl*.

WELCOME TO QUETZALCOATL

We are not wasted. We are not left out.
Quetzalcoatl has come!
There is nothing more to ask for.
Quetzalcoatl has come!

He threw the Fish in the boat.
The cock rose, and crew over the waters.
The naked one climbed in.
Quetzalcoatl has come!

Quetzalcoatl loves the shade of trees.
Give him trees! Call back the trees!
We are like trees, tall and rustling.
Quetzalcoatl is among the trees.

Do not tell me my face is shining.
Quetzalcoatl has come!
Over my head his noiseless eagle
Fans a flame.

Tie my spotted shoes for dancing,
The snake has kissed my heel.
Like a volcano my hips are moving
With fire, and my throat is full.

Blue daylight sinks in my hair.
The star comes out between the two
Wonders, shines out of everywhere,
Saying without speech: Look you!

Ah, Quetzalcoatl!
Put sleep as black as beauty in the secret of my belly.
Put star-oil over me.
Call me a man.

Even as she read, she could hear the people outside singing it, as the reed-flutes unthreaded the melody time after time. This strange dumb people of Mexico was opening its voice at last. It was as if a stone had been rolled off them all, and she heard their voice for the first time, deep, wild, with a certain exultance and menace.

'The naked one climbed in.
Quetzalcoatl has come!'

She could hear the curious defiance and exultance in the men's voices. Then a woman's voice, clear almost as a star itself, went up the road at the verse:

> 'Blue daylight sinks in my hair.
> The star comes out between the two
> Wonders ...'

Strange! The people had opened hearts at last. They had rolled the stone of their heaviness away, a new world had begun. Kate was frightened. It was dusk. She laid her hand on Cipriano's knee, lost. And he leaned and put his dark hand against her cheek, breathing silently.

'To-day,' he said softly, 'we have done well.'

She felt for his hand. All was so dark. But oh, so deep, so deep and beyond her, the vast, soft, living heat! So beyond her!

> 'Put sleep so black as beauty in the secret of my belly.
> Put star-oil over me.'

She could almost feel her soul appealing to Cipriano for this sacrament.

They sat side by side in darkness, as the night fell, and he held his hand loosely on hers. Outside, the people were still singing. Some were dancing round the drum. On the church-towers, where the bells had been, there were fires flickering, and white forms of men, the noise of a heavy drum, then again, the chant. In the yard before the church doors a fire was blazing, and men of Huitzilopochtli stood watching two of their men, naked save for a breech-cloth and the scarlet feathers on their head, dancing the old spear-dance, whooping challenge in the firelight.

Ramón came in, in his white clothes. He pulled off his big hat, and stood looking down at Carlota. She no longer made noises, and her eyes were turned up horribly, showing the whites. Ramón closed his eyes a moment, and turned away, saying nothing. He came to the window, where Cipriano still sat in his impenetrable but living silence, that satisfied where all speech had failed, holding Kate's hand loosely. Nor did he let go her hand.

Ramón looked out, at the fires in the church towers, the fire before the church doors, the little fires on the beach by the lake; and the figures of men in white, the figures of women in dark rebozos, with full white skirts, the two naked dancers, the standing crowd, the occasional scarlet serapes of Huitzilopochtli, the white and blue of Quetzalcoatl, the creeping away of a motor-car, the running of boys, the men clustering round the drum, to sing.

'It is life,' he said, 'which is the mystery. Death is hardly mysterious in comparison.'

There was a knocking. The doctor had come again, and a sister to nurse the dying woman. Softly the sister paced round the room and bent over her charge.

Cipriano and Kate went away in a boat over the dark lake, away from all the fires and the noise, into the deep darkness of the lake beyond, to Jamiltepec. Kate felt she wanted to be covered with deep and living darkness, the deeps where Cipriano could lay her.

> *Put sleep as black as beauty in the secret of my belly.*
> *Put star-oil over me.*

And Cipriano, as he sat in the boat with her, felt the inward sun rise darkly in him, diffusing through him; and felt the mysterious flower of her woman's femaleness slowly opening to him, as a sea-anemone opens deep under the sea, with infinite soft fleshliness. The hardness of self-will was gone, and the soft anemone of her deeps blossomed for him of itself, far down under the tides.

Ramón remained behind in the hotel, in the impenetrable sanctuary of his own stillness. Carlota remained unconscious. There was a consultation of doctors; to no effect. She died at dawn, before her boys could arrive from Mexico; as a *canoa* was putting off from the shore with a little breeze, and the passengers were singing the Song of Welcome to Quetzalcoatl, unexpectedly, upon the pale water.

CHAPTER XXII

The Living Huitzilopochtli

THEY buried Doña Carlota in Sayula, and Kate, though a woman, went also to the funeral. Don Ramón followed the coffin, in his white clothes and big hat with the Quetzalcoatl sign. His boys went with him; and there were many strangers, men, in black.

The boys looked odd young shoots, in their black suits with short breeches and bare knees. They were both round-faced and creamy brown in complexion, both had a touch of fairness. The elder, Pedro, was more like Don Ramón; but his hair was softer, more fluffy than his father's, with a hint of brown. He was sulky and awkward, and kept his head ducked. The younger boy, Cyprian, had the fluffy, up-standing brown hair and the startled hazel eyes of his mother.

They had come in a motor-car with their aunt, from Guadalajara, and were returning straight to town. In her will, the mother had named guardians in place of the father, stating that the father would consent. And her considerable fortune she had left in trust for the boys. But the father was one of the trustees.

Ramón sat in his room in the hotel, overlooking the lake, and his two boys sat on the cane settee opposite him.

'What do you want to do, my sons?' said Ramón. 'To go back with your Aunt Margarita, and return to school in the United States?'

The boys remained a while in sulky silence.

'Yes!' said Cyprian at last, his brown hair seeming to fluff up with indignation. 'That is what our mother wished us to do. So, of course, we shall do it.'

'Very well!' said Ramón quietly. 'But remember I am your father, and my door, and my arms, and my heart will always be open to you, when you come.'

The elder boy shuffled with his feet, and muttered, without looking up:

'We cannot come, papa!'

'Why not, child?'

The boy looked up at him with brown eyes as challenging as his own.

'You, papa, you call yourself The Living Quetzalcoatl?'

'Yes.'

'But, papa, our father is called Ramón Carrasco.'

'It is also true,' said Ramón, smiling.

'We,' said Pedro, rather heavily, 'are not the children of the Living Quetzalcoatl, papa. We are Carrasco y de Lara.'

'Good names both,' said Ramón.

'Never,' said the young Cyprian, his eyes flashing, 'never can we love you, papa. You are our enemy. You killed our mother.'

'No, no!' said Ramón. 'That you must not say. Your mother sought her own death.'

'Mama loved you much, much, much!' cried Cyprian, the tears rising to his eyes. 'Always she loved you and prayed for you —' He began to cry.

'And I, my son?' said Ramón.

'You hated her and killed her! Oh, mama! Mama! Oh, mama! I want my mother!' he wept.

'Come to me, little one!' said Ramón softly, holding out his hands.

'No!' cried Cyprian, stamping his foot and flashing his eyes through his tears. 'No! No!'

The elder boy hung his head and was crying too. Ramón had the little, perplexed frown of pain on his brow. He looked from side to side, as if for some issue. Then he gathered himself together.

'Listen, my sons,' he said. 'You also will be men; it will not be long. While you are little boys, you are neither men nor women. But soon, the change will come, and you will have to be men. And then you will know that a man must be a man. When his soul tells him to do a thing, he must do it. When you are men, you must listen carefully to your own souls, and be sure to be true. Be true to your own souls; there is nothing else for a man to do.'

'*Je m'en fiche de ton âme, mon père!*'[1] said Cyprian, with one of his flashes into French. It was a language he often spoke with his mother.

'That you may, my boy,' said Ramón. 'But I may not.'

'Papa!' put in the elder boy. 'Is your soul different from mama's soul?'

'Who knows?' said Ramón. 'I understand it differently.'

'Because mama always prayed for your soul.'

'And I, in my way, pray for hers, child. If her soul comes back to me, I will take it into my heart.'

'Mama's soul,' said Cyprian, 'will go straight into Paradise.'

'Who knows, child! Perhaps the Paradise for the souls of the dead is the hearts of the living.'

'I don't understand what you say.'

'It is possible,' said Ramón, 'that even now the only Paradise for the soul of your mother is in my heart.'

The two boys stared at him with open eyes.

'Never will I believe that,' said Cyprian.

'Or it may be in *thy* heart,' said Ramón. 'Hast thou a place in *thy* heart for the soul of thy mother?'

The young Cyprian stared with bewildered hazel eyes.

'The soul of my mother goes direct to Paradise, because she is a saint,' he asserted flatly.

'Which Paradise, my son?'

'The only one. Where God is.'

'And where is that?'

There was a pause.

'In the sky,' said Cyprian, stubbornly.

'It is very far and very empty. But I believe, my son, that the hearts of living men are the very middle of the sky. And there God is; and Paradise; inside the hearts of living men and women. And there the souls of the dead come to rest, there, at the very centre, where the blood turns and returns; that is where the dead sleep best.'

There was a very blank pause.

'And wilt thou go on saying thou art the Living Quetzalcoatl?' said Cyprian.

'Surely! And when you are a little older, perhaps you will come to me and say it too.'

'Never! Thou hast killed our mother, and we shall hate thee. When we are men we ought to kill thee.'

'Nay, that is bombast, child! Why wilt thou listen only to servants and priests and people of that sort? Are they not thy inferiors, since thou art my son, and thy mother's son? Why dost thou take the talk of servants and inferiors into thy mouth? Hast thou no room for the speech of brave men? Thou wilt not kill me, neither will thy brother. For I would not allow you, even if you wished it. And you do not wish it. Talk no more of this empty lackey-talk to me, Cyprian, for I will not hear it. Art thou already a little lackey, or a priest? Come, thou art vulgar. Thou are a little vulgarian. We had better speak English; or thy French. Castilian is too good a language to turn into this currish talk.'

Ramón rose and went to the window to look out at the lake. The drums on the church were sounding for midday, when every man should glance at the sun, and stand silent with a little prayer.

'The sun has climbed the hill, the day is on the downward slope.
Between the morning and the afternoon, stand I here with my soul, and lift it up.
My soul is heavy with sunshine, and steeped with strength.
The sunbeams have filled me like a honeycomb,
It is the moment of fulness,
And the top of the morning.'

Ramón turned and repeated the Mid-day verse to his boys. They listened in confused silence.

'Come!' he said. 'Why are you confused? If I talked to you about your new boots, or ten pesos, you would not be confused. But if I speak of the sun and your own souls filled from the sun like honeycombs, you sulk. You had better go back to your school in America, to learn to be business men. You had better say to everybody: Oh, no! we have no father! Our mother died, but we never had a father. We are children of an immaculate conception, so we should make excellent business men.'

'I shall be a priest,' said Cyprian.

'And I a doctor,' said Pedro.

'Very good! Very good! *Shall-be* is far from *am*, and tomorrow is another day. Come to me when your heart tells you to come. You are my little boys, whatever you say, and I shall stroke your hair and laugh at you. Come! Come here!'

He looked at them, and they dared not refuse to obey, his power was so much greater than theirs.

He took his eldest son in his arms and stroked his head.

'There!' he said. 'Thou art my eldest son, and I am thy father, who calls himself The Living Quetzalcoatl. When they say: "Is it thy father who calls himself The Living Quetzalcoatl?" – say to them: "Yes, he is my father." And when they ask you what you think of such a father, say: "I am young, and I do not understand him yet. But I do not judge my father without understanding him." Wilt thou say that, my boy, Pedro, my son?' And Ramón stroked the boy's hair with the gentleness and tenderness which filled the child with a sort of awe.

'Yes, papa! I will say that,' said the boy, relieved.

'It is well,' said Ramón, laying his hand on the child's head for a moment, like a blessing.

Then he turned to the younger son.

'Come then,' he said, 'and let me stroke thy upstanding hair.'

'If I love thee, I cannot love mama!' said Cyprian.

'Nay, is thy heart so narrow? Love not at all, if it makes thee petty.'

'But I do not want to come to thee, papa.'

'Then stay away, my son, and come when thou dost want it.'

'I do not think thou lovest me, papa.'

'Nay, when thou art an obstinate monkey, I love thee not. But when thy real manhood comes upon thee, and thou art brave and daring, rather than rash and impudent, then thou wilt be lovable. How can I love thee if thou art not lovable?'

'Mama always loved me.'

'She called thee her own. I do not call thee mine own. Thou art thyself. When thou art lovable, I can love thee. When thou art rash and impudent, nay, I cannot. The mill will not spin when the wind does not blow.'

The boys went away. Ramón watched them as they stood in their black clothes and bare knees upon the jetty, and his heart yearned over them.

'Ah, the poor little devils!' he said to himself. And then:

'But I can do no more than keep my soul like a castle for them, to be a stronghold to them when they need it – if ever they do.'

These days Kate often sat by the lake shore, in the early light of the morning. Between the rains, the day came very clear, she could see every wrinkle in the great hills opposite, and the fold, or pass, through which a river came, away at Tuliapan, was so vivid to her she felt she had walked it. The red birds looked as if rains had freshened even their poppy-buds, and in the morning frogs were whirring.

But the world was somehow different; all different. No jingle of bells from the church, no striking of the clock. The clock was taken away.

And instead, the drums. At dawn, the heavy drum rolling its sound on the air. Then the sound of the Dawn-Verse chanted from the tower, in a strong man's voice:

'The dark is dividing, the sun is coming past the wall.
Day is at hand.
Lift your hand, say Farewell! say Welcome!
Then be silent.
Let the darkness leave you, let the light come into you,
Man in the twilight.'

The voice, and the great drum ceased. And in the dawn the men
who had risen stood silent, with arm uplifted, in the moment of change,
the women covered their faces and bent their heads. All was changeless
still for the moment of change.

Then the light drum rattled swiftly, as the first sparkle of the bright
sun flashed in sheer light from the crest of the great hills. The day
had begun. People of the world moved on their way.

At about nine o'clock the light drum rattled quickly, and the voice
in the tower cried:

'Half-way! Half-way up the slope of the morning!'

There was the heavy drum at noon, the light drum again at about
three o'clock, with the cry:

'Half-way! Half-way down the slope of afternoon.'

And at sunset again, the great drum rolling, and the voice crying:

'Leave off! Leave off! Leave off!
Lift your hand, say Farewell! say Welcome!
Man in the twilight.
The sun is in the outer porch, cry to him: Thanks! Oh, Thanks!
Then be silent.
You belong to the night.'

And again in the sunset everywhere men stood with lifted faces and
hands, and women covered their faces and stood with bowed heads,
all was changeless still for the moment of change.

Then the lighter drums suddenly beat, and people moved on into
the night.

The world was different, different. The drums seemed to leave the
air soft and vulnerable, as if it were alive. Above all, no clang of metal
on metal, during the moments of change.

'Metal for resistance.
Drums for the beating heart.
The heart ceases not.'

This was one of Ramón's little verses.

Strange, the change that was taking place in the world. Always the air had a softer, more velvety silence, it seemed alive. And there were no hours. Dawn and noon and sunset, mid-morning, or the up-slope middle, and mid-afternoon, or the down-slope middle, this was the day, with the watches of the night. They began to call the four watches of the day the watch of the rabbit, the watch of the hawk, the watch of the turkey-buzzard and the watch of the deer. And the four quarters of the night were the watch of the frog, the watch of the fire-fly, the watch of the fish, the watch of the squirrel.

'I shall come for you,' wrote Cipriano to her, 'when the deer is thrusting his last foot towards the forest.'

That meant, she knew, in the last quarter of the hours of the deer; something after five o'clock.

It was as if, from Ramón and Cipriano, from Jamiltepec and the lake region, a new world was unfolding, unrolling, as softly and subtly as twilight falling and removing the clutter of day. It was a soft, twilit newness slowly spreading and penetrating the world, even into the cities. Now, even in the cities the blue serapes of Quetzalcoatl were seen, and the drums were heard at the Hours, casting a strange mesh of twilight over the clash of bells and the clash of traffic. Even in the capital the big drum rolled again, and men, even men in city clothes, would stand still with uplifted faces and arm upstretched, listening for the noon-verse, which they knew in their hearts, and trying not to hear the clash of metal.

> 'Metal for resistance.
> Drums for the beating heart.'

But it was a world of metal, and a world of resistance. Cipriano, strangely powerful with the soldiers, in spite of the hatred he aroused in other officials, was for meeting metal with metal. For getting Montes to declare: The Religion of Quetzalcoatl is the religion of Mexico, official and declared. – Then backing up the declaration with the army.

But no! no! said Ramón. Let it spread of itself. And wait awhile, till you can be declared the living Huitzilopochtli, and your men can have the red and black blanket, with the snake-curve. Then perhaps we can have the open wedding with Caterina, and she will be a mother among the gods.

All the time, Ramón tried as far as possible to avoid arousing resistance and hate. He wrote open letters to the clergy, saying:

'Who am I, that I should be enemy of the One Church? I am catholic of catholics. I would have One Church of all the world, with Rome for the Central City, if Rome wish.

'But different peoples must have different Saviours, as they have different speech and different colour. The final mystery is one mystery. But the manifestations are many.

'God must come to Mexico in a blanket and in huaraches, else He is no God of the Mexicans, they cannot know Him. Naked, all men are but men. But the touch, the look, the word that goes from one naked man to another is the mystery of living. We live by manifestations.

'And men are fragile, and fragments, and strangely grouped in their fragmentariness. The invisible God has done it to us, darkened some faces and whitened others, and grouped us in groups, even as the zopilote is a bird, and the parrot of the hot lands is a bird, and the little oriole is a bird. But the angel of the zopilotes must be a zopilote, and the angel of the parrots a parrot. And to one, the dead carcase will ever smell good; to the other, the fruit.

'Priests who will come to me do not forsake either faith or God. They change their manner of speech and vestments, as the peon calls with one cry to the oxen, and with another cry to the mules. Each responds to its own call in its own way –'

To the socialists and agitators he wrote:

'What do you want? Would you make all men as you are? And when every peon in Mexico wears an American suit of clothes and shiny black shoes, and looks for life in the newspaper and for his manhood to the government, will you be satisfied? Did the government, then, give you your manhood, that you expect it to give it to these others?

'It is time to forget. It is time to put away the grudge and the pity. No man was ever the better for being pitied, and every man is the worse for a grudge.

'We can do nothing with life, except live it.

'Let us seek life where it is to be found. And, having found it, life will solve the problems. But every time we deny the living life, in order to solve a problem, we cause ten problems to spring up where was one before. Solving the problems of the people, we lose the people in a poisonous forest of problems.

'Life makes, and moulds, and changes the problem. The problem will always be there, and will always be different. So nothing can be solved, even by life and living, for life dissolves and resolves, solving it leaves alone.

'Therefore we turn to life; and from the clock to the sun and from metal to membrane.

'This way we hope the problem will dissolve, since it can never be solved. When men seek life first, they will not seek land nor gold. The land will lie on the lap of the gods, where men lie. And if the old communal system[2] comes back, and the village and the land are one, it will be very good. For truly, no man can possess lands.

'But when we are deep in a bog, it is no use attempting to gallop. We can only wade out with toil. And in our haste to have a child, it is no good tearing the babe from the womb.

'Seek life, and life will bring the change.

'Seek life itself, even pause at dawn and at sunset, and life will come back into us and prompt us through the transitions.

'Lay forcible hands on nothing, only be ready to resist, if forcible hands should be laid on you. For the new shoots of life are tender, and better ten deaths than that they should be torn or trampled down by the bullies of the world. When it comes to fighting for the tender shoots of life, fight as the jaguar fights for her young, as the she-bear for her cubs.

'That which is life is vulnerable, only metal is invulnerable. Fight for the vulnerable unfolding of life. But for that, fight never to yield.'

Cipriano, too, was always speaking to his soldiers, always with the same cry:

'We are men! We are fighters!

'But what can we do?

'Shall we march to simple death?

'No! No! We must march to life.

'The gringos are here. We have let them come. We must let them stay, for we cannot drive them out. With guns and swords and bayonets we can never drive them out, for they have a thousand where we have one. And if they come in peace, let them stay in peace.

'But we have not lost Mexico yet. We have not lost each other.

'We are the blood of America. We are the blood of Montezuma.[3]

'What is my hand for? Is it to turn the handle of a machine alone?

'My hand is to salute the God of Mexicans, beyond the sky.

'My hand is to touch the hand of a brave man.

'My hand is to hold a gun.

'My hand is to make the corn grow out of the ground.

'What are my knees for?

'My knees are to hold me proud and erect.

'My knees are for marching on my way.

'My knees are the knees of a man.

'Our god is Quetzalcoatl of the blue sky, and Huitzilopochtli red at the gates, watching.

'Our gods hate a kneeling man. They shout *Ho! Erect!*

'Then what can we do?

'Wait!

'I am a man, naked inside my clothes as you are.

'Am I a big man? Am I a tall and powerful man, from Tlaxcala, for example.

'I am not. I am little. I am from the south. I am small –

'Yet am I not your general?

'Why?

'Why am I a general, and you only soldiers?

'I will tell you.

'I found the other strength.

'There are two strengths; the strength which is the strength of oxen and mules and iron, of machines and guns, and of men who cannot get the second strength.

'Then there is the second strength. It is the strength you want. And you can get it, whether you are small or big. It is the strength that comes from behind the sun. And you can get it; you can get it here!' – he struck his breast – 'and here!' – he struck his belly – 'and here!' – he struck his loins. 'The strength that comes from back of the sun.'

When Cipriano was roused, his eyes flashed, and it was as if dark feathers, like pinions, were starting out of him, out of his shoulders and back, as if these dark pinions clashed and flashed like a roused eagle. His men seemed to see him, as by second sight, with the demonish clashing and dashing of wings, like an old god. And they murmured, their eyes flashing:

'It is Cipriano! It is he! We are Ciprianistos, we are his children.'

'We are men! We are men!' cried Cipriano.

'But listen. There are two kinds of men. There are men with the second strength, and men without it.

'When the first gringos came, we lost our second strength. And the padres taught us: Submit! Submit!

'The gringos had got the second strength!

'How?

'Like cunning ones, they stole it on the sly. They kept very still, like a tarantula in his hole. Then when neither sun nor moon nor stars knew he was there, Biff! – the tarantula sprang across, and bit, and left the poison and sucked the secret.

'So they got the secrets of the air and the water, and they got the secrets out of the earth. So the metals were theirs, and they made guns and machines and ships, and they made trains and telegrams and radio.

'Why? Why did they make all these things? How could they do it?

'Because, by cunning, they had got the secret of the second strength, which comes from behind the sun.

'And we had to be slaves, because we had only got the first strength, we had lost the second strength.

'Now we are getting it back. We have found our way again to the secret sun behind the sun. There sat Quetzalcoatl, and at last Don Ramón found him. There sits the red Huitzilopochtli, and *I* have found him. For *I* have found the second strength.

'When he comes, all you who strive shall find the second strength.

'And when you have it, where will you feel it?

'Not here!' – and he struck his forehead. 'Not where the cunning gringos have it, in the head, and in their books. Not we. We are men, we are not spiders.

'We shall have it here!' – he struck his breast – 'and here!' – he struck his belly – 'and here!' – he struck his loins.

'Are we men? Can we not get the second strength? Can we not? Have we lost it forever?

'I say no! Quetzalcoatl is among us. I have found the red Huitzilopochtli. The second strength!

'When you walk or sit, when you work or lie down, when you eat or sleep, think of the second strength, that you must have it.

'Be very quiet. It is shy as a bird in a dark tree.

'Be very clean, clean in your bodies and your clothes. It is like a star, that will not shine in dirt.

'Be very brave, and do not drink till you are drunk, nor soil yourself with bad women, nor steal. Because a drunken man has lost his second strength, and a man loses his strength in bad women, and a thief is a coward, and the red Huitzilopochtli hates a coward.

'Try! Try for the second strength. When we have it, the others will lose it.'

Cipriano struggled hard with his army. The curse of any army is the having nothing to do. Cipriano made all his men cook and wash for themselves, clean and paint the barracks, make a great garden to grow vegetables, and plant trees wherever there was water. And he himself took a passionate interest in what they did. A dirty tunic, a sore foot, a badly-made huarache did not escape him. But even when they cooked their meals he went among them.

'Give me something to eat,' he would say. 'Give me an enchilada!'

Then he praised the cooking, or said it was bad.

Like all savages, they liked doing small things. And, like most Mexicans, once they were a little sure of what they were doing, they loved doing it well.

Cipriano was determined to get some discipline into them. Discipline is what Mexico needs, and what the whole world needs. But it is the discipline from the inside that matters. The machine discipline, from the outside, breaks down.

He had the wild Indians from the north beat their drums in the barracks-yard, and start the old dances again. The dance, the dance which has meaning, is a deep discipline in itself. The old Indians of the north still have the secret of animistic dancing. They dance to gain power; power over the *living* forces or potencies of the earth. And these dances need intense dark concentration, and immense endurance.

Cipriano encouraged the dances more than anything. He learned them himself, with curious passion. The shield and spear dance, the knife dance, the dance of ambush and the surprise dance, he learned them in the savage villages of the north, and he danced them in the barracks-yard, by the bonfire, at night, when the great doors were shut.

Then, naked saved for a black breech-cloth, his body smeared with oil and red earth-powder, he would face some heavy naked Indian and with shield and spear dance the dance of the two warriors, champions in the midst of the dense ring of soldiers. And the silent, rhythmic concentration of this duel in subtlety and rapidity kept the feet softly beating with the drum, the naked body suave and subtle, circling with suave, primitive stealth, then crouching and leaping like a panther, with the spear poised, to a clash of shields, parting again with the crowing yell of defiance and exultance.

In this dance, no one was more suave and sudden than Cipriano. He could swerve along the ground with bent, naked back, as invisible as a lynx, circling round his opponent, his feet beating and his suave body subtly lilting to the drum. Then in a flash he was in the air, his spear pointing down at the collar-bone of his enemy and gliding over his shoulder, as the opponent swerved under, and the war-yell resounded. The soldiers in the deep circle watched, fascinated, uttering the old low cries.

And as the dance went on, Cipriano felt his strength increase and surge inside him. When all his limbs were glistening with sweat, and his spirit was at last satisfied, he was at once tired and surcharged with extraordinary power. Then he would throw his scarlet and dark serape around him, and motion other men to fight, giving his spear and shield to another officer or soldier, going himself to sit down on the ground and watch, by the firelight. And then he felt his limbs and his whole body immense with power, he felt the black mystery of power go out of him over all his soldiers. And he sat there imperturbable, in silence, holding all those black-eyed men in the splendour of his own, silent self. His own dark consciousness seemed to radiate through their flesh and their bones, they were conscious, not through themselves but through him. And as a man's instinct is to shield his own head, so that instinct was to shield Cipriano, for he was the most precious part of themselves to them. It was in him they were supreme. They got their splendour from his power and their greatest consciousness was his consciousness diffusing them.

'I am not of myself,' he would say to them. 'I am of the red Huitzilopochtli and the power from behind the sun. And you are not of yourselves. Of yourselves you are nothing. You are of me, my men.'

He encouraged them to dance naked, with the breech-cloth, to rub themselves with the red earth-powder, over the oil.

'This is the oil of the stars. Rub it well into your limbs and you will be strong as the starry sky. This is the red blood of volcanoes. Rub yourselves with it, you will have the power of the fire of the volcanoes, from the centre of the earth.'

He encouraged them to dance the silent, concentrated dances to the drum, to dance for hours, gathering power and strength.

'If you know how to tread the dance, you can tread deeper and deeper till you touch the middle of the earth with your foot. And when you touch the middle of the earth, you will have such power in your belly and your breast, no man will be able to overcome you. Get the second strength. Get it, get it out of the earth, get it from behind the sun. Get the second strength.'

He made long, rapid marches across the wild Mexican country, and through the mountains, moving light and swift. He liked to have his men camping in the open, with no tents: but the watch set, and the stars overhead. He pursued the bandits with swift movements. He stripped his captives and tied them up. But if it seemed a brave man, he would swear him in. If it seemed to him a knave, a treacherous cur, he stabbed him to the heart, saying:

'I am the red Huitzilopochtli, of the knife.'

Already he had got his own small, picked body of men out of the ignominious drab uniform, dressed in white with the scarlet sash and the scarlet ankle cords, and carrying the good, red and black serape. And his men must be clean. On the march they would stop by some river, with the order for every man to strip and wash, and wash his clothing. Then the men, dark and ruddy, moved about naked, while the white clothing of strong white cotton dried on the earth. They moved on again, glittering with the peculiar whiteness of cotton clothes in Mexico, gun at their backs, serape and small pack on their backs, wearing the heavy straw hats with the scarlet crowns on their heads.

'They must move!' he said to his officers. 'They must learn again to move swiftly and untiringly, with the old power. They must not lie about. In the sleep hours, let them sleep. In the waking, let them work, or march, or drill, or dance.'

He divided his regiment up into little companies of a hundred each, with a centurion and a sergeant in command. Each company of a hundred must learn to act in perfect unison, freely and flexibly. 'Perfect your hundred,' Cipriano insisted, 'and I will perfect your thousands and your tens of thousands.'

'Listen!' he said. 'For us, no trench and cannon warfare. My men are no cannon-fodder, nor trench-dung. Where cannon are, we move away. Our hundreds break up, and we attack where the cannon are not. That we are swift, that we are silent, that we have no burdens, and that the second strength is in us: that is all. We intend to put up no battle-front, but to attack at our own moment, and at a thousand points.'

And always he reiterated:

'If you can get the power from the heart of the earth, and the power from behind the sun; if you can summon the power of the red Huitzilo-pochtli into you, nobody can conquer you. Get the second strength.'

Ramón was pressing Cipriano now openly to assume the living Huitzilopochtli.

'Come!' he said. 'It is time you let General Viedma be swallowed up in the red Huitzilopochtli. Don't you think?'

'If I know what it means,' said Cipriano.

They were sitting on the mats in Ramón's room, in the heat before the rain came, towards the end of the rainy season.

'Stand up!' said Ramón.

Cipriano stood up at once, with that soft, startling alertness in his movement.

Ramón came quickly to him, placed one of his hands over Cipriano's eyes, closing them. Ramón stood behind Cipriano, who remained motionless in the warm dark, his consciousness reeling in strange concentric waves, towards a centre where it suddenly plunges into the bottomless deeps, like sleep.

'Cipriano?' – the voice sounded so far off.

'Yes.'

'Is it dark?'

'It is dark.'

'Is it alive? Is the darkness alive?'

'Surely it is alive.'

'Who lives?'

'I.'

'Where?'

'I know not. In the living darkness.'

Ramón then bound Cipriano's eyes and head with a strip of black fur. Then again, with a warm, soft pressure, he pressed one naked hand over Cipriano's naked breast, and one between his shoulders. Cipriano stood in profound darkness, erect and silent.

'Cipriano?'

'Yes.'

'Is it dark in your heart?'

'It is coming dark.'

Ramón felt the thud of the man's heart slowly slackening. In Cipriano, another circle of darkness had started slowly to revolve, from his heart. It swung in widening rounds, like a greater sleep.

'Is it dark?'

'It is dark.'

'Who lives?'

'I.'

Ramón bound Cipriano's arms at his sides, with a belt of fur round the breast. Then he put his one hand over the navel, his other hand in the small of the other man's back, pressing with slow, warm, powerful pressure.

'Cipriano?'

'Yes.'

The voice and the answer going farther and farther away.

'Is it dark?'

'No, my Lord.'

Ramón knelt and pressed his arms close round Cipriano's waist, pressing his black head against his side. And Cipriano began to feel as if his mind, his head were melting away in the darkness, like a pearl in black wine, the other circle of sleep began to swing, vast. And he was a man without a head, moving like a dark wind over the face of the dark waters.

'Is it perfect?'

'It is perfect.'

'Who lives?'

'Who – !'

Cipriano no longer knew.

Ramón bound him fast round the middle, then, pressing his head against the hip, folded the arms round Cipriano's loins, closing with his hands the secret places.

'Cipriano?'

'Yes.'

'Is it all dark?'

But Cipriano could not answer. The last circle was sweeping round, and the breath upon the waters was sinking into the waters, there was no more utterance. Ramón kneeled with pressed head and arms and hands, for some moments still. Then he bound the loins, binding the wrists to the hips.

Cipriano stood rigid and motionless. Ramón clasped the two knees with his hands, till they were warm, and he felt them dark and asleep like two living stones, or two eggs. Then swiftly he bound them together, and grasped the ankles, as one might grasp the base of a young tree, as it emerges from the earth. Crouching on the earth, he gripped them in an intense grip, resting his head on the feet. The moments passed, and both men were unconscious.

Then Ramón bound the ankles, lifted Cipriano suddenly, with a sleep-moving softness, laid him on the skin of a big mountain-lion, which was spread upon the blankets, threw over him the red and black serape of Huitzilopochtli, and lay down at his feet, holding Cipriano's feet to his own abdomen.

And both men passed into perfect unconsciousness, Cipriano within the womb of undisturbed creation, Ramón in the death sleep.

How long they were both dark, they never knew. It was twilight. Ramón was suddenly aroused by the jerking of Cipriano's feet. He sat up, and took the blanket off Cipriano's face.

'Is it night?' said Cipriano.

'Almost night,' said Ramón.

Silence followed, while Ramón unfastened the bonds, beginning at the feet. Before he unbound the eyes, he closed the window, so the room was almost dark. Then he unfastened the last binding, and Cipriano sat up, looking, then suddenly covering his eyes.

'Make it quite dark!' he said.

Ramón closed the shutters, and the room was complete night. Then he returned and sat on the mat by Cipriano. Cipriano was asleep again. After a while, Ramón left him.

He did not see him again till dawn. Then Ramón found him going down to the lake, to swim. The two men swam together, while the sun rose. With the rain, the lake was colder. They went to the house to rub oil in their limbs.

Cipriano looked at Ramón with black eyes which seemed to be looking at all space.

'I went far,' he said.

'To where there is no beyond?' said Ramón.

'Yes, there.'

And in a moment or two, Cipriano was wrapped in his blanket again, and asleep.

He did not wake till the afternoon. Then he ate, and took a boat, and rowed down the lake to Kate. He found her at home. She was surprised to see him, in his white clothes and with his serape of Huitzilo-pochtli.

'I am going to be the living Huitzilopochtli,' he said.

'Are you? When? Does it feel queer?' – Kate was afraid of his eyes, they seemed inhuman.

'On Thursday. The day of Huitzilopochtli is to be Thursday. Won't you sit beside me, and be wife of me when I am a god?'

'But do you feel you *are* a god?' she asked, querulous.

He turned his eyes on her strangely.

'I have been,' he said. 'And I have come back. But I belong there, where I went.'

'Where?'

'Where there is no beyond, and the darkness sinks into the water, and waking and sleeping are one thing.'

'No,' said Kate, afraid. 'I never understood mystical things. They make me uneasy.'

'Is it mystical when I come in to you?'

'No,' said Kate. 'Surely that is physical.'

'So is the other, only further. Won't you be the bride of Huitzilo-pochtli?' he asked again.

'Not so soon,' said Kate.

'Not so soon!' he re-echoed.

There was a pause.

'Will you come back with me to Jamiltepec now?' he asked.

'Not now,' she said.

'Why not now?'

'Oh, I don't know. – You treat me as if I had no life of my own,' she said. 'But I have.'

'A life of your own? Who gave it you? Where did you get it?'

'I don't know. But I have got it. And I must live it. I can't be just swallowed up.'

'Why, Malintzi?'[4] he said, giving her a name. 'Why can't you?'

'Be just swallowed up?' she said. 'Well, I just can't.'

'I am the living Huitzilopochtli,' he said. 'And I am swallowed up. I thought, so could you be, Malintzi.'

'No! Not quite!' she said.

'Not quite! Not quite! Not now! Not just now! How often you say *Not*, to-day! – I must go back to Ramón.'

'Yes. Go back to him. You only care about him, and your living Quetzalcoatl and your living Huitzilopochtli. – I am only a woman.'

'No, Malintzi, you are more. You are more than Kate, you are Malintzi.'

'I am not! I am only Kate, and I am only a woman. I mistrust all that other stuff.'

'I am more than just a man, Malintzi. – Don't you see that?'

'No!' said Kate. 'I don't see it. Why *should* you be more than just a man?'

'Because I am the living Huitzilopochtli. Didn't I tell you? You've got dust in your mouth to-day, Malintzi.'

He went away, leaving her rocking in anger on her terrace, in love again with her old self, and hostile to the new thing. She was thinking of London and Paris and New York, and all the people there.

'Oh!' she cried to herself, stifling. 'For heaven's sake let me get out of this, and back to simple human people. I loathe the very sound of Quetzalcoatl and Huitzilopochtli. I would die rather than be mixed up in it any more. Horrible, really, both Ramón and Cipriano. And they want to put it over me, with their high-flown bunk, and their Malintzi. Malintzi! I am Kate Forrester, really. I am neither Kate Leslie nor Kate Tylor. I am sick of these men putting names over me. I was born Kate Forrester, and I shall die Kate Forrester. I want to go home. Loathsome, really, to be called Malintzi. – I've had it put over me.'

CHAPTER XXIII

Huitzilopochtli's Night

THEY had the Huitzilopochtli ceremony at night, in the wide yard in front of the church. The guard of Huitzilopochtli, in serapes of black, red, and yellow stripes, striped like tigers or wasps, stood holding torches of blazing ocote. A tall bonfire was built, but unkindled, in the centre of the yard.

In the towers where the bells had been, fires were blazing and the heavy drum of Huitzilopochtli went rolling its deep, sinister notes. It had been sounding all the while since the sun went down.

The crowd gathered under the trees, outside the gates in front of the church. The church doors were closed.

There was a bang of four firework cannons exploding simultaneously, then four rockets shot up into the sky, leaning in the four directions, and exploding in showers of red, green, white, and yellow.

The church doors opened, and Cipriano appeared, in his brilliant serape of Huitzilopochtli, and with three green parrot feathers erect on his brow. He was carrying a torch. He stooped and lit the big bonfire, then plucked out four blazing brands and tossed them to four of his men, who stood waiting, naked save for their black breech-cloths. The men caught the brands as they flew, and ran in the four directions, to kindle the four bonfires that waited, one in each corner of the yard.

The guard had taken off their blankets and blouses, and were naked to the red sash. The lighter drum began to beat for the dance, and the dance began, the half-naked men throwing their blazing torches whirling in the air, catching them as they came down, dancing all the while. Cipriano, in the centre, threw up brand after brand from the fire.

Now that he was stripped of his blanket, his body was seen painted in horizontal bars of red and black, while from his mouth went a thin green line, and from his eyes a band of yellow.

The five fires, built hollow of little towers of ocote faggots, sent pure flame in a rush up to the dark sky, illuminating the dancing men, who sang in deep voices as they danced.

The fires rushed rapidly upwards in flame. The drum beat without ceasing. And the men of Huitzilopochtli danced on, like demons. Meanwhile the crowd sat in the old Indian silence, their black eyes glittering in the firelight. And gradually the fires began to die down, the white façade of the church, that had danced also to the yellow flames, began to go bluish above, merging into the night, rose-coloured below, behind the dark shapes that danced to the sinking fires.

Suddenly the dance ceased, the men threw their serapes around them, and sat down. Little ocote fires upon the cane tripods flickered here and there, in a silence that lasted for some minutes. Then the drum sounded, and a man began to sing, in a clear, defiant voice, the *First Song of Huitzilopochtli*:

> 'I am Huitzilopochtli,
> The Red Huitzilopochtli,
> The blood-red.
>
> I am Huitzilopochtli,
> Yellow of the sun,
> Sun in the blood.
>
> I am Huitzilopochtli,
> White of the bone,
> Bone in the blood.
>
> I am Huitzilopochtli,
> With a blade of grass between my teeth.
>
> I am Huitzilopochtli, sitting in the dark.
> With my redness staining the body of the dark.
>
> I watch by the fire.
> I wait behind men.
>
> In the stillness of my night
> The cactus sharpens his thorn.
> The grass feels with his roots for the other sun.
>
> Deeper than the roots of the mango tree
> Down in the centre of the earth
> Is the yellow, serpent-yellow shining of my sun.
>
> Oh, beware of him!
> Oh, beware of me!

Who runs athwart my serpent-flame
Gets bitten and must die.

I am the sleeping and waking
Of the anger of the manhood of men.
I am the leaping and quaking
Of fire bent back again.'

The song came to an end. There was a pause. Then all the men
of Huitzilopochtli took it up again, changing the 'I' into 'He'.

'He is Huitzilopochtli,
The Red Huitzilopochtli,
The blood-red.

He is Huitzilopochtli,
Yellow of the sun,
Sun in the blood.

He is Huitzilopochtli,
White of the bone,
Bone in the blood.

He is Huitzilopochtli,
With a blade of green grass between his teeth.

He is Huitzilopochtli, sitting in the dark,
With his redness staining the body of the night.

He is watching by the fire.
Waiting behind men.

In the stillness of his night
Cactuses sharpen their thorns.
Grass feels downwards with his roots.

Deeper than the roots of the mango tree
Down in the centre of the earth
Shines the yellow, serpent-yellow shining of the sun.

Oh, men, take care, take care!
Take care of him and it.
Nor run aslant his rays.
Who is bitten, dies.

He is Huitzilopochtli, sleeping or waking
Serpent in the bellies of men.

Huitzilopochtli, leaping and quaking
Fire of the passion of men.'

The big fires had all died down. Only the little flames on the tripods lit up the scene with a ruddy glow. The guard withdrew to the outer wall of the yard, holding bayonets erect. The big drum was going alone, slowly.

The yard was now a clear space, with the glowing red heaps of the bonfires, and the ocote flames flapping. And now was seen a platform erected against the white wall of the church.

In the silence the big doors of the church opened, and Cipriano came out, in his bright serape, holding in his hand a bunch of black leaves, or feathers, and with a tuft of scarlet feathers, black-tipped, rising from the back of his head. He mounted the platform and stood facing the crowd, the light of a torch on his face and on the brilliant feathers that rose like flames from the back of his head.

After him came a strange procession: a peon in floppy white clothes, led prisoner between two of the guards of Huitzilopochtli: who wore their serapes with red and black and yellow and white and green stripes: then another peon prisoner: then another: in all, five, the fifth one tall, limping, and with a red cross painted on the breast of his white jacket. Last of all came a woman-prisoner, likewise between two guards, her hair flowing loose, over a red tunic.

They mounted the platform. The peons, prisoners, were placed in a row, their guards behind them. The limping peon was apart, with his two guards behind him: the woman again was apart, her two guards behind her.

The big drum ceased, and a bugle rang out, a long, loud triumphant note, repeated three times. Then the kettle-drums, or the small tom-toms like kettle-drums, rattled fierce as hail.

Cipriano lifted his hand, and there was silence.

Out of the silence he began to speak, in his short, martial sentences:

'Man that is man is more than a man.
No man is man till he is more than a man.
Till the power is in him
Which is not his own.

The power is in me from behind the sun,
And from middle earth.

I am Huitzilopochtli.
I am dark as the sunless under-earth,
And yellow as the fire that consumes,
And white as bone,
And red as blood.

But I touched the hand of Quetzalcoatl.
And between our fingers rose a blade of green grass.
I touched the hand of Quetzalcoatl.
Lo! I am lord of the watches of the night
And the dream of the night rises from me like a red feather.

I am the watcher, and master of the dream.
In the dream of the night I see the grey dogs prowling.
Prowling to devour the dream.

In the night the soul of a coward creeps out of him
Like a grey dog whose mouth is foul with rabies,
Creeping among the sleeping and the dreaming, who are lapped in my dark,
And in whom the dream sits up like a rabbit, lifting long ears tipped with night,
On the dream-slopes browsing like a deer in the dusk.

In the night I see the grey dogs creeping, out of the sleeping men
Who are cowards, who are liars, who are traitors, who have no dreams
That prick their ears like a rabbit, or browse in the dark like deer,
But whose dreams are dogs, grey dogs with yellow mouths.
From the liars, from the thieves, from the false and treacherous and mean
I see the grey dogs creeping out, where my deer are browsing in the dark.
Then I take my knife, and throw it upon the grey dog.
And lo! it sticks between the ribs of a man!
The house of the grey dog!

Beware! Beware!
Of the men and the women who walk among you.
You know not how many are houses of grey dogs.
Men that seem harmless, women with fair words,
Maybe they kennel the grey dog.'

The drums began to beat and the singer began to sing, clear and pure:

The Song of the Grey Dog

'When you sleep and know it not
The grey dog creeps among you.
In your sleep, you twist, your soul hurts you.
The grey dog is chewing your entrails.

Then call on Huitzilopochtli:
The grey dog caught me at the cross-roads
As I went down the road of sleep
And crossed the road of the uneasy.

The grey dog leapt at my entrails.
Huitzilopochtli, call him off.
Lo! the Great One answers. *Track him down!*
Kill him in his unclean house.

Down the road of the uneasy
You track the grey dog home
To his house in the heart of a traitor,
A thief, a murderer of dreams.

And you kill him there with one stroke,
Crying: *Huitzilopochtli, is this well done?*
That your sleep be not as a cemetery
Where dogs creep unclean.'

The song ceased, and there was silence. Then Cipriano beckoned to the men to bring forward the peon with the black cross painted on his front and back. He limped forward.

Cipriano: 'What man is that, limping?'

Guards: 'It is Guillermo, overseer of Don Ramón, who betrayed Don Ramón, his master.'

Cipriano: 'Why does he limp?'

Guards: 'He fell from the window on to the rocks.'

Cipriano: 'What made him wish to betray his master?'

Guards: 'His heart is a grey dog, and a woman, a grey bitch, enticed him forth.'

Cipriano: 'What woman enticed the grey dog forth?'

The guards came forward with the woman.

Guards: 'This woman, Maruca, my Lord, with the grey bitch heart.'

Cipriano: 'Is it she, indeed?'

Guards: 'It is she.'

Cipriano: 'The grey dog, and the grey bitch, we kill, for their mouths are yellow with poison? Is it well, men of Huitzilopochtli?'

Guards: 'It is very well, my Lord.'

The guards stripped the peon Guillermo of his white clothes, leaving him naked, in a grey loin-cloth, with a grey-white cross painted on his naked breast. The woman, too, had a grey-white cross painted on her body. She stood in a short petticoat of grey wool.

Cipriano: 'The grey dog and the grey bitch shall run no more about the world. We will bury their bodies in quick-lime, till their souls are eaten, and their bodies, and nothing is left. For lime is the thirsty bone that swallows even a soul and is not slaked. – Bind them with the grey cords, put ash on their heads.'

The guards quickly obeyed. The prisoners, ash-grey, gazed with black, glittering eyes, making not a sound. A guard stood behind each of them. Cipriano gave a sign, and quick as lightning the guards had got the throats of the two victims in a grey cloth, and with a sharp jerk had broken their necks, lifting them backwards in one movement. The grey cloths they tied hard and tight round the throats, laying the twitching bodies on the floor.

Cipriano turned to the crowd:

> 'The Lords of Life are the Masters of Death.
> Blue is the breath of Quetzalcoatl.
> Red is Huitzilopochtli's blood.
> But the grey dog belongs to the ash of the world.
> The Lords of Life are the Masters of Death.
> Dead are the grey dogs.
> Living are the Lords of Life.
> Blue is the deep sky and the deep water
> Red is the blood and the fire.
> Yellow is the flame.
> The bone is white and alive.
> The hair of night is dark over our faces.
> But the grey dogs are among the ashes.
> The Lords of Life are the Masters of Death.'

Then he turned once more, to the other, imprisoned peons.

Cipriano: 'Who are these four?'

Guards: 'Four who came to kill Don Ramón.'

Cipriano: 'Four men, against one man?'

Guards: 'They were more than four, my Lord.'

Cipriano: 'When many men come against one, what is the name of the many?'

Guards: 'Cowards, my Lord.'

Cipriano: 'Cowards it is. They are less than men. Men that are less than men are not good enough for the light of the sun. If men that are men will live, men that are less than men must be put away, lest they multiply too much. Men that are more than men have the judgment of men that are less than men. Shall they die?'

Guards: 'They shall surely die, my Lord.'

Cipriano: 'Yet my hand has touched the hand of Quetzalcoatl, and among the black leaves one sprung green, with the colour of Malintzi.'

An attendant came and lifted Cipriano's serape over his head, leaving his body bare to the waist. The guards likewise took off their serapes.

Cipriano lifted up his fist, in which he held a little tuft of black feathers, or leaves.

Then he said slowly:

'Huitzilopochtli gives the black blade of death.
Take it bravely.
Take death bravely.
Go bravely across the border, admitting your mistake.

Determine to go on and on, till you enter the Morning Star.
Quetzalcoatl will show you the way.
Malintzi of the green dress will open the door.
In the fountain you will lie down.
If you reach the fountain, and lie down
And the fountain covers your face, forever,
You will have departed forever from your mistake.

And the man that is more than a man in you
Will wake at last from the clean forgetting
And stand up, and look about him,
Ready again for the business of being a man.

But Huitzilopochtli touched the hand of Quetzalcoatl
And one green leaf sprang among the black.
The green leaf of Malintzi
Who pardons once, and no more.'

Cipriano turned to the four peons. He held out his fist with the four black twigs, to the first. This first one, a little man, peered at the leaves curiously.

'There is no green one,' he said sceptically.

'Good!' said Cipriano. 'Then receive a black.'

And he handed him a black leaf.

'I knew it,' said the man, and he threw the leaf away with contempt and defiance.

The second man drew a black leaf. He stood gazing at it, as if fascinated, turning it round.

The third man drew a leaf whose lower half was green.

'See!' said Cipriano. 'The green leaf of Malintzi!'

And he handed the last black leaf to the last man.

'Have I got to die?' said the last man.

'Yes.'

'I don't want to die, *Patrón*.'

'You played with death, and it has sprung upon you.'

The eyes of the three men were blindfolded with black cloths, their blouses and pantaloons were taken away. Cipriano took a bright, thin dagger.

'The Lords of Life are Masters of Death,' he said in a loud, clear voice.

And swift as lightning he stabbed the blindfolded men to the heart, with three swift, heavy stabs. Then he lifted the red dagger and threw it down.

'The Lords of Life are Masters of Death,' he repeated.

The guards lifted the bleeding bodies one by one, and carried them into the church. There remained only the one prisoner, with the green leaf.

'Put the green leaf of Malintzi between his brows; for Malintzi pardons once, and no more,' said Cipriano.

'Yes, my Lord!' replied the guard.

And they led the man away into the church.

Cipriano followed, the last of his guard after him.

In a few minutes the drums began to beat and men came slowly streaming into the church. Women were not admitted. All the interior was hung with red and black banners. At the side of the chancel was a new idol: a heavy, seated figure of Huitzilopochtli, done in black lava stone. And round him burned twelve red candles. The idol held the bunch of black strips, or leaves, in his hand. And at his feet lay the five dead bodies.

The fire on the altar was flickering high, to the dark statue of Quetzalcoatl. On his little throne Ramón sat, wearing his blue and white colours of Quetzalcoatl. There was another corresponding throne next him, but it was empty. Six of the guard of Quetzalcoatl stood by Ramón: but Huitzilopochtli's side of the chancel was empty save for the dead.

The hard drums of Huitzilopochtli were beating incessantly outside, with a noise like madness. Inside was the soft roll of the drum of Quetzalcoatl. And the men from the crowd outside thronged slowly in, between the guard of Quetzalcoatl.

A flute sounded the summons to close the doors. The drums of Quetzalcoatl ceased, and from the towers was heard again the wild bugle of Huitzilopochtli.

Then down the centre of the church, in silence, bare-foot, came the procession of Huitzilopochtli, naked save for the black loin-cloths and the paint, and the scarlet feathers of the head-dresses. Cipriano had his face painted with a white jaw, a thin band of green stretched from his mouth, a band of black across his nose, yellow from his eyes, and scarlet on his brow. One green feather rose from his forehead, and behind his head a beautiful head-dress of scarlet feathers. A band of red was painted round his breast, yellow round his middle. The rest was ash-grey.

After him came his guard, their faces red, black, and white, their bodies painted as Cipriano's, and a scarlet feather rising from the back of their head. The hard, dry drum of Huitzilopochtli beat monotonously.

As the Living Huitzilopochtli came near the altar steps, the Living Quetzalcoatl rose and came to meet him. The two saluted, each covering his eyes with his left hand for a moment, then touching fingers with the right hand.

Cipriano stood before the statue of Huitzilopochtli, dipped his hand in a stone bowl, and giving the loud cry or whoop of Huitzilopochtli, lifted up his red hand. His guard uttered the loud cry, and quickly filed past, each man dipping his hand and raising his wet, red fist. The hard drums of Huitzilopochtli rattled like madness in the church, then fell suddenly silent.

Ramón: 'Why is your hand red, Huitzilopochtli, my brother?'

Cipriano: 'It is the blood of the treacherous, Oh Quetzalcoatl.'

Ramón: 'What have they betrayed?'

Cipriano: 'The yellow sun and the heart of darkness; the hearts of men, and the buds of women. While they lived, the Morning Star could not be seen.'

Ramón: 'And are they verily dead?'

Cipriano: 'Verily dead, my Lord.'

Ramón: 'Their blood is shed?'

Cipriano: 'Yes, my Lord, save that the grey dogs shed no blood. Two died the bloodless death of the grey dogs, three died in blood.'

Ramón: 'Give me the blood of the three, my brother Huitzilopochtli, to sprinkle the fire.'

Cipriano brought the stone bowl, and the little bunch of black leaves from Huitzilopochtli's idol. Ramón slowly, gently, sprinkled a little blood on the fire, with the black leaves.

Ramón: 'Darkness, drink the blood of expiation.

Sun, swallow up the blood of expiation.

Rise, Morning Star, between the divided sea.'

He gave back the bowl and the leaves to Huitzilopochtli, who placed them by the black idol.

Ramón: 'Thou who didst take the lives of the three, Huitzilopochtli, my brother, what wilt thou do with the souls?'

Cipriano: 'Even give them to thee, my Lord, Quetzalcoatl, my Lord of the Morning Star.'

Ramón: 'Yea, give them to me and I will wrap them in my breath and send them the longest journey, to the sleep and the far awakening.'

Cipriano: 'My Lord is lord of two ways.'

The naked, painted guard of Huitzilopochtli came and carried the dead bodies of the three stabbed men, carried them on red biers, and laid them at the foot of the Quetzalcoatl statue.

Ramón: 'So, there is a long way to go, past the sun to the gate of the Morning Star. And if the sun is angry he strikes swifter than a jaguar, and the whirr of the winds is like an angry eagle, and the upper waters strike in wrath like silver-coloured snakes. Ah, three souls, make peace now with the sun and winds and waters, and go in courage, with the breath of Quetzalcoatl around you like a cloak. Fear not and shrink not and fail not; but come to the end of the longest journey, and let the fountain cover your face. So shall all at length be made new.'

When he had spoken to the dead, Ramón took incense and threw it on the fire, so clouds of blue smoke arose. Then with a censer he swung the blue smoke over the dead. Then he unfolded three blue cloths and covered the dead. Then the guards of Quetzalcoatl lifted the biers, and the flute of Quetzalcoatl sounded.

'Salute the Morning Star!' cried Ramón, turning to the light beyond the statue of Quetzalcoatl, and throwing up his right arm in the Quetzalcoatl prayer. Every man turned to the light and threw up his arm in the passion. And the silence of the Morning Star filled the church.

The drum of Quetzalcoatl sounded: the guards slowly moved away with the three blue-wrapped dead.

Then came the voice of the Living Huitzilopochtli:

'Upon the dead grey dogs the face of Quetzalcoatl cannot look. Upon the corpses of grey dogs rises no Morning Star. But the fire of corpses shall consume them.'

There was a sharp rattle of the dry drums of Huitzilopochtli. Ramón remained with his back to the church, his arm upraised to the Morning Star. And the guard of Huitzilopochtli lifted the strangled bodies, laid them on biers, covered them with grey cloths, and bore them away.

The bugle of Huitzilopochtli sounded.

Cipriano: 'The dead are on their way. Quetzalcoatl helps them on the longest journey. – But the grey dogs sleep within the quicklime, in the slow corpse-fire. – It is finished.'

Ramón dropped his arm and turned to the church. All men dropped their hands. The soft drums of Quetzalcoatl sounded, mingling with the hard drums of Huitzilopochtli. Then both guards began to sing together:

HUITZILOPOCHTLI'S WATCH

'Red Huitzilopochtli
Keeps day and night apart.

Huitzilopochtli the golden
Guards life from death, and death from life.

No grey-dogs, cowards, pass him.
No spotted traitors crawl by,
False fair ones cannot slip through
Past him, from the one to the other.

Brave men have peace at nightfall,
True men look up at the dawn,
Men in their manhood walk out
Into blue day, past Huitzilopochtli.

> Red Huitzilopochtli
> Is the purifier.
>
> Black Huitzilopochtli
> Is doom.
>
> Huitzilopochtli golden
> Is the liberating fire.
>
> White Huitzilopochtli
> Is washed bone.
>
> Green Huitzilopochtli
> Is Malintzi's blade of grass.'

At the beginning of each stanza, the Guard of Huitzilopochtli struck their left palm with their scarlet right fist, and the drums gave a great crash, a terrific splash of noise. When the song ended, the drums gradually died down, like subsiding thunder, leaving the hearts of men re-echoing.

Ramón: 'Why is your hand so red, Huitzilopochtli?'

Cipriano: 'With the blood of slain men, Brother.'

Ramón: 'Must it always be red?'

Cipriano: 'Till green-robed Malintzi brings her water-bowl.'

The bugle and the flute both sounded. The guard of Huitzilopochtli put out the red candles, one by one, the guard of Quetzalcoatl extinguished the blue candles. The church was dark, save for the small but fierce blue-white light beyond the Quetzalcoatl statue, and the red smouldering on the altar.

Ramón began slowly to speak:

> 'The dead are on their journey, the way is dark.
> There is only the Morning Star.
> Beyond the white of whiteness,
> Beyond the blackness of black,
> Beyond spoken day,
> Beyond the unspoken passion of night,
> The light which is fed from two vessels
> From the black oil and the white
> Shines at the gate.
>
> A gate to the innermost place
> Where the Breath and the Fountains commingle,
> Where the dead are living, and the living are dead.

The deeps that life cannot fathom,
The Source and the End, of which we know
Only that it is, and its life is our life and our death.
All men cover their eyes
Before the unseen.
All men be lost in silence,
Within the noiseless.'

The church was utterly still, all men standing with a hand pressed over their eyes.

Till there was one note of a silver gong, and the green candles of Malintzi were being lighted in the altar place. – Ramón's voice was heard again:

'Like the green candles of Malintzi
Like a tree in new leaf.
The rain of blood is fallen, is gone into the earth.

The dead have gone the long journey
Beyond the star.
Huitzilopochtli has thrown his black mantle
To those who would sleep.
When the blue wind of Quetzalcoatl
Waves softly,
When the water of Malintzi falls
Making a greenness:

Count the red grains of the Huitzilopochtli
Fire in your hearts, O men.
And blow the ash away.

For the living live,
And the dead die.
But the fingers of all touch the fingers of all
In the Morning Star.'

CHAPTER XXIV

Malintzi

WHEN the women were shut out of the church, Kate went home gloomy and uneasy. The executions shocked and depressed her. She knew that Ramón and Cipriano did deliberately what they did: they believed in their deeds, they acted with all their conscience. And as men, probably they were right.

But they seemed nothing but men. When Cipriano said: *Man that is man is more than a man*, he seemed to be driving the male significance to its utmost, and beyond, with a sort of demonism. It seemed to her all terrible *will*, the exertion of pure, awful will.

And deep in her soul came a revulsion against this manifestation of pure will. It was fascinating also. There was something dark and lustrous and fascinating to her in Cipriano, and in Ramón. The black, relentless power, even passion of the will in men! The strange, sombre, lustrous beauty of it! She knew herself under the spell.

At the same time, as is so often the case with any spell, it did not bind her completely. She was spell-bound, but not utterly acquiescent. In one corner of her soul was revulsion and a touch of nausea.

Ramón and Cipriano no doubt were right for themselves, for their people and country. But for herself, ultimately, ultimately she belonged elsewhere. Not to this terrible, natural *will* which seemed to beat its wings in the very air of the American continent. Always will, will, will, without remorse or relenting. This was America to her: all the Americas. Sheer will!

The Will of God! She began to understand that once fearsome phrase. At the centre of all things, a dark, momentous Will sending out its terrific rays and vibrations, like some vast octopus. And at the other end of the vibration, men, created men, erect in the dark potency, answering Will with will, like gods or demons.

It was wonderful too. But where was woman, in this terrible inter-change of will? Truly only a subservient, instrumental thing: the soft stone on which the man sharpened the knife of his relentless volition:

the soft lode-stone to magnetize his blade of steel and keep all its molecules alive in the electric flow.

Ah yes, it was wonderful. It was, as Ramón said, a manifestation, a manifestation of the Godhead. But to the Godhead as a sheer and awful Will she could not respond.

Joachim, letting himself be bled to death for people who would profit nothing by his sacrifice, he was the other extreme. The black and magnificent pride of will which comes out of the volcanic earth of Mexico had been unknown to him. He was one of the white, self-sacrificing gods. Hence her bitterness. And hence, naturally, the spell of beauty and lustrous satisfaction which Cipriano could cast over her. She was in love with him, when he was with her; in his arms, she was quite gone in his spell. She was the deep, slumbrous lodestone which set all his bones glittering with the energy of relentless pride. And she herself derived a great gratification in the embrace, a sense of passive, downward-sinking power, profound.

Yet she could not be purely this, this thing of sheer reciprocity. Surely, though her woman's nature was reciprocal to his male, surely it was more than that! Surely he and she were not two potent and reciprocal currents between which the Morning Star flashed like a spark out of nowhere. Surely this was not it? Surely she had one tiny Morning Star inside her, which was herself, her own very soul and star-self!

But he would never admit this. The tiny star of her very self he would never see. To him she was but the answer to his call, the sheath for his blade, the cloud to his lightning, the earth to his rain, the fuel to his fire.

Alone, she was nothing. Only as the pure female corresponding to his pure male, did she signify.

As an isolated individual, she had little or no significance. As a woman on her own, she was repulsive, and even evil, to him. She was not real till she was reciprocal.

To a great extent this was true, and she knew it. To a great extent, the same was true of him, and without her to give him the power, he too would not achieve his own manhood and meaning. With her or without her, he would be beyond ordinary men, because the power was in him. But failing her, he would never make his ultimate achievement, he would never be whole. He would be chiefly an instrument.

He knew this too: though perhaps not well enough. He would strive to keep her, to have her, for his own fulfilment. He would not let her go.

But that little star of her own single self, would he ever recognise that? Nay, did he even recognise any single star of his own being? Did he not conceive of himself as a power and a potency on the face of the earth, an embodied will, like a rushing dark wind? And hence, inevitably, she was but the stone of rest to his potency, his bed of sleep, the cave and lair of his male will.

What else? To him there was nothing else. The star! Don Ramón's Morning Star was something that sprung between him and her and hung shining, the strange third thing that was both of them and neither of them, between his night and her day.

Was it true? Was she nothing, nothing, by herself? And he, alone, failing his last manhood, without her was he nothing, or next to nothing? As a fig tree which grows up, but never comes to flower.

Was this thing true, the same of both of them? – that alone, they were next to nothing? Each of them, separate, next to nothing. Apart in a sort of grey, mechanical twilight, without a star?

And together, in strange reciprocity, flashing darkly till the Morning Star rose between them?

He would say to her, as Ramón had said of Carlota: 'Soul! No, you have no soul of your own. You have at best only half a soul. It takes a man and a woman together to make a soul. The soul is the Morning Star, emerging from the two. One alone cannot have a soul.'

This Ramón said. And she knew it conveyed what Cipriano really felt. Cipriano could not see Kate as a being by herself. And if he lived a thousand more years, he would never see her as such. He would see her only as reciprocal to himself. As the balance of him, and the correspondence on the other side of heaven.

'Let the Morning Star rise between us,' he would say. 'Alone you are nothing, and I am *manqué*. But together we are the wings of the Morning.'

Was it true? Was this the final answer to man's assertion of individuality?

Was it true? And was it her sacred duty to sit beside him in the green dress of Malintzi, in the church, the goddess admitting her halfness? Her halfness! Was there no star of the single soul? Was that all an illusion?

Was the individual an illusion? Man, any man, every man, by himself just a fragment, knowing no Morning Star? And every woman the same; by herself, starless and fragmentary. Even in the relation to the innermost God, still fragmentary and unblest.

Was it true, that the gate was the Morning Star, the only entrance to the Innermost? And the Morning Star rises between the two, and between the many, but never from one alone.

And was a man but a dark and arrowy will, and woman the bow from which the arrow is shot? The bow without the arrow was as nothing, and the arrow without the bow only a short-range dart, ineffectual?

Poor Kate, it was hard to have to reflect this. It meant a submission she had never made. It meant the death of her individual self. It meant abandoning so much, even her own very foundations. For she had believed truly that every man and every woman alike was founded on the individual.

Now, must she admit that the individual was an illusion and a falsification? There was no such animal. Except in the mechanical world. In the world of machines, the individual machine is effectual. The individual, like the perfect being, does not and cannot exist, in the vivid world. We are all fragments. And at the best, halves. The only whole thing is the Morning Star. Which can only rise between two: or between many.

And men can only meet in the light of the Morning Star.

She thought again of Cipriano and the executions, and she covered her hands over her face. Was this the knife to which she must be sheath? Was it such a star of power and relentlessness that must rise between her and him? Him naked and painted, with his soldiers, dancing and sweating and shouting among them. Herself unseen and nowhere!

As she sat rocking in her terrible loneliness and misgiving, she heard the drums on the towers, and the sound of rockets. She went to the gate. Over the church, in the night sky, hung a spangling cloud of red and blue fire, the colours of Huitzilopochtli and Quetzalcoatl. The night of Huitzilopochtli would be over. The sky was dark again, and there were all the stars, beyond, far, far beyond where the spangling had been.

She went indoors again, to retire. The servants had all run out to see the rockets. Ezequiel would be in with the men in church.

She heard footsteps on the gravel walk, and suddenly Cipriano stood in the doorway, in his white clothes. He took off his hat, quickly. His black eyes were sparkling, almost blazing to her, with a flashing of light such as she had never seen. There were still smears of paint on his face. In the blazing of his eyes he seemed to be smiling to her, but in a dazzling, childish way.

'Malintzi,' he said to her in Spanish. 'Oh, come! Come and put on the green dress. I cannot be the Living Huitzilopochtli without a bride. I cannot be it, Malintzi!'

He stood before her, flickering and flashing and strangely young, vulnerable, as young and boyish as flame. She saw that when the fire came free in him, he would be like this always, flickering, flashing with a flame of virgin youth. Now, not will at all. Sensitive as a boy. And calling her only with his boyish flame. The living, flickering, fiery *Wish*. This was first. The *Will* she had seen was subsidiary and instrumental, the *Wish* in armour.

She had been so used to fighting for her own soul with individualistic men, that for a moment she felt old, and uncertain. The strange, flashing vulnerability in him, the nakedness of the living Wish, disconcerted her. She was used to men who had themselves well in hand, and were seeking their own ends as individuals.

'Where do you want me to come?' she said.

'To the church,' he said. 'It is mine to-night. I am Huitzilopochtli: but I cannot be it alone,' he added with quick, wistful, watchful smile, as if all his flesh were flickering with delicate fire.

Kate wrapped herself in a dark tartan shawl and went with him. He stepped quickly, in the short, Indian way. The night was very dark. Down on the beach some fireworks were flaming, and the people were all watching.

They entered the yard of the church from the back, by the priest's little gate. Soldiers were already rolled up in their blankets, sleeping under the wall. Cipriano opened the little vestry door. Kate passed into the darkness. He followed, lighting a candle.

'My soldiers know I am watching to-night in the church,' he said. 'They will keep guard.'

The body of the church was quite dark, but the bluish white light burned above the statue of Quetzalcoatl, giving not much light.

Cipriano lifted his candle to the black statue of Huitzilopochtli. Then he turned to Kate, his black eyes flashing.

'I am Huitzilopochtli, Malintzi,' he said in his low, Indian Spanish. 'But I cannot be it without you. Stay with me, Malintzi. Say you are the bride of the Living Huitzilopochtli.'

'Yes!' she replied, 'I say it.'

Convulsive flames of joy and triumph seemed to go over his face. He lit two candles in front of Huitzilopochtli.

'Come!' he said. 'Put on the green dress.'

He took her to the vestry, where were many folded serapes, and the silver bowl and other implements of the church, and left her while she put on the dress of Malintzi she had worn when Ramón married them.

When she stepped out she found Cipriano naked and in his paint, before the statue of Huitzilopochtli, on a rug of jaguar skins.

'I am the living Huitzilopochtli,' he murmured to her in a sort of ecstasy.

'You are Malintzi,' he said. 'The bride of Huitzilopochtli.'

The convulsion of exultance went over his face. He took her hand in his left hand, and they stood facing the bluish light.

'Cover your face!' he said to her.

They covered their faces in the salute.

'Now salute Quetzalcoatl.' And he flung up his arm. She held out her left hand, in the woman's salute.

Then they turned to the statue of Huitzilopochtli.

'Salute Huitzilopochtli!' he said, bringing his right fist down with a smash in the palm of his left hand. But this was the male salute. He taught her to press her hands together in front of her breast, then shoot them out towards the idol.

Then he put a little lamp of earthenware between the feet of Huitzilopochtli. From the right knee of the idol he took a little black vessel of oil, making her take a little white vessel from the god's left knee.

'Now,' he said, 'together we fill the lamp.'

And together they poured the oil from their little pitchers, into the saucer-shaped lamp.

'Now together we light it,' he said.

He took one of the two candles burning before the black idol, she took the other, and with the flames dripping and leaping together, they kindled the floating wick of the lamp. It burned in a round blue bud, then rose higher.

'Blow out your candle,' he said. 'It is our Morning Star.'

They blew out the two candles. It was almost dark now, with the slow light, like a snow-drop, of their united lives floating between the feet of Huitzilopochtli, and the everlasting light burning small and bluish beyond the statue of Quetzalcoatl.

At the foot of the altar, beside the chair of Huitzilopochtli, a third chair was placed.

'Sit in your throne of Malintzi,' he said to her.

They sat side by side, his hand holding her hand, in complete silence, looking down the dark church. He had placed tufts of greenish flowers, like thin, greenish lilac, above her chair, and their perfume was like a dream, strong, overpoweringly sweet on the darkness.

Strange how naïve he was! He was not like Ramón, rather ponderous and deliberate in his ceremonials. Cipriano in his own little deeds to-night with her, was naïve like a child. She could hardly look at that bud of light which he said meant their united lives, without a catch at her heart. It burned so soft and round, and he had such an implicit, childish satisfaction in its symbol. It all gave him a certain wild, childish joy. The strange convulsions like flames of joy and gratification went over his face!

'Ah, God!' she thought. 'There are more ways than one of becoming like a little child.'

The flaminess and the magnificence of the beginning: this was what Cipriano wanted to bring to his marriage. The reeling, powerful perfume of those invisible green flowers, that the peons call *buena de noche*: good by night.

Strange – that which he brought to marriage was something flamey and unabashed, forever virginal. Not, as she had always known in men, yearning and seeking his own ends. Naïvely bringing his flame to her flame.

As she sat in that darkened church in the intense perfume of flowers, in the seat of Malintzi, watching the bud of her life united with his, between the feet of the idol, and feeling his dark hand softly holding her own, with the soft, deep Indian heat, she felt her own childhood coming back on her. The years seemed to be reeling away in great circles, falling away from her.

Leaving her sitting there like a girl in her first adolescence. The Living Huitzilopochtli! Ah, easily he was the living Huitzilopochtli. More than anything. More than Cipriano, more than a male man, he was the living Huitzilopochtli. And she was the goddess bride, Malintzi of the green dress.

Ah, yes, it was childish. But it was actually so. She was perhaps fourteen years old, and he was fifteen. And he was the young Huitzilo-pochtli, and she was the bride Malintzi, the bride-girl. She had seen it. When the flame came up in him and licked him all over, he was young and vulnerable as a boy of fifteen, and he would always be so, even when he was seventy.

And this was her bridegroom. Here at last he was not a *will*. When he came clothed in his own free flame, it was not *will* that clothed him. Let him be a general, an executioner, what he liked, in the world. The flame of their united lives was a naked bud of flame. Their marriage was a young, vulnerable flame.

So he sat in silence, on his throne, holding her hand in silence till the years reeled away from her in fleeing circles, and she sat, as every real woman can sit, no matter at what age, a girl again, and for him, a virgin. He held her hand in silence, till she was Malintzi, and virgin for him, and when they looked at one another, and their eyes met, the two flames rippled in oneness. She closed her eyes, and was dark.

Then later, when she opened her eyes and saw the bud of flame just above her, and the black idol invisibly crouching, she heard his strange voice, the voice of a boy hissing in naïve ecstasy, in Spanish:

'Miel! Miel de Malintzi! – Honey of Malintzi!'

And she pressed him to her breast, convulsively. His innermost flame was always virginal, it was always the first time. And it made her again always a virgin girl. She could feel their two flames flowing together.

How else, she said to herself, is one to begin again, save by re-finding one's virginity? And when one finds one's virginity, one realises one is among the gods. He is of the gods, and so am I. Why should I judge him!

So, when she thought of him and his soldiers, tales of swift cruelty she had heard of him: when she remembered his stabbing the three helpless peons, she thought: Why should I judge him? He is of the gods. And when he comes to me he lays his pure, quick flame to mine, and every time I am a young girl again, and every time he takes the flower of my virginity, and I his. It leaves me insouciant like a young

girl. What do I care if he kills people? His flame is young and clean.
He is Huitzilopochtli, and I am Malintzi. What do I care, what Cipriano
Viedma does or doesn't do? Or even what Kate Leslie does or doesn't
do!

Teresa

RAMÓN somewhat surprised Kate by marrying again, a couple of months or so after the death of Doña Carlota. The new bride was a young woman of about twenty-eight, called Teresa. There was a very quiet civil wedding, and Ramón brought his new wife to Jamiltepec.

He had known her since she was a child, for she was the daughter of the famous hacienda of Las Yemas, some twelve miles inland from Jamiltepec. Don Tomás, her father, had been a staunch friend of the Carrascos.

But Don Tomás had died a year ago, leaving the large, flourishing tequila hacienda to his three children, to be administered by Teresa. Teresa was the youngest. Her two brothers had reverted to the usual wasteful, spendthrift, brutal Mexican way. Therefore Don Tomás, in order to save the hacienda from their destructive hands, had especially appointed Teresa *administrador*, and had got the brothers' consent to this. After all, they were shiftless ne'er-do-wells, and had never shown the slightest desire to help in the rather burdensome business of managing a large tequila hacienda, during their father's lifetime. Teresa had been the one. And during her father's illness the whole charge had devolved on her, while her brothers wasted themselves and their substance in the squashy prostitution-living of Mexicans of their class, away in the cities.

No sooner was the father dead, however, and Teresa in charge, than home came the two brothers, big with their intention to be hacendados. By simple brute force they ousted their sister, gave orders over her head, jeered at her, and in crushing her united for once with each other. They were putting her back into her place as a woman – that is to say, back into a secluded sort of prostitution, to which, in their eyes, women belonged.

But they were bullies, and, as bullies, cowards. And like so many Mexicans of that class, soft and suicidal towards themselves. They made friends with judges and generals. They rode about in resplendent charro dress, and had motor-loads of rather doubtful visitors.

Against their soft, sensuous brutality Teresa could do nothing, and she knew it. They were all soft and sensual, or sensuous, handsome in their way, open-handed, careless, but bullies, with no fear at the middle of them.

'Make yourself desirable, and get a husband for yourself,' they said to her.

In their eyes, her greatest crime was that she did not make herself desirable to men of their sort. That she had never had a man, that she was not married, made her almost repulsive to them. What was woman for, but for loose, soft, prostitutional sex?

'Do you want to wear the trousers?' they jeered at her. 'No, Señorita! Not while there are two men on the place, you are not going to wear the trousers. No, Señorita! The trousers, the men wear them. The women keep under their petticoats that which they are women for.'

Teresa was used to these insults. But they made her soul burn.

'You, do you want to be an American woman?' they said to her. 'Go off to America, then, and bob your hair and wear breeches. Buy a ranch there, and get a husband to take your orders. Go!'

She went to her lawyers, but they held up their hands. And she went to Ramón, whom she had known since she was a child.

It would have meant a hopeless and ruinous law-suit, to get the brothers ejected from the hacienda. It would have meant the rapid ruin of the estate. Ramón instead asked Teresa to marry him, and he carefully arranged her dowry, so that she should always have her own provision.

'It is a country where men despise sex, and live for it,' said Ramón. 'Which is just suicide.'

Ramón came with his wife, to see Kate. Teresa was rather small, pale, with a lot of loose black hair and big, wide black eyes. Yet in her quiet bearing and her well-closed mouth there was an air of independence and authority. She had suffered great humiliation at the hands of her brothers, there was still a certain wanness round her eyes, the remains of tears of anger and helpless indignation, and the bitterness of insulted sex. But now she loved Ramón with a wild, virgin loyalty. That, too, was evident. He had saved her sex from the insult, restored it to her in its pride and its beauty. And in return, she felt an almost fierce reverence for him.

But with Kate she was shy and rather distant: a little afraid of the travelled, experienced, rather assertive white-skinned woman, the woman of the other race. She sat in Kate's salon in her simple white dress with a black gauze rebozo, her brown hands motionless in her lap, her dark neck erect, her dark, slender, well-shaped cheek averted. She seemed, Kate thought, rather like a little sempstress.

But Kate was reckoning without that strange quiescent power of authority which Teresa also possessed, in her slight, dark body. And without the black, flashing glances which rested on her from time to time, from Teresa's eyes, full of searching fierceness and fiery misgiving. A fiery soul, in such a demure, slight, dark body. Sometimes a muted word came from her mouth, and a constrained smile moved her lips. But her burning eyes never changed. She did not even look at Ramón.

'How much do you charge per word, Chica?' he asked her, with a sort of soft fondness.

Then her dark eyes flashed at him, and her mouth gave a little smile. It was evident she was hopelessly in love with him, in a sort of trance or muse of love. And she maintained such a cold sort of blankness towards Kate.

'She despises me,' thought Kate, 'because I can't be in love as she is.'

And for one second Kate envied Teresa. The next second, she despised her. 'The harem type –'

Well, it was Ramón's nature to be a sort of Sultan. He looked very handsome in his white clothes, very serene and pasha-like in his assurance, yet at the same time, soft, pleasant, something boyish also in his physical well-being. In his soft yet rather pasha-like way, he was mixing a cocktail of gin and vermouth and lime. Teresa watched him from the corner of her eye. And at the same time, she watched Kate, the potential enemy, the woman who talked with men on their own plane.

Kate rose to get spoons. At the same moment, he stepped back from the low table where he was squeezing a lime, so that he came into slight collision with her. And Kate noticed again, how quick and subtle was his physical evasion of her, the soft, almost liquid, hot quickness of sliding out of contact with her. His natural voluptuousness avoided her as a flame leans away from a draught.

She flushed slightly. And Teresa saw the quick flush under the fair, warm-white skin, the leap of yellow light, almost like anger, into

Kate's grey-hazel eyes. The moment of evasion of two different blood-streams.

And Teresa rose and went to Ramón's side, bending over and looking in the tumblers, asking, with that curious affected childishness of dark women:

'What do you put in?'

'Look!' said Ramón. And with the same curious male childishness of dark men, he was explaining the cocktail to her, giving her a little gin in a spoon, to taste.

'It is an impure tequila,' she said naïvely.

'At eight pesos a bottle?' he laughed.

'So much! It is much!'

She looked into his eyes for a second, and saw all his face go darker, warmer, as if his flesh were fusing soft towards her. Her small head poised the prouder. She had got him back.

'Harem tricks!' said Kate to herself. And she was somewhat impatient, seeing the big, portentous Ramón enveloped in the toils of this little dark thing. She resented being made so conscious of his physical presence, his full, male body inside his thin white clothes, the strong, yet soft shoulders, the full, rich male thighs. It was as if she herself, also, being in the presence of this Sultan, should succumb as part of the harem.

What a curious will the little dark woman had! What a subtle female power inside her rather skinny body! She had the power to make him into a big, golden full glory of a man. Whilst she herself became almost inconspicuous, save for her big black eyes lit with a tigerish power.

Kate watched in wonder. She herself had known men who made her feel a queen, who made her feel as if the sky rested on her bosom and her head was among the stars. She knew what it was to rise grander and grander, till she filled the universe with her womanhood.

Now she saw the opposite taking place. This little bit of a black-eyed woman had an almost uncanny power to make Ramón great and gorgeous in the flesh, whilst she herself became inconspicuous, almost *invisible*, save for her great black eyes. Like a sultan, he was, like a full golden fruit in the sun, with a strange and magnificent presence, glamour. And then, by some mysterious power in her dark little body, the skinny Teresa held him most completely.

And this was what Ramón wanted. And it made Kate angry, angry.

The big, fluid male, gleaming, was somewhat repulsive to her. And the tense little female with her pale-dark face, wan under her great, intense, black eyes, having all her female being tense in an effort to exalt this big glistening man, this enraged Kate. She could not bear the glistening smile in Ramón's dark eyes, a sort of pasha satisfaction. And she could not bear the erect, tense little figure of the dark woman, using her power in this way.

This hidden, secretive power of the dark female! Kate called it harem, and self-prostitution. But was it? Yes, surely it was the *slave* approach. Surely she wanted nothing but sex from him, like a prostitute! The ancient mystery of the female power, which consists in glorifying the blood-male.

Was it right? Kate asked herself. Wasn't it degrading for a woman? And didn't it make the man either soft and sensuous, or else hatefully autocratic?

Yet Kate herself had convinced herself of one thing, finally: that the clue to all living and to all moving-on into new living lay in the vivid blood-relation between man and woman. A man and a woman in this togetherness were the clue to all present living and future possibility. Out of this clue of togetherness between a man and a woman, the whole of the new life arose. It was the quick of the whole.

And the togetherness needed a balance. Surely it needed a balance! And did not this Teresa throw herself entirely into the male balance, so that all the weight was on the man's side?

Ramón had not wanted Kate. Ramón got what he wanted – this black little creature, who was so servile to him and so haughty in her own power. Ramón had never wanted Kate: except as a friend, a clever friend. As a woman, no! – He wanted this little viper of a Teresa.

Cipriano wanted Kate. The little general, the strutting little soldier, he wanted Kate: just for moments. He did not really want to marry her. He wanted the moments, no more. She was to give him his moments, and then he was off again, to his army, to his men. It was what he wanted.

It was what she wanted too. Her life was her own! It was not her métier to be fanning the blood in a man, to make him almighty and blood-glamorous. Her life was her own!

She rose and went to her bedroom to look for a book she had pro-

mised Ramón. She could not bear the sight of him in love with Teresa
any longer. The heavy, mindless smile on his face, the curious glisten
of his eyes, and the strange, heavy, lordly *aplomb* of his body affected
her like a madness. She wanted to run.

This was what they were, these people! Savages, with the impossible
fluid flesh of savages, and that savage way of dissolving into an awful
black mass of desire. Emerging with the male conceit and haughtiness
swelling his blood and making him feel endless. While his eyes glistened
with a haughty blackness.

The trouble was, that the power of the world, which she had known
until now only in the eyes of blue-eyed men, who made queens of
their women – even if they hated them for it in the end – was now
fading in the blue eyes, and dawning in the black. In Ramón's eyes
at this moment was a steady, alien gleam of pride, and daring, and
power, which she knew was masterly. The same was in Cipriano's quick
looks. The power of the world was dying in the blond men, their bravery
and their supremacy was leaving them, going into the eyes of the dark
men, who were rousing at last.

Joachim, the eager, clever, fierce, sensitive genius, who could look
into her soul, and laugh into her soul, with his blue eyes: he had died
under her eyes. And her children were not even his children.

If she could have fanned his blood as Teresa now fanned the blood
of Ramón, he would never have died.

But it was impossible. Every dog has his day. – And every race.

Teresa came tapping timidly.

'May I come?'

'Do!' said Kate, rising from her knees and leaving little piles of books
all round the book-trunk.

It was a fairly large room, with doors opening on to the patio and
the sun-hard garden, smooth mango trees rising like elephant's trunks
out of the ground, green grass after the rains, chickens beneath the
ragged banana leaves. A red bird splashed in the basin of water, opening
and shutting brown wings above his pure scarlet, vivid.

But Teresa looked at the room, not out of doors. She smelt the smell
of cigarettes and saw the many cigarette stumps in the agate tray by
the bed. She saw the littered books, the scattered jewellery, the brilliant
New-Mexican rugs on the floor, the Persian curtain hung behind the
bed, the handsome, coloured bedcover, the dresses of dark silk and

bright velvet flung over a trunk, the folded shawls with their long fringe, the scattered shoes, white, grey, pale-brown, dark-brown, black, on the floor, the tall Chinese candlesticks. The room of a woman who lived her own life, for her own self.

Teresa was repelled, uneasy, and fascinated.

'How nice this is!' she said, touching the glowing bedcover.

'A friend made it for me, in England.'

Teresa looked with wonder at everything, especially at the tangle of jewellery on the dressing-table.

'Don't you like those red stones!' said Kate, kneeling again to put the books back, and looking at the brown neck bent absorbedly over the jewels. Thin shoulders, with a soft, dark skin, in a bit of a white dress! And loosely folded masses of black hair held by tortoise-shell pins. – An insignificant little thing, humble, Kate thought to herself.

But she knew really that Teresa was neither insignificant nor humble. Under that soft brown skin, and in that stooping female spine was a strange old power to call up the blood in a man, and glorify it, and, in some way, keep it for herself.

On the sewing-table was a length of fine Indian muslin which Kate had bought in India, and did not know what to do with. It was a sort of yellow-peach colour, beautiful, but it did not suit Kate. Teresa was fingering the gold-thread selvedge.

'It is not organdie?' she said.

'No, muslin. Hand-made muslin from India. – Why don't you take it. It doesn't suit me. It would be perfect for you.'

She rose and held the fabric against Teresa's dark neck, pointing to the mirror. Teresa saw the warm-yellow muslin upon herself, and her eyes flashed.

'No!' she said. 'I couldn't take it.'

'Why not? It doesn't suit me. I've had it lying about for a year now, and was wondering whether to cut it up for curtains. Do have it.'

Kate could be imperious, almost cruel in her giving.

'I can't take it from you!'

'Of course you can!'

Ramón appeared in the doorway, glancing round the room, and at the two women.

'Look!' said Teresa, rather confused. 'The Señora wants to give

me this Indian muslin.' – She turned to him shyly, with the fabric held
to her throat.

'You look very well in it,' he said, his eyes resting on her.

'The Señora ought not to give it to me.'

'The Señora would not give it you unless she wished to.'

'Then!' said Teresa to Kate. 'Many thanks! But many thanks!'

'It is nothing,' said Kate.

'But Ramón says it suits me.'

'Yes, doesn't it suit her!' cried Kate to him. 'It was made in India
for someone as dark as she is. It *does* suit her.'

'Very pretty!' said Ramón.

He had glanced round the room, at the different attractive things
from different parts of the world, and at the cigarette ends in the agate
bowl: the rather weary luxury and disorder, and the touch of barrenness,
of a woman living her own life.

She did not know what he was thinking. But to herself she thought:
This is the man I defended on that roof. This is the man who lay
with a hole in his back, naked and unconscious under the lamp. He
didn't look like a Sultan then.

Teresa must have divined something of her thought, for she said,
looking at Ramón:

'Señora! But for you Ramón would have been killed. Always I think
of it.'

'Don't think of it,' said Kate. 'Something else would have happened.
Anyhow it wasn't I, it was destiny.'

'Ah, but you were the destiny!' said Teresa.

'Now there is a hostess, won't you come and stay some time at
Jamiltepec?' said Ramón.

'Oh, do! Do come!' cried Teresa.

'But do you really want me?' said Kate, incredulous.

'Yes! Yes!' cried Teresa.

'She needs a woman-friend,' said Ramón gently.

'Yes, I do!' she cried. 'I have never had a true, *true* woman-friend:
only when I was at school, and we were girls.'

Kate doubted very much her own capacity for being a *true*, true
woman-friend to Teresa. She wondered what the two of them saw in
her. As what did they see her?

'Yes, I should like to come for a few days,' she replied.

'Oh, yes!' cried Teresa. 'When will you come?'

The day was agreed.

'And we will write the Song of Malintzi,' said Ramón

'Don't do that!' cried Kate quickly.

He looked at her, in his slow, wondering way. He could make her feel, at moments, as if she were a sort of child and as if he were a ghost.

Kate went to Jamiltepec, and before the two women knew it, almost, they were making dresses for Teresa, cutting up the pineapple-coloured muslin. Poor Teresa, for a bride she had a scanty wardrobe: nothing but her rather pathetic black dresses that somehow made her look poor, and a few old white dresses. She had lived for her father – who had a good library of Mexicana and was all his life writing a history of the State of Jalisco – and for the hacienda. And it was her proud boast that Las Yemas was the only hacienda, within a hundred miles range, which had not been smashed at all during the revolutions that followed the flight of Porfirio Diaz.

Teresa had a good deal of the nun in her. But that was because she was deeply passionate, and deep passion tends to hide within itself, rather than expose itself to vulgar contact.

So Kate pinned the muslin over the brown shoulders, wondering again at the strange, uncanny softness of the dark skin, the heaviness of the black hair. Teresa's family, the Romeros, had been in Mexico since the early days of the Conquest.

Teresa wanted long sleeves.

'My arms are so thin!' she murmured, hiding her slender brown arms with a sort of shame. 'They are not beautiful like yours.'

Kate was a strong, full-developed woman of forty, with round, strong white arms.

'No!' she said to Teresa. 'Your arms are not thin: they are exactly right for your figure, and pretty and young and brown.'

'But make the sleeves long, to the wrist,' pleaded Teresa.

And Kate did so, realising it became the other woman's nature better.

'The men here don't like little thin women,' said Teresa, wistfully.

'One doesn't care what *the men* like,' said Kate. 'Do you think Don Ramón wishes you were a plump partridge?'

Teresa looked at her with a smile in her dark, big bright eyes, that were so quick, and in many ways so unseeing.

'Who knows!' she said. And in her quick, mischievous smile it was evident she would like also, sometimes, to be a plump partridge.

Kate now saw more of the hacienda life than she had done before. When Ramón was at home, he consulted his overseer, or administrator, every morning. But already Teresa was taking this work off his hands. She would see to the estate.

Ramón was a good deal absent, either in Mexico or in Guadalajara, or even away in Sonora. He was already famous and notorious throughout the country, his name was a name to conjure with. But underneath the rather ready hero-worship of the Mexicans, Kate somehow felt their latent grudging. Perhaps they took more satisfaction in ultimately destroying their heroes, than in temporarily raising them high. The real perfect moment was when the hero was downed.

And to Kate, sceptic as she was, it seemed much more likely that they were sharpening the machete to stick in Ramón's heart, when he got a bit too big for them, than anything else. Though, to be sure, there was Cipriano to reckon with. And Cipriano was a little devil whom they quite rightly feared. And Cipriano, for once, was faithful. He was, to himself, Huitzilopochtli, and to this he would maintain a demonish faith. He was Huitzilopochtli, Ramón was Quetzalcoatl. To Cipriano this was a plain and living fact. And he kept his army keen as a knife. Even the President would not care to run counter to Cipriano. And the President was a brave man too.

'One day,' he said, 'we will put Quetzalcoatl in Puebla Cathedral, and Huitzilopochtli in Mexico Cathedral and Malintzi in Guadalupe.' The day will come, Ramón.'

'We will see that it comes,' Ramón replied.

But Ramón and Montes suffered alike from the deep, devilish animosity the country sent out in silence against them. It was the same, whoever was in power: the Mexicans seemed to steam with invisible, grudging hate, the hate of demons foiled in their own souls, whose only motive is to foil everything, everybody, in the everlasting hell of cramped frustration.

This was the dragon of Mexico, that Ramón had to fight. Montes, the President, had it to fight the same. And it shattered his health. Cipriano also had it up against him. But he succeeded best. With his drums, with his dances round the fire, with his soldiers kept keen as knives he drew real support from his men. He grew stronger and more brilliant.

Ramón also, at home in his own district, felt the power flow into him from his people. He was their chief, and by his effort and his power he had almost overcome their ancient, fathomless resistance. Almost he had *awed* them back into the soft mystery of living, awed them until the tension of their resistant, malevolent wills relaxed. At home, he would feel his strength upon him.

But away from home, and particularly in the city of Mexico, he felt himself bled, bled, bled by the subtle, hidden malevolence of the Mexicans, and the ugly negation of the greedy, mechanical foreigners, birds of prey forever alighting in the cosmopolitan capital.

While Ramón was away, Kate stayed with Teresa. The two women had this in common, that they felt it was better to stand faithfully behind a really brave man, than to push forward into the ranks of cheap and obtrusive women. And this united them. A certain deep, ultimate faithfulness in each woman, to her own man who needed her fidelity, kept Kate and Teresa kindred to one another.

The rainy season had almost passed, though throughout September and even in October occasional heavy downpours fell. But the wonderful Mexican autumn, like a strange, inverted spring, was upon the land. The waste places bloomed with pink and white cosmos, the strange wild trees flowered in a ghostly way, forests of small sunflowers shone in the sun, the sky was a pure, pure blue, the floods of sunshine lay tempered on the land, that in part was flooded with water, from the heavy rains.

The lake was very full, strange and uneasy, and it had washed up a bank of the wicked water-hyacinths along all its shores. The wild-fowl were coming from the north, clouds of wild ducks like dust in the high air, sprinkling the water like weeds. Many, many wild fowl, grebe, cranes, and white gulls of the inland seas, so that the northern mystery seemed to have blown so far south. There was a smell of water in the land, and a sense of soothing. For Kate firmly believed that part of the horror of the Mexican people came from the unsoothed dryness of the land and the untempered crudity of the flat-edged sunshine. If only there could be a softening of water in the air, and a haze above trees, the unspoken and unspeakable malevolence would die out of the human hearts.

Kate rode out often with Teresa to see the fields. The sugar-cane in the inner valley was vivid green, and rising tall, tall. The peons were beginning to cut it with their sword-like machetes, filling the bullock-wagons, to haul the cane to the factory in Sayula. On the dry hill-slopes the spikey tequila plant – a sort of maguey – flourished in its iron wickedness. Low wild cactuses put forth rose-like blossoms, wonderful and beautiful for such sinister plants. The beans were gathered from the bean-fields, some gourds and squashes still sprawled their uncanny weight across the land. Red chiles hung on withering plants, red tomatoes sank to the earth. Some maize still reared its flags, there was still young corn to eat on the cob. The banana crop was small, the children came in with the little wild yellow tejocote apples, for making preserves. Teresa was making preserves, even with the late figs and peaches. On the trees, the ponderous mango trees, some fruit was again orange-yellow and ripe, but the most still hung in strings, heavy and greenish and dropping like the testes of bulls.

It was autumn in Mexico, with wild duck on the waters, and hunters with guns, and small wild doves in the trees. Autumn in Mexico, and the coming of the dry season, with the sky going higher and higher, pure pale blue, the sunset arriving with a strange flare of crystal yellow light. With the coffee berries turning red on the struggling bushes under the trees, and bougainvillea in the strong light glowing with a glow of magenta colour so deep you could plunge your arms deep in it. With a few hummingbirds in the sunshine, and the fish in the waters gone wild, and the flies, that steamed black in the first rains, now passing away again.

Teresa attended to everything, and Kate helped. Whether it was a sick peon in one of the little houses, or the hosts of bees from the hives under the mangoes, or the yellow, yellow beeswax to be made into little bowlfuls, or the preserves, or the garden, or the calves, or the bit of butter and the little fresh cheeses made of strands of curd, or the turkeys to be overlooked: she saw to it along with Teresa. And she wondered at the steady, urgent, efficient *will* which had to be exerted all the time. Everything was kept going by a heavy exertion of will. If once the will of the master broke, everything would break, and ruin would overtake the place almost at once. No real relaxation, ever. Always the sombre, insistent will.

Ramón arrived home one evening in November, from a long journey to Sonora. He had come overland from Tepic, and twice had been stopped by floods. The rains, so late, were very unusual. He was tired and remote-seeming. Kate's heart stood still a moment as she thought: He goes so remote, as if he might go away altogether into death.

It was cloudy again, with lightning beating about on the horizons. But all was very still. She said good-night early, and wandered down her own side of the terrace, to the look-out at the end, which looked on to the lake. Everything was dark, save for the intermittent pallor of lightning.

And she was startled to see, in a gleam of lightning, Teresa sitting with her back to the wall of the open terrace, Ramón lying with his head in her lap, while she slowly pushed her fingers through his thick black hair. They were as silent as the night.

Kate gave a startled murmur and said:

'I'm so sorry! I didn't know you were here.'

'I wanted to be under the sky!' said Ramón, heaving himself to rise.

'Oh, *don't* move!' said Kate. 'It was stupid of me to come here. You are tired.'

'Yes,' he said, sinking again. 'I am tired. These people make me feel I have a hole in the middle of me. So I have come back to Teresa.'

'Yes!' said Kate. 'One isn't the Living Quetzalcoatl for nothing. Of course they eat holes in you. – Really, is it worth it? – To give yourself to be eaten away by them.'

'It must be so,' he said. 'The change has to be made. And some man has to make it. I sometimes wish it wasn't I.'

'So do I wish it. So does Teresa. One wonders if it isn't better to be just a man,' said Kate.

But Teresa said nothing.

'One does what one must. And after all, one is always just a man,' he said. 'And if one has wounds – à la guerre comme à la guerre!'[2]

His voice came out of the darkness like a ghost.

'Ah!' sighed Kate. 'It makes one wonder what a man is, that he must needs expose himself to the horrors of all the other people.'

There was silence for a moment.

'Man is a column of blood, with a voice in it,' he said. 'And when the voice is still, and he is only a column of blood, he is better.'

She went away to her room sadly, hearing the sound of infinite exhaustion in his voice. As if he had a hole, a wound in the middle of him. She could almost feel it, in her own bowels.

And if, with his efforts, he killed himself? – Then, she said, Cipriano would come apart, and it would be all finished.

Ah, why should a man have to make these efforts on behalf of a beastly, malevolent people who weren't worth it! Better let the world come to an end, if that was what it wanted.

She thought of Teresa soothing him, soothing him and saying nothing. And him like a great helpless, wounded thing! It was rather horrible, really. Herself, she would have to expostulate, she would have to try to prevent him. Why should men damage themselves with this useless struggling and fighting, and then come home to their women to be restored!

To Kate, the fight simply wasn't worth one wound. Let the beastly world of man come to an end, if that was its destiny, as soon as possible. Without lifting a finger to prevent it. – Live one's own precious life, that was given but once, and let the rest go its own hellish way.

She would have *had* to try to prevent Ramón from giving himself to destruction this way. She was willing for him to be ten Living Quetzalcoatls. But not to expose himself to the devilish malevolence of people.

Yet he would do it. Even as Joachim had done. And Teresa, with her silence and her infinitely soft administering, she would heal him far better than Kate, with her expostulation and her opposition.

'Ah!' said Kate to herself. 'I'm glad Cipriano is a soldier, and doesn't get wounds in his *soul*.'

At the same time, she knew that without Ramón, Cipriano was just an instrument, and not ultimately interesting to her.

In the morning, Teresa appeared alone to breakfast. She seemed very calm, hiding her emotions in her odd, brown, proud little way.

'How is Ramón?' said Kate.

'He is sleeping,' said Teresa.

'Good! He seemed to me almost done up, last night.'

'Yes.' – The black eyes looked at Kate, wide with unshed tears and courage, and a beautiful deep, remote light.

'I *don't* believe in a man's sacrificing himself in this way,' said Kate. 'And I don't.'

Teresa still looked her full in the eyes.

'Ah!' she said. 'He doesn't sacrifice himself. He feels he must do as he does. And if he must, I must help him.'

'But then you are sacrificing yourself to *him*, and I don't believe in that either,' said Kate.

'Oh, no!' replied Teresa quickly, and a little flush burned in her cheek, and her dark eyes flashed. 'I am not sacrificing myself to Ramón. If I can give him – sleep – when he needs it – that is not sacrifice. It is –' She did not finish, but her eyes flashed, and the flush burned darker.

'It is love, I know,' said Kate. 'But it exhausts you too.'

'It is not simply love,' flashed Teresa proudly. 'I might have loved more than one man: many men are lovable. But Ramón! – My soul is with Ramón.' – The tears rose to her eyes. 'I do not want to talk about it,' she said, rising. 'But you must not touch me there, and judge me.'

She hurried out of the room, leaving Kate somewhat dismayed. Kate sighed, thinking of going home.

But in an hour Teresa appeared again, putting her cool, soft, snake-like little hand on Kate's arm.

'I am sorry if I was rude,' she said.

'No,' said Kate. 'Apparently it is I who am wrong.'

'Yes, I think you are,' said Teresa. 'You think there is only love. Love is only such a little bit.'

'And what is the rest?'

'How can I tell you if you do not know? – But do you think Ramón is no more to me than a lover?'

'A husband!' said Kate.

'Ah!' Teresa put her head aside with an odd impatience. 'Those little words! Those little words! Nor either a husband. – He is my life.'

'Surely it is better for one to live one's own life!'

'No! It is like seed. It is no good till it is given. I know. I kept my own life for a long time. As you keep it longer, it dies. And I tried to give it to God. But I couldn't, quite. Then they told me, if I married Ramón and had any part in the Quetzalcoatl heresy, my soul would be damned. – But something made me know it was not true. I even knew he needed my soul. – Ah, Señora –' a subtle smile came on Teresa's pale face – 'I have lost my soul to Ramón. – What more can I say!'

'And what about his soul?'

'It comes home to me – *here*!' She put her hand over her womb.

Kate was silent for a time.

'And if he betrays you?' she said.

'Ah, Señora!' said Teresa. 'Ramón is not just a lover. He is a brave man, and he doesn't betray his own blood. And it is his soul that comes home to me. – And I would struggle to my last breath to give him sleep, when he came home to me with his soul, and needed it,' she flashed. Then she added, murmuring to herself: 'No, thank God! I have not got a life of my own! I have been able to give it to a man who is more than a man, as they say in their Quetzalcoatl language. And now it needn't die inside me, like a bird in a cage. – Oh, yes, Señora! If he goes to Sinaloa and the west coast, my soul goes with him and takes part in it all. It does not let him go alone. And he does not forget that he has my soul with him. I know it. – No, Señora! You must not criticise me or pity me.'

'Still!' said Kate. 'It still seems to me it would be better for each one to keep her own soul, and be responsible for it.'

'If it were possible!' said Teresa. 'But you can no more keep your own soul inside you for yourself, without its dying, than you can keep the seed of your womb. Until a man gives you his seed, the seed of your womb is nothing. And the man's seed is nothing to him. – And until you give your soul to a man, and he takes it, your soul is nothing to you. – And when a man has taken your whole soul. – Ah, do not talk to me about betraying. A man only betrays because he has been given *a part*, and not the whole. And a woman only betrays because only the part has been taken from her, and not the whole. That is all about betrayal. I know. – But when the whole is given, and taken, betrayal can't exist. What I am to Ramón, I am. And what he is to me, he is. I do not care what he does. If he is away from me, he does as he wishes. So long as he will always keep safe what I am to him.'

Kate did not like having to learn lessons from this little waif of a Teresa. Kate was a woman of the world, handsome and experienced. She was accustomed to homage. Other women usually had a slight fear of her, for she was powerful and ruthless in her own way.

Teresa also feared her a little, as a woman of the world. But as an intrinsic woman, not at all. Trenched inside her own fierce and proud little soul, Teresa looked on Kate as on one of those women of the outside world, who make a very splendid show, but who are not so sure of the real secret of womanhood, and the innermost power. All Kate's handsome, ruthless female power was second-rate to Teresa, compared with her own quiet, deep passion of connection with Ramón.

Yes, Kate was accustomed to looking on other women as inferiors. But the tables were suddenly turned. Even as, in her soul, she knew Ramón to be a greater man than Cipriano, suddenly she had to question herself, whether Teresa was not a greater woman than she.

Teresa! A greater woman than Kate? What a blow! Surely it was impossible!

Yet there it was. Ramón had wanted to marry Teresa, not Kate. And the flame of his marriage with Teresa she saw both in his eyes and in Teresa's. A flame that was not in Kate's eyes.

Kate's marriage with Cipriano was curious and momentary. When Cipriano was away, Kate was her old individual self. Only when Cipriano was present, and then only sometimes, did the connection overwhelm her.

When Teresa turned and looked at her with this certain flame, touched with indignation, Kate quailed. Perhaps for the first time in her life she quailed and felt abashed: repentant.

Kate even knew that Teresa felt a little repugnance for her: for the foreign white woman who talked as cleverly as a man and who never gave her soul: who did not believe in giving her soul. All these well-dressed, beautiful women from America or England, Europe, they all kept their souls for themselves, in a sort of purse, as it were.

Teresa was determined that Kate should leave off treating her, very, very indefinably, as an inferior. It was how all the foreign women treated the Mexican women. Because the foreign women were their own mistresses! They even tried to be condescending to Ramón.

But Ramón! He could look at them and make them feel small, feel really nothing, in spite of all their money and their experience and their air of belonging to the ruling races. The ruling races! Wait! Ramón was a challenge to all that. Let those rule who can.

'You did not sleep?' Teresa said to Kate.

'Not very well,' said Kate.

'No, you look as if you had not slept very well. – Under your eyes.'

Kate smoothed the skin under her eyes, querulously.

'One gets that look in Mexico,' she said. 'It's not an easy country to keep your youth in. – You are looking well.'

'Yes, I am very well.'

Teresa had a new, soft bloom on her dark skin, something frail and tender, which she did not want to have to defend against another woman.

'I think I will go home now Ramón has come,' said Kate.

'Oh, why? Do you wish to?'

'I think I'd better.'

'Then I will go with you to Sayula. In the boat, no?'

Kate put her few things together. She had slept badly. The night had been black, black, with something of horror in it. As when the bandits had attacked Ramón. She could see the scar in his back, in the night. And the drumming crash of falling water, menacing and horrible, seemed to keep up for hours.

In her soul, Kate felt Teresa's contempt for her way of wifehood.

'I have been married too,' Kate had said. 'To a very exceptional man, whom I *loved*.'

'Ah, yes!' said Teresa. 'And he died.'

'He wanted to die.'

'Ah, yes! He wanted to die.'

'I did my level best to prevent him from wearing himself out.'

'Ah, yes, to prevent him.'

'What else could I have done?' flashed Kate in anger.

'If you could have given him your life, he would not even have wanted to die.'

'I *did* give him my life. I loved him – oh, you will never know. – But he didn't *want* my soul. He believed I should keep a soul of my own.'

'Ah, yes, men are like that, when they are merely men. When a man is *warm* and brave – then he wants the woman to give him her soul, and he keeps it in *his* womb, so he is more than a mere man, a single man. I know it. I know where my soul is. It is in Ramón's womb, the womb of a man, just as his seed is in my womb, the womb of a woman. He is a man, and a column of blood. I am a woman, and a valley of blood. I shall not contradict him. How can I? My soul is inside him, and I am far from contradicting him when he is trying with all his might to do something that *he* knows about. He won't die, and they won't kill him. No! The stream flows into him from the heart of the world: and from me. – I tell you, because you saved his life, and therefore we belong to the same thing, you and I and he – and

Cipriano. But you should not misjudge me. That other way of women, where a woman keeps her own soul – ah, what is it but weariness!'

'And the men?'

'Ah! if there are men whose souls are warm and brave, how they comfort one's womb, Caterina!'

Kate hung her head, stubborn and angry at being put down from her eminence. – The slave morale! she said to herself. The miserable old trick of a woman living just for the sake of a man. Only living to send her soul with him, inside his precious body. And to carry his precious seed in her womb! Herself, apart from this, nothing.

Kate wanted to make her indignation thorough, but she did not quite succeed. Somewhere, secretly and angrily, she envied Teresa her dark eyes with the flame in them and their savage assurance. She envied her her serpent-delicate fingers. And above all, she envied her, with repining, the comfort of a living man permanent in her womb. And the secret, savage indomitable pride in her own womanhood, that rose from this.

In the warm morning after the rain, the frogs were whirring frantically. Across the lake, the mountains were blue black, and little pieces of white, fluffy vapour wandered low across the trees. Clouds were along the mountain-tops, making a level sky-line of whitish softness the whole length of the range. On the lonely, fawn-coloured water, one sail was blowing.

'It is like Europe – like the Tyrol to-day,' said Kate wistfully.

'Do you love Europe very much?' asked Teresa.

'Yes, I think I love it.'

'And must you go back to it?'

'I think so. Soon! To my mother and my children.'

'Do they want you very much?'

'Yes!' said Kate, rather hesitant. Then she added: 'Not *very* much, really. But I want them.'

'What for? – I mean,' Teresa added, 'do you long for them?'

'Sometimes,' said Kate, the tears coming to her eyes.

The boat rowed on in silence.

'And Cipriano?' Teresa asked timidly.

'Ah!' said Kate shortly. 'He is such a stranger to me.'

Teresa was silent for some moments.

'I think a man is always a stranger to a woman,' said Teresa. 'Why should it not be so?'

'But you,' said Kate, 'haven't any children.'

'Ramón has. – And he says: "I cast my bread upon the waters. It is my children too. And if they return to me after many days, I shall be glad." – Is it not the same for you?'

'Not quite!' said Kate. 'I am a woman, I am not a man.'

'I, if I have children,' said Teresa, 'I shall try to cast my bread upon the waters, so my children come to me that way. I hope I shall. I hope I shall not try to fish them out of life for myself, with a net. I have a very great fear of love. It is so personal. Let each bird fly with its own wings, and each fish swim its own course. – Morning brings more than love. And I want to be true to the morning.'

CHAPTER XXVI

Kate Is a Wife

KATE was glad to get back to her own house, and to be more or less alone. She felt a great change was being worked in her, and if it worked too violently, she would die. It was the end of something, and the beginning of something, far, far inside her: in her soul and womb. The men, Ramón and Cipriano, caused the change, and Mexico. Because the time had come. – Nevertheless if what was happening happened too rapidly, or violently, she felt she would die. So, from time to time she had to withdraw from contact, to be alone.

She would sit alone for hours on the shore, under a green willow tree that hung its curtains of pale-green fronds, on the beach. The lake was much fuller and higher up the shore, softer, more mysterious. There was a smell of the piles of water-hyacinth decaying at the water's edges. Distance seemed farther away. The near conical hills were dotted with green bushes, like a Japanese drawing. Bullock-wagons with solid wheels came rolling to the village, high with sugar cane, drawn by eight oxen with ponderous heads and slowly swinging horns, while a peon walked in front, with the guiding-stick on the cross-beam of the yoke. So slow, so massive, yet with such slight control!

She had a strange feeling, in Mexico, of the old prehistoric humanity, the dark-eyed humanity of the days, perhaps, before the glacial period.[1] When the world was colder, and the seas emptier, and all the land-formation was different. When the waters of the world were piled in stupendous glaciers on the high places, and high, high upon the poles. When great plains stretched away to the oceans, like Atlantis and the lost continents of Polynesia, so that seas were only great lakes, and the soft, dark-eyed people of that world could walk around the globe. Then there was a mysterious, hot-blooded, soft-footed humanity with a strange civilisation of its own.

Till the glaciers melted, and drove the peoples to the high places, like the lofty plateaux of Mexico, separated them into cut-off nations.

Sometimes, in America, the shadow of that old pre-Flood world was so strong, that the day of historic humanity would melt out of Kate's consciousness, and she would begin to approximate to the old mode of consciousness, the old, dark will, the unconcern for death, the subtle, dark consciousness, non-cerebral, but vertebrate. When the mind and the power of man was in his blood and his back-bone, and there was the strange, dark inter-communication between man and man and man and beast, from the powerful spine.

The Mexicans were still this. That which is aboriginal in America still belongs to the way of the world before the Flood, before the mental-spiritual world came into being. In America, therefore, the mental-spiritual life of white people suddenly flourishes like a great weed let loose in virgin soil. Probably it will as quickly wither. A great death come. And after that, the living result will be a new germ, a new conception of human life, that will arise from the fusion of the old blood-and-vertebrate consciousness with the white man's present mental-spiritual consciousness. The sinking of both beings, into a new being.

Kate was more Irish than anything, and the almost deathly mysticism of the aboriginal Celtic or Iberian people lay at the bottom of her soul. It was a residue of memory, something that lives on from the pre-Flood world, and cannot be killed. Something older, and more ever-lastingly potent, than our would-be fair-and-square world.

She knew more or less what Ramón was trying to effect: this fusion! She knew what it was that made Cipriano more significant to her than all her past, her husbands and her children. It was the leap of the old, antediluvian blood-male into unison with her. And for this, without her knowing, her innermost blood had been thudding all the time.

Ireland would not and could not forget that other old, dark, sumptuous living. The Tuatha De Danaan[2] might be under the western sea. But they are under the living blood, too, never quite to be silenced. Now they have to come forth again, to a new connection. And the scientific, fair-and-square Europe has to mate once more with the old giants.

But the change, Kate felt, must not come on her too soon and too suddenly, or it would rupture her and she would die. The old way has its horror. The heavy-footed, *à terre* spirit of aboriginal Mexico could be so horrible to her, as to make her wicked. The slow, indomitable kind of existing and persisting, without hope or élan, which is in the aboriginal American, sometimes made her feel she would go mad. The sullen will persisting over the slow, dark centuries, counting the individual existence a trifle! A tenacity of demons, less than human. And a sudden ferocity, a sudden lust of death rousing incalculable and terrible.

People who never really changed. Men who were not faithful to life, to the living actuality. Faithful to some dark necessity out of the past. The actual present suddenly collapsing in the souls of the men and the women, and the old, black, volcanic lava bursting up in violence, followed by a lava-rock indifference.

The hope! The hope! Would it ever be possible to revive the hope in these black souls, and achieve the marriage which is the only step to the new world of man?

But meanwhile, a strange, almost torn nausea would come over Kate, and she felt she must go away, to spare herself. The strange, reptilian insistence of her very servants. *Blood is one blood. We are all of one blood-stream.* Something aboriginal and tribal, and almost worse than death to the white individual. Out of the dark eyes and the powerful spines of these people, all the time the unknown assertion: *The blood is one blood.* It was a strange, overbearing insistence, a claim of blood-unison.

Kate was of a proud old family. She had been brought up with the English-Germanic idea of the *intrinsic* superiority of the hereditary aristocrat. Her blood was different from the common blood, another, finer fluid.

But in Mexico, none of this. Her criada Juana, the aguador who carried the water, the boatman who rowed her on the lake, all looked at her with one look in their eyes. *The blood is one blood. In the blood, you and I are undifferentiated.* She saw it in their eyes, she heard it in their words, it tinged their deference and their mockery. And sometimes it made her feel physically sick: this overbearing blood-familiarity.

And sometimes, when she tried to hold herself up, in the proud old assertion: *My blood is my own. Noli me tangere,*[3] she would see the terrible ancient hatred in their eyes, the hatred which leads them to atrocities and fearful maimings.

They would defer to her spirit, her knowledge, her understanding. They would give her deference, and a sort of grudging reverence for this. She belonged to the ruling races, the clever ones. But back again they demanded her acquiescence to the primeval assertion: *The blood is one blood. We are one blood.* It was the assertion that swept away all individualism, and left her immersed, drowned in the grand sea of the living blood, in immediate contact with all these men and all these women.

To this she must submit. Or they would persist in the slow revenge.

And she could not submit, off-hand. It had to be a slow, organic process. Anything sudden or violent would destroy her.

Now she understood Ramón's assertion: Man is a column of blood: Woman is a valley of blood. It was the primeval oneness of mankind, the opposite of the oneness of the spirit.

But Kate had always looked upon her blood as absolutely her own, her individual own. Her spirit she shared, in the spirit she communed. But her blood stayed by her in individuality.

Now she was confronted by the other great assertion: The blood is one blood. — It meant a strange, marginless death of her individual self.

Now she understood why Ramón and Cipriano wore the white clothes and the sandals, and were naked, or half-naked, as living gods. It was the acquiescence in the primitive assertion. It was the renewal of the old, terrible bond of the blood-unison of man, which made blood-sacrifice so potent a factor of life. The blood of the individual is given back to the great blood-being, the god, the nation, the tribe.

Now she understood the strange unison she could always feel between Ramón and his men, and Cipriano and his men. It was the soft, quaking, deep communion of blood-oneness. Sometimes it made her feel sick. Sometimes it made her revolt. But it was the power she could not get beyond.

Because, admitting his blood-unison, Ramón at the same time claimed a supremacy, even a godliness. He was a man, as the lowest of his peons was a man. At the same time, rising from the same pool of blood, from the same roots of manhood as they, and being, as they were, a man of the pulsing blood, he was still something more. Not in the blood nor in the spirit lay his individuality and his supremacy, his godhead. But in a star within him, an inexplicable star which rose out of the dark sea and shone between the flood and the great sky. The mysterious star which unites the vast universal blood with the universal breath of the spirit, and shines between them both.

Not the rider on the white horse: nor the rider on the red. That which is beyond the riders and the horses, the inexplicable mystery of the star whence no horseman comes and to which no horseman can arrive. The star which is a man's innermost clue, which rules the power of the blood on the one hand, and the power of the spirit on the other.

For this, the only thing which is supreme above all power in a man, and at the same time, is power; which far transcends knowledge; the strange star between the sky and the waters of the first cosmos: this is man's divinity.

And some men are not divine at all. They have only faculties. They are slaves, or they should be slaves.

But many a man has his own spark of divinity, and has it quenched, blown out by the winds of force or ground out of him by machines.

And when the spirit and the blood in man begin to go asunder, bringing the great death, most stars die out.

Only the man of a great star, a great divinity, can bring the opposites together again, in a new unison.

And this was Ramón, and this was his great effort: to bring the great opposites into contact and into unison again. And this is the god-power in man. By this power you shall know the god in man. By none other.

Ramón was a man as the least of his peons was a man, with the beating heart and the secret loins and the lips closed on the same secret of manhood. And he was human as Kate was human, with the same yearning of the spirit, for pure knowledge and communion, the soul in the greatness of its comprehending.

But only he had that starry power for bringing together the two great human impulses to a point of fusion, for being the bird between the vast wings of the dual-created power to which man has access and in which man has his being. The Morning Star, between the breath of dawn and the deeps of the dark.

Men had tried to murder him with knives. Carlota would have murdered him with her spirit. Each half separately wanted to commit the murder of him.

But he kept himself beyond. He was the living Quetzalcoatl, and the tiny sparkle of a star was rising in his own men, in his own woman.

The star between the two wings of power: that alone was divinity in a man, and final manhood.

Kate had a message from Cipriano to say he was coming out to stay in the Villa Aragon. The Villa Aragon was the chief house on the lake, in small but rather beautiful grounds with tufts of palm-trees and heavy hedges of jasmine, a garden kept always green by constant watering. The house was built rather like a little castle, absurd, yet its deep, spacious verandahs opening on to the slopes and knolls of the tree-clustered garden, above the lake, were pleasant.

Cipriano arrived very pleased, his black eyes shining with the boyish look. He wanted Kate to marry him, go through the Mexican civil marriage, and install herself in the Villa Aragon. She hesitated. She knew she must go back to Europe, to England and Ireland, very soon. The necessity was imperative. The sense of menace that Mexico put over her, and the feeling of inner nausea, was becoming too much to bear. She felt she could not stand it, unless she went away to relax for a time.

This she told to Cipriano. And his face fell.

'It doesn't matter to me very much whether I marry or not, before I go,' she said. 'But I must go soon – soon.'

'How soon?'

'By January.'

His face lightened again.

'Then marry me before you go,' he said. 'Next week.'

She agreed, with curious indifference, and he, his eyes flashing again like a boy's, moved quickly, to make the necessary legal preparations.

She did not care whether she married or not. In one essential sense, she had married Cipriano already. He was first and foremost a soldier, swift to come to her, and swift to go. She would always be a good deal alone.

And him alone, just as a man and a soldier, she could marry easily enough. It was this terrible Mexico that frightened her with a sense of doom.

The Quetzalcoatl movement had spread in the country, but sinisterly. The Archbishop had declared against it, Ramón and Cipriano and their adherents were excommunicated. An attempt had been made to assassinate Montes.

The adherents of Quetzalcoatl in the capital had made the Church of San Juan Bautisto, which was called the Church of the Black Saviour, their Metropolitan House of Quetzalcoatl. The Archbishop, a choleric man, had summoned his fervent followers to march in procession to this Church of San Juan, now called the House of Quetzalcoatl, and seize it and restore it to the Catholic Church. The government, knowing it would have to fight sooner or later, arrested the Archbishop and broke up the procession after some bloodshed.

Then a kind of war began. The Knights of Cortés brought out their famous hidden stores of arms, not very impressive, after all, and a clerical mob, headed by a fanatical priest, surged into the Zócalo. Montes had the guns turned on them. But it looked like the beginnings of a religious war. In the streets the white and blue serapes of Quetzalcoatl and the scarlet and black serapes of Huitzilopochtli were seen in bands, marching to the sound of tom-toms, and holding up the curious round banners, made of feather-work, of Quetzalcoatl, and the tall scarlet signs of Huitzilopochtli, long poles with the soft club of scarlet feathers at the top, tufted with a black point. – In the churches, the priests were still inflaming the orthodox to a holy war. In the streets, priests who had gone over to Quetzalcoatl were haranguing the crowd.

It was a wild moment. In Zacatecas General Narciso Beltran had declared against Montes and for the Church. But Cipriano with his Huitzilopochtli soldiers had attacked with such swiftness and ferocity, Beltran was taken and shot, his army disappeared.

Then Montes declared the old Church illegal in Mexico, and caused a law to be passed, making the religion of Quetzalcoatl the national religion of the Republic. All churches were closed. All priests were compelled to take an oath of allegiance to the Republic, or condemned to exile.[4] The armies of Huitzilopochtli and the white and blue serapes of Quetzalcoatl appeared in all the towns and villages of the Republic. Ramón laboured ceaselessly. Cipriano appeared in unexpected flashes, in unexpected places. He managed to rouse the most discontented States, Vera Cruz, Tamaulipas, Yucatan, to a sort of religious frenzy. Strange baptisms took place in the sea, and a scarlet and black tower of Huitzilopochtli rose along the shores.

The whole country was thrilling with a new thing, with a release of new energy. But there was a sense of violence and crudity in it all, a touch of horror.

The Archbishop was deported, no more priests were seen in the streets. Only the white and blue and earth-coloured serapes of Quetzalcoatl, and the scarlet and black of Huitzilopochtli, were seen among the crowds. There was a great sense of release, almost of exuberance.

This is why Cipriano came to Kate with those black, flashing, boyish eyes. He was in a strange state of triumph. Kate was frightened, and she felt curiously hollow. Even the queer, new, flashing triumph and the sense of a new thing on the face of the earth could not quite save her. She belonged too much to the old world of Europe, she could not, could not make herself over so quickly. But she felt that if she could go back to Ireland, and let her life and her body *pause* for a time, then she could come back and take her share.

For it was not her spirit alone which was changing, it was her body, and the constitution of her very blood. She could feel it, the terrible katabolism and metabolism in her blood, changing her even as a creature, changing her to another creature.

And if it went too fast, she would die.

So, she was legally married to Cipriano, and she went to live with him in the Villa Aragon, for a month. After a month, she would sail away, alone, to Ireland. He agreed too.

It was strange, to be married to him. He made her go all vague and quiet, as if she sank away heavy and still, away from the surface of life, and lay deep in the under-life.

The strange, heavy, *positive* passivity. For the first time in her life she felt absolutely at rest. And talk, and thought, had become trivial, superficial to her: as the ripples on the surface of the lake are as nothing, to the creatures that live away below in the unwavering deeps.

In her soul, she was still and proud. If only the body had not suffered the unbearable nausea of change. She had sunk to a final rest, within a great, opened-out cosmos. The universe had opened out to her new and vast, and she had sunk to the deep bed of pure rest. She had become almost like Teresa in sureness.

Yet the process of change within her blood was terrible to her.

Cipriano was happy, in his curious Indian way. His eyes kept that flashing, black, dilated look of a boy looking newly on a strange, almost uncanny wonder of life. He did not look very definitely at Kate, or even take much definite notice of her. He did not like talking to her, in any serious way. When she wanted to talk seriously, he flashed a cautious, dark look at her, and went away.

He was aware of things that she herself was hardly conscious of. Chiefly, of the curious irritant quality of talk. And this he avoided. Curious as it may seem, he made her aware of her own old desire for frictional, irritant sensation. She realised how all her old love had been frictional, charged with the fire of irritation and the spasms of frictional voluptuousness.

Cipriano, curiously, by refusing to share any of this with her, made it become external to her. Her strange seething feminine will and desire subsided in her and swept away, leaving her soft and powerfully potent, like the hot springs of water that gushed up so noiseless, so soft, yet so powerful, with a sort of secret potency.

She realised, almost with wonder, the death in her of the Aphrodite of the foam:[5] the seething, frictional, ecstatic Aphrodite. By a swift dark instinct, Cipriano drew away from this in her. When, in their love, it came back on her, the seething electric female ecstasy, which knows such spasms of delirium, he recoiled from her. It was what she used to call her 'satisfaction'. She had loved Joachim for this, that again, and again, and again he could give her this orgiastic 'satisfaction', in spasms that made her cry aloud.

But Cipriano would not. By a dark and powerful instinct he drew away from her as soon as this desire rose again in her, for the white ecstasy of frictional satisfaction, the throes of Aphrodite of the foam. She could see that to him, it was repulsive. He just removed himself, dark and unchangeable, away from her.

And she, as she lay, would realise the worthlessness of this foam-effervescence, its strange externality to her. It seemed to come upon her from without, not from within. And succeeding the first moment of disappointment, when this sort of 'satisfaction' was denied her, came the knowledge that she did not really want it, that it was really nauseous to her.

And he, in his dark, hot silence would bring her back to the new, soft, heavy, hot flow, when she was like a fountain gushing noiseless and with urgent softness from the volcanic deeps. Then she was open to him soft and hot, yet gushing with a noiseless soft power. And there was no such thing as conscious 'satisfaction'. What happened was dark and untellable. So different from the beak-like friction of Aphrodite of the foam, the friction which flares out in circles of phosphorescent ecstasy, to the last wild spasm which utters the involuntary cry, like a death-cry, the final love-cry. This she had known, and known to the end, with Joachim. And now this too was removed from her. What she had with Cipriano was curiously beyond her knowing: so deep and hot and flowing, as it were subterranean. She had to yield before it.

She could not grip it into one final spasm of white ecstasy which was like sheer knowing.

And as it was in the love-act, so it was with him. She could not *know* him. When she tried to know him, something went slack in her, and she had to leave off. She had to let be. She had to leave him, dark and hot and potent, along with the things that *are*, but are not known. The presence. And the stranger. This he was always to her.

There was hardly anything to say to him. And there was no personal intimacy. He kept his privacy round him like a cloak, and left her immune within her own privacy. He was a stranger to her, she to him. He accepted the fact absolutely, as if nothing else were possible. She, sometimes, felt it strange. She had so craved for intimacy, *insisted* on intimacy.

Now she found herself accepting him finally and forever as the stranger in whose presence she lived. It was his impersonal presence which enveloped her. She lived in his aura, and he, she knew, lived in hers, with nothing said, and no personal or spiritual intimacy whatever. A mindless communion of the blood.

Therefore, when he had to go away, it did not matter so very much. His presence was something he left with her, and he took her presence along with him. And somehow, there was no need for emotions.

He had to leave early one morning, for Mexico. The dawn came perfect and clear. The sun was not yet on the lake, but it caught the mountains beyond Tuliapan, and they shone magically distinct, as if some magic light were focussed on them. The green furrows of the mountain-sides were as if in her own hand. Two white gulls, flying, suddenly got the light, and glittered. But the full, soft, noiseless dun lake was pallid, unlit.

She thought of the sea. The Pacific was not very far away. The sea seemed to have retreated entirely out of her consciousness. Yet she knew she needed its breath again.

Cipriano was going down to bathe. She saw him walk out on the masonry of the square basin which was their own tiny harbour. He threw off his wrap and stood dark in silhouette against the pale, unlit water. How dark he was! Dark as a Malay. Curious that his body was as dark, almost, as his face. And with that strange archaic fulness of physique, with the full chest and the full, yet beautiful buttocks of men on old Greek coins.

He dropped off the edge of masonry and waded out in the dim, soft, uncanny water. And at that moment the light tipped over the edge of the mountain and spilled gold upon the surface of the lake. And instantly he was red as fire. The sunshine was not red, the sun was too high for that. It was golden with morning. But as it flushed along the surface of the lake it caught the body of Cipriano and he was red as fire, as a piece of pure fire.

The Sons of the Morning! The column of blood! A Red Indian. She looked at him in wonder, as he moved pure red and luminous further into the lake, unconscious. As if on fire!

The Sons of the Morning! She let her effort at knowing slip away from her once more, and remained without effort, within the communion.

It was his race, too. She had noticed before how the natives shone pure red when morning or evening light caught them, rather level. As fires they stood in the water. The Red Indian.

He went away, with his man, on horseback. And she watched him ride over the brow of the road, sitting dark and still on his silky, roan horse. He loved a red horse. And there was a curious motionlessness about him as he rode horseback, an old, male pride, and at the same time the half-ghostly, dark invisibility of the Indian, sitting close upon the horse as if he and it belonged to one birth.

He was gone, and for a while she felt the old nostalgia for his presence. Not for him, exactly. Not even to see him or touch him or speak to him. Only to feel him about.

Then quickly she recovered. She adjusted herself to the presence he left behind with her. As soon as he had *really* gone, and the act of going was over, his presence came back to her.

She walked a little while by the shore, beyond the breakwater wall. She loved to be alone: a great deal alone, with a garden and the lake and the morning.

'I am like Teresa, really,' she said to herself.

Suddenly before her she saw a long, dark soft rope, lying over a pale boulder. But her soul was softly alert, at once. It was a snake, with a subtle pattern along its soft dark back, lying there over a big stone, with its head sunk down to earth.

It felt her presence, too, for suddenly, with incredible soft quickness, it contracted itself down the boulder, and she saw it entering a little gap in the bottom of the wall.

The hole was not very big. And as it entered it quickly looked back, poising its little, dark, wicked, pointed head, and flickering a dark tongue. Then it passed on, slowly easing its dark length into the hole.

When it had all gone in, Kate could see the last fold still, and the flat little head resting on the fold, like the devil with his chin on his arms, looking out of a loop-hole. So the wicked sparks of the eyes looked out at her, from within the recess. Watching out of its own invisibility.

So she wondered over it, as it lay in its hidden places. At all the unseen things in the hidden places of the earth. And she wondered if it was disappointed at not being able to rise higher in creation: to be able to run on four feet, and not keep its belly on the ground.

Perhaps not! Perhaps it had its own peace. She felt a certain reconciliation between herself and it.

CHAPTER XXVII

Here!

SHE and Teresa visited one another along the lake. There was a kinship and a gentleness between them, especially now Kate was going away for a while.

There was a certain autumnal purity and lull on the lake. The moisture still lingered, the bushes on the wild hills were green in puffs. Sunlight lay in a rich gleam on the mountains, and shadows were deep and velvety. The green almost covered the rocks and the pinkish land. Bright green the sugar cane, red the ploughed earth, dark the trees with white specks of villages here and there. And over the wild places, a sprinkle of bushes, then stark grey rock still coming out.

The sky was very high and pure. In the morning came the sound of drums, and on the motionless, crystal air the cry for the pauses of the day. And always the day seemed to be pausing and unfolding again to the greater mystery. The universe seemed to have opened vast and soft and delicate with life.

There was something curiously soothing even in the full, pale, dove-brown water of the lake. A boat was coming over, with its sail hollowed out like a shell, pearly white, and its sharp black canoe-beak slipping past the water. It looked like the boat of Dionysos coming with a message, and the vine sprouting.[1]

Kate could hardly remember now the dry rigid pallor of the heat, when the whole earth seemed to crepitate viciously with dry malevolence: like memory gone dry and sterile, hellish.

Ramón and Teresa came along the lake, and rowed into the basin. It was a morning when the shadows on the mountains were almost corn-flower blue.

'Yet you must go away?' Ramón said to her.

'For a little while. You don't think I am Lot's wife,[2] do you?'

'No!' laughed Ramón. 'I think you're Cipriano's.'

'I am really. But I want to go back for a little while.'

'Ah yes! Better go and then come again. Tell them in your Ireland to do as we have done here.'

'But how?'

'Let them find themselves again, and their own universe, and their own gods. Let them substantiate their own mysteries. The Irish have been so wordy about their far-off heroes and green days of the heroic gods. Now tell them to substantiate them, as we have tried to substantiate Quetzalcoatl and Huitzilopochtli.'

'I will tell them,' she said. 'If there is anybody to listen.'

'Yes!' he said.

He watched the white sail blowing nearer.

'But why do you go away?' he asked her, after a silence.

'You don't care, do you?' she said.

There was a dead pause.

'Yes, I care,' he said.

'But why?'

Again it was some time before he answered.

'You are one of us, we need you,' he said.

'Even when I don't do anything? – and when I get a bit bored with living Quetzalcoatls – and the rest, and wish for a simple Don Ramón?' she replied.

He laughed suddenly.

'What is a simple Don Ramón?' he said. 'A simple Don Ramón has a living Quetzalcoatl inside him. But you help all the same.'

'You go ahead so grandly, one would not think you needed help: especially from a mere woman who – who after all is only the wife of your friend.'

They were sitting on a bench under a red-flowering poinsettia whose huge scarlet petal-leaves spread out like sharp plumes.

'The wife of my friend!' he said. 'What could you be better?'

'Of course,' she said, more than equivocal.

He was leaning his arms on his knees, and looking out to the lake, abstract, and remote. There was a certain worn look on his face, and the vulnerability which always caught at Kate's heart. She realised again the isolation and the deadly strain his effort towards a new way of life put upon him. Yet he had to do it.

This again gave her a feeling of helplessness, a woman's utter helplessness with a man who goes out to the beyond. She had to stifle her resentment, and her dislike of his 'abstract' efforts.

'Do you feel awfully sure of yourself?' she said.

'Sure of myself?' he re-echoed. 'No! Any day I may die and disappear from the face of the earth. I not only know it, I *feel* it. So why should I be sure of *myself*?'

'Why should you die?' she said.

'Why should anybody ever die? – even Carlota!'

'Ah! – her hour had come!'

'Can you set one's hour as one sets an alarm clock?'

Kate paused.

'And if you're not sure of yourself, what are you sure of?' she challenged.

He looked at her with dark eyes which she could not understand.

'I am sure – sure –' his voice tailed off into vagueness, his face seemed to go grey and peaked, as a dead man's, only his eyes watched her blackly, like a ghost's. Again she was confronted with the suffering ghost of the man. And she was a woman, powerless before this suffering ghost which was still in the flesh.

'You don't think you are wrong, do you?' she asked, in cold distress.

'No! I am not wrong. Only maybe I can't hold out,' he said.

'And then what?' she said, coldly.

'I shall go my way, alone.' There seemed to be nothing left of him but the black, ghostly eyes that gazed on her. He began to speak Spanish.

'It hurts me in my soul, as if I were dying,' he said.

'But why?' she cried. 'You are not ill?'

'I feel as if my soul were coming undone.'

'Then don't let it,' she cried, in fear and repulsion.

But he only gazed with those fixed, blank eyes. A sudden deep stillness came over her; a sense of power in herself.

'You should forget for a time,' she said gently, compassionately laying her hand on his. What was the good of trying to understand him or wrestle with him? She was a woman. He was a man, and – and – and therefore not quite real. Not true to life.

He roused himself suddenly from her touch, as if he had come awake, and he looked at her with keen, proud eyes. Her motherly touch had roused him like a sting.

'Yes!' he said. 'It is true!'

'Of course it is!' she replied. 'If you want to be so – so abstract and Quetzalcoatlian, then bury your head sometimes, like an ostrich in the sand, and forget.'

'So!' he said, smiling. 'You are angry again!'

'It's not so simple,' she said. 'There is a conflict in me. And you won't let me go away for a time.'

'We can't even prevent you,' he said.

'Yes, but you are against my going – you don't let me go in peace.'

'Why must you go?' he said.

'I must,' she said. 'I must go back to my children, and my mother.'

'It is a necessity in you?' he said.

'Yes!'

The moment she had admitted the necessity, she realised it was a certain duplicity in herself. It was as if she had two selves: one, a new one, which belonged to Cipriano and to Ramón, and which was her sensitive, desirous self: the other hard and finished, accomplished, belonging to her mother, her children, England, her whole past. This old accomplished self was curiously invulnerable and insentient, curiously hard and 'free'. In it, she was an individual and her own mistress. The other self was vulnerable, and organically connected with Cipriano, even with Ramón and Teresa, and so was not 'free' at all.

She was aware of a duality in herself, and she suffered from it. She could not definitely commit herself, either to the old way of life, or to the new. She reacted from both. The old was a prison, and she loathed it. But in the new way she was not her own mistress at all, and her egoistic will recoiled.

'That's just it!' she said. 'It *is* a necessity in me, and you want to prevent me.'

'No! No!' said Ramón. 'I hope not.'

'Yes! You put a weight on me, and paralyse me, to prevent me from going,' she said.

'We must not do that,' he said. 'We must leave you, and not come near you for a time, if you feel it is so.'

'Why? Why can't you be friendly? Why can't you be *with* me in my going? Why can't you *want* me to go, since I must go?'

He looked at her with dispassionate eyes.

'I can't do that,' he said. 'I don't believe in your going. It is a turning back: there is something renegade in it. – But we are all complicated. And if you *feel* you must go back for a time, go! It isn't terribly important. You have chosen, really. I am not afraid for you.'

It was a great relief to her to hear this: because she was terribly afraid for herself. She could never be sure, never be *whole* in her connection with Cipriano and Ramón. Yet she said, mocking slightly:

'Why *should* you be afraid for me?'

'Aren't you sometimes afraid for yourself?' he asked.

'Never!' she said. 'I'm absolutely sure about myself.'

They had been sitting in the garden of the Villa Aragon, under the poinsettia tree with the huge scarlet petal-leaves, like soft red quill feathers. The morning was becoming hot. The lake had gone still, with the fallen wind. Everything was still. Save the long scarlet of the poinsettia.

Christmas was coming! The poinsettia reminded Kate of it.

Christmas! Holly-berries! England! Presents! Food! – If she hurried, she could be in England for Christmas. It felt so safe, so familiar, so normal, the thought of Christmas at home, in England, with her mother. And all the exciting things she could tell to the people at home! And all the exciting gossip she could hear! In the distance, it looked very attractive. – She still had a qualm as to what the actual return would be like.

'One can have too much of a good thing,' she said to Ramón.

'What good thing in particular?' he asked her.

'Oh – Quetzalcoatl and all that!' she said. 'One can have too much of it.'

'It may be,' he said, rising and going quietly away; so quietly, he was gone before she knew. And when she realised he had gone like that, she flushed with anger. But she sat on under the poinsettia tree, in the hot, still November sun, looking with anger at the hedge of jasmine, with its pure white flowers, and its sere, withered flowers, and its pinkish buds among the dark leaves. Where had she heard something about jasmine? 'And the jasmine flowers between us!'

Oh! how tired she was of all that!

Teresa came down the garden slope.

'You are still sitting here?' she exclaimed.

'Where else should I be?' Kate answered.

'I don't know. – Ramón has gone to Sayula, to see the Jefe. He wouldn't wait for us, to come with us in the boat.'

'I suppose he was in a hurry,' said Kate.

'How fine these Noche Buenas are!' said Teresa, looking at the brilliant spread of the red poinsettias.

'They are your Christmas flower, aren't they?' said Kate.

'Yes – the flowers of the Noche Buena –'

'How awful, Christmas with hibiscus and poinsettia! It makes me long to see mistletoe among the oranges, in a fruiterer's shop in Hampstead.'

'Why that?' laughed Teresa.

'Oh!' Kate sighed petulantly. 'To get back to simple life. To see the buses rolling on the mud in Piccadilly, on Christmas Eve, and the wet pavements crowded with people under the brilliant shops.'

'Is that life, to you?' asked Teresa.

'Yes! Without all this abstraction, and *will*. Life is good enough for me if I am allowed to live and be myself.'

'It is time Cipriano should come home,' said Teresa.

But this made Kate rise from her seat, with sudden impatience. She would not have this thing put over her! She would break free, and show them!

She went with Teresa to the village. The air seemed mysteriously alive, with a new Breath. But Kate felt out of it. The two women sat under a tree on the beach at Sayula, talking a little, and watching the full expanse of the dove-pale lake.

A black boat with a red-painted roof and a tall mast was moored to the low breakwater-wall, which rose about a yard high, from the shallow water. On the wall stood loose little groups of white-clad men, looking into the black belly of the ship. And perched immobile in silhouette against the lake, was a black-and-white cow, and a huge monolithic black-and-white bull. The whole silhouette frieze motionless, against the far water that was coloured brown like turtle doves.

It was near, yet seemed strange and remote. Two peons fixed a plank gangway up to the side of the boat. Then they began to shove the cow towards it. She pawed the new broad planks tentatively, then, with that slow Mexican indifference, she lumbered unwillingly on to the gangway. They edged her slowly to the end, where she looked down into the boat. And at last, she dropped neatly into the hold.

Now the group of men broke into motion, for the huge and spangled bull. A tall old Mexican, in fawn, skin-tight trousers and little leather jacket, and a huge felt hat heavily embroidered with silver, gently took the ring in the bull's nose, gently lifted the wedge of the bull's head, so the great soft throat was uplifted. A peon behind put his head down, and with all his might began shoving the mighty, living flanks of the bull. The slim-legged, high-hatted old Mexican pulled evenly at the nose-ring. And with a calm and weighty poise, the bull stepped along the crest of the wall, delicately and impassively, to the plank gangway. There he stopped.

The peons began to re-group. The one behind, with his red sash tied so determinedly over his white hips, ceased to shove, the slim-legged Mexican let go the ring.

Then two peons passed a rope loosely round the haunches of the bull. The high-hatted farmer stepped on to the planks, and took the nose-ring again, very gently. He pulled softly. The bull lifted its head, but held back. It struck the planks with an unwilling foot. Then it stood, spangled with black on its whiteness, like a piece of the sky, immobile.

The farmer pulled once more at the ring. Two men were pulling the rope, pressing in the flanks of the immovable, passive, spangled monster. Two peons, at the back, with their heads down and their red-sashed, flexible loins thrust out behind, shoved with all their strength in the soft flanks of the mighty creature.

And all was utterly noiseless and changeless; against the fulness of the pale lake, this silent, monumental group of life.

Then the bull stepped slowly, imperturbably, yet against its will, on to the loose planks, and was edged slowly along, to the brink of the boat. There he waited.

He stood huge and silvery, dappled like the sky, with black snake markings down his haunches, looming massive above the red roof of the *canoa*. How would he ever duck to that roof, and drop under, into the darkness of the ship?

He lowered his head, and looked into the hold. The men behind shoved his living flanks. He took no heed, but lowered his head and looked again. The men pushed with all their might, in the dense Mexican silence.

Slowly, carefully, the bull crouched himself, made himself small, and with a quick, massive little movement dropped his forefeet down into the body of the boat, leaving his huge hind-quarters heaved up behind. There was a shuffle and a little stagger down below, then the soft thud as his hind-feet leaped down. He had gone.

The planks were taken away. A peon ran to unfasten the mooring rope from the stones of the shore. There was a strange thudding of soft feet within the belly of the boat. Men in the water were pushing the ship's black stern, to push her off. But she was heavy. Slowly, casually they pulled the stones from under her flat bottom, and flung them aside. Slowly she edged, swayed, moved a little, and was afloat.

The men climbed in. The two peons on the ship's rims were poling her out, pressing their poles and walking heavily till they reached the stern, then lifting their poles and running to the high prow. She slid slowly out, on to the lake.

Then quickly they hoisted the wide white sail. The sail thrust up her horn and curved in a whorl to the wind. The ship was going across the waters, with her massive, sky-spangled cargo of life invisible.

All so still and soft and remote.

'And will Ramón want you to sit beside him in the church as the bride of Quetzalcoatl – with some strange name?' Kate asked of Teresa.

'I don't know,' said Teresa. 'Later, he says, when the time comes for them to have a goddess.'

'And will you mind?'

'For myself, I am afraid of it. But I understand that Ramón wants it. He says it is accepting the greater responsibility of one's existence. And I think that is true. If there is God in me, and God as woman, then I must accept this part of myself also, and put on the green dress, and be for the time the God-woman, since it is true of me also. I think it is true. Ramón says we must make it manifest. When I think of my brothers, I know we must. So I shall think of the God that beats invisible, like the heart of all the world. So when I have to wear the green dress, and sit before all the people in the church, I shall look away to the heart of all the world, and try to be my sacred self, because it is necessary, and the right thing to do. It is right. I would not do it if I thought it was not right.'

'But I thought the green dress was for the Bride of Huitzilopochtli!' said Kate.

'Ah yes!' Teresa caught herself up. 'Mine is the black dress with the white edges, and the red clouds.'

'Would you rather have the green?' Kate asked. 'Have it if you would. I am going away.'

Teresa glanced up at her quickly.

'The green is for the wife of Huitzilopochtli,' she said, as if numbed.

'I can't see that it matters,' said Kate.

Teresa looked at her with quick, dark eyes.

'Different men must have different wives,' she said. 'Cipriano would never want a wife like me.'

'And different women must have different husbands,' said Kate. 'Ramón would always be too abstract and overbearing for me.'

Teresa flushed slowly, looking down at the ground.

'Ramón needs far too much submission from a woman, to please me,' Kate added. 'He takes too much upon himself.'

Teresa looked up quickly, and raised her head proudly, showing her brownish throat like a rearing, crested snake.

'How do you know that Ramón needs submission from a woman?' she said. 'How do you know? He has not asked any submission from you. – And you are wrong. He does not ask submission from me. He wants me to give myself gently to him. And then he gives himself back to me far more gently than I give myself to him. Because a man like that is more gentle than a woman. He is not like Cipriano. Cipriano is a soldier. But Ramón is gentle. You are mistaken in what you say.'

Kate laughed a little.

'And you are a soldier among women, fighting all the time,' Teresa continued. 'I am not such. But some women must be soldiers in their spirit, and they need soldier husbands. That is why you are Malintzi, and your dress is green. You would always fight. You would fight with yourself, if you were alone in the world.'

It was very still by the lake. They were waiting for Ramón.

A man was stripping palm-stalks, squatting in silence under a tree, in his white clothes, his black head bent forward. Then he went to wet his long strips in the lake, returning with them dangling.

Then he sat down again, and deftly, silently, with the dark, childlike absorption of the people, took up his work. He was mending a chair bottom. When Kate watched him, he glanced up with a flash of black eyes, saluting her. And she felt a strange power surge in her limbs, from the flash of living recognition and deference in his eyes. As if his deference were a sort of flame of life, rich in him when he saw her.

A roan horse speckled with white was racing prancing along the shore, neighing frantically. His mane flowed in the wind, his feet struck the pebbles as he ran, and again he opened his long nose and neighed anxiously. Away up the shore he ran. What had he lost?

A peon had driven a high-wheeled wagon, drawn by four mules, deep into the lake, till the water was above the high axles of the wheels, almost touching the bed of the cart. It looked like a dark square boat drawn by four soft, dark sea-horses which slowly waved their long dark ears like leaves, while the peon, in white with his big hat proudly balanced, stood erect. The mules deep in the water stepped gently, curving to the shore.

It was winter, but like spring by the lake. White and yellow calves, new and silky, were skipping, butting up their rear ends, lifting their tails, trotting side by side down to the water, to sniff at it suspiciously.

In the shadow of a great tree a mother-ass was tethered, and her foal lay in the shadow, a little thing black as ink, curled up, with fluffy head erect and great black ears spreading up, like some jet-black hare full of witch-craft.

'How many days?' called Kate to the peon, who had come out of the straw hut.

He gave her the flash of his dark eyes, in a sort of joy of deference. And she felt her breast surge with living pride.

'Last night, *Patrona*!' he smiled in answer.

'So new! So new! He doesn't get up, can't he?'

The peon went round, put his arm under the foal and lifted it to its feet. There it straddled on high, in amaze, upon its black legs like bent hair-pins.

'How nice it is!' cried Kate in delight, and the peon laughed at her with a soft, grateful flame, touched with reverence.

The ink-black ass-foal did not understand standing up. It rocked on its four loose legs, and wondered. Then it hobbled a few steps, to smell at some green, growing maize. It smelled and smelled and smelled, as if all the dark aeons were stirring awake in its nostrils.

Then it turned, and looked with its bushy-velvet face straight at Kate, and put out a pink tongue at her. She laughed aloud. It stood wondering, dazed. Then it put out its tongue again. She laughed at it. It gave an awkward little skip, which surprised its own self very much. Then it ventured forward again, and all unexpectedly even to itself, exploded into another little skip.

'Already it dances!' cried Kate. 'And it came into the world only last night.'

'Yes, already it dances!' reiterated the peon.

After bethinking itself for a time, the ass-foal walked uncertainly towards the mother. She was a well-liking grey-and-brown she-ass, rather glossy and self-assured. The ass-foal straight found the udder, and was drinking.

Glancing up, Kate met again the peon's eyes, with their black, full flame of life heavy with knowledge and with a curious re-assurance. The black foal, the mother, the drinking, the new life, the mystery of the shadowy battlefield of creation; and the adoration of the full-breasted, glorious woman beyond him: all this seemed in the primitive black eyes of the man.

'Adiós!' said Kate to him, lingeringly.

'Adiós, Patrona!' he replied, suddenly lifting his hand high, in the Quetzalcoatl salute.

She walked across the beach to the jetty, feeling the life surging vivid and resistant within her. 'It is sex,' she said to herself. 'How wonderful sex can be, when men keep it powerful and sacred, and it fills the world! Like sunshine through and through one! – But I'm not going to submit, even there. Why should one give in, to anything!'

Ramón was coming down towards the boat, the blue symbol of Quetzalcoatl in his hat. And at that moment the drums began to sound for mid-day, and there came the mid-day call, clear and distinct, from the tower. All the men on the shore stood erect, and shot up their right hands to the sky. The women spread both palms to the light. Everything was motionless, save the moving animals.

Then Ramón went on to the boat, the men saluting him with the Quetzalcoatl salute as he came near.

'It is wonderful, really,' said Kate, as they rowed over the water, 'how – how splendid one can feel in this country! As if one were still genuinely of the nobility.'

'Aren't you?' he said.

'Yes, I am. But everywhere else it is denied. Only here one feels the full force of one's nobility. The natives still worship it.'

'At moments,' said Ramón. 'Later, they will murder you and violate you, for having worshipped you.'

'Is it inevitable?' she said flippantly.

'I think so,' he replied. 'If you lived here alone in Sayula, and queened it for a time, you would get yourself murdered – or worse – by the people who had worshipped you.'

'I don't think so,' she said.

'I know,' he replied.

'Why?' she said, obstinate.

'Unless one gets one's nobility from the gods and turns to the middle of the sky for one's power, one will be murdered at last.'

'I do get my nobility that way,' she said.

But she did not quite believe it. And she made up her mind still more definitely, to go away.

She wrote to Mexico City, and engaged a berth from Vera Cruz to Southampton: she would sail on the last day of November. Cipriano came home on the seventeenth, and she told him what she had done. He looked at her with his head a little on one side, with a queer boyish judiciousness, but she could not tell at all what he felt.

'You are going already?' he said in Spanish.

And then she knew, at last, that he was offended. When he was offended he never spoke English at all, but spoke Spanish just as if he were addressing another Mexican.

'Yes,' she said. 'On the thirtieth.'

'And when do you come back?' he asked.

'Quién sabe! – Who knows!' she retorted.

He let his black eyes rest on her face for some minutes, watching her, unchanging and incomprehensible. He was thinking, superficially, that if he liked, he could use the law and have her prevented from leaving the country – or even from leaving Sayula – since she was legally married to him. There was the old fixity of Indian anger, glinting fixed and relentless in the depths of his eyes. And then the almost invisible change in his face, as the hidden emotion sank down and the stoic indifference, the emotionlessness of centuries, and the stoic kind of tolerance came over him. She could almost feel the waves of successive shadow and coldness go through his blood, his mind hardly aware at all. And again a fear of losing his contact melted her heart.

It was somehow, to her, beautiful, to feel shadows, and cold gleams, and a hardness like stone, then the strange heavy inertia of the tropical mid-day, the stupor of the sun, moving upon him while he stood motionless, watching her. In the end it was that weird, sultry, tropical stupor of the hot hours, a heat-swoon of sheer indifference.

'Como quieres tu!' he said. 'As you wish.'

And she knew he had already released her, in the dark, sultry stupor of his blood. He would make no further effort after her. This also was the doom of his race.

He took a boat and went down to Jamiltepec, to Ramón: as she knew he would.

She was alone, as usual. It occurred to her, that she herself willed this aloneness. She could not relax and be with these people. She could not relax and be with anybody. She always had to recoil upon her own individuality, as a cat does.

Sex, sexual correspondence, did it matter so very much to her? It might have mattered more, if she had not had it. But she had had it – and very finally and consummately, with Cipriano. So she knew all about it. It was as if she had conquered another territory, another field of life. The conqueress! And now she would retire to the lair of her own individuality, with the prey.

Suddenly, she saw herself as men often saw her: the great cat, with its spasms of voluptuousness and its lifelong lustful enjoyment of its own isolated, isolated individuality. Voluptuously to enjoy a contact. Then with a lustful feline gratification, to break the contact, and roam alone in a sense of power. Each time, to seize a sort of power, purring upon her own isolated individuality.

She knew so many women like that. They played with love and intimacy as a cat with a mouse. In the end, they quickly ate up the love mouse, then trotted off with a full belly and a voluptuous sense of power.

Only sometimes the love-mouse refused to be digested, and there was life-long dyspepsia. Or, like Cipriano, turned into a sort of serpent, that reared and looked at her with glittering eyes, then slid away into the void, leaving her blank, the sense of power gone out of her.

Another thing, she had observed, with a touch of horror. One after the other, her women 'friends', the powerful love-women, at the age of forty, forty-five, fifty, they lost all their charm and allure, and turned into real grimalkins,[3] greyish, avid, and horrifying, prowling around looking for prey that became scarcer and scarcer. As human beings they went to pieces. And they remained these grey-ribbed grimalkins, dressed in elegant clothes, the grimalkin howl even passing into their smart chatter.

Kate was a wise woman, wise enough to take a lesson.

It is all very well for a woman to cultivate her ego, her individuality.

It is all very well for her to despise love, or to love love as a cat loves a mouse, that it plays with as long as possible, before devouring it to vivify her own individuality and voluptuously fill the belly of her own ego.

'Woman has suffered far more from the suppression of her ego than from sex suppression,' says a woman writer, and it may well be true. But look, only look at the modern women of fifty and fifty-five, those who have cultivated their ego to the top of their bent! Usually, they are grimalkins to fill one with pity or with repulsion.

Kate knew all this. And as she sat alone in her villa, she remembered it again. She had had her fling, even here in Mexico. And these men would let her go again. She was no prisoner. She could carry off any spoil she had captured.

And then what! To sit in a London drawing-room, and add another to all the grimalkins? To let the peculiar grimalkin-grimace come on her face, the most weird grimalkin-twang come into her voice? Horror! Of all the horrors, perhaps the grimalkin women, her contemporaries, were the most repellent to her. Even the horrid old tom-cat men of the civilised roof gutters, did not fill her with such sickly dread.

'No!' she said to herself. 'My ego and my individuality are not worth *that* ghastly price. I'd better abandon some of my ego, and sink some of my individuality, rather than go like that.'

After all, when Cipriano touched her caressively, all her body flowered. That was the greater sex, that could fill all the world with lustre, and which she dared not think about, its power was so much greater than her own will. But on the other hand when she spread the wings of her own ego, and sent forth her own spirit, the world could look very wonderful to her, when she was alone. But after a while, the wonder faded, and a sort of jealous emptiness set in.

'I must have both,' she said to herself. 'I must not recoil against Cipriano and Ramón, they make my blood blossom in my body. I say they are limited. But then one must be limited. If one tries to be unlimited, one becomes horrible. Without Cipriano to touch me and limit me and submerge my will, I shall become a horrible, elderly female. I ought to *want* to be limited. I ought to be *glad* if a man will limit me with a strong will and a warm touch. Because what I call my greatness, and the vastness of the Lord behind me, lets me fall through a hollow floor of nothingness, once there is no man's hand there, to hold me warm and limited. Ah yes! Rather than become elderly and a bit grisly, I will make my submission; as far as I need, and no further.'

She called a man-servant, and set off down the lake in a row-boat. It was a very lovely November morning, the world had not yet gone dry again. In the sharp folds of the steep mountain slopes to the north-east, the shadows were pure corn-flower blue. Below was the lingering delicacy of green, already drying. The lake was full still, but subsided, and the water-hyacinths had drifted away. Birds flew low in the still-ness. It was very full and still, in the strong, hot light. Some maize-fields showed sere stubble, but the palo-blanco flowers were out, and the mesquite bushes were frail green, and there were wafts of perfume from the little yellow flower-balls, like cassia.

'Why should I go away!' said Kate. 'Why should I see the buses on the mud of Piccadilly, on Christmas Eve, and the crowds of people on the wet pavements, under the big shops like great caves of light? I may as well stay here, where my soul is less dreary. I shall have to tell Ramón I am sorry for the things I said. I won't carp at them. After all, there is another kind of vastness here, with the sound of drums, and the cry of Quetzalcoatl.'

Already she could see the yellow and reddish, tower-like upper storey of Jamiltepec, and the rich, deep fall of magenta bougainvillea, from the high wall, with the pale spraying of plumbago flowers, and many loose creamy-coloured roses.

'Están tocando!'⁴ said her boatman quietly, looking up at her with dark, pregnant eyes.

He had heard already the sound of the light drum, at Jamiltepec. The boat rowed softly: and there came a sound of a man's voice singing in the morning.

Her boatman lifted an oar, as a signal to the house. And as the boat rounded the curve into the basin, a man-servant in white clothes came running down to the little jetty. In the changeless sunshine was a scent, perhaps of datura and of roses, and an eternal Mexican silence, which the noise of the drum, and the voice of singing, did not disturb.

'Is Don Cipriano here?' asked Kate.

'Está!' murmured the man, with a slight motion towards Ramón's balcony, whence the singing came. 'Shall I say you have come?'

He did not lift his voice above the murmur.

'No!' said Kate. 'I shall sit here in the garden a while, before I come up.'

'Then I will leave open the door,' said the man, 'and you can come up when you will.'

Kate sat on a seat under a big tree. A creeping plant, with great snake-like cords, and big sulphur-and-brown trumpet flowers, hung above. She listened to the singing. It was Ramón, teaching one of the singers.

Ramón had not a very good voice. He sang quietly, as if to the inner air, with very beautiful, simple expression. But Kate could not catch the words.

'Ya?' said Ramón, when he had finished.

'Ya, Patrón!' said the man, the singer.

And he began, in his strong, pure voice that caught at the very bowels, to sing another of the Hymns.

> 'My way is not thy way, and thine is not mine.
> But come, before we part
> Let us separately go to the Morning Star,
> And meet there.
>
> I do not point you to my road, nor yet
> Call: "Oh come!"
> But the Star is the same for both of us,
> Winsome.
>
> The good ghost of me goes down the distance
> To the Holy Ghost.
> Oh you, in the tent of the cloven flame
> Meet me, you I like most.
>
> Each man his own way forever, but towards
> The hoverer between;
> Who opens his flame like a tent-flap,
> As we slip in unseen.
>
> A man cannot tread like a woman,
> Nor a woman step out like a man.
> The ghost of each through the leaves of shadow
> Moves as it can.
>
> But the Morning Star and the Evening Star
> Pitch tents of flame
> Where we foregather like gypsies, none knowing
> How the other came.

I ask for nothing except to slip
In the tent of the Holy Ghost
And be there in the house of the cloven flame,
Guest of the Host.

Be with me there, my woman,
Be bodily there.
Then let the flame wrap round us
Like a snare.

Be there along with me, O men!
Reach across the hearth,
And laugh with me while the woman rests
For all we are worth.'

The man had sung this hymn over several times, halting and forgetting, his pure, burning voice faltering out; then the low, rather husky voice of Ramón, with a subtler intensity, coming in, as if heard from the centre of a shell; then again the sudden ripping sound of the true singer's tenor, going like a flame through the blood.

Her mozo, a man-servant, had followed her into the garden, and sat at a distance on his heels, under a tree, with his back to the trunk, like a crouching shadow clothed in white. His toes spread dark and hard, in his open huaraches, and the black braid of his hat-string hung against his dark cheek. For the rest he was pure white, the white cotton tight on his thighs.

When the singing had finished above, and the drum was silent, and even the voices speaking in low tones were silent, her mozo looked up at Kate, with his black hat-string dangling at his chin, his black eyes shining, and a timid sort of smile on his face.

'Está muy bien, Patrona?' he said shyly. 'It is good, isn't it, Mistress?'

'It is very good,' she replied, with the infallible echo. But there were conflicting feelings in her breast, and the man knew it.

He looked so young, when he smiled that gay, shy, excited little smile. Something of the eternal child in him. But a child that could harden in an instant into a savage man, revengeful and brutal. And a man always fully sex-alive, for the moment innocent in the fulness of sex, not in the absence. And Kate thought to herself, as she had thought before, that there were more ways than one of 'becoming again as a little child'. [5]

But the man had a sharp, watchful look in the corner of his eye: to see if she were feeling some covert hostility. He wanted her to acquiesce in the hymn, in the drum, in the whole mood. Like a child he wanted her to acquiesce. But if she were going to be hostile, he would be quick to be first in the hostility. Her hostile judgement would make a pure enemy of him.

Ah, all men were alike!

At that moment the man stood up, with soft suddenness, and she heard Cipriano's voice from the balcony above:

'What is it, Lupe?'

'Está la Patrona,' answered the servant.

Kate rose to her feet and looked up. She saw the head and the naked shoulders of Cipriano above the parapet of the balcony.

'I will come up,' she said.

And slowly she went through the great iron gates into the passage-way. Lupe, following, bolted the doors behind her.

On the terrace above she found Ramón and Cipriano both with their upper bodies naked, waiting for her in silence. She was embarrassed.

'I waited to hear the new hymn,' she said.

'And how does it seem to you?' said Ramón, in Spanish.

'I like it,' she said.

'Let us sit down,' said Ramón, still in Spanish. He and she sat in the cane rocking-chairs: Cipriano stood by the wall of the terrace.

She had come to make a sort of submission: to say she didn't want to go away. But finding them both in the thick of their Quetzalcoatl mood, with their manly breasts uncovered, she was not very eager to begin. They made her feel like an intruder. She did not pause to realise that she *was* one.

'We don't meet in your Morning Star, apparently, do we!' she said, mocking, but with a slight quaver.

A deeper silence seemed suddenly to hold the two men.

'And I suppose a woman is really *de trop*, even there, when two men are together.'

But she faltered a bit in the saying. Cipriano, she knew, was baffled and stung when she taunted him.

Ramón answered her, with the gentleness that could come straight out of his heart: but still in Spanish:

'Why, Cousin, what is it?'

Her lip quivered, as she suddenly said:

'I don't really want to go away from you.'

Ramón looked swiftly at Cipriano, then said:

'I know you don't.'

But the gentle protective tone of his voice only made Kate rebel again. She brimmed over with sudden tears, crying:

'You don't really want me.'

'Yes, I want you! – Verdad! Verdad!' exclaimed Cipriano, in his low, secret, almost muttering voice.

And even amid her tears, Kate was thinking to herself: *What a fraud I am! I know all the time it is I who don't altogether want them. I want myself to myself. But I can fool them so that they shan't find out.*

For she heard the hot, phallic passion in Cipriano's voice.

Then came the voice of Ramón, like a chill:

'It is you who don't want,' he said, in English this time. 'You needn't commit yourself to *us*. Listen to your own best desire.'

'And if it tells me to go away?' she flashed, defiant through the end of her tears.

'Then go! Oh certainly go!'

Suddenly her tears came afresh.

'I knew you didn't really want me,' she wept.

Then Cipriano's voice said, with a hot, furtive softness of persuasion:

'You are not his! He would not tell you!'

'That is very true,' said Ramón. 'Don't listen to me!'

He spoke in Spanish. And Kate glanced up sharply through her tears, to see him going quietly, but swiftly, away.

She wiped her face, suddenly calm. Then she looked with wet eyes at Cipriano. He was standing erect and alert, like a little fighting male, and his eyes glowed black and uncannily as he met her wet, limpid glance.

Yes, she was a bit afraid of him too, with his inhuman black eyes.

'You don't want me to go, do you?' she pleaded.

A slow, almost foolish smile came over his face, and his body was slightly convulsed. Then came his soft-tongued Indian speech, as if all his mouth were soft, saying in Spanish, but with the 'r' sound almost lost:

'*Yo! Yo!*' – his eyebrows lifted with queer mock surprise, and a little convulsion went through his body again. '*Te quiero mucho! Mucho te quiero! Mucho! Mucho!* I like you very much! Very much!'

It sounded so soft, so soft-tongued, of the soft, wet, hot blood, that she shivered a little.

'You won't let me go!' she said to him.

Notes

CHAPTER I

1 (p. 39). The character of Owen Rhys is based on Witter Bynner (1881–1968), an American poet who, along with his friend and secretary Willard Johnson (see note 3 below) accompanied the Lawrences on their first visit to Mexico, March–July 1923. See Bynner's vitriolic but informative account of their relationship, *Journey with Genius: Recollections and Reflections Concerning the D. H. Lawrences* (John Day, N.Y., 1951; Peter Nevill, 1953).

2 (p. 39). i.e. westwards from central Mexico City probably to Avenida Insurgentes, a major artery, down which Kate and her friends must go to reach the Plaza México bull-ring. Chapultepec is a large public park in the city.

3 (p. 39). The character of Bud Villiers is based on Willard 'Spud' Johnson (1897–1968), an American journalist. He and Witter Bynner (see note 1 above) travelled with the Lawrences on their first trip to Mexico in 1923; Johnson typed at least part of the manuscript of the first version of *The Plumed Serpent*, in Chapala.

4 (p. 43). Freely translated: hired music plays sour notes (or off-key); *mal tono* also means [in] bad taste.

5 (p. 43). Kate's attitudes toward the Mexican working class (especially the *mestizo* or Mexican of mixed blood), so at odds with the ethos of the Mexican revolution, were Lawrence's as well, as his letters of this period demonstrate. Kate's aristocratic origins may resemble somewhat those of Frieda Lawrence, but her views on such matters are all too clearly the views of one reacting against his origins as a Nottinghamshire miner's son.

6 (p. 44). 'Very well, sir, very well!'

7 (p. 46). These would seem to be the *alguaciles* (mounted bailiffs) who head the traditional promenade (*paseo de las cuadrillas*) of participants before the first bull enters, and who formally petition the authorities for permission to begin the bull-fight; however, the horsemen are later identified as *picadores* (not as a rule dressed gaily) whose job is to 'pic' the bull with the *vara* or barbed shaft in the first third (*tercio*) of the three-part *corrida*. Here and throughout, Lawrence's account of the bull-fight, effective as it is in creating a mood, is full of inaccuracies. He attended a bull-fight at the then-new Plaza México in Mexico City on 1 April 1923, and, like his protagonist, left in disgust before the end of the first *corrida*. Six months later, during his second trip to Mexico, he attended another bull-fight, near Tepic, remaining this time till the end.

8 (p. 46). Toreadors are professional bullfighters; the preferred term is *torero*; Hemingway, in *Death in the Afternoon* (Scribner's, N.Y., 1932; Jonathan Cape, 1932), says that *toreador* is a 'Frenchification ... not used in Spanish except to

refer slightingly to a French bull-fighter'. In Lawrence's description these four men turn out to be the matadors; as a rule, however, there are only three matadors in a bull-fight, each one facing two bulls.

9 (p. 47). The image of the picador on the 'lean old horse' momentarily reminds Kate of Cervantes' picaresque old knight and his ramshackle mount, Rocinante.

10 (p. 47). See Revelation 6:1–8.

11 (p. 47). A few years after Lawrence's visit to the bull-fight there was a change in the rules designed to prevent this sort of thing from happening; the picadors' horses were fitted with a protective covering called a *peto*. Hemingway's account of the subtle disadvantages of the *peto* is most illuminating. See *Death in the Afternoon* (n.p., glossary entries for '*peto*' and '*pica*').

12 (p. 49). The bull was sacred to the Roman Mithraic mystery cults (*c.* 100 B.C.–300 A.D.), its blood spilt in initiation rites to ensure the continuance of natural fecundity. The Roman mystery-god derived from the ancient Persian sun-god Mithras, whose myth includes a bull-slaying episode to which the subsequent ritual sacrifices presumably corresponded. The bull was similarly involved in the Dionysian rituals of ancient Crete, where, furthermore, bull-fighting originated.

13 (p. 51). Hemingway comments: 'Writers ... who tell of the public [at a bull-fight] applauding the death of the horses are wrong. The public is applauding the force and bravery of the bull, which has killed those horses, not their death ... The writer is looking at the horses and the public is looking at the bull. It is the lack of understanding of this viewpoint in the public which has made the bull-fight unexplainable to non-Spaniards.' See *Death in the Afternoon*, p. 404 (caption to penultimate photograph).

14 (p. 51). In Greek myth Orpheus descends into the underworld in an attempt to recover his dead wife Eurydice. Having charmed Pluto, the Lord of Hades, with his wondrous music, Orpheus is permitted to return with Eurydice on the condition that he will not look at her until they reach the upper world. He turns to see her a moment too soon and loses her again to death. See Ovid, *Metamorphoses* X, 1–152.

15 (p. 53). 'Let's See Who [lit., what] Leaves.' Cantinas and pulque shops in Mexico often have quaint or humorous names. That this one strikes Kate as 'sinisterly named' says more about her humour than that of the natives.

16 (p. 53). Literally, 'with permission?'; here, 'excuse me'. The phrase is an example of the often elaborate social courtesies common in Mexico. It is used whenever one is about to do anything that could conceivably be taken as a liberty or an imposition.

17 (p. 54). Fictional name for the Hotel Monte Carlo, inexpensive Italian-owned hotel on Calle Uruguay where the Lawrences stayed in downtown Mexico City. One may find it there still.

18 (p. 56). A famous restaurant chain in Mexico City noted for its excellent soda-fountain concoctions; long a haven for tourists eager for a respite from traditional Mexican cuisine. In Lawrence's day the Sanborn's in question would have been the historic House of Tiles on Avenida Madero, located one block from

the Palace of Fine Arts in central Mexico City, not far from the Hotel Monte Carlo (San Remo).

CHAPTER II

1 (p. 58). As with other factual details in Lawrence's account of the bull-fight, the accuracy of this is doubtful. As a rule, there are six bulls in a bull-fight, two for each matador.

2 (p. 60). In Greek mythology, Argus was a giant with a hundred eyes, used by Zeus' jealous wife Hera as a watchman because he could sleep with some of his eyes closed while keeping guard with the rest.

3 (p. 62). This character is based on Mrs Zelia Nuttall (1853– 1933), a noted English archaeologist who entertained the Lawrences several times in her home (once the home of Pedro de Alvarado, the conquistador) in Coyoacán. Her book, *The Fundamental Principles of Old and New World Religions* (1901), which she gave to Lawrence personally, was one of his most important sources of information about the mythology of the Mexican Indians before the Conquest.

4 (p. 62). Fictional name for Coyoacán, in Lawrence's day a suburban village to the south of Mexico City.

5 (p. 63). Southern suburbs of Mexico City. Xochimilco is the site of the famous 'floating gardens' dating back to the pre-Columbian era.

6 (p. 66). i.e. during the Porfirian period (see note 20, Ch. III), 1876–1910, characterized by relative political stability, fiscal efficiency, prolific foreign investment, and material prosperity for the privileged few – all qualities that conservative members of the foreign colony such as those at Mrs Norris's tea-party would appreciate. The period was also marked, however, by flagrant violations of social justice, especially for the peons: the apportioning of millions of acres of land to *hacendados* at the expense of the traditional *ejidal* communities (see note 2, Ch. XXII), the exploitation of Mexican natural resources by foreign interests, the mockery of democratic principles of government, the brutality of the state militia called *rurales*, and the widespread imposition of debt peonage in rural areas.

7 (p. 67). This character is based on Plutarco Elías Calles (1877–1945), dictator of Mexico between 1924 and 1934, though technically out of office after 1928. Generally regarded as the leader of the left wing of the revolutionary party, Calles, once in power, began (in the words of Mrs Norris, on p. 67) to 'change his views'. Dubbed the 'supreme chief of the revolution' in 1928, he soon thereafter placated foreign interests, subverted the labour movement, declared the agrarian reform programme a failure, and sanctioned the machinations of a pro-Calles Fascist group, the Gold Shirts, which persecuted political rivals, Catholics and minority groups. Calles assumed office in December 1924 during Lawrence's third trip to Mexico, when *The Plumed Serpent* was rewritten.

8 (p. 68). Probably an allusion (one of several to follow) to the rebellion headed by General Adolfo de la Huerta (*c.* 1882–1955), against the naming of Plutarco Elías Calles (see note 7 above) as the successor to President Álvaro Obregón. In

September 1923 De la Huerta, at the urging of military leaders opposed to Calles, resigned his post in the Obregón cabinet and three months later began his rebellion, which attracted strong support in several parts of the country, including Oaxaca. By spring the rebellion was successfully suppressed, and De la Huerta was exiled to California. But when Lawrence arrived in Oaxaca, in the autumn of 1924, the signs of violence and chaos stemming from this episode of the revolution were abundant – especially to one so prepared to find them as Lawrence was. (See Introduction, pp. 21–2.)

9 (p. 68). 'Good day, sir! Come in! Do you want anything?'

10 (p. 69). Very likely a reference to Oaxaca, where the Lawrences lived from November 1924 to February 1925 and where the novel was rewritten.

11 (p. 69). Mister So-and-So; *Fulano de Tal* = John Doe.

12 (p. 70). The 'brown Virgin', patron saint of Mexico; her shrine at the hill of Tepeyac, and her image there (according to tradition miraculous in origin), have for over four and a half centuries been the object of the most intense devotion – even during the anti-clerical persecution no one dared to profane this symbol of Mexican spirituality. (See Introduction, p. 16.)

13 (p. 71). The famous twin volcanoes, located south-east of Mexico City. In Nahuatl (the dominant language group of the Mexican central plateau before the Conquest), Ixtaccihuatl means 'the white woman' and Popocatepetl means 'the smoking mountain', both names derived from legendary Aztec lovers.

14 (p. 73). 'Not long live Christ the King! but long live Death the King! Let's go! Viva!' *Viva Cristo Rey!* was the rallying cry of the reactionary *cristeros* during the bitter church–state feuds of the 1920s and early 1930s (see note 4, Ch. xxvi).

15 (p. 73). 'Don' (with a capital) is the title of respect used before first names of men; the female equivalent is 'Doña'.

16 (p. 74). *Real* = crown, a Spanish coin; a *tostón*, in colonial South America, was a silver coin worth four silver reals. Hence, one able to drink four times the pulque may transmute hope into paradise.

17 (p. 74). The magical formula used by Ali Baba in the *Arabian Nights* to open the secret door of the robbers' cave.

18 (p. 75). Refers to Article 27 in the Mexican Constitution of 1917 which provided a sweeping new definition of property ('property is not a right but a social function') empowering the government to confiscate it when necessary to promote public welfare. Thus the large property concessions made to *hacendados* and foreigners during the Porfirian period were now vulnerable to repossession, partition, and redistribution by the state (an innovation that Evelyn Waugh later termed 'robbery under law'). The principal beneficiaries of the law were, at least in theory, the *ejido* communities (see note 2, Ch. xxii). Although the agrarian question was perhaps the most volatile social issue involved in the Mexican revolution – the *cause célèbre* of such figures as Emiliàno Zapata – the law was not seriously enforced until the administration of Lázaro Cárdenas, 1934–40. Lawrence's own views of the agrarian reform were probably coloured by an incident recounted to him by Zelia Nuttall (see note 3 above) during his last trip to Mexico, in autumn 1924. Mrs Nuttall told him of the recent murder in ambush of her friend Rosalie Evans, who had defied the new law for six years by

defending her haciendas against repartition by the government. The Evans case was notorious among the reactionary foreign element in Mexico at the time. Though Lawrence was no proponent of private property, he was sceptical about the reform efforts of the revolution, referring in his letters to the leaders as 'self-seeking bolsheviks'.

19 (p. 75). She was raised a bluestocking; i.e. with literary or bookish interests.

20 (p. 76). A major artery on the east side of Manhattan, parallel to Park Avenue.

21 (p. 78). The underworld or kingdom of the dead in Greek and Roman mythology (see note 14, Ch. 1).

CHAPTER III

1 (p. 81). See note 13, Ch. 11.

2 (p. 82). The advanced ancient civilization that dominated the Mexican central plateau from *c.* A.D. 900 (after the fall of Teotihuacán; see note 5, Ch. 1v) to the mid twelfth century. The word in Nahuatl means 'master builders'. Their religion centered on the opposition between the benevolent god Quetzalcoatl (see note 12 below) and the malevolent Tezcatlipoca (see note 19 below), both subsequently appropriated by the conquering Aztecs, in whose hands the old religion degenerated into a totalitarian cult of sun-worship with wholesale human sacrifices. Though aware of this distinction, Lawrence tends to emphasize the Aztec rather than the more appealing Toltec interpretation of the gods in Don Ramón's religious movement.

3 (p. 82). 'It is finished'; see John 19:30.

4 (p. 83). Refers to Plaza de la Constitución, better known as the Zócalo, the large public square located in the central section of downtown Mexico City; it is surrounded by old government buildings and, on the northern side, flanked by the enormous National Cathedral, built on the ruins of the great Aztec temples of Tenochtitlán.

5 (p. 84). Diego Rivera (1886–1957), the most famous of the Mexican muralists who, from the 1920s on, painted the walls of public buildings with scenes depicting Mexican history from the standpoint of the revolution.

6 (p. 84). To shock the bourgeois.

7 (p. 85). The reference is almost certainly to José Clemente Orozco (1883–1949), who, along with Diego Rivera and David Alfaro Siqueiros, led the Mexican renaissance in the arts during the 1920s and 1930s. Orozco's painting, fiercely executed, treats social themes from a radical revolutionary viewpoint. Though Lawrence's disapprobation of Mexican revolutionary art is very evident in this scene, the muralists' preoccupation with the epic myth of indigenous reconquest – and with the Indian as chief protagonist – political dogma aside, is roughly parallel to Lawrence's own schema in the novel.

8 (p. 85). The character García is probably based on Miguel Covarrubias (1902–57), Mexican painter and caricaturist, whom Lawrence met in Mexico City in April 1923.

9 (p. 86). Excuse for contention; ground for war.

10 (p. 88). The first reference to the main setting of the novel; Sayula is Lawrence's fictional name for Chapala, a village resort on the northern shore of Lake Chapala, thirty-two miles south-east of Guadalajara in the state of Jalisco. The first draft of *The Plumed Serpent* was written in Chapala in May–June 1923 (see Introduction, pp. 15–18). Lake Chapala, the largest natural lake in Mexico, has now been officially declared a dead lake because of industrial pollution.

11 (p. 89). Aztec god of rain and fertility.

12 (p. 90). Pronounced *kĕtz·äll·KŌ·öttle*; the essential meaning of the name is as given in the text. He was the principal god of the Toltecs (see note 2 above); originally the personification of the trade winds, hence the bringer of spring rains and fertility, he became the god of learning, civilisation and priesthood – and, in some myths, the creator of mankind. Some archaeologists and historians argue that he was an historical personage, a great ninth-century Toltec priest-king, a view worth mentioning here only because of Don Ramón's insistence upon human 'manifestations' of the gods. Whether as actual person or as legend, the fair-skinned and bearded Quetzalcoatl was venerated for more than five centuries as a benevolent culture-hero and god incarnate. He was credited with the discovery of maize, the arts, science and the calendar; he opposed the practice of human sacrifice and, as priest, emphasised the importance of chastity, contemplation and spiritual detachment. Thus when his rival, the evil wizard Tezcatlipoca (see note 19 below), tricked him into getting drunk and sleeping with a woman, the anguished Quetzalcoatl decided to leave his people. He travelled east to the Gulf coast where, promising to return one day, he immolated himself by fire (another version has him sailing away on a raft of serpents), descended into the land of death (where he revivified dead human bones), and ascended into the heavens as the star Venus (see note 2, Ch. v). See Laurette Séjourné, *Burning Water: Thought and Religion in Ancient Mexico* (Vanguard, N.Y., 1956; Thames & Hudson, 1957). Lawrence's principal sources for materials about pre-Columbian Mexico were Lewis Spence (see note 1, Ch. XXVI), *The Gods of Mexico* (1923); Zelia Nuttall (see note 3, Ch. 11), *Fundamental Principles of Old and New World Religions* (1901); and the *Anales del Museo Nacional de México*.

13 (p. 91). Of all the precedents that could be named for this view of the corresponding life cycles of individual men, nations and divinities, two seem especially apt here. First, as the novel explicitly indicates, there is the cyclical pattern of conquest and counter-conquest embodied in Mexican history, involving the imposition of a new religion as well as a new social order, both of which (in the novel) have 'grown old' and are in need of a 'rebirth' of some sort. Second, the basis in myth and ritual of the pattern of 'dying and reborn gods' – symbolically parallel to human and natural cycles of fertility – is a central idea in Sir J. G. Frazer's *The Golden Bough* (1907–15), which Lawrence had been reading as early as 1915.

14 (p. 93). Refers to a notorious literary forgery perpetrated by James Macpherson, whose pseudo-Celtic 'Ossianic' poems (1760–65) exploited the fashion-

able romantic interest in 'primitive' antiquities; hence Kate's 'gift' here is that of artifice.

15 (p. 94). This character is probably based, in part, on Luis Quintanilla, a French-born Mexican poet and academic and, later, a diplomat of note. He and Lawrence became friends during Lawrence's third visit to Mexico (November 1924–March 1925).

16 (p. 94). Pronounced *weet·see·lō·POACHED·lee*; the name in Nahuatl means 'Humming Bird' (a symbol of resurrection). He was the principal Aztec deity, the god of war, who guided the Aztec migration south from the mythical Aztlán (hence their name) and who revealed the site of their island city, Tenochtitlán. He was also the god of the sun and of fire, and human sacrifices (often prisoners of war) were made to him so as to perpetuate his life and tutelary influence. At the moment of his birth his jealous siblings attacked him, but Huitzilopochtli, literally a born warrior, killed them all and saved his mother, the earth-goddess Coatlicue. This myth has been interpreted as a prophetic rationale for the extension by force of the Aztec empire in the fifteenth century.

17 (p. 94). 'The jewel is in the lotus, *Om*!' The mystic formula of the Tibetans and northern Buddhists, used as a ritual charm. The lotus represents universal being; the jewel, the individuality of the utterer; *Om* is the mystic equivalent for the name of the godhead.

18 (p. 94). A stellar and also an agricultural goddess of the Aztecs, possibly of Chichimecan (pre-Aztec) origin. Apart from its sound, the name recurs as a candidate for Don Ramón's pantheon because, as L. D. Clark has observed, 'she was one of the few Aztec goddesses with any attractive qualities at all, from a European point of view. The rest vary from unsavory to abominable.' (*Dark Night of the Body: D. H. Lawrence's 'The Plumed Serpent'*, University of Texas Press, 1964, p. 123).

19 (p. 94). 'Lord of the Smoking Mirror', ancient deity of the Toltecs (see note 2 above). He was associated with the night, moon and stars, and identified with the forces of evil and destruction in various forms. His linked opposite was Quetzalcoatl (see note 12 above), the god of light, wind and benevolence, with whom he carried on a running feud culminating in the temptation and self-expulsion of Quetzalcoatl from the Toltec capital, Tollán (Tula). In Don Ramón's pantheon, as in the Aztec, Huitzilopochtli (see note 16 above) supersedes Tezcatlipoca.

20 (p. 95). The dictator of Mexico from 1876 to 1911, when the revolution headed by Francisco I. Madero drove Díaz into exile in France (see note 6, Ch. 11).

21 (p. 96). Actually a good deal less; though such figures are always suspect, the percentage usually given is around thirty per cent. The racial theory expounded here and elsewhere in the novel runs directly counter to that of the Mexican revolution. Although indigenism played an important part in early revolutionary ideology, the fact is that the revolution – following the lead of poet-philosopher José Vasconcelos (1882–1959) – essentially represented the interests of '*la raza*', i.e. Mexicans of mixed blood, who constitute the vast majority of the population. In the spring of 1923 Lawrence directed a tirade of abuse against

Vasconcelos (then Minister of Education in the Obregón administration) when a meeting between the two men was cancelled at the last minute. It has been suggested that Vasconcelos was the chief model for the character of Don Ramón.

22 (p. 96). A very interesting possibility, since it was the Tlaxcalans who, themselves defeated in battle by the Spaniards, formed an alliance with the outnumbered conquistadors crucial to the defeat of the Aztecs, long the bitter enemies of the Tlaxcalans. The latter, along with Cortés' Tabascan Indian mistress Malinche (see note 4, Ch. XXII), are popularly regarded as the proto-typical traitors of the homeland and lackeys to foreign interests. Don Ramón's racial heritage would seem to associate him with the foreign conquistador rather than with the novel's indigenous movement rallying round the tom-toms of Quetzalcoatl.

23 (p. 97). Juárez (1806–72), born of Zapotecan parents, was orphaned at the age of three and soon after taken in by a wealthy family in the city. In time his keen ambition to raise his station in life was recognised, and he was sent to a Franciscan seminary to be educated, it was hoped, for the priesthood. A voracious reader with an independent cast of mind, Juárez distinguished himself as a student but finally chose to read the law (including the Enlightenment thinkers) rather than become a cleric. Entering politics, he became governor of Oaxaca, aligning himself with the liberals against the dictator Santa Anna, and was a chief proponent of the Reform Law of 1857, which severely limited the secular powers of the Catholic Church in Mexico. When the liberals defeated the conservative forces in 1861, he became the first 'citizen' president. The French intervention (1864–7) offered him his greatest challenge, but his eventual victory over Maximilian demonstrated the widespread support of the emergent middle-class *mestizo* and helped to forge the national consciousness of Mexico.

24 (p. 101). Cipriano's early background, recounted in the next few paragraphs, resembles that of Benito Juárez (see note 23 above).

25 (p. 104). The Virgin of Solitude is the patronness of Oaxaca State and also of sailors. Her white hands, in an attitude of mournful supplication, are fre-quently emphasised in representations of her. Kate's whiteness, as well as her penchant for solitude (and, here, her grief), make this a fitting association which helps to explain the ascetic Cipriano's immediate fascination for her and her subsequent promotion to goddess in Ramón's pantheon.

CHAPTER IV

1 (p. 108). Pulque, a white, thick, rather sweet drink rich in vitamins, is one of the oldest and most popular of Mexican intoxicating beverages, dating back to about A.D. 1000. Made from the fermented juice of the maguey or agave plant, pulque was considered a sacred drink by the indigenous peoples of Mexico. Elaborate rituals and taboos (vestiges of which survive in remote areas) accom-panied its production and use. Lawrence's references to its 'phallic' properties seem to be accurate. *Agua miel* (honey-water) is the nectar that gathers within

the plant after its bud has been pierced with a long lance; the juice is later removed to ferment – with the aid of a specially prepared 'pulque seed' – in large vats. According to Frances Toor, *A Treasury of Mexican Folkways* (Crown, N.Y., 1947), in some regions only men are permitted to enter the vat-rooms, while women, especially those who are pregnant, may not approach them.

2 (p. 111). Moloch (or Molech) was an Ammonite god whose worship required parents to sacrifice their children by forcing them to pass 'through the fire to Molech'. See II Kings 23:10.

3 (p. 111). In the direction opposite, the wrong way; also, 'contrary to the apparent course of the sun (considered as . . . causing disaster)' (*OED*).

4 (p. 112). Hernán Cortés (1485–1547), Spanish conquistador, architect of the Conquest of Mexico – both military and religious. Despite his 'iron will', which in Lawrence's eyes would link Cortés with all that is objectionable in America, Cortés' life after the defeat of the Aztecs is a pathetic tale of error, neglect, and great personal disappointment. In this respect he exemplifies Lawrence's view that the dark 'No!' of the American continent ultimately nullifies the white will.

5 (p. 112). Important archaeological zone some thirty miles north-east of Mexico City. In Nahuatl, Teotihuacán means 'City of the Gods'. Site of massive pyramids to the sun and the moon and the citadel containing the famed temple of Quetzalcoatl, it was the commercial and religious centre of the valley of Mexico, its culture flourishing from about A.D. 300–900. Lawrence visited Teotihuacán in April 1923 (see Introduction, p. 15).

6 (p. 112). City in central Mexico, about nine miles west of Puebla City. The Holy City of the Aztec confederation, it was said to have some 100,000 inhabitants and 400 Aztec temples and shrines before the Conquest, including flat-topped Tepanapa Pyramid, believed to be the largest in the world. Cortés destroyed the city and vowed to build a church on the ruins of each pagan shrine. Lawrence visited Cholula in April 1923.

7 (p. 112). Archaeological site in south-east Mexico, some twenty-five miles east and south of Oaxaca City. In Nahuatl the name means 'Abode of the Dead'; probably built in the thirteenth century, Mitla was a burial ground for the Zapotecan Indians. The ruin is best known for the distinctive decorations on its wall panels – intricate carved mosaics and friezes of various interlocking geometrical designs. Lawrence visited Milta *c.* December 1924, during his third trip to Mexico (see Introduction, p. 22).

8 (p. 113). Archetypal symbol of unified being. Its ubiquity as a motif in the myths of the world (much emphasised by Frazer, see note 13, Ch. 111), where it is often associated with god incarnate, and in Kabbalistic lore, where the arboreal roots and branches stand for various interconnected realms of being has induced Joseph Campbell to identify it with the World Navel, 'the centre of the symbolic circle of the universe . . . the umbilical point through which the energies of eternity break into time' (*The Hero with a Thousand Faces*, Princeton University Press, N. J., 1949, pp. 40–41). In *The Plumed Serpent* a similar significance gathers around such symbols as the lake, the 'centreless' Indian eyes, and the legendary antediluvian world (see note 1, Ch. XXVI).

CHAPTER V

1 (p. 115). Orilla is the fictional name for El Fuerte, a village on Lake Chapala; the real hotel (where Lawrence stopped in April 1923) was called the Ribera.

2 (p. 125). Venus, associated with the apotheosis of Quetzalcoatl by the Toltecs. Quetzalcoatl (see note 12, Ch. III) means 'Plumed Serpent' but can also be interpreted as 'Precious Twin', a reference to the double aspect of Venus, which rises in the east, disappears, and then reappears in the west as the evening star – the interval of absence being linked with the death and departure of Quetzalcoatl from his people, the Toltecs. In this aspect the 'Lord of the Two Ways' represents death and rebirth.

3 (p. 127). Sea monsters in Greek mythology; Scylla, who has six heads and the body of a dog, lives in a cave on a rocky island opposite Charybdis, whose cave is a large whirlpool. Through the dangerous straits between them Odysseus and his mariners sail, losing six men to the voracious Scylla (see Homer's *Odyssey*, X).

4 (p. 129). Since Díaz fled from Mexico in 1911 (see note 20, Ch. III), and since Montes (Calles) is about to assume office (see note 7, Ch. II), the time of the story is probably 1924, April to November.

CHAPTER VI

1 (p. 135). See note 3, Ch. IV.

2 (p. 144). 'No, child, there is no more.'

3 (p. 145). 'How pretty! How pretty, child! Look how pretty!'

CHAPTER VII

1 (p. 147). Five of spades! King of hearts!

2 (p. 156). This scene is based on a visit Lawrence made to the Jicarilla Apache reservation in northern New Mexico, in September 1922; Kate's feelings strongly resemble those of Lawrence as described in 'Indians and an Englishman' (*Phoenix: The Posthumous Papers of D. H. Lawrence*, ed. Edward D. McDonald, pp. 97–9).

3 (p. 160). See note 8, Ch. IV.

4 (p. 161). Abbreviated form of Latin dictum, *Verbum sapienti sat est*, a word to the wise is enough; a hint will suffice to any intelligent person.

CHAPTER VIII

1 (p. 169). Baron Alexander von Humboldt (1769–1859), German statesman, naturalist and explorer. From 1799 to 1804 he made a scientific expedition to the Spanish colonies in the New World. His four-volume *Political Essay on the Kingdom of New Spain* (1811) and *Vues des cordillères et monumens des peuples*

indigènes de l'Amerique (1810), the latter familiar to Lawrence, provided northern Europeans with a wealth of important information about colonial Mexico.

2 (p. 171). In ancient Greek religion, the primordial goat-god of the wild – a fertility god who watched over forests, flocks and herds. He loved to frighten unwary travellers (hence the word *panic*; see preceding lines). In 'Pan in America' (written in 1924) Lawrence identified Pan with the Christian devil and with the aboriginal spirit of place in America, embodied in the 'heathen' Red Indians who terrorised the first Puritan settlers in the New World. Though obscured by centuries of white abstractions such as the Puritans' God and Emerson's Over-Soul, Pan survives in America, according to Lawrence. Later in *The Plumed Serpent*, Cipriano becomes identified with the 'ancient phallic mystery' of Pan (see, e.g., p. 347).

CHAPTER IX

1 (p. 177). Now then! Now then! Ah, child, I have no memory!

2 (p. 179). Juana's son Ezequiel is the sole example in the novel of a peasant who has been affected (however superficially) by the reforms attempted by the agrarian laws of the revolution (see note 18, Ch. 11).

CHAPTER X

1 (p. 190). See note 18, Ch. 11.

2 (p. 194). Ramón's villa, located four miles west of Sayula, is modelled on El Manglar, a deserted villa in Chapala.

3 (p. 195). Here, used as a greeting. This usage is common in Mexico when one is passing someone walking in the opposite direction.

4 (p. 196). Lit., sweet doing nothing; blissful idleness.

5 (p. 198). 'Beautiful – yes! Yes, lovely!'

6 (p. 200). Doroteo Arango 'Pancho' Villa (c. 1877–1923), famous revolutionary general from the north of Mexico; popularly regarded as a kind of Robin Hood, his legend (like that of his contemporary Emiliano Zapata) was perpetuated in numerous ballads and tales. Villa was assassinated on 20 July 1923, about a fortnight after Lawrence had finished working on the first draft of his novel in Chapala.

7 (p. 201). Lit., old game; old-fashioned.

8 (p. 203). Count Leo Tolstoy (1828–1910), the Russian novelist and philosopher, created a sensation by deciding, after a profound religious conversion, to give up his wealth and position, preferring the simpler life of a Russian peasant (moujik). Like Don Ramón, Tolstoy dressed in peasant garb, attacked religious and political orthodoxy, founded a new religious cult, and came into severe conflict with his wife and children because of his heterodoxy (he was excommunicated, as Ramón will be).

CHAPTER XII

1 (p. 219). Salome, daughter of Herodias, danced before Herod (her uncle and stepfather) to obtain the head of John the Baptist. See Mark 6:17–28.

2 (p. 220). Fictional name for Tizapán, a village on the southern shore, opposite Chapala.

CHAPTER XIII

1 (p. 230). 'Is the rain coming?' 'I believe so, sire.'

2 (p. 232). In *The Priest of Love: A Life of D. H. Lawrence* (Farrar, Straus & Giroux, N.Y., 1974; Penguin, 1976), pp. 371–2, Harry T. Moore discusses the similarity between many of the Hymns to Quetzalcoatl and the hymns Lawrence had heard as a child in the miners' chapel. This hymn in particular strongly resembles the Protestant hymn 'Someone Will Enter the Pearly Gate', one verse of which may be quoted:

> Someone will knock when the door is shut,
> By-and-by, by-and-by,
> Hear a voice saying: I know you not.
> Shall you? Shall I?
> Shall you? Shall I?

See Lawrence's essay 'Hymns in a Man's Life' (1928), in *Phoenix II*, ed. Warren Roberts and Harry T. Moore (Viking, N.Y., 1970), pp. 597–601.

3 (p. 237). Archaic form of *zopilote*, vulture.

4 (p. 240). On the alert.

5 (p. 241). When it [a pear] is spoiling.

6 (p. 243). 'Who knows! That remains to be seen.' 'And will continue so to remain.'

CHAPTER XIV

1 (p. 247). See note 23, Ch. III.

2 (p. 252). Baroja (1879–1956) was a prolific and popular Basque novelist and member of the famed 'generation of 98' in Spain. His best-known novel cycles include *La lucha por la vida* (The Struggle for Life, 1904–24) and the 22-volume *Memórias de un hombre de acción* (Memories of a Man of Action).

3 (p. 252). 'I am the spirit that always denies' (Goethe, *Faust*, Part I, line 1338); a paraphrase of Satan's name – lit., 'adversary'.

CHAPTER XVI

1 (p. 267). Fictional village, its name possibly derived from a cross between the actual place-names Tlaquepaque (famous pottery-making village on the

outskirts of Guadalajara) and Jocotepec, a village at the western end of Lake Chapala, less than fifteen miles from Chapala.

2 (p. 267). Fictional villages, the former probably based on Ocotlán, on the lake to the north-east of Chapala; Jaramay is derived from Jamay, on the eastern edge of the lake, some fifty miles from Chapala.

3 (p. 268). The descriptions of the market scenes here and elsewhere in the novel probably derive from Lawrence's stay in Oaxaca, where the weekly native market is one of the most remarkable in Mexico, rather than from Chapala, where the weekends are given over to tourists and fun-seekers from the city. For a sharply contrasting description by Lawrence of the Oaxacan market, see the 'Market Day' sketch in *Mornings in Mexico* (1927).

4 (p. 274). See note 18, Ch. III.

5 (p. 281). 'Very tiny [ones]!'

CHAPTER XVII

1 (p. 284). A fictional group of pro-Catholic fanatics similar to the *cristeros* who terrorized the Mexican countryside in the late 1920s (see note 4, Ch. XXVI). Lawrence's choice of a name for his terrorists is apt in its dual suggestion of medieval European Christianity and the Spanish deracination of indigenous America – both alien to the expressed spirit of Don Ramón's movement.

2 (p. 285). Son of Wotan, and the second god in the Norse pantheon; god of thunder, hence of might and war.

3 (p. 285). In Norse mythology, the supreme god; god of wisdom, poetry, magic, agriculture and war. More commonly named Odin; Lawrence generally preferred the forms used by Richard Wagner in *The Ring of the Nibelung*.

4 (p. 285). In Norse mythology, the great tree of the world, binding together the sky, the earth and the lower world. It is an evergreen, an ash; at its top is an eagle, at the bottom a serpent, with a squirrel running between to arouse strife (see note 8, Ch. IV).

5 (p. 285). Evergreen plant parasitic on the deciduous oak tree, hence symbolic of the mysterious interrelation of eternal and temporal life. The use of mistletoe in Druidic fertility rites and its significance in the myth of Balder are discussed by Frazer in the last part of *The Golden Bough*. The cross-cultural grouping of mythical figures in this paragraph owes much to Frazer and his followers in the Cambridge school, with several of whose works Lawrence was familiar (see note 13, Ch. III).

6 (p. 285). A legendary race of superhuman heroes who invaded Ireland, overthrew the Firbolgs and were themselves overthrown by the Gaels, who later worshipped them as gods.

7 (p. 285). In Greek myth, the messenger of the gods; known for his cunning, dexterity and swiftness, he is also the god of travellers and crossroads.

8 (p. 285). Phoenician goddess of fertility, beauty and love; the supreme goddess in the Phoenician pantheon (called Astarte by the Greeks and Romans), comparable to Ishtar, Aphrodite and Venus.

9 (p. 285). See note 12, Ch. I.

10 (p. 285). Supreme god of post-Vedic Hindu mythology; creator of the universe, later 'broken' into a divine trinity with Vishnu (the Preserver) and Shiva (the Destroyer), constituting the other aspects of the originally unitary godhead.

11 (p. 285). The reference is vague (unlike the others in this list) and alters, in the lines following, to 'the Greatest Dragon'. In Chinese mythology the generic dragon figure is often (though far from exclusively) associated with lightning, hence with rain and fecundity. Frazer (see note 13, Ch. 111) speaks of Chinese paper dragons carried in ritual processions to bring rain, and the context permits the inference that the dragon figure is a symbolic substitute for a primal 'dragon', i.e. divine king. Though none is identified by name in Frazer, other sources mention the Dragon-King Lung-Wang, who assumed human form. (See J. Hackin *et al.*, *Asiatic Mythology*, Crescent Books, N.Y., n.d.; Harrap, 1932.) As a winged reptile, the dragon has obvious affinities with Quetzalcoatl.

12 (p. 286). Goddess of fertility and love, wife of Wotan; usually spelled 'Freyja' (see note 3 above).

13 (p. 286). i.e. Ashtaroth; see note 8 above.

14 (p. 286). See note 8, Ch. IV.

15 (p. 287). 'Sheer monkeys! ... and what they do, sheer monkeyshine'; possibly also a play on *mōneda* (coin), hence 'small change'. Since the prefix *mono*-means one or single in Spanish as in English, *puros monos* may connote, to a polyglot like Ramón, the idea of the isolate self (or an aggregate of separate selves), motivated by will.

16 (p. 287). Monkeys and no more.

17 (p. 292). You are all monkeys!

18 (p. 292). 'Come on, let's amuse ourselves!' The latter verb form subtly repeats the motif of this scene, *monos* (monkeys).

19 (p. 293). 'Very hot, child, very hot!'

20 (p. 297). A fiction. In the autumn of 1922 and again in the spring and summer of 1924, Lawrence had visited the ceremonials of the Pueblo Indians at the Apache, Hopi, and Navajo reservations in the American south-west (see Introduction, p. 20). These he described, lyrically, in three sketches in *Mornings in Mexico*. The ritual dances described in *The Plumed Serpent* are all either transplants from the Pueblos of the north or inventions.

21 (p. 298). This is the only reference in the novel to that peculiar Mexican fiesta, the Day of the Dead (November 2). Unlike Malcolm Lowry, who set his entire story on that day in *Under the Volcano* (1947), Lawrence chose not to mention the macabre fiesta when his story moves (in Chapter XXV) into November. For Lawrence's reflections on the Day of the Dead, however, see Witter Bynner, *Journey with Genius* (John Day, N.Y., 1951), p. 42.

22 (p. 298). This 'scandal' is cleverly conceived. The exploding of papier-mâché Judas figures on the Saturday morning before Easter (commemorating his hanging) points to Judas's essential function as scapegoat in the elaborate festivities of Holy Week in Mexico. That Judas is represented as 'the old-fashioned *patrón*', in white rather than Indian garb (a point stressed even more

by Aldous Huxley in *Beyond the Mexique Bay*, 1934), carries implications as to the modern counterpart of Judas. Replacing the sacred images with these Judases not only anticipates Ramón's *auto da fé* in Chapter XVIII, it also links him with both the betrayer of Christ and the modern conquistador, the landowner and foreigner against whom the revolution was directed.

23 (p. 298). Like Juárez (see note 23, Ch. III) half a century before, revolutionary ideologues saw the Catholic Church as a prime opponent to progressive social reform in Mexico (notwithstanding individual clerics such as Fathers Hidalgo and Morelos, heroes of the War for Independence from Spain). The Church's support of reactionary leaders like Díaz and Victoriano Huerta and its coolness towards organised labour, agrarian reform, and the spirit of *mexicanismo* – all these demonstrated the need to extend the anti-clerical legislation of the Reform. Consequently, in the Constitution of 1917, the 'charter' of the revolution, there were more stringent prohibitions against Church ownership of property (even the churches themselves were declared state property); priests were forbidden to form or head political parties and were required to register with the government authorities; all primary education was to be secular, and parochial schools were outlawed; aliens were not allowed to serve as clerics; state legislatures were empowered to determine the number of priests in their jurisdiction; and religious activities outside the churches were forbidden. These provisions – which were anti-clerical rather than anti-religious – were not in fact enforced until 1926, when the Calles regime and the Church engaged openly in a long and bitter feud, which Lawrence was so perceptive as to foresee (see note 4, Ch. XXVI).

CHAPTER XVIII

1 (p. 304). *Auto da fé*, lit., means an act of faith (Portuguese); historically, it referred to the judicial 'act' or sentencing of heretics during the Inquisition, especially to public burning.

2 (p. 304). Lit., the coackroach; title of an amusing folksong made popular during the revolution. Unlike the coackroach in the actual song, who cannot walk and finally dies because it has no marijuana to smoke, Don Ramón 'don't smoke' or drink, yet he hallucinates that he is the successor of the Christian God. The last line of Lawrence's parody, if sung to the authentic tune, does not scan.

CHAPTER XIX

1 (p. 326). A fictional village; name probably derived from Ajijic, then a sleepy fishing village about five miles west of Chapala, on the lake.

2 (p. 334). 'He's coming! Don Ramón is coming! He's coming!'

3 (p. 337). 'The English (i.e. English-speaking) lady.'

4 (p. 339). See note 1, Ch. XVII, and note 4, Ch. XXVI.

CHAPTER XX

1 (p. 347). See note 2, Ch. VIII.

2 (p. 348). An echo of Coleridge's 'Kubla Khan' (*c.* 1797–8):

> A savage place! as holy and enchanted
> As e'er beneath a waning moon was haunted
> By woman wailing for her demon lover!
>
> (lines 14–16)

3 (p. 350). The first step matters most.

4 (p. 352). See note 16, Ch. III.

5 (p. 352). See note 18, Ch. III.

6 (p. 364). 'But such a little pale blue flower. And it opened in my shade, friend.' 'You are a man of great good fortune.' 'True.'

CHAPTER XXI

1 (p. 373). 'Hear ye! Hear ye!', etc.

2 (p. 378). For a fuller presentation of this schema (which may owe something to the 'Fourfold Vision', the recovery of which represents the apocalypse in Blake's *Jerusalem*), see Lawrence's *Fantasia of the Unconscious* (1922).

3 (p. 380). Doña Carlota's dementia, her fanatically 'maternal' attitude towards her husband, her Catholicism, and of course her name – all these suggest a parallel with the empress Carlotta (1840–1927), wife of Maximilian (see note 23, Ch. III).

4 (p. 383). In *The Merchant of Venice* (1595), IV, i, Shylock the usurer is granted his claim for 'a pound of flesh' from a debtor, as long as he does not 'shed one drop of Christian blood' in the cutting of it.

CHAPTER XXII

1 (p. 390). 'I don't give a damn about your soul, my father!'

2 (p. 397). Refers to the *ejido* system of communal-land ownership which, in its original form, dates back to the pre-Columbian period. The *ejidos* were to become an important aspect of the revolution's land reform policy, especially in the 1930s (see note 18, Ch. 11).

3 (p. 397). Montezuma II (?1480–1520), Emperor of the Aztecs (*c.* 1502–20), was killed by the Spanish conquistadors under Cortés. Montezuma's fanatical devotion to Quetzalcoatl, whose return had been prophesied (see note 12, Ch. III), worked to Cortés' advantage.

4 (p. 406). Why Malintzi indeed, when Itzpapalotl (see note 18, Ch. III) had been the choice of the goddess's name until now? From what follows it is evident that Malintzi is to assume the role of fertility goddess (or First Woman of same) in the new pantheon. Malintzi is the Nahuatl equivalent of the Spanish name

Marina, and the Indian word was hispanicized later to Malinche. This woman was anything but an Aztec goddess: it was Malinche, the Nahua princess given as concubine and translator to Cortés, who conspired with the Spaniards in the overthrow of the indigenous Indian nations. Even today she is wryly termed the mother of the 'new' Mexican race of mixed blood, her descendants known as *hijos de la chingada* (sons of the whore). See Octavio Paz, *The Labyrinth of Solitude: Life and Thought in Mexico*, trans. Lysander Kemp (Grove Press, 1961), Ch. IV.

CHAPTER XXV

1 (p. 440). Actually, such a substitution would amount to an unthinkable heresy in Mexico, more shocking even than the replacement of the images of Christ and the saints with that of Judas (see note 22, Ch. XVII). On Guadalupe, see note 12, Ch. II.

2 (p. 443). One must take things as they come.

CHAPTER XXVI

1 (p. 451). The idea of a prelapsarian paradise, a potent image in all mythologies, was important to the later Lawrence. Specifically the Atlantis myth, which for him represented the 'old mode of consciousness ... dark ... noncerebral, but vertebrate', underlay his symbolic interpretation of America (see Introduction, pp. 12–13). Although the association of America with Atlantis dates back to the sixteenth century, the particular link between ancient Mexico and Atlantis was probably suggested to Lawrence by the occult speculations of Lewis Spence (see note 12, Ch. III). In an article in the *D. H. Lawrence Review*, 13 (Spring, 1980), Michael Ballin argues that Lawrence may have read Spence's articles on the Atlantean link between Celtic Ireland and the Mexico of Quetzalcoatl, articles that appeared in the *Occult Review* between 1915 and 1923. This hypothesis would enhance the significance of the 'foreignness' not only of the fair-skinned Quetzalcoatl (subsequently linked by the Aztecs with the alien conquistadors) but also that of his modern representative, Don Ramón. Moreover, as the subsequent paragraphs explicitly state, Kate's sympathy with the Quetzalcoatl movement derives in part from her Irish background with its 'residue of memory' of the antediluvian world as preserved in Celtic mysticism.

2 (p. 452). See note 6, Ch. XVII.

3 (p. 453). 'Touch me not'; the resurrected Christ's injunction to Mary Magdalene, who, after first mistaking Him for a gardener, finally recognizes Him as the Master. The complete statement (John 20:17) is worth quoting in connection with the 'great change' being worked in Kate: 'Touch me not; for I am not yet ascended to my father.'

4 (p. 457). Whatever misgivings one might have as to the thematic validity

of these developments as the outcome of Lawrence's *fictional* revolution, they epitomize his uncanny ability to anticipate, in essence, the course of actual events. In 1925 President Calles (see note 7, Ch. 11) covertly supported a plan to form a Mexican Catholic Church, with a native Mexican patriarch, allied to the revolutionary government; in February of that year he even compelled the orthodox clergy to 'donate' a church to the new schismatic sect (see John W. F. Dulles, *Yesterday in Mexico*, University of Texas Press, 1961, p. 300). When the episcopacy objected and the conservative press subsequently renewed its protest against the anti-clerical articles of the Constitution of 1917 (see note 23, Ch. XVII), Calles retaliated by enforcing the letter of the law – including oaths of allegiance – and then some. Rather than comply with Calles' strictures, the clergy went on strike on 31 July 1926: for three years there were no formal Catholic services in Mexico. In January 1927 the *cristero* rebellion (see note 1, Ch. XVII), fomented largely by creoles rather than by Indians, began a series of brutal attacks and counter-attacks that continued until mid 1929, when a compromise made possible (temporarily) the reopening of the churches; or at least those that had not been destroyed or converted to secular functions. The persecution of the clergy was renewed in 1931–2 and continued to flourish in certain provinces until the end of the decade, the occasion for Graham Greene's novel *The Power and the Glory* (1940).

5 (p. 459). i.e. clitoral orgasm. In Greek mythology Aphrodite is the goddess of fertility, sexual love and beauty and the mother of Eros. She was born from the foam of the sea (aphros = sea foam).

CHAPTER XXVII

1 (p. 463). One of the Homeric Hymns tells of how Dionysos, the Greek god of wine, is abducted by Tyrrhenian pirates who, unaware of his identity, think to obtain a great ransom. But their chains cannot hold him, wine flows in streams over the deck, a vine with clusters of grapes sprouts from the mast, and the pirates leap overboard and are changed to dolphins (see *Homeric Hymns* VII, 1–57). Hence the 'message' brought by the boat is the annunciation of the god Dionysos, one of whose epithets is 'far-crying Dionysos'. Lawrence's description strongly resembles a well-known representation of Dionysos painted on a cup by Exekias (*c.* 540 B.C.) – as bearded seafarer, on a vine-sprouting boat surrounded by dolphins. See Walter F. Otto, *Dionysus: Myth and Cult*, trans. Robert B. Palmer (Indiana University Press, 1965), Plate 10. Lawrence would make use, tellingly, of similar imagery in his unfinished tale, 'The Flying Fish', which he dictated to Frieda during the last, death-haunted weeks in Mexico. This beautiful fragment was published posthumously in *Phoenix*.

2 (p. 463). She, her husband, and two daughters were to be spared from the Lord's destruction of Sodom and Gomorrah: 'Escape for thy life,' the angels told them; 'look not behind thee, neither stay thou in all the plain.' But Lot's wife looked back (compare Orpheus: see note 14, Ch. 1) and was turned into a pillar of salt (see Genesis 19:15–26).

3 (p. 475). A grimalkin is an old she-cat, associated with witches (cf. *Macbeth*, I, i: 'I come, Graymalkin').

4 (p. 477). 'They are playing' [music].

5 (p. 479). Matthew 18:3: 'Verily I say unto you, Except ye be converted, and become as little children, ye shall not enter into the kingdom of heaven.'

Glossary

(All words here are Spanish unless otherwise indicated. F. indicates French. In general, foreign words translated in the text or in the notes are not included here. Exceptions are made for words and phrases used frequently or with multiple meanings.)

adiós goodbye
adónde? Where to?
aguador water carrier
alacrán scorpion
alameda park; tree-lined walk
ambiente atmosphere, environment
amigo friend
bágari a kind of catfish; *bagre*
banderillas long darts, wrapped in coloured paper, placed in pairs into the bull's hump of muscle above the neck, during the second part of the bull-fight
banderilleros bull-fighters who prepare the bull for the matador by placing the banderillas
bienvenido welcome
bonito pretty
bon mot [F.] jest, witticism
botes jars, pots
calabacita pumpkin, squash
caldo broth, bouillon
camote sweet potato
canaille [F.] rabble, riffraff
canóa canoe, launch
cargador stevedore, longshoreman
centavo cent
charal a small fish
charro horseman, Mexican cowboy
cine motion picture theatre
cuartelazos military insurrections
despedida farewell, parting
de trop [F.] unwelcome
dueña chaperone (female)
dulce sweet, candy
elegancia elegance; gentry
enchilada typical Mexican food consisting of a soft tortilla wrapped around chicken, beef, beans, or cheese and covered with any one of a variety of sauces, usually highly seasoned

entonces well then, so then

esposa wife

farouche [F.] shy, unpolished, lacking in social graces; but also wild, fierce, savage

fiesta party, holiday

fonda inn, restaurant

Gachupines Spaniards living in Mexico; a derogatory epithet, especially during the Mexican revolution

hacendado landed gentry, rancher

hacienda country estate, large ranch

hola hello

insouciance [F.] unconcern, without care or worry

jefatura headquarters

jefe chief, boss

joie de vivre [F.] zest for living

metate flat stone used for grinding corn, chiles, vegetables, etc.

mío(a) mine

mire! look!

mozo manservant

muchas gracias many thanks

mundo world

nieve sherbet, ice

novedades novelties, knick-knacks

obrero worker, manual labourer

ocote resinous pine, highly inflammable, used by Indians for torches

olla jar, pot; dim.: *ollita*

orilla bank, edge, shore

oubliette [F.] pit or dungeon; also, oblivion

palo blanco lit., white timber; tropical tree with whitish wood or bark

patrón boss, sponsor, patron, sire

patrona mistress, boss, patroness, madam

pelado literally, peeled, plucked; a destitute peon; denotes a social class in Mexico; often, in Mexico, used as a term of abuse

picador mounted bull-fighter who 'pics' the bull with a sharp lance, in the first of three 'acts' of a bull-fight, to prepare the bull for the matador

pitahaya cactus fruit

planta nursery; pl.: potted plants

plaza central park or square; marketplace

plaza de toros bull-ring

poncho a blanket or cloak with a hole in the middle to fit over the head

pulquería a shop, usually in the city, where pulque (see note 1, Ch. IV) is sold

rancheros ranch-style eggs, i.e., scrambled, usually with spicy seasoning added

rebozo Mexican shawl, worn by peasant women

rey king

salón parlour

santísima holiest one (female), epithet for the Virgin

santo saint

El Señor the Lord

serape colourful Mexican blanket or shawl

sinvergüenza one who is without honour and without shame

tamales traditional Mexican dish made of fried chopped meat, crushed peppers, seasoning, wrapped in corn husks or thick dough, and steamed

tapa [Polynes.] native Polynesian cloth, unwoven, made from specially prepared tree-bark

tepache pulque mixed with fruit juice, usually pineapple; sometimes brown sugar or honey is substituted for fruit juice

toreo the art of bull-fighting

torero bull-fighter, including *picadores*, *banderilleros* and *matadores*

toro bull

tren train

tu second person sing. pronoun: you (familiar form of address)

verdad truth

ya already

yo I

zopilote turkey buzzard, a New World vulture (*Cathartes aura*)

Select Bibliography

The following books and articles are particularly helpful to the student of *The Plumed Serpent*. (Titles cited in the Introduction are not included here.)

David Cavitch, *D. H. Lawrence and the New World* (Oxford University Press, 1969)

L. D. Clark, *The Dark Night of the Body: D. H. Lawrence's 'The Plumed Serpent'* (University of Texas Press, 1964). Still the single most informative study of the novel and its backgrounds

—, *The Minoan Distance: The Symbolism of Travel in D. H. Lawrence* (University of Arizona Press, 1980). Especially useful for its discussion of the Chapala version of the novel

James C. Cowan, *D. H. Lawrence's American Journey: A Study in Literature and Myth* (Case Western Reserve University Press, 1970)

Reloy Garcia, 'The Quest for Paradise in the Novels of D. H. Lawrence', in *D. H. Lawrence Review*, III (1970), 93–112

Graham Hough, *The Dark Sun: A Study of D. H. Lawrence* (Duckworth, 1956)

Aldous Huxley, *Beyond the Mexique Bay: A Traveller's Journal* (1934; reprinted in Collected Edition, Chatto & Windus, 1949). The final chapter contains an important and perceptive critique by Lawrence's friend and one-time disciple

Jascha Kessler, 'Descent into Darkness: Myth in *The Plumed Serpent*', in *A D. H. Lawrence Miscellany*, ed. Harry T. Moore (Southern Illinois University Press, 1959), pp. 239–61

D. H. Lawrence, *Mornings in Mexico* (Penguin, 1960). An indispensable companion to the novel

Patricia Merivale, 'D. H. Lawrence and the Modern Pan Myth', in *Texas Studies in Literature and Language*, VI (Autumn, 1964), 299–305

Jeffrey Meyers, '*The Plumed Serpent* and the Mexican Revolution', in *Journal of Modern Literature*, IV (September, 1974), 55–72

Edward Nehls, ed., *D. H. Lawrence: A Composite Biography*, Vol. II (University of Wisconsin Press, 1958). Contains an extremely useful compilation of comments about Lawrence in Mexico by those who knew him there (e.g. Witter Bynner, Willard Johnson, Carelton Beals, Frederick W. Leighton, Idella Purnell, Kai Gótzsche, Dorothy Brett, Luis Quintanilla, and Edward Weston), interspersed with extracts from Lawrence's letters

Ross Parmenter, Introduction to *Mornings in Mexico* (Peregrine Smith, Utah, 1982)

Octavio Paz, *The Labyrinth of Solitude: Life and Thought in Mexico*, trans. Lysander Kemp (Grove Press, N.Y. and London, 1961)

Jorge Ruffinelli, *El Otro México: México en la obra de B. Traven, D. H. Lawrence, y Malcolm Lowry* (Editorial Nueva Imagen, Mexico City, 1978). The most comprehensive Spanish-language treatment to date

Keith Sagar, *D. H. Lawrence: A Calendar of His Works* (University of Texas Press, 1979). A highly informative chronology of Lawrence's travels and works (with a checklist of the locations of all extant manuscripts), based on the latest research

Laurette Séjourné, *Burning Water: Thought and Religion in Ancient Mexico* (Vanguard, N.Y., 1956; Thames and Hudson, 1957)

Leslie Byrd Simpson, *Many Mexicos*, 3rd edn, revised (University of California Press, 1952). An excellent short history

William York Tindall, *D. H. Lawrence and Susan His Cow* (Columbia University Press, N.Y., 1939). A study of Lawrence's primitivist and theosophical reading and thought

John B. Vickery, '"The Plumed Serpent" and the Eternal Paradox', *Criticism*, V (Spring, 1963), 119–34. Perhaps the best analysis of the character of Don Ramón Carrasco

Eliseo Vivas, *D. H. Lawrence: The Failure and the Triumph of Art* (Indiana University Press, 1960)

Ronald G. Walker, *Infernal Paradise: Mexico and the Modern English Novel* (University of California Press, 1978)

Frank Waters, 'Quetzalcoatl Versus D. H. Lawrence's *Plumed Serpent*', in *Western American Literature*, 3 (1968), 103–13

George Woodcock, 'Mexico and the English Novelist', in *Western Review*, XXI (Autumn, 1956), 21–32

FOR THE BEST IN PAPERBACKS, LOOK FOR THE Ⓟ

In every corner of the world, on every subject under the sun, Penguin represents quality and variety – the very best in publishing today.

For complete information about books available from Penguin – including Puffins, Penguin Classics and Arkana – and how to order them, write to us at the appropriate address below. Please note that for copyright reasons the selection of books varies from country to country.

In the United Kingdom: Please write to *Dept E.P., Penguin Books Ltd, Harmondsworth, Middlesex, UB7 0DA.*

If you have any difficulty in obtaining a title, please send your order with the correct money, plus ten per cent for postage and packaging, to *PO Box No 11, West Drayton, Middlesex*

In the United States: Please write to *Dept BA, Penguin, 299 Murray Hill Parkway, East Rutherford, New Jersey 07073*

In Canada: Please write to *Penguin Books Canada Ltd, 2801 John Street, Markham, Ontario L3R 1B4*

In Australia: Please write to the *Marketing Department, Penguin Books Australia Ltd, P.O. Box 257, Ringwood, Victoria 3134*

In New Zealand: Please write to the *Marketing Department, Penguin Books (NZ) Ltd, Private Bag, Takapuna, Auckland 9*

In India: Please write to *Penguin Overseas Ltd, 706 Eros Apartments, 56 Nehru Place, New Delhi, 110019*

In the Netherlands: Please write to *Penguin Books Netherlands B.V., Postbus 195, NL–1380AD Weesp*

In West Germany: Please write to *Penguin Books Ltd, Friedrichstrasse 10–12, D–6000 Frankfurt/Main 1*

In Spain: Please write to *Alhambra Longman S.A., Fernandez de la Hoz 9, E–28010 Madrid*

In Italy: Please write to *Penguin Italia s.r.l., Via Como 4, I-20096 Pioltello (Milano)*

In France: Please write to *Penguin Books Ltd, 39 Rue de Montmorency, F-75003 Paris*

In Japan: Please write to *Longman Penguin Japan Co Ltd, Yamaguchi Building, 2–12–9 Kanda Jimbocho, Chiyoda-Ku, Tokyo 101*

FOR THE BEST IN PAPERBACKS, LOOK FOR THE 🐧

CLASSICS OF THE TWENTIETH CENTURY

The Outsider   Albert Camus

Meursault leads an apparently unremarkable bachelor life in Algiers, until his involvement in a violent incident calls into question the fundamental values of society. 'The protagonist of *The Outsider* is undoubtedly the best achieved of all the central figures of the existential novel' – *Listener*

Dark as the Grave wherein my Friend is Laid   Malcolm Lowry

A Dantesque descent into hell: into Lowry's infernal landscape of Mexico – the Mexico of his masterpiece, *Under the Volcano* – and into Lowry's own personal abyss, reverberating with mental terrors and spiritual chasms.

I'm Dying Laughing   Christina Stead

A dazzling novel set in the 1930s and 1940s when fashionable Hollywood Marxism was under threat from the savage repression of McCarthyism. 'The Cassandra of the modern novel in English … reading her seems like plunging into the mess of life itself' – Angela Carter

The Desert of Love   François Mauriac

Two men, father and son, share a passion for the same woman – attractive, intelligent and proud, but an outcast from respectable society because of her position as a 'kept woman'. 'He writes with an intense, almost tempestuous force about the life of the emotions' – Olivia Manning

The Expelled and Other Novellas   Samuel Beckett

Rich in verbal and situational humour, these four stories offer the reader a fascinating insight into Beckett's preoccupation with the helpless individual consciousness, a preoccupation which has remained constant throughout his work.

Chance Acquaintances and Julie de Carneilhan   Colette

Two contrasting works in one volume. Colette's last full-length novel, *Julie de Carneilhan* was 'as close a reckoning with the elements of her second marriage as she ever allowed herself'. In *Chance Acquaintances*, Colette visits a health resort, accompanied only by her cat.

CLASSICS OF THE TWENTIETH CENTURY

Petersburg   Andrei Bely

'The most important, most influential and most perfectly realized Russian novel written in the twentieth century' (*The New York Times Book Review*), *Petersburg* is an exhilarating search for the identity of the city, presaging Joyce's search for Dublin in *Ulysses*.

The Miracle of the Rose   Jean Genet

Within a squalid prison lies a world of total freedom, in which chains become garlands of flowers – and a condemned prisoner is discovered to have in his heart a rose of monstrous size and beauty. Of this profoundly shocking novel Sartre wrote: 'Genet holds the mirror up to us: we must look at it and see ourselves.'

Labyrinths   Jorge Luis Borges

Seven parables, ten essays and twenty-three stories, including Borges's classic 'Tlön, Uqbar; Orbis Tertius', a new world where external objects are whatever each person wants, and 'Pierre Menard', the man who rewrote *Don Quixote* word for word without ever reading the original.

The Vatican Cellars   André Gide

Admired by the Dadaists, denounced as nihilist, defended by its author as a satirical farce: five interlocking books explore a fantastic conspiracy to kidnap the Pope and place a Freemason on his throne. *The Vatican Cellars* teases and subverts as only the finest satire can.

The Rescue   Joseph Conrad

'The air is thick with romance like a thunderous sky...' 'It matters not how often Mr Conrad tells the story of the man and the brig. Out of the million stories that life offers the novelist, this one is founded upon truth. And it is only Mr Conrad who is able to tell it us' – Virginia Woolf

Southern Mail/Night Flight   Antoine de Saint-Exupéry

Both novels in this volume are concerned with the pilot's solitary struggle with the elements, his sensation of insignificance amid the stars' timelessness and the sky's immensity. Flying and writing were inextricably linked in the author's life and he brought a unique sense of dedication to both.

FOR THE BEST IN PAPERBACKS, LOOK FOR THE 🐧

CLASSICS OF THE TWENTIETH CENTURY

Thirst for Love Yukio Mishima

Before her husband's death Etsuko had already learnt that jealousy is useless unless it can be controlled. Love, hatred, and a new, secret passion – she can control them all as long as there is hope. But as that hope fades, her frustrated desire gathers a momentum that can be checked only by an unspeakable act of violence.

The Collected Dorothy Parker

Dorothy Parker, more than any of her contemporaries, captured in her writing the spirit of the Jazz Age. Here, in a single volume, is the definitive Dorothy Parker: poetry, prose, articles and reviews. 'A good, fat book ... greatly to be welcomed' – Richard Ingrams

Remembrance of Things Past (3 volumes) Marcel Proust

'What an extraordinary world it is, the universe that Proust created! Like all great novels, À la Recherche has changed and enlarged our vision of the "real" world in which we live' – Peter Quennell. Terence Kilmartin's flawless translation is 'as near to the real Proust as we can hope for' – Angus Wilson

The Sword of Honour Trilogy Evelyn Waugh

A glorious fusion of comedy, satire and farcical despair, Waugh's magnificently funny trilogy is also a bitter attack on a world where chivalry and nobility were betrayed at every hand. 'Unquestionably the finest novels to have come out of the war' – Cyril Connolly

Buddenbrooks Thomas Mann

Published in 1902, Mann's 'immortal masterpiece' was already a classic before it was banned and burned by Hitler. 'The richness and complexity ... the interplay of action and ideas ... has never been surpassed in German fiction' – J. P. Stern

Sanctuary William Faulkner

Faulkner draws America's Deep South exactly as he saw it – seething with life and corruption. In Sanctuary he asserts a compulsive and unsparing vision of human nature.

FOR THE BEST IN PAPERBACKS, LOOK FOR THE 🐧

D. H. LAWRENCE IN PENGUIN

D. H. Lawrence is acknowledged as one of the greatest writers of the twentieth century. Nearly all his works have been published by Penguin.

NOVELS

Aaron's Rod	Lady Chatterley's Lover
The Lost Girl	The Plumed Serpent
The Rainbow	Sons and Lovers
The Trespasser	The White Peacock
Women in Love	Kangaroo
The First Lady Chatterley	John Thomas and Lady Jane
The Boy in the Bush	

SHORT STORIES

The Prussian Officer	England, My England
Love Among the Haystacks	The Woman Who Rode Away
The Princess	The Mortal Coil

Three Novellas: The Fox/The Ladybird/The Captain's Doll
St Mawr *and* The Virgin and the Gipsy
Selected Short Stories

TRAVEL BOOKS AND OTHER WORKS

Mornings in Mexico	Fantasia of the Unconscious *and*
Studies in Classic	Psychoanalysis and the
American Literature	Unconscious
Apocalypse	D. H. Lawrence and Italy

POETRY

D. H. Lawrence: The Complete Poems
Edited and Introduced by Vivian de Sola Pinto and F. Warren Roberts